Best-loved
Folktales
OF THE WORLD

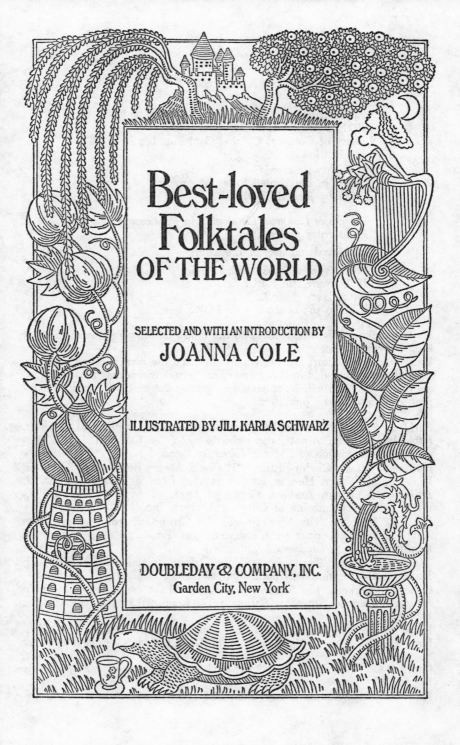

Best-loved Folktales
OF THE WORLD

SELECTED AND WITH AN INTRODUCTION BY
JOANNA COLE

ILLUSTRATED BY JILL KARLA SCHWARZ

DOUBLEDAY & COMPANY, INC.
Garden City, New York

For Philip

Copyright © 1982 by Joanna Cole
ISBN: 0-385-18520-0
Library of Congress Catalog Card Number 81–43288
First Edition

All Rights Reserved
Printed in the United States of America
Design by Jeanette Portelli

Library of Congress Cataloging in Publication Data
Main entry under title:

Best-loved folktales of the world.

    1. Tales. 2. Fairy tales. I. Cole, Joanna.
II. Schwarz, Jill Karla.
GR74.B47   398.2
ISBN 0-385-18520-0   AACR2

Grateful acknowledgment is made to the following for permission to reprint their copyrighted material.

Every reasonable effort has been made to trace the ownership of all copyrighted stories included in this volume. Any errors which may have occurred are inadvertent and will be corrected in subsequent editions, provided notification is sent to the publisher.

Kathleen Arnott. "The Rubber Man" from *African Myths and Legends*, retold by Kathleen Arnott, copyright © 1962 by Kathleen Arnott. Reprinted by permission of Oxford University Press.

Nathan Ausubel. "Chelm Justice," "It Could Always Be Worse," "Saint on Horse," and "When Hershel Eats" reprinted from *A Treasury of Jewish Folklore* by Nathan Ausubel. Copyright 1948, © 1976 by Crown Publishers, Inc. By permission of Crown Publishers, Inc.

Ellen C. Babbitt. "The Monkey and the Crocodile" from *Jakata Tales: Animal Stories*, copyright 1912, renewed 1940. Reprinted by permission of Prentice-Hall, Inc., Englewood Cliffs, N.J.

"Younde Goes to Town" from *West African Folktales* by William H. Barker, 1917. Reprinted by permission of Harrap Limited.

Genevieve Barlow. "The Search for the Magic Lake" reprinted from *Latin American Tales* by Genevieve Barlow, 1966. Reprinted by permission of the author.

Ralph Steele Boggs and Mary Gould Davis. "Don Demonio's Mother-in-Law" and "Toñino and the Fairies" from *Three Golden Oranges and Other Spanish Folktales* by Ralph Steele Boggs and Mary Gould Davis. Longmans, Green & Co. Copyright 1936, © 1964. Used by permission of Ralph Steele Boggs.

Leslie Bonnett. "Simple Wang" from *Chinese Folk and Fairy Tales*. Copy-

Thief," "The Farmer and His Hired Help," "The Magic Brocade," and "The Tale of the Oki Islands" from *Folk and Fairy Tales of Far-off Lands* by Eric and Nancy Protter. Copyright © 1965 by Eric Protter. Reprinted by permission of JCA Literary Agency, Inc.

Paul Radin and James Johnson Sweeney. "The Origin of Death" reprinted from *African Folktales and Sculptures*, edited by Paul Radin and James Johnson Sweeney, copyright 1952, © 1954, 1964, by permission of Princeton University Press.

Arthur Ransome. "The Firebird, the Horse of Power and the Princess Vasilissa," "The Fool of the World and the Flying Ship," and "Salt" from *Old Peter's Russian Tales* by Arthur Ransome. Copyright 1916 by Arthur Ransome. Reprinted by permission of Hamish Hamilton Ltd.

R. S. Rattray. "How Spider Obtained the Sky-God's Stories" from *Akan-Ashanti Folk Tales*, collected and translated by R. S. Rattray (1930). Reprinted by permission of Oxford University Press.

Moss Roberts. "The King's Favorite" by Han Fei Tzu; "The Groom's Crimes" by Yen Tzu Ch'un Ch'iu; "Drinking Companions" by P'u Sung-ling; "A Clever Judge" by Chang Shih-nan from *Chinese Fairy Tales and Fantasies*, edited and translated by Moss Roberts. Copyright © 1979 by Moss Roberts. Reprinted by permission of Pantheon Books, a Division of Random House, Inc.

Milton Rugoff. "Raven Brings Light" from *A Harvest of World Folk Tales*, edited by Milton Rugoff. Copyright 1949 by Viking Press, © renewed 1977 by Milton Rugoff. Reprinted by permission of Viking Penguin, Inc.

Jacqueline Simpson. "The Seal Skin" by Jacqueline Simpson reprinted from *Icelandic Folktales and Legends*, copyright © 1972, by permission of University of California Press and B. T. Batsford Ltd.

Edwin W. Smith and A. M. Dale. "Why There Are Cracks in Tortoise's Shell" reprinted from *The Ila-speaking Peoples of Northern Rhodesia* by Edwin W. Smith and A. M. Dale, copyright 1920, by permission of Macmillan, London and Basingstoke.

Dan Storm. "Señor Coyote and the Dogs" reprinted from *Picture Tales from Mexico* by Dan Storm, copyright 1941 by Frederick A. Stokes, Inc., by permission of Mark Storm.

Bitite Vinklers. "The Bul-Bul Bird" and "God and the Devil Share the Harvest" translated from the Latvian by Bitite Vinklers from A. Lerchis-Puskaitis, *Latviesu Tautas Pasakas Un Teikas* (*Latvian Folktales and Legends*), 7 vols., 1891–1902. Copyright © 1982 by Bitite Vinklers. Reprinted by permission of the translator.

Mai Vo-Dinh. "The Fly" and "The Little Lizard's Sorrow" from *The Toad Is the Emperor's Uncle, Animal Folktales from Viet-Nam* by Mai Vo-Dinh. Copyright © 1970 by Sung Ngo-Dinh. Reprinted by permission of the author.

Diane Wolkstein. "The Magic Orange Tree" from *The Magic Orange Tree and Other Haitian Folktales*, collected by Diane Wolkstein. Copyright © 1978 by Diane Wolkstein. Reprinted by permission of Alfred A. Knopf, Inc.

Acknowledgments

I WISH TO THANK the following friends and associates, who suggested tales, gave me leads, lent me books, listened to stories and provided me with encouragement and moral support: Melvyn D. Baron, Harvey Birenbaum, Ashley Bryan, Stephanie Calmenson, Patricia Connolly, Madeleine Edmondson, Jack Flam, Marie Macfarlane, Jane Mobley, Yuri Salzman, Peter Spier and Robert V. Stone.

I am especially grateful to Dr. Lester M. Golden, who encouraged my interest in fairy tales and shared with me his understanding of their symbols.

Thanks go to Bitite Vinklers for making the new translations of the Latvian tales.

Thanks also to Suzanne Konowitz of the Cultural Service of the French Embassy, to the Consulate General of the Netherlands and to the Norwegian Information Service for responding helpfully to my queries; to Carol Christiansen and Florence Eichin at Doubleday for help with copyright and permissions; to Marianne Koch for editorial assistance; and, of course, to Barbara Greenman for being an editor after my own heart and always putting the book first.

JOANNA COLE

CONTENTS

British Isles

Scandinavia and Northern Europe

The Pacific

Caribbean and West Indies

Central and South America

Introduction

ENJOYING THE WORLD'S FOLKTALES

FOLKTALES AND FAIRY TALES are usually the first stories we hear as children, and almost no others can equal their power to involve us so totally. When Little Red Riding Hood says to the wolf, "What big eyes you have, Grandmother," the young child, listening with wide eyes herself, gives a shiver of delight tinged with fear. And when Jack wakes to find that the worthless beans of yesterday have grown into a magic beanstalk, every child is as eager as Jack to find out what is at the top.

But, although the tales are especially loved by children, the familiar nursery stories form only a small portion of the world's tales, most of which were not originally intended for children alone. In past times, folktales were told in family or village groups, some stories told mainly to children, some to mixed groups, and some only to the adults of the community.

Because they are the products of preliterate societies, the folktales, unlike our modern novels and short stories, were not invented by a single author and printed in a book to be read unchanged forever. Instead, they were passed by word of mouth from one teller to another, never told twice in exactly the same way. This oral tradition made for a unique intimacy between teller and listeners, and the give and take with the audience no doubt influenced the form of the tales. Thus the stories express the wishes, hopes, and fears of many people, rather than the concerns of a particular writer, and they deal with universal human dilemmas that span differences of age, culture, and geography.

When heard again and again throughout a lifetime, the tales served not only to entertain but to transmit the values and wisdom of the culture, imbue a strong sense of right and wrong, and provide a reservoir of vivid images that became part of the individual's imagination and even of his everyday language.

In modern times, such gifts are not usually received at the knee of a village storyteller, but can be obtained by reading. It is hoped that this collection will offer tales for everyone, for it was planned to be shared by families and to be read by people of all ages.

Many of the two hundred tales in this book may be appreciated by the youngest children. Stories like *Teeny-Tiny*, from England, *The Monkey and the Crocodile*, from India, and *The Three Billy-Goats Gruff*, from Norway, can be read aloud to preschoolers. Older children will enjoy more complex tales like the Irish hero tale *The Birth of Fin MacCoul*, the love story from ancient Greece *Eros and Psyche*, and the West African and Caribbean trickster tales about Anansi, the spider-hero. Subtle tales like *The Tiger's Whisker*, from Korea, and *The Little Lizard's Sorrow*, from Vietnam, hold surprises and pleasures for the most sophisticated readers, who will find as they read that almost all the tales can be read with fascination at many levels.

The Index of Categories of Tales (pp. 781–788) will help not only in selecting tales of interest to a particular reader, but also in choosing stories to appeal to younger children and in finding tales that lend themselves especially well to reading aloud or story-telling.

In preparing this anthology, I made every effort to choose tales that are favorites in the cultures from which they came. I drew not only on my own knowledge and on my reading in the literature about folktales, but I also asked friends, associates, folklorists, national embassies, librarians, and storytellers for suggestions.

I also tried to stay as close as possible to the oral tradition of the folktales, selecting stories that came originally from the lips of a storyteller rather than the pen of a writer. To be sure, many of the stories in the book were retold by authors and editors to make them more suitable for the printed page. Some of the tales come from literary sources like *The Arabian Nights*, the *Uncle Remus* stories of Joel Chandler Harris or the *Fables* of Aesop; in these cases, however, the stories are known to have been modeled closely on folktales and the spirit of the telling has been kept. Other stories were taken down word for word from storytellers by professional tale collectors who retained the style of the original teller. This kind of faithful rendering, now used by all modern folklorists, was invented in the early nineteenth century by two German scholars who possessed an extraordinary love for the tales of their people.

Jakob and Wilhelm Grimm, known to most of us as the Brothers Grimm, devoted their lives to collecting tales from native storytellers in Germany, and in 1812 they published the first volume of *Kinder- und*

Hausmärchen, popularly known in translation as *Grimms' Fairy Tales.**
A few years later, the Grimms put out a second volume, making a total
of 211 tales, which include a majority of the favorite tales known to
people in the Western world today.

The Grimms' work in Germany had a profound influence on the rest
of Europe. Not only was their collection widely translated, but scholars
in other countries began to follow their lead and collect the folktales of
their own nations. It was not long before almost every European country had a folklore society, dedicated to preserving not only folktales, but
other folk literature as well: songs, poems, games, proverbs, folk reme-
dies, weatherlore and the like.

After a time, the science of folklore spread to Asia, Africa and the
Americas, so that at present, tales have been published from almost everywhere. And as the tales accumulated, something amazing began to
emerge: despite the cultural variation one would naturally expect in stories from different places, there were uncanny similarities in tales from
countries as far away from each other as India and Ireland. For instance, there are so many versions of the Cinderella story in the world
that in 1893 a book was published that analyzed no fewer than 345 of
them! And most of the other major folktale themes as well are told in
hundreds of versions from one country to another.

To account for the existence of similar stories everywhere, some
scholars believed that the world's tales originally spread from one
source by diffusion; that is, the plots were thought to have originated in
India and traveled via pilgrims, merchants and immigrants to local storytellers elsewhere, who adopted the stories as their own, changing details in the telling, but keeping the bones of the tales intact.

Another theory was that the stories sprang up simultaneously in
different countries because the material of the folktales is universal.
The themes were said to be those concerning human beings everywhere
and the stories were bound to be invented wherever communities devel-
oped.

Today most folklorists hold a kind of combination view; that is, some
themes do seem to be universal, and stories centering around these arise
independently in different places. But other specific plots have spread
from a variety of places by diffusion.

---

* In common usage "fairy tale" is used interchangeably with "folktale."
The term "fairy tale" is probably an attempt to translate the German word
märchen, which means an ordinary folktale set in an unnamed, faraway
place at an unspecified time in the past when magical events still happened.

Thus scholars will admit that people everywhere have stories of giants, witches and ogres, as well as of supernatural helpers, of culture heroes who bring gifts from the gods, of tricksters who practice deceptions and of fools and noodleheads who allow us to laugh at our own or others' foibles. It seems reasonable that general themes like these would arise in any culture.

But often a tale appears in different countries with the same series of very specific details: for instance, the same old woman helper is met on the road *and* a similar magic object is given to the hero *and* identical tasks are performed with the aid of the object. It seems impossible that a story like this—even down to the order of events and often the dialogue—could have been invented separately by storytellers in different places, and in such a case, folklorists would assume the tale was spread by diffusion.

In either case, whether a story has traveled or whether it was told independently, it is clear that those themes and plots that are widespread are those that have been entertaining and meaningful to many people in many places. These are the themes I have tried to include in the selection of tales in this book. For the sake of variety, however, an effort has been made to avoid excessive duplication of tale types. For some themes, I have included the tale best known to English-speaking readers. For others, the most familiar version has been omitted and a variant included from another culture. For instance, readers will recognize the Turkish tale *The Three Hares* as a version of the familiar *The Three Little Pigs*.

In other cases, however, several variations of the same tale do appear. It will be of interest to many readers, I suspect, to read a few of the many Cinderella stories mentioned above. Therefore, I have included, in addition to the French version known to most of us, four other variations: *Ashenputtel*, from the Grimms, in which the role of the girl's fairy godmother is filled by a magic tree growing on her mother's grave; *The Magic Orange Tree*, from Haiti, which also features a tree and omits mention of the famous slipper or the handsome prince; *The Indian Cinderella*, a Canadian Indian tale that has mythical elements; and *Thousand-Furs*, a variation in which the story is told without the wicked stepmother or stepsisters.

There are a few other cases of repetition of tales, including: *Bastianelo*, from Italy, and *Not a Pin to Choose Between Them*, from Norway, both noodlehead stories about a man who sets out to find three people as foolish as his wife; *Eros and Psyche*, the lyrical tale from ancient Greek and Roman sources, which is echoed in the Norwegian *East of the Sun and West of the Moon* and in the famous *Beauty and the Beast*, from France; and *Rumpelstiltskin*, represented in both the German version and the droll English *Tom Tit Tot*, in which the impish helper wants for his reward not the queen's baby, but the queen herself.

Even when the entire tale type is not repeated, isolated themes, or motifs, as they are called by folklorists, often reappear. For instance, the motif of a suitor winning the hand of a princess by making her laugh (or speak) is found in *The Golden Goose*, from the Grimms, *Lazy Jack*, from England, and *Intelligence and Luck*, from Czechoslovakia. And the motif of the false bride, in which the heroine temporarily loses the hero to a treacherous rival, appears in several tales, including *The Goosegirl* and *Darling Roland*, both from the Grimms. In these cases, the overall plots of the stories are quite different from each other.

It is hoped that these repetitions will prove more entertaining than monotonous, for the variation of details sets a new mood and renders each tale unique. And for those who would like to study the tales further, there is no end to the comparisons that might be made.

Studying the tales, however, is not at all necessary for appreciating them; for folk and fairy tales have gifts to offer those who read them, and these gifts are given generously, without effort and often without even awareness on the reader's part. Many commentators on the psychological meaning of fairy tales have written about specific stories in terms of an individual's development from childhood through adolescence to adulthood. A case can be made that tales of development can serve as guides for those who are themselves growing.

The fairy tale hero often starts out as a lad, the heroine as a girl, and by the end of the story he or she is a grown man or woman ready to marry and assume an independent life. Yet nothing in the tale has been mentioned of years passing or of physical growth occurring. Only if we look closely can we see that the events of the story, especially their magical aspects, parallel the maturation process.

The heroes and heroines of fairy tales often begin not only as children, but as disadvantaged children. A boy may be the youngest of three brothers, considered a simpleton by everyone and unable to measure up to the cleverness of his older brothers (see *The Queen Bee*, from the Grimms, *The Forest Bride*, from Finland, or *Salt*, from Russia). A girl is often a stepdaughter in the lowest position in the family (see *Ashenputtel* or *Mother Holle*, from the Grimms). This low status can be seen as representing the child's own image of himself as a weak dependent in a world where others are more competent and powerful. A child may in fact be bright, beloved and confident, but in the earliest years, he still needs others to care for him, still is at a disadvantage with older children and still looks forward with longing to the time when he too will be grown up. We all know something of how it feels to be the youngest son or the cinder-girl of fairy tales.

It is from this humble starting point that the tale unfolds and the magical events chronicle the struggle of the hero to attain an autonomous position in the world. This struggle is usually represented by a quest to perform some "impossible" task or tasks. Ashenputtel must sort out beans and lentils thrown among the ashes; the Fool of the World, in the Russian tale, must build a flying ship; the youngest daughter must find a castle that lies East of the Sun and West of the Moon. Sometimes the protagonists despair of being able to complete the task, just as it sometimes seems impossible to all of us to accomplish something that requires not only effort but growth as well. Despite the despair, however, they attempt to succeed and are able to do so with the aid of magical helpers, which take the form of supernatural beings or talking animals.

The magical helper is one of the most misunderstood characters in fairy tales, often seen as someone who fulfills all the hero's desires while the hero stands idly by. Usually, however, the protagonist is not passive at all: the youngest daughter in *East of the Sun and West of the Moon* is already on her quest when the magical helpers assist her; the Fool of the World acquires his helpers on the way to perform the tasks required of him; and the same is true of the Raja's Son in the Indian tale, who gets animal helpers on the way to Princess Labam's kingdom.

Even more, it is often the actions of the hero and heroine that win the assistance of the magical helper once he is found. By aiding the helpless or performing an act of kindness, the heroes engage in a positive way with others and establish a relationship with potential helpers. This they do in an unselfconscious, openhearted way, and their style is many times contrasted in the tales with that of other lads and maidens, who either refuse to connect with others (like the older brothers in *The Queen Bee*) or do so in a false, manipulative way for the sake of some desired end or reward (like the ugly sister in the Grimms' *Mother Holle* or the wicked woman in the modern Greek story *The Twelve Months*).

The heroes' relationships with the magical helpers can be understood as their willingness to partake of what their surroundings have to offer, their acceptance of good fortune when it comes their way, and even their reliance on parts of their own nature not under their conscious control. Theirs is an attitude of trust, or faith, in the world, without which life is a bleak business indeed.

Thus, whether or not they are the cleverest or most highly favored of youths, the heroes and heroines of the tales sow the seeds for their own success by engaging with the world in a receptive, creative manner. And the happy ending of the tales, far from being an unrealistic "fairy tale" fantasy, as some would have it, shows that maturity and independence will surely come to those who have such an attitude toward themselves and life. This piece of wisdom, at the core of the developmental tales, gives the young a sense of hope when they identify with the characters, and explains how the tales—as fantastic as they are—can serve as a very real model of personal growth for people today, who may seem far removed from a world in which folk wisdom has much meaning.

The wisdom or the kernel of truth in a folk story, moreover, is not confined to the more serious tales of quests and tasks. Even the humorous tales, which at first glance seem to be told for entertainment alone, impart meaning to listeners.

The humorous trickster tales, for example, which form a large part of the world's tales, have something serious to say about the rights of the "little guy." The trickster is so often pitted against a bully or an unjust authority that questions of justice and power are frequently at the heart of the tales. In the African tale *A Tug-of-War*, the clever tortoise triumphs over two larger animals. Even though he resorts to a sly deception, we side with him because he shows that size and strength should not be an excuse for disregarding the small and weak. In the American Indian tale *The Theft of Fire*, the trickster-hero Manabozho steals a spark of fire from the powerful old man, who, being greedy and indifferent to the needs of others, is hoarding all fire for himself. Because the tales reinforce our concept of justice, they instruct us; and because we see that the trickster has right on his side, we identify with him even when he does not follow the letter of the law.

Sometimes, however, the usually clever trickster is not so clever. He shows up in many tales as a greedy fool, a fellow who is so eager to gratify his own selfish wishes that he ends up completely humiliating himself. Examples of this type of trickster tale can be found in *The Rubber Man*, from Africa, and *Anansi Play with Fire, Anansi Get Burned*, from the Caribbean. In these tales, the trickster serves as an object lesson, demonstrating the folly of placing one's own desires before any other considerations.

Almost every other type of humorous tale, no matter how trivial it may seem on the surface, has a message about human behavior. The noodlehead stories, for instance, set us laughing at extreme cases of foolishness, but usually we ourselves are guilty of the same behavior in milder form. In *The Two Old Women's Bet*, from the southern United States, one wife tricks her foolish husband into believing that he is dead, while another woman convinces her spouse that he is wearing elegant clothes when he is actually naked. All of us laugh at the noodleheads, but on some level we recognize how few of us trust the evidence of our own senses when society conspires to convince us otherwise.

Even fantastic tales of magic and the supernatural can impart wisdom for those who are willing to listen. Two apparently disparate stories, *The Brownie of Blednock*, from Scotland, and *The Woman and the Children of the Sycamore Tree*, from Africa, deal with the question of how to accept supernatural help. In the Scottish legend, a helpful fairy suddenly disappears after years of service when a farm wife pays it wages. And in the African tale, a woman who obtained children by magic from sycamore fruits loses them instantly when she mentions their origin. As different as these tales are on the surface, both admonish us to keep an attitude of healthy respect for Lady Fortune and warn us not to tamper with sources of magic. Such tales may give us insight into archaic superstitions, but they can give us much more if we understand them symbolically. For who has not had experiences like those of the women in the tales? How often have we found ourselves tongue-tied when we paid extra attention to our speech? And how many artists, becoming suddenly overconscious of their art, have found themselves unable to work? The folktales tell us that to try to control the sources of our own "magic" is to destroy our natural connection with it and to make it disappear.

It is clear that there is more to a folktale than just a good story, but the tales are good stories first and foremost. It is not necessary to be aware of their subtlety to enjoy them. In fact, it is better to read them just for the fun, excitement, and adventure they offer. The deeper meanings actually speak to us more clearly when we forget to look for them. You may find that if you read aloud or tell tales as a family, even the youngest children will become interested in spite of themselves. And parents, in reading with their children, will recapture a sense of wonder because they are sharing the age-old plots with someone who is hearing them for the first time.

JOANNA COLE

West Europe

Beauty and the Beast

1. CINDERELLA

(*France*)

ONCE UPON A TIME there was a worthy man who married for his second wife the haughtiest, proudest woman that had ever been seen. She had two daughters, who possessed their mother's temper and resembled her in everything. Her husband, on the other hand, had a young daughter, who was of an exceptionally sweet and gentle nature. She got this from her mother, who had been the nicest person in the world.

The wedding was no sooner over than the stepmother began to display her bad temper. She could not endure the excellent qualities of this young girl, for they made her own daughters appear more hateful than ever. She thrust upon her all the meanest tasks about the house. It was she who had to clean the plates and the stairs, and sweep out the rooms of the mistress of the house and her daughters. She slept on a wretched mattress in a garret at the top of the house, while the sisters had rooms with parquet flooring, and beds of the most fashionable style, with mirrors in which they could see themselves from top to toe.

The poor girl endured everything patiently, not daring to complain to her father. The latter would have scolded her, because he was entirely ruled by his wife. When she had finished her work she used to sit among the cinders in the corner of the chimney, and it was from this habit that she came to be commonly known as Cinder-clod. The younger of the two sisters, who was not quite so spiteful as the elder, called her Cinderella. But her wretched clothes did not prevent Cinderella from being a hundred times more beautiful than her sisters, for all their resplendent garments.

It happened that the king's son gave a ball, and he invited all persons of high degree. The two young ladies were invited among others, for they cut a considerable figure in the country. Not a little pleased were they, and the question of what clothes and what mode of dressing the hair would become them best took up all their time. And all this meant fresh trouble for Cinderella, for it was she who went over her sisters' linen and ironed their ruffles. They could talk of nothing else but the fashions in clothes.

"For my part," said the elder, "I shall wear my dress of red velvet, with the Honiton lace."

"I have only my everyday petticoat," said the younger, "but to make up for it I shall wear my cloak with the golden flowers and my necklace of diamonds, which are not so bad."

They sent for a good hairdresser to arrange their double-frilled caps, and bought patches at the best shop.

They summoned Cinderella and asked her advice, for she had good taste. Cinderella gave them the best possible suggestions, and even offered to dress their hair, to which they gladly agreed.

While she was thus occupied they said:

"Cinderella, would you not like to go to the ball?"

"Ah, but you fine young ladies are laughing at me. It would be no place for me."

"That is very true, people would laugh to see a cinder-clod in the ballroom."

Anyone else but Cinderella would have done their hair amiss, but she was good-natured, and she finished them off to perfection. They were so excited in their glee that for nearly two days they ate nothing. They broke more than a dozen laces through drawing their stays tight in order to make their waists more slender, and they were perpetually in front of a mirror.

At last the happy day arrived. Away they went, Cinderella watching them as long as she could keep them in sight. When she could no longer see them she began to cry. Her godmother found her in tears, and asked what was troubling her.

"I should like—I should like——"

She was crying so bitterly that she could not finish the sentence.

Said her godmother, who was a fairy:

"You would like to go to the ball, would you not?"

"Ah, yes," said Cinderella, sighing.

"Well, well," said her godmother, "promise to be a good girl and I will arrange for you to go."

She took Cinderella into her room and said:

"Go into the garden and bring me a pumpkin."

Cinderella went at once and gathered the finest that she could find. This she brought to her godmother, wondering how a pumpkin could help in taking her to the ball.

Her godmother scooped it out, and when only the rind was left, struck it with her wand. Instantly the pumpkin was changed into a beautiful coach, gilded all over.

Then she went and looked in the mouse-trap, where she found six mice all alive. She told Cinderella to lift the door of the mouse-trap a little, and as each mouse came out she gave it a tap with her wand, whereupon it was transformed into a fine horse. So that here was a fine team of six dappled mouse-gray horses.

But she was puzzled to know how to provide a coachman.

"I will go and see," said Cinderella, "if there is not a rat in the rat-trap. We could make a coachman of him."

"Quite right," said her godmother, "go and see."

Cinderella brought in the rat-trap, which contained three big rats. The fairy chose one specially on account of his elegant whiskers.

As soon as she had touched him he turned into a fat coachman with the finest mustachios that ever were seen.

"Now go into the garden and bring me the six lizards which you will find behind the water-butt."

No sooner had they been brought than the godmother turned them into six lackeys, who at once climbed up behind the coach in their braided liveries, and hung on there as if they had never done anything else all their lives.

Then said the fairy godmother:

"Well, there you have the means of going to the ball. Are you satisfied?"

"Oh, yes, but am I to go like this in my ugly clothes?"

Her godmother merely touched her with her wand, and on the instant her clothes were changed into garments of gold and silver cloth, bedecked with jewels. After that her godmother gave her a pair of glass slippers, the prettiest in the world.

Thus altered, she entered the coach. Her godmother bade her not to stay beyond midnight whatever happened, warning her that if she remained at the ball a moment longer, her coach would again become a pumpkin, her horses mice, and her lackeys lizards, while her old clothes would reappear upon her once more.

She promised her godmother that she would not fail to leave the ball before midnight, and away she went, beside herself with delight.

The king's son, when he was told of the arrival of a great princess whom nobody knew, went forth to receive her. He handed her down from the coach, and led her into the hall where the company was assembled. At once there fell a great silence. The dancers stopped, the violins played no more, so rapt was the attention which everybody bestowed upon the superb beauty of the unknown guest. Everywhere could be heard in confused whispers:

"Oh, how beautiful she is!"

The king, old man as he was, could not take his eyes off her, and whispered to the queen that it was many a long day since he had seen anyone so beautiful and charming.

All the ladies were eager to scrutinize her clothes and the dressing of her hair, being determined to copy them on the morrow, provided they could find materials so fine, and tailors so clever.

The king's son placed her in the seat of honor, and at once begged the privilege of being her partner in a dance. Such was the grace with which she danced that the admiration of all was increased.

A magnificent supper was served, but the young prince could eat nothing, so taken up was he with watching her. She went and sat beside her sisters, and bestowed numberless attentions upon them. She made them share with her the oranges and lemons which the king had given her—greatly to their astonishment, for they did not recognize her.

While they were talking, Cinderella heard the clock strike a quarter to twelve. She at once made a profound curtsy to the company, and departed as quickly as she could.

As soon as she was home again she sought out her godmother, and having thanked her, declared that she wished to go upon the morrow once more to the ball, because the king's son had invited her.

While she was busy telling her godmother all that had happened at the ball, her two sisters knocked at the door. Cinderella let them in.

"What a long time you have been in coming!" she declared, rubbing her eyes and stretching herself as if she had only just awakened. In real truth she had not for a moment wished to sleep since they had left.

"If you had been at the ball," said one of the sisters, "you would not be feeling weary. There came a most beautiful princess, the most beautiful that has ever been seen, and she bestowed numberless attentions upon us, and gave us her oranges and lemons."

Cinderella was overjoyed. She asked them the name of the princess, but they replied that no one knew it, and that the king's son was so distressed that he would give anything in the world to know who she was.

Cinderella smiled, and said she must have been beautiful indeed.

"Oh, how lucky you are. Could I not manage to see her? Oh, please, Javotte, lend me the yellow dress which you wear every day."

"Indeed!" said Javotte, "that is a fine idea. Lend my dress to a grubby cinder-clod like you—you must think me mad!"

Cinderella had expected this refusal. She was in no way upset, for she would have been very greatly embarrassed had her sister been willing to lend the dress.

The next day the two sisters went to the ball, and so did Cinderella, even more splendidly attired than the first time.

The king's son was always at her elbow, and paid her endless compliments.

The young girl enjoyed herself so much that she forgot her godmother's bidding completely, and when the first stroke of midnight fell upon her ears, she thought it was no more than eleven o'clock.

She rose and fled as nimbly as a fawn. The prince followed her, but could not catch her. She let fall one of her glass slippers, however, and this the prince picked up with tender care.

When Cinderella reached home she was out of breath, without coach, without lackeys, and in her shabby clothes. Nothing remained of all her splendid clothes save one of the little slippers, the fellow to the one which she had let fall.

Inquiries were made of the palace doorkeepers as to whether they had seen a princess go out, but they declared they had seen no one leave except a young girl, very ill-clad, who looked more like a peasant than a young lady.

When her two sisters returned from the ball, Cinderella asked them if they had again enjoyed themselves, and if the beautiful lady had been there. They told her that she was present, but had fled away when midnight sounded, and in such haste that she had let fall one of her little glass slippers, the prettiest thing in the world. They added that the king's son, who picked it up, had done nothing but gaze at it for the rest of the ball, from which it was plain that he was deeply in love with its beautiful owner.

They spoke the truth. A few days later, the king's son caused a proclamation to be made by trumpeters, that he would take for wife the owner of the foot which the slipper would fit.

They tried it first on the princesses, then on the duchesses and the whole of the Court, but in vain. Presently they brought it to the home of the two sisters, who did all they could to squeeze a foot into the slipper. This, however, they could not manage.

Cinderella was looking on and recognized her slipper:

"Let me see," she cried, laughingly, "if it will not fit me."

Her sisters burst out laughing, and began to gibe at her, but the equerry who was trying on the slipper looked closely at Cinderella. Observing that she was very beautiful he declared that the claim was quite a fair one, and that his orders were to try the slipper on every maiden. He bade Cinderella sit down, and on putting the slipper to her little foot he perceived that the latter slid in without trouble, and was molded to its shape like wax.

Great was the astonishment of the two sisters at this, and greater still when Cinderella drew from her pocket the other little slipper. This she likewise drew on.

At that very moment her godmother appeared on the scene. She gave a tap with her wand to Cinderella's clothes, and transformed them into a dress even more magnificent than her previous ones.

The two sisters recognized her for the beautiful person whom they had seen at the ball, and threw themselves at her feet, begging her pardon for all the ill-treatment she had suffered at their hands.

Cinderella raised them, and declaring as she embraced them that she pardoned them with all her heart, bade them to love her well in future.

She was taken to the palace of the young prince in all her new array. He found her more beautiful than ever, and was married to her a few days afterward.

Cinderella was as good as she was beautiful. She set aside apartments in the palace for her two sisters, and married them the very same day to two gentlemen of high rank about the Court.

2. BEAUTY AND THE BEAST
(France)

ONCE UPON A TIME, in a very far-off country, there lived a merchant who had been so fortunate in all his undertakings that he was enormously rich. As he had, however, six sons and six daughters, he found that his money was not too much to let them all have everything they fancied, as they were accustomed to do.

But one day a most unexpected misfortune befell them. Their house caught fire and was speedily burned to the ground, with all the splendid furniture, the books, pictures, gold, silver, and precious goods it contained; and this was only the beginning of their troubles. Their father, who had until this moment prospered in all ways, suddenly lost every ship he had upon the sea, either by dint of pirates, shipwreck, or fire. Then he heard that his clerks in distant countries, whom he trusted entirely, had proved unfaithful; and at last from great wealth he fell into the direst poverty.

All that he had left was a little house in a desolate place at least a hundred leagues from the town in which he had lived, and to this he was forced to retreat with his children, who were in despair at the idea of leading such a different life. Indeed, the daughters at first hoped that their friends, who had been so numerous while they were rich, would insist on their staying in their houses now they no longer possessed one. But they soon found that they were left alone, and that their former friends even attributed their misfortunes to their own extravagance, and showed no intention of offering them any help. So nothing was left for them but to take their departure to the cottage, which stood in the midst of a dark forest, and seemed to be the most dismal place upon the face of the earth. As they were too poor to have any servants, the girls had to work hard, like peasants, and the sons, for their part, cultivated the fields to earn their living. Roughly clothed, and living in the simplest way, the girls regretted unceasingly the luxuries and amusements of their former life; only the youngest tried to be brave and cheerful. She had been as sad as anyone when misfortune first overtook her father, but, soon recovering her natural gaiety, she set to work to make the best of things, to amuse her father and brothers as well as she could, and to try to persuade her sisters to join her in dancing and singing. But they would do nothing of the sort, and, because she was not as doleful as themselves, they declared that this miserable life was all she was fit for. But she was really far prettier and cleverer than they were; indeed, she was so lovely that she was always called Beauty. After two years, when they were all beginning to get used to their new life, something happened to disturb their tranquility. Their father received the news that one of his ships, which he had believed to be lost, had come safely into port with a rich cargo. All the sons and daughters at once thought that their poverty was at an end, and wanted to set out directly for the town; but their father, who was more prudent, begged them to wait a little, and, though it was harvest-time, and he could ill be spared, determined to go himself first, to make inquiries. Only the youngest daughter had any doubt but that they would soon again be as rich as they were before, or at least rich enough to live comfortably in some town where they would find amusement and gay companions once more. So they all loaded their father with commissions for jewels and dresses which it would have taken a fortune to buy; only Beauty, feeling sure that it was of no use, did not ask for anything. Her father, noticing her silence, said: "And what shall I bring for you, Beauty?"

"The only thing I wish for is to see you come home safely," she answered.

But this reply vexed her sisters, who fancied she was blaming them for having asked for such costly things. Her father, however, was pleased, but as he thought that at her age she certainly ought to like pretty presents, he told her to choose something.

"Well, dear father," she said, "as you insist upon it, I beg that you will bring me a rose. I have not seen one since we came here, and I love them so much."

So the merchant set out and reached the town as quickly as possible, but only to find that his former companions, believing him to be dead, had divided between them the goods which the ship had brought; and after six months of trouble and expense he found himself as poor as when he started, having been able to recover only just enough to pay the cost of his journey. To make matters worse, he was obliged to leave the town in the most terrible weather, so that by the time he was within a few leagues of his home he was almost exhausted with cold and fatigue. Though he knew it would take some hours to get through the forest, he was so anxious to be at his journey's end that he resolved to go on; but night overtook him, and the deep snow and bitter frost made it impossible for his horse to carry him any further. Not a house was to be seen; the only shelter he could get was the hollow trunk of a great tree, and there he crouched all the night, which seemed to him the longest he had ever known. In spite of his weariness the howling of the wolves kept him awake, and even when at last the day broke he was not much better off, for the falling snow had covered up every path, and he did not know which way to turn.

At length he made out some sort of track, and though at the beginning it was so rough and slippery that he fell down more than once, it presently became easier, and led him into an avenue of trees which ended in a splendid castle. It seemed to the merchant very strange that no snow had fallen in the avenue, which was entirely composed of orange trees, covered with flowers and fruit. When he reached the first court of the castle he saw before him a flight of agate steps, and went up them, and passed through several splendidly furnished rooms. The pleasant warmth of the air revived him, and he felt very hungry; but there seemed to be nobody in all this vast and splendid palace whom he could ask to give him something to eat. Deep silence reigned everywhere, and at last, tired of roaming through empty rooms and galleries, he stopped in a room smaller than the rest, where a clear fire was burning and a couch was drawn up cozily close to it. Thinking that this must be prepared for someone who was expected, he sat down to wait till he should come, and very soon fell into a sweet sleep.

When his extreme hunger wakened him after several hours, he was still alone; but a little table, upon which was a good dinner, had been drawn up close to him, and, as he had eaten nothing for twenty-four hours, he lost no time in beginning his meal, hoping that he might soon have an opportunity of thanking his considerate entertainer, whoever it might be. But no one appeared, and even after another long sleep, from which he awoke completely refreshed, there was no sign of anybody, though a fresh meal of dainty cakes and fruit was prepared upon the little table at his elbow. Being naturally timid, the silence began to terrify him, and he resolved to search once more through all the rooms; but it was of no use. Not even a servant was to be seen; there was no sign of life in the palace! He began to wonder what he should do, and to amuse himself by pretending that all the treasures he saw were his own, and considering how he would divide them among his children. Then he went down into the garden, and though it was winter everywhere else, here the sun shone, and the birds sang, and the flowers bloomed, and the air was soft and sweet. The merchant, in ecstasies with all he saw and heard, said to himself:

"All this must be meant for me. I will go this minute and bring my children to share all these delights."

In spite of being so cold and weary when he reached the castle, he had taken his horse to the stable and fed it. Now he thought he would saddle it for his homeward journey, and he turned down the path which led to the stable. This path had a hedge of roses on each side of it, and the merchant thought he had never seen or smelled such exquisite flowers. They reminded him of his promise to Beauty, and he stopped and had just gathered one to take to her when he was startled by a strange noise behind him. Turning around, he saw a frightful Beast, which seemed to be very angry and said, in a terrible voice:

"Who told you that you might gather my roses? Was it not enough that I allowed you to be in my palace and was kind to you? This is the way you show your gratitude, by stealing my flowers! But your insolence shall not go unpunished." The merchant, terrified by these furious words, dropped the fatal rose, and, throwing himself on his knees, cried: "Pardon me, noble sir. I am truly grateful to you for your hospitality, which was so magnificent that I could not imagine that you would be offended by my taking such a little thing as a rose." But the Beast's anger was not lessened by this speech.

"You are very ready with excuses and flattery," he cried; "but that will not save you from the death you deserve."

"Alas!" thought the merchant, "if my daughter Beauty could only know what danger her rose has brought me into!"

And in despair he began to tell the Beast all his misfortunes, and the reason of his journey, not forgetting to mention Beauty's request.

"A king's ransom would hardly have procured all that my other daughters asked," he said; "but I thought that I might at least take Beauty her rose. I beg you to forgive me, for you see I meant no harm."

The Beast considered for a moment, and then he said, in a less furious tone:

"I will forgive you on one condition—that is, that you will give me one of your daughters."

"Ah!" cried the merchant, "if I were cruel enough to buy my own life at the expense of one of my children's, what excuse could I invent to bring her here?"

"No excuse would be necessary," answered the Beast. "If she comes at all she must come willingly. On no other condition will I have her. See if any one of them is courageous enough, and loves you well enough to come and save your life. You seem to be an honest man, so I will trust you to go home. I give you a month to see if one of your daughters will come back with you and stay here, to let you go free. If none of them is willing, you must come alone, after bidding them good-bye forever, for then you will belong to me. And do not imagine that you can hide from me, for if you fail to keep your word I will come and fetch you!" added the Beast grimly.

The merchant accepted this proposal, though he did not really think any of his daughters would be persuaded to come. He promised to return at the time appointed, and then, anxious to escape from the presence of the Beast, he asked permission to set off at once. But the Beast answered that he could not go until the next day.

"Then you will find a horse ready for you," he said. "Now go and eat your supper, and await my orders."

The poor merchant, more dead than alive, went back to his room, where the most delicious supper was already served on the little table which was drawn up before a blazing fire. But he was too terrified to eat, and only tasted a few of the dishes, for fear the Beast should be angry if he did not obey his orders. When he had finished he heard a great noise in the next room, which he knew meant that the Beast was coming. As he could do nothing to escape his visit, the only thing that remained was to seem as little afraid as possible; so when the Beast appeared and asked roughly if he had supped well, the merchant answered humbly that he had, thanks to his host's kindness. Then the Beast warned him to remember their agreement, and to prepare his daughter exactly for what she had to expect.

"Do not get up tomorrow," he added, "until you see the sun and hear a golden bell ring. Then you will find your breakfast waiting for you here, and the horse you are to ride will be ready in the courtyard. He will also bring you back again when you come with your daughter a month hence. Farewell. Take a rose to Beauty, and remember your promise!"

The merchant was only too glad when the Beast went away, and though he could not sleep for sadness, he lay down until the sun rose. Then, after a hasty breakfast, he went to gather Beauty's rose, and mounted his horse, which carried him off so swiftly that in an instant he had lost sight of the palace, and he was still wrapped in gloomy thoughts when it stopped before the door of the cottage.

His sons and daughters, who had been very uneasy at his long absence, rushed to meet him, eager to know the result of his journey, which, seeing him mounted upon a splendid horse and wrapped in a rich mantle, they supposed to be favorable. But he hid the truth from them at first, only saying sadly to Beauty as he gave her the rose:

"Here is what you asked me to bring you; you little know what it has cost."

But this excited their curiosity so greatly that presently he told them his adventures from beginning to end, and then they were all very unhappy. The girls lamented loudly over their lost hopes, and the sons declared that their father should not return to this terrible castle, and began to make plans for killing the Beast if it should come to fetch him. But he reminded them that he had promised to go back. Then the girls were very angry with Beauty, and said it was all her fault, and that if she had asked for something sensible this would never have happened, and complained bitterly that they should have to suffer for her folly.

Poor Beauty, much distressed, said to them:

"I have indeed caused this misfortune, but I assure you I did it innocently. Who could have guessed that to ask for a rose in the middle of summer would cause so much misery? But as I did the mischief it is only just that I should suffer for it. I will therefore go back with my father to keep his promise."

At first nobody would hear of this arrangement, and her father and brothers, who loved her dearly, declared that nothing should make them let her go; but Beauty was firm. As the time drew near she divided all her little possessions between her sisters, and said good-bye to everything she loved, and when the fatal day came she encouraged and cheered her father as they mounted together the horse which had brought him back. It seemed to fly rather than gallop, but so smoothly that Beauty was not frightened; indeed, she would have enjoyed the journey if she had not feared what might happen to her at the end of it. Her father still tried to persuade her to go back, but in vain. While they were talking the night fell, and then, to their great surprise, wonderful colored lights began to shine in all directions, and splendid fireworks blazed out before them; all the forest was illuminated by them, and even felt pleasantly warm, though it had been bitterly cold before. This lasted until they reached the avenue of orange trees, where were statues holding flaming torches, and when they got nearer to the palace they saw that it was illuminated from the roof to the ground, and music sounded softly from the courtyard. "The Beast must be very hungry," said Beauty, trying to laugh, "if he makes all this rejoicing over the arrival of his prey."

But, in spite of her anxiety, she could not help admiring all the wonderful things she saw.

The horse stopped at the foot of the flight of steps leading to the terrace, and when they had dismounted her father led her to the little room he had been in before, where they found a splendid fire burning, and the table daintily spread with a delicious supper.

The merchant knew that this was meant for them, and Beauty, who was rather less frightened now that she had passed through so many rooms and seen nothing of the Beast, was quite willing to begin, for her long ride had made her very hungry. But they had hardly finished their meal when the noise of the Beast's footsteps was heard approaching, and Beauty clung to her father in terror, which became all the greater when she saw how frightened he was. But when the Beast really appeared, though she trembled at the sight of him, she made a great effort to hide her horror, and saluted him respectfully.

This evidently pleased the Beast. After looking at her he said, in a tone that might have struck terror into the boldest heart, though he did not seem to be angry:

"Good evening, old man. Good evening, Beauty."

The merchant was too terrified to reply, but Beauty answered sweetly:

"Good evening, Beast."

"Have you come willingly?" asked the Beast. "Will you be content to stay here when your father goes away?"

Beauty answered bravely that she was quite prepared to stay.

"I am pleased with you," said the Beast. "As you have come of your own accord, you may stay. As for you, old man," he added, turning to the merchant, "at sunrise tomorrow you will take your departure. When the bell rings get up quickly and eat your breakfast, and you will find the same horse waiting to take you home; but remember that you must never expect to see my palace again."

Then turning to Beauty, he said:

"Take your father into the next room, and help him to choose everything you think your brothers and sisters would like to have. You will find two traveling-trunks there; fill them as full as you can. It is only just that you should send them something very precious as a remembrance of yourself."

Then he went away, after saying, "Good-bye, Beauty. Good-bye, old man"; and though Beauty was beginning to think with great dismay of her father's departure, she was afraid to disobey the Beast's orders; and they went into the next room, which had shelves and cupboards all around it. They were greatly surprised at the riches it contained. There were splendid dresses fit for a queen, with all the ornaments that were to be worn with them; and when Beauty opened the cupboards she was quite dazzled by the gorgeous jewels that lay in heaps upon every shelf. After choosing a vast quantity, which she divided between her sisters— for she had made a heap of the wonderful dresses for each of them—she opened the last chest, which was full of gold.

"I think, father," she said, "that, as the gold will be more useful to you, we had better take out the other things again, and fill the trunks with it." So they did this; but the more they put in, the more room there seemed to be, and at last they put back all the jewels and dresses they had taken out, and Beauty even added as many more of the jewels as she could carry at once; and then the trunks were not too full, but they were so heavy that an elephant could not have carried them!

"The Beast was mocking us," cried the merchant; "he must have pretended to give us all these things, knowing that I could not carry them away."

"Let us wait and see," answered Beauty. "I cannot believe that he meant to deceive us. All we can do is to fasten them up and leave them ready."

So they did this and returned to the little room, where, to their astonishment, they found breakfast ready. The merchant ate his with a good appetite, as the Beast's generosity made him believe that he might perhaps venture to come back soon and see Beauty. But she felt sure that her father was leaving her forever, so she was very sad when the bell rang sharply for the second time, and warned them that the time was come for them to part. They went down into the courtyard, where two horses were waiting, one loaded with the two trunks, the other for him to ride. They were pawing the ground in their impatience to start, and the merchant was forced to bid Beauty a hasty farewell; and as soon as he was mounted he went off at such a pace that she lost sight of him in an instant. Then Beauty began to cry, and wandered sadly back to her own room. But she soon found that she was very sleepy, and as she had nothing better to do she lay down and instantly fell asleep. And then she dreamed that she was walking by a brook bordered with trees, and lamenting her sad fate, when a young prince, handsomer than anyone she had ever seen, and with a voice that went straight to her heart, came and said to her, "Ah, Beauty! you are not so unfortunate as you suppose. Here you will be rewarded for all you have suffered elsewhere. Your every wish shall be gratified. Only try to find me out, no matter how I may be disguised, as I love you dearly, and in making me happy you will find your own happiness. Be as truehearted as you are beautiful, and we shall have nothing left to wish for."

"What can I do, Prince, to make you happy?" said Beauty.

"Only be grateful," he answered, "and do not trust too much to your eyes. And, above all, do not desert me until you have saved me from my cruel misery."

After this she thought she found herself in a room with a stately and beautiful lady, who said to her:

"Dear Beauty, try not to regret all you have left behind you, for you are destined to a better fate. Only do not let yourself be deceived by appearances."

Beauty found her dreams so interesting that she was in no hurry to awake, but presently the clock roused her by calling her name softly twelve times, and then she got up and found her dressing table set out with everything she could possibly want; and when her toilet was finished she found dinner was waiting in the room next to hers. But dinner does not take very long when you are all by yourself, and very soon she sat down cozily in the corner of a sofa, and began to think about the charming Prince she had seen in her dream.

"He said I could make him happy," said Beauty to herself.

"It seems, then, that this horrible Beast keeps him a prisoner. How can I set him free? I wonder why they both told me not to trust to appearances? I don't understand it. But, after all, it was only a dream, so why should I trouble myself about it? I had better go and find something to do to amuse myself."

So she got up and began to explore some of the many rooms of the palace.

The first she entered was lined with mirrors, and Beauty saw herself reflected on every side, and thought she had never seen such a charming room. Then a bracelet which was hanging from a chandelier caught her eye, and on taking it down she was greatly surprised to find that it held a portrait of her unknown admirer, just as she had seen him in her dream. With great delight she slipped the bracelet on her arm, and went on into a gallery of pictures, where she soon found a portrait of the same handsome Prince, as large as life, and so well painted that as she studied it he seemed to smile kindly at her. Tearing herself away from the portrait at last, she passed through into a room which contained every musical instrument under the sun, and here she amused herself for a long while in trying some of them, and singing until she was tired. The next room was a library, and she saw everything she had ever wanted to read, as well as everything she had read, and it seemed to her that a whole lifetime would not be enough even to read the names of the books, there were so many. By this time it was growing dusk, and wax candles in diamond and ruby candlesticks were beginning to light themselves in every room.

Beauty found her supper served just at the time she preferred to have it, but she did not see anyone or hear a sound, and, though her father had warned her that she would be alone, she began to find it rather dull.

But presently she heard the Beast coming, and wondered tremblingly if he meant to eat her up now.

However, as he did not seem at all ferocious, and only said gruffly:

"Good evening, Beauty," she answered cheerfully and managed to conceal her terror. Then the Beast asked her how she had been amusing herself, and she told him all the rooms she had seen.

Then he asked if she thought she could be happy in his palace; and Beauty answered that everything was so beautiful that she would be very hard to please if she could not be happy. And after about an hour's talk Beauty began to think that the Beast was not nearly so terrible as she had supposed at first. Then he got up to leave her, and said in his gruff voice:

"Do you love me, Beauty? Will you marry me?"

"Oh! what shall I say?" cried Beauty, for she was afraid to make the Beast angry by refusing.

"Say 'yes' or 'no' without fear," he replied.

"Oh! no, Beast," said Beauty hastily.

"Since you will not, good night, Beauty," he said. And she answered:

"Good night, Beast," very glad to find that her refusal had not provoked him. And after he was gone she was very soon in bed and asleep, and dreaming of her unknown Prince. She thought he came and said to her:

"Ah, Beauty! why are you so unkind to me? I fear I am fated to be unhappy for many a long day still."

And then her dreams changed, but the charming Prince figured in them all; and when morning came her first thought was to look at the portrait and see if it was really like him, and she found that it certainly was.

This morning she decided to amuse herself in the garden, for the sun shone, and all the fountains were playing; but she was astonished to find that every place was familiar to her, and presently she came to the brook where the myrtle trees were growing where she had first met the Prince in her dream, and that made her think more than ever that he must be kept a prisoner by the Beast. When she was tired she went back to the palace, and found a new room full of materials for every kind of work—ribbons to make into bows, and silks to work into flowers. Then there was an aviary full of rare birds, which were so tame that they flew to Beauty as soon as they saw her, and perched upon her shoulders and her head.

"Pretty little creatures," she said, "how I wish that your cage was nearer to my room, that I might often hear you sing!"

So saying she opened a door, and found to her delight that it led into her own room, though she had thought it was quite the other side of the palace.

There were more birds in a room farther on, parrots and cockatoos that could talk, and they greeted Beauty by name; indeed, she found them so entertaining that she took one or two back to her room, and they talked to her while she was at supper; after which the Beast paid her his usual visit, and asked the same questions as before, and then with a gruff good night he took his departure, and Beauty went to bed to dream of her mysterious Prince. The days passed swiftly in different amusements, and after a while Beauty found out another strange thing in the palace, which often pleased her when she was tired of being alone. There was one room which she had not noticed particularly; it was empty, except that under each of the windows stood a very comfortable chair; and the first time she had looked out of the window it had seemed to her that a black curtain prevented her from seeing anything outside. But the second time she went into the room, happening to be tired, she sat down in one of the chairs, when instantly the curtain was rolled aside, and a most amusing pantomime was acted before her; there were dances, and colored lights, and music, and pretty dresses, and it was all so gay that Beauty was in ecstasies. After that she tried the other seven windows in turn, and there was some new and surprising entertainment to be seen from each of them, so that Beauty never could feel lonely any more. Every evening after supper the Beast came to see her, and always before saying good night asked her in his terrible voice:

"Beauty, will you marry me?"

And it seemed to Beauty, now she understood him better, that when she said, "No, Beast," he went away quite sad. But her happy dreams of the handsome young Prince soon made her forget the poor Beast, and the only thing that at all disturbed her was to be constantly told to distrust appearances, to let her heart guide her, and not her eyes, and many other equally perplexing things, which, consider as she would, she could not understand.

So everything went on for a long time, until at last, happy as she was, Beauty began to long for the sight of her father and her brothers and sisters; and one night, seeing her look very sad, the Beast asked her what was the matter. Beauty had quite ceased to be afraid of him. Now she knew that he was really gentle in spite of his ferocious looks and his dreadful voice. So she answered that she was longing to see her home once more. Upon hearing this the Beast seemed sadly distressed, and cried miserably.

"Ah! Beauty, have you the heart to desert an unhappy Beast like this? What more do you want to make you happy? Is it because you hate me that you want to escape?"

"No, dear Beast," answered Beauty softly, "I do not hate you, and I should be very sorry never to see you any more, but I long to see my father again. Only let me go for two months, and I promise to come back to you and stay for the rest of my life."

The Beast, who had been sighing dolefully while she spoke, now replied:

"I cannot refuse you anything you ask, even though it should cost me my life. Take the four boxes you will find in the room next to your own, and fill them with everything you wish to take with you. But remember your promise and come back when the two months are over, or you may have cause to repent it, for if you do not come in good time you will find your faithful Beast dead. You will not need any chariot to bring you back. Only say good-bye to all your brothers and sisters the night before you come away, and when you have gone to bed turn this ring round upon your finger and say firmly: 'I wish to go back to my palace and see my Beast again.' Good night, Beauty. Fear nothing, sleep peacefully, and before long you shall see your father once more."

As soon as Beauty was alone she hastened to fill the boxes with all the rare and precious things she saw about her, and only when she was tired of heaping things into them did they seem to be full.

Then she went to bed, but could hardly sleep for joy. And when at last she did begin to dream of her beloved Prince she was grieved to see him stretched upon a grassy bank sad and weary, and hardly like himself.

"What is the matter?" she cried.

But he looked at her reproachfully, and said:

"How can you ask me, cruel one? Are you not leaving me to my death perhaps?"

"Ah! don't be so sorrowful," cried Beauty; "I am only going to assure my father that I am safe and happy. I have promised the Beast faithfully that I will come back, and he would die of grief if I did not keep my word!"

"What would that matter to you?" said the Prince. "Surely you would not care?"

"Indeed I should be ungrateful if I did not care for such a kind

Beast," cried Beauty indignantly. "I would die to save him from pain. I assure you it is not his fault that he is so ugly."

Just then a strange sound woke her—someone was speaking not very far away; and opening her eyes she found herself in a room she had never seen before, which was certainly not nearly so splendid as those she was used to in the Beast's palace. Where could she be? She got up and dressed hastily, and then saw that the boxes she had packed the night before were all in the room. While she was wondering by what magic the Beast had transported them and herself to this strange place she suddenly heard her father's voice, and rushed out and greeted him joyfully. Her brothers and sisters were all astonished at her appearance, as they had never expected to see her again, and there was no end to the questions they asked her. She had also much to hear about what had happened to them while she was away, and of her father's journey home. But when they heard that she had only come to be with them for a short time, and then must go back to the Beast's palace forever, they lamented loudly. Then Beauty asked her father what he thought could be the meaning of her strange dreams, and why the Prince constantly begged her not to trust to appearances. After much consideration he answered: "You tell me yourself that the Beast, frightful as he is, loves you dearly, and deserves your love and gratitude for his gentleness and kindness; I think the Prince must mean you to understand that you ought to reward him by doing as he wishes you to, in spite of his ugliness."

Beauty could not help seeing that this seemed very probable; still, when she thought of her dear Prince who was so handsome, she did not feel at all inclined to marry the Beast. At any rate, for two months she need not decide, but could enjoy herself with her sisters. But though they were rich now, and lived in a town again, and had plenty of acquaintances, Beauty found that nothing amused her very much; and she often thought of the palace, where she was so happy, especially as at home she never once dreamed of her dear Prince, and she felt quite sad without him.

Then her sisters seemed to have got quite used to being without her, and even found her rather in the way, so she would not have been sorry when the two months were over but for her father and brothers, who begged her to stay, and seemed so grieved at the thought of her departure that she had not the courage to say good-bye to them. Every day when she got up she meant to say it at night, and when night came she put it off again, until at last she had a dismal dream which helped her to make up her mind. She thought she was wandering in a lonely path in the palace gardens, when she heard groans which seemed to come from some bushes hiding the entrance of a cave, and running quickly to see what could be the matter, she found the Beast stretched out upon his side, apparently dying. He reproached her faintly with being the cause of his distress, and at the same moment a stately lady appeared, and said very gravely:

"Ah! Beauty, you are only just in time to save his life. See what happens when people do not keep their promises! If you had delayed one day more, you would have found him dead."

Beauty was so terrified by this dream that the next morning she announced her intention of going back at once, and that very night she said good-bye to her father and all her brothers and sisters, and as soon as she was in bed she turned her ring round upon her finger, and said firmly:

"I wish to go back to my palace and see my Beast again," as she had been told to do.

Then she fell asleep instantly, and only woke up to hear the clock saying, "Beauty, Beauty," twelve times in its musical voice, which told her at once that she was really in the palace once more. Everything was just as before, and her birds were so glad to see her! but Beauty thought she had never known such a long day, for she was so anxious to see the Beast again that she felt as if suppertime would never come.

But when it did come and no Beast appeared she was really frightened; so, after listening and waiting for a long time, she ran down into the garden to search for him. Up and down the paths and avenues ran poor Beauty, calling him in vain, for no one answered, and not a trace of him could she find; until at last, quite tired, she stopped for a minute's rest, and saw that she was standing opposite the shady path she had seen in her dream. She rushed down it, and, sure enough, there was the cave, and in it lay the Beast—asleep, as Beauty thought. Quite glad to have found him, she ran up and stroked his head, but to her horror he did not move or open his eyes.

"Oh! he is dead; and it is all my fault," said Beauty, crying bitterly.

But then, looking at him again, she fancied he still breathed, and, hastily fetching some water from the nearest fountain, she sprinkled it over his face, and to her great delight he began to revive.

"Oh! Beast, how you frightened me!" she cried. "I never knew how much I loved you until just now, when I feared I was too late to save your life."

"Can you really love such an ugly creature as I am?" said the Beast faintly. "Ah! Beauty, you only came just in time. I was dying because I thought you had forgotten your promise. But go back now and rest; I shall see you again by and by."

Beauty, who had half expected that he would be angry with her, was reassured by his gentle voice, and went back to the palace, where supper was awaiting her; and afterward the Beast came in as usual, and talked about the time she had spent with her father, asking if she had enjoyed herself, and if they had all been very glad to see her.

Beauty answered politely, and quite enjoyed telling him all that had happened to her. And when at last the time came for him to go, and he asked, as he had so often asked before:

"Beauty, will you marry me?" she answered softly:

"Yes, dear Beast."

As she spoke a blaze of light sprang up before the windows of the palace; fireworks crackled and guns banged, and across the avenue of orange trees, in letters all made of fireflies, was written: LONG LIVE THE PRINCE AND HIS BRIDE.

Turning to ask the Beast what it could all mean, Beauty found that he had disappeared, and in his place stood her long-loved Prince! At the same moment the wheels of a chariot were heard upon the terrace, and two ladies entered the room. One of them Beauty recognized as the stately lady she had seen in her dreams; the other was also so grand and queenly that Beauty hardly knew which to greet first.

But the one she already knew said to her companion:

"Well, Queen, this is Beauty, who has had the courage to rescue your son from the terrible enchantment. They love one another, and only your consent to their marriage is wanting to make them perfectly happy."

"I consent with all my heart," cried the Queen. "How can I ever thank you enough, charming girl, for having restored my dear son to his natural form?"

And then she tenderly embraced Beauty and the Prince, who had meanwhile been greeting the Fairy and receiving her congratulations.

"Now," said the Fairy to Beauty, "I suppose you would like me to send for all your brothers and sisters to dance at your wedding?"

And so she did, and the marriage was celebrated the very next day with the utmost splendor, and Beauty and the Prince lived happily ever after.

3. PUSS IN BOOTS

(France)

THERE WAS A MILLER who left no more estate to the three sons he had than his mill, his ass, and his cat. The partition was soon made. Neither the scrivener nor attorney was sent for. They would soon have eaten up all the poor patrimony. The eldest had the mill, the second the ass, and the youngest nothing but the cat.

The poor young fellow was quite comfortless at having so poor a lot.

"My brothers," said he, "may get their living handsomely enough by joining their stocks together; but, for my part, when I have eaten up my cat, and made me a muff of his skin, I must die of hunger."

The Cat, who heard all this, but made as if he did not, said to him with a grave and serious air:

"Do not thus afflict yourself, my good master; you have nothing else to do but to give me a bag, and get a pair of boots made for me, that I may scamper through the dirt and the brambles, and you shall see that you have not so bad a portion of me as you imagine."

The Cat's master did not build very much upon what he said; he had, however, often seen him play a great many cunning tricks to catch rats and mice; as when he used to hang by the heels, or hide himself in the meal, and make as if he were dead; so that he did not altogether despair of his affording him some help in his miserable condition. When the Cat had what he asked for, he booted himself very gallantly, and, putting his bag about his neck, he held the strings of it in his two fore paws, and went into a warren where was great abundance of rabbits. He put bran and sow-thistle into his bag, and, stretching out at length, as if he had been dead, he waited for some young rabbits, not yet acquainted with the deceits of the world, to come and rummage his bag for what he had put into it.

Scarce was he lain down but he had what he wanted: a rash and foolish young rabbit jumped into his bag, and Monsieur Puss, immediately drawing close the strings, took and killed him without pity. Proud of his prey, he went with it to the palace, and asked to speak with his Majesty. He was shown upstairs into the King's apartment, and, making a low reverence, said to him:

"I have brought you, sir, a rabbit of the warren, which my noble Lord, the Master of Carabas" (for that was the title which Puss was pleased to give his master) "has commanded me to present to your Majesty from him."

"Tell thy master," said the King, "that I thank him, and that he does me a great deal of pleasure."

Another time he went and hid himself among some standing corn, holding still his bag open; and, when a brace of partridges ran into it, he drew the strings, and so caught them both. He went and made a present of these to the King, as he had done before of the rabbit which he took in the warren. The King, in like manner, received the partridges with great pleasure, and ordered him some money, to drink.

The Cat continued for two or three months thus to carry his Majesty, from time to time, game of his master's taking. One day in particular, when he knew for certain that he was to take the air along the riverside, with his daughter, the most beautiful princess in the world, he said to his master:

"If you will follow my advice your fortune is made. You have nothing else to do but go and wash yourself in the river, in that part I shall show you, and leave the rest to me."

The Marquis of Carabas did what the Cat advised him to, without knowing why or wherefore. While he was washing the King passed by, and the Cat began to cry out:

"Help! help! My Lord Marquis of Carabas is going to be drowned."

At this noise the King put his head out of the coach window, and, finding it was the Cat who had so often brought him such good game, he commanded his guards to run immediately to the assistance of his Lordship the Marquis of Carabas. While they were drawing the poor Marquis out of the river, the Cat came up to the coach and told the King that, while his master was washing, there came by some rogues, who went off with his clothes, though he had cried out: "Thieves! thieves!" several times, as loud as he could.

This cunning Cat had hidden them under a great stone. The King immediately commanded the officers of his wardrobe to run and fetch one of his best suits for the Lord Marquis of Carabas.

The King caressed him after a very extraordinary manner, and as the fine clothes he had given him extremely set off his good mien (for he was well made and very handsome in his person), the King's daughter took a secret inclination to him, and the Marquis of Carabas had no sooner cast two or three respectful and somewhat tender glances but she fell in love with him to distraction. The King would needs have him come into the coach and take part of the airing. The Cat, quite overjoyed to see his project begin to succeed, marched on before, and, meeting with some countrymen, who were mowing a meadow, he said to them:

"Good people, you who are mowing, if you do not tell the King that the meadow you mow belongs to my Lord Marquis of Carabas, you shall be chopped as small as herbs for the pot."

The King did not fail asking of the mowers to whom the meadow they were mowing belonged.

"To my Lord Marquis of Carabas," answered they altogether, for the Cat's threats had made them terribly afraid.

"You see, sir," said the Marquis, "this is a meadow which never fails to yield a plentiful harvest every year."

The Master Cat, who went still on before, met with some reapers, and said to them:

"Good people, you who are reaping, if you do not tell the King that all this corn belongs to the Marquis of Carabas, you shall be chopped as small as herbs for the pot."

The King, who passed by a moment after, would needs know to whom all that corn, which he then saw, did belong.

"To my Lord Marquis of Carabas," replied the reapers, and the King was very well pleased with it, as well as the Marquis, whom he congratulated thereupon. The Master Cat, who went always before, said the same words to all he met, and the King was astonished at the vast estates of my Lord Marquis of Carabas.

Monsieur Puss came at last to a stately castle, the master of which was an ogre, the richest had ever been known; for all the lands which the King had then gone over belonged to this castle. The Cat, who had taken care to inform himself who this ogre was and what he could do, asked to speak with him, saying he could not pass so near his castle without having the honor of paying his respects to him.

The ogre received him as civilly as an ogre could do, and made him sit down.

"I have been assured," said the Cat, "that you have the gift of being able to change yourself into all sorts of creatures you have a mind to;

you can, for example, transform yourself into a lion, or elephant, and the like."

"That is true," answered the ogre very briskly; "and to convince you, you shall see me now become a lion."

Puss was so sadly terrified at the sight of a lion so near him that he immediately got into the gutter, not without abundance of trouble and danger, because of his boots, which were of no use at all to him in walking upon the tiles. A little while after, when Puss saw that the ogre had resumed his natural form, he came down, and owned he had been very much frightened.

"I have been moreover informed," said the Cat, "but I know not how to believe it, that you have also the power to take on you the shape of the smallest animals; for example, to change yourself into a rat or a mouse; but I must own to you I take this to be impossible."

"Impossible!" cried the ogre; "you shall see that presently."

And at the same time he changed himself into a mouse, and began to run about the floor. Puss no sooner perceived this but he fell upon him and ate him up.

Meanwhile the King, who saw, as he passed, this fine castle of the ogre's, had a mind to go into it. Puss, who heard the noise of his Majesty's coach running over the drawbridge, ran out, and said to the King:

"Your Majesty is welcome to this castle of my Lord Marquis of Carabas."

"What! my Lord Marquis," cried the King, "and does this castle also belong to you? There can be nothing finer than this court and all the stately buildings which surround it; let us go into it, if you please."

The Marquis gave his hand to the Princess, and followed the King, who went first. They passed into a spacious hall, where they found a magnificent collation, which the ogre had prepared for his friends, who were that very day to visit him, but dared not to enter, knowing the King was there. His Majesty was perfectly charmed with the good qualities of my Lord Marquis of Carabas, as was his daughter, who had fallen violently in love with him, and, seeing the vast estate he possessed, said to him, after having drunk five or six glasses:

"It will be owing to yourself only, my Lord Marquis, if you are not my son-in-law."

The Marquis, making several low bows, accepted the honor which his Majesty conferred upon him, and forthwith, that very same day, married the Princess.

Puss became a great lord, and never ran after mice any more but only for his diversion.

4. BLUE BEARD

(*France*)

THERE WAS A MAN who had fine houses, both in town and country, a deal of silver and gold plate, embroidered furniture, and coaches gilded all over with gold. But this man was so unlucky as to have a blue beard, which made him so frightfully ugly that all the women and girls ran away from him.

One of his neighbors, a lady of quality, had two daughters who were perfect beauties. He desired of her one of them in marriage, leaving to her choice which of the two she would bestow on him. They would neither of them have him, and sent him backward and forward from one another, not being able to bear the thoughts of marrying a man who had a blue beard, and what besides gave them disgust and aversion was his having already been married to several wives, and nobody ever knew what became of them.

Blue Beard, to engage their affection, took them, with the lady their mother and three or four ladies of their acquaintance, with other young people of the neighborhood, to one of his country seats, where they stayed a whole week.

There was nothing then to be seen but parties of pleasure, hunting, fishing, dancing, mirth, and feasting. Nobody went to bed, but all passed the night in rallying and joking with each other. In short, everything succeeded so well that the youngest daughter began to think the master of the house not to have a beard so very blue, and that he was a mighty civil gentleman.

As soon as they returned home, the marriage was concluded. About a month afterward, Blue Beard told his wife that he was obliged to take a country journey for six weeks at least, about affairs of very great consequence, desiring her to divert herself in his absence, to send for her friends and acquaintances, to carry them into the country, if she pleased, and to make good cheer wherever she was.

"Here," said he, "are the keys of the two great wardrobes, wherein I have my best furniture; these are of my silver and gold plate, which is not every day in use; these open my strongboxes, which hold my money, both gold and silver; these my caskets of jewels; and this is the master-key to all my apartments. But for this little one here, it is the key of the closet at the end of the great gallery on the ground floor. Open them all; go into all and every one of them, except that little closet, which I forbid you, and forbid it in such a manner that, if you happen to open it, there's nothing but what you may expect from my just anger and resentment."

She promised to observe, very exactly, whatever he had ordered; then he, after having embraced her, got into his coach and proceeded on his journey.

Her neighbors and good friends did not stay to be sent for by the new married lady, so great was their impatience to see all the rich furniture of her house, not daring to come while her husband was there, because of his blue beard, which frightened them. They ran through all the rooms, closets, and wardrobes, which were all so fine and rich that they seemed to surpass one another.

After that they went up into the two great rooms, where were the best and richest furniture; they could not sufficiently admire the number and beauty of the tapestry, beds, couches, cabinets, stands, tables, and looking glasses, in which you might see yourself from head to foot; some of them were framed with glass, others with silver, plain and gilded, the finest and most magnificent ever were seen.

They ceased not to extol and envy the happiness of their friend, who in the meantime in no way diverted herself in looking upon all these rich things, because of the impatience she had to go and open the closet on the ground floor. She was so much pressed by her curiosity that, without considering that it was very uncivil to leave her company, she went down a little back staircase, and with such excessive haste that she had twice or thrice like to have broken her neck.

Being come to the closet door, she made a stop for some time, thinking upon her husband's orders, and considering what unhappiness might attend her if she was disobedient; but the temptation was so strong she could not overcome it. She then took the little key, and opened it, trembling, but could not at first see anything plainly, because the windows were shut. After some moments she began to perceive that the floor was all covered over with clotted blood, on which lay the bodies of several dead women, ranged against the walls. (These were all the

wives whom Blue Beard had married and murdered, one after another.)
She thought she should have died for fear, and the key, which she
pulled out of the lock, fell out of her hand.

After having somewhat recovered her surprise, she took up the key,
locked the door, and went upstairs into her chamber to recover herself;
but she could not, so much was she frightened. Having observed that
the key of the closet was stained with blood, she tried two or three
times to wipe it off, but the blood would not come out; in vain did she
wash it, and even rub it with soap and sand, the blood still remained,
for the key was magical and she could never make it quite clean; when
the blood was gone off from one side, it came again on the other.

Blue Beard returned from his journey the same evening, and said he
had received letters upon the road, informing him that the affair he
went about was ended to his advantage. His wife did all she could to
convince him she was extremely glad of his speedy return.

Next morning he asked her for the keys, which she gave him, but
with such a trembling hand that he easily guessed what had happened.

"What!" said he, "is not the key of my closet among the rest?"

"I must certainly," said she, "have left it above upon the table."

"Fail not," said Blue Beard, "to bring it me presently."

After several goings backward and forward she was forced to bring
him the key. Blue Beard, having very attentively considered it, said to
his wife,

"How comes this blood upon the key?"

"I do not know," cried the poor woman, paler than death.

"You do not know!" replied Blue Beard. "I very well know. You were
resolved to go into the closet, were you not? Mighty well, madam; you
shall go in, and take your place among the ladies you saw there."

Upon this she threw herself at her husband's feet, and begged his
pardon with all the signs of a true repentance, vowing that she would
never more be disobedient. She would have melted a rock, so beautiful
and sorrowful was she; but Blue Beard had a heart harder than any
rock!

"You must die, madam," said he, "and that presently."

"Since I must die," answered she (looking upon him with her eyes all
bathed in tears), "give me some little time to say my prayers."

"I give you," replied Blue Beard, "half a quarter of an hour, but not
one moment more."

When she was alone she called out to her sister, and said to her:

"Sister Anne" (for that was her name), "go up, I beg you, upon the
top of the tower, and look if my brothers are not coming; they prom-

ised me that they would come today, and if you see them, give them a sign to make haste."

Her sister Anne went up upon the top of the tower, and the poor afflicted wife cried out from time to time:

"Anne, sister Anne, do you see anyone coming?"

And sister Anne said:

"I see nothing but the sun, which makes a dust, and the grass, which looks green."

In the meanwhile Blue Beard, holding a great saber in his hand, cried out as loud as he could bawl to his wife:

"Come down instantly, or I shall come up to you."

"One moment longer, if you please," said his wife; and then she cried out very softly, "Anne, sister Anne, do you see anybody coming?"

And sister Anne answered:

"I see nothing but the sun, which makes a dust, and the grass, which is green."

"Come down quickly," cried Blue Beard, "or I will come up to you."

"I am coming," answered his wife; and then she cried, "Anne, sister Anne, do you not see anyone coming?"

"I see," replied sister Anne, "a great dust, which comes on this side here."

"Are they my brothers?"

"Alas! no, my dear sister, I see a flock of sheep."

"Will you not come down?" cried Blue Beard.

"One moment longer," said his wife, and then she cried out: "Anne, sister Anne, do you see nobody coming?"

"I see," said she, "two horsemen, but they are yet a great way off."

"God be praised," replied the poor wife joyfully: "they are my brothers; I will make them a sign, as well as I can, for them to make haste."

Then Blue Beard bawled out so loud that he made the whole house tremble. The distressed wife came down, and threw herself at his feet, all in tears, with her hair about her shoulders.

"This signifies nothing," says Blue Beard; "you must die"; then, taking hold of her hair with one hand, and lifting up the sword with the other, he was going to take off her head. The poor lady, turning about to him, and looking at him with dying eyes, desired him to afford her one little moment to recollect herself.

"No, no," said he, "recommend thyself to God," and was just ready to strike . . .

At this very instant there was such a loud knocking at the gate that

Blue Beard made a sudden stop. The gate was opened, and presently entered two horsemen, who, drawing their swords, ran directly to Blue Beard. He knew them to be his wife's brothers, one a dragoon, the other a musketeer; so that he ran away immediately to save himself; but the two brothers pursued so close that they overtook him before he could get to the steps of the porch, when they ran their swords through his body and left him dead. The poor wife was almost as dead as her husband, and had not strength enough to rise and welcome her brothers.

Blue Beard had no heirs, and so his wife became mistress of all his estate. She made use of one part of it to marry her sister Anne to a young gentleman who had loved her a long while; another part to buy captains' commissions for her brothers, and the rest to marry herself to a very worthy gentleman, who made her forget the ill time she had passed with Blue Beard.

5. THE WHITE CAT
(France)

ONCE UPON A TIME there was a king who had three sons, who were all so clever and brave that he began to be afraid that they would want to reign over the kingdom before he was dead. Now the King, though he felt that he was growing old, did not at all wish to give up the government of his kingdom while he could still manage it very well, so he thought the best way to live in peace would be to divert the minds of his sons by promises which he could always get out of when the time came for keeping them.

So he sent for them all, and, after speaking to them kindly, he added: "You will quite agree with me, my dear children, that my great age makes it impossible for me to look after my affairs of state as carefully as I once did. I begin to fear that this may affect the welfare of my subjects, therefore I wish that one of you should succeed to my crown; but in return for such a gift as this it is only right that you should do something for me. Now, as I think of retiring into the country, it seems to me that a pretty, lively, faithful little dog would be very good company for me; so, without any regard for your ages, I promise that the one who brings me the most beautiful little dog shall succeed me at once."

The three Princes were greatly surprised by their father's sudden fancy for a little dog, but as it gave the two younger ones a chance they would not otherwise have had of being king, and as the eldest was too polite to make any objection, they accepted the commission with pleasure. They bade farewell to the King, who gave them presents of silver and precious stones, and appointed to meet them at the same hour, in the same place, after a year had passed, to see the little dogs they had brought for him.

Then they went together to a castle which was about a league from the city, accompanied by all their particular friends, to whom they gave a grand banquet, and the three brothers promised to be friends always, to share whatever good fortune befell them, and not to be parted by any envy or jealousy; and so they set out, agreeing to meet at the same castle at the appointed time, to present themselves before the King together. Each one took a different road, and the two eldest met with many adventures; but it is about the youngest that you are going to hear. He was young, and gay, and handsome, and knew everything that a prince ought to know; and as for his courage, there was simply no end to it.

Hardly a day passed without his buying several dogs—big and little, greyhounds, mastiffs, spaniels, and lapdogs. As soon as he had bought a pretty one he was sure to see a still prettier, and then he had to get rid of all the others and buy that one, as, being alone, he found it impossible to take thirty or forty thousand dogs about with him. He journeyed from day to day, not knowing where he was going, until at last, just at nightfall, he reached a great, gloomy forest. He did not know his way, and, to make matters worse, it began to thunder, and the rain poured down. He took the first path he could find, and after walking for a long time he fancied he saw a faint light, and began to hope that he was coming to some cottage where he might find shelter for the night. At length, guided by the light, he reached the door of the most splendid castle he could have imagined. This door was of gold covered with carbuncles, and it was the pure red light which shone from them that had shown him the way through the forest. The walls were of the finest porcelain in all the most delicate colors, and the Prince saw that all the stories he had ever read were pictured upon them; but as he was quite terribly wet, and the rain still fell in torrents, he could not stay to look about any more, but came back to the golden door. There he saw a deer's foot hanging by a chain of diamonds, and he began to wonder who could live in this magnificent castle.

"They must feel very secure against robbers," he said to himself. "What is to hinder anyone from cutting off that chain and digging out those carbuncles, and making himself rich for life?"

He pulled the deer's foot, and immediately a silver bell sounded and the door flew open, but the Prince could see nothing but numbers of hands in the air, each holding a torch. He was so much surprised that he stood quite still, until he felt himself pushed forward by other hands, so that, though he was somewhat uneasy, he could not help going on. With his hand on his sword, to be prepared for whatever might happen, he entered a hall paved with lapis-lazuli, while two lovely voices sang:

> "The hands you see floating above
> Will swiftly your bidding obey;
> If your heart dreads not conquering Love,
> In this place you may fearlessly stay."

The Prince could not believe that any danger threatened him when he was welcomed in this way, so, guided by the mysterious hands, he went toward a door of coral, which opened of its own accord, and he found himself in a vast hall of mother-of-pearl, out of which opened a number of other rooms, glittering with thousands of lights, and full of such beautiful pictures and precious things that the Prince felt quite bewildered. After passing through sixty rooms the hands that conducted him stopped, and the Prince saw a most comfortable-looking armchair drawn up close to the chimney corner; at the same moment the fire lighted itself, and the pretty, soft, clever hands took off the Prince's wet, muddy clothes, and presented him with fresh ones made of the richest stuffs, all embroidered with gold and emeralds. He could not help admiring everything he saw, and the deft way in which the hands waited on him, though they sometimes appeared so suddenly that they made him jump.

When he was quite ready—and I can assure you that he looked very different from the wet and weary Prince who had stood outside in the rain, and pulled the deer's foot—the hands led him to a splendid room, upon the walls of which were painted the histories of Puss in Boots and a number of other famous cats. The table was laid for supper with two golden plates, and golden spoons and forks, and the sideboard was covered with dishes and glasses of crystal set with precious stones. The Prince was wondering who the second place could be for, when suddenly in came about a dozen cats carrying guitars and rolls of music, who took their places at one end of the room, and under the direction of a cat who beat time with a roll of paper began to mew in every imaginable key, and to draw their claws across the strings of the guitars, making the strangest kind of music that could be heard. The Prince hastily stopped up his ears, but even then the sight of these comical musicians sent him into fits of laughter.

"What funny thing shall I see next?" he said to himself, and instantly the door opened, and in came a tiny figure covered by a long black veil. It was conducted by two cats wearing black mantles and carrying swords, and a large party of cats followed, who brought in cages full of rats and mice.

The Prince was so much astonished that he thought he must be dreaming, but the little figure came up to him and threw back its veil, and he saw that it was the loveliest little white cat it is possible to imagine. She looked very young and very sad, and in a sweet little voice that went straight to his heart she said to the Prince:

"King's son, you are welcome; the Queen of the Cats is glad to see you."

"Lady Cat," replied the Prince, "I thank you for receiving me so kindly, but surely you are no ordinary pussycat? Indeed, the way you speak and the magnificence of your castle prove it plainly."

"King's son," said the White Cat, "I beg you to spare me these compliments, for I am not used to them. But now," she added, "let supper be served, and let the musicians be silent, as the Prince does not understand what they are saying."

So the mysterious hands began to bring in the supper, and first they put on the table two dishes, one containing stewed pigeons and the other a fricassee of fat mice. The sight of the latter made the Prince feel as if he could not enjoy his supper at all; but the White Cat seeing this assured him that the dishes intended for him were prepared in a separate kitchen, and he might be quite certain that they contained neither rats nor mice; and the Prince felt so sure that she would not deceive him that he had no more hesitation in beginning. Presently he noticed that on the little paw that was next him the White Cat wore a bracelet containing a portrait, and he begged to be allowed to look at it. To his great surprise he found it represented an extremely handsome young man, who was so like himself that it might have been his own portrait! The White Cat sighed as he looked at it, and seemed sadder than ever, and the Prince dared not ask any questions for fear of displeasing her; so he began to talk about other things, and found that she was interested in all the subjects he cared for himself, and seemed to know quite well what was going on in the world. After supper they went into another room, which was fitted up as a theater, and the cats acted and danced for their amusement, and then the White Cat said good night to him, and the hands conducted him into a room he had not seen before, hung with tapestry worked with butterflies' wings of every color; there were mirrors that reached from the ceiling to the floor, and a little white bed with curtains of gauze tied up with ribbons. The Prince went to bed in silence, as he did not quite know how to begin a conversation with the hands that waited on him, and in the morning he was awakened by a noise and confusion outside his window, and the hands came and quickly dressed him in hunting costume. When he looked out all the cats were assembled in the courtyard, some leading greyhounds, some blowing horns, for the White Cat was going out hunting. The hands led a wooden horse up to the Prince, and seemed to expect him to mount it, at which he was very indignant; but it was no use for him to object, for he speedily found himself upon its back, and it pranced gaily off with him.

The White Cat herself was riding a monkey, which climbed even up to the eagles' nests when she had a fancy for the young eaglets. Never was there a pleasanter hunting party, and when they returned to the castle the Prince and the White Cat supped together as before, but when they had finished she offered him a crystal goblet, which must have contained a magic draught, for, as soon as he had swallowed its contents, he forgot everything, even the little dog that he was seeking for the King, and only thought how happy he was to be with the White Cat! And so the days passed, in every kind of amusement, until the year was nearly gone. The Prince had forgotten all about meeting his brothers: he did not even know what country he belonged to; but the White Cat knew when he ought to go back, and one day she said to him:

"Do you know that you have only three days left to look for the little dog for your father, and your brothers have found lovely ones?"

Then the Prince suddenly recovered his memory, and cried:

"What can have made me forget such an important thing? My whole fortune depends upon it; and even if I could in such a short time find a dog pretty enough to gain me a kingdom, where should I find a horse who could carry me all that way in three days?" And he began to be very vexed. But the White Cat said to him: "King's son, do not trouble yourself; I am your friend, and will make everything easy for you. You can still stay here for a day, as the good wooden horse can take you to your country in twelve hours."

"I thank you, beautiful Cat," said the Prince; "but what good will it do me to get back if I have not a dog to take to my father?"

"See here," answered the White Cat, holding up an acorn; "there is a prettier one in this than in the Dog-star!"

"Oh! White Cat dear," said the Prince, "how unkind you are to laugh at me now!"

"Only listen," she said, holding the acorn to his ear.

And inside it he distinctly heard a tiny voice say: "Bow-wow!"

The Prince was delighted, for a dog that can be shut up in an acorn must be very small indeed. He wanted to take it out and look at it, but the White Cat said it would be better not to open the acorn till he was before the King, in case the tiny dog should be cold on the journey. He thanked her a thousand times, and said good-bye quite sadly when the time came for him to set out.

"The days have passed so quickly with you," he said, "I only wish I could take you with me now."

But the White Cat shook her head and sighed deeply in answer.

After all the Prince was the first to arrive at the castle where he had agreed to meet his brothers, but they came soon after, and stared in amazement when they saw the wooden horse in the courtyard jumping like a hunter.

The Prince met them joyfully, and they began to tell him all their adventures; but he managed to hide from them what he had been doing, and even led them to think that a turnspit dog which he had with him was the one he was bringing for the King. Fond as they all were of one another, the two eldest could not help being glad to think that their dogs certainly had a better chance. The next morning they started in the same chariot. The elder brothers carried in baskets two such tiny, fragile dogs that they hardly dared to touch them. As for the turnspit, he ran after the chariot, and got so covered with mud that one could hardly see what he was like at all. When they reached the palace everyone crowded round to welcome them as they went into the King's great hall; and when the two brothers presented their little dogs nobody could decide which was the prettier. They were already arranging between themselves to share the kingdom equally, when the youngest stepped forward, drawing from his pocket the acorn the White Cat had given him. He opened it quickly, and there upon a white cushion they saw a dog so small that it could easily have been put through a ring. The Prince laid it upon the ground, and it got up at once and began to dance. The King did not know what to say, for it was impossible that anything could be prettier than this little creature. Nevertheless, as he was in no hurry to part with his crown, he told his sons that, as they had been so successful the first time, he would ask them to go once again, and seek by land and sea for a piece of muslin so fine that it could be drawn through the eye of a needle. The brothers were not very willing to set out again, but the two eldest consented because it gave them another chance, and they started as before. The youngest again mounted the wooden horse, and rode back at full speed to his beloved White Cat. Every door of the castle stood wide open, and every window and turret was illuminated, so it looked more wonderful than before. The hands hastened to meet him, and led the wooden horse off to the stable, while he hurried in to find the White Cat. She was asleep in a little basket on a white satin cushion, but she very soon started up when she heard the Prince, and was overjoyed at seeing him once more.

"How could I hope that you would come back to me, King's son?" she said. And then he stroked and petted her, and told her of his successful journey, and how he had come back to ask her help, as he believed that it was impossible to find what the King demanded. The White Cat looked serious, and said she must think what was to be done, but that, luckily, there were some cats in the castle who could spin very well, and if anybody could manage it they could, and she would set them the task herself.

And then the hands appeared carrying torches, and conducted the Prince and the White Cat to a long gallery which overlooked the river, from the windows of which they saw a magnificent display of fireworks of all sorts; after which they had supper, which the Prince liked even better than the fireworks, for it was very late, and he was hungry after his long ride. And so the days passed quickly as before; it was impossible to feel dull with the White Cat, and she had quite a talent for inventing new amusements—indeed, she was cleverer than a cat has any right to be. But when the Prince asked her how it was that she was so wise, she only said:

"King's son, do not ask me; guess what you please. I may not tell you anything."

The Prince was so happy that he did not trouble himself at all about the time, but presently the White Cat told him that the year was gone, and that he need not be at all anxious about the piece of muslin, as they had made it very well.

"This time," she added, "I can give you a suitable escort"; and on looking out into the courtyard the Prince saw a superb chariot of burnished gold, enameled in flame color with a thousand different devices. It was drawn by twelve snow-white horses, harnessed four abreast; their trappings were of flame-colored velvet, embroidered with diamonds. A hundred chariots followed, each drawn by eight horses, and filled with officers in splendid uniforms, and a thousand guards surrounded the procession. "Go!" said the White Cat, "and when you appear before the King in such state he surely will not refuse you the crown which you deserve. Take this walnut, but do not open it until you are before him, then you will find in it the piece of stuff you asked me for."

"Lovely Blanchette," said the Prince, "how can I thank you properly for all your kindness to me? Only tell me that you wish it, and I will give up forever all thought of being king, and will stay here with you always."

"King's son," she replied, "it shows the goodness of your heart that you should care so much for a little white cat, who is good for nothing but to catch mice; but you must not stay."

So the Prince kissed her little paw and set out. You can imagine how fast he traveled when I tell you that they reached the King's palace in just half the time it had taken the wooden horse to get there. This time the Prince was so late that he did not try to meet his brothers at their castle, so they thought he could not be coming, and were rather glad of it, and displayed their pieces of muslin to the King proudly, feeling sure of success. And indeed the stuff was very fine, and would go through the eye of a very large needle; but the King, who was only too glad to make a difficulty, sent for a particular needle, which was kept among the Crown jewels, and had such a small eye that everybody saw at once that it was impossible that the muslin should pass through it. The Princes were angry, and were beginning to complain that it was a trick, when suddenly the trumpets sounded and the youngest Prince came in. His father and brothers were quite astonished at his magnificence, and after he had greeted them he took the walnut from his pocket and opened it, fully expecting to find the piece of muslin, but instead there was only a hazel nut. He cracked it, and there lay a cherry stone. Everybody was looking on, and the King was chuckling to himself at the idea of finding the piece of muslin in a nutshell.

However, the Prince cracked the cherry stone, but everyone laughed when he saw it contained only its own kernel. He opened that and found a grain of wheat, and in that was a millet seed. Then he himself began to wonder, and muttered softly:

"White Cat, White Cat, are you making fun of me?"

In an instant he felt a cat's claw give his hand quite a sharp scratch, and hoping that it was meant as an encouragement he opened the millet seed, and drew out of it a piece of muslin four hundred ells long, woven with the loveliest colors and most wonderful patterns; and when the needle was brought it went through the eye six times with the greatest ease! The King turned pale, and the other Princes stood silent and sorrowful, for nobody could deny that this was the most marvelous piece of muslin that was to be found in the world.

Presently the King turned to his sons, and said, with a deep sigh:

"Nothing could console me more in my old age than to realize your willingness to gratify my wishes. Go then once more, and whoever at the end of a year can bring back the loveliest princess shall be married to her, and shall, without further delay, receive the crown, for my successor must certainly be married." The Prince considered that he had earned the kingdom fairly twice over, but still he was too well bred to argue about it, so he just went back to his gorgeous chariot, and, surrounded by his escort, returned to the White Cat faster than he had come. This time she was expecting him, the path was strewn with flowers, and a thousand braziers were burning scented woods which perfumed the air. Seated in a gallery from which she could see his arrival, the White Cat waited for him. "Well, King's son," she said, "here you are once more, without a crown." "Madam," said he, "thanks to your generosity I have earned one twice over; but the fact is that my father is so loath to part with it that it would be no pleasure to me to take it."

"Never mind," she answered; "it's just as well to try and deserve it. As you must take back a lovely princess with you next time I will be on the lookout for one for you. In the meantime let us enjoy ourselves; to-night I have ordered a battle between my cats and the river rats, on purpose to amuse you." So this year slipped away even more pleasantly than the preceding ones. Sometimes the Prince could not help asking the White Cat how it was she could talk.

"Perhaps you are a fairy," he said. "Or has some enchanter changed you into a cat?"

But she only gave him answers that told him nothing. Days go by so quickly when one is very happy that it is certain the Prince would never have thought of its being time to go back, when one evening as they sat together the White Cat said to him that if he wanted to take a lovely princess home with him the next day he must be prepared to do as she told him.

"Take this sword," she said, "and cut off my head!"

"I!" cried the Prince, "I cut off your head! Blanchette darling, how could I do it?"

"I entreat you to do as I tell you, King's son," she replied.

The tears came into the Prince's eyes as he begged her to ask him anything but that—to set him any task she pleased as a proof of his devotion, but to spare him the grief of killing his dear Pussy. But nothing he could say altered her determination, and at last he drew his sword, and desperately, with a trembling hand, cut off the little white head. But imagine his astonishment and delight when suddenly a lovely princess stood before him, and, while he was still speechless with amazement, the door opened and a goodly company of knights and ladies entered, each carrying a cat's skin! They hastened with every sign of joy to the Princess, kissing her hand and congratulating her on being once more restored to her natural shape. She received them graciously, but after a few minutes begged that they would leave her alone with the Prince, to whom she said:

"You see, Prince, that you were right in supposing me to be no ordinary cat. My father reigned over six kingdoms. The Queen, my mother, whom he loved dearly, had a passion for traveling and exploring, and when I was only a few weeks old she obtained his permission to visit a certain mountain of which she had heard many marvelous tales, and set out, taking with her a number of her attendants. On the way they had to pass near an old castle belonging to the fairies. Nobody had ever been into it, but it was reported to be full of the most wonderful things, and my mother remembered to have heard that the fairies had in their garden such fruits as were to be seen and tasted nowhere else. She began to wish to try them for herself, and turned her steps in the direction of the garden. On arriving at the door, which blazed with gold and jewels, she ordered her servants to knock loudly, but it was useless; it seemed as if all the inhabitants of the castle must be asleep or dead. Now the more difficult it became to obtain the fruit, the more the Queen was determined that have it she would. So she ordered that they should bring ladders, and get over the wall into the garden; but though the wall did not look very high, and they tied the ladders together to make them very long, it was quite impossible to get to the top.

"The Queen was in despair, but as night was coming on she ordered that they should encamp just where they were, and went to bed herself, feeling quite ill, she was so disappointed. In the middle of the night she was suddenly awakened, and saw to her surprise a tiny, ugly old woman seated by her bedside, who said to her:

"'I must say that we consider it somewhat troublesome of your Majesty to insist upon tasting our fruit; but, to save you any annoyance, my sisters and I will consent to give you as much as you can carry away, on one condition—that is, that you shall give us your little daughter to bring up as our own.'

"'Ah! my dear madam,' cried the Queen, 'is there nothing else that you will take for the fruit? I will give you my kingdoms willingly.'

"'No,' replied the old fairy, 'we will have nothing but your little daughter. She shall be as happy as the day is long, and we will give her everything that is worth having in fairyland, but you must not see her again until she is married.'

"'Though it is a hard condition,' said the Queen, 'I consent, for I shall certainly die if I do not taste the fruit, and so I should lose my little daughter either way.'

"So the old fairy led her into the castle, and, though it was still the middle of the night, the Queen could see plainly that it was far more beautiful than she had been told, ("which you can easily believe, Prince," said the White Cat, "when I tell you that it was this castle that we are now in.") 'Will you gather the fruit yourself, Queen?' said the old fairy, 'or shall I call it to come to you?'

"'I beg you to let me see it come when it is called,' cried the Queen; 'that will be something quite new.' The old fairy whistled twice, then she cried:

"'Apricots, peaches, nectarines, cherries, plums, pears, melons, grapes, apples, oranges, lemons, gooseberries, strawberries, raspberries, come!'

"And in an instant they came tumbling in, one over another, and yet they were neither dusty nor spoiled, and the Queen found them quite as good as she had fancied them. You see they grew upon fairy trees.

"The old fairy gave her golden baskets in which to take the fruit away, and it was as much as four hundred mules could carry. Then she reminded the Queen of her agreement, and led her back to the camp, and next morning she went back to her kingdom; but before she had gone very far she began to repent of her bargain, and when the King came out to meet her she looked so sad that he guessed that something had happened, and asked what was the matter. At first the Queen was afraid to tell him, but when, as soon as they reached the palace, five frightful little dwarfs were sent by the fairies to fetch me, she was obliged to confess what she had promised. The King was very angry, and had the Queen and myself shut up in a great tower and safely guarded, and drove the little dwarfs out of his kingdom; but the fairies sent a great dragon who ate up all the people he met, and whose breath burned up everything as he passed through the country; and at last, after trying in vain to rid himself of the monster, the King, to save his subjects, was obliged to consent that I should be given up to the fairies. This time they came themselves to fetch me, in a chariot of pearl drawn by seahorses, followed by the dragon, who was led with chains of diamonds. My cradle was placed between the old fairies, who loaded me with caresses, and away we whirled through the air to a tower which they had built on purpose for me. There I grew up surrounded with everything that was beautiful and rare, and learning everything that is ever taught to a princess, but without any companions but a parrot and a little dog, who could both talk; and receiving every day a visit from one of the old fairies, who came mounted upon the dragon. One day, however, as I sat at my window I saw a handsome young prince, who seemed to have been hunting in the forest which surrounded my prison, and who was standing and looking up at me. When he saw that I observed him he saluted me with great deference. You can imagine that I was delighted to have someone new to talk to, and in spite of the height of my window our conversation was prolonged till night fell, then my prince reluctantly bade me farewell. But after that he came again many times, and at last I consented to marry him, but the question was how I was to escape from my tower. The fairies always supplied me with flax for my spinning, and by great diligence I made enough cord for a ladder that would reach to the foot of the tower; but, alas! just as my prince was helping me to descend it, the crossest and ugliest of the old fairies flew in. Before he had time to defend himself my unhappy lover was swallowed up by the dragon. As for me, the fairies, furious at having their plans defeated, for they intended me to marry the king of the dwarfs and I utterly refused, changed me into a white cat. When they brought me here I found all the lords and ladies of my father's court awaiting me under the same enchantment, while the people of lesser rank had been made invisible, all but their hands.

"As they laid me under the enchantment the fairies told me all my history, for until then I had quite believed that I was their child, and warned me that my only chance of regaining my natural form was to win the love of a prince who resembled in every way my unfortunate lover."

"And you have won it, lovely Princess," interrupted the Prince.

"You are indeed wonderfully like him," resumed the Princess—"in voice, in features, and everything; and if you really love me all my troubles will be at an end."

"And mine too," cried the Prince, throwing himself at her feet, "if you will consent to marry me."

"I love you already better than anyone in the world," she said; "but now it is time to go back to your father, and we shall hear what he says about it."

So the Prince gave her his hand and led her out, and they mounted the chariot together; it was even more splendid than before, and so was the whole company. Even the horses' shoes were of rubies with diamond nails, and I suppose that is the first time such a thing was ever seen.

As the Princess was as kind and clever as she was beautiful, you may imagine what a delightful journey the Prince found it, for everything the Princess said seemed to him quite charming.

When they came near the castle where the brothers were to meet, the Princess got into a chair carried by four of the guards; it was hewn out of one splendid crystal, and had silken curtains, which she drew around her that she might not be seen.

The Prince saw his brothers walking upon the terrace, each with a lovely princess, and they came to meet him, asking if he had also found a wife. He said that he had found something much rarer—a little white cat! At which they laughed very much, and asked him if he was afraid of being eaten up by mice in the palace. And then they set out together for the town. Each prince and princess rode in a splendid carriage; the horses were decked with plumes of feathers, and glittered with gold. After them came the youngest prince, and last of all the crystal chair, at which everybody looked with admiration and curiosity. When the courtiers saw them coming they hastened to tell the King.

"Are the ladies beautiful?" he asked anxiously.

And when they answered that nobody had ever before seen such lovely princesses he seemed quite annoyed.

However, he received them graciously, but found it impossible to choose between them.

Then turning to his youngest son he said:

"Have you come back alone, after all?"

"Your Majesty," replied the Prince, "will find in that crystal chair a little white cat, which has such soft paws, and mews so prettily, that I am sure you will be charmed with it."

The King smiled, and went to draw back the curtains himself, but at a touch from the Princess the crystal shivered into a thousand splinters, and there she stood in all her beauty; her fair hair floated over her shoulders and was crowned with flowers, and her softly falling robe was of the purest white. She saluted the King gracefully, while a murmur of admiration rose from all around.

"Sire," she said, "I am not come to deprive you of the throne you fill so worthily. I have already six kingdoms, permit me to bestow one upon you, and upon each of your sons. I ask nothing but your friendship, and your consent to my marriage with your youngest son; we shall still have three kingdoms left for ourselves."

The King and all the courtiers could not conceal their joy and astonishment, and the marriages of the three Princes were celebrated at once. The festivities lasted several months, and then each king and queen departed to their own kingdom and lived happily ever after.

6. DRAKESTAIL
(France)

DRAKESTAIL WAS VERY LITTLE, that is why he was called Drakestail; but tiny as he was he had brains, and he knew what he was about, for having begun with nothing he ended by amassing a hundred crowns. Now the King of the country, who was very extravagant and never kept any money, having heard that Drakestail had some, went one day in his own person to borrow his hoard, and, my word, in those days Drakestail was not a little proud of having lent money to the King. But after the first and second year, seeing that they never even dreamed of paying the interest, he became uneasy, so much so that at last he resolved to go and see His Majesty himself, and get repaid. So one fine morning

Drakestail, very spruce and fresh, takes the road, singing: "Quack, quack, quack, when shall I get my money back?"

He had not gone far when he met friend Fox, on his rounds that way.

"Good morning, neighbor," says the friend, "where are you off to so early?"

"I am going to the King for what he owes me."

"Oh! take me with thee!"

Drakestail said to himself: "One can't have too many friends." . . . "I will," says he, "but going on all-fours you will soon be tired. Make yourself quite small, get into my throat—go into my gizzard and I will carry you."

"Happy thought!" says friend Fox.

He takes bag and baggage, and, presto! is gone like a letter into the post.

And Drakestail is off again, all spruce and fresh, still singing: "Quack, quack, quack, when shall I have my money back?"

He had not gone far when he met his lady friend Ladder, leaning on her wall.

"Good morning, my duckling," says the lady friend, "whither away so bold?"

"I am going to the King for what he owes me."

"Oh! take me with thee!"

Drakestail said to himself: "One can't have too many friends." . . . "I will," says he, "but with your wooden legs you will soon be tired. Make yourself quite small, get into my throat—go into my gizzard and I will carry you."

"Happy thought!" says my friend Ladder, and nimble, bag and baggage, goes to keep company with friend Fox.

And "Quack, quack, quack." Drakestail is off again, singing and spruce as before. A little farther he meets his sweetheart, my friend River, wandering quietly in the sunshine.

"Thou, my cherub," says she, "whither so lonesome, with arching tail, on this muddy road?"

"I am going to the King, you know, for what he owes me."

"Oh! take me with thee!"

Drakestail said to himself: "We can't be too many friends." . . . "I will," says he, "but you who sleep while you walk will soon be tired. Make yourself quite small, get into my throat—go into my gizzard and I will carry you."

"Ah! happy thought!" says my friend River.

She takes bag and baggage, and glug, glug, glug, she takes her place between friend Fox and my friend Ladder.

And "Quack, quack, quack." Drakestail is off again singing.

A little farther on he meets comrade Wasp's-nest, maneuvering his wasps.

"Well, good morning, friend Drakestail," said comrade Wasp's-nest, "where are we bound for so spruce and fresh?"

"I am going to the King for what he owes me."

"Oh! take me with thee!"

Drakestail said to himself, "One can't have too many friends." . . . "I will," says he, "but with your battalion to drag along, you will soon be tired. Make yourself quite small, go into my throat—get into my gizzard and I will carry you."

"By Jove! that's a good idea!" says comrade Wasp's-nest.

And left file! he takes the same road to join the others with all his party. There was not much more room, but by closing up a bit they managed. . . . And Drakestail is off again singing.

He arrived thus at the capital, and threaded his way straight up the High Street, still running and singing "Quack, quack, quack, when shall I get my money back?" to the great astonishment of the good folks, till he came to the King's palace.

He strikes with the knocker: "Toc! toc!"

"Who is there?" asks the porter, putting his head out of the wicket.

" 'Tis I, Drakestail. I wish to speak to the King."

"Speak to the King! . . . That's easily said. The King is dining, and will not be disturbed."

"Tell him that it is I, and I have come he well knows why."

The porter shuts his wicket and goes up to say it to the King, who was just sitting down to dinner with a napkin round his neck, and all his ministers.

"Good, good!" said the King laughing. "I know what it is! Make him come in, and put him with the turkeys and chickens."

The porter descends.

"Have the goodness to enter."

"Good!" says Drakestail to himself, "I shall now see how they eat at court."

"This way, this way," says the porter. "One step further. . . . There, there you are."

"How? what? in the poultry yard?"

Imagine how angry Drakestail was!

"Ah! so that's it," says he. "Wait! I will compel you to receive me. Quack, quack, quack, when shall I get my money back?" But turkeys and chickens are creatures who don't like people that are not as themselves. When they saw the newcomer and how he was made, and when they heard him crying too, they began to look black at him.

"What is it? what does he want?"

Finally they rushed at him all together, to overwhelm him with pecks.

"I am lost!" said Drakestail to himself, when by good luck he remembers his comrade friend Fox, and he cries:

> "Reynard, Reynard, come out of your earth,
> Or Drakestail's life is of little worth."

Then friend Fox, who was only waiting for these words, hastens out, throws himself on the wicked fowls, and quick! quack! he tears them to pieces; so much so that at the end of five minutes there was not one left alive. And Drakestail, quite content, began to sing again, "Quack, quack, quack, when shall I get my money back?"

When the King who was still at table heard this refrain, and the poultry woman came to tell him what had been going on in the yard, he was terribly annoyed.

He ordered them to throw this tail of a drake into the well, to make an end of him.

And it was done as he commanded. Drakestail was in despair of getting himself out of such a deep hole, when he remembered his lady friend, the Ladder.

> "Ladder, Ladder, come out of thy hold,
> Or Drakestail's days will soon be told."

My friend Ladder, who was only waiting for these words, hastens out, leans her two arms on the edge of the well, then Drakestail climbs nimbly on her back, and hop! he is in the yard, where he begins to sing louder than ever.

When the King, who was still at table and laughing at the good trick he had played his creditor, heard him again reclaiming his money, he became livid with rage.

He commanded that the furnace should be heated, and this tail of a drake thrown into it, because he must be a sorcerer.

The furnace was soon hot, but this time Drakestail was not so afraid; he counted on his sweetheart, my friend River.

> "River, River, outward flow,
>   Or to death Drakestail must go."

My friend River hastens out, and errouf! throws herself into the furnace, which she floods, with all the people who had lighted it; after which she flowed growling into the hall of the palace to the height of more than four feet.

And Drakestail, quite content, begins to swim, singing deafeningly, "Quack, quack, quack, when shall I get my money back?"

The King was still at table, and thought himself quite sure of his game; but when he heard Drakestail singing again, and when they told him all that had passed, he became furious and got up from table brandishing his fists.

"Bring him here, and I'll cut his throat! bring him here quick!" cried he.

And quickly two footmen ran to fetch Drakestail.

"At last," said the poor chap, going up the great stairs, "they have decided to receive me."

Imagine his terror when on entering he sees the King as red as a turkey cock, and all his ministers attending him standing sword in hand. He thought this time it was all up with him. Happily, he remembered that there was still one remaining friend, and he cried with dying accents:

> "Wasp's-nest, Wasp's-nest, make a sally,
>   Or Drakestail nevermore may rally."

Hereupon the scene changes.

"Bzz, bzz, bayonet them!" The brave Wasp's-nest rushes out with all his wasps. They threw themselves on the infuriated King and his ministers, and stung them so fiercely in the face that they lost their heads, and not knowing where to hide themselves they all jumped pell-mell from the window and broke their necks on the pavement.

Behold Drakestail much astonished, all alone in the big saloon and master of the field. He could not get over it.

Nevertheless, he remembered shortly what he had come for to the palace, and improving the occasion, he set to work to hunt for his dear money. But in vain he rummaged in all the drawers; he found nothing; all had been spent.

And ferreting thus from room to room he came at last to the one with the throne in it, and feeling fatigued, he sat himself down on it to think over his adventure. In the meanwhile the people had found their King and his ministers with their feet in the air on the pavement, and they had gone into the palace to know how it had occurred. On entering the throne-room, when the crowd saw that there was already someone on the royal seat, they broke out in cries of surprise and joy:

"The King is dead, long live the King!
Heaven has sent us down this thing."

Drakestail, who was no longer surprised at anything, received the acclamations of the people as if he had never done anything else all his life.

A few of them certainly murmured that a Drakestail would make a fine King; those who knew him replied that a knowing Drakestail was a more worthy King than a spendthrift like him who was lying on the pavement. In short, they ran and took the crown off the head of the deceased, and placed it on that of Drakestail, whom it fitted like wax.

Thus he became King.

"And now," said he after the ceremony, "ladies and gentlemen, let's go to supper. I am so hungry!"

7. THE DOCTOR AND HIS PUPIL
(France)

THERE WAS ONCE a poor man who had a twelve-year-old son. He sent him to find work.

The boy departed wearing a jacket that was red in front and white behind. He passed in front of a castle; it was the residence of a doctor, who happened to be standing at the window. As he needed a servant, the master of the castle called the boy.

"What are you looking for in these parts?"

"Since I'd like to make a living, I'm looking for work."

"Do you know how to read?"

"Yes, for I've been to school for six months."

"Then you won't do."

The boy went away; but in a few days he came back with his jacket on backward and passed once more in front of the castle. Again the master was at his window.

"What are you looking for in these parts?"

"I'd like to make a living; I'm looking for work."

"Do you know how to read?"

"No, for I've never been to school."

"Well, then, come in; I'll hire you. I'll give you one hundred francs a year and board."

The boy entered and his master gave him something to eat. Then he showed him his book of secrets and gave him a duster.

"You will dust my book carefully every day, and that's all you'll have to do."

Then the doctor left on a trip and was gone a whole year. The boy took advantage of this absence to read his master's book and get acquainted with the doctor's skills.

The physician returned. He was very happy with his servant and departed for another year. During this second absence, the boy learned half of the book by heart.

The doctor returned and was so happy with his servant that he doubled his wages and departed for another year. During this third absence the young man learned the remainder of the book by heart. When his master returned he left the doctor's employ to return to his parents, who were as poor as ever.

On the eve of the village fair the young man said to his father: "Tomorrow go into the stable; you will find a beautiful horse that you must take to the fair. Sell him, but above all be sure to keep the halter."

The next day the father entered the stable and found a magnificent horse. He took it to the fair and buyers hastened around to admire the handsome animal. The father sold it for a good price, but he kept the halter and put it in his pocket. Then he set out on the road to his village and shortly he heard footsteps behind him: it was his son who, having transformed himself into a horse and then retransformed himself into his natural shape while the buyer of the horse was celebrating in the tavern, was hastening to catch up with his father. And both were delighted with the fine deal they had made.

After a time there was no more money left in the house.

"Don't worry about it," said the boy to his father. "I'll see that you get more. Go in the stable tomorrow; you will find a steer that you can take to the fair. But when you sell it be sure to keep the rope that you are leading it with."

All took place at the fair as before, and the boy caught up with his father, whose appetite had been whetted by this money which was so easily earned, and who now proposed to take his son again to the next fair in the form of a horse.

But the doctor, by consulting his book, had become aware of what his former servant was doing. He went to the fair, recognized the horse, and bought it. He took the father to the inn to conclude the bargain and made him drink a great deal so that he forgot to keep the halter.

The doctor took the horse quickly away to a blacksmith. "Give him a good shoeing," he advised.

The horse was tied to the door. The children came out of school and a group of them came to hang around the blacksmith shop. The horse extended its muzzle toward a child and whispered to him:

"Untie me!"

The child was afraid and withdrew a bit; but the horse repeated: "Child, untie me!"

The schoolboy approached and untied him. Immediately the horse transformed itself into a hare and ran away. The doctor saw it and turned six boys into hunting dogs. The hare came to the edge of a reservoir, jumped in, and turned into a carp. The doctor arrived, bought all the fish in the reservoir, and had it fished clean. He recognized the carp and was about to grab it when it turned into a lark. He turned into an eagle and pursued the lark, which flew over a castle and fell down the chimney, where it turned into a grain of wheat, which rolled under the table in the bedroom of the girl of the castle.

The day passed. In the evening when the girl had gone to bed, the young man said:

"Mademoiselle, if you wish—"

The girl, hearing his voice, cried out to her parents, who came at once.

"What's the matter?"

"There's someone talking in here!"

But the young man turned back into a grain of wheat and rolled under the table. The parents turned on the lights, looked everywhere, and, finding nothing, departed.

The young man took his own shape and made more advances. The girl cried and her parents returned.

"There's been more talking in the room."

"Have you gone mad?" said the father.

"Well! Go to bed here if you want to hear it."

The father stayed a moment, then went away. The young man reappeared and the girl ended by acceding to him.

"Nights I shall sleep with you and days you may wear me as an engagement ring on your finger."

But the doctor found out all that was going on by consulting his books. He caused the father to become ill and came as a doctor to cure him.

"Heal me and I will pay you well," said the father.

"All I want is the ring on your daughter's finger."

The father promised. But the young man was aware of what was going on.

"The doctor is going to ask you for your ring," he said to the girl. "Don't give it to him; let it fall on the floor."

When the father was cured he called his daughter and told her to give the ring to the doctor. She took it off and let it fall; the ring turned into grains of wheat, which scattered out on the floor. The doctor turned into a rooster to pick them up. The young man turned into a fox and ate the rooster.

8. SNOW-WHITE
(Germany)

IT WAS THE MIDDLE of winter, and the snowflakes were falling like feathers from the sky, and a queen sat at her window working, and her embroidery frame was of ebony. And as she worked, gazing at times out on the snow, she pricked her finger, and there fell from it three drops of blood on the snow. And when she saw how bright and red it looked, she said to herself, "Oh, that I had a child as white as snow, as red as blood, and as black as the wood of the embroidery frame!"

Not very long after she had a daughter, with skin as white as snow, lips as red as blood, and hair as black as ebony, and she was named Snow-White. And when she was born the Queen died.

After a year had gone by the King took another wife, a beautiful

woman, but proud and overbearing, and she could not bear to be
surpassed in beauty by anyone. She had a magic looking glass, and she
used to stand before it, and look in it, and say:

> "Looking glass upon the wall,
> Who is fairest of us all?"

And the looking glass would answer:

> "You are fairest of them all."

And she was contented, for she knew that the looking glass spoke the
truth.

Now, Snow-White was growing prettier and prettier, and when she
was seven years old she was as beautiful as day, far more so than the
Queen herself. So one day when the Queen went to her mirror and
said:

> "Looking glass upon the wall,
> Who is fairest of us all?"

It answered:

> "Queen, you are full fair, 'tis true,
> But Snow-White fairer is than you."

This gave the Queen a great shock, and she became yellow and green
with envy, and from that hour her heart turned against Snow-White,
and she hated her. And envy and pride like ill weeds grew in her heart
higher every day, until she had no peace day or night. At last she sent
for a huntsman, and said:

"Take the child out into the woods, so that I may set eyes on her no
more. You must put her to death, and bring me her heart for a token."

The huntsman consented, and led her away; but when he drew his
cutlass to pierce Snow-White's innocent heart, she began to weep, and
to say:

"Oh, dear huntsman, do not take my life; I will go away into the
wild wood, and never come home again."

And as she was so lovely the huntsman had pity on her, and said,

"Away with you then, poor child"; for he thought the wild animals
would be sure to devour her, and it was as if a stone had been rolled
away from his heart when he spared to put her to death. Just at that
moment a young wild boar came running by, so he caught and killed it,
and taking out its heart, he brought it to the Queen for a token. And it
was salted and cooked, and the wicked woman ate it up, thinking that
there was an end of Snow-White.

Now, when the poor child found herself quite alone in the wild woods, she felt full of terror, even of the very leaves on the trees, and she did not know what to do for fright. Then she began to run over the sharp stones and through the thornbushes, and the wild beasts after her, but they did her no harm. She ran as long as her feet would carry her; and when the evening drew near she came to a little house, and she went inside to rest. Everything there was very small, but as pretty and clean as possible. There stood the little table ready laid, and covered with a white cloth, and seven little plates, and seven knives and forks, and drinking cups. By the wall stood seven little beds, side by side, covered with clean white quilts. Snow-White, being very hungry and thirsty, ate from each plate a little porridge and bread, and drank out of each little cup a drop of wine, so as not to finish up one portion alone. After that she felt so tired that she lay down on one of the beds, but it did not seem to suit her; one was too long, another too short, but at last the seventh was quite right; and so she lay down upon it, committed herself to heaven, and fell asleep.

When it was quite dark, the masters of the house came home. They were seven dwarfs, whose occupation was to dig underground among the mountains. When they had lighted their seven candles, and it was quite light in the little house, they saw that someone must have been in, as everything was not in the same order in which they left it. The first said:

"Who has been sitting in my little chair?"

The second said:

"Who has been eating from my little plate?"

The third said:

"Who has been taking my little loaf?"

The fourth said:

"Who has been tasting my porridge?"

The fifth said:

"Who has been using my little fork?"

The sixth said:

"Who has been cutting with my little knife?"

The seventh said:

"Who has been drinking from my little cup?"

Then the first one, looking round, saw a hollow in his bed, and cried:

"Who has been lying on my bed?"

And the others came running, and cried:

"Someone has been on our beds too!"

But when the seventh looked at his bed, he saw little Snow-White lying there asleep. Then he told the others, who came running up, crying out in their astonishment, and holding up their seven little candles to throw a light upon Snow-White.

"O goodness! O gracious!" cried they, "what beautiful child is this?" and were so full of joy to see her that they did not wake her, but let her sleep on. And the seventh dwarf slept with his comrades, an hour at a time with each, until the night had passed.

When it was morning, and Snow-White awoke and saw the seven dwarfs, she was very frightened; but they seemed quite friendly, and asked her what her name was, and she told them; and then they asked how she came to be in their house. And she related to them how her stepmother had wished her to be put to death, and how the huntsman had spared her life, and how she had run the whole day long, until at last she had found their little house. Then the dwarfs said:

"If you will keep our house for us, and cook, and wash, and make the beds, and sew and knit, and keep everything tidy and clean, you may stay with us, and you shall lack nothing."

"With all my heart," said Snow-White; and so she stayed, and kept the house in good order. In the morning the dwarfs went to the mountain to dig for gold; in the evening they came home, and their supper had to be ready for them. All the day long the maiden was left alone, and the good little dwarfs warned her, saying:

"Beware of your stepmother, she will soon know you are here. Let no one into the house."

Now the Queen, having eaten Snow-White's heart, as she supposed, felt quite sure that now she was the first and fairest, and so she came to her mirror, and said:

"Looking glass upon the wall,
Who is fairest of us all?"

And the glass answered:

"Queen, thou art of beauty rare,
But Snow-White living in the glen
With the seven little men
Is a thousand times more fair."

Then she was very angry, for the glass always spoke the truth, and she knew that the huntsman must have deceived her, and that Snow-White must still be living. And she thought and thought how she could manage to make an end of her, for as long as she was not the fairest in the land, envy left her no rest. At last she thought of a plan; she painted her face and dressed herself like an old peddler woman, so that no one would have known her. In this disguise she went across the seven mountains, until she came to the house of the seven little dwarfs, and she knocked at the door and cried:

"Fine wares to sell! fine wares to sell!"

Snow-White peeped out of the window and cried:

"Good day, good woman, what have you to sell?"

"Good wares, fine wares," answered she, "laces of all colors"; and she held up a piece that was woven of variegated silk.

"I need not be afraid of letting in this good woman," thought Snow-White, and she unbarred the door and bought the pretty lace.

"What a figure you are, child!" said the old woman, "come and let me lace you properly for once."

Snow-White, suspecting nothing, stood up before her, and let her lace her with the new lace; but the old woman laced so quick and tight that it took Snow-White's breath away, and she fell down as dead.

"Now you have done with being the fairest," said the old woman as she hastened away.

Not long after that, toward evening, the seven dwarfs came home, and were terrified to see their dear Snow-White lying on the ground, without life or motion; they raised her up, and when they saw how tightly she was laced they cut the lace in two; then she began to draw breath, and little by little she returned to life. When the dwarfs heard what had happened they said:

"The old peddler woman was no other than the wicked queen; you must beware of letting anyone in when we are not here!"

And when the wicked woman got home she went to her glass and said:

> "Looking glass against the wall,
> Who is fairest of us all?"

And it answered as before:

> "Queen, thou art of beauty rare,
> But Snow-White living in the glen
> With the seven little men
> Is a thousand times more fair."

When she heard that she was so struck with surprise that all the blood left her heart, for she knew that Snow-White must still be living.

"But now," said she, "I will think of something that will be her ruin." And by witchcraft she made a poisoned comb. Then she dressed herself up to look like another different sort of old woman. So she went across the seven mountains and came to the house of the seven dwarfs, and knocked at the door and cried:

"Good wares to sell! good wares to sell!"

Snow-White looked out and said:

"Go away, I must not let anybody in."

"But you are not forbidden to look," said the old woman, taking out the poisoned comb and holding it up. It pleased the poor child so much that she was tempted to open the door; and when the bargain was made the old woman said:

"Now, for once your hair shall be properly combed."

Poor Snow-White, thinking no harm, let the old woman do as she would, but no sooner was the comb put in her hair than the poison began to work, and the poor girl fell down senseless.

"Now, you paragon of beauty," said the wicked woman, "this is the end of you," and went off. By good luck it was now near evening, and the seven little dwarfs came home. When they saw Snow-White lying on the ground as dead, they thought directly that it was the step-mother's doing, and looked about, found the poisoned comb, and no sooner had they drawn it out of her hair than Snow-White came to herself, and related all that had passed. Then they warned her once more to be on her guard, and never again to let anyone in at the door.

And the Queen went home and stood before the looking glass and said:

> "Looking glass against the wall,
> Who is fairest of us all?"

And the looking glass answered as before:

> "Queen, thou art of beauty rare,
> But Snow-White living in the glen
> With the seven little men
> Is a thousand times more fair."

When she heard the looking glass speak thus she trembled and shook with anger.

"Snow-White shall die," cried she, "though it should cost me my own life!" And then she went to a secret lonely chamber, where no one was likely to come, and there she made a poisonous apple. It was beautiful to look upon, being white with red cheeks, so that anyone who should see it must long for it, but whoever ate even a little bit of it must die. When the apple was ready she painted her face and clothed herself like a peasant woman, and went across the seven mountains to where the seven dwarfs lived. And when she knocked at the door Snow-White put her head out of the window and said:

"I dare not let anybody in; the seven dwarfs told me not."

"All right," answered the woman; "I can easily get rid of my apples elsewhere. There, I will give you one."

"No," answered Snow-White, "I dare not take anything."

"Are you afraid of poison?" said the woman, "look here, I will cut the apple in two pieces; you shall have the red side, I will have the white one."

For the apple was so cunningly made, that all the poison was in the rosy half of it. Snow-White longed for the beautiful apple, and as she saw the peasant woman eating a piece of it she could no longer refrain, but stretched out her hand and took the poisoned half. But no sooner had she taken a morsel of it into her mouth than she fell to the earth as dead. And the Queen, casting on her a terrible glance, laughed aloud and cried:

"As white as snow, as red as blood, as black as ebony! this time the dwarfs will not be able to bring you to life again."

And when she went home and asked the looking glass:

> "Looking glass against the wall,
> Who is fairest of us all?"

at last it answered:

"You are the fairest now of all."

Then her envious heart had peace, as much as an envious heart can have.

The dwarfs, when they came home in the evening, found Snow-White lying on the ground, and there came no breath out of her mouth, and she was dead. They lifted her up, sought if anything poisonous was to be found, cut her laces, combed her hair, washed her with water and wine, but all was of no avail, the poor child was dead, and remained dead. Then they laid her on a bier, and sat all seven of them around it, and wept and lamented three whole days. And then they would have buried her, but that she looked still as if she were living, with her beautiful blooming cheeks. So they said:

"We cannot hide her away in the black ground." And they had made a coffin of clear glass, so as to be looked into from all sides, and they laid her in it, and wrote in golden letters upon it her name, and that she was a king's daughter. Then they set the coffin out upon the mountain, and one of them always remained by it to watch. And the birds came too, and mourned for Snow-White, first an owl, then a raven, and lastly, a dove.

Now, for a long while Snow-White lay in the coffin and never changed, but looked as if she were asleep, for she was still as white as snow, as red as blood, and her hair was as black as ebony. It happened, however, that one day a king's son rode through the wood and up to the dwarfs' house, which was near it. He saw on the mountain the coffin, and beautiful Snow-White within it, and he read what was written in golden letters upon it. Then he said to the dwarfs:

"Let me have the coffin, and I will give you whatever you like to ask for it."

But the dwarfs told him that they could not part with it for all the gold in the world. But he said:

"I beseech you to give it me, for I cannot live without looking upon Snow-White; if you consent I will bring you to great honor, and care for you as if you were my brethren."

When he so spoke the good little dwarfs had pity upon him and gave him the coffin, and the King's son called his servants and bid them carry it away on their shoulders. Now it happened that as they were going along they stumbled over a bush, and with the shaking the bit of poisoned apple flew out of her throat. It was not long before she opened her eyes, threw up the cover of the coffin, and sat up, alive and well.

"Oh dear! where am I?" cried she. The King's son answered, full of joy, "You are near me," and, relating all that had happened, he said:

"I would rather have you than anything in the world; come with me to my father's castle and you shall be my bride."

And Snow-White was kind, and went with him, and their wedding was held with pomp and great splendor.

But Snow-White's wicked stepmother was also bidden to the feast, and when she had dressed herself in beautiful clothes she went to her looking glass and said:

> "Looking glass upon the wall,
> Who is fairest of us all?"

The looking glass answered:

> "O Queen, although you are of beauty rare,
> The young bride is a thousand times more fair."

Then she railed and cursed, and was beside herself with disappointment and anger. First she thought she would not go to the wedding; but then she felt she should have no peace until she went and saw the bride. And when she saw her she knew her for Snow-White, and could not stir from the place for anger and terror. For they had ready red-hot iron shoes, in which she had to dance until she fell down dead.

9. THE BRAVE LITTLE TAILOR
(Germany)

ONE SUMMER MORNING a little tailor was sitting on his board near the window, and working cheerfully with all his might, when an old woman came down the street crying:

"Good jelly to sell! good jelly to sell!"

The cry sounded pleasant in the little tailor's ears, so he put his head out of the window, and called out:

"Here, my good woman—come here, if you want a customer."

So the poor woman climbed the steps with her heavy basket, and was obliged to unpack and display all her pots to the tailor. He looked at every one of them, and lifting all the lids, applied his nose to each, and said at last:

"The jelly seems pretty good; you may weigh me out four half ounces, or I don't mind having a quarter of a pound."

The woman, who had expected to find a good customer, gave him what he asked for, but went off angry and grumbling.

"This jelly is the very thing for me," cried the little tailor; "it will give me strength and cunning"; and he took down the bread from the cupboard, cut a whole round of the loaf, and spread the jelly on it, laid it near him, and went on stitching more gallantly than ever. All the while the scent of the sweet jelly was spreading throughout the room, where there were quantities of flies, who were attracted by it and flew to partake.

"Now, then, who asked you to come?" said the tailor, and drove the unbidden guests away. But the flies, not understanding his language, were not to be got rid of like that, and returned in larger numbers than before. Then the tailor, not being able to stand it any longer, took from his chimney corner a ragged cloth, and saying,

"Now, I'll let you have it!" beat it among them unmercifully. When he ceased, and counted the slain, he found seven lying dead before him.

"This is indeed somewhat," he said, wondering at his own gallantry; "the whole town shall know this."

So he hastened to cut out a belt, and he stitched it, and put on it in large capitals "Seven at one blow!"

"—The town, did I say!" said the little tailor; "the whole world shall know it!" And his heart quivered with joy, like a lamb's tail.

The tailor fastened the belt round him, and began to think of going out into the world, for his workshop seemed too small for his worship. So he looked about in all the house for something that would be useful to take with him, but he found nothing but an old cheese, which he put in his pocket. Outside the door he noticed that a bird had got caught in the bushes, so he took that and put it in his pocket with the cheese. Then he set out gallantly on his way, and as he was light and active he felt no fatigue. The way led over a mountain, and when he reached the topmost peak he saw a terrible giant sitting there, and looking about him at his ease. The tailor went bravely up to him, called out to him, and said,

"Comrade, good day! there you sit looking over the wide world! I am on the way thither to seek my fortune: have you a fancy to go with me?"

The giant looked at the tailor contemptuously, and said:

"You little rascal! you miserable fellow!"

"That may be!" answered the little tailor, and undoing his coat he showed the giant his belt; "you can read there whether I am a man or not!"

The giant read: "Seven at one blow!" and thinking it meant men that the tailor had killed, felt at once more respect for the little fellow. But as he wanted to prove him, he took up a stone and squeezed it so hard that water came out of it.

"Now you can do that," said the giant, "that is, if you have the strength for it."

"That's not much," said the little tailor, "I call that play," and he put his hand in his pocket and took out the cheese and squeezed it, so that the whey ran out of it.

"Well," said he, "what do you think of that?"

The giant did not know what to say to it, for he could not have believed it of the little man. Then the giant took up a stone and threw it so high that it was nearly out of sight.

"Now, little fellow, suppose you do that!"

"Well thrown," said the tailor; "but the stone fell back to earth again—I will throw you one that will never come back." So he felt in his pocket, took out the bird, and threw it into the air. And the bird, when it found itself at liberty, took wing, flew off, and returned no more.

"What do you think of that, comrade?" asked the tailor.

"There is no doubt that you can throw," said the giant; "but we will see if you can carry."

He led the little tailor to a mighty oak tree which had been felled, and was lying on the ground, and said:

"Now, if you are strong enough, help me to carry this tree out of the wood."

"Willingly," answered the little man; "you take the trunk on your shoulders, I will take the branches with all their foliage, that is much the most difficult."

So the giant took the trunk on his shoulders, and the tailor seated himself on a branch, and the giant, who could not see what he was doing, had the whole tree to carry, and the little man on it as well. And the little man was very cheerful and merry, and whistled the tune: *"There were three tailors riding by,"* as if carrying the tree was mere child's play. The giant, when he had struggled on under his heavy load a part of the way, was tired out, and cried:

"Look here, I must let go the tree."

The tailor jumped off quickly, and taking hold of the tree with both arms, as if he were carrying it, said to the giant:

"You see you can't carry the tree though you are such a big fellow!"

They went on together a little farther, and presently they came to a cherry tree, and the giant took hold of the topmost branches, where the ripest fruit hung, and pulling them downward, gave them to the tailor to hold, bidding him eat. But the little tailor was much too weak to hold the tree, and as the giant let go, the tree sprang back, and the tailor was caught up into the air. And when he dropped down again without any damage, the giant said to him,

"How is this? Haven't you strength enough to hold such a weak sprig as that?"

"It is not strength that is lacking," answered the little tailor; "how should it to one who has slain seven at one blow! I just jumped over the tree because the hunters are shooting down there in the bushes. You jump it too, if you can."

The giant made the attempt, and not being able to vault the tree, he remained hanging in the branches, so that once more the little tailor got the better of him. Then said the giant:

"As you are such a gallant fellow, suppose you come with me to our den, and stay the night."

The tailor was quite willing, and he followed him. When they reached the den there sat some other giants by the fire, and all gladly welcomed him. The little tailor looked round and thought:

"There is more elbowroom here than in my workshop."

And the giant showed him a bed, and told him he had better lie down upon it and go to sleep. The bed was, however, too big for the tailor, so he did not stay in it, but crept into a corner to sleep. As soon as it was midnight the giant got up, took a great staff of iron and beat the bed through with one stroke, and supposed he had made an end of that grasshopper of a tailor. Very early in the morning the giants went into the wood and forgot all about the little tailor, and when they saw him coming after them alive and merry, they were terribly frightened, and, thinking he was going to kill them, they ran away in all haste.

So the little tailor marched on, always following his nose. And after he had gone a great way he entered the courtyard belonging to a king's palace, and there he felt so overpowered with fatigue that he lay down and fell asleep. In the meanwhile came various people, who looked at him very curiously, and read on his belt, "Seven at one blow!"

"Oh!" said they, "why should this great lord come here in time of peace? What a mighty champion he must be."

Then they went and told the King about him, and they thought that if war should break out what a worthy and useful man he would be, and that he ought not to be allowed to depart at any price. The King then summoned his council, and sent one of his courtiers to the little tailor to beg him, so soon as he should wake up, to consent to serve in the King's army. So the messenger stood and waited at the sleeper's side until his limbs began to stretch, and his eyes to open, and then he carried his answer back. And the answer was:

"That was the reason for which I came," said the little tailor. "I am ready to enter the King's service."

So he was received into it very honorably, and a separate dwelling set apart for him.

But the rest of the soldiers were very much set against the little tailor, and they wished him a thousand miles away.

"What shall be done about it?" they said among themselves; "if we pick a quarrel and fight with him then seven of us will fall at each blow. That will be of no good to us."

So they came to a resolution, and went all together to the King to ask for their discharge.

"We never intended," said they, "to serve with a man who kills seven at a blow."

The King felt sorry to lose all his faithful servants because of one man, and he wished that he had never seen him, and would willingly get rid of him if he might. But he did not dare to dismiss the little tailor for fear he should kill all the King's people, and place himself upon the throne. He thought a long while about it, and at last made up his mind what to do. He sent for the little tailor, and told him that as he was so great a warrior he had a proposal to make to him. He told him that in a wood in his dominions dwelled two giants, who did great damage by robbery, murder, and fire, and that no man dared go near them for fear of his life.

But that if the tailor should overcome and slay both these giants the King would give him his only daughter in marriage, and half his kingdom as dowry, and that a hundred horsemen should go with him to give him assistance.

"That would be something for a man like me!" thought the little tailor, "a beautiful princess and half a kingdom are not to be had every day," and he said to the King:

"Oh, yes, I can soon overcome the giants, and yet have no need of the hundred horsemen; he who can kill seven at one blow has no need to be afraid of two."

So the little tailor set out, and the hundred horsemen followed him. When he came to the border of the wood he said to his escort:

"Stay here while I go to attack the giants."

Then he sprang into the wood, and looked about him right and left. After a while he caught sight of the two giants; they were lying down under a tree asleep, and snoring so that all the branches shook. The little tailor, all alive, filled both his pockets with stones and climbed up into the tree, and made his way to an overhanging bough, so that he could seat himself just above the sleepers; and from there he let one stone after another fall on the chest of one of the giants. For a long time the giant was quite unaware of this, but at last he waked up and pushed his comrade, and said:

"What are you hitting me for?"

"You are dreaming," said the other, "I am not touching you." And they composed themselves again to sleep, and the tailor let fall a stone on the other giant.

"What can that be?" cried he. "What are you casting at me?"

"I am casting nothing at you," answered the first, grumbling.

They disputed about it for a while, but as they were tired, they gave it up at last, and their eyes closed once more. Then the little tailor began his game anew, picked out a heavier stone and threw it down with force upon the first giant's chest.

"This is too much!" cried he, and sprang up like a madman and struck his companion such a blow that the tree shook above them. The other paid him back with ready coin, and they fought with such fury that they tore up trees by their roots to use for weapons against each other, so that at last they both of them lay dead upon the ground. And now the little tailor got down.

"Another piece of luck!" said he, "that the tree I was sitting in did not get torn up too, or else I should have had to jump like a squirrel from one tree to another."

Then he drew his sword and gave each of the giants a few hacks in the breast, and went back to the horsemen and said,

"The deed is done, I have made an end of both of them: but it went hard with me, in the struggle they rooted up trees to defend themselves, but it was of no use, they had to do with a man who can kill seven at one blow."

"Then are you not wounded?" asked the horsemen.

"Nothing of the sort!" answered the tailor, "I have not turned a hair."

The horsemen still would not believe it, and rode into the wood to see, and there they found the giants wallowing in their blood, and all about them lying the uprooted trees.

The little tailor then claimed the promised boon, but the King repented him of his offer, and he sought again how to rid himself of the hero.

"Before you can possess my daughter and the half of my kingdom," said he to the tailor, "you must perform another heroic act. In the wood lives a unicorn who does great damage; you must secure him."

"A unicorn does not strike more terror into me than two giants. Seven at one blow!—that is my way," was the tailor's answer.

So, taking a rope and an ax with him, he went out into the wood, and told those who were ordered to attend him to wait outside. He had not far to seek, the unicorn soon came out and sprang at him, as if he would make an end of him without delay. "Softly, softly," said he, "most haste, worst speed," and remained standing until the animal came quite near, then he slipped quietly behind a tree. The unicorn ran with all his might against the tree and stuck his horn so deep into the trunk that he could not get it out again, and so was taken.

"Now I have you," said the tailor, coming out from behind the tree, and, putting the rope round the unicorn's neck, he took the ax, set free the horn, and when all his party were assembled he led forth the animal and brought it to the King.

The King did not yet wish to give him the promised reward, and set him a third task to do. Before the wedding could take place the tailor was to secure a wild boar which had done a great deal of damage in the wood.

The huntsmen were to accompany him.

"All right," said the tailor, "this is child's play."

But he did not take the huntsmen into the wood, and they were all the better pleased, for the wild boar had many a time before received them in such a way that they had no fancy to disturb him. When the boar caught sight of the tailor he ran at him with foaming mouth and gleaming tusks to bear him to the ground, but the nimble hero rushed into a chapel which chanced to be near, and jumped quickly out of a window on the other side. The boar ran after him, and when he got inside the door shut after him, and there he was imprisoned, for the creature was too big and unwieldy to jump out of the window too. Then the little tailor called the huntsmen that they might see the prisoner with their own eyes; and then he betook himself to the King, who now, whether he liked it or not, was obliged to fulfill his promise, and give him his daughter and the half of his kingdom. But if he had known that the great warrior was only a little tailor he would have taken it still more to heart. So the wedding was celebrated with great splendor and little joy, and the tailor was made into a king.

One night the young queen heard her husband talking in his sleep and saying,

"Now, boy, make me that waistcoat and patch me those breeches, or I will lay my yard measure about your shoulder!"

And so, as she perceived of what low birth her husband was, she went to her father the next morning and told him all, and begged him to set her free from a man who was nothing better than a tailor. The King bade her be comforted, saying,

"Tonight leave your bedroom door open, my guard shall stand outside, and when he is asleep they shall come in and bind him and carry him off to a ship, and he shall be sent to the other side of the world."

So the wife felt consoled, but the King's waterbearer, who had been listening all the while, went to the little tailor and disclosed to him the whole plan.

"I shall put a stop to all this," said he.

At night he lay down as usual in bed, and when his wife thought that he was asleep, she got up, opened the door and lay down again. The little tailor, who only made believe to be asleep, began to murmur plainly.

"Now, boy, make me that waistcoat and patch me those breeches, or I will lay my yard measure about your shoulders! I have slain seven at one blow, killed two giants, caught a unicorn, and taken a wild boar, and shall I be afraid of those who are standing outside my room door?"

And when they heard the tailor say this, a great fear seized them; they fled away as if they had been wild hares, and none of them would venture to attack him.

And so the little tailor all his lifetime remained a king.

10. ASHENPUTTEL
(Germany)

THE WIFE OF A rich man fell ill, and when she felt that she was nearing her end, she called her only daughter to her bedside, and said:

"Dear child, continue devout and good, then God will always help you, and I will look down upon you from heaven, and watch over you."

Thereupon she closed her eyes, and breathed her last.

The maiden went to her mother's grave every day and wept, and she continued to be devout and good. When the winter came, the snow spread a white covering on the grave, and when the sun of spring had unveiled it again, the husband took another wife. The new wife brought home with her two daughters, who were fair and beautiful to look upon, but base and black at heart.

Then began a sad time for the unfortunate stepchild.

"Is this stupid goose to sit with us in the parlor?" they said.

"Whoever wants to eat bread must earn it; go and sit with the kitchenmaid."

They took away her pretty clothes, and made her put on an old gray frock, and gave her wooden clogs.

"Just look at the proud princess, how well she's dressed," they laughed, as they led her to the kitchen. There, the girl was obliged to do hard work from morning till night, to get up at daybreak, carry water, light the fire, cook, and wash. Not content with that, the sisters inflicted on her every vexation they could think of; they made fun of her, and tossed the peas and lentils among the ashes, so that she had to sit down and pick them out again. In the evening, when she was worn out with work, she had no bed to go to, but had to lie on the hearth among the cinders. And because, on account of that, she always looked dusty and dirty, they called her Ashenputtel.

It happened one day that the father had a mind to go to the fair. So he asked both his stepdaughters what he should bring home for them.

"Fine clothes," said one.

"Pearls and jewels," said the other.

"But you, Ashenputtel?" said he, "what will you have?"

"Father, break off for me the first twig which brushes against your hat on your way home."

Well, for his two stepdaughters he brought beautiful clothes, pearls and jewels, and on his way home, as he was riding through a green copse, a hazel twig grazed against him and knocked his hat off. Then he broke off the branch and took it with him.

When he got home he gave his stepdaughters what they had asked for, and to Ashenputtel he gave the twig from the hazel bush.

Ashenputtel thanked him, and went to her mother's grave and planted the twig upon it; she wept so much that her tears fell and watered it. And it took root and became a fine tree.

Ashenputtel went to the grave three times every day, wept and prayed, and every time a little white bird came and perched upon the tree, and when she uttered a wish, the little bird threw down to her what she had wished for.

Now it happened that the King proclaimed a festival, which was to last three days, and to which all the beautiful maidens in the country were invited, in order that his son might choose a bride.

When the two stepdaughters heard that they were also to be present, they were in high spirits, called Ashenputtel, and said:

"Brush our hair and clean our shoes, and fasten our buckles, for we are going to the feast at the King's palace."

Ashenputtel obeyed, but wept, for she also would gladly have gone to the ball with them, and begged her stepmother to give her leave to go.

"You, Ashenputtel!" she said. "Why, you are covered with dust and dirt. You go to the festival! Besides you have no clothes or shoes, and yet you want to go to the ball."

As she, however, went on asking, her stepmother said:

"Well, I have thrown a dishful of lentils into the cinders, if you have picked them all out in two hours you shall go with us."

The girl went through the back door into the garden, and cried, "Ye gentle doves, ye turtle doves, and all ye little birds under heaven, come and help me,

> "The good into a dish to throw,
> The bad into your crops can go."

Then two white doves came in by the kitchen window, and were followed by the turtle doves, and finally all the little birds under heaven flocked in, chirping, and settled down among the ashes. And the doves gave a nod with their little heads, peck, peck, peck; and then the rest began also, peck, peck, peck, and collected all the good beans into the dish. Scarcely had an hour passed before they had finished, and all flown out again.

Then the girl brought the dish to her stepmother, and was delighted to think that now she would be able to go to the feast with them.

But she said, "No, Ashenputtel, you have no clothes, and cannot dance; you will only be laughed at."

But when she began to cry, the stepmother said:

"If you can pick out two whole dishes of lentils from the ashes in an hour, you shall go with us."

And she thought, "She will never be able to do that."

When her stepmother had thrown the dishes of lentils among the ashes, the girl went out through the back door, and cried, "Ye gentle doves, ye turtle doves, and all ye little birds under heaven, come and help me,

"The good into a dish to throw,
The bad into your crops can go."

Then two white doves came in by the kitchen window, and were followed by the turtle doves, and all the other little birds under heaven, and in less than an hour the whole had been picked up, and they had all flown away.

Then the girl carried the dish to her stepmother, and was delighted to think that she would now be able to go to the ball.

But she said, "It's not a bit of good. You can't go with us, for you've got no clothes, and you can't dance. We should be quite ashamed of you."

Thereupon she turned her back upon her, and hurried off with her two proud daughters.

As soon as everyone had left the house, Ashenputtel went out to her mother's grave under the hazel tree, and cried:

"Shiver and shake, dear little tree,
Gold and silver shower on me."

Then the bird threw down to her a gold and silver robe, and a pair of slippers embroidered with silk and silver. With all speed she put on the robe and went to the feast. But her stepsisters and their mother did not recognize her, and supposed that she was some foreign princess, so beautiful did she appear in her golden dress. They never gave a thought to Ashenputtel, but imagined that she was sitting at home in the dirt picking the lentils out of the cinders.

The Prince came up to the stranger, took her by the hand, and danced with her. In fact, he would not dance with anyone else, and never let go of her hand. If anyone came up to ask her to dance, he said, "This is my partner."

She danced until nightfall, and then wanted to go home; but the Prince said, "I will go with you and escort you."

For he wanted to see to whom the beautiful maiden belonged. But she slipped out of his way and sprang into the pigeon house.

Then the Prince waited till her father came, and told him that the unknown maiden had vanished into the pigeon house.

The old man thought, "Could it be Ashenputtel?" And he had an ax brought to him, so that he might break down the pigeon house, but there was no one inside.

When they went home, there lay Ashenputtel in her dirty clothes among the cinders, and a dismal oil lamp was burning in the chimney corner. For Ashenputtel had quietly jumped down out of the pigeon house and ran back to the hazel tree. There she had taken off her beautiful clothes and laid them on the grave, and the bird had taken them away again. Then she had settled herself among the ashes on the hearth in her old gray frock.

On the second day, when the festival was renewed, and her parents and stepsisters had started forth again, Ashenputtel went to the hazel tree, and said:

> "Shiver and shake, dear little tree,
> Gold and silver shower on me."

Then the bird threw down a still more gorgeous robe than on the previous day. And when she appeared at the festival in this robe, everyone was astounded by her beauty.

The King's son had waited till she came, and at once took her hand, and she danced with no one but him. When others came forward and invited her to dance, he said, "This is my partner."

At nightfall she wished to leave; but the Prince went after her, hoping to see into what house she went, but she sprang out into the garden behind the house. There stood a fine big tree on which the most delicious pears hung. She climbed up among the branches as nimbly as a squirrel, and the Prince could not make out what had become of her.

But he waited till her father came, and then said to him, "The unknown maiden has slipped away from me, and I think that she has jumped into the pear tree."

The father thought, "Can it be Ashenputtel?" And he had the ax brought to cut down the tree, but there was no one on it. When they went home and looked into the kitchen, there lay Ashenputtel among the cinders as usual; for she had jumped down on the other side of the tree, taken back the beautiful clothes to the bird on the hazel tree, and put on her old gray frock.

On the third day, when her parents and stepsisters had started, Ashenputtel went again to her mother's grave, and said:

> "Shiver and shake, dear little tree,
> Gold and silver shower on me."

Then the bird threw down a dress which was so magnificent that no one had ever seen the like before, and the slippers were entirely of gold. When she appeared at the festival in this attire, they were all speechless with astonishment. The Prince danced only with her, and if anyone else asked her to dance, he said, "This is my partner."

When night fell and she wanted to leave, the Prince was more desirous than ever to accompany her, but she darted away from him so quickly that he could not keep up with her. But the Prince had used a stratagem, and had caused the steps to be covered with cobbler's wax. The consequence was, that as the maiden sprang down them, her left slipper remained sticking there. The Prince took it up. It was small and dainty, and entirely made of gold.

The next morning he went with it to Ashenputtel's father, and said to him, "No other shall become my wife but she whose foot this golden slipper fits."

The two sisters were delighted at that, for they both had beautiful feet. The eldest went into the room intending to try on the slipper, and her mother stood beside her. But her great toe prevented her getting it on, her foot was too long.

Then her mother handed her a knife, and said, "Cut off the toe; when you are Queen you won't have to walk any more."

The girl cut off her toe, forced her foot into the slipper, stifled her pain, and went out to the Prince. Then he took her up on his horse as his bride, and rode away with her.

However, they had to pass the grave on the way, and there sat the two doves on the hazel tree, and cried:

> "Prithee, look back, prithee, look back,
>   There's blood on the track,
>   The shoe is too small,
>   At home the true bride is waiting thy call."

Then he looked at her foot and saw how the blood was streaming from it. So he turned his horse round and carried the false bride back to her home, and said that she was not the right one; the second sister must try the shoe.

Then she went into the room, and succeeded in getting her toes into the shoe, but her heel was too big.

Then her mother handed her a knife, and said, "Cut a bit off your heel; when you are Queen you won't have to walk any more."

The maiden cut a bit off her heel, forced her foot into the shoe, stifled her pain, and went out to the Prince.

Then he took her up on his horse as his bride, and rode off with her.

As they passed the grave, the two doves were sitting on the hazel tree, and crying:

> "Prithee, look back, prithee, look back,
> There's blood on the track,
> The shoe is too small,
> At home the true bride is waiting thy call."

He looked down at her foot and saw that it was streaming with blood, and there were deep red spots on her stockings. Then he turned his horse and brought the false bride back to her home.

"This is not the right one either," he said. "Have you no other daughter?"

"No," said the man. "There is only a daughter of my late wife's, a puny, stunted drudge, but she cannot possibly be the bride."

The Prince said that she must be sent for.

But the mother answered, "Oh, no, she is much too dirty; she mustn't be seen on any account."

He was, however, absolutely determined to have his way, and they were obliged to summon Ashenputtel.

When she had washed her hands and face, she went up and curtsied to the Prince, who handed her the golden slipper.

Then she sat down on a bench, pulled off her wooden clog and put on the slipper, which fitted to a nicety.

And when she stood up and the Prince looked into her face, he recognized the beautiful maiden that he had danced with, and cried: "This is the true bride!"

The stepmother and the two sisters were dismayed and turned white with rage; but he took Ashenputtel on his horse and rode off with her.

As they rode past the hazel tree the two white doves cried:

> "Prithee, look back, prithee, look back,
> No blood's on the track,
> The shoe's *not* too small,
> You carry the true bride home to your hall."

And when they had said this they both came flying down, and settled on Ashenputtel's shoulders, one on the right, and one on the left, and remained perched there.

When the wedding was going to take place, the two false sisters came and wanted to curry favor with her, and take part in her good fortune. As the bridal party was going to the church, the eldest was on the right side, the youngest on the left, and the doves picked out one of the eyes of each of them.

Afterward, when they were coming out of the church, the elder was on the left, the younger on the right, and the doves picked out the other eye of each of them. And so for their wickedness and falseness they were punished with blindness for the rest of their days.

11. RAPUNZEL
(Germany)

THERE ONCE LIVED a man and his wife who had long wished for a child, but in vain. Now there was at the back of their house a little window which overlooked a beautiful garden full of the finest vegetables and flowers; but there was a high wall all round it, and no one ventured into it, for it belonged to a witch of great might, and of whom all the world was afraid. One day when the wife was standing at the window, and looking into the garden, she saw a bed filled with the finest lettuce; and it looked so fresh and green that she began to wish for some; and at length she longed for it greatly. This went on for days, and as she knew she could not get the lettuce, she pined away, and grew pale and miserable.

Then the man was uneasy, and asked, "What is the matter, dear wife?" "Oh," answered she, "I shall die unless I can have some of that lettuce to eat that grows in the garden at the back of our house." The man, who loved her very much, thought to himself, "Rather than lose my wife I will get some lettuce, cost what it will."

So in the twilight he climbed over the wall into the witch's garden, plucked hastily a handful of lettuce and brought it to his wife. She made a salad of it at once, and ate of it to her heart's content. But she liked it so much, and it tasted so good, that the next day she longed for it thrice as much as she had done before; if she was to have any rest the man must climb over the wall once more. So he went in the twilight again; and as he was climbing back, he saw, all at once, the witch standing before him, and was terribly frightened, as she cried, with angry eyes, "How dare you climb over into my garden like a thief, and steal my lettuce! It shall be the worse for you!"

"Oh," answered he, "be merciful rather than just; I have only done it through necessity; for my wife saw your lettuce out of the window, and became possessed with so great a longing that she would have died if she could not have had some to eat."

Then the witch said, "If it is all as you say, you may have as much lettuce as you like, on one condition—the child that will come into the world must be given to me. It shall go well with the child, and I will care for it like a mother."

In his distress of mind the man promised everything; and when the time came when the child was born the witch appeared, and, giving the child the name of Rapunzel (which is the same as lettuce), she took it away with her.

Rapunzel was the most beautiful child in the world. When she was twelve years old the witch shut her up in a tower in the midst of a wood, and it had neither steps nor door, only a small window above. When the witch wished to be let in, she would stand below and would cry, "Rapunzel, Rapunzel! Let down your hair!"

Rapunzel had beautiful long hair that shone like gold. When she heard the voice of the witch she would undo the fastening of the upper window, unbind the plaits of her hair, and let it down twenty ells below, and the witch would climb up by it.

After they had lived thus a few years it happened that as the King's son was riding through the wood, he came to the tower; and as he drew near he heard a voice singing so sweetly that he stood still and listened. It was Rapunzel in her loneliness trying to pass away the time with sweet songs. The King's son wished to go in to her, and sought to find a door in the tower, but there was none. So he rode home, but the song had entered into his heart, and every day he went into the wood and listened to it.

Once, as he was standing there under a tree, he saw the witch come up, and listened while she called out, "Oh Rapunzel, Rapunzel! Let down your hair."

Then he saw how Rapunzel let down her long tresses, and how the witch climbed up by them and went in to her, and he said to himself, "Since that is the ladder, I will climb it, and seek my fortune." And the next day, as soon as it began to grow dusk, he went to the tower and cried, "Oh Rapunzel, Rapunzel! Let down your hair." And she let down her hair, and the King's son climbed up by it.

Rapunzel was greatly terrified when she saw that a man had come in to her, for she had never seen one before; but the King's son began speaking so kindly to her, and told how her singing had entered into his heart, so that he could have no peace until he had seen her herself. Then Rapunzel forgot her terror, and when he asked her to take him for her husband, and she saw that he was young and beautiful, she thought to herself, "I certainly like him much better than old mother Gothel," and she put her hand into his hand, saying, "I would willingly go with you, but I do not know how I shall get out. When you come, bring each time a silken rope, and I will make a ladder, and when it is quite ready I will get down by it out of the tower, and you shall take me away on your horse."

They agreed that he should come to her every evening, as the old woman came in the daytime. So the witch knew nothing of all this until once Rapunzel said to her unwittingly, "Mother Gothel, how is it that you climb up here so slowly, and the King's son is with me in a moment?"

"O wicked child," cried the witch, "what is this I hear! I thought I had hidden you from all the world, and you have betrayed me!"

In her anger she seized Rapunzel by her beautiful hair, struck her several times with her left hand, and then grasping a pair of shears in her right—snip, snap—the beautiful locks lay on the ground. And she was so hardhearted that she took Rapunzel and put her in a waste and desert place, where she lived in great woe and misery.

The same day on which she took Rapunzel away she went back to the tower in the evening and made fast the severed locks of hair to the window hasp, and the King's son came and cried, "Rapunzel, Rapunzel! Let down your hair."

Then she let the hair down, and the King's son climbed up, but instead of his dearest Rapunzel he found the witch looking at him with wicked, glittering eyes.

"Aha!" cried she, mocking him, "you came for your darling, but the sweet bird sits no longer in the nest, and sings no more; the cat has got her, and will scratch out your eyes as well! Rapunzel is lost to you; you will see her no more."

The King's son was beside himself with grief, and in his agony he sprang from the tower; he escaped with life, but the thorns on which he fell put out his eyes. Then he wandered blind through the wood, eating nothing but roots and berries, and doing nothing but lament and weep for the loss of his dearest wife.

So he wandered several years in misery until at last he came to the desert place where Rapunzel lived with her twin children that she had borne, a boy and a girl. At first he heard a voice that he thought he knew, and when he reached the place from which it seemed to come Rapunzel knew him, and fell on his neck and wept. And when her tears touched his eyes they became clear again, and he could see with them as well as ever.

Then he took her to his kingdom, where he was received with great joy, and there they lived long and happily.

12. THE DEVIL'S THREE GOLD HAIRS
(Germany)

ONCE THERE WAS a very poor woman who was delighted when her son was born with a caul enveloping his head. This was supposed to bring good fortune, and it was predicted that he would marry the King's daughter when he became nineteen. Soon after, a King came to the village, but no one knew that it was the King. When he asked for news, they told him that a few days before a child had been born in the village, with a caul, and it was prophesied that he would be very lucky. Indeed, it had been said that in his nineteenth year he would have the King's daughter for his wife.

The King, who had a wicked heart, was very angry when he heard this; but he went to the parents in a most friendly manner, and said to them kindly, "Good people, give up your child to me. I will take the greatest care of him."

At first they refused; but when the stranger offered them a large amount of gold, and then mentioned that if their child was born to be lucky everything must turn out for the best with him, they willingly at last gave him up.

The King placed the child in a box and rode away with it for a long distance, till he came to deep water, into which he threw the box containing the child, saying to himself as he rode away, "From this unwelcome suitor have I saved my daughter."

But the box did not sink; it swam like a boat on the water, and so high above it that not a drop got inside. It sailed on to a spot about two miles from the chief town of the King's dominions, where there were a mill and a weir, which stopped it, and on which it rested.

The miller's man, who happened to be standing near the bank, fortunately noticed it, and thinking it would most likely contain something valuable, drew it on shore with a hook; but when he opened it, there lay a beautiful baby, who was quite awake and lively.

He carried it in to the miller and his wife, and as they had no children they were quite delighted, and said Heaven had sent the little boy as a gift to them. They brought him up carefully, and he grew to manhood clever and virtuous.

It happened one day that the King was overtaken by a thunderstorm while passing near the mill, and stopped to ask for shelter. Noticing the youth, he asked the miller if that tall young man was his son.

"No," he replied; "he is a foundling. Nineteen years ago a box was seen sailing on the mill stream by one of our men, and when it was caught in the weir he drew it out of the water and found the child in it."

Then the King knew that this must be the child of fortune, and therefore the one which he had thrown into the water. He hid his vexation, however, and presently said kindly, "I want to send a letter to the Queen, my wife; if that young man will take it to her I will give him two gold pieces for his trouble."

"We are at the King's service," replied the miller, and called to the young man to prepare for his errand. Then the King wrote a letter to the Queen, containing these words: "As soon as the boy who brings this letter arrives, let him be killed, and I shall expect to find him dead and buried when I come back."

The youth was soon on his way with this letter. He lost himself, however, in a large forest. But when darkness came on he saw in the distance a glimmering light, which he walked to, and found a small house. He entered and saw an old woman sitting by the fire, quite alone. She appeared frightened when she saw him, and said: "Where do you come from, and what do you want?"

"I am come from the mill," he replied, "and I am carrying a letter to the wife of the King, and, as I have lost my way, I should like very much to stay here during the night."

"You poor young man," she replied, "you are in a den of robbers, and when they come home they may kill you."

"They may come when they like," said the youth; "I am not afraid; but I am so tired that I cannot go a step further." Then he stretched himself on a bench and fell fast asleep.

Soon after the robbers came home, and asked angrily what that youth was lying there for.

"Ah," said the old woman, "he is an innocent child who has lost himself in the wood, and I took him in out of compassion. He is carrying a letter to the Queen, which the King has sent."

Then the robbers went softly to the sleeping youth, took the letter from his pocket, and read in it that as soon as the bearer arrived at the palace he was to lose his life. Then pity arose in the hardhearted robbers, and their chief tore up the letter and wrote another, in which it was stated that as soon as the boy arrived he should be married to the King's daughter. Then they left him to lie and rest on the bench till the next morning, and when he awoke they gave him the letter and showed him the road he was to take.

As soon as he reached the palace and sent in the letter, the Queen read it, and she acted in exact accordance with what was written—ordered a grand marriage feast, and had the Princess married at once to the fortunate youth. He was very handsome and amiable, so that the King's daughter soon learned to love him very much, and was quite happy with him.

Not long after, when the King returned home to his castle, he found the prophecy respecting the child of fortune fulfilled, and that he was married to a King's daughter. "How has this happened?" said he. "I have in my letter given very different orders!"

Then the Queen gave him the letter, and said: "You may see for yourself what is stated there."

The King read the letter and saw very clearly that it was not the one he had written. He asked the youth what he had done with the letter he had entrusted to him, and where he had brought the other from. "I know not," he replied, "unless it was changed during the night while I slept in the forest."

Full of wrath, the King said, "You shall not get off so easily, for whoever marries my daughter must first bring me three golden hairs from the head of the demon of the Black Forest. If you bring them to me before long, then shall you keep my daughter as a wife, but not otherwise."

Then said the child of fortune, "I will fetch these golden hairs very quickly; I am not the least afraid of the demon." Thereupon he said farewell, and started on his travels. His way led him to a large city, and as he stood at the gate and asked admission, a watchman said to him, "What trade do you follow, and how much do you know?" "I know everything," he replied.

"Then you can do us a favor," answered the watchman, "if you can tell why our master's fountain, from which wine used to flow, is dried up, and never gives us even water now." "I will tell you when I come back," he said; "only wait till then."

He traveled on still further, and came by and by to another town, where the watchman also asked him what trade he followed, and what he knew. "I know everything," he answered.

"Then," said the watchman, "you can do us a favor, and tell us why a tree in our town, which once bore golden apples, now only produces leaves." "Wait till I return," he replied, "and I will tell you."

On he went again, and came to a broad river, over which he must pass in a ferryboat, and the ferryman asked him the same question about his trade and his knowledge. He gave the same reply, that he knew everything.

"Then," said the man, "you can do me a favor, and tell me how it is that I am obliged to go backward and forward in my ferryboat every day, without a change of any kind." "Wait till I come back," he replied, "then you shall know all about it."

As soon as he reached the other side of the water he found the entrance to the Black Forest, in which was the demon's cove. It was very dark and gloomy, and the demon was not at home; but his old mother was sitting in a large armchair, and she looked up and said, "What do you want? You don't look wicked enough to be one of us."

"I just want three golden hairs from the demon's head," he replied; "otherwise my wife will be taken away from me."

"That is asking a great deal," she replied; "for if the demon comes home and finds you here, he will have no mercy on you. However, if you will trust me, I will try to help you."

Then she turned him into an ant, and said: "Creep into the folds of my gown; there you will be safe."

"Yes," he replied, "that is all very good; but I have three things besides that I want to know. First, why a well, from which formerly wine used to flow, should be dry now, so that not even water can be got from it. Secondly, why a tree that once bore golden apples should now produce nothing but leaves. And, thirdly, why a ferryman is obliged to row forward and back every day, without ever leaving off."

"These are difficult questions," said the old woman; "but keep still and quiet, and when the demon comes in, pay great attention to what he says, while I pull the golden hairs out of his head."

Late in the evening the demon came home, and as soon as he entered he declared that the air was not clear. "I smell the flesh of man," he said, "and I am sure that there is someone here." So he peeped into all the corners, and searched everywhere, but could find nothing.

Then his old mother scolded him well, and said, "Just as I have been sweeping, and dusting, and putting everything in order, then you come home and give me all the work to do over again. You have always the smell of something in your nose. Do sit down and eat your supper."

The demon did as she told him, and when he had eaten and drunk enough, he complained of being tired. So his mother made him lie down so that she could place his head in her lap; and he was soon so comfortable that he fell fast asleep and snored.

Then the old woman lifted up a golden hair, twitched it out, and laid it by her side. "Oh!" screamed the demon, waking up; "what was that for?" "I have had a bad dream," answered she, "and it made me catch hold of your hair."

"What did you dream about?" asked the demon. "Oh, I dreamed of a well in a marketplace from which wine once used to flow, but now it is dried up, and they can't even get water from it. Whose fault is that?" "Ah, they ought to know that there sits a toad under a stone in the well, and if he were dead wine would again flow."

Then the old woman combed his hair again, till he slept and snored so loud that the windows rattled, and she pulled out the second hair. "What are you about now?" asked the demon in a rage. "Oh, don't be angry," said the woman; "I have had another dream."

"What was this dream about?" he asked. "Why, I dreamed that in a certain country there grows a fruit tree which used to bear golden apples, but now it produces nothing but leaves. What is the cause of this?" "Why, don't they know," answered the demon, "that there is a mouse gnawing at the root? Were it dead the tree would again bear golden apples; and if it gnaws much longer the tree will wither and dry up. Bother your dreams; if you disturb me again, just as I am comfortably asleep, you will have a box on the ear."

Then the old woman spoke kindly to him, and smoothed and

combed his hair again, till he slept and snored. Then she seized the third golden hair and pulled it out.

The demon, on this, sprang to his feet, roared out in a greater rage than ever, and would have done some mischief in the house, but she managed to appease him this time also, and said: "How can I help my bad dreams?" "And whatever did you dream?" he asked, with some curiosity. "Well, I dreamed about a ferryman, who complains that he is obliged to take people across the river, and is never free." "Oh, the stupid fellow!" replied the wizard, "he can very easily ask any person who wants to be ferried over to take the oar in his hand, and he will be free at once."

Then the demon laid his head down once more; and as the old mother had pulled out the three golden hairs, and got answers to all the three questions, she let the old fellow rest and sleep in peace till the morning dawned.

As soon as he had gone out next day, the old woman took the ant from the folds of her dress and restored the lucky youth to his former shape. "Here are the three golden hairs for which you wished," said she; "and did you hear all the answers to your three questions?" "Yes," he replied, "every word, and I will not forget them." "Well, then, I have helped you out of your difficulties, and now get home as fast as you can."

After thanking the old woman for her kindness, he turned his steps homeward, full of joy that everything had succeeded so well.

When he arrived at the ferry the man asked for the promised answer. "Ferry me over first," he replied, "and then I will tell you."

So when they reached the opposite shore he gave the ferryman the demon's advice, that the next person who came and wished to be ferried over should have the oar placed in his hand, and from that moment he would have to take the ferryman's place.

Then the youth journeyed on till he came to the town where the unfruitful tree grew, and where the watchman was waiting for his answer. To him the young man repeated what he had heard, and said, "Kill the mouse that is gnawing at the root; then will your tree again bear golden apples."

The watchman thanked him, and gave him in return for his information two asses laden with gold, which were led after him. He very soon arrived at the city which contained the dried-up fountain. The sentinel came forward to receive his answer. Said the youth, "Under a stone in the fountain sits a toad; it must be searched for and killed; then will wine again flow from it." To show how thankful he was for this advice, the sentinel also ordered two asses laden with gold to be sent after him.

At length the child of fortune reached home with his riches, and his wife was overjoyed at seeing him again, and hearing how well he had succeeded in his undertaking. He placed before the King the three golden hairs he had brought from the head of the black demon; and when the King saw these and the four asses laden with gold he was quite satisfied, and said, "Now that you have performed all the required conditions, I am quite ready to sanction your marriage with my daughter; but, my dear son-in-law, tell me how you obtained all this gold. It is indeed a very valuable treasure; where did you find it?" "I crossed the river in a ferryboat, and on the opposite shore I found the gold lying in the sand."

"Can I find some if I go?" asked the King eagerly. "Yes, as much as you please," replied he. "There is a ferryman there who will row you over, and you can fill a sack in no time."

The greedy old King set out on his journey in all haste, and when he came near the river he beckoned to the ferryman to row him over the river.

The man told him to step in, and just as they reached the opposite shore he placed the rudder oar in the King's hand, and sprang out of the boat; and so the King became a ferryman as a punishment for his sins.

I wonder if he still goes on ferrying people over the river! It is very likely, for no one has ever been persuaded to touch the oar since he took it.

13. DARLING ROLAND
(Germany)

ONCE UPON A TIME there was a woman who was a real witch, and she had two daughters; one was ugly and wicked, but she loved her because she was her own daughter. The other was good and lovely, but she hated her for she was only her foster child.

Now, this foster child had a beautiful apron which the other daughter envied, and she said to her mother that have it she must and would. "Just wait quietly, my child," said her mother. "You shall have it. Tonight, when she is asleep, I will go and chop off your sister's head. Only take care to lie on the further side of the bed, against the wall, and push her well to this side."

Now, all this would certainly have come to pass if the poor girl had not been standing in a corner, and heard what they said. She was not even allowed to go near the door all day, and when bedtime came the witch's daughter got into bed first, so as to lie at the further side; but when she was asleep the other gently changed places with her, and put herself next the wall.

In the middle of the night the witch crept up holding an ax in her right hand, while with her left she felt if there was anyone there. Then she seized the ax with both hands, struck—and struck off her own child's head.

When she had gone away, the maiden got up, and went to the house of her sweetheart, Roland, and knocked at his door. When he came out, she said to him, "Listen, dear Roland; we must quickly fly. My foster mother tried to kill me, but she hit her own child instead. When day comes, and she sees what she has done, we shall be lost."

"But," said Roland, "you must first get her magic wand, or we shall not be able to escape if she comes after us."

The maiden fetched the magic wand, and then she took her foster sister's head, and dropped three drops of blood from it—one by the bed, one in the kitchen, and one on the stairs. After that, she hurried away with her sweetheart, Roland.

When the old witch got up in the morning she called her daughter in order to give her the apron, but she did not come. Then she called, "Where are you?"

"Here on the stairs," answered one drop of blood.

The witch went on to the stairs, but saw nothing, so she called again: "Where are you?"

"Here in the kitchen warming myself," answered the second drop of blood.

The witch went into the kitchen, but found nothing, then she called again: "Where are you?"

"Here in bed, sleeping," answered the third drop of blood.

So she went into the bedroom, and there she found her own child, whose head she had chopped off herself.

The witch flew into a violent passion, and sprang out of the window. As she could see for many miles around, she soon discovered the maiden hurrying away with Roland.

"That won't be any good," she cried. "However far you may go, you won't escape me."

She put on her seven-league boots, and before long she overtook them. When the maiden saw her coming, she changed her sweetheart into a lake, with the magic wand, and herself into a duck swimming in it. The witch stood on the shore, and threw breadcrumbs into the water, and did everything she could think of to entice the duck ashore. But it was all to no purpose, and she was obliged to go back at night without having accomplished her object.

When she had gone away, the maiden and Roland resumed their own shapes, and they walked the whole night till break of day.

Then the maiden changed herself into a beautiful rose in the middle of a briar hedge, and Roland into a fiddler. Before long the witch came striding along, and said to the fiddler, "Good fiddler, may I pick this beautiful rose?"

"By all means," he said, "and I will play to you."

As she crept into the hedge, in great haste to pick the flower (for she knew well who the flower was), Roland began to play, and she had to dance, whether she liked or not, for it was a magic dance. The quicker he played, the higher she had to jump, and the thorns tore her clothes to ribbons, and scratched her till she bled. He would not stop a moment, so she had to dance till she fell down dead.

When the maiden was freed from the spell, Roland said, "Now I will go to my father and order the wedding."

"Then I will stay here in the meantime," said the maiden. "And so that no one shall recognize me while I am waiting, I will change myself into a common red stone."

So Roland went away, and the maiden stayed in the field, as a stone, waiting his return.

But when Roland reached home, he fell into the snares of another woman, who made him forget all about his love. The poor maiden waited a long, long time, but when he did not come back, she became very sad, and changed herself into a flower, and thought, "Somebody at least will tread upon me."

Now it so happened that a shepherd was watching his sheep in the field, and saw the flower, and he picked it because he thought it was so pretty. He took it home and put it carefully away in a chest. From that time forward a wonderful change took place in the shepherd's hut. When he got up in the morning, all the work was done; the tables and benches were dusted, the fire was lighted, and the water was carried in. At dinnertime, when he came home, the table was laid, and a well-cooked meal stood ready. He could not imagine how it all came about, for he never saw a creature in his house, and nobody could be hidden in the tiny hut. He was much pleased at being so well served, but at last he got rather frightened, and went to a wise woman to ask her advice. The wise woman said, "There is magic behind it. You must look carefully about the room, early in the morning, and whatever you see, throw a white cloth over it, and the spell will be broken."

The shepherd did what she told him, and next morning, just as the day broke, he saw his chest open, and the flower come out. So he sprang up quickly, and threw a white cloth over it. Immediately the spell was broken, and a lovely maiden stood before him, who confessed that she had been the flower, and it was she who had done all the work of his hut. She also told him her story, and he was so pleased with her that he asked her to marry him.

But she answered, "No; I want my sweetheart Roland. Though he has forsaken me, I will always be true to him."

She promised not to go away, however, but to go on with the housekeeping for the present.

Now the time came for Roland's marriage to be celebrated. According to old custom, a proclamation was made that every maiden in the land should present herself to sing at the marriage in honor of the bridal pair.

When the faithful maiden heard this, she grew very sad, so sad that she thought her heart would break. She had no wish to go to the marriage, but the others came and fetched her. But each time as her turn came to sing, she slipped behind the others till she was the only one left, and she could not help herself.

As soon as she began to sing, and her voice reached Roland's ears, he sprang up and cried, "That is the true bride, and I will have no other."

Everything that he had forgotten came back, and his heart was filled with joy. So the faithful maiden was married to her sweetheart, Roland; all her grief and pain were over, and only happiness lay before her.

14. THE FISHERMAN AND HIS WIFE
(Germany)

THERE WAS ONCE a fisherman, who lived with his wife in a miserable little hovel close to the sea. He went to fish every day, and he fished and fished, and at last one day, as he was sitting looking deep down into the shining water, he felt something on his line. When he hauled it up there was a big flounder on the end of the line. The flounder said to him, "Listen, fisherman, I beg you not to kill me: I am no common flounder, I am an enchanted prince! What good will it do you to kill me? I shan't be good to eat; put me back into the water, and leave me to swim about."

"Ho! ho!" said the fisherman, "you need not make so many words about it. I am quite ready to put back a flounder that can talk." And so saying, he put back the flounder into the shining water, and it sank down to the bottom, leaving a streak of blood behind it.

Then the fisherman got up and went back to his wife in the hovel. "Husband," she said, "have you caught nothing today?"

"No," said the man; "all I caught was one flounder and he said he was an enchanted prince, so I let him go swim again."

"Did you not wish for anything then?" asked the goodwife.

"No," said the man; "what was there to wish for?"

"Alas!" said his wife, "isn't it bad enough always to live in this wretched hovel! You might at least have wished for a nice clean cottage. Go back and call him, tell him I want a pretty cottage: he will surely give us that."

"Alas!" said the man, "what am I to go back there for?"

"Well," said the woman, "it was you who caught him and let him go again; for certain he will do that for you. Be off now!"

The man was still not very willing to go, but he did not want to vex his wife, and at last he went back to the sea.

He found the sea no longer bright and shining, but dull and green. He stood by it and said—

"Flounder, flounder in the sea,
Prithee, hearken unto me:
My wife, Ilsebil, must have her own will,
And sends me to beg a boon of thee."

The flounder came swimming up, and said, "Well, what do you want?"

"Alas!" said the man, "I had to call you, for my wife said I ought to have wished for something as I caught you. She doesn't want to live in our miserable hovel any longer, she wants a pretty cottage."

"Go home again then," said the flounder, "she has her wish fully."

The man went home and found his wife no longer in the old hut, but a pretty little cottage stood in its place, and his wife was sitting on a bench by the door.

She took him by the hand, and said, "Come and look in here—isn't this much better?"

They went inside and found a pretty sitting room, and a bedroom with a bed in it, a kitchen and a larder furnished with everything of the best in tin and brass and every possible requisite. Outside there was a little yard with chickens and ducks, and a little garden full of vegetables and fruit.

"Look!" said the woman, "is not this nice?"

"Yes," said the man, "and so let it remain. We can live here very happily."

"We will see about that," said the woman. With that they ate something and went to bed.

Everything went well for a week or more, and then said the wife, "Listen, husband, this cottage is too cramped, and the garden is too small. The flounder could have given us a bigger house. I want to live in a big stone castle. Go to the flounder, and tell him to give us a castle."

"Alas, wife," said the man, "the cottage is good enough for us: what should we do with a castle?"

"Never mind," said his wife, "but go to the flounder, and he will manage it."

"Nay, wife," said the man, "the flounder gave us the cottage. I don't want to go back; as likely as not he'll be angry."

"Go, all the same," said the woman. "He can do it easily enough, and willingly into the bargain. Just go!"

The man's heart was heavy, and he was very unwilling to go. He said to himself, "It's not right." But at last he went.

He found the sea was no longer green; it was still calm, but dark violet and gray. He stood by it and said—

"Flounder, flounder in the sea,
  Prithee, hearken unto me:
  My wife, Ilsebil, must have her own will,
  And sends me to beg a boon of thee."

"Now, what do you want?" said the flounder.

"Alas," said the man, half scared, "my wife wants a big stone castle."

"Go home again," said the flounder, "she is standing at the door of it."

Then the man went away thinking he would find no house, but when he got back he found a great stone palace, and his wife standing at the top of the steps, waiting to go in.

She took him by the hand and said, "Come in with me."

With that they went in and found a great hall paved with marble slabs, and numbers of servants in attendance, who opened the great doors for them. The walls were hung with beautiful tapestries, and the rooms were furnished with golden chairs and tables, while rich carpets covered the floors, and crystal chandeliers hung from the ceilings. The tables groaned under every kind of delicate food and the most costly wines. Outside the house there was a great courtyard, with stabling for horses, and cows, and many fine carriages. Beyond this there was a great garden filled with the loveliest flowers, and fine fruit-trees. There was also a park, half a mile long, and in it were stags and hinds, and hares, and everything of the kind one could wish for.

"Now," said the woman, "is not this worth having?"

"Oh, yes," said the man, "and so let it remain. We will live in this beautiful palace and be content."

"We will think about that," said his wife, "and sleep upon it."

With that they went to bed.

Next morning the wife woke up first; day was just dawning, and from her bed she could see the beautiful country around her. Her husband was still asleep, but she pushed him with her elbow, and said, "Husband, get up and peep out of the window. See here, now, could we not be King over all this land? Go to the flounder. We will be King."

"Alas, wife," said the man, "what should we be King for? I don't want to be King."

"Ah," said his wife, "if you will not be King, I will. Go to the flounder. I will be King."

"Alas, wife," said the man, "whatever do you want to be King for? I don't like to tell him."

"Why not?" said the woman. "Go you must. I will be King."

So the man went; but he was quite sad because his wife would be King.

"It is not right," he said; "it is not right."

When he reached the sea, he found it dark, gray, and rough, and evil smelling. He stood there and said—

> "Flounder, flounder in the sea,
> Prithee, hearken unto me:
> My wife, Ilsebil, must have her own will,
> And sends me to beg a boon of thee."

"Now, what does she want?" said the flounder.

"Alas," said the man, "she wants to be King now."

"Go back. She is King already," said the flounder.

So the man went back, and when he reached the palace he found that it had grown much larger, and a great tower had been added with handsome decorations. There was a sentry at the door, and numbers of soldiers were playing drums and trumpets. As soon as he got inside the house, he found everything was marble and gold; and the hangings were of velvet, with great golden tassels. The doors of the saloon were thrown wide open, and he saw the whole court assembled. His wife was sitting on a lofty throne of gold and diamonds; she wore a golden crown, and carried in one hand a scepter of pure gold. On each side of her stood her ladies in a long row, every one a head shorter than the next.

He stood before her, and said: "Alas, wife, are you now King?"

"Yes," she said; "now I am King."

He stood looking at her for some time, and then he said: "Ah, wife, it is a fine thing for you to be King; now we will not wish to be anything more."

"Nay, husband," she answered, quite uneasily; "I find the time hangs very heavy on my hands. I can't bear it any longer. Go back to the flounder. King I am, but I must also be Emperor."

"Alas, wife," said the man, "why do you now want to be Emperor?"

"Husband," she answered, "go to the flounder. Emperor I will be."

"Alas, wife," said the man, "Emperor he can't make you, and I won't ask him. There is only one emperor in the country; and Emperor the flounder cannot make you, that he can't."

"What?" said the woman. "I am King, and you are but my husband. To him you must go, and that right quickly. If he can make a king, he can also make an emperor. Emperor I will be, so go quickly."

He had to go, but he was quite frightened. And as he went, he thought, "This won't end well; Emperor is too shameless. The flounder will make an end of the whole thing."

With that he came to the sea, but now he found it quite black, and heaving up from below in great waves. It tossed to and fro, and a sharp wind blew over it, and the man trembled. So he stood there, and said—

> "Flounder, flounder in the sea,
> Prithee, hearken unto me:
> My wife, Ilsebil, must have her own will,
> And sends me to beg a boon of thee."

"What does she want now?" said the flounder.

"Alas, flounder," he said, "my wife wants to be Emperor."

"Go back," said the flounder. "She is Emperor."

So the man went back, and when he got to the door, he found that the whole palace was made of polished marble, with alabaster figures and golden decorations. Soldiers marched up and down before the doors, blowing their trumpets and beating their drums. Inside the palace, counts, barons, and dukes walked about as attendants, and they opened to him the doors, which were of pure gold.

He went in, and saw his wife sitting on a huge throne made of solid gold. It was at least two miles high. She had on her head a great golden crown set with diamonds three yards high. In one hand she held the scepter, and in the other the orb of empire. On each side of her stood the gentlemen-at-arms in two rows, each one a little smaller than the other, from giants two miles high down to the tiniest dwarf no bigger than my little finger. She was surrounded by princes and dukes.

Her husband stood still, and said: "Wife, are you now Emperor?"

"Yes," said she; "now I am Emperor."

Then he looked at her for some time, and said: "Alas, wife, how much better off are you for being Emperor?"

"Husband," she said, "what are you standing there for? Now I am Emperor, I mean to be Pope! Go back to the flounder."

"Alas, wife," said the man, "what will you not want? Pope you cannot be. There is only one Pope in Christendom. That's more than the flounder can do."

"Husband," she said, "Pope I will be; so go at once. I must be Pope this very day."

"No, wife," he said, "I dare not tell him. It's no good; it's too monstrous altogether. The flounder cannot make you Pope."

"Husband," said the woman, "don't talk nonsense. If he can make an emperor, he can make a pope. Go immediately. I am Emperor, and you are but my husband, and you must obey."

So he was frightened, and went; but he was quite dazed. He shivered and shook, and his knees trembled.

A great wind arose over the land, the clouds flew across the sky, and it grew as dark as night; the leaves fell from the trees, and the water foamed and dashed upon the shore. In the distance the ships were being tossed to and fro on the waves, and he heard them firing signals of distress. There was still a little patch of blue in the sky among the dark clouds, but toward the south they were red and heavy, as in a bad storm. In despair, he stood and said—

> "Flounder, flounder in the sea,
> Prithee, hearken unto me:
> My wife, Ilsebil, must have her own will,
> And sends me to beg a boon of thee."

"Now, what does she want?" said the flounder.

"Alas," said the man, "she wants to be Pope!"

"Go back. Pope she is," said the flounder.

So back he went, and he found a great church surrounded with palaces. He pressed through the crowd, and inside he found thousands and thousands of lights, and his wife, entirely clad in gold, was sitting on a still higher throne, with three golden crowns upon her head, and she was surrounded with priestly state. On each side of her were two rows of candles, the biggest as thick as a tower, down to the tiniest little taper. Kings and emperors were on their knees before her, kissing her shoe.

"Wife," said the man, looking at her, "are you now Pope?"

"Yes," said she; "now I am Pope."

So there he stood gazing at her, and it was like looking at a shining sun.

"Alas, wife," he said, "are you better off for being Pope?"

At first she sat as stiff as a post, without stirring. Then he said: "Now, wife, be content with being Pope; higher you cannot go."

"I will think about that," said the woman, and with that they both went to bed. Still she was not content, and could not sleep for her inordinate desires. The man slept well and soundly, for he had walked about a great deal in the day; but his wife could think of nothing but what further grandeur she could demand. When the dawn reddened the sky she raised herself up in bed and looked out of the window, and when she saw the sun rise, she said:

"Ha! can I not cause the sun and the moon to rise? Husband!" she cried, digging her elbow into his side, "wake up and go to the flounder. I will be Lord of the Universe."

Her husband, who was still more than half asleep, was so shocked that he fell out of bed. He thought he must have heard wrong. He rubbed his eyes, and said:

"Alas, wife, what did you say?"

"Husband," she said, "if I cannot be Lord of the Universe, and cause the sun and moon to set and rise, I shall not be able to bear it. I shall never have another happy moment."

She looked at him so wildly that it caused a shudder to run through him.

"Alas, wife," he said, falling on his knees before her, "the flounder can't do that. Emperor and Pope he can make, but that is indeed beyond him. I pray you, control yourself and remain Pope."

Then she flew into a terrible rage. Her hair stood on end; she kicked him and screamed—

"I won't bear it any longer; will you go!"

Then he pulled on his trousers and tore away like a madman. Such a storm was raging that he could hardly keep his feet: houses and trees quivered and swayed, and mountains trembled, and the rocks rolled into the sea. The sky was pitchy black; it thundered and lightened, and the sea ran in black waves mountains high, crested with white foam. He shrieked out, but could hardly make himself heard—

> "Flounder, flounder in the sea,
> Prithee, hearken unto me:
> My wife, Ilsebil, must have her own will,
> And sends me to beg a boon of thee."

"Now, what does she want?" asked the flounder.

"Alas," he said, "she wants to be Lord of the Universe."

"Now she must go back to her old hovel; and there she is." So there they are to this very day.

15. THE FROG PRINCE
(Germany)

LONG AGO, WHEN WISHES often came true, there lived a King whose daughters were all handsome, but the youngest was so beautiful that the sun himself, who has seen everything, was bemused every time he shone over her because of her beauty. Near the royal castle there was a great dark wood, and in the wood under an old linden tree was a well; and when the day was hot, the King's daughter used to go forth into the wood and sit by the brink of the cool well, and if the time seemed long, she would take out a golden ball, and throw it up and catch it again, and this was her favorite pastime.

Now it happened one day that the golden ball, instead of falling back into the maiden's little hand which had sent it aloft, dropped to the ground near the edge of the well and rolled in. The King's daughter followed it with her eyes as it sank, but the well was deep, so deep that the bottom could not be seen. Then she began to weep, and she wept and wept as if she could never be comforted.

And in the midst of her weeping she heard a voice saying to her, "What ails you, King's daughter? Your tears would melt a heart of stone."

And when she looked to see where the voice came from, there was nothing but a frog stretching his thick ugly head out of the water. "Oh, is it you, old waddler?" said she; "I weep because my golden ball has fallen into the well."

"Never mind, do not weep," answered the frog; "I can help you; but what will you give me if I fetch up your ball again?"

"Whatever you like, dear frog," said she; "any of my clothes, my pearls and jewels, or even the golden crown that I wear."

"Your clothes, your pearls and jewels, and your golden crown are not for me," answered the frog; "but if you would love me, and have me for your companion and play-fellow, and let me sit by you at table, and eat from your plate, and drink from your cup, and sleep in your little bed—

if you would promise all this, then would I dive below the water and fetch you your golden ball again."

"Oh yes," she answered; "I will promise it all, whatever you want; if you will only get me my ball again." But she thought to herself, "What nonsense he talks! as if he could do anything but sit in the water and croak with the other frogs, or could possibly be anyone's companion."

But the frog, as soon as he heard her promise, drew his head under the water and sank down out of sight, but after a while he came to the surface again with the ball in his mouth, and he threw it on the grass.

The King's daughter was overjoyed to see her pretty plaything again, and she caught it up and ran off with it.

"Stop, stop!" cried the frog; "take me up too; I cannot run as fast as you!"

But it was of no use, for croak, croak after her as he might, she would not listen to him, but made haste home, and very soon forgot all about the poor frog, who had to betake himself to his well again.

The next day, when the King's daughter was sitting at table with the King and all the court, and eating from her golden plate, there came something pitter-patter up the marble stairs, and then there came a knocking at the door, and a voice crying, "Youngest King's daughter, let me in!"

And she got up and ran to see who it could be, but when she opened the door, there was the frog sitting outside. Then she shut the door hastily and went back to her seat, feeling very uneasy.

The King noticed how quickly her heart was beating, and said, "My child, what are you afraid of? Is there a giant standing at the door ready to carry you away?" "Oh no," answered she; "no giant, but a horrid frog." "And what does the frog want?" asked the King.

"O dear father," answered she, "when I was sitting by the well yesterday, and playing with my golden ball, it fell into the water, and while I was crying for the loss of it, the frog came and got it again for me on condition I would let him be my companion, but I never thought that he could leave the water and come after me; but now there he is outside the door, and he wants to come in to me."

And then they all heard him knocking the second time and crying,

> "Youngest King's daughter,
> Open to me!
> By the well water
> What promised you me?
> Youngest King's daughter
> Now open to me!"

"That which you have promised must you perform," said the King; "so go now and let him in."

So she went and opened the door, and the frog hopped in, following at her heels, till she reached her chair. Then he stopped and cried, "Lift me up to sit by you."

But she delayed doing so until the King ordered her. When once the frog was on the chair, he wanted to get on the table, and there he sat and said, "Now push your golden plate a little nearer, so that we may eat together."

And so she did, but everybody might see how unwilling she was, and the frog feasted heartily, but every morsel seemed to stick in her throat.

"I have had enough now," said the frog at last, "and as I am tired, you must carry me to your room, and make ready your silken bed, and we will lie down and go to sleep."

Then the King's daughter began to weep, and was afraid of the cold frog, that nothing would satisfy him but he must sleep in her pretty clean bed. Now the King grew angry with her, saying, "That which you have promised in thy time of necessity, must you now perform."

So she picked up the frog with her finger and thumb, carried him upstairs and put him in a corner, and when she had lain down to sleep, he came creeping up, saying, "I am tired and want sleep as much as you; take me up, or I will tell your father."

Then she felt beside herself with rage, and picking him up, she threw him with all her strength against the wall, crying, "Now will you be quiet, you horrid frog!"

But as he fell, he ceased to be a frog, and became all at once a Prince with beautiful kind eyes. And it came to pass that, with her father's consent, they became bride and bridegroom. And he told her how a wicked witch had bound him by her spells, and how no one but she alone could have released him, and that they two would go together to his father's kingdom. And there came to the door a carriage drawn by eight white horses, with white plumes on their heads, and with golden harness, and behind the carriage was standing faithful Henry, the servant of the young Prince.

Now, faithful Henry had suffered such care and pain when his master was turned into a frog, that he had been obliged to wear three iron bands over his heart, to keep it from breaking with trouble and anxiety. When the carriage started to take the Prince to his kingdom, and faithful Henry had helped them both in, he got up behind, and was full of joy at his master's deliverance. And when they had gone a part of the way, the Prince heard a sound at the back of the carriage, as if something had broken, and he turned round and cried, "Henry, the wheel must be breaking!" but Henry answered,

> *"The wheel does not break,*
> *'Tis the band round my heart*
> *That, to lessen its ache,*
> *When I grieved for your sake,*
> *I bound round my heart."*

Again, and yet once again there was the same sound, and the Prince thought it must be the wheel breaking. But it was the breaking of the other bands from faithful Henry's heart, because he was so relieved and happy.

16. THE GOOSEGIRL
(Germany)

THERE WAS ONCE an old queen whose husband had been dead for many years, and she had a very beautiful daughter. When she grew up she was betrothed to a prince in a distant country. When the time came for the maiden to be sent into this distant country to be married, the old queen packed up quantities of clothes and jewels, gold and silver, cups and ornaments, and, in fact, everything suitable to a royal outfit, for she loved her daughter very dearly.

She also sent a waiting-woman to travel with her, and to put her hand into that of the bridegroom. They each had a horse. The Princess's horse was called Falada, and it could speak.

When the hour of departure came, the old queen went to her bedroom, and with a sharp little knife cut her finger and made it bleed. Then she held a piece of white cloth under it, and let three drops of blood fall onto it. This cloth she gave to her daughter, and said, "Dear child, take good care of this; it will stand you in good stead on the journey." They then bade each other a sorrowful farewell. The Princess hid the piece of cloth in her bosom, mounted her horse, and set out to her bridegroom's country.

When they had ridden for a time the Princess became very thirsty, and said to the waiting-woman, "Get down and fetch me some water in my cup from the stream. I must have something to drink."

"If you are thirsty," said the waiting-woman, "dismount yourself, lie down by the water and drink. I don't choose to be your servant."

So, in her great thirst, the Princess dismounted and stooped down to the stream and drank, as she might not have her golden cup. The poor Princess said, "Alas!" and the drops of blood answered, "If your mother knew this, it would break her heart."

The royal bride was humble, so she said nothing, but mounted her horse again. Then they rode several miles further; but the day was warm, the sun was scorching, and the Princess was soon very thirsty again.

When they reached a river she called out again to her waiting-woman, "Get down, and give me some water in my golden cup!"

She had forgotten all about the rude words which had been said to her. But the waiting-woman answered more haughtily than ever, "If you want to drink, get the water for yourself. I won't be your servant."

Being very thirsty, the Princess dismounted, and knelt by the flowing water. She cried, and said, "Ah me!" and the drops of blood answered, "If your mother knew this it would break her heart."

While she stooped over the water to drink, the piece of cloth with the drops of blood on it fell out of her bosom, and floated away on the stream; but she never noticed this in her great fear. The waiting-woman, however, had seen it, and rejoiced at getting more power over the bride, who, by losing the drops of blood, had become weak and powerless.

Now, when she was about to mount her horse Falada again, the waiting-woman said, "By rights, Falada belongs to me; this jade will do for you!"

The poor little princess was obliged to give way. Then the waiting-woman, in a harsh voice, ordered her to take off her royal robes, and to put on her own mean garments. Finally, she forced her to swear before heaven that she would not tell a creature at the court what had taken place. Had she not taken the oath she would have been killed on the spot. But Falada saw all this and marked it.

The waiting-woman then mounted Falada and put the real bride on her poor jade, and they continued their journey.

There was great rejoicing when they arrived at the castle. The Prince hurried toward them, and lifted the waiting-woman from her horse, thinking she was his bride. She was led upstairs, but the real princess had to stay below.

The old king looked out of the window and saw the delicate, pretty little creature standing in the courtyard; so he went to the bridal apartment and asked the bride about her companion, who was left standing in the courtyard, and wished to know who she was.

"I picked her up on the way, and brought her with me for company. Give the girl something to do to keep her from idling."

But the old king had no work for her, and could not think of anything. At last he said, "I have a little lad who looks after the geese; she may help him."

The boy was called little Conrad, and the real bride was sent with him to look after the geese.

Soon after, the false bride said to the Prince, "Dear husband, I pray you do me a favor."

He answered, "That will I gladly."

"Well, then, let the knacker be called to cut off the head of the horse I rode; it angered me on the way."

Really, she was afraid that the horse would speak, and tell of her treatment of the Princess. So it was settled, and the faithful Falada had to die.

When this came to the ear of the real Princess, she promised the knacker a piece of gold if he would do her a slight service. There was a great dark gateway to the town, through which she had to pass every morning and evening. Would he nail up Falada's head in this gateway, so that she might see him as she passed?

The knacker promised to do as she wished, and when the horse's head was cut off, he hung it up in the dark gateway. In the early morning, when she and Conrad went through the gateway, she said in passing—

"Alas, Falada, hanging there!"

Then the head answered,

"Alas, young Queen, how ill you fare!
If this your tender mother knew,
Her heart would surely break in two."

Then they passed on out of the town, right into the fields, with the geese. When they reached the meadow, the Princess sat down on the grass and let down her hair. It shone like pure gold, and when little Conrad saw it, he was so delighted that he wanted to pluck some out; but she said—

> "Blow, blow, little breeze,
> And Conrad's hat seize.
> Let him join in the chase
> While away it is whirled,
> Till my tresses are curled
> And I rest in my place."

Then a strong wind sprang up, which blew away Conrad's hat right over the fields, and he had to run after it. When he came back, she had finished combing her hair, and it was all put up again; so he could not get a single hair. This made him very sulky, and he would not say another word to her. And they tended the geese till evening, when they went home.

Next morning, when they passed under the gateway, the Princess said—

> "Alas, Falada, hanging there!"

Falada answered,

> "Alas, young Queen, how ill you fare!
> If this your tender mother knew,
> Her heart would surely break in two."

Again, when they reached the meadows, the Princess undid her hair and began combing it. Conrad ran to pluck some out; but she said quickly—

> "Blow, blow, little breeze,
> And Conrad's hat seize.
> Let him join in the chase
> While away it is whirled,
> Till my tresses are curled
> And I rest in my place."

The wind sprang up and blew Conrad's hat far away over the fields, and he had to run after it. When he came back the hair was all put up again, and he could not pull a single hair out. And they tended the geese till the evening. When they got home Conrad went to the old king, and said, "I won't tend the geese with that maiden again."

"Why not?" asked the King.

"Oh, she vexes me every day."

The old king then ordered him to tell what she did to vex him.

Conrad said, "In the morning, when we pass under the dark gateway with the geese, she talks to a horse's head which is hung up on the wall. She says—

'Alas, Falada, hanging there!'

And the head replies,

'Alas, young Queen, how ill you fare!
If this your tender mother knew,
Her heart would surely break in two.'"

Then Conrad went on to tell the King all that happened in the meadow, and how he had to run after his hat in the wind.

The old king ordered Conrad to go out next day as usual. Then he placed himself behind the dark gateway, and heard the Princess speaking to Falada's head. He also followed her into the field, and hid himself behind a bush, and with his own eyes he saw the Goosegirl and the lad come driving the geese into the field. Then, after a time, he saw the girl let down her hair, which glittered in the sun. Directly after this, she said—

"Blow, blow, little breeze,
And Conrad's hat seize.
Let him join in the chase
While away it is whirled,
Till my tresses are curled
And I rest in my place."

Then came a puff of wind, which carried off Conrad's hat and he had to run after it. While he was away, the maiden combed and did up her hair; and all this the old king observed. Thereupon he went away unnoticed; and in the evening, when the Goosegirl came home, he called her aside and asked why she did all these things.

"That I may not tell you, nor may I tell any human creature; for I have sworn it under the open sky, because if I had not done so I should have lost my life."

He pressed her sorely, and gave her no peace, but he could get nothing out of her. Then he said, "If you won't tell me, then tell your sorrows to the iron stove there"; and he went away.

She crept up to the stove, and, beginning to weep and lament, unburdened her heart to it, and said: "Here I am, forsaken by all the world, and yet I am a princess. A false waiting-woman brought me to such a pass that I had to take off my royal robes. Then she took my place with my bridegroom, while I have to do mean service as a goosegirl. If my mother knew it she would break her heart."

The old king stood outside by the pipes of the stove, and heard all that she said. Then he came back, and told her to go away from the stove. He caused royal robes to be put upon her, and her beauty was a marvel. The old king called his son, and told him that he had a false bride—she was only a waiting-woman; but the true bride was here, the so-called Goosegirl.

The young prince was charmed with her youth and beauty. A great banquet was prepared, to which all the courtiers and good friends were bidden. The bridegroom sat at the head of the table, with the Princess on one side and the waiting-woman at the other; but she was dazzled, and did not recognize the Princess in her brilliant apparel.

When they had eaten and drunk and were all very merry, the old king put a riddle to the waiting-woman. "What does a person deserve who deceives his master?" telling the whole story, and ending by asking, "What doom does he deserve?"

The false bride answered, "No better than this. He must be put stark naked into a barrel stuck with nails, and be dragged along by two white horses from street to street till he is dead."

"That is your own doom," said the King, "and the judgment shall be carried out."

When the sentence was fulfilled, the young prince married his true bride, and they ruled their kingdom together in peace and happiness.

17. TOM THUMB
(Germany)

A POOR PEASANT sat one evening by his hearth and poked the fire, while his wife sat opposite spinning. He said: "What a sad thing it is that we have no children; our home is so quiet, while other folk's houses are noisy and cheerful."

"Yes," answered his wife, and she sighed; "even if it were an only one, and if it were no bigger than my thumb, I should be quite content; we would love it with all our hearts."

Now, some time after this, she had a little boy who was strong and healthy, but was no bigger than a thumb. Then they said: "Well, our wish is fulfilled, and, small as he is, we will love him dearly"; and because of his tiny stature they called him Tom Thumb. They let him want for nothing, yet still the child grew no bigger, but remained the same size as when he was born. Still, he looked out on the world with intelligent eyes, and soon showed himself a clever and agile creature, who was lucky in all he attempted.

One day, when the peasant was preparing to go into the forest to cut wood, he said to himself: "I wish I had someone to bring the cart after me."

"O father!" said Tom Thumb, "I will soon bring it. You leave it to me; it shall be there at the appointed time."

Then the peasant laughed, and said: "How can that be? You are much too small even to hold the reins."

"That doesn't matter, if only mother will harness the horse," answered Tom. "I will sit in his ear and tell him where to go."

"Very well," said the father; "we will try it for once."

When the time came, the mother harnessed the horse, set Tom in his ear, and then the little creature called out "Gee-up" and "Whoa" in turn, and directed it where to go. It went quite well, just as though it were being driven by its master; and they went the right way to the wood. Now it happened that while the cart was turning a corner, and Tom was calling to the horse, two strange men appeared on the scene.

"My goodness," said one, "what is this? There goes a cart, and a driver is calling to the horse, but there is nothing to be seen."

"There is something queer about this," said the other; "we will follow the cart and see where it stops."

The cart went on deep into the forest, and arrived quite safely at the place where the wood was cut.

When Tom spied his father, he said: "You see, father, here I am with the cart; now lift me down." The father held the horse with his left hand, and took his little son out of its ear with the right. Then Tom sat down quite happily on a straw.

When the two strangers noticed him, they did not know what to say for astonishment.

Then one drew the other aside, and said: "Listen, that little creature might make our fortune if we were to show him in the town for money. We will buy him."

So they went up to the peasant, and said: "Sell us the little man; he shall be well looked after with us."

"No," said the peasant; "he is the delight of my eyes, and I will not sell him for all the gold in the world."

But Tom Thumb, when he heard the bargain, crept up by the folds of his father's coat, placed himself on his shoulder, and whispered in his ear: "Father, let me go; I will soon come back again."

Then his father gave him to the two men for a fine piece of gold.

"Where will you sit?" they asked him.

"Oh, put me on the brim of your hat, then I can walk up and down and observe the neighborhood without falling down."

They did as he wished, and when Tom had said good-bye to his father, they went away with him.

They walked on till it was twilight, when the little man said: "You must lift me down."

"Stay where you are," answered the man on whose head he sat.

"No," said Tom; "I will come down. Lift me down immediately."

The man took off his hat and set the little creature in a field by the wayside. He jumped and crept about for a time, here and there among the sods, then slipped suddenly into a mouse hole which he had discovered.

"Good evening, gentlemen, just you go home without me," he called out to them in mockery.

They ran about and poked with sticks into the mouse hole, but all in vain. Tom crept further and further back, and, as it soon got quite dark, they were forced to go home, full of anger, and with empty purses.

When Tom noticed that they were gone, he crept out of his underground hiding place again. "It is dangerous walking in this field in the dark," he said. "One might easily break one's leg or one's neck." Luckily, he came to an empty snail shell. "Thank goodness," he said; "I can pass the night in safety here," and he sat down.

Not long after, just when he was about to go to sleep, he heard two men pass by. One said: "How shall we set about stealing the rich parson's gold and silver?"

"I can tell you," interrupted Tom.

"What was that?" said one robber in a fright. "I heard someone speak."

They remained standing and listened.

Then Tom spoke again: "Take me with you and I will help you."

"Where are you?" they asked.

"Just look on the ground and see where the voice comes from," he answered.

At last the thieves found him, and lifted him up. "You little urchin, are *you* going to help us?"

"Yes," he said; "I will creep between the iron bars in the pastor's room, and will hand out to you what you want."

"All right," they said, "we will see what you can do."

When they came to the parsonage, Tom crept into the room, but called out immediately with all his strength to the others: "Do you want everything that is here?"

The thieves were frightened, and said: "Do speak softly, and don't wake anyone."

But Tom pretended not to understand, and called out again: "What do you want? Everything?"

The cook, who slept above, heard him and sat up in bed and listened. But the thieves were so frightened that they retreated a little way. At last they summoned up courage again, and thought to themselves, "The little rogue wants to tease us." So they came back and whispered to him: "Now, do be serious, and hand us out something."

Then Tom called out again, as loud as he could, "I will give you everything if only you will hold out your hands."

The maid, who was listening intently, heard him quite distinctly, jumped out of bed, and stumbled to the door. The thieves turned and fled, running as though wild huntsmen were after them. But the maid, seeing nothing, went to get a light. When she came back with it, Tom, without being seen, slipped out into the barn, and the maid, after she had searched every corner and found nothing, went to bed again, thinking she had been dreaming with her eyes and ears open.

Tom Thumb climbed about in the hay, and found a splendid place to sleep. There he determined to rest till day came, and then to go home to his parents. But he had other experiences to go through first. This world is full of trouble and sorrow!

The maid got up in the gray dawn to feed the cows. First she went into the barn, where she piled up an armful of hay, the very bundle in which poor Tom was asleep. But he slept so soundly that he knew nothing till he was almost in the mouth of the cow, who was eating him up with the hay.

"Heavens!" he said, "however did I get into this mill?" but he soon saw where he was, and the great thing was to avoid being crushed between the cow's teeth. At last, whether he liked it or not, he had to go down the cow's throat.

"The windows have been forgotten in this house," he said. "The sun does not shine into it, and no light has been provided."

Altogether he was very ill-pleased with his quarters, and, worst of all, more and more hay came in at the door, and the space grew narrower and narrower. At last he called out, in his fear, as loud as he could, "Don't give me any more food. Don't give me any more food."

The maid was just milking the cow, and when she heard the same voice as in the night, without seeing anyone, she was frightened, and slipped from her stool and spilled the milk. Then, in the greatest haste, she ran to her master, and said: "Oh, your reverence, the cow has spoken!"

"You are mad," he answered; but he went into the stable himself to see what was happening.

Scarcely had he set foot in the cow shed before Tom began again, "Don't bring me any more food."

Then the pastor was terrified too, and thought that the cow must be bewitched; so he ordered it to be killed. It was accordingly slaughtered, but the stomach, in which Tom was hidden, was thrown into the manure heap. Tom had the greatest trouble in working his way out. Just as he stuck out his head, a hungry wolf ran by and snapped up the whole stomach with one bite. But still Tom did not lose courage. "Perhaps the wolf will listen to reason," he said. So he called out, "Dear wolf, I know where you can find a fine meal."

"Where is it to be had?" asked the wolf.

"Why, in such and such a house," answered Tom. "You must squeeze through the grating of the store-room window, and there you will find cakes, bacon, and sausages, as many as you can possibly eat"; and he went on to describe his father's house.

The wolf did not wait to hear this twice, and at night forced himself in through the grating, and ate to his heart's content. When he was satisfied, he wanted to go away again; but he had grown so fat that he could not get out the same way. Tom had reckoned on this, and began to make a great commotion inside the wolf's body, struggling and screaming with all his might.

"Be quiet," said the wolf; "you will wake up the people of the house."

"All very fine," answered Tom. "You have eaten your fill, and now I am going to make merry"; and he began to scream again with all his might.

At last his father and mother woke up, ran to the room, and looked through the crack of the door. When they saw a wolf, they went away, and the husband fetched his ax, and the wife a scythe.

"You stay behind," said the man, as they came into the room. "If my blow does not kill him, you must attack him and rip up his body."

When Tom Thumb heard his father's voice, he called out: "Dear father, I am here, inside the wolf's body."

Full of joy, his father cried, "Heaven be praised! Our dear child is found again," and he bade his wife throw aside the scythe that it might not injure Tom.

Then he gathered himself together, and struck the wolf a blow on the head, so that it fell down lifeless. Then with knifes and shears they ripped up the body, and took their little boy out.

"Ah," said his father, "what trouble we have been in about you."

"Yes, father, I have traveled about the world, and I am thankful to breathe fresh air again."

"Wherever have you been?" they asked.

"Down a mouse hole, in a cow's stomach, and in a wolf's maw," he answered; "and now I shall stay with you."

"And we will never sell you again, for all the riches in the world," they said, kissing and fondling their dear child.

Then they gave him food and drink, and had new clothes made for him, as his own had been spoiled in his travels.

18. THE WOLF AND THE SEVEN LITTLE KIDS
(Germany)

THERE WAS ONCE an old nanny-goat who had seven kids, and she was just as fond of them as is a mother of her children. One day she was going into the woods to fetch some food for them, so she called them all up to her, and said—

"My dear children, I am going out into the woods. Beware of the wolf! If once he gets into the house, he will eat you up, skin, and hair, and all. The rascal often disguises himself, but you will know him by his rough voice and his black feet."

The kids said, "Oh, we will be very careful, dear mother. You may be quite happy about us."

Bleating tenderly, the old goat went off to her work. Before long, someone knocked at the door, and cried—

"Open the door, dear children! Your mother has come back and brought something for each of you."

But the kids knew quite well by the voice that it was the wolf.

"We won't open the door," they cried. "You are not our mother. She has a soft gentle voice; but yours is rough, and we are quite sure that you are the wolf."

So he went away to a shop and bought a lump of chalk, which he ate, and it made his voice quite soft. He went back, knocked at the door again, and cried—

"Open the door, dear children. Your mother has come back and brought something for each of you."

But the wolf had put one of his paws on the windowsill, where the kids saw it, and cried—

"We won't open the door. Our mother has not got a black foot as you have; you are the wolf."

Then the wolf ran to a baker and said, "I have bruised my foot; please put some dough on it." And when the baker had put some dough on his foot, he ran to the miller and said, "Strew some flour on my foot."

The miller thought, "The old wolf is going to take somebody in," and refused.

But the wolf said, "If you don't do it, I will eat you up."

So the miller was frightened, and whitened his paws. People are like that, you know.

Now the wretch went for the third time to the door, and knocked, and said—

"Open the door, children. Your dear mother has come home, and has brought something for each of you out of the wood."

The kids cried, "Show us your feet first, that we may be sure you are our mother."

He put his paws on the windowsill, and when they saw that they were white, they believed all he said, and opened the door.

Alas! It was the wolf who walked in. They were terrified, and tried to hide themselves. One ran under the table, the second jumped into bed, the third into the oven, the fourth ran into the kitchen, the fifth got into the cupboard, the sixth into the washtub, and the seventh hid in the tall clock case. But the wolf found them all but one, and made short work of them. He swallowed one after the other, except the youngest one in the clock case, whom he did not find. When he had satisfied his appetite, he took himself off, and lay down in a meadow outside, where he soon fell asleep.

Not long after the old nanny-goat came back from the woods. Oh! what a terrible sight met her eyes! The house door was wide open, tables, chairs, and benches were overturned, the washing bowl was smashed to atoms, the covers and pillows torn from the bed. She searched all over the house for her children, but nowhere were they to be found. She called them by name, one by one, but no one answered. At last, when she came to the youngest, a tiny voice cried:

"I am here, dear mother, hidden in the clock case."

She brought him out, and he told her that the wolf had come and devoured all the others.

You may imagine how she wept over her children.

At last, in her grief, she went out, and the youngest kid ran by her side. When they went into the meadow, there lay the wolf under a tree, making the branches shake with his snores. They examined him from every side, and they could plainly see movements within his distended body.

"Ah, heavens!" thought the goat, "is it possible that my poor children whom he ate for his supper, should be still alive?"

She sent the kid running to the house to fetch scissors, needles, and thread. Then she cut a hole in the monster's side, and, hardly had she begun, when a kid popped out its head, and as soon as the hole was big enough, all six jumped out, one after the other, all alive, and without having suffered the least injury, for, in his greed, the monster had swallowed them whole. You may imagine the mother's joy. She hugged them, and skipped about like a tailor on his wedding day. At last she said:

"Go and fetch some big stones, children, and we will fill up the brute's body while he is asleep."

Then the seven kids brought a lot of stones, as fast as they could carry them, and stuffed the wolf with them till he could hold no more. The old mother quickly sewed him up, without his having noticed anything, or even moved.

At last, when the wolf had had his sleep out, he got up, and, as the stones made him feel very thirsty, he wanted to go to a spring to drink. But as soon as he moved the stones began to roll about and rattle inside him. Then he cried—

> "What's the rumbling and tumbling
> That sets my stomach grumbling?
> I thought 'twas six kids, flesh and bones,
> Now find it's nought but rolling stones."

When he reached the spring, and stooped over the water to drink, the heavy stones dragged him down, and he was drowned miserably.

When the seven kids saw what had happened, they came running up, and cried aloud—"The wolf is dead, the wolf is dead!" and they and their mother capered and danced round the spring in their joy.

19. LITTLE RED RIDING HOOD
(Germany)

THERE WAS ONCE a sweet little maiden, who was loved by all who knew her; but she was especially dear to her grandmother, who did not know how to make enough of the child. Once she gave her a little red velvet cloak. It was so becoming, and she liked it so much, that she would never wear anything else; and so she got the name of Little Red Riding Hood.

One day her mother said to her: "Come here, Little Red Riding Hood, take this cake and a bottle of wine to grandmother, she is weak and ill, and they will do her good. Go quickly, before it gets hot, and don't loiter by the way, or run, or you will fall down and break the bottle, and there would be no wine for grandmother. When you get there, don't forget to say, 'Good morning,' prettily, without staring about you."

"I will do just as you tell me," Little Red Riding Hood promised her mother.

Her grandmother lived away in the woods, a good half-hour from the village. When she got to the wood, she met a wolf; but Little Red Riding Hood did not know what a wicked animal he was, so she was not a bit afraid of him.

"Good morning, Little Red Riding Hood," he said.

"Good morning, wolf," she answered.

"Whither away so early, Little Red Riding Hood?"

"To grandmother's."

"What have you got in your basket?"

"Cake and wine; we baked yesterday, so I'm taking a cake to granny; she wants something to make her well."

"Where does your grandmother live, Little Red Riding Hood?"

"A good quarter of an hour further into the wood. Her house stands under three big oak trees, near a hedge of nut trees which you must know," said Little Red Riding Hood.

The wolf thought: "This tender little creature will be a plump morsel; she will be nicer than the old woman. I must be cunning, and snap them both up."

He walked along with Little Red Riding Hood for a while, then he said: "Look at the pretty flowers, Little Red Riding Hood. Why don't you look about you? I don't believe you even hear the birds sing, you are just as solemn as if you were going to school: everything else is so gay out here in the woods."

Little Red Riding Hood raised her eyes, and when she saw the sunlight dancing through the trees, and all the bright flowers, she thought: "I'm sure granny would be pleased if I took her a bunch of fresh flowers. It is still quite early, I shall have plenty of time to pick them."

So she left the path, and wandered off among the trees to pick the flowers. Each time she picked one, she always saw another prettier one further on. So she went deeper and deeper into the forest.

In the meantime the wolf went straight off to the grandmother's cottage, and knocked at the door.

"Who is there?"

"Little Red Riding Hood, bringing you a cake and some wine. Open the door!"

"Press the latch!" cried the old woman. "I am too weak to get up."

The wolf pressed the latch, and the door sprang open. He went straight in and up to the bed without saying a word, and ate up the poor old woman. Then he put on her nightdress and nightcap, got into bed and drew the curtains.

Little Red Riding Hood ran about picking flowers till she could carry no more, and then she remembered her grandmother again. She was astonished when she got to the house to find the door open, and when she entered the room everything seemed so strange.

She felt quite frightened, but she did not know why. "Generally I like coming to see grandmother so much," she thought. She cried: "Good morning, grandmother," but she received no answer.

Then she went up to the bed and drew the curtain back. There lay her grandmother, but she had drawn her cap down over her face, and she looked very odd.

"O grandmother, what big ears you have got," she said.

"The better to hear with, my dear."

"Grandmother, what big eyes you have got."

"The better to see with, my dear."

"What big hands you have got, grandmother."

"The better to catch hold of you with, my dear."

"But, grandmother, what big teeth you have got."

"The better to eat you up with, my dear."

Hardly had the wolf said this, than he made a spring out of bed, and devoured poor Little Red Riding Hood. When the wolf had satisfied himself, he went back to bed and he was soon snoring loudly.

A huntsman went past the house, and thought, "How loudly the old lady is snoring; I must see if there is anything the matter with her."

So he went into the house, and up to the bed, where he found the wolf fast asleep. "Do I find you here, you old sinner?" he said. "Long enough have I sought you."

He raised his gun to shoot, when it just occurred to him that perhaps the wolf had eaten up the old lady, and that she might still be saved. So he took a knife and began cutting open the sleeping wolf. At the first cut he saw the little red cloak, and after a few more slashes, the little girl sprang out, and cried: "Oh, how frightened I was, it was so dark inside the wolf!" Next the old grandmother came out, alive, but hardly able to breathe.

Little Red Riding Hood brought some big stones with which they filled the wolf, so that when he woke and tried to spring away, they dragged him back, and he fell down dead.

They were all quite happy now. The huntsman skinned the wolf, and took the skin home. The grandmother ate the cake and drank the wine which Little Red Riding Hood had brought, and she soon felt quite strong. Little Red Riding Hood thought: "I will never again wander off into the forest as long as I live, if my mother forbids it."

20. THE JUNIPER TREE

(Germany)

A LONG, LONG time ago, perhaps as much as two thousand years, there was a rich man, and he had a beautiful and pious wife, and they loved each other very much, and they had no children, though they wished greatly for some, and the wife prayed for one day and night. Now, in the courtyard in front of their house stood a juniper tree; and one day in winter the wife was standing beneath it, and paring an apple, and as she pared it she cut her finger, and the blood fell upon the snow.

"Ah," said the woman, sighing deeply, and looking down at the blood, "if only I could have a child as red as blood, and as white as snow!"

And as she said these words, her heart suddenly grew light, and she felt sure she should have her wish. So she went back to the house, and when a month had passed the snow was gone; in two months everything was green; in three months the flowers sprang out of the earth; in four months the trees were in full leaf, and the branches were thickly entwined; the little birds began to sing, so that the woods echoed, and the blossoms fell from the trees; when the fifth month had passed the wife stood under the juniper tree, and it smelled so sweet that her heart leaped within her, and she fell on her knees for joy; and when the sixth month had gone, the fruit was thick and fine, and she remained still; and the seventh month she gathered the berries and ate them eagerly, and was sick and sorrowful; and when the eighth month had passed she called to her husband, and said, weeping, "If I die, bury me under the juniper tree."

Then she was comforted and happy until the ninth month had passed, and then she bore a child as white as snow and as red as blood, and when she saw it her joy was so great that she died.

Her husband buried her under the juniper tree, and he wept sore;

time passed, and he became less sad; and after he had grieved a little more he left off, and then he took another wife.

His second wife bore him a daughter, and his first wife's child was a son, as red as blood and as white as snow. Whenever the wife looked at her daughter she felt great love for her, but whenever she looked at the little boy, evil thoughts came into her heart, of how she could get all her husband's money for her daughter, and how the boy stood in the way; and so she took great hatred to him, and drove him from one corner to another, and gave him a buffet here and cuff there, so that the poor child was always in disgrace; when he came back after school hours there was no peace for him.

Once, when the wife went into the room upstairs, her little daughter followed her, and said, "Mother, give me an apple."

"Yes, my child," said the mother, and gave her a fine apple out of the chest, and the chest had a great heavy lid with a strong iron lock.

"Mother," said the little girl, "shall not my brother have one too?"

That was what the mother expected; and she said, "Yes, when he comes back from school."

And when she saw from the window that he was coming, an evil thought crossed her mind, and she snatched the apple, and took it from her little daughter, saying, "You shall not have it before your brother."

Then she threw the apple into the chest, and shut the lid. Then the little boy came in at the door, and she said to him in a kind tone, but with evil looks, "My son, will you have an apple?"

"Mother," said the boy, "how terrible you look! Yes, give me an apple!"

Then she spoke as kindly as before, holding up the cover of the chest, "Come here and take out one for yourself."

And as the boy was stooping over the open chest, crash went the lid down, so that his head flew off among the red apples. But then the woman felt great terror, and wondered how she could escape the blame. And she went to the chest of drawers in her bedroom and took a white handkerchief out of the nearest drawer, and fitting the head to the neck, she bound them with a handkerchief, so that nothing should be seen, and set him on a chair before the door with the apple in his hand.

Then came little Marjory into the kitchen to her mother, who was standing before the fire stirring a pot of hot water.

"Mother," said Marjory, "my brother is sitting before the door and he has an apple in his hand, and looks very pale; I asked him to give me the apple, but he did not answer me; it seems very strange." "Go again to him," said the mother, "and if he will not answer you, give him a box on the ear."

So Marjory went again and said, "Brother, give me the apple."

But as he took no notice, she gave him a box on the ear, and his head fell off, at which she was greatly terrified, and began to cry and scream, and ran to her mother, and said, "Oh mother! I have knocked my brother's head off!" and cried and screamed, and would not cease.

"Oh Marjory!" said her mother, "what have you done? But keep quiet, that no one may see there is anything the matter; it can't be helped now; we will put him out of the way safely."

When the father came home and sat down to table, he said, "Where is my son?" But the mother was filling a great dish full of black broth, and Marjory was crying bitterly, for she could not refrain. Then the father said again, "Where is my son?" "Oh," said the mother, "he is gone into the country to his great-uncle's to stay for a little while." "What should he go for?" said the father, "and without bidding me good-bye, too!" "Oh, he wanted to go so much, and he asked me to let him stay there six weeks; he will be well taken care of." "Dear me," said the father, "I am quite sad about it; it was not right of him to go without bidding me good-bye."

With that he began to eat, saying, "Marjory, what are you crying for? Your brother will come back some time."

After a while he said, "Well, wife, the food is very good; give me some more."

And the more he ate the more he wanted, until he had eaten it all up, and he threw the bones under the table. Then Marjory went to her chest of drawers, and took one of her best handkerchiefs from the bottom drawer, and picked up all the bones from under the table and tied them up in her handkerchief, and went out at the door crying bitterly. She laid them in the green grass under the juniper tree, and immediately her heart grew light again, and she wept no more.

Then the juniper tree began to wave to and fro, and the boughs drew together and then parted, just like a clapping of hands for joy; then a cloud rose from the tree, and in the midst of the cloud there burned a fire, and out of the fire a beautiful bird arose, and, singing most sweetly, soared high into the air; and when he had flown away, the juniper tree remained as it was before, but the handkerchief full of bones was gone. Marjory felt quite glad and lighthearted, just as if her brother were still alive. So she went back merrily into the house and had her dinner.

The bird, when it flew away, perched on the roof of a goldsmith's house, and began to sing,

> "It was my mother who murdered me;
> It was my father who ate of me;
> It was my sister Marjory
> Who all my bones in pieces found;
> Them in a handkerchief she bound,
> And laid them under the juniper tree.
> Kywitt, kywitt, kywitt, I cry,
> Oh what a beautiful bird am I!"

The goldsmith was sitting in his shop making a golden chain, and when he heard the bird, who was sitting on his roof and singing, he started up to go and look, and as he passed over his threshold he lost one of his slippers; and he went into the middle of the street with a slipper on one foot and only a sock on the other; with his apron on, and the gold chain in one hand and the pincers in the other; and so he stood in the sunshine looking up at the bird.

"Bird," said he, "how beautifully you sing; do sing that piece over again." "No," said the bird, "I do not sing for nothing twice; if you will give me that gold chain I will sing again." "Very well," said the goldsmith, "here is the gold chain; now do as you said."

Down came the bird and took the gold chain in his right claw, perched in front of the goldsmith, and sang,

> "It was my mother who murdered me;
> It was my father who ate of me;
> It was my sister Marjory
> Who all my bones in pieces found;
> Them in a handkerchief she bound,
> And laid them under the juniper tree.
> Kywitt, kywitt, kywitt, I cry,
> Oh what a beautiful bird am I!"

Then the bird flew to a shoemaker's, and perched on his roof, and sang,

> "It was my mother who murdered me;
> It was my father who ate of me;
> It was my sister Marjory
> Who all my bones in pieces found;
> Them in a handkerchief she bound,
> And laid them under the juniper tree.
> Kywitt, kywitt, kywitt, I cry,
> Oh what a beautiful bird am I!"

When the shoemaker heard, he ran out of his door in his shirt sleeves and looked up at the roof of his house, holding his hand to shade his eyes from the sun. "Bird," said he, "how beautifully you sing!" Then he called in at his door, "Wife, come out directly; here is a bird singing beautifully. Just listen."

Then he called his daughter, all his children, and acquaintance, both young men and maidens, and they came up the street and gazed on the bird, and saw how beautiful it was with red and green feathers, and round its throat was as it were gold, and its eyes twinkled in its head like stars.

"Bird," said the shoemaker, "do sing that piece over again." "No," said the bird, "I may not sing for nothing twice; you must give me something." "Wife," said the man, "go into the shop; on the top shelf stands a pair of red shoes; bring them here." So the wife went and brought the shoes. "Now bird," said the man, "sing us that piece again."

And the bird came down and took the shoes in his left claw, and flew up again to the roof, and sang,

> "It was my mother who murdered me;
> It was my father who ate of me;
> It was my sister Marjory
> Who all my bones in pieces found;
> Them in a handkerchief she bound,
> And laid them under the juniper tree.
> Kywitt, kywitt, kywitt, I cry,
> Oh what a beautiful bird am I!"

And when he had finished he flew away, with the chain in his right claw and the shoes in his left claw, and he flew till he reached a mill, and the mill went "clip-clap, clip-clap, clip-clap." And in the mill sat twenty miller's-men hewing a millstone—"hick-hack, hick-hack, hick-hack," while the mill was going "clip-clap, clip-clap, clip-clap." And the bird perched on a linden tree that stood in front of the mill, and sang,

> "It was my mother who murdered me";

Here one of the men looked up.

> "It was my father who ate of me";

Then two more looked up and listened.

> "It was my sister Marjory"

Here four more looked up.

> "*Who all my bones in pieces found;*
> *Them in a handkerchief she bound,*"

Now there were only eight left hewing.

> "*And laid them under the juniper tree.*"

Now only five.

> "*Kywitt, kywitt, kywitt, I cry,*"

Now only one.

> "*Oh what a beautiful bird am I!*"

At length the last one left off, and he only heard the end.

"Bird," said he, "how beautifully you sing; let me hear it all. Sing that again!" "No," said the bird, "I may not sing it twice for nothing; if you will give me the millstone I will sing it again." "Indeed," said the man, "if it belonged to me alone you should have it." "All right," said the others, "if he sings again he shall have it."

Then the bird came down, and all the twenty millers heaved up the stone with poles—"yo! heave-ho! yo! heave-ho!" and the bird stuck his head through the hole in the middle, and with the millstone round his neck he flew up to the tree and sang,

> "*It was my mother who murdered me;*
> *It was my father who ate of me;*
> *It was my sister Marjory*
> *Who all my bones in pieces found;*
> *Them in a handkerchief she bound,*
> *And laid them under the juniper tree.*
> *Kywitt, kywitt, kywitt, I cry,*
> *Oh what a beautiful bird am I!*"

And when he had finished, he spread his wings, having in the right claw the chain, and in the left claw the shoes, and round his neck the millstone, and he flew away to his father's house.

In the parlor sat the father, the mother, and Marjory at the table; the father said, "How lighthearted and cheerful I feel." "Nay," said the mother, "I feel very low, just as if a great storm were coming."

But Marjory sat weeping; and the bird came flying, and perched on the roof.

"Oh," said the father, "I feel so joyful, and the sun is shining so bright; it is as if I were going to meet with an old friend." "Nay," said the wife, "I am terrified, my teeth chatter, and there is fire in my veins," and she tore open her dress to get air; and Marjory sat in a corner and wept, with her plate before her, until it was quite full of tears. Then the bird perched on the juniper tree, and sang,

> "It was my mother who murdered me";

And the mother stopped her ears and hid her eyes, and would neither see nor hear; nevertheless, the noise of a fearful storm was in her ears, and in her eyes a quivering and burning as of lightning.

> "It was my father who ate of me";

"Oh, mother!" said the father, "there is a beautiful bird singing so finely, and the sun shines, and everything smells as sweet as cinnamon."

> "It was my sister Marjory"

Marjory hid her face in her lap and wept, and the father said, "I must go out to see the bird." "Oh do not go!" said the wife, "I feel as if the house were on fire."

But the man went out and looked at the bird.

> "Who all my bones in pieces found;
> Them in a handkerchief she bound,
> And laid them under the juniper tree.
> Kywitt, kywitt, kywitt, I cry,
> Oh what a beautiful bird am I!"

With that the bird let fall the gold chain upon his father's neck, and it fitted him exactly. So he went indoors and said, "Look what a beautiful chain the bird has given me!"

Then his wife was so terrified that she fell down on the floor, and her cap came off. Then the bird began again to sing,

> "It was my mother who murdered me";

"Oh," groaned the mother, "that I were a thousand fathoms under ground, so as not to be obliged to hear it."

> "It was my father who ate of me";

Then the woman lay as if she were dead.

> "It was my sister Marjory"

"Oh," said Marjory, "I will go out, too, and see if the bird will give me anything." And so she went.

> "Who all my bones in pieces found;
> Them in a handkerchief she bound,"

Then he threw the shoes down to her.

> "And laid them under the juniper tree.
> Kywitt, kywitt, kywitt, I cry,
> Oh what a beautiful bird am I!"

And poor Marjory all at once felt happy and joyful, and put on her red shoes, and danced and jumped for joy. "Oh dear," said she, "I felt so sad before I went outside, and now my heart is so light! He is a charming bird to have given me a pair of red shoes."

But the mother's hair stood on end, and looked like flame, and she said, "Even if the world is coming to an end, I must go out for a little relief."

Just as she came outside the door, crash went the millstone on her head, and crushed her flat. The father and daughter rushed out, and saw smoke and flames of fire rise up; but when that had gone by, there stood the little brother; and he took his father and Marjory by the hand, and they felt very happy and content, and went indoors, and sat at the table, and had their dinner.

21. THE GOLDEN GOOSE
(Germany)

THERE WAS ONCE a man who had three sons. The youngest of them was called Simpleton; he was scorned and despised by the others, and kept in the background.

The eldest son was going into the forest to cut wood, and before he started, his mother gave him a nice sweet cake and a bottle of wine to take with him, so that he might not suffer from hunger or thirst. In the wood he met a little, old, gray man, who bade him good day, and said, "Give me a bit of the cake in your pocket, and let me have a drop of your wine. I am so hungry and thirsty."

But the clever son said: "If I give you my cake and wine, I shan't have enough for myself. Be off with you."

He left the little man standing there, and went on his way. But he had not been long at work, cutting down a tree, before he made a false stroke, and dug the ax into his own arm, and he was obliged to go home to have it bound up.

Now, this was no accident; it was brought about by the little gray man.

The second son now had to go into the forest to cut wood, and, like the eldest, his mother gave him a sweet cake and a bottle of wine. In the same way the little gray man met him, and asked for a piece of his cake and a drop of his wine. But the second son made the same sensible answer, "If I give you any, I shall have the less for myself. Be off out of my way," and he went on.

His punishment, however, was not long delayed. After a few blows at the tree, he hit his own leg, and had to be carried home.

Then Simpleton said, "Let me go to cut the wood, father."

But his father said, "Your brothers have only come to harm by it; you had better leave it alone. You know nothing about it." But Simpleton begged so hard to be allowed to go that at last his father said, "Well, off you go then. You will be wiser when you have hurt yourself."

His mother gave him a cake which was only mixed with water and baked in the ashes, and a bottle of sour beer. When he reached the forest, like the others, he met the little gray man.

"Give me a bit of the cake in your pocket and a drop of your wine. I am so hungry and thirsty," said the little man.

Simpleton answered, "I only have a cake baked in the ashes, and some sour beer; but, if you like such fare, we will sit down and eat it together."

So they sat down; but when Simpleton pulled out his cake it was a sweet, nice cake, and his sour beer was turned into good wine. So they ate and drank, and the little man said, "As you have such a good heart, and are willing to share your goods, I will give you good luck. There stands an old tree; cut it down, and you will find something at the roots."

The Simpleton went there, and hewed away at the tree, and when it fell he saw, sitting among the roots, a goose with feathers of pure gold. He lifted it out and took it with him to an inn where he intended to stay the night.

The landlord had three daughters who, when they saw the goose, were curious to know what wonderful kind of bird it was, and ended by longing for one of its golden feathers. The eldest thought, "I will wait for a good opportunity, and then I will pull out one of its feathers for myself"; and so, when the Simpleton was gone out, she seized the goose by its wing—but there her finger and hand had to stay, held fast. Soon after came the second sister with the same idea of plucking out one of the golden feathers for herself; but scarcely had she touched her sister than she also was obliged to stay, held fast. Lastly came the third with the same intentions; but the others screamed out, "Stay away! for heaven's sake stay away!" But she did not see why she should stay away, and thought, "If they do so, why should not I?" and went towards them. But when she reached her sisters there she stopped, hanging on with them. And so they had to stay, all night.

The next morning the Simpleton took the goose under his arm and went away, unmindful of the three girls that hung on to it. The three had to run after him, left and right, wherever his legs carried him. In the midst of the fields they met the parson, who, when he saw the procession, said, "Shame on you, girls, running after a young fellow through the fields like this," and forthwith he seized hold of the youngest by the hand to drag her away, but hardly had he touched her when he too was obliged to run after them himself.

Not long after the sexton came that way, and seeing the respected parson following at the heels of the three girls, he called out, "Ho, your reverence, whither away so quickly? You forget that we have another christening today"; and he seized hold of him by his gown; but no sooner had he touched him than he was obliged to follow on too. As the five tramped on, one after another, two peasants with their hoes came up from the fields, and the parson cried out to them, and begged them to come and set him and the sexton free, but no sooner had they touched the sexton than they had to follow on too; and now there were seven following the Simpleton and the goose.

By and by they came to a town where a King reigned, who had an only daughter who was so serious that no one could make her laugh; therefore the King had given out that whoever should make her laugh should have her in marriage. The Simpleton, when he heard this, went with his goose and his hangers-on into the presence of the King's daughter, and as soon as she saw the seven people following always one after the other, she burst out laughing, and seemed as if she could never stop. And so the Simpleton earned a right to her as his bride; but the King did not like him for a son-in-law and made all kinds of objections, and said he must first bring a man who could drink up a whole cellar of wine.

The Simpleton thought that the little gray man would be able to help him, and went out into the forest, and there, on the very spot where he felled the tree, he saw a man sitting with a very sad countenance. The Simpleton asked him what was the matter, and he answered, "I have a great thirst, which I cannot quench: cold water does not agree with me; I have indeed drunk up a whole cask of wine; but what is a drop like that on a burning stone?"

"Well, there I can help you," said Simpleton. "Come with me, and you shall soon have enough to drink and to spare."

He led him to the King's cellar, and the man set to upon the great casks, and he drank and drank till his sides ached, and by the end of the day the cellar was empty.

Then again Simpleton demanded his bride. But the King was annoyed that a wretched fellow called "Simpleton" should have his daughter, and he made new conditions. He was now to find a man who could eat up a mountain of bread.

Simpleton did not reflect long, but went straight to the forest, and there in the selfsame place sat a man tightening a strap round his body, and making a very miserable face. He said: "I have eaten up a whole ovenful of rolls, but what is the good of that when anyone is as hungry as I am. I am never satisfied. I have to tighten my belt every day if I am not to die of hunger."

Simpleton was delighted, and said: "Get up and come with me. You shall have enough to eat."

And he took him to the court, where the King had caused all the flour in the kingdom to be brought together, and a huge mountain of bread to be baked. The man from the forest sat down before it and began to eat, and at the end of the day the whole mountain had disappeared.

Now, for the third time, Simpleton asked for his bride. But again the King tried to find an excuse, and demanded a ship which could sail on land as well as at sea.

"As soon as you sail up in it, you shall have my daughter," he said.

Simpleton went straight to the forest, and there sat the little gray man to whom he had given his cake. The little man said: "I have eaten and drunk for you, and now I will give you the ship, too. I do it all because you were merciful to me."

Then he gave him the ship which could sail on land as well as at sea, and when the King saw it he could no longer withhold his daughter. The marriage was celebrated, and, at the King's death, the Simpleton inherited the kingdom, and lived long and happily with his wife.

22. THOUSAND-FURS
(Germany)

A KING ONCE HAD a wife with golden hair who was so beautiful that none on earth could be found equal to her. It happened that she fell ill, and as soon as she knew she must die, she sent for the King and said to him, "After my death I know you will marry another wife; but you must promise me that, however beautiful she may be, if she is not as beautiful as I am and has not golden hair like mine you will not marry her."

The King had no sooner given his promise than she closed her eyes and died.

For a long time he refused to be comforted, and thought it was impossible he could ever take another wife. At length his counselors came to him, and said, "A King should not remain unmarried; we ought to have a Queen."

So he at last consented, and then messengers were sent far and wide to find a bride whose beauty should equal that of the dead Queen. But none was to be found in the whole world; for even when equally beautiful they had not golden hair. So the messengers returned without obtaining what they sought.

Now, the King had a daughter who was quite as beautiful as her dead mother, and had also golden hair. She had all this while growing up, and very soon the King noticed how exactly she resembled her dead mother. So he sent for his counselors, and said to them, "I will marry my daughter; she is the image of my dead wife, and no other bride can be found to enable me to keep my promise to her."

When the counselors heard this, they were dreadfully shocked, and said, "It is forbidden for a father to marry his daughter; nothing but evil could spring from such a sin, and the kingdom will be ruined."

When the King's daughter heard of her father's proposition she was greatly alarmed, the more so as she saw how resolved he was to carry out his intention. She hoped, however, to be able to save him and herself from such ruin and disgrace, so she said to him, "Before I consent to your wish I shall require three things—a dress as golden as the sun, another as silvery as the moon, and a third as glittering as the stars; and besides this, I shall require a mantle made of a thousand skins of rough fur sewn together, and every animal in the kingdom must give a piece of his skin toward it."

"Ah!" she thought, "I have asked for impossibilities, and I hope I shall be able to make my father give up his wicked intentions."

The King, however, was not to be diverted from his purpose. All the most skillful young women in the kingdom were employed to weave the three dresses, one to be as golden as the sun, another as silvery as the moon, and the third as glittering as the stars. He sent hunters into the forest to kill the wild animals and bring home their skins, of which the mantle was to be made; and at last when all was finished he brought them and laid them before her, and then said, "Tomorrow our marriage shall take place."

Then the King's daughter saw that there was no hope of changing her father's heart, so she determined to run away from the castle.

In the night, when everyone slept, she rose and took from her jewel case a gold ring, a gold spinning wheel, and a golden hook. The three dresses of the sun, moon, and stars she folded in so small a parcel that they were placed in a walnut shell; then she put on the fur mantle, stained her face and hands black with walnut juice, and committing herself to the care of Heaven, she left her home.

After traveling the whole night she came at last to a large forest, and feeling very tired she crept into a hollow tree and went to sleep. The sun rose, but she still slept on, and did not awake till nearly noon.

It happened on this very day that the King to whom the wood belonged was hunting in the forest, and when his hounds came to the tree they sniffed about, and ran round and round the tree barking loudly. The King called to his hunters, and said, "Just go and see what wild animal the dogs are barking at."

They obeyed, and quickly returning told the King that in the hollow tree was a most beautiful creature, such as they had never seen before, that the skin was covered with a thousand different sorts of fur, and that it was fast asleep.

"Then," said the King, "go and see if you can capture it alive. Then bind it on the wagon and bring it home."

While the hunters were binding the maiden she awoke, and full of terror cried out to them, "I am only a poor child, forsaken by my father and mother; take pity on me, and take me with you!" "Well," they replied, "you may be useful to the cook, Thousand-Furs. Come with us; you can at least sweep up the ashes."

So they seated her on the wagon and took her home to the King's castle. They showed her a little stable under the steps, where no daylight ever came, and said, "Thousand-Furs, here you can live and sleep." So the King's daughter was sent into the kitchen to fetch the wood, draw the water, stir the fire, pluck the fowls, look after the vegetables, sweep the ashes, and do all the hard work.

Poor Thousand-Furs, as they called her, lived for a long time most miserably, and the beautiful King's daughter knew not when it would end or how. It happened, however, after a time that a festival was to take place in the castle, so she said to the cook, "May I go out for a little while to see the company arrive? I will stand outside the door." "Yes, you may go," he replied, "but in half an hour I shall want you to sweep up the ashes and put the kitchen in order."

Then she took her little oil lamp, went into the stable, threw off the fur coat, washed the nut stains from her face and hands, so that her full beauty appeared before the day. After this she opened the nutshell and took out the dress that was golden as the sun, and put it on. As soon as she was quite dressed she went out and presented herself at the entrance of the castle as a visitor. No one recognized her as Thousand-Furs; they thought she was a King's daughter, and sent and told the King of her arrival. He went to receive her, offered her his hand, and while they danced together he thought in his heart, "My eyes have never seen any maiden before so beautiful as this."

As soon as the dance was over she bowed to the King, and before he could look round she had vanished, no one knew where. The sentinel at the castle gate was called and questioned, but he had not seen anyone pass.

But she had run to her stable, quickly removed her dress, stained her face and hands, put on her fur coat, and was again Thousand-Furs. When she entered the kitchen and began to do her work and sweep up the ashes, the cook said, "Leave that alone till tomorrow; I want you to cook some soup for the King. I will also taste a little when it is ready. But do not let one of your hairs fall in, or you will get nothing to eat in future from me."

Then the cook went out, and Thousand-Furs made the King's soup as nicely as she could, and cut bread for it, and when it was ready she fetched from her little stable her gold ring and laid it in the dish in which the soup was prepared.

After the King had left the ballroom he called for the soup, and while eating it thought he had never tasted better soup in his life. But when the dish was nearly empty he saw to his surprise a gold ring lying at the bottom, and could not imagine how it came there. Then he ordered the cook to come to him, and he was in a terrible fright when he heard the order. "You must certainly have let a hair fall into the soup; if you have, I shall thrash you!" he said.

As soon as he appeared the King said, "Who cooked this soup?" "I cooked it," he replied. "That is not true," said the King. "This soup is made quite differently and much better than you ever made it."

Then the cook was obliged to confess that Thousand-Furs had made the soup. "Go and send her to me," said the King.

As soon as she appeared the King said to her, "Who are you, maiden?" She replied, "I am a poor child, without father or mother." He asked again, "Why are you in my castle?" "Because I am trying to earn my bread by helping the cook," she replied. "How came this ring in the soup?" he said again. "I know nothing about the ring!" she replied.

When the King found he could learn nothing from Thousand-Furs, he sent her away. A little time after this there was another festival, and Thousand-Furs had again permission from the cook to go and see the visitors. "But," he added, "come back in half an hour and cook for the King the soup that he is so fond of."

She promised to return, and ran quickly into her little stable, washed off the stains, and took out of the nutshell her dress, silvery as the moon, and put it on. Then she appeared at the castle like a King's daughter, and the King came to receive her with great pleasure; he was so glad to see her again, and while the dancing continued the King kept her as his partner. When the ball ended she disappeared so quickly that the King could not imagine what had become of her. But she had rushed down to her stable, made herself again the rough little creature that was called Thousand-Furs, and went into the kitchen to cook the soup.

While the cook was upstairs she fetched the golden spinning wheel and dropped it into the soup as soon as it was ready. The King again ate it with great relish; it was as good as before, and when he sent for the cook and asked who made it, he was obliged to own that it was Thousand-Furs. She was also ordered to appear before the King, but he could get nothing out of her, excepting that she was a poor child, and knew nothing of the golden spinning wheel.

At the King's third festival everything happened as before. But the cook said, "I will let you go and see the dancing room this time, Thousand-Furs; but I believe you are a witch, for although the soup is good, and the King says it is better than I can make it, there is always something dropped into it which I cannot understand." Thousand-Furs did not stop to listen; she ran quickly to her little stable, washed off the nut stains, and this time dressed herself in the dress that glittered like the stars. When the King came as before to receive her in the hall, he thought he had never seen such a beautiful woman in his life. While they were dancing he contrived, without being noticed by the maiden, to slip a gold ring on her finger, and he had given orders that the dancing should continue longer than usual. When it ended, he wanted to hold her hand still, but she pulled it away, and sprang so quickly among the people that she vanished from his eyes.

She ran out of breath to her stable under the steps, for she knew that she had remained longer away than half an hour, and there was not time to take off her dress, so she threw on her fur cloak over it, and in her haste she did not make her face black enough, nor hide her golden hair properly; her hands also remained white. However, when she entered the kitchen, the cook was still away, so she prepared the King's soup, and dropped into it the golden hook.

The King, when he found another trinket in his soup, sent immediately for Thousand-Furs, and as she entered the room he saw the ring on her white finger which he had placed there. Instantly he seized her hand and held her fast, but in her struggles to get free the fur mantle opened and the star-glittering dress was plainly seen. The King caught the mantle and tore it off, and as he did so her golden hair fell over her shoulders, and she stood before him in her full splendor, and felt that she could no longer conceal who she was. Then she wiped the soot and stains from her face, and was as beautiful to the eyes of the King as any woman upon earth.

"You shall be my dear bride," said the King, "and we will never be parted again, although I know not who you are."

Then she told him her past history, and all that had happened to her, and he found that she was, as he thought, a King's daughter. Soon after the marriage was celebrated, and they lived happily till their death.

23. RUMPELSTILTSKIN
(Germany)

THERE WAS ONCE a miller who was poor, but he had one beautiful daughter. It happened one day that he came to speak with the King, and, to give himself consequence, he told him that he had a daughter who could spin gold out of straw. The King said to the miller, "That is an art that pleases me well; if your daughter is as clever as you say, bring her to my castle tomorrow, that I may put her to the proof."

When the girl was brought to him, he led her into a room that was quite full of straw, and gave her a wheel and spindle, and said, "Now set to work, and if by the early morning you have not spun this straw to gold you shall die." And he shut the door himself, and left her there alone.

And so the poor miller's daughter was left there sitting, and could not think what to do for her life: she had no notion how to set to work to spin gold from straw, and her distress grew so great that she began to weep. Then all at once the door opened, and in came a little man, who said, "Good evening, miller's daughter; why are you crying?" "Oh!" answered the girl, "I have got to spin gold out of straw, and I don't understand the business."

Then the little man said, "What will you give me if I spin it for you?" "My necklace," said the girl.

The little man took the necklace, seated himself before the wheel, and whirr, whirr, whirr! three times round and the bobbin was full; then he took up another, and whirr, whirr, whirr! three times round, and that was full; and so he went on till the morning, when all the straw had been spun, and all the bobbins were full of gold. At sunrise came the King, and when he saw the gold he was astonished and very much rejoiced, for he was very avaricious. He had the miller's daughter taken into another room filled with straw, much bigger than the last, and told her that as she valued her life she must spin it all in one night.

The girl did not know what to do, so she began to cry, and then the door opened, and the little man appeared and said, "What will you give me if I spin all this straw into gold?" "The ring from my finger," answered the girl.

So the little man took the ring, and began again to send the wheel whirring round, and by the next morning all the straw was spun into glistening gold. The King was rejoiced beyond measure at the sight, but as he could never have enough of gold, he had the miller's daughter taken into a still larger room full of straw, and said, "This, too, must be spun in one night, and if you accomplish it you shall be my wife." For he thought, "Although she is but a miller's daughter, I am not likely to find anyone richer in the whole world."

As soon as the girl was left alone, the little man appeared for the third time and said, "What will you give me if I spin the straw for you this time?" "I have nothing left to give," answered the girl. "Then you must promise me the first child you have after you are Queen," said the little man.

"But who knows whether that will happen?" thought the girl; but as she did not know what else to do in her necessity, she promised the little man what he desired, upon which he began to spin, until all the straw was gold. And when in the morning the King came and found all done according to his wish, he caused the wedding to be held at once, and the miller's pretty daughter became a Queen.

In a year's time she brought a fine child into the world, and thought no more of the little man; but one day he came suddenly into her room, and said, "Now give me what you promised me."

The Queen was terrified greatly, and offered the little man all the riches of the kingdom if he would only leave the child; but the little man said, "No, I would rather have something living than all the treasures of the world."

Then the Queen began to lament and to weep, so that the little man had pity upon her. "I will give you three days," said he, "and if at the end of that time you cannot tell my name, you must give up the child to me."

Then the Queen spent the whole night in thinking over all the names that she had ever heard, and sent a messenger through the land to ask far and wide for all the names that could be found. And when the little man came next day, beginning with Caspar, Melchior, Baltha-zar, she repeated all she knew, and went through the whole list, but after each the little man said, "That is not my name."

The second day the Queen sent to inquire of all the neighbors what the servants were called, and told the little man all the most unusual and singular names, saying, "Perhaps you are Roast-ribs, or Sheep-shanks, or Spindleshanks?" But he answered nothing but "That is not my name."

The third day the messenger came back again, and said, "I have not been able to find one single new name; but as I passed through the woods I came to a high hill, and near it was a little house, and before the house burned a fire, and round the fire danced a comical little man, and he hopped on one leg and cried,

> 'Today I bake; tomorrow I brew my beer;
> The next day I will bring the Queen's child here.
> Ah! lucky 'tis that not a soul doth know
> That Rumpelstiltskin is my name, ho! ho!' "

You cannot think how pleased the Queen was to hear that name, and soon afterward, when the little man walked in and said, "Now, Mrs. Queen, what is my name?" she said at first, "Are you called Jack?" "No," answered he. "Are you called Harry?" she asked again. "No," answered he. And then she said, "Then perhaps your name is Rumpel-stiltskin!"

"The devil told you that! the devil told you that!" cried the little man, and in his anger he stamped with his right foot so hard that it went into the ground above his knee; then he seized his left foot with both his hands in such a fury that he split in two, and there was an end of him.

24. MOTHER HOLLE
(Germany)

A WIDOW HAD two daughters; one was pretty and industrious, the other was ugly and lazy. And as the ugly one was her own daughter, she loved her much the best, and the pretty one was made to do all the work, and be the drudge of the house. Every day the poor girl had to sit by a well on the high road and spin until her fingers bled. Now it happened once that as the spindle was bloody, she dipped it into the well to wash it; but it slipped out of her hand and fell in. Then she began to cry, and ran to her stepmother, and told her of her misfortune; and her stepmother scolded her without mercy, and said in her rage, "As you have let the spindle fall in, you must go and fetch it out again!"

Then the girl went back again to the well, not knowing what to do, and in the despair of her heart she jumped down into the well the same way the spindle had gone. After that she knew nothing; and when she came to herself she was in a beautiful meadow, and the sun was shining on the flowers that grew round her. And she walked on through the meadow until she came to a baker's oven that was full of bread; and the bread called out to her, "Oh, take me out, take me out, or I shall burn; I am baked enough already!"

Then she drew near, and with the baker's peel she took out all the loaves one after the other. And she went farther on till she came to a tree weighed down with apples, and it called out to her, "Oh, shake me, shake me, we apples are all of us ripe!" Then she shook the tree until the apples fell like rain, and she shook until there were no more to fall; and when she had gathered them together in a heap, she went on farther.

At last she came to a little house, and an old woman was peeping out of it, but she had such great teeth that the girl was terrified and about to run away, only the old woman called her back. "What are you afraid of, my dear child? Come and live with me, and if you do the housework well and orderly, things shall go well with you. You must take great pains to make my bed well, and shake it up thoroughly, so that the feathers fly about, and then in the world it snows, for I am Mother Holle."*

As the old woman spoke so kindly, the girl took courage, consented, and went to her work. She did everything to the old woman's satisfaction, and shook the bed with such a will that the feathers flew about like snowflakes; and so she led a good life, had never a cross word, but boiled and roast meat every day. When she had lived a long time with Mother Holle, she began to feel sad, not knowing herself what ailed her; at last she began to think she must be homesick; and although she was a thousand times better off than at home where she was, yet she had a great longing to go home. At last she said to her mistress, "I am homesick, and although I am very well off here, I cannot stay any longer; I must go back to my own home."

Mother Holle answered, "It pleases me well that you should wish to go home, and, as you have served me faithfully, I will undertake to send you there!"

She took her by the hand and led her to a large door standing open, and as she was passing through it there fell upon her a heavy shower of gold, and the gold hung all about her, so that she was covered with it.

"All this is yours, because you have been so industrious," said Mother Holle; and, besides that, she returned to her her spindle, the very same that she had dropped in the well. And then the door was shut again, and the girl found herself back again in the world, not far from her mother's house; and as she passed through the yard the cock stood on the top of the well and cried,

> "Cock-a-doodle doo!
> Our golden girl has come home too!"

Then she went in to her mother, and as she had returned covered with gold she was well received.

So the girl related all her history, and what had happened to her, and when the mother heard how she came to have such great riches she began to wish that her ugly and idle daughter might have the same good fortune. So she sent her to sit by the well and spin; and in order to make her spindle bloody she put her hand into the thorn hedge.

---

* In Hesse, when it snows, they still say, "Mother Holle is making her bed."

Then she threw the spindle into the well, and jumped in herself. She found herself, like her sister, in the beautiful meadow, and followed the same path, and when she came to the baker's oven, the bread cried out, "Oh, take me out, take me out, or I shall burn; I am quite done already!"

But the lazy-bones answered, "I have no desire to black my hands," and went on farther. Soon she came to the apple tree, who called out, "Oh, shake me, shake me, we apples are all of us ripe!" But she answered, "That is all very fine, suppose one of you should fall on my head," and went on farther.

When she came to Mother Holle's house she did not feel afraid, as she knew beforehand of her great teeth, and entered into her service at once. The first day she put her hand well to the work, and was industrious, and did everything Mother Holle bade her, because of the gold she expected; but the second day she began to be idle, and the third day still more so, so that she would not get up in the morning. Neither did she make Mother Holle's bed as it ought to have been made, and did not shake it for the feathers to fly about. So that Mother Holle soon grew tired of her, and gave her warning, at which the lazy thing was well pleased, and thought that now the shower of gold was coming; so Mother Holle led her to the door, and as she stood in the doorway, instead of the shower of gold a great kettle full of pitch was emptied over her.

"That is the reward for your service," said Mother Holle, and shut the door. So the lazy girl came home all covered with pitch, and the cock on the top of the well, seeing her, cried,

> "Cock-a-doodle doo!
> Our dirty girl has come home too!"

And the pitch remained sticking to her fast, and never, as long as she lived, could it be got off.

25. SLEEPING BEAUTY
(Germany)

A LONG TIME AGO there lived a king and queen, who said every day, "If only we had a child"; but for a long time they had none.

It fell out once, as the Queen was bathing, that a frog crept out of the water onto the land, and said to her: "Your wish shall be fulfilled; before a year has passed you shall bring a daughter into the world."

The frog's words came true. The Queen had a little girl who was so beautiful that the King could not contain himself for joy, and prepared a great feast. He invited not only his relations, friends, and acquaintances, but the fairies, in order that they might be favorably and kindly disposed toward the child. There were thirteen of them in the kingdom, but as the King had only twelve golden plates for them to eat from, one of the fairies had to stay at home.

The feast was held with all splendor, and when it came to an end the fairies all presented the child with a magic gift. One gave her virtue, another beauty, a third riches, and so on, with everything in the world that she could wish for.

When eleven of the fairies had said their say, the thirteenth suddenly appeared. She wanted to revenge herself for not having been invited. Without greeting anyone, or even glancing at the company, she called out in a loud voice: "The Princess shall prick herself with a spindle in her fifteenth year and shall fall down dead"; and without another word she turned and left the hall.

Everyone was terror-struck, but the twelfth fairy, whose wish was still unspoken, stepped forward. She could not cancel the curse, but could only soften it, so she said: "It shall not be death, but a deep sleep lasting a hundred years, into which your daughter shall fall."

The King was so anxious to guard his dear child from the misfortune, that he sent out a command that all the spindles in the whole kingdom should be burned.

As time went on all the promises of the fairies came true. The Princess grew up so beautiful, modest, kind, and clever that everyone who saw her could not but love her. Now it happened that on the very day when she was fifteen years old the King and Queen were away from home, and the Princess was left quite alone in the castle. She wandered about over the whole place, looking at rooms and halls as she pleased, and at last she came to an old tower. She ascended a narrow, winding staircase and reached a little door. A rusty key was sticking in the lock, and when she turned it the door flew open. In a little room sat an old woman with a spindle, spinning her flax busily.

"Good day, Granny," said the Princess; "what are you doing?"

"I am spinning," said the old woman, and nodded her head.

"What is the thing that whirls around so merrily?" asked the Princess; and she took the spindle and tried to spin too.

But she had scarcely touched it before the curse was fulfilled, and she pricked her finger with the spindle. The instant she felt the prick she fell upon the bed which was standing near, and lay still in a deep sleep which spread over the whole castle.

The King and Queen, who had just come home and had stepped into the hall, went to sleep, and all their courtiers with them. The horses went to sleep in the stable, the dogs in the yard, the doves on the roof, the flies on the wall; yes, even the fire flickering on the hearth grew still and went to sleep, and the roast meat stopped crackling; the cook, who was pulling the scullion's hair because he had made some mistake, let him go and went to sleep. The wind dropped, and on the trees in front of the castle not a leaf stirred.

But round the castle a hedge of briar roses began to grow up; every year it grew higher, till at last it surrounded the whole castle so that nothing could be seen of it, not even the flags on the roof.

But there was a legend in the land about the lovely sleeping Briar Rose, as the King's daughter was called, and from time to time princes came and tried to force a way through the hedge into the castle. They found it impossible, for the thorns, as though they had hands, held them fast, and the princes remained caught in them without being able to free themselves, and so died a miserable death.

After many, many years a prince came again to the country and heard an old man tell of the castle which stood behind the briar hedge, in which a most beautiful maiden called Briar Rose had been asleep for the last hundred years, and with her slept the King, Queen, and all her courtiers. He knew also, from his grandfather, that many princes had already come and sought to pierce through the briar hedge, and had remained caught in it and died a sad death.

Then the young prince said, "I am not afraid; I am determined to go and look upon the lovely Briar Rose."

The good old man did all in his power to dissuade him, but the Prince would not listen to his words.

Now, however, the hundred years were just ended, and the day had come when Briar Rose was to wake up again. When the Prince approached the briar hedge it was in blossom, and was covered with beautiful large flowers which made way for him of their own accord and let him pass unharmed, and then closed up again into a hedge behind him.

In the courtyard he saw the horses and brindled hounds lying asleep, on the roof sat the doves with their heads under their wings: and when he went into the house the flies were asleep on the walls, and near the throne lay the King and Queen; in the kitchen was the cook, with his hand raised as though about to strike the scullion, and the maid sat with the black fowl in her lap which she was about to pluck.

He went on further, and all was so still that he could hear his own breathing. At last he reached the tower, and opened the door into the little room where Briar Rose was asleep. There she lay, looking so beautiful that he could not take his eyes off her; he bent down and gave her a kiss. As he touched her Briar Rose opened her eyes and looked lovingly at him. Then they went down together; and the King woke up, and the Queen, and all the courtiers, and looked at each other with astonished eyes. The horses in the stable stood up and shook themselves, the hounds leaped about and wagged their tails, the doves on the roof lifted their heads from under their wings, looked around, and flew into the fields; the flies on the walls began to crawl again, the fire in the kitchen roused itself and blazed up and cooked the food, the meat began to crackle, and the cook boxed the scullion's ears so soundly that he screamed aloud, while the maid finished plucking the fowl. Then the wedding of the Prince and Briar Rose was celebrated with all splendor, and they lived happily till they died.

26. THE QUEEN BEE
(Germany)

TWO KING'S SONS once started to seek adventures, and fell into a wild, reckless way of living, and gave up all thoughts of going home again. Their third and youngest brother, who was called Witling, and had remained behind, started off to seek them; and when at last he found them, they jeered at his simplicity in thinking that he could make his way in the world, while they who were so much cleverer were unsuccessful. But they all three went on together until they came to an ant-hill, which the two eldest brothers wished to stir up, that they might see the little ants hurry about in their fright and carrying off their eggs, but Witling said:

"Leave the little creatures alone, I will not suffer them to be disturbed."

And they went on farther until they came to a lake, where a number of ducks were swimming about. The two eldest brothers wanted to catch a couple and cook them, but Witling would not allow it, and said, "Leave the creatures alone, I will not suffer them to be killed."

And then they came to a bee's-nest in a tree, and there was so much honey in it that it overflowed and ran down the trunk. The two eldest brothers then wanted to make a fire beneath the tree, that the bees might be stifled by the smoke, and then they could get at the honey. But Witling prevented them, saying,

"Leave the little creatures alone, I will not suffer them to be stifled."

At last the three brothers came to a castle where there were in the stables many horses standing, all of stone, and the brothers went through all the rooms until they came to a door at the end secured with three locks, and in the middle of the door a small opening through which they could look into the room. And they saw a little gray-haired man sitting at a table. They called out to him once, twice, and he did not hear, but at the third time he got up, undid the locks, and came out. Without speaking a word he led them to a table loaded with all sorts of good things, and when they had eaten and drunk he showed to each his bed-chamber. The next morning the little gray man came to the eldest brother, and beckoning him, brought him to a table of stone, on which were written three things directing by what means the castle could be delivered from its enchantment. The first thing was, that in the wood under the moss lay the pearls belonging to the Princess—a thousand in number—and they were to be sought for and collected, and if he who should undertake the task had not finished it by sunset—if but one pearl were missing—he must be turned to stone. So the eldest brother went out, and searched all day, but at the end of it he had only found one hundred; just as was said on the table of stone came to pass and he was turned into stone. The second brother undertook the adventure next day, but it fared with him no better than with the first; he found two hundred pearls, and was turned into stone.

And so at last it was Witling's turn, and he began to search in the moss; but it was a very tedious business to find the pearls, and he grew so out of heart that he sat down on a stone and began to weep. As he was sitting thus, up came the ant-king with five thousand ants, whose lives had been saved through Witling's pity, and it was not very long before the little insects had collected all the pearls and put them in a heap.

Now the second thing ordered by the table of stone was to get the key of the Princess's sleeping-chamber out of the lake.

And when Witling came to the lake, the ducks whose lives he had saved came swimming, and dived below, and brought up the key from the bottom. The third thing that had to be done was the most difficult, and that was to choose out the youngest and loveliest of the three princesses, as they lay sleeping. All bore a perfect resemblance each to the other, and only differed in this, that before they went to sleep each one had eaten a different sweetmeat—the eldest a piece of sugar, the second a little sirup, and the third a spoonful of honey. Now the Queen-bee of those bees that Witling had protected from the fire came at this moment, and trying the lips of all three, settled on those of the one that had eaten honey, and so it was that the King's son knew which to choose. Then the spell was broken; everyone awoke from stony sleep, and took their right form again.

And Witling married the youngest and loveliest princess, and became king after her father's death. But his two brothers had to put up with the two other sisters.

27. THE BREMEN TOWN MUSICIANS
(*Germany*)

A CERTAIN MAN had a donkey which for many years carried sacks to the mill without tiring. At last, however, its strength was worn out; it was no longer of any use for work. Accordingly its master began to ponder as to how best to cut down its keep; but the donkey, seeing there was mischief in the air, ran away and started on the road to Bremen; there he thought he could become a town musician.

When he had been traveling a short time, he fell in with a hound, who was lying panting on the road as though he had run himself off his legs.

"Well, what are you panting so for, Growler?" said the donkey.

"Ah," said the hound, "just because I am old, and every day I get weaker, and also because I can no longer keep up with the pack, my master wanted to kill me, so I took my departure. But now, how am I to earn my bread?"

"Do you know what?" said the donkey. "I am going to Bremen, and shall there become a town musician; come with me and take your part in the music. I shall play the lute, and you shall beat the kettle drum."

The hound agreed, and they went on.

A short time after they came upon a cat, sitting in the road, with a face as long as a wet week.

"Well, what has been crossing you, Whiskers?" asked the donkey.

"Who can be cheerful when he is out at elbows?" said the cat. "I am getting on in years, and my teeth are blunted and I prefer to sit by the stove and purr instead of hunting round after mice. Just because of this my mistress wanted to drown me. I made myself scarce, but now I don't know where to turn."

"Come with us to Bremen," said the donkey. "You are a great hand at serenading, so you can become a town musician."

The cat consented, and joined them.

Next the fugitives passed by a yard where a barn-door fowl was sitting on the door, crowing with all its might.

"You crow so loud you pierce one through and through," said the donkey. "What is the matter?"

"Why! didn't I prophesy fine weather for Lady Day, when Our Lady washes the Christ Child's little garment and wants to dry it? But, notwithstanding this, because Sunday visitors are coming tomorrow, the mistress has no pity, and she has ordered the cook to make me into soup, so I shall have my neck wrung tonight. Now I am crowing with all my might while I have the chance."

"Come along, Red-comb," said the donkey; "you had much better come with us. We are going to Bremen, and you will find a much better fate there. You have a good voice, and when we make music together, there will be quality in it."

The rooster allowed himself to be persuaded, and they all four went off together. They could not, however, reach the town in one day, and by evening they arrived at a wood, where they determined to spend the night. The donkey and the hound lay down under a big tree; the cat and the rooster settled themselves in the branches, the rooster flying right up to the top, which was the safest place for him. Before going to sleep he looked round once more in every direction; suddenly it seemed to him that he saw a light burning in the distance. He called out to his comrades that there must be a house not far off, for he saw a light.

"Very well," said the donkey, "let us set out and make our way to it, for the entertainment here is very bad."

The hound thought some bones or meat would suit him too, so they set out in the direction of the light, and soon saw it shining more clearly, and getting bigger and bigger, till they reached a brightly lighted robbers' den. The donkey, being the tallest, approached the window and looked in.

"What do you see, old Jackass?" asked the rooster.

"What do I see?" answered the donkey; "why, a table spread with delicious food and drink, and robbers seated at it enjoying themselves."

"That would just suit us," said the rooster.

"Yes; if we were only there," answered the donkey.

Then the animals took counsel as to how to set about driving the robbers out. At last they hit upon a plan.

The donkey was to take up his position with his forefeet on the windowsill, the hound was to jump on his back, the cat to climb up onto the hound, and last of all the rooster flew up and perched on the cat's head. When they were thus arranged, at a given signal they all began to perform their music; the donkey brayed, the hound barked, the cat mewed, and the rooster crowed; then they dashed through the window, shivering the panes. The robbers jumped up at the terrible noise; they thought nothing less than that a demon was coming in upon them, and fled into the wood in the greatest alarm. Then the four animals sat down to table, and helped themselves according to taste, and ate as though they had been starving for weeks. When they had finished they extinguished the light, and looked for sleeping places, each one to suit his nature and taste.

The donkey lay down on a pile of straw, the hound behind the door, the cat on the hearth near the warm ashes, and the rooster flew up to the rafters. As they were tired from the long journey, they soon went to sleep.

When midnight was past, and the robbers saw from a distance that the light was no longer burning, and that all seemed quiet, the chief said:

"We ought not to have been scared by a false alarm," and ordered one of the robbers to go and examine the house.

Finding all quiet, the messenger went into the kitchen to kindle a light, and taking the cat's glowing, fiery eyes for live coals, he held a match close to them so as to light it. But the cat would stand no nonsense; it flew at his face, spat and scratched. He was terribly frightened and ran away.

He tried to get out by the back door, but the hound, who was lying there, jumped up and bit his leg. As he ran across the pile of straw in front of the house, the donkey gave him a good sound kick with his hind legs, while the rooster, who had awakened at the uproar quite fresh and gay, cried out from his perch: "Cock-a-doodle-doo." Thereupon the robber ran back as fast as he could to his chief, and said: "There is a gruesome witch in the house, who breathed on me and scratched me with her long fingers. Behind the door there stands a man with a knife, who stabbed me; while in the yard lies a black monster, who hit me with a club; and upon the roof the judge is seated, and he called out, 'Bring the rogue here,' so I hurried away as fast as fast as I could."

Thenceforward the robbers did not venture again to the house, which, however, pleased the four Bremen musicians so much that they never wished to leave it again.

And he who last told the story has hardly finished speaking yet.

28. HANSEL AND GRETEL
(*Germany*)

CLOSE TO A LARGE forest there lived a woodcutter with his wife and his two children. The boy was called Hansel, and the girl Gretel. They were always very poor, and had very little to live on; and at one time, when there was famine in the land, he could no longer procure daily bread.

One night he lay in bed worrying over his troubles, and he sighed and said to his wife: "What is to become of us? How are we to feed our poor children when we have nothing for ourselves?"

"I'll tell you what, husband," answered the woman, "tomorrow morning we will take the children out quite early into the thickest part of the forest. We will light a fire, and give each of them a piece of bread; then we will go to our work and leave them alone. They won't be able to find their way back, and so we shall be rid of them."

"Nay, wife," said the man; "we won't do that. I could never find it in my heart to leave my children alone in the forest; the wild animals would soon tear them to pieces."

"What a fool you are!" she said. "Then we must all four die of hunger. You may as well plane the boards for our coffins at once."

She gave him no peace till he consented. "But I grieve over the poor children all the same," said the man.

The two children could not go to sleep for hunger either, and they heard what their stepmother said to their father.

Gretel wept bitterly, and said: "All is over with us now!"

"Be quiet, Gretel!" said Hansel. "Don't cry; I will find some way out of it."

When the old people had gone to sleep, he got up, put on his little coat, opened the door, and slipped out. The moon was shining brightly, and the white pebbles round the house shone like newly minted coins.

Hansel stooped down and put as many into his pockets as they would hold.

Then he went back to Gretel, and said: "Take comfort, little sister, and go to sleep. God won't forsake us." And then he went to bed again.

When the day broke, before the sun had risen, the woman came and said: "Get up, you lazy-bones; we are going into the forest to fetch wood."

Then she gave them each a piece of bread, and said: "Here is something for your dinner, but mind you don't eat it before, for you'll get no more."

Gretel put the bread under her apron, for Hansel had the stones in his pockets. Then they all started for the forest.

When they had gone a little way, Hansel stopped and looked back at the cottage, and he did the same thing again and again.

His father said: "Hansel, what are you stopping to look back at? Take care, and put your best foot foremost."

"O Father!" said Hansel, "I am looking at my white cat, it is sitting on the roof, wanting to say good-bye to me."

"Little fool! that's no cat, it's the morning sun shining on the chimney," said the mother.

But Hansel had not been looking at the cat, he had been dropping a pebble onto the ground each time he stopped. When they reached the middle of the forest, their father said:

"Now, children, pick up some wood, I want to make a fire to warm you."

Hansel and Gretel gathered the twigs together and soon made a huge pile. Then the pile was lighted, and when it blazed up, the woman said: "Now lie down by the fire and rest yourselves while we go and cut wood; when we have finished we will come back to fetch you."

Hansel and Gretel sat by the fire, and when dinnertime came they each ate their little bit of bread, and they thought their father was quite near because they could hear the sound of an ax. It was no ax, however, but a branch which the man had tied to a dead tree, and which blew backward and forward against it. They sat there such a long time that they got tired, their eyes began to close, and they were soon fast asleep.

When they woke it was dark night. Gretel began to cry: "How shall we ever get out of the wood!"

But Hansel comforted her, and said: "Wait a little till the moon rises, then we will soon find our way."

When the full moon rose, Hansel took his little sister's hand, and they walked on, guided by the pebbles, which glittered like newly coined money. They walked the whole night, and at daybreak they found themselves back at their father's cottage.

They knocked at the door, and when the woman opened it and saw Hansel and Gretel, she said: "You bad children, why did you sleep so long in the wood? We thought you did not mean to come back any more."

But their father was delighted, for it had gone to his heart to leave them behind alone.

Not long after they were again in great destitution, and the children heard the woman at night in bed say to their father: "We have eaten up everything again but half a loaf, and then we are at the end of everything. The children must go away; we will take them further into the forest so that they won't be able to find their way back. There is nothing else to be done."

The man took it much to heart, and said: "We had better share our last crust with the children."

But the woman would not listen to a word he said, she only scolded and reproached him. Anyone who once says A must also say B and as the father had given in the first time, he had to do so the second. The children were again wide awake and heard what was said.

When the old people went to sleep Hansel again got up, meaning to go out and get some more pebbles, but the woman had locked the door and he couldn't get out. But he consoled his little sister, and said:

"Don't cry, Gretel; go to sleep. God will help us."

In the early morning the woman made the children get up, and gave them each a piece of bread, but it was smaller than the last. On the way to the forest Hansel crumbled it up in his pocket, and stopped every now and then to throw a crumb onto the ground.

"Hansel, what are you stopping to look about you for?" asked his father.

"I am looking at my dove which is sitting on the roof and wants to say good-bye to me," answered Hansel.

"Little fool!" said the woman, "that is no dove, it is the morning sun shining on the chimney."

Nevertheless, Hansel strewed the crumbs from time to time on the ground. The woman led the children far into the forest where they had never been in their lives before. Again they made a big fire, and the woman said:

"Stay where you are, children, and when you are tired you may go to sleep for a while. We are going further on to cut wood, and in the evening when we have finished we will come back and fetch you."

At dinnertime Gretel shared her bread with Hansel, for he had crumbled his up on the road. Then they went to sleep, and the evening passed, but no one came to fetch the poor children.

It was quite dark when they woke up, and Hansel cheered his little sister, and said: "Wait a bit, Gretel, till the moon rises, then we can see the breadcrumbs which I scattered to show us the way home."

When the moon rose they started, but they found no breadcrumbs, for all the thousands of birds in the forest had pecked them up and eaten them.

Hansel said to Gretel: "We shall soon find the way."

But they could not find it. They walked the whole night, and all the next day from morning till night, but they could not get out of the wood.

They were very hungry, for they had nothing to eat but a few berries which they found. They were so tired that their legs would not carry them any further, and they lay down under a tree and went to sleep.

When they woke in the morning, it was the third day since they had left their father's cottage. They started to walk again, but they only got deeper and deeper into the wood, and if no help came they must perish.

At midday they saw a beautiful snow-white bird sitting on a tree. It sang so beautifully that they stood still to listen to it. When it stopped, it fluttered its wings and flew around them. They followed it till they came to a little cottage, on the roof of which it settled itself.

When they got quite near, they saw that the little house was made of bread, and it was roofed with cake; the windows were transparent sugar.

"This will be something for us," said Hansel. "We will have a good meal. I will have a piece of the roof, Gretel, and you can have a bit of the window, it will be nice and sweet."

Hansel stretched up and broke off a piece of the roof to try what it was like. Gretel went to the window and nibbled at that. A gentle voice called out from within:

> "Nibbling, nibbling like a mouse,
> Who's nibbling at my little house?"

The children answered:

> "The wind, the wind doth blow
> From heaven to earth below,"

and went on eating without disturbing themselves. Hansel, who found the roof very good, broke off a large piece for himself; and Gretel pushed a whole round pane out of the window, and sat down on the ground to enjoy it.

All at once the door opened and an old, old woman, supporting herself on a crutch, came hobbling out. Hansel and Gretel were so frightened, that they dropped what they held in their hands.

But the old woman only shook her head, and said: "Ah, dear children, who brought you here? Come in and stay with me; you will come to no harm."

She took them by the hand and led them into the little house. A nice dinner was set before them, pancakes and sugar, milk, apples, and nuts. After this she showed them two little white beds into which they crept, and felt as if they were in Heaven.

Although the old woman appeared to be so friendly, she was really a wicked old witch who was on the watch for children, and she had built the bread house on purpose to lure them to her. Whenever she could get a child into her clutches she cooked it and ate it, and considered it a grand feast. Witches have red eyes, and can't see very far, but they have keen scent like animals, and can perceive the approach of human beings.

When Hansel and Gretel came near her, she laughed wickedly to herself, and said scornfully: "Now I have them, they shan't escape me."

She got up early in the morning, before the children were awake, and when she saw them sleeping, with their beautiful rosy cheeks, she murmured to herself: "They will be dainty morsels."

She seized Hansel with her bony hand and carried him off to a little stable, where she shut him up with a barred door; he might shriek as loud as he liked, she took no notice of him. Then she went to Gretel and shook her till she woke, and cried:

"Get up, little lazy-bones, fetch some water and cook something nice for your brother; he is in the stable, and has to be fattened. When he is nice and fat, I will eat him."

Gretel began to cry bitterly, but it was no use, she had to obey the witch's orders. The best food was now cooked for poor Hansel, but Gretel only had the shells of crayfish.

The old woman hobbled to the stable every morning, and cried: "Hansel, put your finger out for me to feel how fat you are."

Hansel put out a little bone, and the old woman, whose eyes were dim, could not see, and thought it was his finger, and she was much astonished that he did not get fat.

When four weeks had passed, and Hansel still kept thin, she became very impatient and would wait no longer.

"Now then, Gretel," she cried, "bustle along and fetch the water. Fat or thin, tomorrow I will kill Hansel and eat him."

Oh, how his poor little sister grieved. As she carried the water, the tears streamed down her cheeks.

"Dear God, help us!" she cried. "If only the wild animals in the forest had devoured us, we should, at least, have died together."

"You may spare your lamentations; they will do you no good," said the old woman.

Early in the morning Gretel had to go out to fill the kettle with water, and then she had to kindle a fire and hang the kettle over it.

"We will bake first," said the old witch. "I have heated the oven and kneaded the dough."

She pushed poor Gretel toward the oven, and said: "Creep in and see if it is properly heated, and then we will put the bread in."

She meant, when Gretel had got in, to shut the door and roast her.

But Gretel saw her intention, and said: "I don't know how to get in. How am I to manage it?"

"Stupid goose!" cried the witch. "The opening is big enough; you can see that I could get into it myself."

She hobbled up, and stuck her head into the oven. But Gretel gave her a push which sent the witch right in, and then she banged the door and bolted it.

"Oh! oh!" she began to howl horribly. But Gretel ran away and left the wicked witch to perish miserably.

Gretel ran as fast as she could to the stable. She opened the door, and cried: "Hansel, we are saved. The old witch is dead."

Hansel sprang out, like a bird out of a cage when the door is set open. How delighted they were. They fell upon each other's necks, and kissed each other, and danced about for joy.

As they had nothing more to fear, they went into the witch's house, and they found chests in every corner full of pearls and precious stones.

"These are better than pebbles," said Hansel, as he filled his pockets.

Gretel said: "I must take something home with me too." And she filled her apron.

"But now we must go," said Hansel, "so that we may get out of this enchanted wood."

Before they had gone very far, they came to a great piece of water.

"We can't get across it," said Hansel; "I see no stepping-stones and no bridge."

"And there are no boats either," answered Gretel. "But there is a duck swimming, it will help us over if we ask it."

So she cried—

"Little duck, that cries quack, quack,
Here Gretel and here Hansel stand.
Quickly, take us on your back,
No path nor bridge is there at hand!"

The duck came swimming toward them, and Hansel got on its back, and told his sister to sit on his knee.

"No," answered Gretel, "it will be too heavy for the duck; it must take us over one after the other."

The good creature did this, and when they had got safely over and walked for a while, the wood seemed to grow more and more familiar to them, and at last they saw their father's cottage in the distance. They began to run, and rushed inside, where they threw their arms around their father's neck. The man had not had a single happy moment since he had deserted his children in the wood, and in the meantime his wife had died.

Gretel shook her apron and scattered the pearls and precious stones all over the floor, and Hansel added handful after handful out of his pockets.

So all their troubles came to an end, and they lived together as happily as possible.

29. THE MERMAN AND THE FARMER
(Germany)

THE MERMAN LOOKS just like any other man; the only difference is that when he opens his mouth, one can see his green teeth. And he always wears a green hat. When a pretty girl walks past his pond, he appears, measures out a length of ribbon, and tosses it to her.

For a time a Merman and a farmer, who lived not far from his lake, enjoyed a good neighborly relationship, and the Merman often visited him. One day the Merman asked the farmer if he would not like to visit him in his house. The farmer agreed and went with him.

Everything under the water was as magnificent as if it had been in a splendid palace on earth. There were rooms, halls, and chambers full of diverse treasures, wealth, and decorations. The Merman led his guest around all of his palace and showed him everything.

Finally, they came to a small room where many pots stood upside down, their openings resting on the floor. When the farmer asked what they were, the Merman replied, "Those are the souls of the drowned. I keep them here under the pots and thus hold them captive so they cannot escape." The farmer remained silent, and later he ascended again to the surface.

For a long time the affair of the drowned souls plagued the farmer, and he paid close attention to the Merman to see when he would leave his watery home. When this came to pass, the farmer who had made careful note of the right path under the water, descended once more into the watery place. He was fortunate enough to find the little room again and he turned up all the pots, one after the other. And so it was that the souls of the drowned rose up through the water to the surface and were delivered.

30. CRAB
(Italy)

THERE WAS ONCE a king who had lost a valuable ring. He looked for it everywhere, but could not find it. So he issued a proclamation that if any astrologer could tell him where it was he would be richly rewarded. A poor peasant by the name of Crab heard of the proclamation. He could neither read nor write, but took it into his head that he wanted to be the astrologer to find the king's ring. So he went and presented himself to the king, to whom he said: "Your Majesty must know that I am an astrologer, although you see me so poorly dressed. I know that you have lost a ring and I will try by study to find out where it is." "Very well," said the king, "and when you have found it, what reward must I give you?" "That is at your discretion, your Majesty." "Go, then, study, and we shall see what kind of an astrologer you turn out to be."

He was conducted to a room, in which he was to be shut up to study. It contained only a bed and a table on which were a large book and writing materials. Crab seated himself at the table and did nothing but turn over the leaves of the book and scribble the paper so that the servants who brought him his food thought him a great man. They were the ones who had stolen the ring, and from the severe glances that the peasant cast at them whenever they entered, they began to fear that they would be found out. They made him endless bows and never opened their mouths without calling him "Mr. Astrologer." Crab, who, although illiterate, was, as a peasant, cunning, all at once imagined that the servants must know about the ring, and this is the way his suspicions were confirmed. He had been shut up in his room turning over his big book and scribbling his paper for a month, when his wife came to visit him. He said to her: "Hide yourself under the bed, and when a servant enters, say: 'That is one'; when another comes, say: 'That is two'; and so on." The woman hid herself. The servants came with the dinner, and hardly had the first one entered when a voice from under the bed said: "That is one." The second one entered; the voice said: "That is two"; and so on. The servants were frightened at hearing that voice, for they did not know where it came from, and held a consultation. One of them said: "We are discovered; if the astrologer denounces us to the king as thieves, we are lost." "Do you know what we must do?" said another. "Let us hear." "We must go to the astrologer and tell him frankly that we stole the ring, and ask him not to betray us, and present him with a purse of money. Are you willing?" "Perfectly."

So they went in harmony to the astrologer, and making him a lower bow than usual, one of them began: "Mr. Astrologer, you have discovered that we stole the ring. We are poor people and if you reveal it to the king, we are undone. So we beg you not to betray us, and accept this purse of money." Crab took the purse and then added: "I will not betray you, but you must do what I tell you, if you wish to save your lives. Take the ring and make that turkey in the courtyard swallow it, and leave the rest to me." The servants were satisfied to do so and departed with a low bow. The next day Crab went to the king and said to him: "Your Majesty must know that after having toiled over a month I have succeeded in discovering where the ring has gone to." "Where is it, then?" asked the king. "A turkey has swallowed it." "A turkey? very well, let us see."

They went for the turkey, opened it, and found the ring inside. The king, amazed, presented the astrologer with a large purse of money and invited him to a banquet. Among the other dishes, there was brought on the table a plate of crabs. Crabs must then have been very rare, because only the king and a few others knew their name. Turning to the peasant the king said: "You, who are an astrologer, must be able to tell me the name of these things which are in this dish." The poor astrologer was very much puzzled, and, as if speaking to himself, but in such a way that the others heard him, he muttered: "Ah! Crab, Crab, what a plight you are in!" All who did not know that his name was Crab rose and proclaimed him the greatest astrologer in the world.

31. BASTIANELO
(Italy)

ONCE UPON A TIME there was a husband and wife who had a son. This son grew up, and said one day to his mother: "Do you know, mother, I would like to marry!" "Very well, marry! whom do you want to take?" He answered: "I want the gardener's daughter." "She is a good girl; take her; I am willing." So he went, and asked for the girl, and her parents gave her to him. They were married, and when they were in the midst of the dinner, the wine gave out. The husband said: "There is no more wine!" The bride, to show that she was a good housekeeper, said: "I will go and get some." She took the bottles and went to the cellar, turned the cock, and began to think: "Suppose I should have a son, and we should call him Bastianelo, and he should die. Oh! how grieved I should be! oh! how grieved I should be!" And thereupon she began to weep and weep; and meanwhile the wine was running all over the cellar.

When they saw that the bride did not return, the mother said: "I will go and see what the matter is." So she went into the cellar, and saw the bride, with the bottle in her hand, and weeping, while the wine was running over the cellar. "What is the matter with you, that you are weeping?" "Ah! my mother, I was thinking that if I had a son, and should name him Bastianelo, and he should die, oh! how I should grieve! oh! how I should grieve!" The mother, too, began to weep, and weep, and weep; and meanwhile the wine was running over the cellar.

When the people at the table saw that no one brought the wine, the groom's father said: "I will go and see what is the matter. Certainly something wrong has happened to the bride." He went and saw the whole cellar full of wine, and the mother and bride weeping. "What is the matter?" he said; "has anything wrong happened to you?" "No," said the bride, "but I was thinking that if I had a son and should call him Bastianelo, and he should die, oh! how I should grieve! oh! how I should grieve!" Then he, too, began to weep, and all three wept; and meanwhile the wine was running over the cellar.

When the groom saw that neither the bride, nor the mother, nor the father came back, he said: "Now I will go and see what the matter is that no one returns." He went into the cellar and saw all the wine running over the cellar. He hastened and stopped the cask, and then asked: "What is the matter, that you are all weeping, and have let the wine run all over the cellar?" Then the bride said: "I was thinking that if I had a son and called him Bastianelo and he should die, oh! how I should grieve! oh! how I should grieve!" Then the groom said: "You stupid fools! are you weeping at this, and letting all the wine run into the cellar? Have you nothing else to think of? It shall never be said that I remained with you! I will roam about the world, and until I find three fools greater than you I will not return home."

He had a bread-cake made, took a bottle of wine, a sausage, and some linen, and made a bundle, which he put on a stick and carried over his shoulder. He journeyed and journeyed, but found no fool. At last he said, worn out: "I must turn back, for I see I cannot find a greater fool than my wife." He did not know what to do, whether to go on or to turn back. "Oh!" he said, "it is better to try and go a little farther." So he went on and shortly he saw a man in his shirtsleeves at a well, all wet with perspiration and water. "What are you doing, sir, that you are so covered with water and in such a sweat?" "Oh! let me alone," the man answered, "for I have been here a long time drawing water to fill this pail and I cannot fill it." "What are you drawing the water in?" he asked him. "In this sieve," he said. "What are you thinking about, to draw water in that sieve? Just wait!" He went to a house nearby, and borrowed a bucket, with which he returned to the well and filled the pail. "Thank you, good man, God knows how long I should have had to remain here!" "Here is one who is a greater fool than my wife."

He continued his journey and after a time he saw at a distance a man in his shirt who was jumping down from a tree. He drew near, and saw a woman under the same tree holding a pair of breeches. He asked them what they were doing, and they said that they had been there a long time, and that the man was trying on those breeches and did not know how to get into them. "I have jumped, and jumped," said the man, "until I am tired out and I cannot imagine how to get into those breeches." "Oh!" said the traveler, "you might stay here as long as you wished, for you would never get into them in this way. Come down and lean against the tree." Then he took his legs and put them in the breeches, and after he had put them on, he said: "Is that right?" "Very good, bless you; for if it had not been for you, God knows how long I should have had to jump." Then the traveler said to himself: "I have seen two greater fools than my wife."

Then he went his way and as he approached a city he heard a great noise. When he drew near he asked what it was, and was told it was a marriage, and that it was the custom in that city for the brides to enter the city gate on horseback, and that there was a great discussion on this occasion between the groom and the owner of the horse, for the bride was tall and the horse high, and they could not get through the gate; so that they must either cut off the bride's head or the horse's legs. The groom did not wish his bride's head cut off, and the owner of the horse did not wish his horse's legs cut off, and hence this disturbance. Then the traveler said: "Just wait," and came up to the bride and gave her a slap that made her lower her head, and then he gave the horse a kick, and so they passed through the gate and entered the city. The groom and the owner of the horse asked the traveler what he wanted, for he had saved the groom his bride, and the owner of the horse his horse. He answered that he did not wish anything and said to himself: "Two and one make three! that is enough; now I will go home." He did so and said to his wife: "Here I am, my wife; I have seen three greater fools than you; now let us remain in peace and think about nothing else." They renewed the wedding and always remained in peace. After a time the wife had a son whom they named Bastianelo, and Bastianelo did not die, but still lives with his father and mother.

32. THE COCK AND THE MOUSE
(*Italy*)

ONCE UPON A TIME there were a cock and a mouse. One day the
mouse said to the cock: "Friend Cock, shall we go and eat some nuts
on yonder tree?" "As you like." So they both went under the tree and
the mouse climbed up at once and began to eat. The poor cock began
to fly, and flew and flew, but could not come where the mouse was.
When it saw that there was no hope of getting there, it said: "Friend
Mouse, do you know what I want you to do? Throw me a nut." The
mouse went and threw one and hit the cock on the head. The poor
cock, with its head all broken and covered with blood, went away to an
old woman. "Old aunt, give me some rags to cure my head." "If you
will give me two hairs I will give you the rags." The cock went away to
a dog. "Dog, give me two hairs; the hairs I will give the old woman; the
old woman will give me rags to cure my head." "If you will give me a
little bread," said the dog, "I will give you the hairs." The cock went
away to a baker. "Baker, give me bread; I will give bread to the dog; the
dog will give hairs; the hairs I will carry to the old woman; the old
woman will give me rags to cure my head." The baker answered: "I will
not give you bread unless you give me some wood." The cock went
away to the forest. "Forest, give me some wood; the wood I will carry
to the baker; the baker will give me some bread; the bread I will give
to the dog; the dog will give me hairs; the hairs I will carry to the old
woman; the old woman will give me rags to cure my head." The forest
answered: "If you will bring me a little water, I will give you some
wood." The cock went away to a fountain. "Fountain, give me water;
water I will carry to the forest; forest will give wood; wood I will carry
to the baker; baker will give bread; bread I will give dog; dog will give
hairs; hairs I will give old woman; old woman will give rags to cure my
head." The fountain gave him water; the water he carried to the forest;
the forest gave him wood; the wood he carried to the baker; the baker

gave him bread; the bread he gave to the dog; the dog gave him the hairs; the hairs he carried to the old woman; the old woman gave him the rags; and the cock cured his head.

33. THE THOUGHTLESS ABBOT
(Italy)

THERE WAS ONCE in a city a priest who became an abbot, and because of his wealth had carriages, horses, grooms, steward, secretary, valet, and many other servants. This abbot thought only of eating, drinking, and sleeping. All the priests and laymen were jealous of him and called him "the thoughtless abbot."

One day the king happened to pass that way and stopped, and all the abbot's enemies went to him straightway and accused the abbot, saying, "Your Majesty, in this town there is a person happier than you, very rich, and lacking nothing in the world, and he is called 'the thoughtless abbot.'"

After reflection the king said to the accusers, "Gentlemen, depart in peace, for I will soon make this abbot think." The king sent directly for the abbot, who had his carriage made ready and went to the king in his coach and four. The king received him kindly, made him sit at his side, and talked about various things with him. Finally he asked him why they called him "the thoughtless abbot," and he replied that it was because he was free from care and that his servants attended to his interests.

Then the king said, "Well, then, Sir Abbot, since you have nothing to do, do me the favor of counting all the stars in the sky, and this within three days and three nights; otherwise you will surely be beheaded." The poor thoughtless abbot, on hearing these words, began to tremble like a leaf, and, taking leave of the king, returned home in mortal fear for his neck.

When mealtime came he could not eat on account of his great anxiety and went out at once on the terrace to look at the sky, but the poor man could not see a single star. When it grew dark, and the stars came out, the abbot began to count them and write it down. But it grew dark and light again without the abbot succeeding in his task. The cook, the steward, the secretaries, the grooms, the coachmen, and everyone else in the house became thoughtful when they saw that their master did not eat or drink and always watched the sky. Not knowing what else to think, they believed that he had gone mad. To make the matter short, the three days passed without the abbot succeeding in counting the stars, and the poor man did not know how to present himself to the king, for he was sure he would behead him. Finally, the last day, an old and trusty servant begged him so long that he told him the whole matter and said, "I have not been able to count the stars, and the king will cut my head off this morning." When the servant had heard all he said, "Do not fear, leave it to me; I will settle everything."

He went and bought a large oxhide, stretched it on the ground, and cut off a piece of the tail, half an ear, and a small piece out of the side, and then said to the abbot, "Now let us go to the king; and when he asks Your Excellency how many stars there are in heaven, Your Excellency will call me; I will stretch the hide on the ground, and Your Excellency will say, 'The stars in heaven are as many as the hairs on this hide; and as there are more hairs than stars, I have been obliged to cut off part of the hide.'"

After the abbot had heard him, he felt relieved, ordered his carriage, and took his servant to the king. When the king saw the abbot he saluted him and then said, "Have you fulfilled my command?"

"Yes, Your Majesty," answered the abbot, "the stars are all counted."

"Then tell me how many they are."

The abbot called his servant, who brought the hide and spread it on the ground, while the king, not knowing how the matter was going to end, continued his questioning.

When the servant had stretched out the hide the abbot said to the king, "Your Majesty, during these three days I have gone mad counting the stars, and they are all counted."

"In short, how many are they?"

"Your Majesty, the stars are as many as the hairs of this hide, and those that were in excess I have had to cut off, and they are so many hundreds of millions; and if you don't believe me, have them counted, for I have brought you the proof."

Then the king remained with his mouth open and had nothing to answer; he said only, "Go and live as long as Noah, without thoughts, for your brains are enough for you." And so speaking, he dismissed him, thanking him, and remaining henceforth his best friend.

The abbot returned home with his servant, delighted and rejoicing. He thanked his servant, made him his steward and intimate friend, and gave him more than an ounce of money a day to live on.

34. DON DEMONIO'S MOTHER-IN-LAW
(Spain)

ONCE UPON A TIME there lived in the little village of La Zubia a widow woman who was known for her long tongue and her short temper. She was thin and brown, her face and body as dried up as a piece of esparto grass. Her voice was as shrill as a cricket's chirp, and her tongue as sharp as a butcher's knife on market day. From the hour when God hung out the daylight till the hour when He drew it in again she was never still.

Now Tía Pía, as she was known to her neighbors, had one daughter who was pretty to look at but so lazy that even an earthquake would not move her. Her name was Pánfila, and what she liked to do best was to put on her dress of red and white muslin and sit, with folded hands, in the window, waiting for a lover to come and marry her. Every handsome youth who passed that way was a possible husband to Pánfila. And more than one of them looked back over his shoulder at her demure face and dark, carefully dressed hair. But when old Tía Pía poked her head around the doorway, each one made off as fast as he could go. Pánfila was not worth the risk of having such a one for a mother-in-law!

Day after day Pánfila sat and looked out the window, and day after day Tía Pía scolded her roundly for her idleness. Wielding her broom vigorously and raising a cloud of dust with every stroke, she would say, "In my day girls did their share of the work of the house." Swish, swish, went the broom! "They did not sit idle with folded hands." Swish, swish! "They did not waste the good daylight waiting for fortune to come to them." Swish, swish! "They thought of something besides a possible sweetheart." Swish, swish! "The sweetheart who comes to such as you will be a good-for-nothing." Swish, swish!

One day Tía Pía called to Pánfila to help her lift from the fire a pot of hot lye. Now it may have been that Tía Pía was too quick in her movements, or it may have been that Pánfila's mind was on a handsome youth who has passed the door that morning and had been frightened away by her mother's voice. Whatever the reason, the pot of lye slipped, and a bit of the hot liquid splashed on Tía Pía's foot. You could have heard her screeching half a mile away!

"It is all your fault," she stormed. "Lazy, worthless creature! You are not worth your salt. You think of nothing but sweethearts! May you marry the Devil himself and be done with it!"

Now not long after this a young stranger appeared in the village of La Zubia. He was tall and dark, courtly in manner, and obviously well off in this world's goods. Over his shoulders he wore a long cape of scarlet silk, and on his head a curious draped cap that no one ever saw him without. He said that he was a traveler from a far country, and he lost no time in making himself popular among the men of the village. The young men were willing enough to be friends with him. He evidently knew a thing or two, and no one need give his own centimos for a glass of *valdepañas* when the stranger was in the village inn! But the old men were less easily won. They muttered among themselves and shook their heads.

"There is something queer about him," said old Tío Blas. "His manners are too good and his hands are too white, and I don't like the look in his eyes."

"He doesn't know a lamb from a kid," muttered old Tío Gil. "He has never been near the church since he came. I saw him hide himself in a doorway the other night when the *cura* went by."

But in spite of this gossip the stranger, who called himself Don Demonio, became a familiar figure in the village. And in no time at all Pánfila, from her window, had fallen in love with him. At first it was only a glance and a smile and a slight gesture of the hand. But Don Demonio, unlike the others, soon showed that he had no fear of old Tía Pía. Her shrill voice seemed only to amuse him, her ugly, wrinkled face to draw his eyes. His manner to her was as courtly as always, and he showered compliments upon her as extravagant as those that he paid Pánfila. By Corpus Christi Day the affair was settled and the marriage arranged.

Now old Tía Pía was as shrewd as she was ugly. She had not forgotten the wish that she had made for Pánfila when the hot lye fell on her toes. Neither was she at all sure that the draped scarlet silk of Don Demonio's cap did not conceal horns! When the wedding day arrived she called Pánfila to her and said, "There is one thing that you must surely do. When you are alone with your husband, see that every door and window is securely locked. See that every crack and cranny in the walls is covered. Cover the chimney even; leave free only the keyhole of the door. Then take an olive branch that has been blessed by the *cura* and switch your husband with it. That is what all brides must do to show that they rule in the home."

Pánfila, who was a meek creature, promised. And the wedding was celebrated with much feasting and rejoicing.

Now the house that Don Demonio had prepared for Pánfila was just outside the village on the road to Granada. When the bride and groom had entered it, no one noticed old Tía Pía stealing along the side of the road with a small, empty glass bottle in her hand.

Inside the house Pánfila had carefully done all that her mother had told her to do. And, having shut the house up as tight as a drum and taken the key from the keyhole, she turned to her husband with the blessed olive branch in her hand. The instant he saw it he went, to her amazement, into a panic of fear and tried to get out of the house. Cringing and whining and begging, his courtly manners completely forgotten, he desperately sought some way of escape, while Pánfila, no longer wondering but now suspicious, followed him about with the olive branch. But there was no way out for Don Demonio except through the keyhole. And he was finally forced to take that way. Driven to it, he at last assumed his own form with the tail and the horns that were rightly his, but he was no higher than a man's little finger! Through the keyhole he slipped before Pánfila's astonished eyes—only to find himself enclosed in a glass bottle!

Old Tía Pía chuckled to herself as she firmly forced in the cork.

"This is one of the times," she said, "when the Devil himself was no match for a woman."

The very next morning old Tía Pía, leaving Pánfila alternately weeping and gazing out the window for another suitor, put the bottle in her pocket, mounted on her donkey, and set out for the Sierra Nevada. It is a long ride to Monte Mulhacén, which is the highest mountain in Spain and is covered with snow the whole year round. But Tía Pía took it, every foot of the way. And there on the top of the mountain she buried the bottle deep in the snow—an element which must have been quite new to his satanic majesty. Then she went back to La Zubia.

Ten years went by—ten years of peace and prosperity for the world. Wives were patient and long-suffering toward their husbands, husbands tender and indulgent toward their wives, children so good that they might have been angels already. Only the lawyers were unhappy, because no man sued his neighbor and time hung heavy on their hands.

Now there passed through the village of La Zubia a gallant soldier of fortune whose name was Ricardo. He chanced to ask his way of old Tía Pía, who still wielded her broom and her tongue as briskly as ever, although Pánfila had long ago married and gone to live in Córdoba. Sharp as her tongue still was, Tía Pía found that she had met her match in Ricardo, who, when she told him that his road lay over the mountains, answered cheerfully, "If the mountains are in my way, old woman, I will ride over them even though I crack my head against heaven's arch."

Now this was an answer that met with Tía Pía's approval, and after a dialogue that left them both breathless, they parted good friends.

Ricardo made his way up the steep, winding *cañada* that led to the top of the mountain. At the top he unsaddled his horse so that it could rest and crop the short grass, and threw himself down under a stunted tree. As he lay there idly, he saw something gleam at his feet. Stooping, he picked up a small glass bottle. Moreover, something inside the bottle moved!

"Now," said Ricardo aloud, "what strange, black insect is this?"

To his surprise a voice—a rather thin and weak voice it is true, but unquestionably a voice—answered from the bottle, "It is no insect," said this voice, "but an honorable and worthy devil, who, owing to the unnatural cunning of his mother-in-law has been shut up in this bottle and buried in this most hateful of elements for ten years. Free me, good soldier, and I will grant you your heart's desire."

"My heart's desire," Ricardo repeated slowly. "As it happens, good sir, I am in love. My heart's desire is the king's youngest daughter, the lovely Princess Blanca."

The Devil flicked his tail. "Nothing could be simpler than to get her for you," he answered contemptuously.

"And how," Ricardo asked, "do you propose to manage it?"

The Devil beat his tiny fists impatiently against the glass. "Let me out of this bottle," he snarled, "and I will manage it with no trouble at all."

But Ricardo was not a soldier of fortune for nothing.

"There is no hurry," he said mildly. "Tell me first just exactly how you propose to get the Princess Blanca for me."

The Devil, seeing what kind of a man he had to deal with, settled himself more comfortably in his bottle and unfolded his plan. He proposed to bewitch the princess with a strange illness in such a way that every doctor in the country would be called to cure her.

"But no doctor will cure her but you," he said, chuckling. "I will see that the king, in desperation, offers her hand in marriage to whoever rids her of the trouble. And then you can step in and, at your command, I will go back to the place that I came from."

Ricardo did not entirely approve of this plan. He did not like to be the cause of suffering to the lovely princess. But the Devil assured him that her pain would be brief, and he finally consented.

"And now," said the Devil, "let me out of this bottle!"

"Not so fast," Ricardo answered coolly. "There is no need for haste. Time enough when we get to the palace." And he slipped the bottle, Devil and all, into the pocket of his coat. "And you might tell me," he went on, "how you got into this fix in the first place."

So as they went down the mountain the Devil told Ricardo the story of Don Demonio and his mother-in-law, and Ricardo laughed until the sides of the mountain rang again.

It soon became known throughout the kingdom that the Princess Blanca suffered from a strange illness, and that the man who cured her would be given her hand in marriage. From far and from near came the doctors, native and foreign, old and young, grave and gay. But not one of them succeeded in ridding the princess of her trouble. Finally Ricardo presented himself at the palace. And a fine figure he made, in his black suit and black cape with a black velvet cap set on his curly hair.

In an upper room of the palace the Princess Blanca lay on her bed with closed eyes and a face as white as a jasmine flower.

"I have come to the end of my patience," the stern old king told Ricardo. "If you cure her before sunset today, she is yours. If you fail to cure her, you will be hanged from the scaffold that is even now being built in the courtyard."

Now this was rather more than Ricardo had bargained for. But he had faith in his compact with the Devil. So he answered calmly, "Leave me alone with the princess, and I will cure her in an hour."

The king and the attendants withdrew. Going over to the bed, Ricardo called upon the Devil to lift the spell and to go back to the place that he came from.

But there was no answer!

For three long hours Ricardo begged and pleaded, blustered and threatened. Once he heard a thin, mocking laugh and a tiny voice that said, "Not so fast! No need for hurry!"

And the Princess Blanca lay scarcely breathing, her eyes closed, her face as white as a jasmine flower. The sun was sinking in the west, and the old king rapping impatiently on the door, before, like a flash, an idea came to Ricardo. He went to the door and opened it, just a little.

"The princess is almost cured," he whispered to the anxious group waiting outside. "Tell them quickly to ring all the bells of every church in the city to celebrate. It will please her."

The king gave the order, and in a short time the air was filled with the clamor of church bells, ringing joyously, a sound that no devil approves. Out from behind Blanca's pillow popped a small, black head with horns, and a harsh, impatient voice demanded, "What is all that noise about?"

And then Ricardo made his master stroke. "That noise," he answered deliberately, "is the sound of the church bells ringing to celebrate the arrival in Granada of old Tía Pía, your mother-in-law."

With a bellow of mingled rage and fear the Devil leaped to the window and was gone, leaving behind him a strong smell of brimstone. While on the bed the color returned to the face of the Princess Blanca, and her gray eyes opened to look, first with wonder and then with shy approval, at Ricardo.

And did old Tía Pía ever know that it was she and none other who had brought happiness to Ricardo and the Princess Blanca?

Probably not. But to the end of her days she chuckled with satisfaction whenever she thought of the part she had played as Don Demonio's mother-in-law.

35. TOÑINO AND THE FAIRIES

(*Spain*)

TOÑINO THE HUNCHBACK was the merriest fellow in all the city of Granada. In spite of the hump on his back and the pain that came to him when the cold winds swept down from the Sierra Nevada, he was always ready with a smile or a jest, or a bit of fun poked at the housewives before whose door he stopped with his herd of goats. From the old grandmother, with her bent back and her wrinkled brown face, to the latest baby, the family would gather around Toñino, and while he milked the goats with his long, skillful fingers, would listen delightedly to his whimsical sayings. The men of Granada liked Toñino, too.

No gathering at the low, white Inn, that stood on the hilltop above the caves where most of the people dwelt, was complete without Toñino. He could sing like a bird, and he knew all the old songs of Spain—ballads of the Cid and of Fernán González, familiar, haunting folk songs and the marching tunes of the soldiers. The first he sang with such fire and passion that even the roughest of his hearers listened spellbound. The second with such a lilting rhythm that, almost unconsciously, heads were set to wagging and feet to dancing.

And, when the merrymaking was over Toñino was always given his full share of the good things to eat and drink. Often he tucked a handful of cakes and an orange or some dried figs and nuts into his pouch to take to old Tía Teresa who lived with him in the cave hollowed out of the hillside. Between the milk of his goats and his gift of song, Toñino and Tía Teresa fared well. And no matter how much his crooked back hurt him neither Tía Teresa nor anyone else ever heard Toñino complain.

One night when the gathering at the Inn had lasted later than usual, Toñino tucked his guitar under his arm and started down the hill toward home. It was St. John's Eve and the June moon hung low in the sky. The high peaks of the Sierra Nevada stood cold and white under it. Even in midsummer, the snow clothed them.

Toñino walked on slowly, the tunes that he had played still singing themselves in his head, his eyes drinking in the beauty of the night. On the slope of the hill, on a little raised terrace, there stood an olive tree, old and gnarled, its leaves silvery white in the moonlight. Just above it, Toñino sat down on the short, dry grass, took off his cap, and let the cool night wind blow through his hair. It had been a long hot day and a long evening, and Toñino was tired. Letting his limbs relax, he rested his head on one outflung arm and went to sleep.

When he awoke the moon had disappeared and the stars blazed low and bright in the sky. Through the stillness there came to Toñino a faint thread of song. At first it was only music. Then, thin and clear, he heard the words:

> "Lunes y martes y miércoles tres,
> Lunes y martes y miércoles tres."
> ("Monday, Tuesday, Wednesday—three,
> Monday, Tuesday, Wednesday—three.")

Now Toñino knew the air—old and wild and filled with an irresistible rhythm. He raised himself on his elbow. Down below him on the terrace under the olive trees the fairies were dancing. There were hundreds of them, tiny fairy men and fairy women. With heads lifted and hands joined they were dancing in a circle around the old tree, flinging their legs high in the air, their tilted, impish faces white in the starlight.

They were so intent on their dance, so lost in the rhythm of their song that they did not even see Toñino. He stared at them in delight and wonder. Often he had heard of the fairies, but never before had he seen them, and their wild grace enchanted him.

> "Lunes y martes y miércoles tres,
> Lunes y martes y miércoles tres,"

—round and round and round the tree, until Toñino grew dizzy with it!

"Hold, my little masters. If you do not know the rest of the song, I will give you a hint of it."

Lifting his guitar, he swept his fingers over the strings and sang in his full, clear voice:

"Lunes y martes y miércoles tres,
Jueves y viernes y sábado seis!"
("Monday, Tuesday, Wednesday—three,
Thursday, Friday, Saturday—six!")

The fairies shouted with joy, and instantly their tiny voices took up the words, singing in unison with Toñino and his guitar until the valley and the surrounding hills rang with the song.

"Lunes y martes y miércoles tres,
Jueves y viernes y sábado seis,"

—higher and shriller and sweeter until the very stars seemed to sing with them.

Suddenly the song ceased, the circle was broken and the fairies, one and all, ran up the slope to Toñino. They swarmed all over and about him, clinging to his fingers with their tiny hands, peering at him with mischievous, slanting eyes.

"A reward, Toñino! A reward!" they cried. "Make a wish and we will grant it!"

Toñino chuckled. "I want no reward, little masters," he answered. "It is enough to have seen you and to have sung with you."

But the fairies insisted. "Make a wish," they shouted. "Any wish. And we will grant it."

Toñino thought for a moment. "There is this hump of mine," he said quaintly. "It is a burden to carry, and it aches when the weather is cold. Could you take it away from me?"

Instantly a thousand little hands were laid on his back and shoulders. His body felt lifted and lightened. A white dawn mist rose from the valley and eddied about him. Through it, ever fainter and sweeter, came the fairy voices:

"Lunes y martes y miércoles tres,
Jueves y viernes y sábado seis." . . .

Toñino rose to his feet, as straight and strong in body as he was blithe in spirit.

There was much excitement among the cave-dwellers in Granada when Toñino's tale was told. Nothing else was talked about for days. No one grudged him his good fortune. And everywhere he went the eyes of the pretty girls of Granada followed him.

Now in a nearby village there lived another hunchback boy whose name was Miguel. He was as cross and resentful as Toñino was merry

and forgiving. To him life itself was as great a burden as the hump that
he carried upon his shoulders. He had hated Toñino always for his
brave spirit, and now that he stood as tall and straight as any man, he
hated him more than ever. In his harsh, complaining voice he questioned Toñino, who told him every word of the story. He even took
him to the hillside and pointed out the ancient olive tree standing
alone on its circular terrace.

"Try it, Miguel," he urged. "Listen carefully to the fairies first so that
you surely get the air and the rhythm of their song. And then sing with
them. Perhaps they will take your hump away, too."

That next night Miguel went out alone to the slope above the olive
tree, and waited for the fairies. And as they had come to Toñino, so
they came to him. He could see them dancing around the tree in a circle. He could hear the thin, sweet voices:

> "Lunes y martes y miércoles tres,
> Jueves y viernes y sábado seis."

Too stupid to catch the lilt of the song, and too impatient to wait
until he did, Miguel—thinking that he was being very clever—shouted
abruptly:

> "Y domingo siete!"
> ("And Sunday—seven!")

Now this was a double insult to the fairies. It rudely broke the
rhythm of their song, and it named that forbidden thing—a holy day.

With a shrill cry of scorn and rage they swarmed upon Miguel. From
some hidden place they dragged out Toñino's hump and fastened it
upon his own. With pointed, impish fingers they poked and pried him,
their light voices mocking him, their long, pale eyes flashing into his. It
was a nightmare to Miguel, and he never quite knew how it ended.

When dawn came he found himself sitting on the hillside under the
old olive tree, with two humps instead of one upon his shoulders. Never
again did he try to see the fairies, and no word of his adventure ever
passed his lips. To all questions he shook his head. Only Toñino
guessed what had happened when Miguel added the last and unwelcome line to the fairies' song.

36. I ATE THE LOAF
(Spain)

TWO CITIZENS AND a rustic, going to Mecca, shared provisions till they reached that place, and then their food failed, so that nothing remained save so much flour as would make a single loaf, and that a small one. The citizens, seeing this, said to each other, "We have too little bread, and our companion eats a great deal. Wherefore we ought to have a plan to take away from him part of the loaf and eat it by ourselves alone."

Accordingly they proposed the following plan to him: to make and bake the loaf, and while it was being baked to sleep, and whoever of them saw the most wonderful things in a dream should eat the loaf alone. These words they spake artfully, as they thought the rustic too simple for inventions of the kind. They made the loaf and baked it, and at length lay down to sleep. But the rustic, more crafty than they thought, whilst his companions were asleep, took the half-baked loaf, ate it up, and again lay down. One of the citizens, as if terrified out of his sleep, awoke and called his companion, who inquired, "What is the matter?" He said, "I have seen a wondrous vision, for it seemed to me that two angels opened the gates of paradise and let me within." Then his companion said to him, "This is a wondrous vision you have seen. But I dreamed that two angels took me and, cleaving the earth, led me to the lower regions." The rustic heard all this and pretended to be asleep; but the citizens, being deceived, and wishing to deceive, called on him to awake. Whereupon the rustic cunningly cried out, as though terrified, "Who are they that call me?" Then they said, "We are your companions." "Have you returned already?" he exclaimed. To this they rejoined, "Where did we go, that we should return?" Then the rustic said, "Now it seemed to me that two angels took one of you, opened the gates of heaven and led him within; then two others took the other, opened the earth, and took him to hell. Seeing this, I thought neither of you would return any more; so I rose and ate the loaf."

37. THE HALF-CHICK
(Spain)

ONCE UPON A TIME there was a handsome black Spanish hen, who had a large brood of chickens. They were all fine, plump little birds, except the youngest, who was quite unlike his brothers and sisters. Indeed, he was such a strange, queer-looking creature, that when he first chipped his shell his mother could scarcely believe her eyes, he was so different from the twelve other fluffy, downy, soft little chicks who nestled under her wings. This one looked just as if he had been cut in two. He had only one leg, and one wing, and one eye, and he had half a head and half a beak. His mother shook her head sadly as she looked at him and said:

"My youngest born is only a half-chick. He can never grow up a tall handsome cock like his brothers. They will go out into the world and rule over poultry yards of their own; but this poor little fellow will always have to stay at home with his mother." And she called him Medio Pollito, which is Spanish for half-chick.

Now though Medio Pollito was such an odd, helpless-looking little thing, his mother soon found that he was not at all willing to remain under her wing and protection. Indeed, in character he was as unlike his brothers and sisters as he was in appearance. They were good, obedient chickens, and when the old hen chicked after them, they chirped and ran back to her side. But Medio Pollito had a roving spirit in spite of his one leg, and when his mother called to him to return to the coop, he pretended that he could not hear, because he had only one ear.

When she took the whole family out for a walk in the fields, Medio Pollito would hop away by himself, and hide among the Indian corn. Many an anxious minute his brothers and sisters had looking for him, while his mother ran to and fro cackling in fear and dismay.

As he grew older he became more self-willed and disobedient, and his manner to his mother was often very rude, and his temper to the other chickens very disagreeable.

One day he had been out for a longer expedition than usual in the fields. On his return he strutted up to his mother with the peculiar little hop and kick which was his way of walking, and cocking his one eye at her in a very bold way he said:

"Mother, I am tired of this life in a dull farmyard, with nothing but a dreary maize field to look at. I'm off to Madrid to see the King."

"To Madrid, Medio Pollito!" exclaimed his mother; "why, you silly chick, it would be a long journey for a grown-up cock, and a poor little thing like you would be tired out before you had gone half the distance. No, no, stay at home with your mother, and some day, when you are bigger, we will go a little journey together."

But Medio Pollito had made up his mind, and he would not listen to his mother's advice, nor to the prayers and entreaties of his brothers and sisters.

"What is the use of our all crowding each other up in this poky little place?" he said. "When I have a fine courtyard of my own at the King's palace, I shall perhaps ask some of you to come and pay me a short visit," and scarcely waiting to say good-bye to his family, away he stumped down the high road that led to Madrid.

"Be sure that you are kind and civil to everyone you meet," called his mother, running after him; but he was in such a hurry to be off, that he did not wait to answer her, or even to look back.

A little later in the day, as he was taking a short cut through a field, he passed a stream. Now the stream was all choked up, and overgrown with weeds and water-plants, so that its waters could not flow freely.

"Oh! Medio Pollito," it cried, as the half-chick hopped along its banks, "do come and help me by clearing away these weeds."

"Help you, indeed!" exclaimed Medio Pollito, tossing his head, and shaking the few feathers in his tail. "Do you think I have nothing to do but to waste my time on such trifles? Help yourself, and don't trouble busy travelers. I am off to Madrid to see the King," and hoppity-kick, hoppity-kick, away stumped Medio Pollito.

A little later he came to a fire that had been left by some gipsies in a wood. It was burning very low, and would soon be out.

"Oh! Medio Pollito," cried the fire, in a weak, wavering voice as the half-chick approached, "in a few minutes I shall go quite out, unless you put some sticks and dry leaves upon me. Do help me, or I shall die!"

"Help you, indeed!" answered Medio Pollito. "I have other things to do. Gather sticks for yourself, and don't trouble me. I am off to Madrid to see the King," and hoppity-kick, hoppity-kick, away stumped Medio Pollito.

The next morning, as he was getting near Madrid, he passed a large chestnut tree, in whose branches the wind was caught and entangled. "Oh! Medio Pollito," called the wind, "do hop up here, and help me to get free of these branches. I cannot come away, and it is so uncomfortable."

"It is your own fault for going there," answered Medio Pollito. "I can't waste all my morning stopping here to help you. Just shake yourself off, and don't hinder me, for I am off to Madrid to see the King," and hoppity-kick, hoppity-kick, away stumped Medio Pollito in great glee, for the towers and roofs of Madrid were now in sight. When he entered the town he saw before him a great splendid house, with soldiers standing before the gates. This he knew must be the King's palace, and he determined to hop up to the front gate and wait there until the King came out. But as he was hopping past one of the back windows the King's cook saw him:

"Here is the very thing I want," he exclaimed, "for the King has just sent a message to say that he must have chicken broth for his dinner," and opening the window he stretched out his arm, caught Medio Pollito, and popped him into the broth pot that was standing near the fire. Oh! how wet and clammy the water felt as it went over Medio Pollito's head, making his feathers cling to his side.

"Water, water!" he cried in his despair, "do have pity upon me and do not wet me like this."

"Ah! Medio Pollito," replied the water, "you would not help me when I was a little stream away on the fields, now you must be punished."

Then the fire began to burn and scald Medio Pollito, and he danced and hopped from one side of the pot to the other, trying to get away from the heat, and crying out in pain:

"Fire, fire! do not scorch me like this; you can't think how it hurts."

"Ah! Medio Pollito," answered the fire, "you would not help me when I was dying away in the wood. You are being punished."

At last, just when the pain was so great that Medio Pollito thought he must die, the cook lifted up the lid of the pot to see if the broth was ready for the King's dinner.

"Look here!" he cried in horror, "this chicken is quite useless. It is burned to a cinder. I can't send it up to the royal table"; and opening the window he threw Medio Pollito out into the street. But the wind caught him up, and whirled him through the air so quickly that Medio Pollito could scarcely breathe, and his heart beat against his side till he thought it would break.

"Oh, wind!" at last he gasped out, "if you hurry me along like this you will kill me. Do let me rest a moment, or——" but he was so breathless that he could not finish his sentence.

"Ah! Medio Pollito," replied the wind, "when I was caught in the branches of the chestnut tree you would not help me; now you are punished." And he swirled Medio Pollito over the roofs of the houses till they reached the highest church in the town, and there he left him fastened to the top of the steeple.

And there stands Medio Pollito to this day. And if you go to Madrid, and walk through the streets till you come to the highest church, you will see Medio Pollito perched on his one leg on the steeple, with his one wing drooping at his side, and gazing sadly out of his one eye over the town.

38. A LEGEND OF SAINT NICHOLAS
(Holland)

NICHOLAS, THE BISHOP of Myra in Asia Minor, was known for his many deeds of kindness. He liked to ride about the town on his white horse, with his faithful servant, Black Piet, walking beside him, and give oranges and toys to the children he met on his way. He cared for the sick, and helped the poor and lonely. People began to speak of him as Saint Nicholas.

The good bishop was particularly fond of entertaining travelers who had been to other lands, and one day a returned voyager told him of Holland. "The cities are full of waterways," he said, "and the houses have stepped roofs. The children wear wooden shoes, and have round, merry faces. There are windmills in the fields, and the ports are full of white-sailed ships."

"I should like to see that country," the bishop said. He clapped his hands to summon his servant. "Black Piet, we are going to Holland. I will take ship tomorrow."

The bishop had the hold of the vessel filled with oranges, and toys, and sugarplums. Of course, his white horse had to go, too. It was winter and the sea was stormy. The winds rose and the waves were so high that the ship listed dangerously.

"We are doomed!" the sailors cried.

Only the bishop was calm. "Fear not," he said. He fell to his knees and prayed, and suddenly the seas were smooth again.

It was the fifth of December when the ship reached the harbor of Amsterdam. As soon as he came ashore a crowd surrounded Bishop Nicholas. The people wanted to stroke his white horse which carried baskets on either side. They wanted to touch the bishop's handsome embroidered robes. They liked his kindly face under the tall miter. And they had never seen anyone like Black Piet.

The children ran beside the bishop as he rode to the market square. There he distributed the good things that filled the baskets. The children clamored for the gifts. But first Bishop Nicholas would say to each one, "Have you been a good child this past year?" If the child said "Yes," he would ask the parents, "Has he truly been a good child this year?"

Those who had been good received the gifts, and those who had not been good found Black Piet shaking a switch at them, so that they ran and hid behind their mothers' skirts.

The crowd followed Bishop Nicholas around the city. "This is a beautiful country," he said. "I have always wanted to see it. And now that I have seen it, I know that I shall come back again."

The children brought sweet hay and carrots to feed the white horse. There was dancing and feasting and singing. Somehow all the people knew that this was a very special visitor, and they were happy to have him in their city. At the end of the day the children of Amsterdam fell asleep, their wooden shoes full of gifts.

As Bishop Nicholas and Black Piet wandered through the quiet streets, they heard the sound of weeping coming from a handsome house. The bishop got off his horse and went close to the house, to listen. "There are two sisters there," he whispered to Black Piet as he peered through one of the windows. "The room is empty. All the furniture is gone. Their eyes are red from weeping. Let us hear what they are saying."

The older sister said, "Where can we go? What can we do? The money our father left us is gone; we have sold all our belongings, we have nothing. Tomorrow we must leave this house, but where can we go?"

The younger sister said, "Do not despair. I will pray God to take care of us." They both bent their heads.

Bishop Nicholas and Black Piet crept away. Late that night, when the sisters were asleep on the bare floor, the bishop came back and silently put a big bag of gold through the window, where they would find it the first thing in the morning.

On the way back to his lodgings, the bishop passed a lowly hovel. He knew that the people in this little hut must be miserably poor, and he wanted to do something for them. But he could not put money through a window, for there were no windows in the hut. And the door was tightly closed against the cold.

The good bishop was puzzled. "How can I get inside to leave money for them?"

Black Piet pointed to the sloping thatched roof. "Why not climb up to the chimney?" And that is what Bishop Nicholas did. Carefully he dropped a handful of gold coins down the chimney, and by a miracle they fell into the stockings which the two children of the household had hung in the fireplace to dry.

Next morning, when they found the coins, the children could not believe their eyes. "It's a gift direct from the good God!" they cried.

But a neighbor, who had seen the bishop clambering over the roof, told them what had happened.

Although everyone hunted over the city for the bringer of gifts and Black Piet, they had disappeared and their ship was gone from the harbor.

But the next year Bishop Nicholas came back, and every year since then he has returned, to bring gifts to the children of Holland on the night of December fifth. When he died, he was made a saint, and the day of his visitation is called Sinterklaas, which is Saint Nicholas in Dutch, and from this we get our Santa Claus.

The beloved bishop became the patron saint of sailors and of the city of Amsterdam; the largest church there is named in his honor. Cakes are made in his image and sold in the streets.

Every year Saint Nicholas visits all the homes in Holland, rich and poor. On the night of December fifth, the children put their wooden shoes in the chimney corner, filled with carrots or hay for his white horse.

39. THE HARE AND THE T
A Fable of Aesop
(Ancient Greece)

THE HARE WAS ONCE boasting of his speed before the other animals. "I have never yet been beaten," said he, "when I put forth my full speed. I challenge anyone here to race with me."

The Tortoise said quietly: "I accept your challenge."

"That is a good joke," said the Hare; "I could dance round you all the way."

"Keep your boasting till you've beaten," answered the Tortoise. "Shall we race?"

So a course was fixed and a start was made. The Hare darted almost out of sight at once, but soon stopped and, to show his contempt for the Tortoise, lay down to have a nap.

The Tortoise plodded on and plodded on, and when the Hare awoke from his nap, he saw the Tortoise just near the winning-post and could not run up in time to save the race. Then said the Tortoise:

"Plodding wins the race."

40. THE FOX AND THE GRAPES
A Fable of Aesop
(*Ancient Greece*)

ONE HOT SUMMER'S DAY a Fox was strolling through an orchard till he came to a bunch of Grapes just ripening on a vine which had been trained over a lofty branch. "Just the thing to quench my thirst," quoth he. Drawing back a few paces, he took a run and a jump, and just missed the bunch. Turning round again with a One, Two, Three, he jumped up, but with no greater success. Again and again he tried after the tempting morsel, but at last had to give it up, and walked away with his nose in the air, saying: "I am sure they are sour."

It is easy to despise what you cannot get.

41. THE GOOSE WITH THE GOLDEN EGGS
A Fable of Aesop
(*Ancient Greece*)

ONE DAY A COUNTRYMAN going to the nest of his Goose found there an egg all yellow and glittering. When he took it up it was as heavy as lead and he was going to throw it away, because he thought a trick had been played upon him. But he took it home on second thoughts, and soon found to his delight that it was an egg of pure gold. Every morning the same thing occurred, and he soon became rich by selling his eggs. As he grew rich he grew greedy; and thinking to get at once all the gold the Goose could give, he killed it and opened it only to find, —nothing.

Greed often overreaches itself.

42. THE MAN, THE BOY AND THE DONKEY
A Fable of Aesop
(*Ancient Greece*)

A MAN AND HIS son were once going with their Donkey to market. As they were walking along by its side a countryman passed them and said: "You fools, what is a Donkey for but to ride upon?"

So the Man put the Boy on the Donkey and they went on their way. But soon they passed a group of men, one of whom said: "See that lazy youngster, he lets his father walk while he rides."

So the Man ordered his Boy to get off, and got on himself. But they hadn't gone far when they passed two women, one of whom said to the other: "Shame on that lazy lout to let his poor little son trudge along."

Well, the Man didn't know what to do, but at last he took his Boy up before him on the Donkey. By this time they had come to the town, and the passersby began to jeer and point at them. The Man stopped and asked what they were scoffing at. The men said: "Aren't you ashamed of yourself for overloading that poor Donkey of yours—you and your hulking son?"

The Man and Boy got off and tried to think what to do. They

thought and they thought, till at last they cut down a pole, tied the Donkey's feet to it, and raised the pole and the Donkey to their shoulders. They went along amid the laughter of all who met them till they came to Market Bridge, when the Donkey, getting one of his feet loose, kicked out and caused the Boy to drop his end of the pole. In the struggle the Donkey fell over the bridge, and his forefeet being tied together he was drowned.

"That will teach you," said an old man who had followed them:

"Please all, and you will please none."

43. EROS AND PSYCHE
(*Ancient Greece*)

A CERTAIN KING had three daughters who were known far and wide for their beauty. The most beautiful of all was the youngest, Psyche. When this youngest princess went into the temples, many people mistook her for Venus herself, and offered her the garlands which they had brought for the goddess of love and beauty.

The real Venus, much vexed by this, determined to be revenged on poor Psyche, who was in no way to blame. One day she told Eros, the god of love, to wound Psyche with one of his golden-pointed arrows, and make her fall in love with some wretched beggar, the most degraded that could be found.

Eros took his arrows and went down to the earth to do his mother's bidding. As soon as he saw Psyche, he was so startled by her wonderful beauty that he wounded himself with his own arrow; consequently, instead of making Psyche fall in love with some ragged beggar, he himself fell in love with Psyche.

Long before this the two elder of the three beautiful sisters had been married to kings' sons, as befitted the rank of princesses; but in spite of her superior beauty, no lovers came to sue for the hand of the youngest sister. The king, suspecting that this might be caused by the wrath of

Venus, inquired of the oracle what he should do. The answer that he received allowed him no longer to doubt the anger of the gods. These were the words of the prophetess:

> "Dress thy daughter like a bride,
> Lead her up the mountainside,
> There an unknown wingèd foe,
> Feared by all who dwell below,
> And even by the gods above,
> Will claim her, as a hawk the dove."

The king was overcome with grief, but did not dare to disobey. Therefore one night Psyche's maids of honor dressed her in wedding garments and a long procession of her father's people escorted her to an exposed rock at the top of a high mountain, where they sadly extinguished their torches, and left her alone in the darkness.

After the last sound of human footsteps had died away, Psyche sat weeping and trembling, fearing every moment that she might hear the rushing wings of some dragon, and feel his claws and teeth. Instead she felt the cool breath and the downy wings of Zephyrus, the west wind, who lifted her gently from the rock, then puffed out his cheeks, and blew her down into a beautiful green valley, where he laid her softly on a bank of violets.

This moonlit valley was so sweet and peaceful that Psyche forgot her fears and fell asleep. When she woke in the morning, she saw a beautiful grove of tall trees, and in the grove a most wonderful palace, with a fountain in front of it. The great arches of the roof were supported by golden columns, and the walls were covered with silver carving, while the floor was a mosaic of precious stones of all colors.

Psyche timidly entered the doors, and wandered through the great rooms, each of which seemed more splendid than the last. She could see no one, but once or twice thought she heard low voices, as if the fairies were talking together. It might have been voices, or it might have been the trickling of water in the fountain.

Presently, she opened the door of a room, where a table was laid ready for a feast. Evidently only one guest was expected, for there was but one chair and one cover. Psyche, half afraid, seated herself in the chair, and the fairies of the palace, or the nymphs, or whatever beings the voices belonged to, came and waited on her, but not one of them could be seen. She enjoyed a most appetizing repast. After the last dish had been whisked away by invisible hands, she heard music—a chorus of singing voices, and then a single voice, accompanied by a lyre, which seemed to play of itself.

As the light faded away, and night came, Psyche began to tremble, for she feared that the owner of the palace might prove to be the winged monster of the oracle, and that he would come to claim her. There were no locks nor bolts, and the doors and windows stood wide open, as if no thief, nor evil creature of any kind, had ever lived.

When it had grown perfectly dark, so dark that she could not see her own hand, Psyche heard the sound of wings, and then footsteps coming down the great hall. The footsteps came lightly and quickly to the low seat where she was sitting, and then a voice which was sweet and musical said to her: "Beautiful Psyche, this palace and all it holds is yours, if you will consent to live here and be my wife. The voices you have heard are the voices of your handmaidens, who will obey any commands that you give them. Every night I will spend here with you; but before day comes, I must fly away. Do not ask to see my face, nor to know who I am. Only trust me; I ask nothing more."

This speech took away Psyche's fear of being immediately eaten, at any rate; but still she could not be quite sure that this voice was not the voice of the monster.

Her mysterious lover came to talk to her every night, as he had said he would do. Sometimes she looked forward to his coming with pleasure; at other times the sound of his wings filled her with terror.

One day, while she was gathering roses within sight of the rock from which Zephyrus had blown her into the valley, she saw her two sisters on this rock, weeping, beating their breasts, and crying out as if mourning for the dead. Hearing her own name, she knew that her sisters must be mourning for her, supposing that she had been devoured on this rock. These sisters of Psyche had not always been kind to her; but she now believed that they had really loved her after all.

That night, when her lover came in the dark, Psyche asked him if she might not see her sisters, and let them know that she was alive and happy. She received an unwilling consent.

The next day the sisters came again to the high rock, and Zephyrus blew them down into the valley, just as he had blown Psyche down. They were very much surprised to see the good fortune that had befallen their little sister, but instead of rejoicing at it, as they should have done, they were envious of her. They asked her a great many questions, and were particularly curious about the owner of the palace. Psyche told them that he was away hunting in the mountains. Then Zephyrus, thinking that they were getting too inquisitive, whisked them away to the rock, and that was the end of their visit.

After a time Psyche grew tired of being so much alone, and wished to see her sisters again. Her lover gave his consent a second time, but warned her not to answer or even to listen to any questions about himself, and told her, above all, that if she ever tried to see him face to face, he should be forced to fly away and leave her, and that the palace also would vanish.

The next day Zephyrus brought the sisters into the valley as before. These envious women had brooded over their sister's superior fortune till their minds were full of wicked thoughts, and between them they made a plan by which they meant to destroy Psyche's happiness. They told her that the owner of the palace was, without doubt, a most horrible winged serpent, the nameless monster of the oracle, and that the people who lived on the mountain had seen him coming down into that valley, every day toward dusk. "Although he seems so kind," said they, "he is only waiting his time to devour you. He knows that you would be terrified by his ugly scales, and this is the reason he never allows you to see him. But listen to the advice of your sisters, who are older and wiser than you. Take this knife, and while your pretended friend is asleep, light a lamp and look at him. If our words prove to be true, strike off his head, and save yourself from an awful death."

With these words her sisters left Psyche the knife and hurried away. When they had gone, poor Psyche could not rid her mind of the fears their words had raised. Her faith was gone. If all were right, why was her lover so anxious to be hidden in the darkness? Why did he fear her sisters' visits? Why did he have wings? Worst of all, she remembered with a shudder that she had once or twice heard a sound like the gliding of a serpent over the marble floors.

Soon it grew dark, and she heard her lover coming. That night she would not talk to him, therefore he went into a chamber where there was a couch, lay down and fell asleep.

Then Psyche, trembling with fear, lighted her lamp, took the knife, and stole to the couch where he lay. The light of the lamp fell full on his face, and Psyche saw no scaly serpent, but Eros, or Love himself, the most beautiful of the gods. Golden curls fell back from his wonderful face; his snow-white wings were folded in sleep, while the down on them—as delicate as that on the wings of a butterfly—stirred faintly, set in motion by his quiet breathing. At his feet lay his bow and arrows.

Psyche dropped her knife, in horror at the deed it might have done.

Then taking up an arrow curiously, she pricked her finger on its golden point. Holding her lamp high above her head, she turned to look at Eros again, and now for the first time in love with Love, gazed at him in an ecstasy of happiness; but her hand trembled, and a drop of hot oil fell on the shoulder of the god. He opened his eyes, looked at her reproachfully, and then flew away without a word. The beautiful palace vanished, and Psyche found herself alone.

Then Psyche began a long search for her lost Eros. She met Pan, Ceres, and Juno, one after another, but none of them could help her. At last she went to Venus herself, thinking that the mother of Love would be kind to her for Love's sake.

Eros, at this time, lay in the palace of Venus, suffering from the wound caused by the burning oil. Venus knew all that had happened, for a gull had flown to her and told her. She was very angry, and as a punishment imposed certain almost impossible tasks upon Psyche.

First, the goddess pointed to a great heap of seeds, the food of the doves that drew her chariot, and of the little sparrows that accompanied her on her journeys. It was composed of wheat, barley, millet, and other kinds of seed, all mixed carelessly together. "Take these," said Venus, "and separate them grain by grain; place each kind by itself, and finish the task before nightfall."

Poor Psyche had no courage to begin the task, but sat with drooping head and folded hands. Then a little ant ran out from under a stone, and called the whole army of the ant people, who came for Love's sake, and quickly separated the seeds, laying each kind by itself.

When Venus came at the close of the day, and saw that Psyche's task was finished, she was very much surprised, and throwing the poor girl a piece of coarse bread, remarked that a harder task would be set for her in the morning. Accordingly, when morning came, Venus took Psyche to the bank of a broad river, and pointing to a grove on the opposite shore, where a flock of sheep with golden wool were feeding, said, "Bring me some of that wool."

Psyche would have plunged immediately into the river, if some reeds on the bank had not whispered to her: "Do not go near those sheep now. They are fierce creatures when the sun is high. Wait till the song of the river has lulled them to sleep; then go and pick all the wool you like from the bushes, where the sheep have left it clinging." So Psyche waited till the sun was low, then crossed the river and came back with her arms full of golden wool.

Venus, seeing Psyche return in safety, was angrier than ever. "You never did this by yourself," said she. "Now we will see whether you are wise and prudent enough to become the bride of Eros. Take this crystal vase, and fill it with water from the Fountain of Forgetfulness."

This fountain was at the very top of a high mountain. The icy water gushed forth from a smooth rock, far higher than anyone could climb, and as it rushed down its narrow channel it shouted, "Fly from me! Beware! You will perish!" On either side of the black stream was a cave, and in each cave lived a fierce dragon. When Psyche came to the place and saw all this, she was so horrified that she could not move or speak. Nevertheless, she accomplished this task also; for Jupiter's eagle, to whom Love had been kind, took the crystal vase and filled it for her at the fountain.

Psyche ran back to Venus with the water, hoping to please her this time. But Venus was still angry. "You are a witch," said she, "or you could not do these things. However, here is one task more. Take this box, carry it down into the underworld, and ask Proserpine if you may not bring back to me some of her beauty."

When Psyche heard this, she felt sure that Venus meant to destroy her, and thinking that it was of no use to struggle longer against the persecutions of the goddess, she climbed up the stairway of a lofty tower, intending to throw herself down from the top. But the stones of the tower cried out to her: "Listen, Psyche! From yonder dark chasm, choked with thorns, a path leads down to the underworld. Take a piece of barley bread in each hand, and two pieces of money in your mouth, then follow this rough path. When you come to the river of the dead, Charon will ferry you over for one of your pieces of money. When you reach the gate of Pluto's palace, where Cerberus keeps watch, give that fierce dog one of the pieces of bread, and he will let you pass. You can then enter the palace where Proserpine is queen. She will give you a portion of her beauty, shutting it into the box, and you can return by the same way, giving the remaining piece of bread to Cerberus, and the remaining piece of money to Charon. One thing more. I charge you, do not, by any means, look into the box."

Psyche was thankful indeed for this advice, and followed it in every particular but one. When she was returning, she forgot the warning about not looking into the box. Since Love had flown away from her, her suffering had been so great that her beauty was nearly gone. Therefore, thinking that it might not be wrong to take a very little of Proserpine's beauty for herself, she raised the lid of the box. Whiff! A strange invisible something rushed from it and overcame her. She fell into a deep sleep, and might never have waked again if Love, cured of his wounds, had not passed by and seen her. The god shook her till she was awake again, then sent her back to his mother with the box, while he flew straight to Mount Olympus, and laid the case before Jupiter.

The king of the gods, after hearing the story, said that Psyche should be made immortal, and should become the bride of Eros.

Mercury was immediately sent to bring Psyche up to Mount Olympus, while the gods all gathered to a great feast. Jupiter himself handed to this mortal maid the cup of sacred nectar, of which whoever drinks will live forever. Psyche drank from the golden cup, and straightway two beautiful butterflylike wings sprang from her shoulders, and she became like the gods in all things.

After this, she was wedded to Eros, who never flew away from her again. Apollo sang, and Venus, her anger forgotten, danced at the wedding.

44. THE TWELVE MONTHS
(Modern Greece)

ONCE UPON A TIME there was a widow woman who had five children, but she was so poor she hadn't so much as a brass farthing. She could find no work to do except once a week, when a gentlewoman of the neighborhood had her in to bake her bread. But for her trouble she did not give her even the corner of a loaf to take for her children to eat, but the poor woman went home with the dough on her hands and there she washed them in clean water and this water she boiled and made gruel and this the children ate. And with this gruel they were satisfied the whole week till their mother went again to make bread at the gentlewoman's house and returned, with hands unwashed, to make them gruel again.

The gentlewoman's children, for all the food they had, so much and so rich, and for all the fresh bread they fed on, were like dried mackerel. But the poor woman's children were filled out and chubby, like plump red mullet. Even the gentlewoman was amazed and spoke about it to her friends.

Her friends said, "The poor woman's children are filled out and chubby because she takes away your children's luck on her hands and gives it to her own children. That is why they get fat and yours grow thinner and dwindle away."

The gentlewoman believed this and when the day came again for making bread, she did not let the poor woman leave with her hands unwashed, but made her wash them clean, so that the luck should stay in her house. And the poor woman came home with tears in her eyes. When her children saw her and saw that she had no dough on her hands, they began to cry. On the one hand, the children wept, and on the other, the mother.

At last, like a grown woman, she steeled herself and calmed her tears, and said to her children, "Dry your eyes, my children, and weep no more, and I'll find a piece of bread for you to eat."

And she went from door to door and barely found someone to give her a stale corner of bread. She dipped it well in water and shared it among her children, and when they had eaten, she put them to bed and they fell asleep. And at midnight she left the house without looking back lest she see her children dying of hunger.

As she walked through the wilderness in the night, she saw a light shining on a high place, and went up toward it. And when she drew close to it, she saw it was a tent, and from the center hung a great candelabra with twelve candles, and underneath it hung a round thing like a ball. She went into the tent and saw twelve young men who were talking over what to do about a certain matter. The tent was round and to the right of the entrance sat three young men with their collars open, and in their hands they carried tender grass and tree blossoms. Next to these young men sat another three, with their sleeves rolled up, and coatless, carrying in their hands dry ears of wheat. Next to these sat another three young men, each with a bunch of grapes in his hand. Next to these sat another three young men, each huddled over himself and wearing a long fur from the neck to the knee.

When the young men saw the woman, they said, "Greetings, good Aunt, be seated."

And after greeting them, the woman sat down. And when she was seated, they asked her how it was she had come to that place. And the poor widow told them of her plight and her troubles. Seeing that the poor woman was hungry, one of those who wore furs got up and laid the table for her to eat, and she saw that he was lame. When the woman had eaten her fill, the young men began to ask her all kinds of things about the country, and the woman answered as well as she could.

At last the three young men that had their collars open said to her, "Now, good Aunt, how do you get on with the months of the year? How do you like March, April, and May?"

"I like them well, my lads," answered the widow, "and indeed, when these months come, the mountains and fields grow green, the earth is gay with all kinds of flowers, and from them comes scent, so that a body feels revived. All the birds begin to sing. The husbandmen see that their fields are green and rejoice in their hearts and make their granaries ready. So we have no complaints against March, April, and May, otherwise God would send fire to burn us for our ingratitude."

Then the next three young men that had their sleeves rolled up and ears of wheat in their hands, asked, "Well, and what have you to say to June, July, and August?"

"Nor can we complain over those three months, because, with the warmth they bring, they ripen the crops and all the fruits. Then the husbandmen reap what they have sown and the gardeners gather their fruit. And indeed the poor are made happy by these months, for they do not need many and costly clothes."

Then the next three young men that carried grapes, "How do you get on with the months of September, October, and November?"

"In those months," answered the woman, "folk gather grapes and make them into wine. And they are good besides in that they tell us that winter is coming, and folk set about getting in wood, coals, and heavy clothing, so as to keep warm."

Then the three young men in furs asked her, "Now, how do you get on with December, January, and February?"

"Ah, those are the months that care for us greatly," said the poor woman, "and we love them very much. And will you ask for why? Here's why! Because folk are by nature insatiable and would like to work the whole year round, so as to earn much, but those winter months come and cause us to draw into a corner and rest ourselves after the summer's labors. Folk love these months because, with their rains and snows, they cause all the seeds and grasses to grow. So, my lads, all the months are good and worthy and each one does his work, may God preserve them. It is us folk who are not good."

Then eleven of the young men made a sign to the first of those who carried grapes, and he went out and very shortly came back with a stoppered jar in his arms and he gave it to the woman, saying, "Come now, Auntie, and take this jar home with you to raise your children on."

Joyfully the woman took the jar on her shoulder, and said to the young men, "May your years be many, my lads."

"May the hour be good to you, good Aunt," they answered, and she went.

Just as dawn was breaking, she came back home and found her children still asleep. She spread out a cloth and emptied the jar onto it. When she saw that it was full of gold pieces she all but went out of her mind for joy. When it was well and truly light, she went to the baker's and bought five or six loaves and an *oka* of cheese and woke her children, washed and tidied them, set them to say their prayers, and then gave them bread and cheese, and the little dears ate until they were truly full. Then she bought a kilo of wheat and took it to the mill and had it ground, made it into dough, and took the loaves to the bakery to bake. And just as she was returning from the bakery, with the board laden with bread on her shoulder, and was almost home, the gentlewoman saw her and suspected that something had happened to her and ran up to her, to learn where she had got the flour to make bread with. The poor woman innocently told her all.

The gentlewoman was envious and made up her mind that she, too, would go to see the young men. So, that night, when her husband and children were asleep, she slipped out of the house and took the road and went on till she found the tent where the twelve months were and greeted them.

And they said to her, "Greetings, mistress, how is it you have consented to visit us?"

"I am poor," she answered, "and I have come to you for help."

"Very good," said the young men, "and how are things where you come from?"

"They might be worse," she answered.

"Well, how do you get on with the months?" they asked next.

"How, indeed," she answered. "Each one is a sore trial. Just as we are getting used to the heat of August, straightway September, October, and November come along and chill us so that this one gets a cough and that one catches a cold. Then the winter months, December, January, and February, come in and freeze us, the roads fill with snow, and we cannot go out, and as for that lame-john of a February . . . !" (Poor February was listening.) "And then those accursed months March, April, and May! They don't consider themselves to be summer months, and all they want is to act like winter ones, so they make the winter last nine months. And we can never go out on the first of May and drink coffee with milk in it and sit on the new grass. Then come the months June, July, and August—they're the ones that are mad to stifle us with sweat by the heat they bring. Indeed, on the fifteenth of August, we are all in a fit of coughing and the bitter winds spoil our linen on the clothesline. What more can I say, lads? Our life with the months (may curses befall them) is a dog's life."

The young man said nothing but made a sign to him who sat in the middle of those bearing grapes.

And he got up and brought in a stoppered jar and gave it to the woman, and said, "Take this jar, and when you get home, lock yourself up in a room alone and empty it out. See that you do not open it on the way."

"I won't," said the woman.

She went and joyfully came home just before dawn. Then she locked herself in a room all alone and spread out a cloth and unstoppered the jar and emptied it out. And what came out of it? Nothing but snakes. They coiled themselves about her and devoured her alive; she left her children motherless, for it is wrong for one to accuse another. But the poor woman, with her true heart and her sweet tongue, went up in the world and became a great lady, and her children flourished. There! That's what they call a happy ending!

British Isles

Jack and the Beanstalk

45. JACK AND THE BEANSTALK
(*England*)

THERE WAS ONCE upon a time a poor widow who had an only son named Jack, and a cow named Milky-white. And all they had to live on was the milk the cow gave every morning which they carried to the market and sold. But one morning Milky-white gave no milk and they didn't know what to do.

"What shall we do, what shall we do?" said the widow, wringing her hands.

"Cheer up, mother, I'll go and get work somewhere," said Jack.

"We've tried that before, and nobody would take you," said his mother; "we must sell Milky-white and with the money start shop, or something."

"All right, mother," says Jack; "it's marketday today, and I'll soon sell Milky-white, and then we'll see what we can do."

So he took the cow's halter in his hand, and off he started. He hadn't gone far when he met a funny-looking old man who said to him: "Good morning, Jack."

"Good morning to you," said Jack, and wondered how he knew his name.

"Well, Jack, and where are you off to?" said the man.

"I'm going to market to sell our cow here."

"Oh, you look the proper sort of chap to sell cows," said the man; "I wonder if you know how many beans make five."

"Two in each hand and one in your mouth," says Jack, as sharp as a needle.

"Right you are," says the man, "and here they are, the very beans themselves," he went on, pulling out of his pocket a number of strange-looking beans. "As you are so sharp," says he, "I don't mind doing a swap with you—your cow for these beans."

"Go along," says Jack; "wouldn't you like it?"

"Ah! you don't know what these beans are," said the man; "if you plant them overnight, by morning they grow right up to the sky."

"Really?" says Jack; "you don't say so."

"Yes, that is so, and if it doesn't turn out to be true you can have your cow back."

"Right," says Jack, and hands him over Milky-white's halter and pockets the beans.

Back goes Jack home, and as he hadn't gone very far it wasn't dusk by the time he got to his door.

"Back already, Jack?" said his mother; "I see you haven't got Milky-white, so you've sold her. How much did you get for her?"

"You'll never guess, mother," says Jack.

"No, you don't say so. Good boy! Five pounds, ten, fifteen, no, it can't be twenty."

"I told you you couldn't guess, what do you say to these beans; they're magical, plant them overnight and——"

"What!" says Jack's mother, "have you been such a fool, such a dolt, such an idiot, as to give away my Milky-white, the best milker in the parish, and prime beef to boot, for a set of paltry beans. Take that! Take that! Take that! And as for your precious beans here they go out of the window. And now off with you to bed. Not a sup shall you drink, and not a bit shall you swallow this very night."

So Jack went upstairs to his little room in the attic, and sad and sorry he was, to be sure, as much for his mother's sake as for the loss of his supper.

At last he dropped off to sleep.

When he woke up, the room looked so funny. The sun was shining into part of it, and yet all the rest was quite dark and shady. So Jack jumped up and dressed himself and went to the window. And what do you think he saw? why, the beans his mother had thrown out of the window into the garden, had sprung up into a big beanstalk which went up and up and up till it reached the sky. So the man spoke truth after all.

The beanstalk grew up quite close past Jack's window, so all he had to do was to open it and give a jump on to the beanstalk which ran up just like a big ladder. So Jack climbed, and he climbed and he climbed and he climbed and he climbed and he climbed and he climbed till at last he reached the sky. And when he got there he found a long broad road going as straight as a dart. So he walked along and he walked along and he walked along till he came to a great big tall house, and on the doorstep there was a great big tall woman.

"Good morning, mum," says Jack, quite polite like. "Could you be so kind as to give me some breakfast?" For he hadn't had anything to eat, you know, the night before and was as hungry as a hunter.

"It's breakfast you want, is it?" says the great big tall woman, "it's breakfast you'll be if you don't move off from here. My man is an ogre and there's nothing he likes better than boys broiled on toast. You'd better be moving on or he'll soon be coming."

"Oh! please, mum, do give me something to eat, mum. I've had nothing to eat since yesterday morning, really and truly, mum," says Jack, "I may as well be broiled as die of hunger."

Well, the ogre's wife was not half so bad after all. So she took Jack into the kitchen, and gave him a hunk of bread and cheese and a jug of milk. But Jack hadn't half finished these when thump! thump! thump! the whole house began to tremble with the noise of someone coming.

"Goodness gracious me! It's my old man," said the ogre's wife, "what on earth shall I do? Come along quick and jump in here." And she bundled Jack into the oven just as the ogre came in.

He was a big one, to be sure. At his belt he had three calves strung up by the heels, and he unhooked them and threw them down on the table and said: "Here, wife, broil me a couple of these for breakfast. Ah! what's this I smell?

> Fee-fi-fo-fum,
> I smell the blood of an Englishman,
> Be he alive or be he dead,
> I'll grind his bones to make my bread."

"Nonsense, dear," said his wife, "you're dreaming. Or perhaps you smell the scraps of that little boy you liked so much for yesterday's dinner. Here, you go and have a wash and tidy up, and by the time you come back your breakfast'll be ready for you."

So off the ogre went, and Jack was just going to jump out of the oven and run away when the woman told him not. "Wait till he's alseep," says she; "he always has a doze after breakfast."

Well, the ogre had his breakfast, and after that he goes to a big chest and takes out of it a couple of bags of gold, and down he sits and counts till at last his head began to nod and he began to snore till the whole house shook again.

Then Jack crept out on tiptoe from his oven, and as he was passing the ogre he took one of the bags of gold under his arm, and off he pelters till he came to the beanstalk, and then he threw down the bag of gold, which of course fell into his mother's garden, and then he climbed down and climbed down till at last he got home and told his mother and showed her the gold and said: "Well, mother, wasn't I right about the beans? They are really magical, you see."

So they lived on the bag of gold for some time, but at last they came to the end of it, and Jack made up his mind to try his luck once more up at the top of the beanstalk. So one fine morning he rose up early, and got on to the beanstalk, and he climbed and he climbed and he climbed and he climbed and he climbed and he climbed till at last he came out on to the road again and up to the great big tall house he had been to before. There, sure enough, was the great big tall woman a-standing on the doorstep.

"Good morning, mum," says Jack, as bold as brass, "could you be so good as to give me something to eat?"

"Go away, my boy," said the big tall woman, "or else my man will eat you up for breakfast. But aren't you the youngster who came here once before? Do you know, that very day, my man missed one of his bags of gold."

"That's strange, mum," says Jack, "I dare say I could tell you something about that, but I'm so hungry I can't speak till I've had something to eat."

Well, the big tall woman was so curious that she took him in and gave him something to eat. But he had scarcely begun munching it as slowly as he could when thump! thump! thump! they heard the giant's footstep, and his wife hid Jack away in the oven.

All happened as it did before. In came the ogre as he did before, said: "Fee-fi-fo-fum," and had his breakfast of three broiled oxen. Then he said: "Wife, bring me the hen that lays the golden eggs." So she brought it, and the ogre said: "Lay," and it laid an egg all of gold. And then the ogre began to nod his head, and to snore till the house shook.

Then Jack crept out of the oven on tiptoe and caught hold of the golden hen, and was off before you could say, "Jack Robinson." But this time the hen gave a cackle which woke the ogre, and just as Jack got out of the house he heard him calling: "Wife, wife, what have you done with my golden hen?"

And the wife said: "Why, my dear?"

But that was all Jack heard, for he rushed off to the beanstalk and climbed down like a house on fire. And when he got home he showed his mother the wonderful hen and said, "Lay," to it; and it laid a golden egg every time he said, "Lay."

Well, Jack was not content, and it wasn't very long before he determined to have another try at his luck up there at the top of the bean-stalk. So one fine morning, he rose up early, and got on to the bean-stalk, and he climbed and he climbed and he climbed and he climbed till he got to the top. But this time he knew better than to go straight to the ogre's house. And when he got near it he waited behind a bush till he saw the ogre's wife come out with a pail to get some water, and then he crept into the house and got into the copper. He hadn't been there long when he heard thump! thump! thump! as before, and in come the ogre and his wife.

"Fee-fi-fo-fum, I smell the blood of an Englishman," cried out the ogre; "I smell him, wife, I smell him."

"Do you, my dearie?" says the ogre's wife. "Then if it's that little rogue that stole your gold and the hen that laid the golden eggs he's sure to have got into the oven." And they both rushed to the oven. But Jack wasn't there, luckily, and the ogre's wife said: "There you are again with your fee-fi-fo-fum. Why of course it's the boy you caught last night that I've just broiled for your breakfast. How forgetful I am, and how careless you are not to know the difference between live and dead after all these years."

So the ogre sat down to the breakfast and ate it, but every now and then he would mutter: "Well, I could have sworn——" and he'd get up and search the larder and the cupboards, and everything, only luckily he didn't think of the copper.

After breakfast was over, the ogre called out: "Wife, wife, bring me my golden harp." So she brought it and put it on the table before him. Then he said: "Sing!" and the golden harp sang most beautifully. And it went on singing till the ogre fell asleep, and commenced to snore like thunder.

Then Jack lifted up the copper lid very quietly and got down like a mouse and crept on hands and knees till he came to the table when up he crawled, caught hold of the golden harp and dashed with it toward the door. But the harp called out quite loud: "Master! master!" and the ogre woke up just in time to see Jack running off with his harp.

Jack ran as fast as he could, and the ogre came rushing after, and would soon have caught him only Jack had a start and dodged him a bit and knew where he was going. When he got to the beanstalk the ogre was not more than twenty yards away when suddenly he saw Jack disappear like, and when he came to the end of the road he saw Jack underneath climbing down for dear life. Well, the ogre didn't like trust-ing himself to such a ladder, and he stood and waited, so Jack got another start. But just then the harp cried out: "Master! master!" and the ogre swung himself down on to the beanstalk which shook with his weight. Down climbs Jack, and after him climbed the ogre. By this time Jack had climbed down and climbed down and climbed down till he was very nearly home. So he called out: "Mother! mother! bring me an ax, bring me an ax." And his mother came rushing out with the ax in her hand, but when she came to the beanstalk she stood stock still with fright for there she saw the ogre with his legs just through the clouds.

But Jack jumped down and got hold of the ax and gave a chop at the beanstalk which cut it half in two. The ogre felt the beanstalk shake and quiver so he stopped to see what was the matter. Then Jack gave another chop with the ax, and the beanstalk was cut in two and began to topple over. Then the ogre fell down and broke his crown, and the beanstalk came toppling after.

Then Jack showed his mother his golden harp, and what with showing that and selling the golden eggs, Jack and his mother became very rich, and he married a great princess, and they lived happy ever after.

46. JACK THE GIANT-KILLER
(England)

WHEN GOOD KING ARTHUR reigned, there lived near the Land's End of England, in the county of Cornwall, a farmer who had one only son called Jack. He was brisk and of a ready lively wit, so that nobody or nothing could worst him.

In those days the Mount of Cornwall was kept by a huge giant named Cormoran. He was eighteen feet in height, and about three yards round the waist, of a fierce and grim countenance, the terror of all the neighboring towns and villages. He lived in a cave in the midst of the Mount, and whenever he wanted food he would wade over to the mainland, where he would furnish himself with whatever came in his way. Everybody at his approach ran out of their houses, while he seized on their cattle, making nothing of carrying half a dozen oxen on his back at a time; and as for their sheep and hogs, he would tie them round his waist like a bunch of tallow-dips. He had done this for many years, so that all Cornwall was in despair.

One day Jack happened to be at the town hall when the magistrates were sitting in council about the giant. He asked: "What reward will be given to the man who kills Cormoran?" "The giant's treasure," they said, "will be the reward." Quoth Jack: "Then let me undertake it."

So he got a horn, shovel, and pickax, and went over to the Mount in the beginning of a dark winter's evening, when he fell to work, and before morning had dug a pit twenty-two feet deep, and nearly as broad, covering it over with long sticks and straw. Then he strewed a little mold over it, so that it appeared like plain ground. Jack then placed himself on the opposite side of the pit, farthest from the giant's lodging, and, just at the break of day, he put the horn to his mouth, and blew, Tantivy, Tantivy. This noise roused the giant, who rushed from his cave, crying: "You incorrigible villain, are you come here to disturb my rest? You shall pay dearly for this. Satisfaction I will have, and this it shall be, I will take you whole and broil you for breakfast." He had no sooner uttered this, than he tumbled into the pit, and made the very foundations of the Mount to shake. "Oh, Giant," quoth Jack, "where are you now? Oh, faith, you are gotten now into Lob's Pound, where I will surely plague you for your threatening words: what do you think now of broiling me for your breakfast? Will no other diet serve you but poor Jack?" Then having tantalized the giant for a while, he gave him a most weighty knock with his pickax on the very crown of his head, and killed him on the spot.

Jack then filled up the pit with earth, and went to search the cave, which he found contained much treasure. When the magistrates heard of this they made a declaration he should henceforth be termed:

JACK THE GIANT-KILLER,

and presented him with a sword and a belt, on which were written these words embroidered in letters of gold:

> HERE'S THE RIGHT VALIANT CORNISH MAN,
> WHO SLEW THE GIANT CORMORAN.

The news of Jack's victory soon spread over all the West of England, so that another giant, named Blunderbore, hearing of it, vowed to be revenged on Jack, if ever he should light on him. This giant was the lord of an enchanted castle situated in the midst of a lonesome wood. Now Jack, about four months afterward, walking near this wood in his journey to Wales, being weary, seated himself near a pleasant fountain and fell fast asleep. While he was sleeping, the giant, coming there for water, discovered him, and knew him to be the far-famed Jack the Giant-Killer by the lines written on the belt. Without ado, he took Jack on his shoulders and carried him toward his castle. Now, as they passed through a thicket, the rustling of the boughs awakened Jack, who was strangely surprised to find himself in the clutches of the giant. His terror was only begun, for, on entering the castle, he saw the ground strewed with human bones, and the giant told him his own would ere long be among them. After this the giant locked poor Jack in an immense chamber, leaving him there while he went to fetch another giant, his brother, living in the same wood, who might share in the meal on Jack.

After waiting some time Jack, on going to the window beheld afar off the two giants coming toward the castle. "Now," quoth Jack to himself, "my death or my deliverance is at hand." Now, there were strong cords in a corner of the room in which Jack was, and two of these he took, and made a strong noose at the end; and while the giants were unlocking the iron gate of the castle he threw the ropes over each of their heads. Then he drew the other ends across a beam, and pulled with all his might, so that he throttled them. Then, when he saw they were black in the face, he slid down the rope, and drawing his sword, slew them both. Then, taking the giant's keys, and unlocking the rooms, he found three fair ladies tied by the hair of their heads, almost starved to death. "Sweet ladies," quoth Jack, "I have destroyed this monster and his brutish brother, and obtained your liberties." This said he presented them with the keys, and so proceeded on his journey to Wales.

Jack made the best of his way by traveling as fast as he could, but lost his road, and was benighted, and could find no habitation until, coming into a narrow valley, he found a large house, and in order to get shelter took courage to knock at the gate. But what was his surprise when there came forth a monstrous giant with two heads; yet he did not appear so fiery as the others were, for he was a Welsh giant, and what he did was by private and secret malice under the false show of friendship. Jack, having told his condition to the giant, was shown into a bedroom, where, in the dead of night, he heard his host in another apartment muttering these words:

"Though here you lodge with me this night,
You shall not see the morning light:
My club shall dash your brains outright!"

"Say'st thou so," quoth Jack; "that is like one of your Welsh tricks, yet I hope to be cunning enough for you." Then, getting out of bed, he laid a billet in the bed in his place, and hid himself in a corner of the room. At the dead time of the night in came the Welsh giant, who struck several heavy blows on the bed with his club, thinking he had broken every bone in Jack's skin. The next morning Jack, laughing in his sleeve, gave him hearty thanks for his night's lodging. "How have you rested?" quoth the giant; "did you not feel anything in the night?" "No," quoth Jack, "nothing but a rat, which gave me two or three slaps with her tail." With that, greatly wondering, the giant led Jack to breakfast, bringing him a bowl containing four gallons of hasty pudding. Being loath to let the giant think it too much for him, Jack put a large leather bag under his loose coat, in such a way that he could convey the pudding into it without its being perceived. Then, telling the giant he would show him a trick, taking a knife, Jack ripped open the bag, and out came all the hasty pudding. Whereupon, saying, "Odds splutters hur nails, hur can do that trick hurself," the monster took the knife, and ripping open his belly, fell down dead.

Now, it happened in these days that King Arthur's only son asked his father to give him a large sum of money, in order that he might go and seek his fortune in the principality of Wales, where lived a beautiful lady possessed with seven evil spirits. The king did his best to persuade his son from it, but in vain; so at last gave way and the prince set out with two horses, one loaded with money, the other for himself to ride upon. Now, after several days' travel, he came to a market town in Wales, where he beheld a vast crowd of people gathered together. The prince asked the reason of it, and was told that they had arrested a corpse for several large sums of money which the deceased owed when he died. The prince replied that it was a pity creditors should be so cruel, and said: "Go bury the dead, and let his creditors come to my lodging, and there their debts shall be paid." They came, in such great numbers that before night he had only twopence left for himself.

Now Jack the Giant-Killer, coming that way, was so taken with the generosity of the prince, that he desired to be his servant. This being agreed upon, the next morning they set forward on their journey together, when, as they were riding out of the town, an old woman called after the prince, saying, "He has owed me twopence these seven years; pray, pay me as well as the rest." Putting his hand to his pocket, the prince gave the woman all he had left, so that after their day's food, which cost what small store Jack had by him, they were without a penny between them.

When the sun got low, the king's son said: "Jack, since we have no money, where can we lodge this night?"

But Jack replied: "Master, we'll do well enough, for I have an uncle lives within two miles of this place; he is a huge and monstrous giant with three heads; he'll fight five hundred men in armor, and make them to fly before him."

"Alas!" quoth the prince, "what shall we do there? He'll certainly chop us up at a mouthful. Nay, we are scarce enough to fill one of his hollow teeth!"

"It is no matter for that," quoth Jack; "I myself will go before and prepare the way for you; therefore stop here and wait till I return." Jack then rode away at full speed, and coming to the gate of the castle, he knocked so loud that he made the neighboring hills resound. The giant roared out at this like thunder: "Who's there?"

Jack answered: "None but your poor cousin Jack."

Quoth he: "What news with my poor cousin Jack?"

He replied: "Dear uncle, heavy news, God wot!"

"Prithee," quoth the giant, "what heavy news can come to me? I am a giant with three heads, and besides thou knowest I can fight five hundred men in armor, and make them fly like chaff before the wind."

"Oh, but," quoth Jack, "here's the king's son a-coming with a thousand men in armor to kill you and destroy all that you have!"

"Oh, cousin Jack," said the giant, "this is heavy news indeed! I will immediately run and hide myself, and thou shalt lock, bolt, and bar me in, and keep the keys until the prince is gone." Having secured the giant, Jack fetched his master, and they made themselves heartily merry whilst the poor giant lay trembling in a vault under the ground.

Early in the morning Jack furnished his master with a fresh supply of gold and silver, and then sent him three miles forward on his journey, at which time the prince was pretty well out of the smell of the giant. Jack then returned, and let the giant out of the vault, who asked what he should give him for keeping the castle from destruction. "Why," quoth Jack, "I want nothing but the old coat and cap, together with the old rusty sword and slippers which are at your bed's head." Quoth the giant: "You know not what you ask; they are the most precious things I have. The coat will keep you invisible, the cap will tell you all you want to know, the sword cuts asunder whatever you strike, and the shoes are of extraordinary swiftness. But you have been very serviceable to me, therefore take them with all my heart." Jack thanked his uncle, and then went off with them. He soon overtook his master and they quickly arrived at the house of the lady the prince sought, who, finding the prince to be a suitor, prepared a splendid banquet for him. After the repast was concluded, she told him she had a task for him. She wiped his mouth with a handkerchief, saying: "You must show me that handkerchief tomorrow morning, or else you will lose your head." With that she put it in her bosom. The prince went to bed in great sorrow, but Jack's cap of knowledge informed him how it was to be obtained. In the middle of the night she called upon her familiar spirit to carry her to Lucifer. But Jack put on his coat of darkness and his shoes of swiftness, and was there as soon as she was. When she entered the place of the demon, she gave the handkerchief to him, and he laid it upon a shelf, whence Jack took it and brought it to his master, who showed it to the lady next day, and so saved his life. On that day, she gave the prince a kiss and told him he must show her the lips tomorrow morning that she kissed last night, or lose his head.

"Ah!" he replied, "if you kiss none but mine, I will."

"That is neither here nor there," she said; "if you do not, death's your portion!"

At midnight she went as before, and was angry with the demon for letting the handkerchief go. "But now," quoth she, "I will be too hard for the king's son, for I will kiss thee, and he is to show me thy lips." Which she did, and Jack, when she was not standing by, cut off Lucifer's head and brought it under his invisible coat to his master, who the next morning pulled it out by the horns before the lady. This broke the enchantment and the evil spirit left her, and she appeared in all her beauty. They were married the next morning, and soon after went to the court of King Arthur, where Jack for his many great exploits, was made one of the Knights of the Round Table.

Jack soon went searching for giants again, but he had not ridden far, when he saw a cave, near the entrance of which he beheld a giant sitting upon a block of timber, with a knotted iron club by his side. His goggle eyes were like flames of fire, his countenance grim and ugly, and his cheeks like a couple of large flitches of bacon, while the bristles of his beard resembled rods of iron wire, and the locks that hung down upon his brawny shoulders were like curled snakes or hissing adders.

Jack alighted from his horse, and, putting on the coat of darkness, went up close to the giant, and said softly: "Oh! are you there? It will not be long before I take you fast by the beard." The giant all this while could not see him, on account of his invisible coat, so that Jack, coming up close to the monster, struck a blow with his sword at his head, but, missing his aim, he cut off the nose instead. At this, the giant roared like claps of thunder, and began to lay about him with his iron club like one stark mad. But Jack, running behind, drove his sword up to the hilt in the giant's back, so that he fell down dead. This done, Jack cut off the giant's head, and sent it, with his brother's also, to King Arthur, by a wagoner he hired for that purpose.

Jack now resolved to enter the giant's cave in search of his treasure, and, passing along through a great many windings and turnings, he came at length to a large room paved with freestone, at the upper end of which was a boiling caldron, and on the right hand a large table, at which the giant used to dine. Then he came to a window, barred with iron, through which he looked and beheld a vast number of miserable captives, who, seeing him, cried out: "Alas! young man, art thou come to be one among us in this miserable den?"

"Ay," quoth Jack, "but pray tell me what is the meaning of your captivity?"

"We are kept here," said one, "till such time as the giants have a wish to feast, and then the fattest among us is slaughtered! And many are the times they have dined upon murdered men!"

"Say you so," quoth Jack, and straightaway unlocked the gate and let them free, who all rejoiced like condemned men at sight of a pardon. Then searching the giant's coffers, he shared the gold and silver equally among them and took them to a neighboring castle, where they all feasted and made merry over their deliverance.

But in the midst of all this mirth a messenger brought news that one Thunderdell, a giant with two heads, having heard of the death of his kinsmen, had come from the northern dales to be revenged on Jack, and was within a mile of the castle, the country people flying before him like chaff. But Jack was not a bit daunted, and said: "Let him come! I have a tool to pick his teeth; and you, ladies and gentlemen, walk out into the garden, and you shall witness this giant Thunderdell's death and destruction."

The castle was situated in the midst of a small island surrounded by a moat thirty feet deep and twenty feet wide, over which lay a drawbridge. So Jack employed men to cut through this bridge on both sides, nearly to the middle; and then, dressing himself in his invisible coat, he marched against the giant with his sword of sharpness. Although the giant could not see Jack, he smelled his approach, and cried out in these words:

> "Fee, fi, fo, fum!
> I smell the blood of an Englishman!
> Be he alive or be he dead,
> I'll grind his bones to make my bread!"

"Say'st thou so," said Jack; "then thou art a monstrous miller indeed."

The giant cried out again: "Art thou that villain who killed my kinsmen? Then I will tear thee with my teeth, suck thy blood, and grind thy bones to powder."

"You'll have to catch me first," quoth Jack, and throwing off his invisible coat, so that the giant might see him, and putting on his shoes of swiftness, he ran from the giant, who followed like a walking castle, so that the very foundations of the earth seemed to shake at every step. Jack led him a long dance, in order that the gentlemen and ladies might see; and at last to end the matter, ran lightly over the drawbridge, the giant, in full speed, pursuing him with his club. Then, coming to the middle of the bridge, the giant's great weight broke it down, and he tumbled headlong into the water, where he rolled and wallowed like a whale. Jack, standing by the moat, laughed at him all the while; but though the giant foamed to hear him scoff, and plunged from place to place in the moat, yet he could not get out to be revenged. Jack at length got a cart rope and cast it over the two heads of the giant, and drew him ashore by a team of horses, and then cut off both his heads with his sword of sharpness, and sent them to King Arthur.

After some time spent in mirth and pastime, Jack, taking leave of the knights and ladies, set out for new adventures. Through many woods he passed, and came at length to the foot of a high mountain. Here, late at night, he found a lonesome house and knocked at the door, which was opened by an aged man with a head as white as snow. "Father," said Jack, "can you lodge a benighted traveler that has lost his way?" "Yes," said the old man, "you are right welcome to my poor cottage." Whereupon Jack entered, and down they sat together, and the old man began to speak as follows: "Son, I see by your belt you are the great conqueror of giants, and behold, my son, on the top of this mountain is an enchanted castle; this is kept by a giant named Galligantua, and he by the help of an old conjurer, betrays many knights and ladies into his castle, where by magic art they are transformed into sundry shapes and forms. But above all, I grieve for a duke's daughter, whom they fetched from her father's garden, carrying her through the air in a burning chariot drawn by fiery dragons, when they secured her within the castle, and transformed her into a white hind. And though many knights have tried to break the enchantment, and work her deliverance, yet no one could accomplish it, on account of two dreadful griffins which are placed at the castle gate and which destroy everyone who comes near. But you, my son, may pass by them undiscovered, where on the gates of the castle you will find engraven in large letters how the spell may be broken." Jack gave the old man his hand, and promised that in the morning he would venture his life to free the lady.

In the morning Jack arose and put on his invisible coat and magic cap and shoes, and prepared himself for the fray. Now, when he had reached the top of the mountain he soon discovered the two fiery griffins, but passed them without fear, because of his invisible coat. When he had got beyond them, he found upon the gates of the castle a golden trumpet hung by a silver chain, under which these lines were engraved:

> WHOEVER SHALL THIS TRUMPET BLOW,
> SHALL SOON THE GIANT OVERTHROW,
> AND BREAK THE BLACK ENCHANTMENT STRAIGHT;
> SO ALL SHALL BE IN HAPPY STATE.

Jack had no sooner read this but he blew the trumpet, at which the castle trembled to its vast foundations, and the giant and conjurer were in horrid confusion, biting their thumbs and tearing their hair, knowing their wicked reign was at an end. Then the giant stooping to take up his club, Jack at one blow cut off his head; whereupon the conjurer, mounting up into the air, was carried away in a whirlwind. Then the enchantment was broken, and all the lords and ladies who had so long been transformed into birds and beasts returned to their proper shapes, and the castle vanished away in a cloud of smoke. This being done, the head of Galligantua was likewise, in the usual manner, conveyed to the Court of King Arthur, where, the very next day, Jack followed, with the knights and ladies who had been delivered. Whereupon, as a reward for his good services, the king prevailed upon the duke to bestow his daughter in marriage on honest Jack. So married they were, and the whole kingdom was filled with joy at the wedding. Furthermore, the king bestowed on Jack a noble castle, with a very beautiful estate thereto belonging, where he and his lady lived in great joy and happiness all the rest of their days.

47. TOM TIT TOT

(England)

ONCE UPON A TIME there was a woman, and she baked five pies. And when they came out of the oven, they were that overbaked the crusts were too hard to eat. So she says to her daughter:

"Darter," says she, "put you them there pies on the shelf, and leave 'em there a little, and they'll come again."—She meant, you know, the crust would get soft.

But the girl, she says to herself: "Well, if they'll come again, I'll eat 'em now." And she set to work and ate 'em all, first and last.

Well, come suppertime the woman said: "Go you, and get one o' them there pies. I dare say they've come again now."

The girl went and she looked, and there was nothing but the dishes. So back she came and says she: "Noo, they ain't come again."

"Not one of 'em?" says the mother.

"Not one of 'em," says she.

"Well, come again, or not come again," said the woman, "I'll have one for supper."

"But you can't, if they ain't come," said the girl.

"But I can," says she. "Go you, and bring the best of 'em."

"Best or worst," says the girl, "I've ate 'em all, and you can't have one till that's come again."

Well, the woman she was done, and she took her spinning to the door to spin, and as she span she sang:

> "My darter ha' ate five, five pies today.
> My darter ha' ate five, five pies today."

The king was coming down the street, and he heard her sing, but what she sang he couldn't hear, so he stopped and said:

"What was that you were singing, my good woman?"

The woman was ashamed to let him hear what her daughter had been doing, so she sang, instead of that:

"My darter ha' spun five, five skeins today.
My darter ha' spun five, five skeins today."

"Stars o' mine!" said the king, "I never heard tell of anyone that could do that."

Then he said: "Look you here, I want a wife, and I'll marry your daughter. But look you here," says he, "eleven months out of the year she shall have all she likes to eat, and all the gowns she likes to get, and all the company she likes to keep; but the last month of the year she'll have to spin five skeins every day, and if she don't I shall kill her."

"All right," says the woman; for she thought what a grand marriage that was. And as for the five skeins, when the time came, there'd be plenty of ways of getting out of it, and likeliest, he'd have forgotten all about it.

Well, so they were married. And for eleven months the girl had all she liked to eat, and all the gowns she liked to get, and all the company she liked to keep.

But when the time was getting over, she began to think about the skeins and to wonder if he had 'em in mind. But not one word did he say about 'em, and she thought he'd wholly forgotten 'em.

However, the last day of the last month he takes her to a room she'd never set eyes on before. There was nothing in it but a spinning wheel and a stool. And says he: "Now, my dear, here you'll be shut in tomorrow with some victuals and some flax, and if you haven't spun five skeins by the night, your head 'll go off."

And away he went about his business.

Well, she was that frightened, she'd always been such a gatless girl, that she didn't so much as know how to spin, and what was she to do tomorrow with no one to come nigh her to help her? She sat down on a stool in the kitchen, and law! how she did cry!

However, all of a sudden she heard a sort of a knocking low down on the door. She upped and oped it, and what should she see but a small little black thing with a long tail. That looked up at her right curious, and that said:

"What are you a-crying for?"

"What's that to you?" says she.

"Never you mind," that said, "but tell me what you're a-crying for."

"That won't do me no good if I do," says she.

"You don't know that," that said, and twirled that's tail round.

"Well," says she, "that won't do no harm, if that don't do no good," and she upped and told about the pies, and the skeins, and everything.

"This is what I'll do," says the little black thing, "I'll come to your window every morning and take the flax and bring it spun at night."

"What's your pay?" says she.

That looked out of the corner of that's eyes, and that said: "I'll give you three guesses every night to guess my name, and if you haven't guessed it before the month's up, you shall be mine."

Well, she thought she'd be sure to guess that's name before the month was up. "All right," says she, "I agree."

"All right," that says, and law! how that twirled that's tail.

Well, the next day, her husband took her into the room, and there was the flax and the day's food.

"Now there's the flax," says he, "and if that ain't spun up this night, off goes your head." And then he went out and locked the door.

He'd hardly gone, when there was a knocking against the window.

She upped and she oped it, and there sure enough was the little old thing sitting on the ledge.

"Where's the flax?" says he.

"Here it be," says she. And she gave it to him.

Well, come the evening a knocking came again to the window. She upped and she oped it, and there was the little old thing with five skeins of flax on his arm.

"Here it be," says he, and he gave it to her.

"Now, what's my name?" says he.

"What, is that Bill?" says she.

"Noo, that ain't," says he, and he twirled his tail.

"Is that Ned?" says she.

"Noo, that ain't," says he, and he twirled his tail.

"Well, is that Mark?" says she.

"Noo, that ain't," says he, and he twirled his tail harder, and away he flew.

Well, when her husband came in, there were the five skeins ready for him. "I see I shan't have to kill you tonight, my dear," says he; "you'll have your food and your flax in the morning," says he, and away he goes.

Well, every day the flax and the food were brought, and every day that there little black impet used to come mornings and evenings. And all the day the girl sat trying to think of names to say to it when it came at night. But she never hit on the right one. And as it got toward the end of the month, the impet began to look so maliceful, and that twirled that's tail faster and faster each time she gave a guess.

At last it came to the last day but one. The impet came at night along with the five skeins, and that said:

"What, ain't you got my name yet?"

"Is that Nicodemus?" says she.

"Noo, 'tain't," that says.

"Is that Sammle?" says she.

"Noo, 'tain't," that says.

"A-well, is that Methusalem?" says she.

"Noo, 'tain't that neither," that says.

Then that looks at her with that's eyes like a coal o' fire, and that says: "Woman, there's only tomorrow night, and then you'll be mine!" And away it flew.

Well, she felt that horrid. However, she heard the king coming along the passage. In he came, and when he sees the five skeins, he says, says he:

"Well, my dear," says he. "I don't see but what you'll have your skeins ready tomorrow night as well, and as I reckon I shan't have to kill you, I'll have supper in here tonight." So they brought supper, and another stool for him, and down the two sat.

Well, he hadn't eaten but a mouthful or so, when he stops and begins to laugh.

"What is it?" says she.

"A-why," says he, "I was out a-hunting today, and I got away to a place in the wood I'd never seen before. And there was an old chalk pit. And I heard a kind of a sort of a humming. So I got off my hobby, and I went right quiet to the pit, and I looked down. Well, what should there be but the funniest little black thing you ever set eyes on. And what was that doing, but that had a little spinning wheel, and that was spinning wonderful fast, and twirling that's tail. And as that span that sang:

"Nimmy nimmy not
My name's Tom Tit Tot."

Well, when the girl heard this, she felt as if she could have jumped out of her skin for joy, but she didn't say a word.

Next day that there little thing looked so maliceful when he came for the flax. And when night came, she heard that knocking against the windowpanes. She opened the window, and that come right in on the ledge. That was grinning from ear to ear, and Oo! that's tail was twirling round so fast.

"What's my name?" that says, as that gave her the skeins.

"Is that Solomon?" she says, pretending to be afeard.

"Noo, 'tain't," that says, and that come further into the room.

"Well, is that Zebedee?" says she again.

"Noo, 'tain't," says the impet. And then that laughed and twirled that's tail till you couldn't hardly see it.

"Take time, woman," that says; "next guess, and you're mine." And that stretched out that's black hands at her.

Well, she backed a step or two, and she looked at it, and then she laughed out, and says she, pointing her finger at it:

> "Nimmy nimmy not
> Your name's Tom
> TIT
> TOT."

Well, when that heard her, that gave an awful shriek and away that flew into the dark, and she never saw it any more.

48. THE BOGGART
(England)

IN THE HOUSE of an honest farmer in Yorkshire, named George Gilbertson, a Boggart had taken up his abode. He here caused a good deal of annoyance, especially by tormenting the children in various ways. Sometimes their bread and butter would be snatched away, or their porringers of bread and milk be capsized by an invisible hand; for the Boggart never let himself be seen; at other times, the curtains of their beds would be shaken backward and forward, or a heavy weight would press on and nearly suffocate them. The parents had often, on hearing their cries, to fly to their aid. There was a kind of closet, formed by a wooden partition on the kitchen stairs, and a large knot having been driven out of one of the deal-boards of which it was made, there remained a hole. Into this one day the farmer's youngest boy stuck the shoehorn, with which he was amusing himself, when immediately it was thrown out again, and struck the boy on the head. The agent was, of course, the Boggart, and it soon became their sport to put the shoe-horn into the hole and have it shot back at them.

The Boggart at length proved such a torment that the farmer and his wife resolved to quit the house and let him have it all to himself. This was put into execution, and the farmer and his family were following the last loads of furniture when a neighbor named John Marshall came up. "Well, Georgey," said he, "and soa you're leaving t'ould house at last?" "Heigh, Johnny, my lad, I'm forced tull it; for that damned Bog-gart torments us soa, we can neither rest neet nor day for't. It seems loike to have such a malice again t'poor bairns, it onmost kills my poor dame here at thoughts on't, and soa, ye see, we're forced to flit loike." He scarce had uttered the words when a voice from a deep upright churn cried out, "Aye, aye, Georgey, we're flitting ye see." "Od damn thee," cried the poor farmer, "if I'd known thou'd been there, I wadn't ha' stirred a peg. Nay, nay, it's no use, Mally," turning to his wife, "we may as weel turn back again to t'ould hoose as be tormented in another that's not so convenient."

49. GOOD AND BAD NEWS
(England)

TWO FRIENDS WHO HAD not seen each other a great while, meeting by chance, one asked the other how he did? He replied, that he was not very well, and was married since they had last met. "That is good news indeed." "Nay, not so very good neither, for I married a shrew." "That is bad, too." "Not so bad, neither, for I had two thousand pounds with her." "That is well again." "Not so well, neither, for I laid it out in sheep, and they all died of the rot." "That was hard, in truth." "Not so hard, neither, for I sold the skins for more than the sheep cost me." "Aye, that made you amends." "Not so much amends, neither, for I laid my money out in a house, and it was burned." "That was a great loss, indeed." "Not so great a loss, neither—for my wife was burned in it."

50. THE HAND OF GLORY
(England)

ONE EVENING, BETWEEN the years 1790 and 1800, a traveler dressed in woman's clothing arrived at the Old Spital Inn, the place where the mail coach changed horses in High Spital, on Bowes Moor. The traveler begged to stay all night, but had to go away so early in the morning, that if a mouthful of food were set ready for breakfast, there was no need the family should be disturbed by her departure. The people of the house, however, arranged that a servant-maid should sit up till the stranger was out of the premises, and then went to bed themselves.

The girl lay down for a nap on the long settle by the fire, but before she shut her eyes, she took a good look at the traveler, who was sitting on the opposite side of the hearth, and spied a pair of men's trousers peeping out from under the gown. All inclination for sleep was now gone; however, with great self-command, she feigned it, closed her eyes, and even began to snore.

On this, the traveler got up, pulled out of his pocket a dead man's hand, fitted a candle to it, lighted the candle, and passed hand and candle several times before the servant-girl's face, saying as he did so, "Let those who are asleep be asleep, and let those who are awake be awake." This done, he placed the light on the table, opened the outer door, went down two or three steps which led from the house to the road, and began to whistle for his companions.

The girl (who had hitherto had presence of mind to remain perfectly quiet) now jumped up, rushed behind the ruffian, and pushed him down the steps. Then she shut the door, locked it, and ran upstairs to try to wake the family, but without success; calling, shouting, and shaking were alike in vain. The poor girl was in despair, for she heard the traveler and his comrades outside the house. So she ran down and seized a bowl of blue [i.e., skimmed milk] and threw it over the hand and candle; after which she went upstairs again, and awoke the sleepers without any difficulty. The landlord's son went to the window, and asked the men outside what they wanted. They answered that if the dead man's hand were but given to them, they would go away quietly, and do no harm to anyone.

This he refused, and fired among them, and the shot must have taken effect, for in the morning stains of blood were traced to a considerable distance.

51. LAZY JACK
(England)

ONCE UPON A TIME there was a boy whose name was Jack, and he lived with his mother on a dreary common. They were very poor, and the old woman got her living by spinning, but Jack was so lazy that he would do nothing but bask in the sun in the hot weather, and sit by the corner of the hearth in the winter time. His mother could not persuade him to do anything for her, and was obliged at last to tell him that if he did not begin to work for his porridge, she would turn him out to get his living as he could.

This threat at length roused Jack, and he went out and hired himself for the day to a neighboring farmer for a penny; but as he was coming home, never having had any money in his possession before, he lost it in passing over a brook. "You stupid boy," said his mother, "you should have put it in your pocket." "I'll do so another time," replied Jack.

The next day Jack went out again, and hired himself to a cowkeeper, who gave him a jar of milk for his day's work. Jack took the jar and put it into the large pocket of his jacket, spilling it all, long before he got home. "Dear me!" said the old woman; "you should have carried it on your head." "I'll do so another time," replied Jack.

The following day Jack hired himself again to a farmer, who agreed to give him a cream cheese for his services. In the evening, Jack took the cheese, and went home with it on his head. By the time he got home the cheese was completely spilled, part of it being lost, and part matted with his hair. "You stupid lout," said his mother, "you should have carried it very carefully in your hands." "I'll do so another time," replied Jack.

The day after this Jack again went out, and hired himself to a baker, who would give him nothing for his work but a large tomcat. Jack took the cat, and began carrying it very carefully in his hands, but in a short time pussy scratched him so much that he was compelled to let it go. When he got home, his mother said to him, "You silly fellow, you should have tied it with a string, and dragged it along after you." "I'll do so another time," said Jack.

The next day Jack hired himself to a butcher, who rewarded his labors by the handsome present of a shoulder of mutton. Jack took the mutton, tied it to a string, and trailed it along after him in the dirt, so that by the time he had got home the meat was completely spoiled. His mother was this time quite out of patience with him, for the next day was Sunday, and she was obliged to content herself with cabbage for her dinner. "You ninnyhammer," said she to her son, "you should have carried it on your shoulder." "I'll do so another time," replied Jack.

On the Monday Jack went once more, and hired himself to a cattle-keeper, who gave him a donkey for his trouble. Although Jack was very strong, he found some difficulty in hoisting the donkey on his shoulders, but at last he accomplished it, and began walking slowly home with his prize. Now it happened that in the course of his journey there lived a rich man with his only daughter, a beautiful girl, but unfortunately deaf and dumb; she had never laughed in her life, and the doctors said she would never recover till somebody made her laugh. Many tried without success, and at last the father, in despair, offered her in marriage to the first man who could make her laugh. This young lady happened to be looking out of the window, when Jack was passing with the donkey on his shoulders, the legs sticking up in the air; and the sight was so comical and strange, that she burst out into a great fit of laughter, and immediately recovered her speech and hearing. Her father was overjoyed, and fulfilled his promise by marrying her to Jack, who was thus made a rich gentleman. They lived in a large house, and Jack's mother lived with them in great happiness until she died.

52. MOLLY WHUPPIE

(England)

ONCE UPON A TIME there was a man and a wife had too many children, and they could not get meat for them, so they took the three youngest and left them in a wood. They traveled and traveled and could see never a house. It began to be dark, and they were hungry. At last they saw a light and made for it; it turned out to be a house. They knocked at the door, and a woman came to it, who said: "What do you want?" They said: "Please let us in and give us something to eat." The woman said: "I can't do that, as my man is a giant, and he would kill you if he comes home." They begged hard. "Let us stop for a little while," said they, "and we will go away before he comes." So she took them in, and set them down before the fire, and gave them milk and bread; but just as they had begun to eat a great knock came to the door, and a dreadful voice said:

> "Fee, fie, fo, fum,
> I smell the blood of some earthly one.

Who have you there wife?" "Eh," said the wife, "it's three poor lassies cold and hungry, and they will go away. Ye won't touch 'em, man." He said nothing, but ate up a big supper, and ordered them to stay all night. Now he had three lassies of his own, and they were to sleep in the same bed with the three strangers. The youngest of the three strange lassies was called Molly Whuppie, and she was very clever. She noticed that before they went to bed the giant put straw ropes round her neck and her sisters', and round his own lassies' necks he put gold chains. So Molly took care and did not fall asleep, but waited till she was sure everyone was sleeping sound. Then she slipped out of the bed, and took the straw ropes off her own and her sisters' necks, and took the gold chains off the giant's lassies. She then put the straw ropes on the giant's lassies and the gold on herself and her sisters, and lay down. And in the middle of the night up rose the giant, armed with a great club, and felt for the necks with the straw. It was dark. He took his own lassies out of bed on to the floor, and battered them until they were dead, and then lay down again, thinking he had managed finely. Molly thought it time she and her sisters were off and away, so she wakened them and told them to be quiet, and they slipped out of the house. They all got out safe, and they ran and ran, and never stopped until morning, when they saw a grand house before them. It turned out to be a king's house: so Molly went in, and told her story to the king. He said: "Well, Molly, you are a clever girl, and you have managed well; but, if you would manage better, and go back, and steal the giant's sword that hangs on the back of his bed, I would give your eldest sister my eldest son to marry." Molly said she would try. So she went back, and managed to slip into the giant's house, and crept in below the bed. The giant came home, and ate up a great supper, and went to bed. Molly waited until he was snoring, and she crept out, and reached over the giant and got down the sword; but just as she got it out over the bed it gave a rattle, and up jumped the giant, and Molly ran out at the door and the sword with her; and she ran, and he ran, till they came to the "Bridge of one hair"; and she got over, but he couldn't, and he says, "Woe worth ye, Molly Whuppie! never you come again." And she says: "Twice yet, carle," quoth she, "I'll come to Spain." So Molly took the sword to the king, and her sister was married to his son.

Well, the king he says: "Ye've managed well, Molly; but if ye would manage better, and steal the purse that lies below the giant's pillow, I would marry your second sister to my second son." And Molly said she would try. So she set out for the giant's house, and slipped in, and hid again below the bed, and waited till the giant had eaten his supper, and was snoring, sound asleep. She slipped out, and slipped her hand below the pillow, and got out the purse; but just as she was going out the giant wakened, and ran after her; and she ran, and he ran, till they came to the "Bridge of one hair," and she got over, but he couldn't, and he said, "Woe worth ye, Molly Whuppie! never you come again." "Once yet, carle," quoth she, "I'll come to Spain." So Molly took the purse to the king, and her second sister was married to the king's second son.

After that the king says to Molly: "Molly, you are a clever girl, but if you would do better yet, and steal the giant's ring that he wears on his finger, I will give you my youngest son for yourself." Molly said she would try. So back she goes to the giant's house, and hides herself below the bed. The giant wasn't long ere he came home, and, after he had eaten a great big supper, he went to his bed, and shortly was snoring loud. Molly crept out and reached over the bed, and got hold of the giant's hand, and she pulled and she pulled until she got off the ring; but just as she got it off the giant got up, and gripped her by the hand, and he says: "Now I have caught you, Molly Whuppie, and, if I had done as much ill to you as ye have done to me, what would ye do to me?"

Molly says: "I would put you into a sack, and I'd put the cat inside wi' you, and the dog aside you, and a needle and thread and a shears, and I'd hang you up upon the wall, and I'd go to the wood, and choose the thickest stick I could get, and I would come home, and take you down, and bang you till you were dead."

"Well, Molly," says the giant, "I'll just do that to you."

So he gets a sack, and puts Molly into it, and the cat and the dog beside her, and a needle and thread and shears, and hangs her up upon the wall, and goes to the wood to choose a stick.

Molly she sings out: "Oh, if ye saw what I see."

"Oh," says the giant's wife, "what do ye see, Molly?"

But Molly never said a word but, "Oh, if ye saw what I see!"

The giant's wife begged that Molly would take her up into the sack till she would see what Molly saw. So Molly took the shears and cut a hole in the sack, and took out the needle and thread with her, and jumped down and helped the giant's wife up into the sack, and sewed up the hole.

The giant's wife saw nothing, and began to ask to get down again; but Molly never minded, but hid herself at the back of the door. Home came the giant, and a great big tree in his hand, and he took down the sack, and began to batter it. His wife cried, "It's me, man"; but the dog barked and the cat mewed, and he did not know his wife's voice. But Molly came out from the back of the door, and the giant saw her, and he after her; and he ran and she ran, till they came to the "Bridge of one hair," and she got over but he couldn't; and he said, "Woe worth you, Molly Whuppie! never you come again." "Never more, carle," quoth she, "will I come again to Spain."

So Molly took the ring to the king, and she was married to his youngest son, and she never saw the giant again.

53. TEENY-TINY

(*England*)

ONCE UPON A TIME there was a teeny-tiny woman lived in a teeny-tiny house in a teeny-tiny village. Now, one day this teeny-tiny woman put on her teeny-tiny bonnet, and went out of her teeny-tiny house to take a teeny-tiny walk. And when this teeny-tiny woman had gone a teeny-tiny way she came to a teeny-tiny gate; so the teeny-tiny woman opened the teeny-tiny gate, and went into a teeny-tiny churchyard. And when this teeny-tiny woman had got into the teeny-tiny churchyard, she saw a teeny-tiny bone on a teeny-tiny grave, and the teeny-tiny woman said to her teeny-tiny self, "This teeny-tiny bone will make me some teeny-tiny soup for my teeny-tiny supper." So the teeny-tiny woman put the teeny-tiny bone into her teeny-tiny pocket, and went home to her teeny-tiny house.

Now when the teeny-tiny woman got home to her teeny-tiny house she was a teeny-tiny bit tired; so she went up her teeny-tiny stairs to her teeny-tiny bed, and put the teeny-tiny bone into a teeny-tiny cupboard. And when this teeny-tiny woman had been to sleep a teeny-tiny time, she was awakened by a teeny-tiny voice from the teeny-tiny cupboard, which said:

"Give me my bone!"

And this teeny-tiny woman was a teeny-tiny frightened, so she hid her teeny-tiny head under the teeny-tiny covers and went to sleep again. And when she had been to sleep again a teeny-tiny time, the teeny-tiny voice again cried out from the teeny-tiny cupboard a teeny-tiny louder,

"GIVE ME MY BONE!"

This made the teeny-tiny woman a teeny-tiny more frightened, so she hid her teeny-tiny head a teeny-tiny further under the teeny-tiny covers. And when the teeny-tiny woman had been to sleep again a teeny-tiny time, the teeny-tiny voice from the teeny-tiny cupboard said again a teeny-tiny louder,

"GIVE ME MY BONE!"

And this teeny-tiny woman was a teeny-tiny bit more frightened, but she put her teeny-tiny head out of the teeny-tiny covers, and said in her loudest teeny-tiny voice, "TAKE IT!"

54. THE THREE WISHES
(England)

ONCE UPON A TIME, and be sure 'twas a long time ago, there lived a poor woodman in a great forest, and every day of his life he went out to fell timber. So one day he started out, and the goodwife filled his wallet and slung his bottle on his back, that he might have meat and drink in the forest. He had marked out a huge old oak, which, thought he, would furnish many and many a good plank. And when he was come to it, he took his ax in his hand and swung it around his head as though he were minded to fell the tree at one stroke. But he hadn't given one blow, when what should he hear but the pitifullest entreating, and there stood before him a fairy who prayed and beseeched him to spare the tree. He was dazed, as you may fancy, with wonderment and affright, and he couldn't open his mouth to utter a word. But he found his tongue at last, and, "Well," said he, "I'll do as you wish."

"You've done better for yourself than you know," answered the fairy, "and to show I'm not ungrateful, I'll grant you your next three wishes, be they what they may." And therewith the fairy was no more to be seen, and the woodman slung his wallet over his shoulder and his bottle at his side, and off he started home.

But the way was long, and the poor man was regularly dazed with the wonderful thing that had befallen him, and when he got home there was nothing in his noddle but the wish to sit down and rest. Maybe, too, 'twas a trick of the fairy's. Who can tell? Anyhow down he sat by the blazing fire, and as he sat he waxed hungry, though it was a long way off suppertime yet.

"Hasn't thou naught for supper, dame?" said he to his wife.

"Nay, not for a couple of hours yet," said she.

"Ah!" groaned the woodman, "I wish I'd a good link of black pudding here before me."

No sooner had he said the word, when clatter, clatter, rustle, rustle, what should come down the chimney but a link of the finest black pudding the heart of man could wish for.

If the woodman stared, the goodwife stared three times as much. "What's all this?" says she.

Then all the morning's work came back to the woodman, and he told his tale right out, from beginning to end, and as he told it the goodwife glowered and glowered, and when he had made an end of it she burst out, "You be but a fool, Jan, you be but a fool; and I wish the pudding were at your nose, I do indeed."

And before you could say, "Jack Robinson," there the goodman sat and his nose was the longer for a noble link of black pudding.

He gave a pull but it stuck, and she gave a pull but it stuck, and they both pulled till they had nigh pulled the nose off, but it stuck and stuck.

"What's to be done now?" said he.

" 'Tisn't so very unsightly," said she, looking hard at him.

Then the woodman saw that if he wished, he must need wish in a hurry; and wish he did, that the black pudding might come off his nose. Well! there it lay in a dish on the table, and if the goodman and goodwife didn't ride in a golden coach, or dress in silk and satin, why, they had at least as fine a black pudding for their supper as the heart of man could desire.

55. DICK WHITTINGTON AND HIS CAT
(*England*)

IN THE REIGN of the famous King Edward III there was a little boy called Dick Whittington, whose father and mother died when he was very young. As poor Dick was not old enough to work, he was very badly off; he got but little for his dinner, and sometimes nothing at all for his breakfast; for the people who lived in the village were very poor indeed, and could not spare him much more than the parings of potatoes, and now and then a hard crust of bread.

Now Dick had heard many, many very strange things about the great city called London; for the country people at that time thought that folks in London were all fine gentlemen and ladies; and that there was singing and music there all day long; and that the streets were all paved with gold.

One day a large wagon and eight horses, all with bells at their heads, drove through the village while Dick was standing by the signpost. He thought that this wagon must be going to the fine town of London; so he took courage, and asked the wagoner to let him walk with him by the side of the wagon. As soon as the wagoner heard that poor Dick had no father or mother, and saw by his ragged clothes that he could not be worse off than he was, he told him he might go if he would, so off they set together.

So Dick got safe to London, and was in such a hurry to see the fine streets paved all over with gold, that he did not even stay to thank the kind wagoner; but ran off as fast as his legs would carry him, through many of the streets, thinking every moment to come to those that were paved with gold; for Dick had seen a guinea three times in his own little village, and remembered what a deal of money it brought in change; so he thought he had nothing to do but to take up some little bits of the pavement, and should then have as much money as he could wish for.

Poor Dick ran till he was tired, and had quite forgot his friend the wagoner; but at last, finding it grow dark, and that every way he turned he saw nothing but dirt instead of gold, he sat down in a dark corner and cried himself to sleep.

Little Dick was all night in the streets; and next morning, being very hungry, he got up and walked about, and asked everybody he met to give him a halfpenny to keep him from starving; but nobody stayed to answer him, and only two or three gave him a halfpenny; so that the poor boy was soon quite weak and faint for the want of victuals.

In this distress he asked charity of several people, and one of them said crossly: "Go to work for an idle rogue." "That I will," says Dick, "I will go to work for you, if you will let me." But the man only cursed at him and went on.

At last a good-natured-looking gentleman saw how hungry he looked. "Why don't you go to work, my lad?" said he to Dick. "That I would, but I do not know how to get any," answered Dick. "If you are willing, come along with me," said the gentleman, and took him to a hayfield, where Dick worked briskly, and lived merrily till the hay was made.

After this he found himself as badly off as before; and being almost starved again, he laid himself down at the door of Mr. Fitzwarren, a rich merchant. Here he was soon seen by the cook-maid, who was an ill-tempered creature, and happened just then to be very busy dressing dinner for her master and mistress; so she called out to poor Dick: "What business have you there, you lazy rogue? there is nothing else but beggars; if you do not take yourself away, we will see how you will like a sousing of some dishwater; I have some here hot enough to make you jump."

Just at that time Mr. Fitzwarren himself came home to dinner; and when he saw a dirty ragged boy lying at the door, he said to him: "Why do you lie there, my boy? You seem old enough to work; I am afraid you are inclined to be lazy."

"No, indeed, sir," said Dick to him, "that is not the case, for I would work with all my heart, but I do not know anybody, and I believe I am very sick for the want of food."

"Poor fellow, get up; let me see what ails you."

Dick now tried to rise, but was obliged to lie down again, being too weak to stand, for he had not eaten any food for three days, and was no longer able to run about and beg a halfpenny of people in the street. So the kind merchant ordered him to be taken into the house, and have a good dinner given him, and be kept to do what work he was able to do for the cook.

Little Dick would have lived very happy in this good family if it had not been for the ill-natured cook. She used to say: "You are under me, so look sharp; clean the spit and the dripping-pan, make the fires, wind up the jack, and do all the scullery work nimbly, or——" and she would shake the ladle at him. Besides, she was so fond of basting, that when she had no meat to baste, she would baste poor Dick's head and shoulders with a broom, or anything else that happened to fall in her way. At last her ill-usage of him was told to Alice, Mr. Fitzwarren's daughter, who told the cook she should be turned away if she did not treat him kinder.

The behavior of the cook was now a little better; but besides this Dick had another hardship to get over. His bed stood in a garret, where there were so many holes in the floor and the walls that every night he was tormented with rats and mice. A gentleman having given Dick a penny for cleaning his shoes, he thought he would buy a cat with it. The next day he saw a girl with a cat, and asked her, "Will you let me have that cat for a penny?" The girl said: "Yes, that I will, master, though she is an excellent mouser."

Dick hid his cat in the garret, and always took care to carry a part of his dinner to her; and in a short time he had no more trouble with the rats and mice, but slept quite sound every night.

Soon after this, his master had a ship ready to sail; and as it was the custom that all his servants should have some chance for good fortune as well as himself, he called them all into the parlor and asked them what they would send out.

They all had something that they were willing to venture except poor Dick, who had neither money nor goods, and therefore could send nothing. For this reason he did not come into the parlor with the rest; but Miss Alice guessed what was the matter, and ordered him to be called in. She then said: "I will lay down some money for him, from my own purse"; but her father told her: "This will not do, for it must be something of his own."

When poor Dick heard this, he said: "I have nothing but a cat which I bought for a penny some time since of a little girl."

"Fetch your cat then, my lad," said Mr. Fitzwarren, "and let her go."

Dick went upstairs and brought down poor puss, with tears in his eyes, and gave her to the captain; "For," he said, "I shall now be kept awake all night by the rats and mice." All the company laughed at Dick's odd venture; and Miss Alice, who felt pity for him, gave him some money to buy another cat.

This, and many other marks of kindness shown him by Miss Alice, made the ill-tempered cook jealous of poor Dick, and she began to use him more cruelly than ever, and always made game of him for sending his cat to sea. She asked him: "Do you think your cat will sell for as much money as would buy a stick to beat you?"

At last poor Dick could not bear this usage any longer, and he thought he would run away from his place; so he packed up his few things, and started very early in the morning, on All-Hallows Day, the first of November. He walked as far as Holloway; and there sat down on a stone, which to this day is called "Whittington's Stone," and began to think to himself which road he should take.

While he was thinking what he should do, the Bells of Bow Church, which at that time were only six, began to ring, and their sound seemed to say to him:

> "Turn again, Whittington,
> Thrice Lord Mayor of London."

"Lord Mayor of London!" said he to himself. "Why, to be sure, I would put up with almost anything now, to be Lord Mayor of London, and ride in a fine coach, when I grow to be a man! Well, I will go back, and think nothing of the cuffing and scolding of the old cook, if I am to be Lord Mayor of London at last."

Dick went back, and was lucky enough to get into the house, and set about his work, before the old cook came downstairs.

We must now follow Miss Puss to the coast of Africa. The ship with the cat on board, was a long time at sea; and was at last driven by the winds on a part of the coast of Barbary, where the only people were the Moors, unknown to the English. The people came in great numbers to see the sailors, because they were of different color to themselves, and treated them civilly; and, when they became better acquainted, were very eager to buy the fine things that the ship was loaded with.

When the captain saw this, he sent patterns of the best things he had to the king of the country; who was so much pleased with them, that he sent for the captain to the palace. Here they were placed, as it is the custom of the country, on rich carpets flowered with gold and silver. The king and queen were seated at the upper end of the room, and a number of dishes were brought in for dinner. They had not sat long, when a vast number of rats and mice rushed in, and devoured all the meat in an instant. The captain wondered at this, and asked if these vermin were not unpleasant.

"Oh yes," said they, "very offensive; and the king would give half his treasure to be freed of them, for they not only destroy his dinner, as you see, but they assault him in his chamber, and even in bed, and so that he is obliged to be watched while he is sleeping, for fear of them."

The captain jumped for joy; he remembered poor Whittington and his cat, and told the king he had a creature on board the ship that would dispatch all these vermin immediately. The king jumped so high at the joy which the news gave him, that his turban dropped off his head. "Bring this creature to me," says he; "vermin are dreadful in a court, and if she will perform what you say, I will load your ship with gold and jewels in exchange for her."

The captain, who knew his business, took this opportunity to set forth the merits of Miss Puss. He told his majesty: "It is not very convenient to part with her, as, when she is gone, the rats and mice may destroy the goods in the ship—but to oblige your majesty, I will fetch her."

"Run, run!" said the queen; "I am impatient to see the dear creature."

Away went the captain to the ship, while another dinner was got ready. He put Puss under his arm, and arrived at the place just in time to see the table full of rats. When the cat saw them, she did not wait for bidding, but jumped out of the captain's arms, and in a few minutes laid almost all the rats and mice dead at her feet. The rest of them in their fright scampered away to their holes.

The king was quite charmed to get rid so easily of such plagues, and the queen desired that the creature who had done them so great a kindness might be brought to her, that she might look at her. Upon which the captain called: "Pussy, pussy, pussy!" and she came to him. He then presented her to the queen, who started back, and was afraid to touch a creature who had made such a havoc among the rats and mice. However, when the captain stroked the cat and called: "Pussy, pussy," the queen also touched her and cried: "Putty, putty," for she had not learned English. He then put her down on the queen's lap, where she purred and played with her majesty's hand, and then purred herself to sleep.

The king, having seen the exploits of Miss Puss, and being informed that her kittens would stock the whole country, and keep it free from rats, bargained with the captain for the whole ship's cargo, and then gave him ten times as much for the cat as all the rest amounted to.

The captain then took leave of the royal party, and set sail with a fair wind for England, and after a happy voyage arrived safe in London.

One morning, early, Mr. Fitzwarren had just come to his counting-house and seated himself at the desk, to count over the cash, and settle the business for the day, when somebody came tap, tap, at the door. "Who's there?" said Mr. Fitzwarren. "A friend," answered the other; "I come to bring you good news of your ship *Unicorn*." The merchant, bustling up in such a hurry that he forgot his gout, opened the door, and who should he see waiting but the captain and factor, with a cabinet of jewels, and a bill of lading; when he looked at this the merchant lifted up his eyes and thanked Heaven for sending him such a prosperous voyage.

They then told the story of the cat, and showed the rich present that the king and queen had sent for her to poor Dick. As soon as the merchant heard this, he called out to his servants:

> "Go send him in, and tell him of his fame;
> Pray call him Mr. Whittington by name."

Mr. Fitzwarren now showed himself to be a good man; for when some of his servants said so great a treasure was too much for him, he answered: "God forbid I should deprive him of the value of a single penny, it is his own, and he shall have it to a farthing."

He then sent for Dick, who at that time was scouring pots for the cook, and was quite dirty. He would have excused himself from coming into the counting-house, saying, "The room is swept, and my shoes are dirty and full of hobnails." But the merchant ordered him to come in.

Mr. Fitzwarren ordered a chair to be set for him, and so he began to think they were making game of him, at the same time said to them: "Do not play tricks with a poor simple boy, but let me go down again, if you please, to my work."

"Indeed, Mr. Whittington," said the merchant, "we are all quite in earnest with you, and I most heartily rejoice in the news that these gentlemen have brought you; for the captain has sold your cat to the King of Barbary, and brought you in return for her more riches than I possess in the whole world; and I wish you may long enjoy them!"

Mr. Fitzwarren then told the men to open the great treasure they had brought with them; and said: "Mr. Whittington has nothing to do but to put it in some place of safety."

Poor Dick hardly knew how to behave himself for joy. He begged his master to take what part of it he pleased, since he owed it all to his kindness. "No, no," answered Mr. Fitzwarren, "this is all your own; and I have no doubt but you will use it well."

Dick next asked his mistress, and then Miss Alice, to accept a part of his good fortune; but they would not, and at the same time told him they felt great joy at his good success. But this poor fellow was too kindhearted to keep it all to himself; so he made a present to the captain, the mate, and the rest of Mr. Fitzwarren's servants; and even to the ill-natured old cook.

After this Mr. Fitzwarren advised him to send for a proper tailor and get himself dressed like a gentleman; and told him he was welcome to live in his house till he could provide himself with a better.

When Whittington's face was washed, his hair curled, his hat cocked, and he was dressed in a nice suit of clothes he was as handsome and genteel as any young man who visited at Mr. Fitzwarren's; so that Miss Alice, who had once been so kind to him, and thought of him with pity, now looked upon him as fit to be her sweetheart; and the more so, no doubt, because Whittington was now always thinking what he could do to oblige her, and making her the prettiest presents that could be.

Mr. Fitzwarren soon saw their love for each other, and proposed to join them in marriage; and to this they both readily agreed. A day for the wedding was soon fixed; and they were attended to church by the Lord Mayor, the court of aldermen, the sheriffs, and a great number of the richest merchants in London, whom they afterward treated with a very rich feast.

History tells us that Mr. Whittington and his lady lived in great splendor, and were very happy. They had several children. He was Sheriff of London, thrice Lord Mayor, and received the honor of knighthood by Henry V.

He entertained this king and his queen at dinner after his conquest of France so grandly, that the king said: "Never had prince such a subject"; when Sir Richard heard this, he said: "Never had subject such a prince."

The figure of Sir Richard Whittington with his cat in his arms, carved in stone, was to be seen till the year 1780 over the archway of the old prison of Newgate, which he built for criminals.

56. THE PIED PIPER
(England)

NEWTOWN, OR FRANCHVILLE, as 'twas called of old, is a sleepy little town, as you all may know, upon the Solent shore. Sleepy as it is now, it was once noisy enough, and what made the noise was—rats. The place was so infested with them as to be scarce worth living in. There wasn't a barn or a corn-rick, a storeroom or a cupboard, but they ate their way into it. Not a cheese but they gnawed it hollow, not a sugar puncheon but they cleared out. Why the very mead and beer in the barrels was not safe from them. They'd gnaw a hole in the top of the tun, and down would go one master rat's tail, and when he brought it up round would crowd all the friends and cousins, and each would have a suck at the tail.

Had they stopped here it might have been borne. But the squeaking and shrieking, the hurrying and scurrying, so that you could neither hear yourself speak nor get a wink of good honest sleep the livelong night! Not to mention that, Mamma must needs sit up, and keep watch and ward over baby's cradle, or there'd have been a big ugly rat running across the poor little fellow's face, and doing who knows what mischief.

Why didn't the good people of the town have cats? Well they did, and there was a fair stand-up fight, but in the end the rats were too many, and the pussies were regularly driven from the field. Poison, I hear you say? Why, they poisoned so many that it fairly bred a plague. Ratcatchers! Why there wasn't a ratcatcher from John o' Groat's house to the Land's End that hadn't tried his luck. But do what they might, cats or poison, terrier or traps, there seemed to be more rats than ever, and every day a fresh rat was cocking his tail or pricking his whiskers.

The Mayor and the town council were at their wits' end. As they were sitting one day in the town hall racking their poor brains, and bewailing their hard fate, who should run in but the town beadle. "Please your Honor," says he, "here is a very queer fellow come to town. I don't rightly know what to make of him." "Show him in," said the Mayor, and in he stepped. A queer fellow, truly. For there wasn't a color of the rainbow but you might find it in some corner of his dress, and he was tall and thin, and had keen piercing eyes.

"I'm called the Pied Piper," he began. "And pray what might you be willing to pay me, if I rid you of every single rat in Franchville?"

Well, much as they feared the rats, they feared parting with their money more, and fain would they have higgled and haggled. But the Piper was not a man to stand nonsense, and the upshot was that fifty pounds were promised him (and it meant a lot of money in those old days) as soon as not a rat was left to squeak or scurry in Franchville.

Out of the hall stepped the Piper, and as he stepped he laid his pipe to his lips and a shrill keen tune sounded through street and house. And as each note pierced the air you might have seen a strange sight. For out of every hole the rats came tumbling. There were none too old and none too young, none too big and none too little to crowd at the Piper's heels and with eager feet and upturned noses to patter after him as he paced the streets. Nor was the Piper unmindful of the little toddling ones, for every fifty yards he'd stop and give an extra flourish on his pipe just to give them time to keep up with the older and stronger of the band.

Up Silver Street he went, and down Gold Street, and at the end of Gold Street is the harbor and the broad Solent beyond. And as he paced along, slowly and gravely, the townsfolk flocked to door and window, and many a blessing they called down upon his head.

As for getting near him there were too many rats. And now that he was at the water's edge he stepped into a boat, and not a rat, as he shoved off into deep water, piping shrilly all the while, but followed him, splashing, paddling, and wagging their tails with delight. On and on he played and played until the tide went down, and each master rat sank deeper and deeper in the slimy ooze of the harbor, until every mother's son of them was dead and smothered.

The tide rose again, and the Piper stepped on shore, but never a rat followed. You may fancy the townsfolk had been throwing up their caps and hurrahing and stopping up rat holes and setting the church bells a-ringing. But when the Piper stepped ashore and not so much as a single squeak was to be heard, the Mayor and the Council, and the townsfolk generally, began to hem and to haw and to shake their heads.

For the town money chest had been sadly emptied of late, and where was the fifty pounds to come from? Such an easy job, too! Just getting into a boat and playing a pipe! Why the Mayor himself could have done that if only he had thought of it.

So he hemmed and hawed and at last, "Come, my good man," said he, "you see what poor folk we are; how can we manage to pay you fifty pounds? Will you not take twenty? When all is said and done, 'twill be good pay for the trouble you've taken."

"Fifty pounds was what I bargained for," said the Piper shortly; "and if I were you I'd pay it quickly. For I can pipe many kinds of tunes, as folk sometimes find to their cost."

"Would you threaten us, you strolling vagabond?" shrieked the Mayor, and at the same time he winked to the Council; "the rats are all dead and drowned," muttered he; and so "You may do your worst, my good man," and with that he turned short upon his heel.

"Very well," said the Piper, and he smiled a quiet smile. With that he laid his pipe to his lips afresh, but now there came forth no shrill notes, as it were, of scraping and gnawing, and squeaking and scurrying, but the tune was joyous and resonant, full of happy laughter and merry play. And as he paced down the streets the elders mocked, but from schoolroom and playroom, from nursery and workshop, not a child but ran out with eager glee and shout following gaily at the Piper's call. Dancing, laughing, joining hands and tripping feet, the bright throng moved along up Gold Street and down Silver Street, and beyond Silver Street lay the cool green forest full of old oaks and wide-spreading beeches. In and out among the oak trees you might catch glimpses of the Piper's many-colored coat. You might hear the laughter of the children break and fade and die away as deeper and deeper into the lone green wood the stranger went and the children followed.

All the while, the elders watched and waited. They mocked no longer now. And watch and wait as they might, never did they set their eyes again upon the Piper in his party-colored coat. Never were their hearts gladdened by the song and dance of the children issuing forth from among the ancient oaks of the forest.

57. MASTER OF ALL MASTERS
(England)

A GIRL ONCE WENT to the fair to hire herself for servant. At last a funny-looking old gentleman engaged her, and took her home to his house. When she got there, he told her that he had something to teach her, for that in his house he had his own names for things.

He said to her: "What will you call me?"

"Master or mister, or whatever you please, sir," says she.

He said: "You must call me 'master of all masters.' And what would you call this?" pointing to his bed.

"Bed or couch, or whatever you please, sir."

"No, that's my 'barnacle.' And what do you call these?" said he, pointing to his pantaloons.

"Breeches or trousers, or whatever you please, sir."

"You must call them 'squibs and crackers.' And what would you call her?" pointing to the cat.

"Cat or kit, or whatever you please, sir."

"You must call her 'white-faced simminy.' And this now," showing the fire, "what would you call this?"

"Fire or flame, or whatever you please, sir."

"You must call it 'hot cockalorum,' and what this?" he went on, pointing to the water.

"Water or wet, or whatever you please, sir."

"No, 'pondalorum' is its name. And what do you call all this?" asked he, as he pointed to the house.

"House or cottage, or whatever you please, sir."

"You must call it 'high topper mountain.'"

That very night the servant woke her master up in a fright and said: "Master of all masters, get out of your barnacle and put on your squibs and crackers. For white-faced simminy has got a spark of hot cockalorum on its tail, and unless you get some pondalorum high topper mountain will be all on hot cockalorum." . . . . That's all.

58. MUNACHAR AND MANACHAR
(*Ireland*)

THERE ONCE LIVED a Munachar and a Manachar, a long time ago, and it is a long time since it was, and if they were alive now they would not be alive then. They went out together to pick raspberries, and as many as Munachar used to pick Manachar used to eat. Munachar said he must go look for a rod to make a gad to hang Manachar, who ate his raspberries every one; and he came to the rod. "What news the day?" said the rod. "It is my own news that I'm seeking. Going looking for a rod, a rod to make a gad, a gad to hang Manachar, who ate my raspberries every one."

"You will not get me," said the rod, "until you get an ax to cut me." He came to the ax. "What news today?" said the ax. "It's my own news I'm seeking. Going looking for an ax, an ax to cut a rod, a rod to make a gad, a gad to hang Manachar, who ate my raspberries every one."

"You will not get me," said the ax, "until you get a flag to edge me." He came to the flag. "What news today?" says the flag. "It's my own news I'm seeking. Going looking for a flag, flag to edge ax, ax to cut a rod, a rod to make a gad, a gad to hang Manachar, who ate my raspberries every one."

"You will not get me," says the flag, "till you get water to wet me." He came to the water. "What news today?" says the water. "It's my own news I'm seeking. Going looking for water, water to wet flag, flag to edge ax, ax to cut a rod, a rod to make a gad, a gad to hang Manachar, who ate my raspberries every one."

"You will not get me," said the water, "until you get a deer who will swim me." He came to the deer. "What news today?" says the deer. "It's my own news I'm seeking. Going looking for a deer, deer to swim water, water to wet flag, flag to edge ax, ax to cut a rod, a rod to make a gad, a gad to hang Manachar, who ate my raspberries every one."

"You will not get me," said the deer, "until you get a hound who will hunt me." He came to the hound. "What news today?" says the hound. "It's my own news I'm seeking. Going looking for a hound, hound to hunt deer, deer to swim water, water to wet flag, flag to edge ax, ax to cut a rod, a rod to make a gad, a gad to hang Manachar, who ate my raspberries every one."

"You will not get me," said the hound, "until you get a bit of butter to put in my claw." He came to the butter. "What news today?" says the butter. "It's my own news I'm seeking. Going looking for butter, butter to go in claw of hound, hound to hunt deer, deer to swim water, water to wet flag, flag to edge ax, ax to cut a rod, a rod to make a gad, a gad to hang Manachar, who ate my raspberries every one."

"You will not get me," said the butter, "until you get a cat who shall scrape me." He came to the cat. "What news today?" said the cat. "It's my own news I'm seeking. Going looking for a cat, cat to scrape butter, butter to go in claw of hound, hound to hunt deer, deer to swim water, water to wet flag, flag to edge ax, ax to cut a rod, a rod to make a gad, a gad to hang Manachar, who ate my raspberries every one."

"You will not get me," said the cat, "until you will get milk which you will give me." He came to the cow. "What news today?" said the cow. "It's my own news I'm seeking. Going looking for a cow, cow to give me milk, milk I will give to the cat, cat to scrape butter, butter to go in claw of hound, hound to hunt deer, deer to swim water, water to wet flag, flag to edge ax, ax to cut a rod, a rod to make a gad, a gad to hang Manachar, who ate my raspberries every one."

"You will not get any milk from me," said the cow, "until you bring me a wisp of straw from those threshers yonder." He came to the threshers. "What news today?" said the threshers. "It's my own news I'm seeking. Going looking for a wisp of straw from ye to give to the cow, the cow to give me milk, milk I will give to the cat, cat to scrape butter, butter to go in claw of hound, hound to hunt deer, deer to swim water, water to wet flag, flag to edge ax, ax to cut a rod, a rod to make a gad, a gad to hang Manachar, who ate my raspberries every one."

"You will not get any wisp of straw from us," said the threshers, "until you bring us the makings of a cake from the miller over yonder." He came to the miller. "What news today?" said the miller. "It's my own news I'm seeking. Going looking for the makings of a cake which I will give the threshers, the threshers to give me a wisp of straw, the wisp of straw I will give to the cow, the cow to give me milk, milk I will give to the cat, cat to scrape butter, butter to go in claw of hound, hound to hunt deer, deer to swim water, water to wet flag, flag to edge ax, ax to cut a rod, a rod to make a gad, a gad to hang Manachar, who ate my raspberries every one."

"You will not get any makings of a cake from me," said the miller, "till you bring me the full of that sieve of water from the river over there."

He took the sieve in his hand and went over to the river, but as often as ever he would stoop and fill it with water, the moment he raised it the water would run out of it again, and sure, if he had been there, from that day till this, he never could have filled it. A crow went flying by him, over his head, "Daub! daub!" said the crow. "My blessings on ye, then," said Munachar, "but it's the good advice you have," and he took the red clay and the daub that was by the brink, and he rubbed it to the bottom of the sieve, until all the holes were filled, and then the sieve held the water, and he brought the water to the miller, and the miller gave him the makings of a cake, and he gave the makings of the cake to the threshers, and the threshers gave him a wisp of straw, and he gave the wisp of straw to the cow, and the cow gave him milk, the milk he gave to the cat, the cat scraped the butter, the butter went into the claw of the hound, the hound hunted the deer, the deer swam the water, the water wet the flag, the flag sharpened the ax, the ax cut the rod, and the rod made a gad, and when he had it ready to hang Manachar he found that Manachar had BURST.

59. THE FIELD OF BOLIAUNS

(*Ireland*)

ONE FINE DAY in harvest—it was indeed Lady-day in harvest, that everybody knows to be one of the greatest holidays in the year—Tom Fitzpatrick was taking a ramble through the ground, and went along the sunny side of a hedge; when all of a sudden he heard a clacking sort of noise a little before him in the hedge. "Dear me," said Tom, "but isn't it surprising to hear the stonechatters singing so late in the season?" So Tom stole on, going on the tops of his toes to try if he could get a sight of what was making the noise, to see if he was right in his guess. The noise stopped; but as Tom looked sharply through the bushes, what should he see in a nook of the hedge but a brown pitcher, that might hold about a gallon and a half of liquor; and by and by a little wee teeny-tiny bit of an old man, with a little *motty* of a cocked hat stuck upon the top of his head, a deeshy-daushy leather apron hanging before him, pulled out a little wooden stool, and stood up upon it, and dipped a little piggin into the pitcher, and took out the full of it, and put it beside the stool, and then sat down under the pitcher, and began to work at putting a heelpiece on a bit of a brogue just fit for himself. "Well, by the powers," said Tom to himself, "I often heard tell of the Lepracauns, and, to tell God's truth, I never rightly believed in them—but here's one of them in real earnest. If I go knowingly to work, I'm a made man. They say a body must never take their eyes off them, or they'll escape."

Tom now stole on a little further, with his eye fixed on the little man just as a cat does with a mouse. So when he got up quite close to him, "God bless your work, neighbor," said Tom.

The little man raised up his head, and "Thank you kindly," said he.

"I wonder you'd be working on the holiday!" said Tom.

"That's my own business, not yours," was the reply.

"Well, maybe you'd be civil enough to tell *us* what you've got in the pitcher there?" said Tom.

"That I will, with pleasure," said he; "it's good beer."

"Beer!" said Tom. "Thunder and fire! where did you get it?"

"Where did I get it, is it? Why, I made it. And what do you think I made it of?"

"Devil a one of me knows," said Tom; "but of malt, I suppose, what else?"

"There you're out. I made it of heath."

"Of heath!" said Tom, bursting out laughing; "sure you don't think me to be such a fool as to believe that?"

"Do as you please," said he, "but what I tell you is the truth. Did you never hear tell of the Danes?"

"Well, what about *them?*" said Tom.

"Why, all the about them there is, is that when they were here they taught us to make beer out of the heath, and the secret's in my family ever since."

"Will you give a body a taste of your beer?" said Tom.

"I'll tell you what it is, young man, it would be fitter for you to be looking after your father's property than to be bothering decent quiet people with your foolish questions. There now, while you're idling away your time here, there's the cows have broke into the oats, and are knocking the corn all about."

Tom was taken so by surprise with this that he was just on the very point of turning round when he recollected himself; so, afraid that the like might happen again, he made a grab at the Lepracaun, and caught him up in his hand; but in his hurry he overset the pitcher, and spilled all the beer, so that he could not get a taste of it to tell what sort it was. He then swore that he would kill him if he did not show him where his money was. Tom looked so wicked and so bloody-minded that the little man was quite frightened; so, says he, "Come along with me a couple of fields off, and I will show you a crock of gold."

So they went, and Tom held the Lepracaun fast in his hand, and never took his eyes from off him, though they had to cross hedges and ditches, and a crooked bit of bog, till at last they came to a great field all full of boliauns, and the Lepracaun pointed to a big boliaun, and says he, "Dig under that boliaun, and you'll get the great crock all full of guineas."

Tom in his hurry had never thought of bringing a spade with him, so he made up his mind to run home and fetch one; and that he might know the place again he took off one of his red garters, and tied it round the boliaun.

Then he said to the Lepracaun, "Swear ye'll not take that garter away from that boliaun." And the Lepracaun swore right away not to touch it.

"I suppose," said the Lepracaun, very civilly, "you have no further occasion for me?"

"No," says Tom; "you may go away now, if you please, and God speed you, and may good luck attend you wherever you go."

"Well, good-bye to you, Tom Fitzpatrick," said the Lepracaun; "and much good may it do you when you get it."

So Tom ran for dear life, till he came home and got a spade, and then away with him, as hard as he could go, back to the field of boliauns; but when he got there, lo and behold! not a boliaun in the field but had a red garter, the very model of his own, tied about it; and as to digging up the whole field, that was all nonsense, for there were more than forty good Irish acres on it. So Tom came home again with his spade on his shoulder, a little cooler than he went, and many's the hearty curse he gave the Lepracaun every time he thought of the neat turn he had served him.

60. THE FISHERMAN'S SON AND THE GRUAGACH OF TRICKS
(Ireland)

THERE WAS AN OLD fisherman once in Erin who had a wife and one son.

The old fisherman used to go about with a fishing rod and tackle to the rivers and lochs and every place where fish resort, and he was killing salmon and other fish to keep the life in himself and his wife and son.

The son was not so keen nor so wise as another, and the father was instructing him every day in fishing, so that if himself should be taken from the world, the son would be able to support the old mother and get his own living.

One day when the father and son were fishing in a river near the sea, they looked out over the water and saw a small dark speck on the waves. It grew larger and larger, till they saw a boat, and when the boat drew near they saw a man sitting in the stern of it.

There was a nice beach near the place where they were fishing. The man brought the boat straight to the beach, and stepping out drew it up on the sand.

They saw then that the stranger was a man of high degree.

After he had put the boat high on the sand, he came to where the two were at work, and said: "Old fisherman, you'd better let this son of yours with me for a year and a day, and I will make a very wise man of him. I am the Gruagach of tricks, and I'll bind myself to be here with your son this day year."

"I can't let him go," said the old fisherman, "till he gets his mother's advice."

"Whatever goes as far as women I'll have nothing to do with," said the Gruagach. "You had better give him to me now, and let the mother alone."

They talked till at last the fisherman promised to let his son go for the year and a day. Then the Gruagach gave his word to have the boy there at the seashore that day year.

The Gruagach and the boy went into the boat and sailed away.

When the year and a day were over, the old fisherman went to the same place where he had parted with his son and the Gruagach, and stood looking over the sea, thinking would he see his son that day.

At last he saw a black spot on the water, then a boat. When it was near he saw two men sitting in the stern of the boat. When it touched land, the two, who were refined in appearance, jumped out, and one of them pulled the boat to the top of the strand. Then that one, followed by the other, came to where the old fisherman was waiting, and asked "What trouble is on you now, my good man?"

"I had a son that wasn't so keen nor so wise as another, and myself and this son were here fishing, and a stranger came, like yourself today, and asked would I let my son with him for a year and a day. I let the son go, and the man promised to be here with him today, and that why I am waiting at this place now."

"Well," said the Gruagach, "am I your son?"

"You are not," said the fisherman.

"Is this man here your son?"

"I don't know him," said the fisherman.

"Well, then, he is all you will have in place of your son," said the Gruagach.

The old man looked again, and knew his son. He caught hold of him and welcomed him home.

"Now," said the Gruagach, "isn't he a better man than he was a year ago?"

"Oh, he's nearly a smart man now!" said the old fisherman.

"Well," said the Gruagach, "will you let him with me for another year and a day?"

"I will not," said the old man; "I want him myself."

The Gruagach then begged and craved till the fisherman promised to let the son with him for a year and a day again. But the old man forgot to take his word of the Gruagach to bring back the son at the end of the time; and when the Gruagach and the boy were in the boat, and had pushed out to sea, the Gruagach shouted to the old man: "I kept my promise to bring back your son today. I haven't given you my word at all now. I'll not bring him back, and you'll never see him again."

The fisherman went home with a heavy and sorrowful heart, and the old woman scolded him all that night till next morning for letting her son go with the Gruagach a second time.

Then himself and the old woman were lamenting a quarter of a year; and when another quarter had passed, he said to her: "I'll leave you here now, and I'll be walking on myself till I wear my legs off up to my knees, and from my knees to my waist, till I find where is my son."

So away went the old man walking, and he used to spend but one night in a house, and not two nights in any house, till his feet were all in blisters. One evening late he came to a hut where there was an old woman sitting at a fire.

"Poor man!" said she, when she laid eyes on him, "it's a great distress you are in, to be so disfigured with wounds and sores. What is the trouble that's on you?"

"I had a son," said the old man, "and the Gruagach of tricks came on a day and took him from me."

"Oh, poor man!" said she. "I have a son with that same Gruagach these twelve years, and I have never been able to get him back or get sight of him, and I'm in dread you'll not be able to get your son either.

But tomorrow, in the morning, I'll tell you all I know, and show you the road you must go to find the house of the Gruagach of tricks."

Next morning she showed the old fisherman the road. He was to come to the place by evening.

When he came and entered the house, the Gruagach shook hands with him, and said: "You are welcome, old fisherman. It was I that put this journey on you, and made you come here looking for your son."

"It was no one else but you," said the fisherman.

"Well," said the Gruagach, "you won't see your son today. At noon tomorrow I'll put a whistle in my mouth and call together all the birds in my place, and they'll come. Among others will be twelve doves. I'll put my hand in my pocket, this way, and take out wheat and throw it before them on the ground. The doves will eat the wheat, and you must pick your son out of the twelve. If you find him, you'll have him; if you don't, you'll never get him again."

After the Gruagach had said these words the old man ate his supper and went to bed.

In the dead of night the old fisherman's son came. "Oh, father!" said he, "it would be hard for you to pick me out among the twelve doves, if you had to do it alone; but I'll tell you. When the Gruagach calls us in, and we go to pick up the wheat, I'll make a ring around the others, walking for myself; and as I go I'll give some of them a tip of my bill, and I'll lift my wings when I'm striking them. There was a spot under one of my arms when I left home, and you'll see that spot under my wing when I raise it tomorrow. Don't miss the bird that I'll be, and don't let your eyes off it; if you do, you'll lose me forever."

Next morning the old man rose, had his breakfast, and kept thinking of what his son had told him.

At midday the Gruagach took his whistle and blew. Birds came to him from every part, and among others the twelve doves.

He took wheat from his pocket, threw it to the doves, and said to the father: "Now pick out your son from the twelve."

The old man was watching, and soon he saw one of the doves walking around the other eleven and hitting some of them a clip of its bill, and then it raised its wings, and the old man saw the spot. The bird let its wings down again, and went to eating with the rest.

The father never let his eyes off the bird. After a while he said to the Gruagach: "I'll have that bird there for my son."

"Well," said the Gruagach, "that is your son. I can't blame you for having him; but I blame your instructor for the information he gave you, and I give him my curse."

So the old fisherman got his son back in his proper shape, and away they went, father and son, from the house of the Gruagach. The old man felt stronger now, and they never stopped traveling a day till they came home.

The old mother was very glad to see her son, and see him such a wise, smart man.

After coming home they had no means but the fishing; they were as poor as ever before.

At this time it was given out at every crossroad in Erin, and in all public places in the kingdom, that there were to be great horse races. Now, when the day came, the old fisherman's son said:

"Come away with me, father, to the races."

The old man went with him, and when they were near the race course, the son said: "Stop here till I tell you this: I'll make myself into the best horse that's here today, and do you take me to the place where the races are to be, and when you take me in, I'll open my mouth, trying to kill and eat every man that'll be near me, I'll have such life and swiftness; and do you find a rider for me that'll ride me, and don't let me go till the other horses are far ahead on the course. Then let me go. I'll come up to them, and I'll run ahead of them and win the race. After that every rich man there will want to buy me of you; but don't you sell me to any man for less than five hundred pounds; and be sure you get that price for me. And when you have the gold, and you are giving me up, take the bit out of my mouth, and don't sell the bridle for any money. Then come to this spot, shake the bridle, and I'll be here in my own form before you."

The son made himself a horse, and the old fisherman took him to the race. He reared and snorted, trying to take the head off every man that came near him.

The old man shouted for a rider. A rider came; he mounted the horse and held him in. The old man didn't let him start till the other horses were well ahead on the course; then he let him go.

The new horse caught up with the others and shot past them. So they had not gone halfway when he was in at the winning-post.

When the race was ended, there was a great noise over the strange horse. Men crowded around the old fisherman from every corner of the field, asking what would he take for the horse.

"Five hundred pounds," said he.

"Here 'tis for you," said the next man to him.

In a moment the horse was sold, and the money in the old man's pocket. Then he pulled the bridle off the horse's head, and made his way out of the place as fast as ever he could.

It was not long till he was at the spot where the son had told him what to do. The minute he came, he shook the bridle, and the son was there before him in his own shape and features.

Oh, but the old fisherman was glad when he had his son with him again, and the money in his pocket!

The two went home together. They had money enough now to live, and quit the fishing. They had plenty to eat and drink, and they spent their lives in ease and comfort till the next year, when it was given out at all the crossroads in Erin, and every public place in the kingdom, that there was to be a great hunting with hounds, in the same place where the races had been the year before.

When the day came, the fisherman's son said: "Come, father, let us go away to this hunting."

"Ah!" said the old man, "what do we want to go for? Haven't we plenty to eat at home, with money enough and to spare? What do we care for hunting with hounds?"

"Oh! they'll give us more money," said the son, "if we go."

The fisherman listened to his son, and away they went. When the two came to the spot where the son had made a horse of himself the year before, he stopped, and said to the father: "I'll make a hound of myself today, and when you bring me in sight of the game, you'll see me wild with jumping and trying to get away; but do you hold me fast till the right time comes, then let go. I'll sweep ahead of every hound in the field, catch the game, and win the prize for you.

"When the hunt is over, so many men will come to buy me that they'll put you in a maze; but be sure you get three hundred pounds for me, and when you have the money, and are giving me up, don't forget to keep my rope. Come to this place, shake the rope, and I'll be here before you, as I am now. If you don't keep the rope, you'll go home without me."

The son made a hound of himself, and the old father took him to the hunting ground.

When the hunt began, the hound was springing and jumping like mad; but the father held him till the others were far out in the field. Then he let him loose, and away went the son.

Soon he was up with the pack, then in front of the pack, and never stopped till he caught the game and won the prize.

When the hunt was over, and the dogs and game brought in, all the people crowded around the old fisherman, saying: "What do you want of that hound? Better sell him; he's no good to you."

They put the old man in a maze, there were so many of them, and they pressed him so hard.

He said at last: "I'll sell the hound; and three hundred pounds is the price I want for him."

"Here 'tis for you," said a stranger, putting the money into his hand.

The old man took the money and gave up the dog, without taking off the rope. He forgot his son's warning.

That minute the Gruagach of tricks called out: "I'll take the worth of my money out of your son now"; and away he went with the hound.

The old man walked home alone that night, and it is a heavy heart he had in him when he came to the old woman without the son. And the two were lamenting their lot till morning.

Still and all, they were better off than the first time they lost their son, as they had plenty of everything, and could live at their ease.

The Gruagach went away home, and put the fisherman's son in a cave of concealment that he had, bound him hand and foot, and tied hard knots on his neck up to the chin. From above there fell on him drops of poison, and every drop that fell went from the skin to the flesh, from the flesh to the bone, from the bone to the marrow, and he sat there under the poison drops, without meat, drink, or rest.

In the Gruagach's house was a servant-maid, and the fisherman's son had been kind to her the time he was in the place before.

On a day when the Gruagach and his eleven sons were out hunting, the maid was going with a tub of dirty water to throw it into the river that ran by the side of the house. She went through the cave of concealment where the fisherman's son was bound, and he asked of her the wetting of his mouth from the tub.

"Oh! the Gruagach would take the life of me," said she, "when he comes home, if I gave you as much as one drop."

"Well," said he, "when I was in this house before, and when I had power in my hands, it's good and kind I was to you; and when I get out of this confinement I'll do you a turn, if you give me the wetting of my mouth now."

The maid put the tub near his lips.

"Oh! I can't stoop to drink unless you untie one knot from my throat," said he.

Then she put the tub down, stooped to him, and loosed one knot from his throat. When she loosed the one knot he made an eel of himself, and dropped into the tub. There he began shaking the water, till he put some of it on the ground, and when he had the place about him wet, he sprang from the tub, and slipped along out under the door. The maid caught him; but could not hold him, he was so slippery. He made his way from the door to the river, which ran near the side of the house.

When the Gruagach of tricks came home in the evening with his eleven sons, they went to take a look at the fisherman's son; but he was not to be seen.

Then the Gruagach called the maid, and taking his sword, said: "I'll take the head off you if you don't tell me this minute what happened while I was gone."

"Oh!" said the maid, "he begged so hard for a drop of dirty water to wet his mouth that I hadn't the heart to refuse, for 'tis good he was to me and kind each time he saw me when he was here in the house before. When the water touched his mouth, he made an eel of himself, spilled water out of the tub, and slipped along over the wet place to the river outside. I caught him to bring him back, but I couldn't hold him; in spite of all I could do, he made away."

The Gruagach dropped his sword, and went to the water side with his sons.

The sons made eleven eels of themselves, and the Gruagach their father was the twelfth. They went around in the water, searching in every place, and there was not a stone in the river that they passed without looking under and around it for the old fisherman's son.

And when he knew that they were after him, he made himself into a salmon; and when they knew he was a salmon, the sons made eleven otters of themselves, and the Gruagach made himself the twelfth.

When the fisherman's son found that twelve otters were after him, he was weak with hunger, and when they had come near, he made himself a whale. But the eleven brothers and their father made twelve cannon whales of themselves, for they had all gone out of the river, and were in the sea now.

When they were coming near him, the fisherman's son was weak from pursuit and hunger, so he jumped up out of the water, and made a swallow of himself; but the Gruagach and his sons became twelve hawks, and chased the swallow through the air; and as they whirled round and darted, they pressed him hard, till all of them came near the castle of the king of Erin.

Now the king had made a summer house for his daughter; and where should she be at this time but sitting on the top of the summer house.

The old fisherman's son dropped down till he was near her; then he fell into her lap in the form of a ring. The daughter of the king of Erin took up the ring, looked at it, and put it on her finger. The ring took her fancy, and she was glad.

When the Gruagach and his sons saw this, they let themselves down at the king's castle, having the form of the finest men that could be seen in the kingdom.

When the king's daughter had the ring on her finger she looked at it and liked it. Then the ring spoke, and said: "My life is in your hands now; don't part from the ring, and don't let it go to any man, and you'll give me a long life."

The Gruagach of tricks and his eleven sons went into the king's castle and played on every instrument known to man, and they showed every sport that could be shown before a king. This they did for three days and three nights. When that time was over, and they were going away, the king spoke up and asked:

"What is the reward that you would like, and what would be pleasing to you from me?"

"We want neither gold nor silver," said the Gruagach; "all the reward we ask of you is the ring that I lost on a time, and which is now on your daughter's finger."

"If my daughter has the ring that you lost, it shall be given to you," said the king.

Now the ring spoke to the king's daughter and said: "Don't part with me for anything till you send your trusted man for three gallons of strong spirits and a gallon of wheat; put the spirits and the wheat together in an open barrel before the fire. When your father says you must give up the ring, do you answer back that you have never left the summer house, that you have nothing on your hand but what is your own and paid for. Your father will say then that you must part with me, and give me up to the stranger. When he forces you in this way, and you can keep me no longer, then throw me into the fire; and you'll see great sport and strange things."

The king's daughter sent for the spirits and the wheat, had them mixed together, and put in an open barrel before the fire.

The king called the daughter in, and asked: "Have you the ring which this stranger lost?"

"I have a ring," said she, "but it's my own, and I'll not part with it. I'll not give it to him nor to any man."

"You must," said the king, "for my word is pledged, and you must part with the ring!"

When she heard this, she slipped the ring from her finger and threw it into the fire.

That moment the eleven brothers made eleven pairs of tongs of themselves; their father, the old Gruagach, was the twelfth pair.

The twelve jumped into the fire to know in what spark of it would they find the old fisherman's son; and they were a long time working and searching through the fire, when out flew a spark, and into the barrel.

The twelve made themselves men, turned over the barrel, and spilled the wheat on the floor. Then in a twinkling they were twelve cocks strutting around.

They fell to and picked away at the wheat to know which one would find the fisherman's son. Soon one dropped on one side, and a second on the opposite side, until all twelve were lying drunk from the wheat.

Then the old fisherman's son made a fox of himself, and the first cock he came to was the old Gruagach of tricks himself. He took the head off the Gruagach with one bite, and the heads off the eleven brothers with eleven other bites.

When the twelve were dead, the old fisherman's son made himself the finest-looking man in Erin, and began to give music and sport to the king; and he entertained him five times better than had the Gruagach and his eleven sons.

Then the king's daughter fell in love with him, and she set her mind on him to that degree that there was no life for her without him.

When the king saw the straits that his daughter was in, he ordered the marriage without delay.

The wedding lasted for nine days and nine nights, and the ninth night was the best of all.

When the wedding was over, the king felt he was losing his strength, so he took the crown off his own head, and put it on the head of the old fisherman's son, and made him king of Erin in place of himself.

The young couple were the luck, and we the stepping-stones. The presents we got at the marriage were stockings of buttermilk and shoes of paper, and these were worn to the soles of our feet when we got home from the wedding.

61. THE THIRTEENTH SON OF THE KING OF ERIN

(Ireland)

THERE WAS A KING in Erin long ago who had thirteen sons, and as they grew up he taught them good learning and every exercise and art befitting their rank.

One day the king went hunting, and saw a swan swimming in a lake with thirteen little ones. She kept driving away the thirteenth, and would not let it come near the others.

The king wondered greatly at this, and when he came home he summoned his Sean dall Glic (old blind sage), and said: "I saw a great wonder today while out hunting—a swan with thirteen cygnets, and she driving away the thirteenth continually, and keeping the twelve with her. Tell me the cause and reason of this. Why should a mother hate her thirteenth little one, and guard the other twelve?"

"I will tell you," said the old blind sage: "All creatures on earth, whether beast or human, which have thirteen young, should put the thirteenth away, and let it wander for itself through the world and find its fate, so that the will of Heaven may work upon it, and not come down on the others. Now you have thirteen sons, and you must give the thirteenth to the Fate."

"Then that is the meaning of the swan on the lake—I must give up my thirteenth son to the Fate?"

"It is," said the old blind sage; "you must give up one of your thirteen sons."

"But how can I give one of them away when I am so fond of all; and which one shall it be?"

"I'll tell you what to do. When the thirteen come home tonight, shut the door against the last that comes."

Now one of the sons was slow, not so keen nor so sharp as another;

but the eldest, who was called Sean Ruadh, was the best, the hero of them all. And it happened that night that he came home last, and when he came his father shut the door against him. The boy raised his hands and said: "Father, what are you going to do with me; what do you wish?"

"It is my duty," said the father, "to give one of my sons to the Fate; and as you are the thirteenth, you must go."

"Well, give me my outfit for the road."

The outfit was brought, Sean Ruadh put it on; then the father gave him a black-haired steed that could overtake the wind before him, and outstrip the wind behind.

Sean Ruadh mounted the steed and hurried away. He went on each day without rest, and slept in the woods at night.

One morning he put on some old clothes which he had in a pack on the saddle, and leaving his horse in the woods, went aside to an opening. He was not long there when a king rode up and stopped before him.

"Who are you, and where are you going?" asked the king.

"Oh!" said Sean Ruadh, "I am astray. I do not know where to go, nor what I am to do."

"If that is how you are, I'll tell you what to do—come with me."

"Why should I go with you?" asked Sean Ruadh.

"Well, I have a great many cows, and I have no one to go with them, no one to mind them. I am in great trouble also. My daughter will die a terrible death very soon."

"How will she die?" asked Sean Ruadh.

"There is an urfeist, a great serpent of the sea, a monster which must get a king's daughter to devour every seven years. Once in seven years this thing comes up out of the sea for its meat. The turn has now come to my daughter, and we don't know what day will the urfeist appear. The whole castle and all of us are in mourning for my wretched child."

"Perhaps someone will come to save her," said Sean Ruadh.

"Oh! there is a whole army of kings' sons who have come, and they all promise to save her; but I'm in dread none of them will meet the urfeist."

Sean Ruadh agreed with the king to serve for seven years, and went home with him.

Next morning Sean Ruadh drove out the king's cows to pasture.

Now there were three giants not far from the king's place. They lived in three castles in sight of each other, and every night each of these giants shouted just before going to bed. So loud was the shout that each let out of himself that the people heard it in all the country around.

Sean Ruadh drove the cattle up to the giant's land, pushed down the wall, and let them in. The grass was very high—three times better than any on the king's pastures.

As Sean Ruadh sat watching the cattle, a giant came running toward him and called out: "I don't know whether to put a pinch of you in my nose, or a bite of you in my mouth!"

"Bad luck to me," said Sean Ruadh, "if I came here but to take the life out of you!"

"How would you like to fight—on the gray stones, or with sharp swords?" asked the giant.

"I'll fight you," said Sean Ruadh, "on the gray stones, where your great legs will be going down, and mine standing high."

They faced one another then, and began to fight. At the first encounter Sean Ruadh put the giant down to his knees among the hard gray stones, at the second he put him to his waist, and at the third to his shoulders.

"Come, take me out of this," cried the giant, "and I'll give you my castle and all I've got. I'll give you my sword of light that never fails to kill at a blow. I'll give you my black horse that can overtake the wind before, and outstrip the wind behind. These are all up there in my castle."

Sean Ruadh killed the giant and went up to the castle, where the housekeeper said to him: "Oh! it is you that are welcome. You have killed the dirty giant that was here. Come with me now till I show you all the riches and treasures."

She opened the door of the giant's storeroom and said: "All these are yours. Here are the keys of the castle."

"Keep them till I come again, and wake me in the evening," said Sean Ruadh, lying down on the giant's bed.

He slept till evening; then the housekeeper roused him, and he drove the king's cattle home. The cows never gave so much milk as that night. They gave as much as in a whole week before.

Sean Ruadh met the king, and asked: "What news from your daughter?"

"The great serpent did not come today," said the king; "but he may come tomorrow."

"Well, tomorrow he may not come till another day," said Sean Ruadh.

Now the king knew nothing of the strength of Sean Ruadh, who was barefoot, ragged, and shabby.

The second morning Sean Ruadh put the king's cows in the second giant's land. Out came the second giant with the same questions and threats as the first, and the cowboy spoke as on the day before.

They fell to fighting; and when the giant was to his shoulders in the hard gray rocks, he said: "I'll give you my sword of light and my brown-haired horse if you'll spare my life."

"Where is your sword of light?" asked Sean Ruadh.

"It is hung up over my bed."

Sean Ruadh ran to the giant's castle, and took the sword, which screamed out when he seized it; but he held it fast, hurried back to the giant, and asked, "How shall I try the edge of this sword?"

"Against a stick," was the reply.

"I see no stick better than your own head," said Sean Ruadh; and with that he swept the head off the giant.

The cowboy now went back to the castle and hung up the sword. "Blessing to you," said the housekeeper; "you have killed the giant! Come, now, and I'll show you his riches and treasures, which are yours forever."

Sean Ruadh found more treasure in this castle than in the first one. When he had seen all, he gave the keys to the housekeeper till he should need them. He slept as on the day before, then drove the cows home in the evening.

The king said: "I have *the* luck since you came to me. My cows give three times as much milk today as they did yesterday."

"Well," said Sean Ruadh, "have you any account of the urfeist?"

"He didn't come today," said the king; "but he may come tomorrow."

Sean Ruadh went out with the king's cows on the third day, and drove them to the third giant's land, who came out and fought a more desperate battle than either of the other two; but the cowboy pushed him down among the gray rocks to his shoulders and killed him.

At the castle of the third giant he was received with gladness by the housekeeper, who showed him the treasures and gave him the keys; but he left the keys with her till he should need them. That evening the king's cows had more milk than ever before.

On the fourth day Sean Ruadh went out with the cows, but stopped at the first giant's castle. The housekeeper at his command brought out the dress of the giant, which was all black. He put on the giant's apparel, black as night, and girded on his sword of light. Then he mounted the black-haired steed, which overtook the wind before, and outstripped the wind behind; and rushing on between earth and sky, he never stopped till he came to the beach, where he saw hundreds upon hundreds of kings' sons, and champions, who were anxious to save the king's daughter, but were so frightened at the terrible urfeist that they would not go near her.

When he had seen the princess and the trembling champions, Sean Ruadh turned his black steed to the castle. Presently the king saw, riding between earth and sky, a splendid stranger, who stopped before him.

"What is that I see on the shore?" asked the stranger. "Is it a fair, or some great meeting?"

"Haven't you heard," asked the king, "that a monster is coming to destroy my daughter today?"

"No, I haven't heard anything," answered the stranger, who turned away and disappeared.

Soon the black horseman was before the princess, who was sitting alone on a rock near the sea. As she looked at the stranger, she thought he was the finest man on earth, and her heart was cheered.

"Have you no one to save you?" he asked.

"No one."

"Will you let me lay my head on your lap till the urfeist comes? Then rouse me."

He put his head on her lap and fell asleep. While he slept, the princess took three hairs from his head and hid them in her bosom. As soon as she had hidden the hairs, she saw the urfeist coming on the sea, great as an island and throwing up water to the sky as he moved. She roused the stranger, who sprang up to defend her.

The urfeist came upon shore, and was advancing on the princess with mouth open and wide as a bridge, when the stranger stood before him and said: "This woman is mine, not yours!"

Then drawing his sword of light, he swept off the monster's head with a blow; but the head rushed back to its place, and grew on again.

In a twinkle the urfeist turned and went back to the sea; but as he went, he said: "I'll be here again tomorrow, and swallow the whole world before me as I come."

"Well," answered the stranger, "maybe another will come to meet you."

Sean Ruadh mounted his black steed, and was gone before the princess could stop him. Sad was her heart when she saw him rush off between the earth and sky more swiftly than any wind.

Sean Ruadh went to the first giant's castle and put away his horse, clothes, and sword. Then he slept on the giant's bed till evening, when the housekeeper woke him, and he drove home the cows. Meeting the king, he asked: "Well, how has your daughter fared today?"

"Oh! the urfeist came out of the sea to carry her away; but a wonderful black champion came riding between earth and sky and saved her."

"Who was he?"

"Oh! there is many a man who says he did it. But my daughter isn't saved yet, for the urfeist said he'd come tomorrow."

"Well, never fear; perhaps another champion will come tomorrow."

Next morning Sean Ruadh drove the king's cows to the land of the second giant, where he left them feeding, and then went to the castle, where the housekeeper met him and said: "You are welcome. I'm here before you, and all is well."

"Let the brown horse be brought; let the giant's apparel and sword be ready for me," said Sean Ruadh.

The apparel was brought, the beautiful blue dress of the second giant, and his sword of light. Sean Ruadh put on the apparel, took the sword, mounted the brown steed, and sped away between earth and air three times more swiftly than the day before.

He rode first to the seashore, saw the king's daughter sitting on the rock alone, and the princes and champions far away, trembling in dread of the urfeist. Then he rode to the king, inquired about the crowd on the seashore, and received the same answer as before. "But is there no man to save her?" asked Sean Ruadh.

"Oh! there are men enough," said the king, "who promise to save her, and say they are brave; but there is no man of them who will stand to his word and face the urfeist when he rises from the sea."

Sean Ruadh was away before the king knew it, and rode to the princess in his suit of blue, bearing his sword of light. "Is there no one to save you?" asked he.

"No one."

"Let me lay my head on your lap, and when the urfeist comes, rouse me."

He put his head on her lap, and while he slept she took out the three hairs, compared them with his hair, and said to herself: "You are the man who was here yesterday."

When the urfeist appeared, coming over the sea, the princess roused the stranger, who sprang up and hurried to the beach.

The monster, moving at a greater speed and raising more water than on the day before, came with open mouth to land. Again Sean Ruadh stood in his way, and with one blow of the giant's sword made two halves of the urfeist. But the two halves rushed together, and were one as before.

Then the urfeist turned to the sea again, and said as he went: "All the champions on earth won't save her from me tomorrow!"

Sean Ruadh sprang to his steed and back to the castle. He went, leaving the princess in despair at his going. She tore her hair and wept for the loss of the blue champion—the one man who had dared to save her.

Sean Ruadh put on his old clothes, and drove home the cows as usual. The king said: "A strange champion, all dressed in blue, saved my daughter today; but she is grieving her life away because he is gone."

"Well, that is a small matter, since her life is safe," said Sean Ruadh.

There was a feast for the whole world that night at the king's castle, and gladness was on every face that the king's daughter was safe again.

Next day Sean Ruadh drove the cows to the third giant's pasture, went to the castle, and told the housekeeper to bring the giant's sword and apparel, and have the red steed led to the door. The third giant's dress had as many colors as there are in the sky, and his boots were of blue glass.

Sean Ruadh, dressed and mounted on his red steed, was the most beautiful man in the world. When ready to start, the housekeeper said to him: "The beast will be so enraged this time that no arms can stop him; he will rise from the sea with three great swords coming out of his mouth, and he could cut to pieces and swallow the whole world if it stood before him in battle. There is only one way to conquer the urfeist, and I will show it to you. Take this brown apple, put it in your bosom, and when he comes rushing from the sea with open mouth, do you throw the apple down his throat, and the great urfeist will melt away and die on the strand."

Sean Ruadh went on the red steed between earth and sky, with thrice the speed of the day before. He saw the maiden sitting on the rock alone, saw the trembling kings' sons in the distance watching to know what would happen, and saw the king hoping for someone to save his daughter; then he went to the princess, and put his head on her lap; when he had fallen asleep, she took the three hairs from her bosom, and looking at them, said: "You are the man who saved me yesterday."

The urfeist was not long in coming. The princess roused Sean Ruadh, who sprang to his feet and went to the sea. The urfeist came up enormous, terrible to look at, with a mouth big enough to swallow the world, and three sharp swords coming out of it. When he saw Sean Ruadh, he sprang at him with a roar; but Sean Ruadh threw the apple into his mouth, and the beast fell helpless on the strand, flattened out and melted away to a dirty jelly on the shore.

Then Sean Ruadh went toward the princess and said: "That urfeist will never trouble man or woman again."

The princess ran and tried to cling to him; but he was on the red steed, rushing away between earth and sky, before she could stop him. She held, however, so firmly to one of the blue glass boots that Sean Ruadh had to leave it in her hands.

When he drove home the cows that night, the king came out, and Sean Ruadh asked: "What news from the urfeist?"

"Oh!" said the king, "I've had the luck since you came to me. A champion wearing all the colors of the sky, and riding a red steed between earth and air, destroyed the urfeist today. My daughter is safe forever; but she is ready to kill herself because she hasn't the man that saved her."

That night there was a feast in the king's castle such as no one had ever seen before. The halls were filled with princes and champions, and each one said: "I am the man that saved the princess!"

The king sent for the old blind sage, and asked, what should he do to find the man who saved his daughter. The old blind sage said—

"Send out word to all the world that the man whose foot the blue glass boot will fit is the champion who killed the urfeist, and you'll give him your daughter in marriage."

The king sent out word to the world to come to try on the boot. It was too large for some, too small for others. When all had failed, the old sage said—

"All have tried the boot but the cowboy."

"Oh! he is always out with the cows; what use in his trying," said the king.

"No matter," answered the old blind sage; "let twenty men go and bring down the cowboy."

The king sent up twenty men, who found the cowboy sleeping in the shadow of a stone wall. They began to make a hay rope to bind him; but he woke up, and had twenty ropes ready before they had one. Then he jumped at them, tied the twenty in a bundle, and fastened the bundle to the wall.

They waited and waited at the castle for the twenty men and the cowboy, till at last the king sent twenty men more, with swords, to know what was the delay.

When they came, this twenty began to make a hay rope to tie the cowboy; but he had twenty ropes made before their one, and no matter how they fought, the cowboy tied the twenty in a bundle, and the bundle to the other twenty men.

When neither party came back, the old blind sage said to the king: "Go up now, and throw yourself down before the cowboy, for he has tied the forty men in two bundles, and the bundles to each other."

The king went and threw himself down before the cowboy, who raised him up and said: "What is this for?"

"Come down now and try on the glass boot," said the king.

"How can I go, when I have work to do here?"

"Oh! nevermind; you'll come back soon enough to do the work."

The cowboy untied the forty men and went down with the king. When he stood in front of the castle, he saw the princess sitting in her upper chamber, and the glass boot on the windowsill before her.

That moment the boot sprang from the window through the air to him, and went on his foot of itself. The princess was downstairs in a twinkle, and in the arms of Sean Ruadh.

The whole place was crowded with kings' sons and champions, who claimed that they had saved the princess.

"What are these men here for?" asked Sean Ruadh.

"Oh! they have been trying to put on the boot," said the king.

With that Sean Ruadh drew his sword of light, swept the heads off every man of them, and threw heads and bodies on the dirt heap behind the castle.

Then the king sent ships with messengers to all the kings and queens of the world—to the kings of Spain, France, Greece, and Lochlin, and to Diarmuid, son of the monarch of light—to come to the wedding of his daughter and Sean Ruadh.

Sean Ruadh, after the wedding, went with his wife to live in the kingdom of the giants, and left his father-in-law on his own land.

62. THE BIRTH OF FIN MAC COUL
(Ireland)

CUMHAL MACART WAS a great champion in the west of Erin, and it was prophesied of him that if ever he married he would meet death in the next battle he fought.

For this reason he had no wife, and knew no woman for a long time; till one day he saw the king's daughter, who was so beautiful that he forgot all fear and married her in secret.

Next day after the marriage, news came that a battle had to be fought.

Now a Druid had told the king that his daughter's son would take the kingdom from him; so he made up his mind to look after the daughter, and not let any man come near her.

Before he went to the battle, Cumhal told his mother everything— told her of his relations with the king's daughter.

He said, "I shall be killed in battle today, according to the prophecy of the Druid, and I'm afraid if his daughter has a son the king will kill the child, for the prophecy is that he will lose the kingdom by the son of his own daughter. Now, if the king's daughter has a son do you hide and rear him, if you can; you will be his only hope and stay."

Cumhal was killed in the battle, and within that year the king's daughter had a son.

By command of his grandfather, the boy was thrown out of the castle window into a loch, to be drowned, on the day of his birth.

The boy sank from sight; but after remaining a while under the water, he rose again to the surface, and came to land holding a live salmon in his hand.

The grandmother of the boy, Cumhal's mother, stood watching on the shore, and said to herself as she saw this: "He is my grandson, the true son of my own child," and, seizing the boy, she rushed away with him and vanished, before the king's people could stop her.

When the king heard that the old woman had escaped with his daughter's son, he fell into a terrible rage, and ordered all the male children born that day in the kingdom to be put to death, hoping in this way to kill his own grandson, and save the crown for himself.

After she had disappeared from the bank of the loch, the old woman, Cumhal's mother, made her way to a thick forest, where she spent that night as best she could. Next day she came to a great oak tree. Then she hired a man to cut out a chamber in the tree.

When all was finished, and there was a nice room in the oak for herself and her grandson, and a whelp of the same age as the boy, and which she had brought with her from the castle, she said to the man: "Give me the ax which you have in your hand, there is something here that I want to fix."

The man gave the ax into her hand, and that minute she swept the head off him, saying: "You'll never tell any man about this place now."

One day the whelp ate some of the fine chippings (*bran*) left cut by the carpenter from the inside of the tree. The old woman said: "You'll be called Bran from this out."

All three lived in the tree together, and the old woman did not take her grandson out till the end of five years; and then he couldn't walk, he had been sitting so long inside.

When the old grandmother had taught the boy to walk, she brought him one day to the brow of a hill from which there was a long slope. She took a switch and said: "Now, run down this place. I will follow and strike you with this switch, and coming up I will run ahead, and you strike me as often as you can."

The first time they ran down, his grandmother struck him many times. In coming up the first time, he did not strike her at all. Every time they ran down she struck him less, and every time they ran up he struck her more.

They ran up and down for three days; and at the end of that time she could not strike him once, and he struck her at every step she took. He had now become a great runner.

When he was fifteen years of age, the old woman went with him to a hurling match between the forces of his grandfather and those of a neighboring king. Both sides were equal in skill; and neither was able to win, till the youth opposed his grandfather's people. Then, he won every game. When the ball was thrown in the air, he struck it coming down, and so again and again—never letting the ball touch the ground till he had driven it through the barrier.

The old king, who was very angry and greatly mortified at the defeat of his people, exclaimed, as he saw the youth, who was very fair and had white hair: "Who is that *fin coul* [white cap]?"

"Ah, that is it; Fin will be his name, and Fin MacCoul he is," said the old woman.

The king ordered his people to seize and put the young man to death, on the spot. The old woman hurried to the side of her grandson. They slipped from the crowd and away they went, a hill at a leap, a glen at a step, and thirty-two miles at a running leap. They ran a long distance, till Fin grew tired; then the old grandmother took him on her back, putting his feet into two pockets which were in her dress, one on each side, and ran on with the same swiftness as before, a hill at a leap, a glen at a step, and thirty-two miles at a running leap.

After a time, the old woman felt the approach of pursuit, and said to Fin: "Look behind, and tell me what you see."

"I see," said he, "a white horse with a champion on his back."

"Oh, no fear," said she; "a white horse has no endurance; he can never catch us, we are safe from him." And on they sped. A second time she felt the approach of pursuit, and again she said: "Look back, and see who is coming."

Fin looked back, and said: "I see a warrior riding on a brown horse."

"Never fear," said the old woman; "there is never a brown horse but is giddy, he cannot overtake us." She rushed on as before. A third time she said: "Look around, and see who is coming now."

Fin looked, and said: "I see a black warrior on a black horse, following fast."

"There is no horse so tough as a black horse," said the grandmother. "There is no escape from this one. My grandson, one or both of us must die. I am old, my time has nearly come. I will die, and you and Bran save yourselves. (Bran had been with them all the time.) Right here ahead is a deep bog; you jump off my back, and escape as best you can. I'll jump into the bog up to my neck; and when the king's men come, I'll say that you are in the bog before me, sunk out of sight, and I'm trying to find you. As my hair and yours are the same color, they will think my head good enough to carry back. They will cut it off, and take it in place of yours, and show it to the king; that will satisfy his anger."

Fin slipped down, took farewell of his grandmother, and hurried on with Bran. The old woman came to the bog, jumped in, and sank to her neck. The king's men were soon at the edge of the bog, and the black rider called out to the old woman: "Where is Fin?"

"He is here in the bog before me, and I'm trying can I find him."

As the horsemen could not find Fin, and thought the old woman's head would do to carry back, they cut it off, and took it with them, saying: "This will satisfy the king."

Fin and Bran went on till they came to a great cave, in which they found a herd of goats. At the further end of the cave was a smoldering fire. The two lay down to rest.

A couple of hours later, in came a giant with a salmon in his hand. This giant was of awful height, he had but one eye, and that in the middle of his forehead, as large as the sun in heaven.

When he saw Fin, he called out: "Here, take this salmon and roast it; but be careful, for if you raise a single blister on it I'll cut the head off you. I've followed this salmon for three days and three nights without stopping, and I never let it out of my sight, for it is the most wonderful salmon in the world."

The giant lay down to sleep in the middle of the cave. Fin spitted the salmon, and held it over the fire.

The minute the giant closed the one eye in his head, he began to snore. Every time he drew breath into his body, he dragged Fin, the spit, the salmon, Bran, and all the goats to his mouth; and every time he drove a breath out of himself, he threw them back to the places they were in before. Fin was drawn time after time to the mouth of the giant with such force, that he was in dread of going down his throat.

When partly cooked, a blister rose on the salmon. Fin pressed the place with his thumb, to know could he break the blister, and hide from the giant the harm that was done. But he burned his thumb, and, to ease the pain, put it between his teeth, and gnawed the skin to the flesh, the flesh to the bone, the bone to the marrow; and when he had tasted the marrow, he received the knowledge of all things. Next moment, he was drawn by the breath of the giant right up to his face, and, knowing from his thumb what to do, he plunged the hot spit into the sleeping eye of the giant and destroyed it.

That instant the giant with a single bound was at the low entrance of the cave, and, standing with his back to the wall and a foot on each side of the opening, roared out: "You'll not leave this place alive."

Now Fin killed the largest goat, skinned him as quickly as he could, then putting the skin on himself he drove the herd to where the giant stood; the goats passed out one by one between his legs. When the great goat came the giant took him by the horns. Fin slipped from the skin, and ran out.

"Oh, you've escaped," said the giant, "but before we part let me make you a present."

"I'm afraid to go near you," said Fin; "if you wish to give me a present, put it out this way, and then go back."

The giant placed a ring on the ground, then went back. Fin took up the ring and put it on the end of his little finger above the first joint. It clung so firmly that no man in the world could have taken it off.

The giant then called out, "Where are you?"

"On Fin's finger," cried the ring. That instant the giant sprang at Fin and almost came down on his head, thinking in this way to crush him to bits. Fin sprang to a distance. Again the giant asked, "Where are you?"

"On Fin's finger," answered the ring.

Again the giant made a leap, coming down just in front of Fin. Many times he called and many times almost caught Fin, who could not escape with the ring on his finger. While in this terrible struggle, not knowing how to escape, Bran ran up and asked:

"Why don't you chew your thumb?"

Fin bit his thumb to the marrow, and then knew what to do. He took the knife with which he had skinned the goat, cut off his finger at the first joint, and threw it, with the ring still on, into a deep bog nearby.

Again the giant called out, "Where are you?" and the ring answered, "On Fin's finger."

Straightaway the giant sprang toward the voice, sank to his shoulders in the bog, and stayed there.

Fin with Bran now went on his way, and traveled till he reached a deep and thick wood, where a thousand horses were drawing timber, and men felling and preparing it.

"What is this?" asked Fin of the overseer of the workmen.

"Oh, we are building a dun (a castle) for the king; we build one every day, and every night it is burned to the ground. Our king has an only daughter; he will give her to any man who will save the dun, and he'll leave him the kingdom at his death. If any man undertakes to save the dun and fails, his life must pay for it; the king will cut his head off. The best champions in Erin have tried and failed; they are now in the king's dungeons, a whole army of them, waiting the king's pleasure. He's going to cut the heads off them all in one day."

"Why don't you chew your thumb?" asked Bran.

Fin chewed his thumb to the marrow, and then knew that on the eastern side of the world there lived an old hag with her three sons, and every evening at nightfall she sent the youngest of these to burn the king's dun.

"I will save the king's dun," said Fin.

"Well," said the overseer, "better men than you have tried and lost their lives."

"Oh," said Fin, "I'm not afraid; I'll try for the sake of the king's daughter."

Now Fin, followed by Bran, went with the overseer to the king. "I hear you will give your daughter to the man who saves your dun," said Fin.

"I will," said the king; "but if he fails I must have his head."

"Well," said Fin, "I'll risk my head for the sake of your daughter. If I fail I'm satisfied." The king gave Fin food and drink; he supped, and after supper went to the dun.

"Why don't you chew your thumb?" said Bran; "then you'll know what to do." He did. Then Bran took her place on the roof, waiting for the old woman's son. Now the old woman in the east told her youngest son to hurry on with his torches, burn the dun, and come back without delay; for the stirabout was boiling and he must not be too late for supper.

He took the torches, and shot off through the air with a wonderful speed. Soon he was in sight of the king's dun, threw the torches upon the thatched roof to set it on fire as usual.

That moment Bran gave the torches such a push with her shoulders, that they fell into the stream which ran around the dun, and were put out. "Who is this," cried the youngest son of the old hag, "who has dared to put out my lights, and interfere with my hereditary right?"

"I," said Fin, who stood in front of him. Then began a terrible battle between Fin and the old woman's son. Bran came down from the dun to help Fin; she bit and tore his enemy's back, stripping the skin and flesh from his head to his heels.

After a terrible struggle such as had not been in the world before that night, Fin cut the head off his enemy. But for Bran, Fin could never have conquered.

The time for the return of her son had passed; supper was ready. The old woman, impatient and angry, said to the second son: "You take torches and hurry on, see why your brother loiters. I'll pay him for this when he comes home! But be careful and don't do like him, or you'll have your pay too. Hurry back, for the stirabout is boiling and ready for supper."

He started off, was met and killed exactly as his brother, except that he was stronger and the battle fiercer. But for Bran, Fin would have lost his life that night.

The old woman was raging at the delay, and said to her eldest son, who had not been out of the house for years (It was only in case of the greatest need that she sent him. He had a cat's head, and was called Pus an Chuine, "Puss of the Corner"; he was the eldest and strongest of all the brothers): "Now take torches, go and see what delays your brothers; I'll pay them for this when they come home."

The eldest brother shot off through the air, came to the king's dun, and threw his torches upon the roof. They had just singed the straw a little, when Bran pushed them off with such force that they fell into the stream and were quenched.

"Who is this," screamed Cat-head, "who dares to interfere with my ancestral right?"

"I," shouted Fin. Then the struggle began fiercer than with the second brother. Bran helped from behind, tearing the flesh from his head to his heels; but at length Cat-head fastened his teeth into Fin's breast, biting and gnawing till Fin cut the head off. The body fell to the ground, but the head lived, gnawing as terribly as before. Do what they could it was impossible to kill it. Fin hacked and cut, but could neither kill nor pull it off. When nearly exhausted, Bran said:

"Why don't you chew your thumb?"

Fin chewed his thumb, and reaching the marrow knew that the old woman in the east was ready to start with torches to find her sons, and burn the dun herself, and that she had a vial of liquid with which she could bring the sons to life; and that nothing could free him from Cat-head but the old woman's blood.

After midnight the old hag, enraged at the delay of her sons, started and shot through the air like lightning, more swiftly than her sons. She threw her torches from afar upon the roof of the dun; but Bran as before hurled them into the stream.

Now the old woman circled around in the air looking for her sons. Fin was getting very weak from pain and loss of blood, for Cat-head was biting at his breast all the time.

Bran called out: "Rouse yourself, oh, Fin; use all your power or we are lost! If the old hag gets a drop from the vial upon the bodies of her sons, they will come to life, and then we're done for."

Thus roused, Fin with one spring reached the old woman in the air and swept the bottle from her grasp; which falling upon the ground was emptied.

The old hag gave a scream which was heard all over the world, came to the ground and closed with Fin. Then followed a battle greater than the world had ever known before that night, or has ever seen since. Water sprang out of gray rocks, cows cast their calves even when they had none, and hard rushes grew soft in the remotest corner of Erin, so desperate was the fighting and so awful, between Fin and the old hag. Fin would have died that night but for Bran.

Just as daylight was coming Fin swept the head off the old woman, caught some of her blood, and rubbed it around Cat-head, who fell off dead.

He rubbed his own wounds with the blood and was cured; then rubbed some on Bran, who had been singed with the torches, and she was as well as ever. Fin, exhausted with fighting, dropped down and fell asleep.

While he was sleeping the chief steward of the king came to the dun, found it standing safe and sound, and seeing Fin lying there asleep knew that he had saved it. Bran tried to waken Fin, pulled and tugged, but could not rouse him.

The steward went to the king, and said: "I have saved the dun, and I claim the reward."

"It shall be given you," answered the king; and straightaway the steward was recognized as the king's son-in-law, and orders were given to make ready for the wedding.

Bran had listened to what was going on, and when her master woke, exactly at midday, she told him of all that was taking place in the castle of the king.

Fin went to the king, and said: "I have saved your dun, and I claim the reward."

"Oh," said the king, "my steward claimed the reward, and it has been given to him."

"He had nothing to do with saving the dun; I saved it," said Fin.

"Well," answered the king, "he is the first man who told me of its safety and claimed the reward."

"Bring him here; let me look at him," said Fin.

He was sent for, and came. "Did you save the king's dun?" asked Fin. "I did," said the steward.

"You did not, and take that for your lies," said Fin; and striking him with the edge of his open hand he swept the head off his body, dashing it against the other side of the room, flattening it like paste on the wall.

"You are the man," said the king to Fin, "who saved the dun; yours is the reward. All the champions, and there is many a man of them, who have failed to save it are in the dungeons of my fortress; their heads must be cut off before the wedding takes place."

"Will you let me see them?" asked Fin.

"I will," said the king.

Fin went down to the men, and found the first champions of Erin in the dungeons. "Will you obey me in all things if I save you from death?" said Fin. "We will," said they. Then he went back to the king and asked:

"Will you give me the lives of these champions of Erin, in place of your daughter's hand?"

"I will," said the king.

All the champions were liberated, and left the king's castle that day. Ever after they followed the orders of Fin, and these were the beginning of his forces and the first of the Fenians of Erin.

63. FIN MACCOUL AND THE FENIANS OF ERIN IN THE CASTLE OF FEAR DUBH
(*Ireland*)

IT WAS THE CUSTOM with Fin MacCoul and the Fenians of Erin, when a stranger from any part of the world came to their castle, not to ask him a question for a year and a day.

On a time, a champion came to Fin and his men, and remained with them. He was not at all pleasant or agreeable.

At last Fin and his men took counsel together; they were much annoyed because their guest was so dull and morose, never saying a word, always silent.

While discussing what kind of man he was, Diarmuid Duivne offered to try him; so one evening when they were eating together, Diarmuid came and snatched from his mouth the hindquarter of a bullock, which he was picking.

Diarmuid pulled at one part of the quarter—pulled with all his strength, but only took the part that he seized, while the other kept the part he held. All laughed; the stranger laughed too, as heartily as any. It was the first laugh they had heard from him.

The strange champion saw all their feats of arms and practiced with them, till the year and a day were over. Then he said to Fin and his men:

"I have spent a pleasant year in your company; you gave me good treatment, and the least I can do now is to give you a feast at my own castle."

No one had asked what his name was up to that time. Fin now asked his name. He answered: "My name is Fear Dubh, of Alba."

Fin accepted the invitation; and they appointed the day for the feast, which was to be in Erin, since Fear Dubh did not wish to trouble them to go to Alba. He took leave of his host and started for home.

When the day for the feast came, Fin and the chief men of the Fenians of Erin set out for the castle of Fear Dubh.

They went, a glen at a step, a hill at a leap, and thirty-two miles at a running leap, till they came to the grand castle where the feast was to be given.

They went in; everything was ready, seats at the table, and every man's name at his seat in the same order as at Fin's castle. Diarmuid, who was always very sportive—fond of hunting, and paying court to women—was not with them; he had gone to the mountains with his dogs.

All sat down, except Conan Maol MacMorna (never a man spoke well of him); no seat was ready for him, for he used to lie on the flat of his back on the floor, at Fin's castle.

When all were seated the door of the castle closed of itself. Fin then asked the man nearest the door, to rise and open it. The man tried to rise; he pulled this way and that, over and hither, but he couldn't get up. Then the next man tried, and the next, and so on, till the turn came to Fin himself, who tried in vain.

Now, whenever Fin and his men were in trouble and great danger it was their custom to raise a cry of distress (a voice of howling), heard all over Erin. Then all men knew that they were in peril of death; for they never raised this cry except in the last extremity.

Fin's son, Fialan, who was three years old and in the cradle, heard the cry, was roused, and jumped up.

"Get me a sword!" said he to the nurse. "My father and his men are in distress; I must go to aid them."

"What could you do, poor little child?"

Fialan looked around, saw an old rusty sword-blade laid aside for ages. He took it down, gave it a snap; it sprang up so as to hit his arm, and all the rust dropped off; the blade was pure as shining silver.

"This will do," said he; and then he set out toward the place where he heard the cry, going a glen at a step, a hill at a leap, and thirty-two miles at a running leap, till he came to the door of the castle, and cried out.

Fin answered from inside, "Is that you, my child?"

"It is," said Fialan.

"Why did you come?"

"I heard your cry, and how could I stay at home, hearing the cry of my father and the Fenians of Erin!"

"Oh, my child, you cannot help us much."

Fialan struck the door powerfully with his sword, but no use. Then one of the men inside asked Fin to chew his thumb, to know what was keeping them in, and why they were bound.

Fin chewed his thumb, from skin to blood, from blood to bone, from bone to marrow, and discovered that Fear Dubh had built the castle by magic, and that he was coming himself with a great force to cut the head off each one of them. (These men from Alba had always a grudge against the champions of Erin.)

Said Fin to Fialan: "Do you go now, and stand at the ford near the castle, and meet Fear Dubh."

Fialan went and stood in the middle of the ford. He wasn't long there when he saw Fear Dubh coming with a great army.

"Leave the ford, my child," said Fear Dubh, who knew him at once. "I have not come to harm your father. I spent a pleasant year at his castle. I've only come to show him honor."

"I know why you have come," answered Fialan. "You've come to destroy my father and all his men, and I'll not leave this ford while I can hold it."

"Leave the ford; I don't want to harm your father, I want to do him honor. If you don't let us pass my men will kill you," said Fear Dubh.

"I will not let you pass so long as I'm alive before you," said Fialan.

The men faced him; and if they did Fialan kept his place, and a battle commenced, the like of which was never seen before that day.

Fialan went through the army as a hawk through a flock of sparrows on a March morning, till he killed every man except Fear Dubh. Fear Dubh told him again to leave the ford, he didn't want to harm his father.

"Oh!" said Fialan, "I know well what you want."

"If you don't leave that place I'll make you leave it!" said Fear Dubh. Then they closed in combat; and such a combat was never seen before between any two warriors. They made springs to rise through the center of hard gray rocks, cows to cast their calves whether they had them or not. All the horses of the country were racing about and neighing in dread and fear, and all created things were terrified at the sound and clamor of the fight, till the weapons of Fear Dubh went to pieces in the struggle, and Fialan made two halves of his own sword.

Now they closed in wrestling. In the first round Fialan put Fear Dubh to his knees in the hard bottom of the river; the second round he put him to his hips, and the third, to his shoulders.

"Now," said he, "I have you," giving him a stroke of the half of his sword, which cut the head off him.

Then Fialan went to the door of the castle and told his father what he had done.

Fin chewed his thumb again, and knew what other danger was coming. "My son," said he to Fialan, "Fear Dubh has a younger brother more powerful than he was; that brother is coming against us now with greater forces than those which you have destroyed."

As soon as Fialan heard these words he hurried to the ford, and waited till the second army came up. He destroyed this army as he had the other, and closed with the second brother in a fight fiercer and more terrible than the first; but at last he thrust him to his armpits in the hard bottom of the river and cut off his head.

Then he went to the castle, and told his father what he had done. A third time Fin chewed his thumb, and said: "My son, a third army more to be dreaded than the other two is coming now to destroy us, and at the head of it is the youngest brother of Fear Dubh, the most desperate and powerful of the three."

Again Fialan rushed off to the ford; and, though the work was greater than before, he left not a man of the army alive. Then he closed with the youngest brother of Fear Dubh, and if the first and second battles were terrible this was more terrible by far; but at last he planted the youngest brother up to his armpits in the hard bottom of the river, and swept the head off him.

Now, after the heat and struggle of combat Fialan was in such a rage that he lost his mind from fury, not having anyone to fight against; and if the whole world had been there before him he would have gone through it and conquered it all.

But having no one to face him he rushed along the riverbank, tearing the flesh from his own body. Never had such madness been seen in any created being before that day.

Diarmuid came now and knocked at the door of the castle, having the dog Bran with him, and asked Fin what had caused him to raise the cry of distress.

"Oh, Diarmuid," said Fin, "we are all fastened in here to be killed. Fialan has destroyed three armies, and Fear Dubh with his two brothers. He is raging now along the bank of the river; you must not go near him, for he would tear you limb from limb. At this moment he wouldn't spare me, his own father; but after a while he will cease from raging and die down; then you can go. The mother of Fear Dubh is coming, and will soon be at the ford. She is more violent, more venomous, more to be dreaded, a greater warrior than her sons. The chief weapon she has are the nails on her fingers; each nail is seven perches long, of the hardest steel on earth. She is coming in the air at this moment with the speed of a hawk, and she has a small vessel, with liquor in it, which has such power that if she puts three drops of it on the mouths of her sons they will rise up as well as ever; and if she brings them to life there is nothing to save us.

"Go to the ford; she will be hovering over the corpses of the three armies to know can she find her sons, and as soon as she sees them she will dart down and give them the liquor. You must rise with a mighty bound upon her, dash the vessel out of her hand and spill the liquor.

"If you can kill her save her blood, for nothing in the world can free us from this place and open the door of the castle but the blood of the old hag. I'm in dread you'll not succeed, for she is far more terrible than all her sons together. Go now; Fialan is dying away, and the old woman is coming; make no delay."

Diarmuid hurried to the ford, stood watching awhile; then he saw high in the air something no larger than a hawk. As it came nearer and nearer he saw it was the old woman. She hovered high in the air over the ford. At last she saw her sons, and was swooping down, when Diarmuid rose with a bound into the air and struck the vial a league out of her hand.

The old hag gave a shriek that was heard to the eastern world, and screamed: "Who has dared to interfere with me or my sons?"

"I," answered Diarmuid; "and you'll not go further till I do to you what has been done to your sons."

The fight began; and if there ever was a fight, before or since, it could not be more terrible than this one; but great as was the power of Diarmuid he never could have conquered but for Bran the dog.

The old woman with her nails stripped the skin and flesh from Diarmuid almost to the vitals. But Bran tore the skin and flesh off the old woman's back from her head to her heels.

From the dint of blood loss and fighting, Diarmuid was growing faint. Despair came on him, and he was on the point of giving way, when a little robin flew near to him, and sitting on a bush, spoke, saying:

"Oh, Diarmuid, take strength; rise and sweep the head off the old hag, or Fin and the Fenians of Erin are no more."

Diarmuid took courage, and with his last strength made one great effort, swept the head off the old hag and caught her blood in a vessel. He rubbed some on his own wounds—they were cured; then he cured Bran.

Straightaway he took the blood to the castle, rubbed drops of it on the door, which opened, and he went in.

All laughed with joy at the rescue. He freed Fin and his men by rubbing the blood on the chairs; but when he came as far as Conan Maol the blood gave out.

All were going away. "Why should you leave me here after you"; cried Conan Maol, "I would rather die at once than stay here for a lingering death. Why don't you, Oscar, and you, Gol MacMorna, come and tear me out of this place; anyhow you'll be able to drag the arms out of me and kill me at once; better that than leave me to die alone."

Oscar and Gol took each a hand, braced their feet against his feet, put forth all their strength and brought him standing; but if they did, he left all the skin and much of the flesh from the back of his head to his heels on the floor behind him. He was covered with blood, and by all accounts was in a terrible condition, bleeding and wounded.

Now there were sheep grazing near the castle. The Fenians ran out, killed and skinned the largest and best of the flock, and clapped the fresh skin on Conan's back; and such was the healing power in the sheep, and the wound very fresh, that Conan's back healed, and he marched home with the rest of the men, and soon got well; and if he did, they sheared off his back wool enough every year to make a pair of stockings for each one of the Fenians of Erin, and for Fin himself.

And that was a great thing to do and useful, for wool was scarce in Erin in those days. Fin and his men lived pleasantly and joyously for some time; and if they didn't, may we.

64. BLACK, BROWN, AND GRAY
(*Ireland*)

ON A DAY Fin MacCoul was near Tara of the Kings, south of Ballyshannon, hunting with seven companies of the Fenians of Erin.

During the day they saw three strange men coming toward them, and Fin said to the Fenians: "Let none of you speak to them, and if they have good manners they'll not speak to you nor to any man till they come to me."

When the three men came up, they said nothing till they stood before Fin himself. Then he asked what their names were and what they wanted. They answered:

"Our names are Dubh, Dun, and Glasán [Black, Brown, and Gray]. We have come to find Fin MacCoul, chief of the Fenians of Erin, and take service with him."

Fin was so well pleased with their looks that he brought them home with him that evening and called them his sons. Then he said, "Every man who comes to this castle must watch the first night for me, and since three of you have come together, each will watch one third of the night. You'll cast lots to see who'll watch first and second."

Fin had the trunk of a tree brought, three equal parts made of it, and one given to each of the men.

Then he said, "When each of you begins his watch he will set fire to his own piece of wood, and so long as the wood burns he will watch."

The lot fell to Dubh to go on the first watch. Dubh set fire to his log, then went out around the castle, the dog Bran with him. He wandered on, going further and further from the castle, and Bran after him. At last he saw a bright light and went toward it. When he came to the place where the light was burning, he saw a large house. He entered the house and when inside saw a great company of most strange-looking men, drinking out of a single cup.

The chief of the party, who was sitting on a high place, gave the cup to the man nearest him; and when he had drunk his fill out of it, he passed it to his neighbor, and so on to the last.

While the cup was going the round of the company, the chief said, "This is the great cup that was taken from Fin MacCoul a hundred years ago; and as much as each man wishes to drink he always gets from it, and no matter how many men there may be, or what they wish for, they always have their fill."

Dubh sat near the door on the edge of the crowd, and when the cup came to him he drank a little, then slipped out and hurried away in the dark; when he came to the fountain at the castle of Fin MacCoul, his log was burned.

As the second lot had fallen on Dun, it was now his turn to watch, so he set fire to his log and went out, in the place of Dubh, with the dog Bran after him.

Dun walked on through the night till he saw a fire. He went toward it, and when he had come near he saw a large house, which he entered; and when inside he saw a crowd of strange-looking men, fighting. They were ferocious, wonderful to look at, and fighting wildly.

The chief, who had climbed on the crossbeams of the house to escape the uproar and struggle, called out to the crowd below: "Stop fighting now; for I have a better gift than the one you have lost this night." And putting his hand behind his belt, he drew out a knife and held it before them, saying: "Here is the wonderful knife, the small knife of division, that was stolen from Fin MacCoul a hundred years ago, and if you cut on a bone with the knife, you'll get the finest meat in the world, and as much of it as ever your hearts can wish for."

Then he passed down the knife and a bare bone to the man next him, and the man began to cut; and off came slices of the sweetest and best meat in the world.

The knife and the bone passed from man to man till they came to Dun, who cut a slice off the bone, slipped out unseen, and made for Fin's castle as fast as his two legs could carry him through the darkness and over the ground.

When he was by the fountain at the castle, his part of the log was burned and his watch at an end.

Now Glasán set fire to his stick of wood and went out on his watch and walked forward till he saw the light and came to the same house that Dubh and Dun had visited. Looking in he saw the place full of dead bodies, and thought, "There must be some great wonder here. If I lie down in the midst of these and put some of them over me to hide myself, I shall be able to see what is going on."

He lay down and pulled some of the bodies over himself. He wasn't there long when he saw an old hag coming into the house. She had but one leg, one arm, and one upper tooth, which was as long as her leg and served her in place of a crutch.

When inside the door she took up the first corpse she met and threw it aside; it was lean. As she went on she took two bites out of every fat corpse she met, and threw every lean one aside.

She had her fill of flesh and blood before she came to Glasán; and as soon as she had that, she dropped down on the floor, lay on her back, and went to sleep.

Every breath she drew, Glasán was afraid she'd drag the roof down on top of his head, and every time she let a breath out of her he thought she'd sweep the roof off the house.

Then he rose up, looked at her, and wondered at the bulk of her body. At last he drew his sword, hit her a slash, and if he did, three young giants sprang forth.

Glasán killed the first giant, the dog Bran killed the second, and the third ran away.

Glasán now hurried back, and when he reached the fountain at Fin's castle, his log of wood was burned, and day was dawning.

When all had risen in the morning, and the Fenians of Erin came out, Fin said to Dubh, "Have you anything new or wonderful to tell me after the night's watching?"

"I have," said Dubh; "for I brought back the drinking cup that you lost a hundred years ago. I was out in the darkness watching. I walked on, and the dog Bran with me till I saw a light. When I came to the light I found a house, and in the house a company feasting. The chief was a very old man, and sat on a high place above the rest. He took out the cup and said: 'This is the cup that was stolen from Fin MacCoul a hundred years ago, and it is always full of the best drink in the world; and when one of you has drunk from the cup pass it on to the next.'

"They drank and passed the cup till it came to me. I took it and hurried back. When I came here, my log was burned and my watch was finished. Here now is the cup for you," said Dubh to Fin MacCoul.

Fin praised him greatly for what he had done, and turning to Dun said: "Now tell us what happened in your watch."

"When my turn came I set fire to the log which you gave me, and walked on; the dog Bran following, till I saw a light. When I came to the light, I found a house in which was a crowd of people, all fighting except one very old man on a high place above the rest. He called to them for peace, and told them to be quiet. 'For,' said he, 'I have a better gift for you than the one you lost this night,' and he took out the small knife of division with a bare bone, and said: 'This is the knife that was stolen from Fin MacCoul, a hundred years ago, and whenever you cut on the bone with the knife, you'll get your fill of the best meat on earth.'

"Then he handed the knife and the bone to the man nearest him, who cut from it all the meat he wanted, and then passed it to his neighbor. The knife went from hand to hand till it came to me, then I took it, slipped out, and hurried away. When I came to the fountain, my log was burned, and here are the knife and bone for you."

"You have done a great work, and deserve my best praise," said Fin. "We are sure of the best eating and drinking as long as we keep the cup and the knife."

"Now what have you seen in your part of the night?" said Fin to Glasán.

"I went out," said Glasán, "with the dog Bran, and walked on till I saw a light, and when I came to the light I saw a house, which I entered. Inside were heaps of dead men, killed in fighting, and I wondered greatly when I saw them. At last I lay down in the midst of the corpses, put some of them over me and waited to see what would happen.

"Soon an old hag came in at the door, she had but one arm, one leg, and the one tooth out of her upper jaw, and that tooth as long as her leg, and she used it for a crutch as she hobbled along. She threw aside the first corpse she met and took two bites out of the second—for she threw every lean corpse away and took two bites out of every fat one. When she had eaten her fill, she lay down on her back in the middle of the floor and went to sleep. I rose up then to look at her, and every time she drew a breath I was in dread she would bring down the roof of the house on the top of my head, and every time she let a breath out of her, I thought she'd sweep the roof from the building, so strong was the breath of the old hag.

"Then I drew my sword and cut her with a blow, but if I did three young giants sprang up before me. I killed the first, Bran killed the second, but the third escaped. I walked away then, and when I was at the fountain outside, daylight had come and my log was burned."

"Between you and me," said Fin, "it would have been as well if you had let the old hag alone. I am greatly in dread the third young giant will bring trouble on us all."

For twenty-one years Fin MacCoul and the Fenians of Erin hunted for sport alone. They had the best of eating from the small knife of division, and the best of drinking from the cup that was never dry.

At the end of twenty-one years Dubh, Dun, and Glasán went away, and one day, as Fin and the Fenians of Erin were hunting on the hills and mountains, they saw a Fear Ruadh (a red-haired man) coming toward them.

"There is a bright-looking man coming this way," said Fin, "and don't you speak to him."

"Oh, what do we care for him?" asked Conan Maol.

"Don't be rude to a stranger," said Fin.

The Fear Ruadh came forward and spoke to no man till he stood before Fin.

"What have you come for?" asked Fin.

"To find a master for twenty-one years."

"What wages do you ask?" inquired Fin.

"No wages but this—that if I die before the twenty-one years have passed, I shall be buried on Light Island."

"I'll give you those wages," said Fin, and he hired the Fear Ruadh for twenty-one years.

He served Fin for twenty years to his satisfaction; but toward the end of the twenty-first year he fell into a decline, became an old man, and died.

When the Fear Ruadh was dead, the Fenians of Erin said that not a step would they go to bury him; but Fin declared that he wouldn't break his word for any man, and must take the corpse to Light Island.

Fin had an old white horse which he had turned out to find a living for himself as he could on the hillsides and in the woods. And now he looked for the horse and found that he had become younger than older in looks since he had put him out. So he took the old white horse and tied a coffin, with the body of the Fear Ruadh in it, on his back. Then they started him on ahead and away he went followed by Fin and twelve men of the Fenians of Erin.

When they came to the temple on Light Island there were no signs of the white horse and the coffin; but the temple was open and in went Fin and the twelve.

There were seats for each man inside. They sat down and rested awhile and then Fin tried to rise but couldn't. He told the men to rise, but the twelve were fastened to the seats, and the seats to the ground, so that not a man of them could come to his feet.

"Oh," said Fin, "I'm in dread there is some evil trick played on us."

At that moment the Fear Ruadh stood before them in all his former strength and youth and said: "Now is the time for me to take satisfaction out of you for my mother and brothers." Then one of the men said to Fin, "Chew your thumb to know is there any way out of this."

Fin chewed his thumb to know what should he do. When he knew, he blew the great whistle with his two hands; which was heard by Donogh Kamcosa and Diarmuid O'Duivne.

The Fear Ruadh fell to and killed three of the men; but before he could touch the fourth Donogh and Diarmuid were there, and put an end to him. Now all were free, and Fin with the nine men went back to their castle south of Ballyshannon.

65. THE BROWNIE OF BLEDNOCK
(Scotland)

DID YOU EVER HEAR how a Brownie came to our village of Blednock, and was frightened away again by a silly young wife, who thought she was cleverer than anyone else, but who did us the worst turn that she ever did anybody in her life, when she made the queer, funny, useful little man disappear?

Well, it was one November evening, in the gloaming, just when the milking was done, and before the bairns were put to bed, and everyone was standing on their doorsteps, having a crack about the bad harvest, and the turnips, and what chances there were of good prices for the bullocks at the Martinmas Fair, when the queerest humming noise started down by the river.

It came nearer and nearer, and everyone stopped their gossip and began to look down the road. And, deed, it was no wonder that they stared, for there, coming up the middle of the highway, was the strangest, most frightsome-looking creature that human eyes had ever seen.

He looked like a little wee, wee man, and yet he looked like a beast, for he was covered with hair from head to foot, and he wore no clothing except a little kilt of green rushes which hung round his waist. His hair was matted, and his head hung forward on his breast, and he had a long blue beard, which almost touched the ground.

His legs were twisted, and knocked together as he walked, and his arms were so long that his hands trailed in the mud.

He seemed to be humming something over and over again, and, as he came near us we could just make out the words, "Hae ye wark for Aiken-Drum?"

Eh, but I can tell you the folk were scared. If it had been the Evil One himself who had come to our quiet little village, I doubt if he would have caused more stir. The bairns screamed, and hid their faces in their mothers' gown-tails, while the lassies, idle huzzies that they were, threw down the pails of milk, which should have been in the milkhouse long ago, if they had not been so busy gossiping; and the very dogs crept in behind their masters, whining, and hiding their tails between their legs. The grown men, who should have known better, and who were not frightened to look the wee man in the face, laughed and hooted at him.

"Did ye ever see such eyes?" cried one.

"His mouth is so big, he could swallow the moon," said another.

"Hech, sirs, but did ye ever see such a creature?" cried the third.

And still the poor little man went slowly up the street, crying wistfully, "Hae ye wark for Aiken-Drum? Any wark for Aiken-Drum?"

Some of us tried to speak to him, but our tongues seemed to be tied, and the words died away on our lips, and we could only stand and watch him with frightened glances, as if we were bewitched.

Old Granny Duncan, the oldest, and the kindest woman in the village, was the first to come to her senses. "He may be a ghost, or a bogle, or a wraith," she said; "or he may only be a harmless Brownie. It is beyond me to say; but this I know that if he be an evil spirit, he will not dare to look on the Holy Book." And with that she ran into her cottage, and brought out the great leatherbound Bible which aye lay on her little table by the window.

She stood on the road, and held it out, right in front of the creature, but he took no more heed of it than if it had been an old songbook, and went slowly on, with his weary cry for work.

"He's just a Brownie," cried Granny Duncan in triumph, "a simple, kindly Brownie. I've heard tell of such folk before, and many a long day's work will they do for the people who treat them well."

Gathering courage from her words, we all crowded round the wee man, and now that we were close to him, we saw that his hairy face was kind and gentle and his tiny eyes had a merry twinkle in them.

"Save us, and help us, creature!" said an old man reprovingly, "but can ye no speak, and tell us what ye want, and where ye come from?"

For answer the Brownie looked all round him, and gave such a groan, that we scattered and ran in all directions, and it was full five minutes before we could pluck up our courage and go close to him again.

But Granny Duncan stood her ground, like a brave old woman that she was, and it was to her that the creature spoke.

"I cannot tell thee from whence I come," he said.

"'Tis a nameless land, and 'tis very different from this land of thine. For there we all learn to serve, while here everyone wishes to be served. And when there is no work for us to do at home, then we sometimes set out to visit thy land, to see if there is any work which we may do there. I must seem strange to human eyes, that I know; but if thou wilt, I will stay in this place awhile. I need not that any should wait on me, for I seek neither wages, nor clothes, nor bedding. All I ask for is the corner of a barn to sleep in, and a cogful of brose set down on the floor at bedtime; and if no one meddles with me, I will be ready to help anyone who needs me. I'll gather your sheep betimes on the hill; I'll take in your harvest by moonlight. I'll sing the bairns to sleep in their cradles, and, though I doubt you'll not believe it, you'll find that the babes will love me. I'll kirn your kirns for you, goodwives, and I'll bake your bread on a busy day; while, as for the men folk, they may find me useful when there is corn to thrash, or untamed colts in the stable, or when the waters are out in flood."

No one quite knew what to say to answer to the creature's strange request. It was an unheard-of-thing for anyone to come and offer their services for nothing, and the men began to whisper among themselves, and to say that it was not canny, and 'twere better to have nothing to do with him.

But up spoke Old Granny Duncan again. "'Tis but a Brownie, I tell you," she repeated, "a poor, harmless Brownie, and many a story have I heard in my young days about the work that a Brownie can do, if he be well treated and let alone. Have we not been complaining all summer about bad times, and scant wages, and a lack of workmen to work the work? And now, when a workman comes ready to your hand, ye will have none of him, just because he is not bonnie to look on."

Still the men hesitated, and the silly young wenches screwed their faces, and pulled their mouths. "But, Granny," cried they, "that is all very well, but if we keep such a creature in our village, no one will come near it, and then what shall we do for sweethearts?"

"Shame on ye," cried Granny impatiently, "and on all you men for encouraging the silly things in their whimsies. It's time that ye were thinking o' other things than bonnie faces and sweethearts. 'Handsome is that handsome does,' is a good old saying; and what about the corn that stands rotting in the fields, an' it past Hallowe'en already? I've heard that a Brownie can stack a whole ten-acre field in a single night."

That settled the matter. The miller offered the creature the corner of his barn to sleep in, and Granny promised to boil the cogful of brose, and send her grandchild, wee Jeannie, down with it every evening, and then we all said good night, and went into our houses, looking over our shoulders as we did so, for fear that the strange little man was following us.

But if we were afraid of him that night, we had a very different song to sing before a week was over. Whatever he was, or whatever he came from, he was the most wonderful worker that men had ever known. And the strange thing was that he did most of it at night. He had the corn safe into the stackyards and the stacks thatched, in the clap of a hand, as the old folk say.

The village became the talk of the countryside, and folk came from all parts to see if they could catch a glimpse of our queer, hairy little visitor; but they were always unsuccessful, for he was never to be seen when one looked for him. One might go into the miller's barn twenty times a day, and twenty times a day find nothing but a heap of straw; and although the cog of brose was aye empty in the morning, no one knew when he came home, or when he supped it.

But wherever there was work to be done, whether it was a sickly bairn to be sung to, or a house to be tidied up; a kirn that would not kirn, or a batch of bread that would not rise; a flock of sheep to be gathered together on a stormy night, or a bundle to be carried home by some weary laborer; Aiken-Drum, as we learned to call him, always got to know of it, and appeared in the nick of time. It looked as if we had all got wishing-caps, for we had just to wish, and the work was done.

Many a time, some poor mother, who had been up with a crying babe all night, would sit down with it in her lap, in front of the fire, in the morning, and fall fast asleep, and when she awoke, she would find that Aiken-Drum had paid her a visit, for the floor would be washed, and the dishes too, and the fire made up, and the kettle put on to boil; but the little man would have slipped away, as if he were frightened of being thanked.

The bairns were the only ones who ever saw him idle, and oh, how they loved him! In the gloaming, or when the school was out, one could see them away down in some corner by the burn-side, crowding round the little dark brown figure, with its kilt of rushes, and one would hear the sound of wondrous low sweet singing, for he knew all the songs that the little ones loved.

So by and by the name of Aiken-Drum came to be a household word among us, and although we so seldom saw him near at hand, we loved him like one of our ain folk.

And he might have been here still, had it not been for a silly, senseless young wife who thought she knew better than everyone else, and who took some idle notion into her empty head that it was not right to make the little man work, and give him no wage.

She dinned this into our heads, morning, noon, and night, and she would not believe us when we told her that Aiken-Drum worked for love, and love only.

Poor thing, she could not understand anyone doing that, so she made up her mind that she, at least, would do what was right, and set us all an example.

"She did not mean any harm," she said afterward, when the miller took her to task for it; but although she might not mean to do any harm, she did plenty, as senseless folk are apt to do when they cannot bear to take other people's advice, for she took a pair of her husband's old, moldy, worn-out breeches, and laid them down one night beside the cogful of brose.

By my faith, if the village folk had not remembered so well what Aiken-Drum had said about wanting no wages, they would have found something better to give him than a pair of worn-out breeks.

Be that as it may, the long and the short of it was, that the dear wee man's feelings were hurt because we would not take his services for nothing, and he vanished in the night, as Brownies are apt to do, so Granny Duncan says, if anyone tries to pay them, and we have never seen him from that day to this, although the bairns declare that they sometimes hear him singing down by the mill, as they pass it in the gloaming, on their way home from school.

66. THE MIDWIFE
(*Scotland*)

THERE WAS ONCE an old midwife fetched by two little men. They took her to a house she did not know, and as they were coming in at the door, they both dipped their hands in a bowl of water, so she did the same. After that she did her work, and a baby boy was born. Then one of the men said, "Just bake us some bannocks before you go. There'll be just enough to do us in the jar there, but mind and put the scrapings of oatmeal from the board back into the jar." Then they went out, and the old wife started baking the bannocks, putting the spare meal back into the jar. But the jar was never emptied. She went on baking and baking, but it was half full, just as it was at the start. Then the woman on the bed said to her:

"You'll never be done if you put the spare meal back. Fling it on the fire."

She did that, and she came to the end of the oatmeal at once. The woman said:

"They'd have had you baking forever, if you hadn't heeded me." So the men came back, and took her home. Some while later she saw one of the little men, and asked him how the baby was. "Do you see me?" he said. "With which eye?"

"With the both." "Did you wash your eyes with our water?" "I just did as you did," said the old wife. "Well, we'll soon cure that," he said, and he blew on her eyes, and she never saw the fairies again.

67. THE WEE, WEE MANNIE

(*Scotland*)

ONCE UPON A TIME, when all big folks were wee ones and all lies were true, there was a wee, wee Mannie that had a big, big Coo.* And out he went to milk her of a morning, and said—

> "Hold still, my Coo, my hinny,
> Hold still, my hinny, my Coo,
> And ye shall have for your dinner
> What but a milk white doo."

But the big, big Coo wouldn't hold still. "Hout!" said the wee, wee Mannie—

> "Hold still, my Coo, my dearie,
> And fill my bucket wi' milk,
> And if ye'll be no contrairy
> I'll gi'e ye a gown o' silk."

But the big, big Coo wouldn't hold still. "Look at that, now!" said the wee, wee Mannie—

> "What's a wee, wee mannie to do,
> Wi' such a big contrairy Coo?"

So off he went to his mother at the house. "Mother," said he, "Coo won't stand still, and wee, wee Mannie can't milk big, big Coo."
"Hout!" says his mother, "take stick and beat Coo."
So off he went to get a stick from the tree, and said—

> "Break, stick, break,
> And I'll gi'e ye a cake."

But the stick wouldn't break, so back he went to the house.

---

* Cow.

"Mother," says he, "Coo won't hold still, stick won't break, wee, wee Mannie can't beat big, big Coo."

"Hout!" says his mother, "go to the Butcher and bid him kill Coo." So off he went to the Butcher, and said—

> "Butcher, kill the big, big Coo,
> She'll gi'e us no more milk noo."

But the Butcher wouldn't kill the Coo without a silver penny, so back the Mannie went to the house. "Mother," says he, "Coo won't hold still, stick won't break, Butcher won't kill without a silver penny, and wee, wee Mannie can't milk big, big Coo."

"Well," said his mother, "go to the Coo and tell her there's a weary, weary lady with long yellow hair weeping for a cup o' milk."

So off he went and told the Coo, but she wouldn't hold still, so back he went and told his mother.

"Well," said she, "tell the Coo there's a fine, fine laddie from the wars sitting by the weary, weary lady with golden hair, and she weeping for a sup o' milk."

So off he went and told the Coo, but she wouldn't hold still, so back he went and told his mother.

"Well," said his mother, "tell the big, big Coo there's a sharp, sharp sword at the belt of the fine, fine laddie from the wars who sits beside the weary, weary lady with the golden hair, and she weeping for a sup o' milk."

And he told the big, big Coo, but she wouldn't hold still.

Then said his mother, "Run quick and tell her that her head's going to be cut off by the sharp, sharp sword in the hands of the fine, fine laddie, if she doesn't give the sup o' milk the weary, weary lady weeps for."

And wee, wee Mannie went off and told the big, big Coo.

And when Coo saw the glint of the sharp, sharp sword in the hand of the fine, fine laddie come from the wars, and the weary, weary lady weeping for a sup o' milk, she reckoned she'd better hold still; so wee, wee Mannie milked big, big Coo, and the weary, weary lady with the golden hair hushed her weeping and got her sup o' milk, and the fine, fine laddie new come from the wars put by his sharp, sharp sword, and all went well that didn't go ill.

68. THE COW ON THE ROOF
(Wales)

SIÔN DAFYDD ALWAYS GRUMBLED that his wife could do nothing properly in the house. Neither a meal nor anything else ever pleased him. At last his wife got tired of his grumbling and one day told him she would go to weed turnips and that he should stay to take care of the baby and the house, to make dinner, and some other things which she used to do. Siôn readily agreed, so that she might have an example.

In setting out to the field, the wife said: "Now, you take care of the baby, feed the hens, feed the pig, turn out the cow to graze, sweep the floor, and make the porridge ready for dinner."

"Don't you bother about all that," said Siôn, "you see to the turnips."

The wife went to the field, Siôn to the house. The baby awoke. For a long time, Siôn rocked the cradle and tried to sing to the child, which seemed to make the poor thing worse. Siôn then remembered the pig, which was squealing very loudly. He went to get some buttermilk to make food for it but spilled it on the kitchen floor. The pig heard the sound of the bucket and made so much noise that Siôn could not stand it.

"You wait a bit, you rascal!" he said to himself, but he meant the pig, "you shall go out to find food for yourself!"

So he opened the door to turn out the pig. Out went the pig like a shot, right between Siôn's legs, throwing him into the dunghill. By the time he got up and tried to scrape a little of the dirt off his clothes, the pig was out of sight. Siôn went into the house. There the pig had gone to lap up the buttermilk from the floor, and had, besides, overthrown another pot of buttermilk and was busy with that.

"You rascal!" shouted Siôn, and catching hold of an ax he struck the pig a blow on the head. The poor pig wobbled like a drunken man, then fell by the door and departed this life.

By this time it was getting late, and Siôn thought of the porridge, but the cow had to be turned out to graze, and he had quite forgotten the hens, poor souls. The field where the cow had to gather its daily bread, as it were, was some distance from the yard, and if Siôn went to take it there, the porridge would never be ready in time. At that moment Siôn happened to remember that there was some fine grass growing on the roof of the house. There was a rise at the back of the house, and the roof reached almost to the ground. Siôn thought the grass on the roof would be a good meal for a cow, and in order to be able to make the porridge as well he took a rope, tied one end round the cow's neck, ran up the roof, and dropped the other end of the rope down the chimney. Then he went to the porridge. So that he might have his two hands free, he tied the end of the rope round his ankle. In grazing on the roof the cow, without thinking, as it were, came to the top and slipped over suddenly. Siôn felt himself being pulled up by the leg, and into the chimney he went, feet first. Somehow, his legs went one on each side of the iron bar from which the kettle was hung over the fire, and there he stuck.

Just at that moment, the wife came back from the turnip field, and was horrified to see the cow dangling in the air. She ran to the door and fell across the dead pig, and without seeing anything else picked up the ax and ran to cut the rope and save the poor cow. Then she ran into the house and the first thing she saw there was Siôn, standing on his head in the porridge.

Scandinavia
and Northern Europe

East of the Sun and West of the Moon

69. EAST OF THE SUN AND WEST OF THE MOON

(Norway)

ONCE ON A TIME there was a poor husbandman who had so many children that he hadn't much of either food or clothing to give them. Pretty children they all were, but the prettiest was the youngest daughter, who was so lovely there was no end to her loveliness.

So one day, 'twas on a Thursday evening late at the fall of the year, the weather was so wild and rough outside, and it was so cruelly dark, and rain fell and wind blew, till the walls of the cottage shook again. There they all sat round the fire busy with this thing and that. But just then, all at once something gave three taps on the windowpane. Then the father went out to see what was the matter; and, when he got out of doors, what should he see but a great big White Bear.

"Good evening to you," said the White Bear.

"The same to you," said the man.

"Will you give me your youngest daughter? If you will, I'll make you as rich as you are now poor," said the Bear.

Well, the man would not be at all sorry to be so rich; but still he thought he must have a bit of a talk with his daughter first; so he went in and told them how there was a great White Bear waiting outside, who had given his word to make them so rich if he could only have the youngest daughter.

The lassie said "No!" outright. Nothing could get her to say anything else; so the man went out and settled it with the White Bear, that he should come again the next Thursday evening and get an answer. Meantime he talked his daughter over, and kept on telling her of all the riches they would get, and how well off she would be herself; and so at last she thought better of it, and washed and mended her rags, made herself as smart as she could, and was ready to start. I can't say her packing gave her much trouble.

Next Thursday evening came the White Bear to fetch her, and she got upon his back with her bundle, and off they went. So, when they had gone a bit of the way, the White Bear said—

"Are you afraid?"

"No!" she wasn't.

"Well! mind and hold tight by my shaggy coat, and then there's nothing to fear," said the Bear.

So she rode a long, long way, till they came to a great steep hill. There, on the face of it, the White Bear gave a knock, and a door opened, and they came into a castle, where there were many rooms all lit up; rooms gleaming with silver and gold; and there too was a table ready laid, and it was all as grand as grand could be. Then the White Bear gave her a silver bell; and when she wanted anything, she was only to ring it, and she would get it at once.

Well, after she had eaten and drunk, and evening wore on, she got sleepy after her journey, and thought she would like to go to bed, so she rang the bell; and she had scarce taken hold of it before she came into a chamber, where there was a bed made, as fair and white as anyone would wish to sleep in, with silken pillows and curtains, and gold fringe. All that was in the room was gold or silver; but when she had gone to bed, and put out the light, a man came and laid himself alongside her. That was the White Bear, who threw off his beast shape at night; but she never saw him, for he always came after she had put out the light, and before the day dawned he was up and off again. So things went on happily for a while, but at last she began to get silent and sorrowful; for there she went about all day alone, and she longed to go home to see her father and mother, and brothers and sisters. So one day, when the White Bear asked what it was that she lacked, she said it was so dull and lonely there, and how she longed to go home to see her father and mother, and brothers and sisters, and that was why she was so sad and sorrowful, because she couldn't get to them.

"Well, well!" said the Bear, "perhaps there's a cure for all this; but you must promise me one thing, not to talk alone with your mother, but only when the rest are by to hear; for she'll take you by the hand and try to lead you into a room alone to talk; but you must mind and not do that, else you'll bring bad luck on both of us."

So one Sunday the White Bear came and said now they could set off to see her father and mother. Well, off they started, she sitting on his back; and they went far and long. At last they came to a grand house, and there her brothers and sisters were running about out of doors at play, and everything was so pretty, 'twas a joy to see.

"This is where your father and mother live now," said the White Bear; "but don't forget what I told you, else you'll make us both unlucky."

"No! bless her, she'd not forget"; and when she had reached the house, the White Bear turned right about and left her.

Then when she went in to see her father and mother, there was such joy, there was no end to it. None of them thought they could thank her enough for all she had done for them. Now, they had everything they wished, as good as good could be, and they all wanted to know how she got on where she lived.

Well, she said, it was very good to live where she did; she had all she wished. What she said beside I don't know; but I don't think any of them had the right end of the stick, or that they got much out of her. But so in the afternoon, after they had done dinner, all happened as the White Bear had said. Her mother wanted to talk with her alone in her bedroom; but she minded what the White Bear had said, and wouldn't go upstairs.

"Oh, what we have to talk about will keep," she said, and put her mother off. But somehow or other, her mother got round her at last, and she had to tell her the whole story. So she said, how every night, when she had gone to bed, a man came and lay down beside her as soon as she had put out the light, and how she never saw him, because he was always up and away before the morning dawned; and how she went about woeful and sorrowing, for she thought she should so like to see him, and how all day long she walked about there alone, and how dull, and dreary, and lonesome it was.

"My!" said her mother; "it may well be a Troll you slept with! But now I'll teach you a lesson how to set eyes on him. I'll give you a bit of candle, which you can carry home in your bosom; just light that while he is asleep, but take care not to drop the tallow on him."

Yes! she took the candle, and hid it in her bosom, and as night drew on, the White Bear came and fetched her away.

But when they had gone a bit of the way, the White Bear asked if all hadn't happened as he had said.

"Well, she couldn't say it hadn't."

"Now, mind," said he, "if you have listened to your mother's advice, you have brought bad luck on us both, and then, all that has passed between us will be as nothing."

"No," she said, "she hadn't listened to her mother's advice."

So when she reached home, and had gone to bed, it was the old story over again. There came a man and lay down beside her; but at dead of night, when she heard he slept, she got up and struck a light, lit the candle, and let the light shine on him, and so she saw that he was the loveliest Prince one ever set eyes on, and she fell so deep in love with him on the spot, that she thought she couldn't live if she didn't give him a kiss there and then. And so she did, but as she kissed him, she dropped three hot drops of tallow on his shirt, and he woke up.

"What have you done?" he cried; "now you have made us both unlucky, for had you held out only this one year, I had been freed. For I have a stepmother who has bewitched me, so that I am a White Bear by day, and a Man by night. But now all ties are snapped between us; now I must set off from you to her. She lives in a castle which stands EAST OF THE SUN AND WEST OF THE MOON, and there, too, is a Princess, with a nose three ells long, and she's the wife I must have now."

She wept and took it ill, but there was no help for it; go he must.

Then she asked if she mightn't go with him.

No, she mightn't.

"Tell me the way, then," she said, "and I'll search you out; *that* surely I may get leave to do."

"Yes, she might do that," he said; "but there was no way to that place. It lay EAST OF THE SUN AND WEST OF THE MOON, and thither she'd never find her way."

So next morning, when she woke up, both Prince and castle were gone, and then she lay on a little green patch, in the midst of the gloomy thick wood, and by her side lay the same bundle of rags she had brought with her from her old home.

So when she had rubbed the sleep out of her eyes, and wept till she was tired, she set out on her way, and walked many, many days, till she came to a lofty crag. Under it sat an old hag, and played with a gold apple which she tossed about. Her the lassie asked if she knew the way to the Prince, who lived with his stepmother in the castle that lay EAST OF THE SUN AND WEST OF THE MOON, and who was to marry the Princess with a nose three ells long.

"How did you come to know about him?" asked the old hag; "but maybe you are the lassie who ought to have had him?"

Yes, she was.

"So, so; it's you, is it?" said the old hag. "Well, all I know about him is, that he lives in the castle that lies EAST OF THE SUN AND WEST OF THE MOON, and thither you'll come, late or never; but still you may have the loan of my horse, and on him you can ride to my next neighbor.

Maybe she'll be able to tell you; and when you get there, just give the horse a switch under the left ear, and beg him to be off home; and, stay, this gold apple you may take with you."

So she got upon the horse, and rode a long long time, till she came to another crag, under which sat another old hag, with a gold carding comb. Her the lassie asked if she knew the way to the castle that lay EAST OF THE SUN AND WEST OF THE MOON, and she answered, like the first old hag, that she knew nothing about it, except it was east of the sun and west of the moon.

"And thither you'll come, late or never; but you shall have the loan of my horse to my next neighbor; maybe she'll tell you all about it; and when you get there, just switch the horse under the left ear, and beg him to be off home."

And this old hag gave her the golden carding comb; it might be she'd find some use for it, she said. So the lassie got up on the horse, and rode a far far way, and a weary time; and so at last she came to another great crag, under which sat another old hag, spinning with a golden spinning wheel. Her, too, she asked if she knew the way to the Prince, and where the castle was that lay EAST OF THE SUN AND WEST OF THE MOON. So it was the same thing over again.

"Maybe it's you who ought to have had the Prince?" said the old hag.

Yes, it was.

But she, too, didn't know the way a bit better than the other two. "East of the sun and west of the moon it was," she knew—that was all.

"And thither you'll come, late or never; but I'll lend you my horse, and then I think you'd best ride to the East Wind and ask him; maybe he knows those parts, and can blow you thither. But when you get to him, you need only give the horse a switch under the left ear, and he'll trot home of himself."

And so, too, she gave her the gold spinning wheel. "Maybe you'll find a use for it," said the old hag.

Then on she rode many many days, a weary time, before she got to the East Wind's house, but at last she did reach it, and then she asked the East Wind if he could tell her the way to the Prince who dwelt east of the sun and west of the moon. Yes, the East Wind had often heard tell of it, the Prince and the castle, but he couldn't tell the way, for he had never blown so far.

"But, if you will, I'll go with you to my brother the West Wind, maybe he knows, for he's much stronger. So, if you will just get on my back, I'll carry you thither."

Yes, she got on his back, and I should just think they went briskly along.

So when they got there, they went into the West Wind's house, and the East Wind said the lassie he had brought was the one who ought to have had the Prince who lived in the castle EAST OF THE SUN AND WEST OF THE MOON; and so she had set out to seek him, and how he had come with her, and would be glad to know if the West Wind knew how to get to the castle.

"Nay," said the West Wind, "so far I've never blown; but if you will, I'll go with you to our brother the South Wind, for he's much stronger than either of us, and he has flapped his wings far and wide. Maybe he'll tell you. You can get on my back, and I'll carry you to him."

Yes! she got on his back, and so they traveled to the South Wind, and weren't so very long on the way, I should think.

When they got there, the West Wind asked him if he could tell her the way to the castle that lay EAST OF THE SUN AND WEST OF THE MOON, for it was she who ought to have had the Prince who lived there.

"You don't say so! That's she, is it?" said the South Wind.

"Well, I have blustered about in most places in my time, but so far have I never blown; but if you will, I'll take you to my brother the North Wind; he is the oldest and strongest of the whole lot of us, and if he don't know where it is, you'll never find anyone in the world to tell you. You can get on my back, and I'll carry you thither."

Yes! she got on his back, and away he went from his house at a fine rate. And this time, too, she wasn't long on her way.

So when they got to the North Wind's house, he was so wild and cross, cold puffs came from him a long way off.

"BLAST YOU BOTH, WHAT DO YOU WANT?" he roared out to them ever so far off, so that it struck them with an icy shiver.

"Well," said the South Wind, "you needn't be so foulmouthed, for here I am, your brother, the South Wind, and here is the lassie who ought to have had the Prince who dwells in the castle that lies EAST OF THE SUN AND WEST OF THE MOON, and now she wants to ask you if you ever were there, and can tell her the way, for she would be so glad to find him again."

"YES, I KNOW WELL ENOUGH WHERE IT IS," said the North Wind; "once in my life I blew an aspen leaf thither, but I was so tired I couldn't blow a puff for ever so many days after. But if you really wish to go thither, and aren't afraid to come along with me, I'll take you on my back and see if I can blow you thither."

Yes! with all her heart; she must and would get thither if it were possible in any way; and as for fear, however madly he went, she wouldn't be at all afraid.

"Very well, then," said the North Wind, "but you must sleep here tonight, for we must have the whole day before us, if we're to get thither at all."

Early next morning the North Wind woke her, and puffed himself up, and blew himself out, and made himself so stout and big, 'twas gruesome to look at him; and so off they went high up through the air, as if they would never stop till they got to the world's end.

Down here below there was such a storm; it threw down long tracts of wood and many houses, and when it swept over the great sea, ships foundered by hundreds.

So they tore on and on—no one can believe how far they went—and all the while they still went over the sea, and the North Wind got more and more weary, and so out of breath he could scarce bring out a puff, and his wings drooped and drooped, till at last he sunk so low that the crests of the waves dashed over his heels.

"Are you afraid?" said the North Wind.

"No!" she wasn't.

But they weren't very far from land; and the North Wind had still so much strength left in him that he managed to throw her up on the shore under the windows of the castle which lay EAST OF THE SUN AND WEST OF THE MOON; but then he was so weak and worn out, he had to stay there and rest many days before he could get home again.

Next morning the lassie sat down under the castle window, and began to play with the gold apple; and the first person she saw was the Long-nose who was to have the Prince.

"What do you want for your gold apple, you lassie?" said the Long-nose, and threw up the window.

"It's not for sale, for gold or money," said the lassie.

"If it's not for sale for gold or money, what is it that you will sell it for? You may name your own price," said the Princess.

"Well! if I may get to the Prince, who lives here, and be with him tonight, you shall have it," said the lassie whom the North Wind had brought.

Yes! she might; that could be done. So the Princess got the gold apple; but when the lassie came up to the Prince's bedroom at night he was fast asleep; she called him and shook him, and between whiles she wept sore; but all she could do she couldn't wake him up. Next morning as soon as day broke, came the Princess with the long nose, and drove her out again.

So in the daytime she sat down under the castle windows and began to card with her golden carding comb, and the same thing happened. The Princess asked what she wanted for it; and she said it wasn't for sale for gold or money, but if she might get leave to go up to the Prince and be with him that night, the Princess should have it. But when she went up she found him fast asleep again, and all she called, and all she shook, and wept, and prayed, she couldn't get life into him; and as soon as the first gray peep of day came, then came the Princess with the long nose, and chased her out again.

So in the daytime the lassie sat down outside under the castle window, and began to spin with her golden spinning wheel, and that, too, the Princess with the long nose wanted to have. So she threw up the window and asked what she wanted for it. The lassie said, as she had said twice before, it wasn't for sale for gold or money; but if she might go up to the Prince who was there, and be with him alone that night, she might have it.

Yes! she might do that and welcome. But now you must know there were some Christian folk who had been carried off thither, and as they sat in their room, which was next the Prince, they had heard how a woman had been in there, and wept and prayed, and called to him two nights running, and they told that to the Prince.

That evening, when the Princess came with her sleepy drink, the Prince made as if he drank, but threw it over his shoulder, for he could guess it was a sleepy drink. So, when the lassie came in, she found the Prince wide awake; and then she told him the whole story how she had come thither.

"Ah," said the Prince, "you've just come in the very nick of time, for tomorrow is to be our wedding day; but now I won't have the Long-nose, and you are the only woman in the world who can set me free. I'll say I want to see what my wife is fit for, and beg her to wash the shirt which has the three spots of tallow on it; she'll say yes, for she doesn't know 'tis you who put them there; but that's a work only for Christian folk, and not for such a pack of Trolls, and so I'll say that I won't have any other for my bride than the woman who can wash them out, and ask you to do it."

So there was great joy and love between them all that night. But next day, when the wedding was to be, the Prince said—

"First of all, I'd like to see what my bride is fit for."

"Yes!" said the stepmother, with all her heart.

"Well," said the Prince, "I've got a fine shirt which I'd like for my wedding shirt, but somehow or other it has got three spots of tallow on it, which I must have washed out; and I have sworn never to take any other bride than the woman who's able to do that. If she can't, she's not worth having."

Well, that was no great thing they said, so they agreed, and she with the long nose began to wash away as hard as she could, but the more she rubbed and scrubbed, the bigger the spots grew.

"Ah!" said the old hag, her mother, "you can't wash; let me try."

But she hadn't long taken the shirt in hand, before it got far worse than ever, and with all her rubbing, and wringing, and scrubbing, the spots grew bigger and blacker, and the darker and uglier was the shirt.

Then all the other Trolls began to wash, but the longer it lasted, the blacker and uglier the shirt grew, till at last it was as black all over as if it had been up the chimney.

"Ah!" said the Prince, "you're none of you worth a straw: you can't wash. Why there, outside, sits a beggar lassie, I'll be bound she knows how to wash better than the whole lot of you. COME IN, LASSIE!" he shouted.

Well, in she came.

"Can you wash this shirt clean, lassie, you?" said he.

"I don't know," she said, "but I think I can."

And almost before she had taken it and dipped it in the water, it was as white as driven snow, and whiter still.

"Yes; you are the lassie for me," said the Prince.

At that the old hag flew into such a rage, she burst on the spot, and the Princess with the long nose after her, and the whole pack of Trolls after her—at least I've never heard a word about them since.

As for the Prince and Princess, they set free all the poor Christian folk who had been carried off and shut up there; and they took with them all the silver and gold, and flitted away as far as they could from the castle that lay EAST OF THE SUN AND WEST OF THE MOON.

70. BOOTS AND THE TROLL
(*Norway*)

ONCE ON A TIME there was a poor man who had three sons. When he died, the two elder set off into the world to try their luck, but the youngest they wouldn't have with them at any price.

"As for you," they said, "you're fit for nothing but to sit and poke about in the ashes."

So the two went off and got places at a palace—the one under the coachman, and the other under the gardener. But Boots, he set off too, and took with him a great kneading trough, which was the only thing his parents left behind them, but which the other two would not bother themselves with. It was heavy to carry, but he did not like to leave it behind, and so, after he had trudged a bit, he too came to the palace, and asked for a place. So they told him they did not want him, but he begged so prettily that at last he got leave to be in the kitchen, and carry in wood and water for the kitchen maid. He was quick and ready, and in a little while everyone liked him; but the two others were dull, and so they got more kicks than halfpence, and grew quite envious of Boots, when they saw how much better he got on.

Just opposite the palace, across a lake, lived a Troll, who had seven silver ducks which swam on the lake, so that they could be seen from the palace. These the king had often longed for; and so the two elder brothers told the coachman—

"If our brother only chose, he has said he could easily get the king those seven silver ducks."

You may fancy it wasn't long before the coachman told this to the king; and the king called Boots before him, and said—

"Your brothers say you can get me the silver ducks; so now go and fetch them."

"I'm sure I never thought or said anything of the kind," said the lad.

"You did say so, and you shall fetch them," said the king, who would hold his own.

"Well, well," said the lad; "needs must, I suppose; but give me a bushel of rye and a bushel of wheat, and I'll try what I can do."

So he got the rye and the wheat, and put them into the kneading trough he had brought with him from home, got in, and rowed across the lake. When he reached the other side he began to walk along the shore, and to sprinkle and strew the grain, and at last he coaxed the ducks into his kneading trough, and rowed back as fast as ever he could.

When he got half over, the Troll came out of his house and set eyes on him.

"HALLOA!" roared out the Troll; "is it you that has gone off with my seven silver ducks?"

"AY! AY!" said the lad.

"Shall you be back soon?" asked the Troll.

"Very likely," said the lad.

So when he got back to the king, with the seven silver ducks, he was more liked than ever, and even the king was pleased to say, "Well done!" But at this his brothers grew more and more spiteful and envious; and so they went and told the coachman that their brother had said if he chose, he was man enough to get the king the Troll's bed quilt, which had a gold patch and a silver patch, and a silver patch and a gold patch; and this time, too, the coachman was not slow in telling all this to the king. So the king said to the lad, how his brothers had said he was good to steal the Troll's bed quilt, with gold and silver patches; so now he must go and do it, or lose his life.

Boots answered, he had never thought or said any such thing; but when he found there was no help for it, he begged for three days to think over the matter.

So when the three days were gone, he rowed over in his kneading trough, and went spying about. At last, he saw those in the Troll's cave come out and hang the quilt out to air, and as soon as ever they had gone back into the face of the rock, Boots pulled the quilt down, and rowed away with it as fast as he could.

And when he was half across, out came the Troll and set eyes on him, and roared out—

"HALLOA! It is you who took my seven silver ducks?"

"AY! AY!" said the lad.

"And now, have you taken my bed quilt, with silver patches and gold patches, and gold patches and silver patches?"

"Ay! ay!" said the lad.

"Shall you come back again?"

"Very likely," said the lad.

But when he got back with the gold and silver patchwork quilt everyone was fonder of him than ever, and he was made the king's body-servant.

At this the other two were still more vexed, and to be revenged, they went and told the coachman—

"Now, our brother has said he is man enough to get the king the gold harp which the Troll has, and that harp is of such a kind that all who listen when it is played grow glad, however sad they may be."

Yes; the coachman went and told the king, and he said to the lad—

"If you have said this you shall do it. If you do it you shall have the Princess and half the kingdom. If you don't, you shall lose your life."

"I'm sure I never thought or said anything of the kind," said the lad; "but if there's no help for it, I may as well try; but I must have six days to think about it."

Yes, he might have six days, but when they were over he must set out.

Then he took a tenpenny nail, a birch pin, and a waxen taper end in his pocket, and rowed across, and walked up and down before the Troll's cave, looking stealthily about him. So when the Troll came out he saw him at once.

"HO, HO!" roared the Troll; "is it you who took my seven silver ducks?"

"Ay! AY!" said the lad.

"And it is you who took my bed quilt, with the gold and silver patches?" asked the Troll.

"Ay! ay!" said the lad.

So the Troll caught hold of him at once, and took him off into the cave in the face of the rock.

"Now, daughter dear," said the Troll, "I've caught the fellow who stole the silver ducks and my bed quilt with gold and silver patches; put him into the fattening coop, and when he's fat we'll kill him, and make a feast for our friends."

She was willing enough, and put him at once into the fattening coop, and there he stayed eight days, fed on the best, both in meat and drink, and as much as he could cram. So, when the eight days were over, the Troll said to his daughter to go down and cut him in his little finger, that they might see if he were fat. Down she came to the coop.

"Out with your little finger!" she said.

But Boots stuck out his tenpenny nail, and she cut at it.

"Nay, nay! he's as hard as iron still," said the Troll's daughter, when she got back to her father; "we can't take him yet."

After another eight days the same thing happened, and this time Boots stuck out his birch pin.

"Well, he's a little better," she said, when she got back to the Troll; "but still he'll be as hard as wood to chew."

But when another eight days were gone, the Troll told his daughter to go down and see if he wasn't fat now.

"Out with your little finger," said the Troll's daughter, when she reached the coop, and this time Boots stuck out the taper end.

"Now he'll do nicely," she said.

"Will he?" said the Troll. "Well, then, I'll just set off and ask the guests; meantime you must kill him, and roast half and boil half."

So when the Troll had been gone a little while, the daughter began to sharpen a great long knife.

"Is that what you're going to kill me with?" asked the lad.

"Yes, it is," said she.

"But it isn't sharp," said the lad. "Just let me sharpen it for you, and then you'll find it easier work to kill me."

So she let him have the knife, and he began to rub and sharpen it on the whetstone.

"Just let me try it on one of your hair plaits; I think it's about right now."

So he got leave to do that; but at the same time that he grasped the plait of hair he pulled back her head, and at one gash cut off the Troll's daughter's head; and half of her he roasted and half of her he boiled, and served it all up.

After that he dressed himself in her clothes, and sat away in the corner.

So when the Troll came home with his guests, he called out to his daughter—for he thought all the time it was his daughter—to come and take a snack.

"No, thank you," said the lad, "I don't care for food, I'm so sad and downcast."

"Oh!" said the Troll, "if that's all, you know the cure; take the harp, and play a tune on it."

"Yes!" said the lad; "but where has it got to; I can't find it."

"Why, you know well enough," said the Troll; "you used it last; where should it be but over the door yonder?"

The lad did not wait to be told twice; he took down the harp, and went in and out playing tunes; but, all at once he shoved off the kneading trough, jumped into it, and rowed off, so that the foam flew around the trough.

After a while the Troll thought his daughter was a long while gone, and went out to see what ailed her; and then he saw the lad in the trough, far, far out on the lake.

"HALLOA! Is it you," he roared, "that took my seven silver ducks?"

"AY, AY!" said the lad.

"Is it you that took my bed quilt, with the gold and silver patches?"

"Yes!" said the lad.

"And now you have taken off my gold harp?" screamed the Troll.

"Yes!" said the lad; "I've got it, sure enough."

"And haven't I eaten you up after all, then?"

"No, no! 'twas your own daughter you ate," answered the lad.

But when the Troll heard that, he was so sorry, he burst; and then Boots rowed back, and took a whole heap of gold and silver with him, as much as the trough could carry. And so, when he came to the palace with the gold harp he got the Princess and half the kingdom, as the king had promised him; and, as for his brothers, he treated them well, for he thought they had only wished his good when they said what they had said.

71. GUDBRAND ON THE HILLSIDE or WHAT THE GOOD MAN DOES IS ALWAYS RIGHT
(*Norway*)

ONCE ON A TIME there was a man whose name was Gudbrand; he had a farm which lay far, far away, upon a hillside, and so they called him Gudbrand on the Hillside.

Now, you must know this man and his goodwife lived so happily together, and understood one another so well, that all the husband did the wife thought so well done, there was nothing like it in the world, and she was always glad whatever he turned his hand to. The farm was their own land, and they had a hundred dollars lying at the bottom of their chest, and two cows tethered up in a stall in their farmyard.

So one day his wife said to Gudbrand—

"Do you know, dear, I think we ought to take one of our cows into town and sell it; that's what I think; for then we shall have some money in hand, and such well-to-do people as we ought to have ready money like the rest of the world. As for the hundred dollars at the bottom of the chest yonder, we can't make a hole in them, and I'm sure I don't know what we want with more than one cow. Besides, we shall gain a little in another way, for then I shall get off with only looking after one cow, instead of having, as now, to feed and litter and water two."

Well, Gudbrand thought his wife talked right good sense, so he set off at once with the cow on his way to town to sell her; but when he got to the town, there was no one who would buy his cow.

"Well, well! never mind," said Gudbrand, "at the worst, I can only go back home again with my cow. I've both stable and tether for her, I should think, and the road is no farther out than in," and with that he began to toddle home with his cow.

But when he had gone a bit of the way, a man met him who had a horse to sell, so Gudbrand thought 'twas better to have a horse than a cow, so he swapped with the man. A little farther on he met a man walking along and driving a fat pig before him, and he thought it better to have a fat pig than a horse, so he swapped with the man. After that he went a little farther, and a man met him with a goat; so he thought it better to have a goat than a pig, and he swapped with the man that owned the goat. Then he went on a good bit till he met a man who had a sheep, and he swapped with him too, for he thought it always better to have a sheep than a goat. After a while he met a man with a goose, and he swapped away the sheep for the goose; and when he had walked a long, long time, he met a man with a cock, and he swapped with him, for he thought in this wise, " 'Tis surely better to have a cock than a goose." Then he went on till the day was far spent, and he began to get very hungry, so he sold the cock for a shilling, and bought food with the money, for, thought Gudbrand on the Hillside, " 'Tis always better to save one's life than to have a cock."

After that he went on home till he reached his nearest neighbor's house, where he turned in.

"Well," said the owner of the house, "how did things go with you in town?"

"Rather so so," said Gudbrand. "I can't praise my luck, nor do I blame it either," and with that he told the whole story from first to last.

"Ah!" said his friend, "you'll get nicely called over the coals, that one can see, when you get home to your wife. Heaven help you, I wouldn't stand in your shoes for something."

"Well," said Gudbrand on the Hillside, "I think things might have gone much worse with me; but now, whether I have done wrong or not, I have so kind a goodwife, she never has a word to say against anything that I do."

"Oh!" answered his neighbor, "I hear what you say, but I don't believe it for all that."

"Shall we lay a bet upon it?" asked Gudbrand on the Hillside. "I have a hundred dollars at the bottom of my chest at home; will you lay as many against them?"

Yes, the friend was ready to bet; so Gudbrand stayed there till evening, when it began to get dark, and then they went together to his house, and the neighbor was to stand outside the door and listen, while the man went in to see his wife.

"Good evening!" said Gudbrand on the Hillside.

"Good evening!" said the goodwife. "Oh, is that you? now God be praised."

Yes! it was he. So the wife asked how things had gone with him in town.

"Oh! only so so," answered Gudbrand; "not much to brag of. When I got to the town there was no one who would buy the cow, so you must know I swapped it away for a horse."

"For a horse," said his wife; "well, that is good of you; thanks with all my heart. We are so well-to-do that we may drive to church, just as well as other people; and if we choose to keep a horse we have a right to get one, I should think. So run out, child, and put up the horse."

"Ah!" said Gudbrand, "but you see I've not got the horse after all; for when I got a bit farther on the road I swapped it away for a pig."

"Think of that, now!" said the wife; "you did just as I should have done myself; a thousand thanks! Now I can have a bit of bacon in the house to set before people when they come to see me, that I can. What do we want with a horse? People would only say we had got so proud that we couldn't walk to church. Go out, child, and put up the pig in the stye."

"But I've not got the pig either," said Gudbrand; "for when I got a little farther on I swapped it away for a milch goat."

"Bless us!" cried his wife, "how well you manage everything! Now I think it over, what should I do with a pig? People would only point at us and say, 'Yonder they eat up all they have got.' No! now I have got a goat, and I shall have milk and cheese, and keep the goat too. Run out, child, and put up the goat."

"Nay, but I haven't got the goat either," said Gudbrand, "for a little farther on I swapped it away, and got a fine sheep instead."

"You don't say so!" cried his wife; "why, you do everything to please me, just as if I had been with you; what do we want with a goat! If I had it I should lose half my time in climbing up the hills to get it down. No! if I have a sheep, I shall have both wool and clothing, and fresh meat in the house. Run out, child, and put up the sheep."

"But I haven't got the sheep any more than the rest," said Gudbrand; "for when I had gone a bit farther I swapped it away for a goose."

"Thank you! thank you! with all my heart," cried his wife; "what should I do with a sheep? I have no spinning wheel, nor carding comb, nor should I care to worry myself with cutting, and shaping, and sewing clothes. We can buy clothes now, as we have always done; and now I shall have roast goose, which I have longed for so often; and, besides, down to stuff my little pillow with. Run out, child, and put up the goose."

"Ah!" said Gudbrand, "but I haven't the goose either; for when I had gone a bit farther I swapped it away for a cock."

"Dear me!" cried his wife, "how you think of everything! just as I should have done myself. A cock! think of that! why it's as good as an eight-day clock, for every morning the cock crows at four o'clock, and we shall be able to stir our stumps in good time. What should we do with a goose? I don't know how to cook it; and as for my pillow, I can stuff it with cotton grass. Run out, child, and put up the cock."

"But after all I haven't got the cock," said Gudbrand; "for when I had gone a bit farther, I got as hungry as a hunter, so I was forced to sell the cock for a shilling, for fear I should starve."

"Now, God be praised that you did so!" cried his wife; "whatever you do, you do it always just after my own heart. What should we do with the cock? We are our own masters, I should think, and can lie abed in the morning as long as we like. Heaven be thanked that I have got you safe back again; you who do everything so well that I want neither cock nor goose; neither pigs nor kine."

Then Gudbrand opened the door and said—

"Well, what do you say now? Have I won the hundred dollars?" and his neighbor was forced to allow that he had.

72. THE GIANT WHO HAD NO HEART IN HIS BODY
(*Norway*)

ONCE ON A TIME there was a King who had seven sons, and he loved them so much that he could never bear to be without them all at once, but one must always be with him. Now, when they were grown up, six were to set off to woo, but as for the youngest, his father kept him at home, and the others were to bring back a princess for him to the palace. So the King gave the six the finest clothes you ever set eyes on, so fine that the light gleamed from them a long way off, and each had his horse, which cost many, many hundred dollars, and so they set off. Now, when they had been to many palaces, and seen many princesses, at last they came to a King who had six daughters; such lovely king's daughters they had never seen, and so they fell to wooing them, each one, and when they had got them for sweethearts, they set off home again, but they quite forgot that they were to bring back with them a sweetheart for Boots, their brother, who stayed at home, for they were over head and ears in love with their own sweethearts.

But when they had gone a good bit on their way, they passed close by a steep hillside, like a wall, where the giant's house was, and there the giant came out, and set his eyes upon them, and turned them all into stone, princes and princesses and all. Now the King waited and waited for his six sons, but the more he waited the longer they stayed away; so he fell into great trouble, and said he should never know what it was to be glad again.

"And if I had not you left," he said to Boots, "I would live no longer, so full of sorrow am I for the loss of your brothers."

"Well, but now I've been thinking to ask your leave to set out and find them again; that's what I'm thinking of," said Boots.

"Nay, nay!" said his father; "that leave you shall never get, for then you would stay away too."

But Boots had set his heart upon it; go he would; and he begged and prayed so long that the King was forced to let him go. Now, you must know the King had no other horse to give Boots but an old broken-down jade, for his six other sons and their train had carried off all his horses; but Boots did not care a pin for that, he sprang up on his sorry old steed.

"Farewell, father," said he; "I'll come back, never fear, and like enough I shall bring my six brothers back with me"; and with that he rode off.

So, when he had ridden awhile, he came to a Raven, which lay in the road and flapped its wings, and was not able to get out of the way, it was so starved.

"Oh, dear friend," said the Raven, "give me a little food, and I'll help you again at your utmost need."

"I haven't much food," said the Prince, "and I don't see how you'll ever be able to help me much; but still I can spare you a little. I see you want it."

So he gave the Raven some of the food he had brought with him.

Now, when he had gone a bit further, he came to a brook, and in the brook lay a great Salmon, which had got upon a dry place, and dashed itself about, and could not get into the water again.

"Oh, dear friend," said the Salmon to the Prince; "shove me out into the water again, and I'll help you again at your utmost need."

"Well!" said the Prince, "the help you'll give me will not be great, I daresay, but it's a pity you should lie there and choke"; and with that he shot the fish out into the stream again.

After that he went a long, long way, and there met him a Wolf, which was so famished that it lay and crawled along the road on its belly.

"Dear friend, do let me have your horse," said the Wolf; "I'm so hungry the wind whistles through my ribs; I've had nothing to eat these two years."

"No," said Boots, "this will never do; first I came to a Raven, and I was forced to give him my food; next I came to a Salmon, and him I had to help into the water again; and now you will have my horse. It can't be done, that it can't, for then I should have nothing to ride on."

"Nay, dear friend, but you can help me," said Graylegs the Wolf; "you can ride upon my back, and I'll help you again in your utmost need."

"Well! the help I shall get from you will not be great, I'll be bound," said the Prince; "but you may take my horse, since you are in such need."

So when the Wolf had eaten the horse, Boots took the bit and put it into the Wolf's jaw, and laid the saddle on his back; and now the Wolf was so strong, after what he had got inside, that he set off with the Prince like nothing. So fast he had never ridden before.

"When we have gone a bit farther," said Graylegs, "I'll show you the Giant's house."

So after a while they came to it.

"See, here is the Giant's house," said the Wolf; "and see, here are your six brothers, whom the Giant has turned into stone; and see here are their six brides, and away yonder is the door, and in at that door you must go."

"Nay, but I daren't go in," said the Prince; "he'll take my life."

"No! no!" said the Wolf; "when you get in you'll find a Princess, and she'll tell you what to do to make an end of the Giant. Only mind and do as she bids you."

Well! Boots went in, but, truth to say, he was very much afraid. When he came in the Giant was away, but in one of the rooms sat the Princess, just as the Wolf had said, and so lovely a Princess Boots had never yet set eyes on.

"Oh! heaven help you! whence have you come?" said the Princess, as she saw him; "it will surely be your death. No one can make an end of the Giant who lives here, for he has no heart in his body."

"Well! well!" said Boots; "but now that I am here, I may as well try what I can do with him; and I will see if I can't free my brothers, who are standing turned to stone out of doors; and you, too, I will try to save, that I will."

"Well, if you must, you must," said the Princess; "and so let us see if we can't hit on a plan. Just creep under the bed yonder, and mind and listen to what he and I talk about. But, pray, do lie as still as a mouse."

So he crept under the bed, and he had scarce got well underneath it, before the Giant came.

"Ha!" roared the Giant, "what a smell of Christian blood there is in the house!"

"Yes, I know there is," said the Princess, "for there came a magpie flying with a man's bone, and let it fall down the chimney. I made all the haste I could to get it out, but all one can do, the smell doesn't go off so soon."

So the Giant said no more about it, and when night came, they went to bed. After they had lain awhile, the Princess said—

"There is one thing I'd be so glad to ask you about, if I only dared."

"What thing is that?" asked the Giant.

"Only where it is you keep your heart, since you don't carry it about you," said the Princess.

"Ah! that's a thing you've no business to ask about; but if you must know, it lies under the doorsill," said the Giant.

"Ho! ho!" said Boots to himself under the bed, "then we'll soon see if we can't find it."

Next morning the Giant got up cruelly early, and strode off to the wood; but he was hardly out of the house before Boots and the Princess set to work to look under the doorsill for his heart; but the more they dug, and the more they hunted, the more they couldn't find it.

"He has balked us this time," said the Princess, "but we'll try him once more."

So she picked all the prettiest flowers she could find, and strewed them over the doorsill, which they had laid in its right place again; and when the time came for the Giant to come home again, Boots crept under the bed. Just as he was well under, back came the Giant.

Snuff—snuff, went the Giant's nose. "My eyes and limbs, what a smell of Christian blood there is in here," said he.

"I know there is," said the Princess, "for there came a magpie flying with a man's bone in his bill, and let it fall down the chimney. I made as much haste as I could to get it out, but I daresay it's that you smell."

So the Giant held his peace, and said no more about it. A little while after, he asked who it was that had strewed flowers about the doorsill.

"Oh, I, of course," said the Princess.

"And, pray, what's the meaning of all this?" said the Giant.

"Ah!" said the Princess, "I'm so fond of you that I couldn't help strewing them, when I knew that your heart lay under there."

"You don't say so," said the Giant; "but after all it doesn't lie there at all."

So when they went to bed again in the evening, the Princess asked the Giant again where his heart was, for she said she would so like to know.

"Well," said the Giant, "if you must know, it lies away yonder in the cupboard against the wall."

"So, so!" thought Boots and the Princess; "then we'll soon try to find it."

Next morning the Giant was away early, and strode off to the wood, and so soon as he was gone Boots and the Princess were in the cupboard hunting for his heart, but the more they sought for it, the less they found it.

"Well," said the Princess, "we'll just try him once more."

So she decked out the cupboard with flowers and garlands, and when the time came for the Giant to come home, Boots crept under the bed again.

Then back came the Giant.

Snuff—snuff! "My eyes and limbs, what a smell of Christian blood there is in here!"

"I know there is," said the Princess; "for a little while since there came a magpie flying with a man's bone in his bill, and let it fall down the chimney. I made all the haste I could to get it out of the house again; but after all my pains, I daresay it's that you smell."

When the Giant heard that, he said no more about it; but a little while after, he saw how the cupboard was all decked about with flowers and garlands; so he asked who it was that had done that? Who could it be but the Princess?

"And, pray, what's the meaning of all this tomfoolery?" asked the Giant.

"Oh, I'm so fond of you, I couldn't help doing it when I knew that your heart lay there," said the Princess.

"How can you be so silly as to believe any such thing?" said the Giant.

"Oh yes; how can I help believing it, when you say it?" said the Princess.

"You're a goose," said the Giant; "where my heart is, you will never come."

"Well," said the Princess; "but for all that, 'twould be such a pleasure to know where it really lies."

Then the poor Giant could hold out no longer, but was forced to say—

"Far, far away in a lake lies an island; on that island stands a church; in that church is a well; in that well swims a duck; in that duck there is an egg, and in that egg there lies my heart—you darling!"

In the morning early, while it was still gray dawn, the Giant strode off to the wood.

"Yes! now I must set off too," said Boots; "if I only knew how to find the way." He took a long, long farewell of the Princess, and when he got out of the Giant's door, there stood the Wolf waiting for him. So Boots told him all that had happened inside the house, and said now he wished to ride to the well in the church, if he only knew the way. So the Wolf bade him jump on his back, he'd soon find the way; and away they went, till the wind whistled after them, over hedge and field, over hill and dale. After they had traveled many, many days, they came at last to the lake. Then the Prince did not know how to get over it, but the Wolf bade him only not be afraid, but stick on, and so he jumped into the lake with the Prince on his back, and swam over to the island. So they came to the church; but the church keys hung high, high up on the top of the tower, and at first the Prince did not know how to get them down.

"You must call on the Raven," said the Wolf.

So the Prince called on the Raven, and in a trice the Raven came, and flew up and fetched the keys, and so the Prince got into the church. But when he came to the well, there lay the duck, and swam about backward and forward, just as the Giant had said. So the Prince stood and coaxed it and coaxed it, till it came to him, and he grasped it in his hand; but just as he lifted it up from the water the duck dropped the egg into the well, and then Boots was beside himself to know how to get it out again.

"Well, now you must call on the Salmon to be sure," said the Wolf; and the king's son called on the Salmon, and the Salmon came and fetched up the egg from the bottom of the well.

Then the Wolf told the Prince to squeeze the egg, and as soon as ever he squeezed it the Giant screamed out.

"Squeeze it again," said the Wolf; and when the Prince did so, the Giant screamed still more piteously, and begged and prayed so prettily to be spared, saying he would do all that the Prince wished if he would only not squeeze his heart in two.

"Tell him, if he will restore to life again your six brothers and their brides, whom he has turned to stone, you will spare his life," said the Wolf. Yes, the Giant was ready to do that, and he turned the six brothers into king's sons again, and their brides into king's daughters.

"Now, squeeze the egg in two," said the Wolf. So Boots squeezed the egg to pieces, and the Giant burst at once.

Now, when he had made an end of the Giant, Boots rode back again on the Wolf to the Giant's house, and there stood all his six brothers alive and merry, with their brides. Then Boots went into the hillside after his bride, and so they all set off home again to their father's house. And you may fancy how glad the old King was when he saw all his seven sons come back, each with his bride— "But the loveliest bride of all is the bride of Boots, after all," said the King, "and he shall sit uppermost at the table, with her by his side."

So he sent out, and called a great wedding feast, and the mirth was both loud and long; and if they have not done feasting, why, they are still at it.

73. THE LAD WHO WENT TO THE NORTH WIND
(Norway)

ONCE ON A TIME there was an old widow who had one son; and as she was poorly and weak, her son had to go up into the safe to fetch meal for cooking; but when he got outside the safe, and was just going down the steps, there came the North Wind, puffing and blowing, caught up the meal, and so away with it through the air. Then the lad went back into the safe for more; but when he came out again on the steps, if the North Wind didn't come again and carry off the meal with a puff; and more than that, he did so the third time. At this the lad got very angry; and as he thought it hard that the North Wind should behave so, he thought he'd just look him up, and ask him to give up his meal.

So off he went, but the way was long, and he walked and walked; but at last he came to the North Wind's house.

"Good day!" said the lad, and "thank you for coming to see us yesterday."

"GOOD DAY!" answered the North Wind, for his voice was loud and gruff, "AND THANKS FOR COMING TO SEE ME. WHAT DO YOU WANT?"

"Oh!" answered the lad, "I only wished to ask you to be so good as to let me have back that meal you took from me on the safe steps, for we haven't much to live on; and if you're to go on snapping up the morsel we have there'll be nothing for it but to starve."

"I haven't got your meal," said the North Wind; "but if you are in such need, I'll give you a cloth which will get you everything you want, if you only say, 'Cloth, spread yourself, and serve up all kind of good dishes!' "

With this the lad was well content. But, as the way was so long he couldn't get home in one day, so he turned into an inn on the way; and when they were going to sit down to supper, he laid the cloth on a table which stood in the corner and said—

"Cloth, spread yourself, and serve up all kind of good dishes."

He had scarce said so before the cloth did as it was bid; and all who stood by thought it a fine thing, but most of all the landlady. So, when all were fast asleep, at dead of night, she took the lad's cloth, and put another in its stead, just like the one he had got from the North Wind, but which couldn't so much as serve up a bit of dry bread.

So, when the lad woke, he took his cloth and went off with it, and that day he got home to his mother.

"Now," said he, "I've been to the North Wind's house, and a good fellow he is, for he gave me this cloth, and when I only say to it, 'Cloth, spread yourself, and serve up all kind of good dishes,' I get any sort of food I please."

"All very true, I daresay," said his mother; "but seeing is believing, and I shan't believe it till I see it."

So the lad made haste, drew out a table, laid the cloth on it, and said—

"Cloth, spread yourself, and serve up all kind of good dishes."

But never a bit of dry bread did the cloth serve up.

"Well," said the lad, "there's no help for it but to go to the North Wind again"; and away he went.

So he came to where the North Wind lived late in the afternoon.

"Good evening!" said the lad.

"Good evening!" said the North Wind.

"I want my rights for that meal of ours which you took," said the lad; "for as for that cloth I got, it isn't worth a penny."

"I've got no meal," said the North Wind; "but yonder you have a ram which coins nothing but golden ducats as soon as you say to it—

" 'Ram, ram! make money!' "

So the lad thought this a fine thing; but as it was too far to get home that day, he turned in for the night to the same inn where he had slept before.

Before he called for anything, he tried the truth of what the North Wind had said of the ram, and found it all right; but when the landlord saw that, he thought it was a famous ram, and, when the lad had fallen asleep, he took another which couldn't coin golden ducats, and changed the two.

Next morning off went the lad; and when he got home to his mother, he said—

"After all, the North Wind is a jolly fellow; for now he has given me a ram which can coin golden ducats if I only say, 'Ram, ram! make money!' "

"All very true, I daresay," said his mother; "but I shan't believe any such stuff until I see the ducats made."

"Ram, ram! make money!" said the lad; but if the ram made anything it wasn't money.

So the lad went back again to the North Wind, and blew him up, and said the ram was worth nothing, and he must have his rights for the meal.

"Well," said the North Wind; "I've nothing else to give you but that old stick in the corner yonder; but it's a stick of that kind that if you say—

" 'Stick, stick! lay on!' it lays on till you say—

" 'Stick, stick! now stop!' "

So, as the way was long, the lad turned in this night too to the landlord; but as he could pretty well guess how things stood as to the cloth and the ram, he lay down at once on the bench and began to snore, as if he were asleep.

Now the landlord, who easily saw that the stick must be worth something, hunted up one which was like it, and when he heard the lad snore, was going to change the two, but just as the landlord was about to take it the lad bawled out—

"Stick, stick! lay on!"

So the stick began to beat the landlord, till he jumped over chairs, and tables, and benches, and yelled and roared—

"Oh my! oh my! bid the stick be still, else it will beat me to death, and you shall have back both your cloth and your ram."

When the lad thought the landlord had got enough, he said—

"Stick, stick! now stop!"

Then he took the cloth and put it into his pocket, and went home with his stick in his hand, leading the ram by a cord round its horns; and so he got his rights for the meal he had lost.

74. THE MASTER THIEF
(Norway)

ONCE UPON A TIME there was a poor cottager who had three sons. He had nothing to leave them when he died, and no money with which to put them to any trade, so that he did not know what to make of them. At last he said he would give them leave to take to anything each liked best, and to go wherever they pleased, and he would go with them a bit of the way; and so he did. He went with them till they came to a place where three roads met, and there each of them chose a road, and their father bade them good-bye, and went back home. I have never heard tell what became of the two elder; but as for the youngest, he went both far and long, as you shall hear.

So it fell out one night as he was going through a great wood that such bad weather overtook him. It blew, and sleeted, and drove so that he could scarce keep his eyes open; and in a trice, before he knew how it was, he got bewildered, and could not find either road or path. But as he went on and on, at last he saw a glimmering of light far far off in the wood. So he thought he would try and get to the light; and after a time he did reach it. There it was in a large house, and the fire was blazing so brightly inside that he could tell the folk had not yet gone to bed; so he went in and saw an old dame bustling about and minding the house.

"Good evening!" said the youth.

"Good evening!" said the old dame.

"Brrr! It's such foul weather out of doors tonight," said he.

"So it is," said she.

"Can I get leave to have a bed and shelter here tonight?" asked the youth.

"You'll get no good by sleeping here," said the old dame; "for if the folk come home and find you here, they'll kill both me and you."

"What sort of folk, then, are they who live here?" asked the youth.

"Oh, robbers! And a bad lot of them too," said the old dame. "They stole me away when I was little, and have kept me as their housekeeper ever since."

"Well, for all that, I think I'll just go to bed," said the youth. "Come what may, I'll not stir out at night in such weather."

"Very well," said the old dame; "but if you stay, it will be the worse for you."

With that the youth got into a bed which stood there, but he dared not go to sleep, and very soon after in came the robbers; so the old dame told them how a stranger fellow had come in whom she had not been able to get out of the house again.

"Did you see if he had any money?" said the robbers.

"Such a one as he money!" said the old dame, "the tramper! Why, if he had clothes to his back, it was as much as he had."

Then the robbers began to talk among themselves what they should do with him; if they should kill him outright, or what else they should do. Meantime the youth got up and began to talk to them, and to ask if they didn't want a servant, for it might be that he would be glad to enter their service.

"Oh," said they, "if you have a mind to follow the trade that we follow, you can very well get a place here."

"It's all one to me what trade I follow," said the youth; "for when I left home father gave me leave to take to any trade I chose."

"Well, have you a mind to steal?" asked the robbers.

"I don't care," said the youth, for he thought it would not take long to learn that trade.

Now there lived a man a little way off who had three oxen. One of these he was to take to the town to sell, and the robbers had heard what he was going to do, so they said to the youth, if he were good to steal the ox from the man by the way without his knowing it, and without doing him any harm, they would give him leave to be their serving-man.

Well, the youth set off, and took with him a pretty shoe with a silver buckle on it, which lay about the house; and he put the shoe in the road along which the man was going with his ox; and when he had done that, he went into the wood and hid himself under a bush. So when the man came by he saw the shoe at once.

"That's a nice shoe," said he. "If I only had the fellow to it, I'd take it home with me, and perhaps I'd put my old dame in a good humor for once." For you must know he had an old wife, so cross and snappish, it was not long between each time that she boxed his ears. But then he bethought him that he could do nothing with the odd shoe unless he had the fellow to it; so he went on his way and let the shoe lie on the road.

Then the youth took up the shoe, and made all the haste he could to get before the man by a shortcut through the wood, and laid it down before him in the road again. When the man came along with his ox, he got quite angry with himself for being so dull as to leave the fellow to the shoe lying in the road instead of taking it with him; so he tied the ox to the fence, and said to himself, "I may just as well run back and pick up the other, and then I'll have a pair of good shoes for my old dame, and so, perhaps, I'll get a kind word from her for once."

So he set off, and hunted and hunted up and down for the shoe, but no shoe did he find; and at length he had to go back with the one he had. But, meanwhile, the youth had taken the ox and gone off with it; and when the man came and saw his ox gone, he began to cry and bewail, for he was afraid his old dame would kill him outright when she came to know that the ox was lost. But just then it came across his mind that he would go home and take the second ox, and drive it to the town, and not let his old dame know anything about the matter. So he did this, and went home and took the ox without his dame's knowing it, and set off with it to the town. But the robbers knew all about it, and they said to the youth, if he could get this ox too, without the man's knowing it, and without his doing him any harm, he should be as good as any one of them. If that were all, the youth said, he did not think it a very hard thing.

This time he took with him a rope, and hung himself up under the armpits to a tree right in the man's way. So the man came along with his ox, and when he saw such a sight hanging there he began to feel a little queer.

"Well," said he, "whatever heavy thoughts you had who have hanged yourself up there, it can't be helped; you may hang for what I care! I can't breathe life into you again"; and with that he went on his way with his ox. Down slipped the youth from the tree, and ran by a footpath, and got before the man, and hung himself up right in his way again.

"Bless me!" said the man, "were you really so heavy at heart that you hanged yourself up there—or is it only a piece of witchcraft that I see before me? Ay, ay! you may hang for all I care, whether you are a ghost, or whatever you are." So he passed on with his ox.

Now the youth did just as he had done twice before; he jumped down from the tree, ran through the wood by a footpath, and hung himself up right in the man's way again. But when the man saw this sight for the third time, he said to himself—

"Well, this is an ugly business! Is it likely now that they should have been so heavy at heart as to hang themselves, all these three? No! I cannot think it is anything else than a piece of witchcraft that I see. But now I'll soon know for certain; if the other two are still hanging there, it must be really so; but if they are not, then it can be nothing but witchcraft that I see."

So he tied up his ox, and ran back to see if the others were still really hanging there. But while he went and peered up into all the trees, the youth jumped down and took his ox and ran off with it. When the man came back and found his ox gone, he was in a sad plight, and, as anyone might know without being told, he began to cry and bemoan; but at last he came to take it easier, and so he thought—

"There's no other help for it than to go home and take the third ox without my dame's knowing it, and to try and drive a good bargain with it, so that I may get a good sum of money for it."

So he went home and set off with the ox, and his old dame knew never a word about the matter. But the robbers, they knew all about it, and they said to the youth, that if he could steal this ox as he had stolen the other two, then he should be master over the whole band. Well, the youth set off, and ran into the wood; and as the man came by with his ox he set up a dreadful bellowing, just like a great ox in the wood. When the man heard that, you can't think how glad he was, for it seemed to him that he knew the voice of his big bullock, and he thought that now he should find both of them again; so he tied up the third ox, and ran off from the road to look for them in the wood; but meantime the youth went off with the third ox. Now, when the man came back and found he had lost this ox too, he was so wild that there was no end to his grief. He cried and roared and beat his breast, and, to tell the truth, it was many days before he dared go home; for he was afraid lest his old dame should kill him outright on the spot.

As for the robbers, they were not very well pleased either, when they had to own that the youth was master over the whole band. So one day they thought they would try their hands at something which he was not man enough to do; and they set off all together, every man Jack of them, and left him alone at home. Now, the first thing that he did when they were all well clear of the house, was to drive the oxen out to the road, so that they might run back to the man from whom he had stolen them; and right glad he was to see them, as you may fancy. Next he took all the horses which the robbers had, and loaded them with the best things he could lay his hands on—gold and silver, and clothes and other fine things; and then he bade the old dame to greet the robbers when they came back, and to thank them for him, and to say that now he was setting off on his travels, and they would have hard work to find him again; and with that, off he started.

After a good bit he came to the road along which he was going when he fell among the robbers, and when he got near home, and could see his father's cottage, he put on a uniform which he had found among the clothes he had taken from the robbers, and which was made just like a general's. So he drove up to the door as if he were any other great man. After that he went in and asked if he could have a lodging. No; that he couldn't at any price.

"How ever should I be able," said the man, "to make room in my house for such a fine gentleman—I who scarce have a rag to lie upon, and miserable rags too?"

"You always were a stingy old hunks," said the youth, "and so you are still, when you won't take your own son in."

"What, you my son!" said the man.

"Don't you know me again?" said the youth. Well, after a little while he did know him again.

"But what have you been turning your hand to, that you have made yourself so great a man in such haste?" asked the man.

"Oh, I'll soon tell you," said the youth. "You said I might take to any trade I chose, and so I bound myself apprentice to a pack of thieves and robbers, and now I've served my time out, and am become a Master Thief."

Now there lived a Squire close by to his father's cottage, and he had such a great house, and such heaps of money, he could not tell how much he had. He had a daughter too, and a smart and pretty girl she was. So the Master Thief set his heart upon having her to wife, and he told his father to go to the Squire and ask for his daughter for him.

"If he asks by what trade I get my living, you can say I'm a Master Thief."

"I think you've lost your wits," said the man, "for you can't be in your right mind when you think of such stuff."

No, he had not lost his wits; his father must and should go to the Squire and ask for his daughter.

"Nay, but I tell you, I daren't go to the Squire and be your spokesman; he who is so rich, and has so much money," said the man.

Yes, there was no help for it, said the Master Thief; he should go whether he would or no; and if he did not go by fair means, he would soon make him go by foul. But the man was still loath to go; so he stepped after him, and rubbed him down with a good birch cudgel, and kept on till the man came crying and sobbing inside the Squire's door.

"How now, my man! what ails you?" said the Squire.

So he told him the whole story; how he had three sons who set off one day, and how he had given them leave to go wherever they would, and to follow whatever calling they chose. "And here now is the youngest come home, and has thrashed me till he has made me come to you and ask for your daughter for him to wife; and he bids me say, besides, that he's a Master Thief." And so he fell to crying and sobbing again.

"Never mind, my man," said the Squire laughing; "just go back and tell him from me he must prove his skill first. If he can steal the roast from the spit in the kitchen on Sunday, while all the household are looking after it, he shall have my daughter. Just go and tell him that."

So he went back and told the youth, who thought it would be an easy job. So he set about and caught three hares alive, and put them into a bag, and dressed himself in some old rags, until he looked so poor and filthy that it made one's heart bleed to see; and then he stole into the passage at the back door of the Squire's house on the Sunday forenoon, with his bag, just like any other beggar boy. But the Squire himself and all his household were in the kitchen watching the roast. Just as they were doing this, the youth let one hare go, and it set off and ran round and round the yard in front of the house.

"Oh, just look at that hare!" said the folk in the kitchen, and were all for running out to catch it.

Yes, the Squire saw it running too. "Oh, let it run," said he; "there's no use in thinking to catch a hare on the spring."

A little while after, the youth let the second hare go, and they saw it in the kitchen, and thought it was the same they had seen before, and still wanted to run out and catch it; but the Squire said again it was no use. It was not long before the youth let the third hare go, and it set off and ran round and round the yard as the others before it. Now, they saw it from the kitchen, and still thought it was the same hare that kept on running about, and were all eager to be out after it.

"Well, it is a fine hare," said the Squire; "come, let's see if we can't lay our hands on it."

So out he ran, and the rest with him—away they all went, the hare before, and they after; so that it was rare fun to see. But meantime the youth took the roast and ran off with it; and where the Squire got a roast for his dinner that day I don't know; but one thing I know, and that is, that he had no roast hare, though he ran after it till he was both warm and weary.

Now it chanced that the Priest came to dinner that day, and when the Squire told him what a trick the Master Thief had played him, he made such game of him that there was no end of it.

"For my part," said the Priest, "I can't think how it could ever happen to me to be made such a fool of by a fellow like that."

"Very well—only keep a sharp lookout," said the Squire; "maybe he'll come to see you before you know a word of it." But the priest stuck to his text—that he did, and made game of the Squire because he had been so taken in.

Later in the afternoon came the Master Thief, and wanted to have the Squire's daughter, as he had given his word. But the Squire began to talk him over, and said, "Oh, you must first prove your skill a little more; for what you did today was no great thing after all. Couldn't you now play a good trick on the Priest, who is sitting in there, and making game of me for letting such a fellow as you twist me round his thumb?"

"Well, as for that, it wouldn't be hard," said the Master Thief. So he dressed himself up like a bird, threw a great white sheet over his body, took the wings of a goose, and tied them to his back, and so climbed up into a great maple which stood in the Priest's garden. And when the Priest came home in the evening, the youth began to bawl out—

"Father Laurence! Father Laurence!"—for that was the Priest's name.

"Who is that calling me?" said the Priest.

"I am an angel," said the Master Thief, "sent from God to let you know that you shall be taken up alive into heaven for your piety's sake. Next Monday night you must hold yourself ready for the journey, for I shall come then to fetch you in a sack; and all your gold and your silver, and all that you have of this world's goods, you must lay together in a heap in your dining room."

Well, Father Laurence fell on his knees before the angel, and thanked him; and the very next day he preached a farewell sermon, and gave it out how there had come down an angel unto the big maple in his garden, who had told him that he was to be taken up alive into heaven for his piety's sake; and he preached and made such a touching discourse, that all who were at church wept, both young and old.

So the next Monday night came the Master Thief like an angel again, and the Priest fell on his knees and thanked him before he was put into the sack; but when he had got him well in, the Master Thief drew and dragged him over stocks and stones.

"OW! OW!" groaned the Priest inside the sack, "wherever are we going?"

"This is the narrow way which leadeth unto the kingdom of heaven," said the Master Thief, who went on dragging him along till he had nearly broken every bone in his body. At last he tumbled him into a goosehouse that belonged to the Squire, and the geese began pecking and pinching him with their bills, so that he was more dead than alive.

"Now you are in the flames of purgatory, to be cleansed and purified for life everlasting," said the Master Thief; and with that he went his way, and took all the gold which the Priest had laid together in his dining room. The next morning, when the goosegirl came to let the geese out, she heard how the Priest lay in the sack, and bemoaned himself in the goosehouse.

"In heaven's name, who's there, and what ails you?" she cried.

"Oh!" said the Priest, "if you are an angel from heaven, do let me out, and let me return again to earth, for it is worse here than in hell. The little fiends keep on pinching me with tongs."

"Heaven help us, I am no angel at all," said the girl, as she helped the Priest out of the sack; "I only look after the Squire's geese, and like enough they are the little fiends which have pinched your reverence."

"Oh!" groaned the Priest, "this is all that Master Thief's doing. Ah! my gold and my silver, and my fine clothes." And he beat his breast, and hobbled home at such a rate that the girl thought he had lost his wits all at once.

Now when the Squire came to hear how it had gone with the Priest, and how he had been along the narrow way, and into purgatory, he laughed till he wellnigh split his sides. But when the Master Thief came and asked for his daughter as he had promised, the Squire put him off again, and said—

"You must do one masterpiece better still, that I may see plainly what you are fit for. Now, I have twelve horses in my stable, and on them I will put twelve grooms, one on each. If you are so good a thief as to steal the horses from under them, I'll see what I can do for you."

"Very well, I daresay I can do it," said the Master Thief; "but shall I really have your daughter if I can?"

"Yes, if you can, I'll do my best for you," said the Squire.

So the Master Thief set off to a shop, and bought brandy enough to fill two pocket flasks, and into one of them he put a sleepy drink, but into the other only brandy. After that he hired eleven men to lie in wait at night behind the Squire's stableyard; and last of all, for fair words and a good bit of money, he borrowed a ragged gown and cloak from an old woman; and so, with a staff in his hand, and a bundle at his back, he limped off, as evening drew on, toward the Squire's stable. Just as he got there they were watering the horses for the night, and had their hands full of work.

"What the devil do you want?" said one of the grooms to the old woman.

"Oh, oh! Brrr! It is so bitter cold," said she, and shivered and shook, and made wry faces. "Brrr! It is so cold, a poor wretch may easily freeze to death"; and with that she fell to shivering and shaking again.

"Oh! for the love of heaven, can I get leave to stay here awhile, and sit inside the stable door?"

"To the devil with your leave," said one. "Pack yourself off this minute, for if the Squire sets his eye on you, he'll lead us a pretty dance."

"Oh! the poor old bag of bones," said another, whose heart took pity on her; "the old hag may sit inside and welcome; such a one as she can do no harm."

And the rest said, some she should stay and some she shouldn't; but while they were quarreling and minding the horses, she crept farther and farther into the stable, till at last she sat herself down behind the door; and when she had got so far, no one gave any more heed to her.

As the night wore on, the men found it rather cold work to sit so still and quiet on horseback.

"Brrr! It is so devilish cold," said one, and beat his arms crosswise.

"That it is," said another; "I freeze so that my teeth chatter."

"If one only had a quid to chew," said a third.

Well! there was one who had an ounce or two; so they shared it between them, though it wasn't much, after all, that each got; and so they chewed and spat, and spat and chewed. This helped them somewhat; but in a little while they were just as bad as ever.

"Brrr!" said one, and shivered and shook.

"Brrr!" said the old woman, and shivered so, that every tooth in her head chattered. Then she pulled out the flask with brandy in it, and her hand shook so that the spirit splashed about in the flask, and then she took such a gulp, that it went "bop" in her throat.

"What's that you've got in your flask, old girl?" said one of the grooms.

"Oh, it's only a drop of brandy, old man," said she.

"Brandy! Well, I never! Do let me have a drop," screamed the whole twelve, one after another.

"Oh, but it is such a little drop," mumbled the old woman, "it will not even wet your mouths round." But they must and would have it; there was no help for it; and so she pulled out the flask with the sleepy drink in it, and put it to the first man's lips; then she shook no more, but guided the flask so that each of them got what he wanted, and the twelfth had not done drinking before the first sat and snored. Then the Master Thief threw off his beggar's rags, and took one groom after the other so softly off their horses, and set them astride on the beams between the stalls; and so he called his eleven men, and rode off with the Squire's twelve horses.

But when the Squire got up in the morning, and went to look after his grooms, they had just begun to come to; and some of them fell to spurring the beams with their spurs, till the splinters flew again, and some fell off, and some still hung on and sat there looking like fools.

"Ho! ho!" said the Squire; "I see very well who has been here; but as for you, a pretty set of blockheads you must be to sit here and let the Master Thief steal the horses from between your legs."

So they all got a good leathering because they had not kept a sharper lookout.

Farther on in the day came the Master Thief again, and told how he had managed the matter, and asked for the Squire's daughter, as he had promised; but the Squire gave him one hundred dollars down, and said he must do something better still.

"Do you think now," said he, "you can steal the horse from under me while I am out riding on his back?"

"Oh, yes! I daresay I could," said the Master Thief, "if I were really sure of getting your daughter."

Well, well, the Squire would see what he could do; and he told the Master Thief a day when he would be taking a ride on a great common where they drilled the troops. So the Master Thief soon got hold of an old worn-out jade of a mare, and set to work, and made traces and collar of withies and broom twigs, and bought an old beggarly cart and a great cask. After that he told an old beggar woman he would give her ten dollars if she would get inside the cask, and keep her mouth agape over the taphole, into which he was going to stick his finger. No harm should happen to her; she should only be driven about a little; and if he took his finger out more than once, she was to have ten dollars more. Then he threw a few rags and tatters over himself, and stuffed himself out, and put on a wig and a great beard of goat's hair, so that no one could know him again, and set off for the common, where the Squire had already been riding about a good bit. When he reached the place, he went along so softly and slowly that he scarce made an inch of way. "Gee up! Gee up!" and so he went on a little; then he stood stock still, and so on a little again; and altogether the pace was so poor it never once came into the Squire's head that this could be the Master Thief.

At last the Squire rode right up to him, and asked if he had seen anyone lurking about in the wood thereabouts.

"No," said the man, "I haven't seen a soul."

"Hark ye, now," said the Squire, "if you have a mind to ride into the wood, and hunt about and see if you can fall upon anyone lurking about there, you shall have the loan of my horse, and a shilling into the bargain, to drink my health for your pains."

"I don't see how I can go," said the man, "for I am going to a wedding with this cask of mead, which I have been to town to fetch, and here the tap has fallen out by the way, and so I must go along holding my finger in the taphole."

"Ride off," said the Squire; "I'll look after your horse and cask."

Well, on these terms the man was willing to go; but he begged the Squire to be quick in putting his finger into the taphole when he took his own out, and to mind and keep it there till he came back. At last the Squire grew weary of standing there with his finger in the taphole, so he took it out.

"Now I shall have ten dollars more!" screamed the old woman inside the cask; and then the Squire saw at once how the land lay, and took himself off home; but he had not gone far before they met him with a fresh horse, for the Master Thief had already been to his house, and told them to send one.

The day after he came to the Squire and would have his daughter, as he had given his word; but the Squire put him off again with fine words, and gave him two hundred dollars, and said he must do one more masterpiece. If he could do that, he should have her. Well, well, the Master Thief thought he could do it, if he only knew what it was to be.

"Do you think, now," said the Squire, "you can steal the sheet off our bed, and the shift off my wife's back. Do you think you could do that?"

"It shall be done," said the Master Thief. "I only wish I was as sure of getting your daughter."

So when night began to fall, the Master Thief went out and cut down a thief who hung on the gallows, and threw him across his shoulders, and carried him off. Then he got a long ladder and set it up against the Squire's bedroom window, and so climbed up, and kept bobbing the dead man up and down, just for all the world like one that was peeping in at the window.

"That's the Master Thief, old lass!" said the Squire, and gave his wife a nudge on the side. "Now see if I don't shoot him, that's all."

So saying, he took up a rifle which he had laid at his bedside.

"No, no! pray don't shoot him after telling him he might come and try," said his wife.

"Don't talk to me, for shoot him I will," said he; and so he lay there and aimed and aimed; but as soon as the head came up before the window, and he saw a little of it, so soon was it down again. At last he thought he had a good aim; "bang" went the gun, down fell the dead body to the ground with a heavy thump, and down went the Master Thief too as fast as he could.

"Well," said the Squire, "it is quite true that I am the chief magistrate in these parts; but people are fond of talking, and it would be a bore if they came to see this dead man's body. I think the best thing to be done is that I should go down and bury him."

"You must do as you think best, dear," said his wife. So the Squire got out of bed and went downstairs, and he had scarce put his foot out of the door before the Master Thief stole in, and went straight upstairs to his wife.

"Why, dear, back already!" said she, for she thought it was her husband.

"Oh yes, I only just put him into a hole, and threw a little earth over him. It is enough that he is out of sight, for it is such a bad night out of doors; by and by I'll do it better. But just let me have the sheet to wipe myself with—he was so bloody—and I have made myself in such a mess with him."

So he got the sheet.

After a while he said—

"Do you know I am afraid you must let me have your night-shift too, for the sheet won't do by itself; that I can see."

So she gave him the shift also. But just then it came across his mind that he had forgotten to lock the house door, so he must step down and look to that before he came back to bed, and away he went with both shift and sheet.

A little while after came the true Squire.

"Why! what a time you've taken to lock the door, dear!" said his wife; "and what have you done with the sheet and shift?"

"What do you say?" said the Squire.

"Why, I am asking what you have done with the sheet and shift that you had to wipe off the blood," said she.

"What, in the Devil's name!" said the Squire, "has he taken me in this time too?"

Next day came the Master Thief and asked for the Squire's daughter, as he had given his word; and then the Squire dared not do anything else than give her to him, and a good lump of money into the bargain; for, to tell the truth, he was afraid lest the Master Thief should steal the eyes out of his head, and that the people would begin to say spiteful things of him if he broke his word. So the Master Thief lived well and happily from that time forward. I don't know whether he stole any more; but if he did, I am quite sure it was only for the sake of a bit of fun.

75. THE THREE BILLYGOATS GRUFF
(*Norway*)

ONCE ON A TIME there were three billygoats, who were to go up to the hillside to make themselves fat, and the name of all three was "Gruff."

On the way up was a bridge over a burn they had to cross; and under the bridge lived a great ugly Troll, with eyes as big as saucers, and a nose as long as a poker.

So first of all came the youngest billygoat Gruff to cross the bridge.

"Trip, trap! trip, trap!" went the bridge.

"WHO'S THAT tripping over my bridge?" roared the Troll.

"Oh, it is only I, the tiniest billygoat Gruff; and I'm going up to the hillside to make myself fat," said the billygoat, with such a small voice.

"Now, I'm coming to gobble you up," said the Troll.

"Oh, no! pray don't take me. I'm too little, that I am," said the billygoat; "wait a bit till the second billygoat Gruff comes, he's much bigger."

"Well, be off with you," said the Troll.

A little while after came the second billygoat Gruff to cross the bridge.

"TRIP, TRAP! TRIP, TRAP! TRIP, TRAP!" went the bridge.

"WHO'S THAT tripping over my bridge?" roared the Troll.

"Oh, it's the second billygoat Gruff, and I'm going up to the hillside to make myself fat," said the billygoat, who hadn't such a small voice.

"Now I'm coming to gobble you up," said the Troll.

"Oh, no! don't take me, wait a little till the big billygoat Gruff comes, he's much bigger."

"Very well! be off with you," said the Troll.

But just then up came the big billygoat Gruff.

"TRIP, TRAP! TRIP, TRAP! TRIP, TRAP!" went the bridge, for

the billygoat was so heavy that the bridge creaked and groaned under him.

"WHO'S THAT tramping over my bridge?" roared the Troll.

"IT'S I! THE BIG BILLYGOAT GRUFF," said the billygoat, who had an ugly hoarse voice of his own.

"Now I'm coming to gobble you up," roared the Troll.

> "Well, come along! I've got two spears,
> And I'll poke your eyeballs out at your ears;
> I've got besides two great, flat stones,
> And I'll crush you to bits, body and bones."

That was what the big billygoat said; and so he flew at the Troll, and poked his eyes out with his horns, and crushed him to bits, body and bones, and tossed him out into the burn, and after that he went up to the hillside. There the billygoats got so fat they were scarce able to walk home again; and if the fat hasn't fallen off them, why, they're still fat; and so—

> "Snip, snap, snout.
> This tale's told out."

76. THE MASTERMAID
(Norway)

ONCE ON A TIME there was a king who had several sons—I don't know how many there were—but the youngest had no rest at home, for nothing else would please him but to go out into the world and try his luck, and after a long time the king was forced to give him leave to go. Now, after he had traveled some days, he came one night to a Giant's house, and there he got a place in the Giant's service. In the morning the Giant went off to herd his goats, and as he left the yard he told the Prince to clean out the stable; "And after you have done that, you needn't do anything else today; for you must know it is an easy master you have come to. But what is set you to do you must do well, and you mustn't think of going into any of the rooms which are beyond that in which you slept, for if you do, I'll take your life."

"Sure enough, it is an easy master I have got," said the Prince to himself, as he walked up and down the room, and caroled and sang, for he thought there was plenty of time to clean out the stable.

"But still it would be good fun just to peep into his other rooms, for there must be something in them which he is afraid lest I should see, since he won't give me leave to go in."

So he went into the first room, and there was a pot boiling on a hook by the wall, but the Prince saw no fire underneath it. I wonder what is inside it, he thought; and then he dipped a lock of his hair into it, and the hair seemed as if it were all turned to copper.

"What a dainty broth," he said; "if one tasted it, he'd look grand inside his gullet"; and with that he went into the next room. There, too, was a pot hanging by a hook, which bubbled and boiled; but there was no fire under that either.

"I may as well try this too," said the Prince, as he put another lock into the pot, and it came out all silvered.

"They haven't such rich broth in my father's house," said the Prince; "but it all depends on how it tastes," and with that he went on into the third room. There, too, hung a pot, and boiled just as he had seen in the two other rooms, and the Prince had a mind to try this too, so he dipped a lock of hair into it, and it came out gilded, so that the light gleamed from it.

" 'Worse and worse,' said the old wife; but I say better and better," said the Prince; "but if he boils gold here, I wonder what he boils in yonder."

He thought he might as well see; so he went through the door into the fourth room. Well, there was no pot in there, but there was a Princess, seated on a bench, so lovely, that the Prince had never seen anything like her in his born days.

"Oh! in Heaven's name," she said, "what do you want here?"

"I got a place here yesterday," said the Prince.

"A place, indeed! Heaven help you out of it."

"Well, after all, I think I've got an easy master; he hasn't set me much to do today, for after I have cleaned out the stable my day's work is over."

"Yes, but how will you do it?" she said; "for if you set to work to clean it like other folk, ten pitchforks full will come in for every one you toss out. But I will teach you how to set to work; you must turn the fork upside down, and toss with the handle, and then all the dung will fly out of itself."

"Yes, he would be sure to do that," said the Prince; and so he sat there the whole day, for he and the Princess were soon great friends, and had made up their minds to have one another, and so the first day of his service with the Giant was not long, you may fancy. But when the evening drew on, she said 'twould be as well if he got the stable cleaned out before the Giant came home; and when he went to the stable he thought he would just see if what she had said were true, and so he began to work like the grooms in his father's stable; but he soon had enough of that, for he hadn't worked a minute before the stable was so full of dung that he hadn't room to stand. Then he did as the Princess bade him, and turned up the fork and worked with the handle, and lo! in a trice the stable was as clean as if it had been scoured. And when he had done his work he went back into the room where the Giant had given him leave to be, and began to walk up and down, and to carol and sing. So after a bit, home came the Giant with his goats.

"Have you cleaned the stable?" asked the Giant.

"Yes, now it's all right and tight, master," answered the Prince.

"I'll soon see if it is," growled the Giant, and strode off to the stable, where he found it just as the Prince had said.

"You've been talking to my Mastermaid, I can see," said the Giant; "for you've not sucked this knowledge out of your own breast."

"Mastermaid!" said the Prince, who looked as stupid as an owl, "what sort of thing is that, master? I'd be very glad to see it."

"Well, well!" said the Giant; "you'll see her soon enough."

Next day the Giant set off with his goats again, and before he went he told the Prince to fetch home his horse, which was out at grass on the hillside, and when he had done that he might rest all the day.

"For you must know it is an easy master you have come to," said the Giant; "but if you go into any of the rooms I spoke of yesterday, I'll wring your head off."

So off he went with his flock of goats.

"An easy master you are indeed," said the Prince; "but for all that, I'll just go in and have a chat with your Mastermaid; may be she'll be as soon mine as yours." So he went in to her, and she asked him what he had to do that day.

"Oh! nothing to be afraid of," said he; "I've only to go up to the hillside to fetch his horse."

"Very well; and how will you set about it?"

"Well, for that matter, there's no great art in riding a horse home. I fancy I've ridden fresher horses before now," said the Prince.

"Ah, but this isn't so easy a task as you think; but I'll teach you how to do it. When you get near it, fire and flame will come out of its nostrils, as out of a tar barrel; but look out, and take the bit which hangs behind the door yonder, and throw it right into his jaws, and he will grow so tame that you may do what you like with him."

Yes! the Prince would mind and do that; and so he sat in there the whole day, talking and chattering with the Mastermaid about one thing and another; but they always came back to how happy they would be if they could only have one another, and get well away from the Giant; and, to tell the truth, the Prince would have clean forgotten both the horse and the hillside, if the Mastermaid hadn't put him in mind of them when evening drew on, telling him he had better set out to fetch the horse before the Giant came home. So he set off, and took the bit which hung in the corner, ran up the hill, and it wasn't long before he met the horse, with fire and flame streaming out of its nostrils. But he watched his time, and as the horse came open-jawed up to him, he threw the bit into its mouth, and it stood as quiet as a lamb. After that it was no great matter to ride it home and put it up, you may fancy; and then the Prince went into his room again, and began to carol and sing.

So the Giant came home again at even with his goats; and the first words he said were—

"Have you brought my horse down from the hill?"

"Yes, master, that I have," said the Prince; "and a better horse I never bestrode; but for all that I rode him straight home, and put him up safe and sound."

"I'll soon see to that," said the Giant, and ran out to the stable, and there stood the horse just as the Prince had said.

"You've talked to my Mastermaid, I'll be bound, for you haven't sucked this out of your own breast," said the Giant again.

"Yesterday master talked of this Mastermaid, and today it's the same story," said the Prince, who pretended to be silly and stupid. "Bless you, master! why don't you show me the thing at once? I should so like to see it only once in my life."

"Oh, if that's all," said the Giant, "you'll see her soon enough."

The third day, at dawn, the Giant went off to the wood again with his goats; but before he went he said to the Prince—

"Today you must go to Hell and fetch my fire-tax. When you have

done that you can rest yourself all day, for you must know it is an easy
master you have come to," and with that off he went.

"Easy master, indeed!" said the Prince. "You may be easy, but you
set me hard tasks all the same. But I may as well see if I can find your
Mastermaid, as you call her. I daresay she'll tell me what to do," and so
in he went to her again.

So when the Mastermaid asked what the Giant had set him to do
that day, he told her how he was to go to Hell and fetch the fire-tax.

"And how will you set about it?" asked the Mastermaid.

"Oh, that you must tell me," said the Prince. "I have never been to
Hell in my life; and even if I knew the way, I don't know how much I
am to ask for."

"Well, I'll soon tell you," said the Mastermaid; "you must go to the
steep rock away yonder, under the hillside, and take the club that lies
there, and knock on the face of the rock. Then there will come out one
all glistening with fire; to him you must tell your errand; and when he
asks you how much you will have, mind you say, 'As much as I can
carry.' "

Yes; he would be sure to say that; so he sat in there with the Mastermaid all that day too; and though evening drew on, he would have sat
there till now, had not the Mastermaid put him in mind that it was
high time to be off to Hell to fetch the Giant's fire-tax before he came
home. So he went on his way, and did just as the Mastermaid had told
him; and when he reached the rock he took up the club and gave a
great thump. Then the rock opened, and out came one whose face glistened, and out of whose eyes and nostrils flew sparks of fire.

"What is your will?" said he.

"Oh! I'm only come from the Giant to fetch his fire-tax," said the
Prince.

"How much will you have then?" said the other.

"I never wish for more than I am able to carry," said the Prince.

"Lucky for you that you did not ask for a whole horseload," said he
who came out of the rock; "but come now into the rock with me, and
you shall have it."

So the Prince went in with him, and you may fancy what heaps and
heaps of gold and silver he saw lying in there, just like stones in a gravel
pit; and he got a load just as big as he was able to carry, and set off
home with it. Now, when the Giant came home with his goats at even,
the Prince went into his room, and began to carol and sing as he had
done the evenings before.

"Have you been to Hell after my fire-tax?" roared the Giant.

"Oh yes; that I have, master," answered the Prince.

"Where have you put it?" said the Giant.

"There stands the sack on the bench yonder," said the Prince.

"I'll soon see to that," said the Giant, who strode off to the bench, and there he saw the sack so full that the gold and silver dropped out on the floor as soon as ever he untied the string.

"You've been talking to my Mastermaid, that I can see," said the Giant; "but if you have, I'll wring your head off."

"Mastermaid!" said the Prince; "yesterday master talked of this Mastermaid, and today he talks of her again, and the day before yesterday it was the same story. I only wish I could see what sort of thing she is! that I do."

"Well, well, wait till tomorrow," said the Giant, "and then I'll take you in to her myself."

"Thank you kindly, master," said the Prince; "but it's only a joke of master's, I'll be bound."

So next day the Giant took him in to the Mastermaid, and said to her—

"Now, you must cut his throat, and boil him in the great big pot you wot of; and when the broth is ready just give me a call."

After that he laid him down on the bench to sleep, and began to snore so, that it sounded like thunder on the hills.

So the Mastermaid took a knife and cut the Prince in his little finger, and let three drops of blood fall on a three-legged stool; and after that she took all the old rags and soles of shoes, and all the rubbish she could lay hands on, and put them into the pot; and then she filled a chest full of ground gold, and took a lump of salt, and a flask of water that hung behind the door, and she took, besides, a golden apple, and two golden chickens, and off she set with the Prince from the Giant's house as fast as they could; and when they had gone a little way, they came to the sea, and after that they sailed over the sea; but where they got the ship from I have never heard tell.

So when the Giant had slumbered a good bit, he began to stretch himself as he lay on the bench, and called out, "Will it be soon done?"

"Only just begun," answered the first drop of blood on the stool.

So the Giant lay down to sleep again, and slumbered a long, long time. At last he began to toss about a little, and cried out—

"Do you hear what I say; will it be soon done?" but he did not look up this time any more than the first, for he was still half asleep.

"Half done," said the second drop of blood.

Then the Giant thought again it was the Mastermaid, so he turned over on his other side, and fell asleep again; and when he had gone on sleeping for many hours, he began to stir and stretch his old bones, and to call out—

"Isn't it done yet?"

"Done to a turn," said the third drop of blood.

Then the Giant rose up, and began to rub his eyes, but he couldn't see who it was that was talking to him, so he searched and called for the Mastermaid, but no one answered.

"Ah, well! I daresay she's just run out of doors for a bit," he thought, and took up a spoon and went up to the pot to taste the broth; but he found nothing but shoe soles, and rags, and such stuff; and it was all boiled up together, so that he couldn't tell which was thick and which was thin. As soon as he saw this, he could tell how things had gone, and he got so angry he scarce knew which leg to stand upon. Away he went after the Prince and the Mastermaid, till the wind whistled behind him; but before long he came to the water and couldn't cross it.

"Never mind," he said; "I know a cure for this. I've only got to call on my stream-sucker."

So he called on his stream-sucker, and he came and stooped down, and took one, two, three gulps; and then the water fell so much in the sea that the Giant could see the Mastermaid and the Prince sailing in their ship.

"Now you must cast out the lump of salt," said the Mastermaid.

So the Prince threw it overboard, and it grew up into a mountain so high, right across the sea, that the Giant couldn't pass it, and the stream-sucker couldn't help him by swilling any more water.

"Never mind," cried the Giant; "there's a cure for this too." So he called on his hill-borer to come and bore through the mountain, that the stream-sucker might creep through and take another swill; but just as they had made a hole through the hill, and the stream-sucker was about to drink, the Mastermaid told the Prince to throw overboard a drop or two out of the flask, and then the sea was just as full as ever, and before the stream-sucker could take another gulp, they reached the land and were saved from the Giant.

So they made up their minds to go home to the Prince's father; but the Prince would not hear of the Mastermaid's walking, for he thought it seemly neither for her nor for him.

"Just wait here ten minutes," he said, "while I go home after the seven horses which stand in my father's stall. It's no great way off, and I shan't be long about it; but I will not hear of my sweetheart walking to my father's palace."

"Ah!" said the Mastermaid, "pray don't leave me, for if you once get home to the palace you'll forget me outright; I know you will."

"Oh!" said he, "how can I forget you; you with whom I have gone through so much, and whom I love so dearly?"

There was no help for it, he must and would go home to fetch the coach and seven horses, and she was to wait for him by the seaside. So at last the Mastermaid was forced to let him have his way; she only said—

"Now, when you get home, don't stop so much as to say good day to anyone, but go straight to the stable and put to the horses, and drive back as quick as you can; for they will all come about you, but do as though you did not see them; and above all things, mind you do not taste a morsel of food, for if you do, we shall both come to grief."

All this the Prince promised; but he thought all the time there was little fear of his forgetting her.

Now, just as he came home to the palace, one of his brothers was thinking of holding his bridal feast, and the bride, and all her kith and kin, were just come to the palace. So they all thronged round him, and asked about this thing and that, and wanted him to go in with them; but he made as though he did not see them, and went straight to the stall and got out the horses, and began to put them to. And when they saw they could not get him to go in, they came out to him with meat and drink, and the best of everything they had got ready for the feast; but the Prince would not taste so much as a crumb, and put to as fast as he could. At last the bride's sister rolled an apple across the yard to him, saying—

"Well, if you won't eat anything else, you may as well take a bite of this, for you must be both hungry and thirsty after so long a journey."

So he took up the apple and bit a piece out of it; but he had scarce done so before he forgot the Mastermaid, and how he was to drive back for her.

"Well, I think I must be mad," he said; "what am I to do with this coach and horses?"

So he put the horses up again, and went along with the others into the palace, and it was soon settled that he should have the bride's sister who had rolled the apple over to him.

There sat the Mastermaid by the seashore, and waited and waited for the Prince, but no Prince came; so at last she went up from the shore, and after she had gone a bit she came to a little hut, which lay by itself in a copse close by the king's palace. She went in and asked if she might lodge there. It was an old dame that owned the hut, and a cross-grained scolding hag she was as ever you saw. At first she would not hear of the Mastermaid's lodging in her house, but at last, for fair words and high rent, the Mastermaid got leave to be there. Now the hut was as dark and dirty as a pigsty, so the Mastermaid said she would smarten it up a little, that their house might look inside like other people's. The old hag did not like this either, and showed her teeth, and was cross; but the Mastermaid did not mind her. She took her chest of gold, and threw a handful or so into the fire, and lo! the gold melted, and bubbled and boiled over out of the grate, and spread itself over the whole hut, till it was gilded both outside and in. But as soon as the gold began to bubble and boil, the old hag got so afraid that she tried to run out as if the Evil One were at her heels; and as she ran out at the door, she forgot to stoop, and gave her head such a knock against the lintel, that she broke her neck, and that was the end of her.

Next morning the Constable passed that way, and you may fancy he could scarce believe his eyes when he saw the golden hut shining and glistening away in the copse; but he was still more astonished when he went in and saw the lovely maiden who sat there. To make a long story short, he fell over head and ears in love with her, and begged and prayed her to become his wife.

"Well, but have you much money?" asked the Mastermaid.

Yes, for that matter, he said, he was not so badly off, and off he went home to fetch the money, and when he came back at even he brought a half-bushel sack, and set it down on the bench. So the Mastermaid said she would have him, since he was so rich; but they were scarce in bed before she said she must get up again—

"For I have forgotten to make up the fire."

"Pray, don't stir out of bed," said the Constable; "I'll see to it."

So he jumped out of bed, and stood on the hearth in a trice.

"As soon as you have got hold of the shovel, just tell me," said the Mastermaid.

"Well, I am holding it now," said the Constable.

Then the Mastermaid said—

"God grant that you may hold the shovel, and the shovel you, and may you heap hot burning coals over yourself till morning breaks."

So there stood the Constable all night long, shoveling hot burning coals over himself; and though he begged, and prayed, and wept, the coals were not a bit colder for that; but as soon as day broke, and he had power to cast away the shovel, he did not stay long, as you may fancy, but set off as if the Evil One or the bailiff were at his heels; and all who met him stared their eyes out at him, for he cut capers as though he were mad, and he could not have looked in worse plight if he had been flayed and tanned, and everyone wondered what had befallen him, but he told no one where he had been, for shame's sake.

Next day the Attorney passed by the place where the Mastermaid lived, and he too saw how it shone and glistened in the copse; so he turned aside to find out who owned the hut; and when he came in and saw the lovely maiden, he fell more in love with her than the Constable, and began to woo her in hot haste.

Well, the Mastermaid asked him, as she had asked the Constable, if he had a good lot of money? and the Attorney said he wasn't so badly off; and as a proof he went home to fetch his money. So at even he came back with a great fat sack of money—I think it was a whole bushel sack—and set it down on the bench; and the long and the short of the matter was, that he was to have her, and they went to bed. But all at once the Mastermaid had forgotten to shut the door of the porch, and she must get up and make it fast for the night.

"What, you do that!" said the Attorney, "while I lie here; that can never be; lie still while I go and do it."

So up he jumped like a pea on a drum-head, and ran out into the porch.

"Tell me," said the Mastermaid, "when you have hold of the door latch."

"I've got hold of it now," said the Attorney.

"God grant, then," said the Mastermaid, "that you may hold the door, and the door you, and that you may go from wall to wall till day dawns."

So you may fancy what a dance the Attorney had all night long; such a waltz he never had before, and I don't think he would much care if he never had such a waltz again. Now he pulled the door forward, and then the door pulled him back, and so he went on, now dashed into one corner of the porch, and now into the other, till he was almost battered to death. At first he began to curse and swear, and then to beg and pray, but the door cared for nothing but holding its own till break of day. As soon as it let go its hold, off set the Attorney, leaving behind him his money to pay for his night's lodging, and forgetting his courtship altogether, for, to tell the truth, he was afraid lest the house door should come dancing after him. All who met him stared and gaped at him, for he too cut capers like a madman, and he could not have looked in worse plight if he had spent the whole night in butting against a flock of rams.

The third day the Sheriff passed that way, and he too saw the golden hut, and turned aside to find out who lived there; and he had scarce set eyes on the Mastermaid before he began to woo her. So she answered him as she had answered the other two. If he had lots of money she would have him; if not, he might go about his business. Well, the Sheriff said he wasn't so badly off, and he would go home and fetch the money; and when he came again at even, he had a bigger sack even than the Attorney—it must have been at least a bushel and a half, and put it down on the bench. So it was soon settled that he was to have the Mastermaid, but they had scarce gone to bed before the Mastermaid said she had forgotten to bring home the calf from the meadow, so she must get up and drive him into the stall. Then the Sheriff swore by all the powers that should never be, and, stout and fat as he was, up he jumped as nimbly as a kitten.

"Well, only tell me when you've got hold of the calf's tail," said the Mastermaid.

"Now I have hold of it," said the Sheriff.

"God grant," said the Mastermaid, "that you may hold the calf's tail, and the calf's tail you, and that you may make a tour of the world together till day dawns."

Well, you may just fancy how the Sheriff had to stretch his legs; away they went, the calf and he, over high and low, across hill and dale, and the more the Sheriff cursed and swore, the faster the calf ran and jumped. At dawn of day the poor Sheriff was well nigh broken-winded, and so glad was he to let go the calf's tail that he forgot his sack of money and everything else. As he was a great man, he went a little slower than the Attorney and the Constable, but the slower he went the more time people had to gape and stare at him; and I must say they made good use of their time, for he was terribly tattered and torn, after his dance with the calf.

Next day was fixed for the wedding at the palace, and the eldest brother was to drive to church with his bride, and the younger, who had lived with the Giant, with the bride's sister. But when they had got into the coach, and were just going to drive off, one of the trace-pins snapped off; and though they made at least three in its place, they all broke, from whatever sort of wood they were made. So time went on and on, and they couldn't get to church, and everyone grew very downcast. But all at once the Constable said, for he too was bidden to the wedding, that yonder, away in the copse, lived a maiden:

"And if you can only get her to lend you the handle of her shovel with which she makes up her fire, I know very well it will hold."

Well! they sent a messenger on the spot, with such a pretty message to the maiden, to know if they couldn't get the loan of her shovel which the Constable had spoken of; and the maiden said "yes," they might have it; so they got a trace-pin which wasn't likely to snap.

But all at once, just as they were driving off, the bottom of the coach tumbled to bits. So they set to work to make a new bottom as they best might; but it mattered not how many nails they put into it, nor of what wood they made it, for as soon as ever they got the bottom well into the coach and were driving off, snap it went in two again, and they were even worse off than when they lost the trace-pin. Just then the Attorney said—for if the Constable was there, you may fancy the Attorney was there too—"Away yonder, in the copse, lives a maiden, and if you could only get her to lend you one half of her porch door, I know it can hold together."

Well! they sent another message to the copse, and asked so prettily if they couldn't have the loan of the gilded porch door which the Attorney had talked of; and they got it on the spot. So they were just setting out; but now the horses were not strong enough to draw the coach, though there were six of them; then they put on eight, and ten, and twelve, but the more they put on, and the more the coachman whipped, the more the coach wouldn't stir an inch. By this time it was far on in the day, and everyone about the palace was in doleful dumps; for to church they must go, and yet it looked as if they should never get there. So at last the Sheriff said that yonder, in the gilded hut in the copse, lived a maiden, and if they could only get the loan of her calf—

"I know it can drag the coach, though it were as heavy as a mountain."

Well, they all thought it would look silly to be drawn to church by a calf, but there was no help for it, so they had to send a third time, and ask so prettily in the King's name, if he couldn't get the loan of the calf the Sheriff had spoken of, and the Mastermaid let them have it on the spot, for she was not going to say "no" this time either. So they put the calf on before the horses, and waited to see if it would do any good, and away went the coach over high and low, and stock and stone, so that they could scarce draw their breath; sometimes they were on the ground, and sometimes up in the air, and when they reached the church, the calf began to run round and round it like a spinning jenny, so that they had hard work to get out of the coach, and into the church. When they went back, it was the same story, only they went faster, and they reached the palace almost before they knew they had set out.

Now when they sat down to dinner, the Prince who had served with the Giant said he thought they ought to ask the maiden who had lent them her shovel handle and porch door, and calf, to come up to the palace.

"For," said he, "if we hadn't got these three things, we should have been sticking here still."

Yes; the King thought that only fair and right, so he sent five of his best men down to the gilded hut to greet the maiden from the King, and to ask her if she wouldn't be so good as to come up and dine at the palace.

"Greet the King from me," said the Mastermaid, "and tell him, if he's too good to come to me, so am I too good to go to him."

So the King had to go himself, and then the Mastermaid went up with him without more ado; and as the King thought she was more than she seemed to be, he sat her down in the highest seat by the side of the youngest bridegroom.

Now, when they had sat a little while at table, the Mastermaid took out her golden apple, and the golden cock and hen, which she had carried off from the Giant, and put them down on the table before her, and the cock and hen began at once to peck at one another, and to fight for the golden apple.

"Oh! only look," said the Prince; "see how those two strive for the apple."

"Yes!" said the Mastermaid; "so we two strove to get away that time when we were together in the hillside."

Then the spell was broken, and the Prince knew her again, and you may fancy how glad he was. But as for the witch who had rolled the apple over to him, he had her torn to pieces between twenty-four horses, so that there was not a bit of her left, and after that they held on with the wedding in real earnest; and though they were still stiff and footsore, the Constable, the Attorney, and the Sheriff kept it up with the best of them.

77. NOT A PIN TO CHOOSE BETWEEN THEM

(Norway)

ONCE ON A TIME there was a man, and he had a wife. Now this couple wanted to sow their fields, but they had neither seed corn nor money to buy it with. But they had a cow, and the man was to drive it into town and sell it, to get money to buy corn for seed. But when it came to the pinch, the wife dared not let her husband start, for fear he should spend the money in drink, so she set off herself with the cow, and took besides a hen with her.

Close by the town she met a butcher, who asked—

"Will you sell that cow, Goody?"

"Yes, that I will," she answered.

"Well, what do you want for her?"

"Oh! I must have five shillings for the cow, but you shall have the hen for ten pound."

"Very good!" said the man; "I don't want the hen, and you'll soon get it off your hands in the town; but I'll give you five shillings for the cow."

Well, she sold her cow for five shillings, but there was no one in the town who would give ten pound for a lean tough old hen, so she went back to the butcher, and said—

"Do all I can, I can't get rid of this hen, master! you must take it too, as you took the cow."

"Well," said the butcher, "come along and we'll see about it." Then he treated her both with meat and drink, and gave her so much brandy that she lost her head, and didn't know what she was about, and fell fast asleep. But while she slept, the butcher took and dipped her into a tar barrel, and then laid her down on a heap of feathers; and when she woke up she was feathered all over, and began to wonder what had befallen her.

"Is it me, or is it not me? No, it can never be me; it must be some great strange bird. But what shall I do to find out whether it is me or not. Oh! I know how I shall be able to tell whether it is me; if the calves come and lick me, and our dog Tray doesn't bark at me when I get home, then it must be me and no one else."

Now, Tray, her dog, had scarce set his eyes on the strange monster which came through the gate, than he set up such a barking, one would have thought all the rogues and robbers in the world were in the yard.

"Ah! deary me!" said she, "I thought so; it can't be me surely." So she went to the straw yard, and the calves wouldn't lick her, when they snuffed in the strong smell of tar.

"No, no!" she said, "it can't be me; it must be some strange outlandish bird."

So she crept up on the roof of the safe and began to flap her arms, as if they had been wings, and was just going to fly off.

When her husband saw all this, out he came with his rifle, and began to take aim at her.

"Oh!" cried his wife, "don't shoot, don't shoot! it is only me."

"If it's you," said her husband, "don't stand up there like a goat on a house top, but come down and let me hear what you have to say for yourself."

So she crawled down again, but she hadn't a shilling to show, for the crown she had got from the butcher she had thrown away in her drunkenness. When her husband heard her story, he said, "You're only twice as silly as you were before," and he got so angry that he made up his mind to go away from her altogether, and never to come back till he had found three other Goodies as silly as his own.

So he toddled off, and when he had walked a little way he saw a Goody, who was running in and out of a newly-built wooden cottage with an empty sieve, and every time she ran in she threw her apron over the sieve, just as if she had something in it, and when she got in she turned it upside down on the floor.

"Why, Goody!" he asked, "what are you doing?"

"Oh," she answered, "I'm only carrying in a little sun; but I don't know how it is, when I'm outside I have the sun in my sieve, but when I get inside, somehow or other I've thrown it away. But in my old cottage I had plenty of sun, though I never carried in the least bit. I only wish I knew someone who would bring the sun inside; I'd give him three hundred dollars and welcome."

"Have you got an ax?" asked the man. "If you have, I'll soon bring the sun inside."

So he got an ax and cut windows in the cottage, for the carpenters had forgotten them; then the sun shone in, and he got his three hundred dollars.

"That was one of them," said the man to himself, as he went on his way.

After a while he passed by a house, out of which came an awful screaming and bellowing; so he turned in and saw a Goody, who was hard at work banging her husband across the head with a beetle, and over his head she had drawn a shirt without any slit for the neck.

"Why, Goody!" he asked, "will you beat your husband to death?"

"No," she said, "I only must have a hole in this shirt for his neck to come through."

All the while the husband kept on screaming and calling out—

"Heaven help and comfort all who try on new shirts! If anyone would teach my Goody another way of making a slit for the neck in my new shirts I'd give him three hundred dollars down, and welcome."

"I'll do it in the twinkling of an eye," said the man, "if you'll only give me a pair of scissors."

So he got a pair of scissors, and snipped a hole in the neck, and went off with his three hundred dollars.

"That was another of them," he said to himself, as he walked along.

Last of all, he came to a farm, where he made up his mind to rest a bit. So when he went in, the mistress asked him—

"Whence do you come, master?"

"Oh!" said he, "I come from Paradise Place," for that was the name of his farm.

"From Paradise Place!" she cried, "you don't say so! Why, then, you must know my second husband Peter, who is dead and gone, God rest his soul!"

For you must know this Goody had been married three times, and as her first and last husbands had been bad, she had made up her mind that the second only was gone to heaven.

"Oh! yes," said the man; "I know him very well."

"Well," asked the Goody, "how do things go with him, poor dear soul?"

"Only middling," was the answer; "he goes about begging from house to house, and has neither food nor a rag to his back. As for money, he hasn't a sixpence to bless himself with."

"Mercy on me!" cried out the Goody; "he never ought to go about such a figure when he left so much behind him. Why, there's a whole cupboardful of old clothes upstairs which belonged to him, besides a great chest full of money yonder. Now, if you will take them with you, you shall have a horse and cart to carry them. As for the horse, he can keep it, and sit on the cart, and drive about from house to house, and then he needn't trudge on foot."

So the man got a whole cartload of clothes, and a chest full of shining dollars, and as much meat and drink as he would; and when he had got all he wanted, he jumped into the cart and drove off.

"That was the third," he said to himself, as he went along.

Now this Goody's third husband was a little way off in a field plowing, and when he saw a strange man driving off from the farm with his horse and cart, he went home and asked his wife who that was that had just started with the black horse.

"Oh, do you mean him?" said the Goody; "why, that was a man from Paradise, who said that Peter, my dear second husband, who is dead and gone, is in a sad plight, and that he goes from house to house begging, and has neither clothes nor money; so I just sent him all those old clothes he left behind him, and the old money box with the dollars in it."

The man saw how the land lay in a trice, so he saddled his horse and rode off from the farm at full gallop. It wasn't long before he was close behind the man who sat and drove the cart; but when the latter saw this he drove the cart into a thicket by the side of the road, pulled out a handful of hair from the horse's tail, jumped up on a little rise in the wood, where he tied the hair fast to a birch, and then lay down under it, and began to peer and stare up at the sky.

"Well, well, if I ever!" he said, as Peter the third came riding up. "No! I never saw the like of this in all my born days!"

Then Peter stood and looked at him for some time, wondering what had come over him; but at last he asked—

"What do you lie there staring at?"

"No," kept on the man, "I never did see anything like it!—here is a man going straight up to heaven on a black horse, and here you see his horse's tail still hanging in this birch; and yonder up in the sky you see the black horse."

Peter looked first at the man, and then at the sky, and said—

"I see nothing but the horsehair in the birch; that's all I see."

"Of course you can't where you stand," said the man; "but just come and lie down here, and stare straight up, and mind you don't take your eyes off the sky; and then you shall see what you shall see."

But while Peter the third lay and stared up at the sky till his eyes filled with tears, the man from Paradise Place took his horse and jumped on its back, and rode off both with it and the cart and horse.

When the hoofs thundered along the road, Peter the third jumped up, but he was so taken aback when he found the man had gone off with his horse, that he hadn't the sense to run after him till it was too late.

He was rather down in the mouth when he got home to his Goody; but when she asked him what he had done with the horse, he said—

"I gave it to the man too for Peter the second, for I thought it wasn't right he should sit in a cart and scramble about from house to house; so now he can sell the cart and buy himself a coach to drive about in."

"Thank you heartily!" said his wife; "I never thought you could be so kind."

Well, when the man reached home, who had got the six hundred dollars and the cartload of clothes and money, he saw that all his fields were plowed and sown, and the first thing he asked his wife was, where she had got the seed corn from.

"Oh," she said, "I have always heard that what a man sows he shall reap, so I sowed the salt which our friends the north country men laid up here with us, and if we only have rain I fancy it will come up nicely."

"Silly you are," said her husband, "and silly you will be so long as you live; but that is all one now, for the rest are not a bit wiser than you. There is not a pin to choose between you."

78. PRINCESS ON THE GLASS HILL
(*Norway*)

ONCE ON A TIME there was a man who had a meadow, which lay high up on the hillside, and in the meadow was a barn, which he had built to keep his hay in. Now, I must tell you there hadn't been much in the barn for the last year or two, for every St. John's night, when the grass stood greenest and deepest, the meadow was eaten down to the very ground the next morning, just as if a whole drove of sheep had been there feeding on it overnight. This happened once, and it happened twice; so at last the man grew weary of losing his crop of hay, and said to his sons—for he had three of them, and the youngest was nicknamed Boots—that now one of them must just go and sleep in the barn in the outlying field when St. John's night came, for it was too good a joke that his grass should be eaten, root and blade, this year, as it had been the last two years. So whichever of them went must keep a sharp lookout; that was what their father said.

Well, the eldest son was ready to go and watch the meadow; trust him for looking after the grass! It shouldn't be his fault if man or beast, or the fiend himself, got a blade of grass. So, when evening came, he set off to the barn, and lay down to sleep; but a little on in the night came such a clatter, and such an earthquake, that walls and roof shook, and groaned, and creaked; then up jumped the lad, and took to his heels as fast as ever he could; nor dared he once look round till he reached home; and as for the hay, why it was eaten up this year just as it had been twice before.

The next St. John's night, the man said again it would never do to lose all the grass in the outlying field year after year in this way, so one of his sons must just trudge off to watch it, and watch it well too. Well, the next oldest son was ready to try his luck, so he set off, and lay down to sleep in the barn as his brother had done before him; but as night wore on there came on a rumbling and quaking of the earth, worse even than on the last St. John's night, and when the lad heard it he got frightened, and took to his heels as though he were running a race.

Next year the turn came to Boots; but when he made ready to go, the other two began to laugh, and to make game of him, saying—

"You're just the man to watch the hay, that you are; you who have done nothing all your life but sit in the ashes and toast yourself by the fire."

But Boots did not care a pin for their chattering, and stumped away, as evening drew on, up the hillside to the outlying field. There he went inside the barn and lay down; but in about an hour's time the barn began to groan and creak, so that it was dreadful to hear.

"Well," said Boots to himself, "if it isn't worse than this, I can stand it well enough."

A little while after came another creak and an earthquake, so that the litter in the barn flew about the lad's ears.

"Oh!" said Boots to himself, "if it isn't worse than this, I daresay I can stand it out."

But just then came a third rumbling, and a third earthquake, so that the lad thought walls and roof were coming down on his head; but it passed off, and all was still as death about him.

"It'll come again, I'll be bound," thought Boots; but no, it did not come again; still it was and still it stayed; but after he had lain a little while he heard a noise as if a horse were standing just outside the barn door, and cropping the grass. He stole to the door, and peeped through a chink, and there stood a horse feeding away. So big, and fat, and grand a horse, Boots had never set eyes on; by his side on the grass lay a saddle and bridle, and a full set of armor for a knight, all of brass, so bright that the light gleamed from it.

"Ho, ho!" thought the lad; "it's you, is it, that eats up our hay? I'll soon put a spoke in your wheel; just see if I don't."

So he lost no time, but took the steel out of his tinderbox, and threw it over the horse; then it had no power to stir from the spot, and became so tame that the lad could do what he liked with it. So he got on its back, and rode off with it to a place which no one knew of, and there he put up the horse. When he got home his brothers laughed, and asked how he had fared.

"You didn't lie long in the barn, even if you had the heart to go so far as the field."

"Well," said Boots, "all I can say is, I lay in the barn till the sun rose, and neither saw nor heard anything; I can't think what there was in the barn to make you both so afraid."

"A pretty story!" said his brothers; "but we'll soon see how you have watched the meadow"; so they set off; but when they reached it, there stood the grass as deep and thick as it had been overnight.

Well, the next St. John's eve it was the same story over again; neither of the elder brothers dared to go out to the outlying field to watch the crop; but Boots, he had the heart to go, and everything happened just as it had happened the year before. First a clatter and an earthquake, then a greater clatter and another earthquake, and so on a third time; only this year the earthquakes were far worse than the year before. Then all at once everything was as still as death, and the lad heard how something was cropping the grass outside the barn door, so he stole to the door, and peeped through a chink; and what do you think he saw? why, another horse standing right up against the wall, and chewing and champing with might and main. It was far finer and fatter than that which came the year before, and it had a saddle on its back, and a bridle on its neck, and a full suit of mail for a knight lay by its side, all of silver, and as grand as you would wish to see.

"Ho, ho!" said Boots to himself; "it's you that gobbles up our hay, is it? I'll soon put a spoke in your wheel," and with that he took the steel out of his tinderbox, and threw it over the horse's crest, which stood as still as a lamb. Well, the lad rode this horse, too, to the hiding place where he kept the other one, and after that he went home.

"I suppose you'll tell us," said one of his brothers, "there's a fine crop this year too, up in the hayfield."

"Well, so there is," said Boots; and off ran the others to see, and there stood the grass thick and deep, as it was the year before; but they didn't give Boots softer words for all that.

Now, when the third St. John's eve came, the two elder still hadn't the heart to lie out in the barn and watch the grass, for they had got so scared at heart the night they lay there before, that they couldn't get over the fright; but Boots, he dared to go; and, to make a long story short, the very same thing happened this time as had happened twice before. Three earthquakes came, one after the other, each worse than the one which went before, and when the last came, the lad danced about with the shock from one barn wall to the other; and after that, all at once, it was still as death. Now when he had lain a little while he heard something tugging away at the grass outside the barn, so he stole again to the door chink, and peeped out, and there stood a horse close outside—far, far bigger and fatter than the two he had taken before.

"Ho, ho!" said the lad to himself, "it's you, is it, that comes here eating up our hay? I'll soon stop that—I'll soon put a spoke in your wheel." So he caught up his steel and threw it over the horse's neck, and in a trice it stood as if it were nailed to the ground, and Boots could do as he pleased with it. Then he rode off with it to the hiding place where he kept the other two, and then went home. When he got home his two brothers made game of him as they had done before, saying they could see he had watched the grass well, for he looked for all the world as if he were walking in his sleep, and many other spiteful things they said, but Boots gave no heed to them, only asking them to go and see for themselves; and when they went, there stood the grass as fine and deep this time as it had been twice before.

Now, you must know that the king of the country where Boots lived had a daughter, whom he would only give to the man who could ride up over the hill of glass, for there was a high, high hill, all of glass, as smooth and slippery as ice, close by the king's palace. Upon the tip-top of the hill the king's daughter was to sit, with three golden apples in her lap, and the man who could ride up and carry off the three golden apples was to have half the kingdom, and the Princess to wife. This the king had stuck up on all the church doors in his realm, and had given it out in many other kingdoms besides. Now, this Princess was so lovely that all who set eyes on her fell over head and ears in love with her whether they would or no. So I needn't tell you how all the princes and knights who heard of her were eager to win her to wife, and half the kingdom beside; and how they came riding from all parts of the world on high prancing horses, and clad in the grandest clothes, for there wasn't one of them who hadn't made up his mind that he, and he alone, was to win the Princess.

So when the day of trial came, which the king had fixed, there was such a crowd of princes and knights under the glass hill, that it made one's head whirl to look at them; and everyone in the country who could even crawl along was off to the hill, for they all were eager to see the man who was to win the Princess. So the two elder brothers set off with the rest; but as for Boots, they said outright he shouldn't go with them, for if they were seen with such a dirty changeling, all begrimed with smut from cleaning their shoes and sifting cinders in the dusthole, they said folk would make game of them.

"Very well," said Boots, "it's all one to me. I can go alone, and stand or fall by myself."

Now when the two brothers came to the hill of glass the knights and princes were all hard at it, riding their horses till they were all in a foam; but it was no good, by my troth; for as soon as ever the horses set foot on the hill, down they slipped, and there wasn't one who could get a yard or two up; and no wonder, for the hill was as smooth as a sheet of glass, and as steep as a house wall. But all were eager to have the Princess and half the kingdom. So they rode and slipped, and slipped and rode, and still it was the same story over again. At last all their horses were so weary that they could scarce lift a leg, and in such a sweat that the lather dripped from them, and so the knights had to give up trying any more. So the king was just thinking that he would proclaim a new trial for the next day, to see if they would have better luck, when all at once a knight came riding up on so brave a steed that no one had ever seen the like of it in his born days, and the knight had mail of brass, and the horse a brass bit in his mouth, so bright that the sunbeams shone from it. Then all the others called out to him he might just as well spare himself the trouble of riding at the hill, for it would lead to no good; but he gave no heed to them, and put his horse at the hill, and went up it like nothing for a good way, about a third of the height; and when he had got so far, he turned his horse round and rode down again. So lovely a knight the Princess thought she had never yet seen; and while he was riding, she sat and thought to herself—

"Would to heaven he might only come up, and down the other side."

And when she saw him turning back, she threw down one of the golden apples after him, and it rolled down into his shoe. But when he got to the bottom of the hill he rode off so fast that no one could tell what had become of him. That evening all the knights and princes were to go before the king, that he who had ridden so far up the hill might show the apple which the princess had thrown, but there was no one who had anything to show. One after the other they all came, but not a man of them could show the apple.

At even the brothers of Boots came home too, and had such a long story to tell about the riding up the hill.

"First of all," they said, "there was not one of the whole lot who could get so much as a stride up; but at last came one who had a suit of brass mail, and a brass bridle and saddle, all so bright that the sun shone from them a mile off. He was a chap to ride, just! He rode a third of the way up the hill of glass, and he could easily have ridden the

whole way up, if he chose; but he turned round and rode down, thinking, maybe, that was enough for once."

"Oh! I should so like to have seen him, that I should," said Boots,
who sat by the fireside, and stuck his feet into the cinders as was his
wont.

"Oh!" said his brothers, "you would, would you? You look fit to keep
company with such high lords, nasty beast that you are, sitting there
among the ashes."

Next day the brothers were all for setting off again, and Boots begged
them this time, too, to let him go with them and see the riding; but no,
they wouldn't have him at any price, he was too ugly and nasty, they
said.

"Well, well!" said Boots; "if I go at all, I must go by myself. I'm not
afraid."

So when the brothers got to the hill of glass, all the princes and
knights began to ride again, and you may fancy they had taken care to
shoe their horses sharp; but it was no good—they rode and slipped, and
slipped and rode, just as they had done the day before, and there was
not one who could get so far as a yard up the hill. And when they had
worn out their horses, so that they could not stir a leg, they were all
forced to give it up as a bad job. So the king thought he might as well
proclaim that the riding should take place the day after for the last
time, just to give them one chance more; but all at once it came across
his mind that he might as well wait a little longer, to see if the knight
in brass mail would come this day too. Well, they saw nothing of him;
but all at once came one riding on a steed, far, far, braver and finer
than that on which the knight in brass had ridden, and he had silver
mail, and a silver saddle and bridle, all so bright that the sunbeams
gleamed and glanced from them far away. Then the others shouted out
to him again, saying he might as well hold hard, and not try to ride up
the hill, for all his trouble would be thrown away; but the knight paid
no heed to them, and rode straight at the hill, and right up it, till he
had gone two thirds of the way, and then he wheeled his horse round
and rode down again. To tell the truth, the Princess liked him still better than the knight in brass, and she sat and wished he might only be
able to come right up to the top, and down the other side; but when
she saw him turning back, she threw the second apple after him, and it
rolled down and fell into his shoe. But as soon as ever he had come
down from the hill of glass, he rode off so fast that no one could see
what became of him.

At even, when all were to go in before the king and the Princess, that he who had the golden apple might show it; in they went, one after the other, but there was no one who had any apple to show, and the two brothers, as they had done on the former day, went home and told how things had gone, and how all had ridden at the hill and none got up.

"But, last of all," they said, "came one in a silver suit, and his horse had a silver saddle and a silver bridle. He was just a chap to ride; and he got two thirds up the hill, and then turned back. He was a fine fellow and no mistake; and the Princess threw the second gold apple to him."

"Oh!" said Boots, "I should so like to have seen him too, that I should."

"A pretty story!" they said. "Perhaps you think his coat of mail was as bright as the ashes you are always poking about, and sifting, you nasty dirty beast."

The third day everything happened as it had happened the two days before. Boots begged to go and see the sight, but the two wouldn't hear of his going with them. When they got to the hill there was no one who could get so much as a yard up it; and now all waited for the knight in silver mail, but they neither saw nor heard of him. At last came one riding on a steed, so brave that no one had ever seen his match; and the knight had a suit of golden mail, and a golden saddle and bridle, so wondrous bright that the sunbeams gleamed from them a mile off. The other knights and princes could not find time to call out to him not to try his luck, for they were amazed to see how grand he was. So he rode right at the hill, and tore up it like nothing, so that the Princess hadn't even time to wish that he might get up the whole way. As soon as ever he reached the top, he took the third golden apple from the Princess' lap, and then turned his horse and rode down again. As soon as he got down, he rode off at full speed, and was out of sight in no time.

Now, when the brothers got home at even, you may fancy what long stories they told, how the riding had gone off that day; and among other things, they had a deal to say about the knight in golden mail.

"He just was a chap to ride!" they said; "so grand a knight isn't to be found in the wide world."

"Oh!" said Boots, "I should so like to have seen him; that I should."

"Ah!" said his brothers, "his mail shone a deal brighter than the glowing coals which you are always poking and digging at; nasty dirty beast that you are."

Next day all the knights and princes were to pass before the king and the Princess—it was too late to do so the night before, I suppose—that he who had the gold apple might bring it forth; but one came after another, first the princes, and then the knights, and still no one could show the gold apple.

"Well," said the king, "someone must have it, for it was something that we all saw with our own eyes, how a man came and rode up and bore it off."

So he commanded that everyone who was in the kingdom should come up to the palace and see if they could show the apple. Well, they all came, one after another, but no one had the golden apple, and after a long time the two brothers of Boots came. They were the last of all, so the king asked them if there was no one else in the kingdom who hadn't come.

"Oh, yes," said they; "we have a brother, but he never carried off the golden apple. He hasn't stirred out of the dust-hole on any of the three days."

"Never mind that," said the king; "he may as well come up to the palace like the rest."

So Boots had to go up to the palace.

"How, now," said the king; "have you got the golden apple? Speak out!"

"Yes, I have," said Boots; "here is the first, and here is the second, and here is the third too," and with that he pulled all three golden apples out of his pocket, and at the same time threw off his sooty rags, and stood before them in his gleaming golden mail.

"Yes!" said the king; "you shall have my daughter, and half my kingdom, for you well deserve both her and it."

So they got ready for the wedding, and Boots got the Princess to wife, and there was great merrymaking at the bridal feast, you may fancy, for they could all be merry though they couldn't ride up the hill of glass; and all I can say is, if they haven't left off their merrymaking yet, why, they're still at it.

79. WHY THE BEAR IS STUMPY-TAILED
(*Norway*)

ONE DAY THE Bear met the Fox, who came slinking along with a string of fish he had stolen.

"Whence did you get those from?" asked the Bear.

"Oh! my Lord Bruin, I've been out fishing and caught them," said the Fox.

So the Bear had a mind to learn to fish too, and bade the Fox tell him how he was to set about it.

"Oh! it's an easy craft for you," answered the Fox, "and soon learned. You've only got to go upon the ice, and cut a hole and stick your tail down into it; and so you must go on holding it there as long as you can. You're not to mind if your tail smarts a little; that's when the fish bite. The longer you hold it there the more fish you'll get; and then all at once out with it, with a cross pull sideways, and with a strong pull too."

Yes; the Bear did as the Fox had said, and held his tail a long, long time down in the hole, till it was fast frozen in. Then he pulled it out with a cross pull, and it snapped short off. That's why Bruin goes about with a stumpy tail this very day.

80. WHY THE SEA IS SALT
(Norway)

ONCE ON A TIME, but it was a long, long time ago, there were two brothers, one rich and one poor. Now, one Christmas Eve, the poor one hadn't so much as a crumb in the house, either of meat or bread, so he went to his brother to ask him for something to keep Christmas with, in God's name. It was not the first time his brother had been forced to help him, and you may fancy he wasn't very glad to see his face, but he said—

"If you will do what I ask you to do, I'll give you a whole flitch of bacon."

So the poor brother said he would do anything, and was full of thanks.

"Well, here is the flitch," said the rich brother, "and now go straight to Hell."

"What I have given my word to do, I must stick to," said the other; so he took the flitch and set off. He walked the whole day, and at dusk he came to a place where he saw a very bright light.

"Maybe this is the place," said the man to himself. So he turned aside, and the first thing he saw was an old, old man, with a long white beard, who stood in an outhouse, hewing wood for the Christmas fire.

"Good even," said the man with the flitch.

"The same to you; whither are you going so late?" said the man.

"Oh! I'm going to Hell, if I only knew the right way," answered the poor man.

"Well, you're not far wrong, for this is Hell," said the old man; "when you get inside they will be all for buying your flitch, for meat is scarce in Hell; but mind you don't sell it unless you get the hand-mill which stands behind the door for it. When you come out, I'll teach you how to handle the mill, for it's good to grind almost anything."

So the man with the flitch thanked the other for his good advice, and gave a great knock at the Devil's door.

When he got in, everything went just as the old man had said. All the devils, great and small, came swarming up to him like ants round an anthill, and each tried to outbid the other for the flitch.

"Well!" said the man, "by rights my old dame and I ought to have this flitch for our Christmas dinner; but since you have all set your hearts on it, I suppose I must give it up to you; but if I sell it at all, I'll have for it that mill behind the door yonder."

At first the Devil wouldn't hear of such a bargain, and chaffered and haggled with the man; but he stuck to what he said, and at last the Devil had to part with his mill. When the man got out into the yard, he asked the old woodcutter how he was to handle the mill; and after he had learned how to use it, he thanked the old man and went off home as fast as he could, but still the clock had struck twelve on Christmas Eve before he reached his own door.

"Wherever in the world have you been?" said his old dame. "Here have I sat hour after hour waiting and watching, without so much as two sticks to lay together under the Christmas brose."

"Oh!" said the man, "I couldn't get back before, for I had to go a long way first for one thing, and then for another; but now you shall see what you shall see."

So he put the mill on the table, and bade it first of all grind lights, then a tablecloth, then meat, then ale, and so on till they had got everything that was nice for Christmas fare. He had only to speak the word, and the mill ground out what he wanted. The old dame stood by blessing her stars, and kept on asking where he had got this wonderful mill, but he wouldn't tell her.

"It's all one where I got it from; you see the mill is a good one, and the millstream never freezes, that's enough."

So he ground meat and drink and dainties enough to last out till Twelfth Day, and on the third day he asked all his friends and kin to his house, and gave a great feast. Now, when his rich brother saw all that was on the table, and all that was behind in the larder, he grew quite spiteful and wild, for he couldn't bear that his brother should have anything.

" 'Twas only on Christmas Eve," he said to the rest, "he was in such straits that he came and asked for a morsel of food in God's name, and now he gives a feast as if he were count or king"; and he turned to his brother and said—

"But whence, in Hell's name, have you got all this wealth?"

"From behind the door," answered the owner of the mill, for he didn't care to let the cat out of the bag. But later on in the evening, when he had got a drop too much, he could keep his secret no longer, and brought out the mill and said—

"There, you see what has gotten me all this wealth"; and so he made the mill grind all kind of things. When his brother saw it, he set his heart on having the mill, and, after a deal of coaxing, he got it; but he had to pay three hundred dollars for it, and his brother bargained to keep it till hay harvest, for he thought, if I keep it till then, I can make it grind meat and drink that will last for years. So you may fancy the mill didn't grow rusty for want of work, and when hay harvest came, the rich brother got it, but the other took care not to teach him how to handle it.

It was evening when the rich brother got the mill home, and next morning he told his wife to go out into the hayfield and toss, while the mowers cut the grass, and he would stay at home and get the dinner ready. So, when dinnertime drew near, he put the mill on the kitchen table and said—

"Grind herrings and broth, and grind them good and fast."

So the mill began to grind herrings and broth; first of all, all the dishes full, then all the tubs full, and so on till the kitchen floor was quite covered. Then the man twisted and twirled at the mill to get it to stop, but for all his twisting and fingering the mill went on grinding, and in a little while the broth rose so high that the man was like to drown. So he threw open the kitchen door and ran into the parlor, but it wasn't long before the mill had ground the parlor full too, and it was only at the risk of his life that the man could get hold of the latch of the house door through the stream of broth. When he got the door open, he ran out and set off down the road, with the stream of herrings and broth at his heels, roaring like a waterfall over the whole farm.

Now, his old dame, who was in the field tossing hay, thought it a long time to dinner, and at last she said—

"Well! though the master doesn't call us home, we may as well go. Maybe he finds it hard work to boil the broth, and will be glad of my help."

The men were willing enough, so they sauntered homeward; but just as they had got a little way up the hill, what should they meet but herrings, and broth, and bread, all running and dashing, and splashing together in a stream, and the master himself running before them for his life, and as he passed them he bawled out—"Would to heaven each of you had a hundred throats! but take care you're not drowned in the broth."

Away he went, as though the Evil One were at his heels, to his brother's house, and begged him for God's sake to take back the mill that instant; for, said he—

"If it grinds only one hour more, the whole parish will be swallowed up by herrings and broth."

But his brother wouldn't hear of taking it back till the other paid him down three hundred dollars more.

So the poor brother got both the money and the mill, and it wasn't long before he set up a farmhouse far finer than the one in which his brother lived, and with the mill he ground so much gold that he covered it with plates of gold; and as the farm lay by the seaside, the golden house gleamed and glistened far away over the sea. All who sailed by put ashore to see the rich man in the golden house, and to see the wonderful mill, the fame of which spread far and wide, till there was nobody who hadn't heard tell of it.

So one day there came a sea captain who wanted to see the mill; and the first thing he asked was if it could grind salt.

"Grind salt!" said the owner; "I should just think it could. It can grind anything."

When the skipper heard that, he said he must have the mill, cost what it would; for if he only had it, he thought he should be rid of his long voyages across stormy seas for a lading of salt. Well, at first the man wouldn't hear of parting with the mill; but the skipper begged and prayed so hard, that at last he let him have it, but he had to pay many, many thousand dollars for it. Now, when the skipper had got the mill on his back, he soon made off with it, for he was afraid lest the man should change his mind; so he had no time to ask how to handle the mill, but got on board his ship as fast as he could, and set sail. When he had sailed a good way off, he brought the mill on deck and said—

"Grind salt, and grind both good and fast."

Well, the mill began to grind salt so that it poured out like water; and when the skipper had got the ship full, he wished to stop the mill, but whichever way he turned it, and however much he tried, it was no good; the mill kept grinding on, and the heap of salt grew higher and higher, and at last down sunk the ship.

There lies the mill at the bottom of the sea, and grinds away at this very day, and that's why the sea is salt.

81. THE TINDERBOX
A tale retold by
Hans Christian Andersen
(Denmark)

A SOLDIER CAME MARCHING along the high road—left, right! left, right! He had his knapsack on his back and a sword by his side, for he had been to the wars and was now returning home.

An old Witch met him on the road. She was very ugly to look at: her underlip hung down to her breast.

"Good evening, Soldier!" she said. "What a fine sword and knapsack you have! You are something like a soldier! You ought to have as much money as you would like to carry!"

"Thank you, old Witch," said the Soldier.

"Do you see that great tree there?" said the Witch, pointing to a tree beside them. "It is hollow within. You must climb up to the top, and then you will see a hole through which you can let yourself down into the tree. I will tie a rope round your waist, so that I may be able to pull you up again when you call."

"What shall I do down there?" asked the Soldier.

"Get money!" answered the Witch. "Listen! When you reach the bottom of the tree you will find yourself in a large hall; it is light there for there are more than three hundred lamps burning. Then you will see three doors, which you can open—the keys are in the locks. If you go into the first room, you will see a great chest in the middle of the floor with a dog sitting upon it; he has eyes as large as saucers, but you needn't trouble about him. I will give you my blue-check apron, which you must spread out on the floor, and then go back quickly and fetch the dog and set him upon it; open the chest and take as much money as you like. It is copper there. If you would rather have silver, you must go into the next room, where there is a dog with eyes as large as mill wheels. But don't take any notice of him; just set him upon my apron, and help yourself to the money. If you prefer gold, you can get that too, if you go into the third room, and as much as you like to carry. But the dog that guards the chest there has eyes as large as the Round Tower at Copenhagen! He is a savage dog, I can tell you; but you needn't be afraid of him either. Only, put him on my apron and he won't touch you, and you can take out of the chest as much gold as you like!"

"Come, this is not bad!" said the Soldier. "But what am I to give you, old Witch; for surely you are not going to do this for nothing?"

"Yes, I am!" replied the Witch. "Not a single farthing will I take! For me you shall bring nothing but an old tinderbox which my grandmother forgot last time she was down there."

"Well, tie the rope round my waist!" said the Soldier.

"Here it is," said the Witch, "and here is my blue-check apron."

Then the Soldier climbed up the tree, let himself down through the hole, and found himself standing, as the Witch had said, underground in the large hall, where the three hundred lamps were burning.

Well, he opened the first door. Ugh! there sat the dog with eyes as big as saucers glaring at him.

"You are a fine fellow!" said the Soldier, and put him on the Witch's apron, took as much copper as his pockets could hold; then he shut the chest, put the dog on it again, and went into the second room. Sure enough there sat the dog with eyes as large as mill wheels.

"You had better not look at me so hard!" said the Soldier. "Your eyes will come out of their sockets!"

And then he set the dog on the apron. When he saw all the silver in the chest, he threw away the copper he had taken, and filled his pockets and knapsack with nothing but silver.

Then he went into the third room. Horrors! the dog there had two eyes, each as large as the Round Tower at Copenhagen, spinning round in his head like wheels.

"Good evening!" said the Soldier and saluted, for he had never seen a dog like this before. But when he had examined him more closely, he thought to himself: "Now then, I've had enough of this!" and put him down on the floor, and opened the chest. Heavens! what a heap of gold there was! With all that he could buy up the whole town, and all the sugar pigs, all the tin soldiers, whips and rocking horses in the whole world. Now he threw away all the silver with which he had filled his pockets and knapsack, and filled them with gold instead—yes, all his pockets, his knapsack, cap and boots even, so that he could hardly walk. Now he was rich indeed. He put the dog back upon the chest, shut the door, and then called up through the tree:

"Now pull me up again, old Witch!"

"Have you got the tinderbox also?" asked the Witch.

"Botheration!" said the Soldier, "I had clean forgotten it!" And then he went back and fetched it.

The Witch pulled him up, and there he stood again on the high road, with pockets, knapsack, cap and boots filled with gold.

"What do you want to do with the tinderbox?" asked the Soldier.

"That doesn't matter to you," replied the Witch. "You have got your money, give me my tinderbox."

"We'll see!" said the Soldier. "Tell me at once what you want to do with it, or I will draw my sword, and cut off your head!"

"No!" screamed the Witch.

The Soldier immediately cut off her head. That was the end of her! But he tied up all his gold in her apron, slung it like a bundle over his shoulder, put the tinderbox in his pocket, and set out toward the town.

It was a splendid town! He turned into the finest inn, ordered the best chamber and his favorite dinner; for now that he had so much money he was really rich.

It certainly occurred to the servant who had to clean his boots that they were astonishingly old boots for such a rich lord. But that was because he had not yet bought new ones; next day he appeared in respectable boots and fine clothes. Now, instead of a common soldier he had become a noble lord, and the people told him about all the grand doings of the town and the King, and what a beautiful Princess his daughter was.

"How can one get to see her?" asked the Soldier.

"She is never to be seen at all!" they told him; "she lives in a great copper castle, surrounded by many walls and towers! No one except the King may go in or out, for it is prophesied that she will marry a common soldier, and the King cannot submit to that."

"I should very much like to see her," thought the Soldier; but he could not get permission.

Now he lived very gaily, went to the theater, drove in the King's garden, and gave the poor a great deal of money, which was very nice of him; he had experienced in former times how hard it is not to have a farthing in the world. Now he was rich, wore fine clothes, and made many friends, who all said that he was an excellent man, a real noble-man. And the Soldier liked that. But as he was always spending money, and never made any more, at last the day came when he had nothing left but two shillings, and he had to leave the beautiful rooms in which he had been living, and go into a little attic under the roof, and clean his own boots, and mend them with a darning needle. None of his friends came to visit him there, for there were too many stairs to climb.

It was a dark evening, and he could not even buy a light. But all at once it flashed across him that there was a little end of tinder in the tin-derbox, which he had taken from the hollow tree into which the Witch had helped him down. He found the box with the tinder in it; but just as he was kindling a light, and had struck a spark out of the tinderbox, the door burst open, and the dog with eyes as large as saucers, which he had seen down in the tree, stood before him and said:

"What does my lord command?"

"What's the meaning of this?" exclaimed the Soldier. "This is a pretty kind of tinderbox, if I can get whatever I want like this. Get me money!" he cried to the dog, and hey, presto! he was off and back again, holding a great purse full of money in his mouth.

Now the Soldier knew what a capital tinderbox this was. If he rubbed once, the dog that sat on the chest of copper appeared; if he rubbed twice, there came the dog that watched over the silver chest; and if he rubbed three times, the one that guarded the gold appeared. Now, the Soldier went down again to his beautiful rooms, and appeared once more in splendid clothes. All his friends immediately recognized him again, and paid him great court.

One day he thought to himself: "It is very strange that no one can get to see the Princess. They all say she is very pretty, but what's the use of that if she has to sit forever in the great copper castle with all the towers? Can I not manage to see her somehow? Where is my tinder-box?" and so he struck a spark, and, presto! there came the dog with eyes as large as saucers.

"It is the middle of the night, I know," said the Soldier; "but I should very much like to see the Princess for a moment."

The dog was already outside the door, and before the Soldier could look round, in he came with the Princess. She was lying asleep on the dog's back, and was so beautiful that anyone could see she was a real Princess. The Soldier really could not refrain from kissing her—he was such a thorough Soldier. Then the dog ran back with the Princess. But when it was morning, and the King and Queen were drinking tea, the

Princess said that the night before she had had such a strange dream about a dog and a Soldier: she had ridden on the dog's back, and the Soldier had kissed her.

"That is certainly a fine story," said the Queen. But the next night one of the ladies-in-waiting was to watch at the Princess' bed, to see if it was only a dream, or if it had actually happened.

The Soldier had an overpowering longing to see the Princess again, and so the dog came in the middle of the night and fetched her, running as fast as he could. But the lady-in-waiting slipped on india-rubber shoes and followed them. When she saw them disappear into a large house, she thought to herself: "Now I know where it is"; and made a great cross on the door with a piece of chalk. Then she went home and lay down, and the dog came back also, with the Princess. But when he saw that a cross had been made on the door of the house where the Soldier lived, he took a piece of chalk also, and made crosses on all the doors in the town; and that was very clever, for now the lady-in-waiting could not find the right house, as there were crosses on all the doors.

Early next morning the King, Queen, ladies-in-waiting, and officers came out to see where the Princess had been.

"There it is!" said the King, when he saw the first door with a cross on it.

"No, there it is, my dear!" said the Queen, when she likewise saw a door with a cross.

"But here is one, and there is another!" they all exclaimed; wherever they looked there was a cross on the door. Then they realized that the sign would not help them at all.

But the Queen was an extremely clever woman, who could do a great deal more than just drive in a coach. She took her great golden scissors, cut up a piece of silk, and made a pretty little bag of it. This she filled with the finest buckwheat grains, and tied it round the Princess' neck; this done, she cut a little hole in the bag, so that the grains would strew the whole road wherever the Princess went.

In the night the dog came again, took the Princess on his back and ran away with her to the Soldier, who was very much in love with her, and would have liked to have been a Prince, so that he might have had her for his wife.

The dog did not notice how the grains were strewn right from the castle to the Soldier's window, where he ran up the wall with the Princess.

In the morning the King and the Queen saw plainly where their daughter had been, and they took the Soldier and put him into prison.

There he sat. Oh, how dark and dull it was there! And they told him: "Tomorrow you are to be hanged." Hearing that did not exactly cheer him, and he had left his tinderbox in the inn.

Next morning he could see through the iron grating in front of his little window how the people were hurrying out of the town to see him hanged. He heard the drums and saw the soldiers marching; all the people were running to and fro. Just below his window was a shoemaker's apprentice, with leather apron and shoes; he was skipping along so merrily that one of his shoes flew off and fell against the wall, just where the Soldier was sitting peeping through the iron grating.

"Oh, shoemaker's boy, you needn't be in such a hurry!" said the Soldier to him. "There's nothing going on till I arrive. But if you will run back to the house where I lived, and fetch me my tinderbox, I will give you four shillings. But you must put your best foot foremost."

The shoemaker's boy was very willing to earn four shillings, and fetched the tinderbox, gave it to the Soldier, and—yes—now you shall hear.

Outside the town a great scaffold had been erected, and all round were standing the soldiers, and hundreds of thousands of people. The King and Queen were sitting on a magnificent throne opposite the judges and the whole council.

The Soldier was already standing on the top of the ladder; but when they wanted to put the rope round his neck, he said that the fulfillment of one innocent request was always granted to a poor criminal before he underwent his punishment. He would so much like to smoke a small pipe of tobacco; it would be his last pipe in this world.

The King could not refuse him this, and so he took out his tinderbox, and rubbed it once, twice, three times. And lo, and behold! there stood all three dogs—the one with eyes as large as saucers, the second with eyes as large as mill wheels, and the third with eyes each as large as the Round Tower of Copenhagen.

"Help me now, so that I may not be hanged!" cried the Soldier. And thereupon the dogs fell upon the judges and the whole council, seized some by the legs, others by the nose, and threw them so high into the air that they fell and were smashed into pieces.

"I won't stand this!" said the King; but the largest dog seized him too, and the Queen as well, and threw them up after the others. This frightened the soldiers, and all the people cried: "Good Soldier, you shall be our King, and marry the beautiful Princess!"

Then they put the Soldier into the King's coach, and the three dogs danced in front, crying "Hurrah!" And the boys whistled and the soldiers presented arms.

The Princess came out of the copper castle, and became Queen; and that pleased her very much.

The wedding festivities lasted for eight days, and the dogs sat at table and made eyes at everyone.

82. PETER BULL
(Denmark)

THERE ONCE LIVED in Denmark a peasant and his wife who owned a very good farm, but had no children. They often lamented to each other that they had no one of their own to inherit all the wealth that they possessed. They continued to prosper, and became rich people, but there was no heir to it all.

One year it happened that they owned a pretty little bull-calf, which they called Peter. It was the prettiest little creature they had ever seen— so beautiful and so wise that it understood everything that was said to it, and so gentle and so full of play that both the man and his wife came to be as fond of it as if it had been their own child.

One day the man said to his wife, "I wonder, now, whether our parish clerk could teach Peter to talk; in that case we could not do better than adopt him as our son, and let him inherit all that we possess."

"Well, I don't know," said his wife, "our clerk is tremendously learned, and knows much more than his Paternoster, and I could almost believe that he might be able to teach Peter to talk, for Peter has a wonderfully good head too. You might at least ask him about it."

Off went the man to the clerk, and asked him whether he thought he could teach a bull-calf that they had to speak, for they wished so much to have it as their heir.

The clerk was no fool; he looked round about to see that no one could overhear them, and said, "Oh, yes, I can easily do that, but you must not speak to anyone about it. It must be done in all secrecy, and the priest must not know of it, otherwise I shall get into trouble, as it is forbidden. It will also cost you something, as some very expensive books are required."

That did not matter at all, the man said; they would not care so very much what it cost. The clerk could have a hundred dollars to begin with to buy the books. He also promised to tell no one about it, and to bring the calf round in the evening.

He gave the clerk the hundred dollars on the spot, and in the evening took the calf round to him, and the clerk promised to do his best with it. In a week's time he came back to the clerk to hear about the calf and see how it was thriving. The clerk, however, said that he could not get a sight of it, for then Peter would long after him and forget all that he had already learned. He was getting on well with his learning, but another hundred dollars were needed, as they must have more books. The peasant had the money with him, so he gave it to the clerk, and went home again with high hopes.

In another week the man came again to learn what progress Peter had made now.

"He is getting on very well," said the clerk.

"I suppose he can't say anything yet?" said the man.

"Oh, yes," said the clerk, "he can say 'Moo' now."

"Do you think he will get on with his learning?" asked the peasant.

"Oh, yes," said the clerk, "but I shall want another hundred dollars for books. Peter can't learn well out of the ones that he has got."

"Well, well," said the man, "what must be spent *shall* be spent."

So he gave the clerk the third hundred dollars for books, and a cask of good old ale for Peter. The clerk drank the ale himself, and gave the calf milk, which he thought would be better for it.

Some weeks passed, during which the peasant did not come round to ask after the calf, being frightened lest it should cost him another hundred dollars, for he had begun to squirm a bit at having to part with so much money. Meanwhile the clerk decided that the calf was as fat as it could be, so he killed it. After he had got all the beef out of the way he went inside, put on his black clothes, and made his way to the peasant's house.

As soon as he had said "Good day" he asked, "Has Peter come home here?"

"No, indeed, he hasn't," said the man; "surely he hasn't run away?"

"I hope," said the clerk, "that he would not behave so contemptibly after all the trouble I have had to teach him, and all that I have spent upon him. I have had to spend at least a hundred dollars of my own money to buy books for him before I got him so far on. He could say anything he liked now, so he said today that he longed to see his parents again. I was willing to give him that pleasure, but I was afraid that he wouldn't be able to find the way here by himself, so I made myself ready to go with him. When we had got outside the house I remembered that I had left my stick inside, and went in again to get it. When I came out again Peter had gone off on his own account. I thought he would be here, and if he isn't I don't know where he is."

The peasant and his wife began to lament bitterly that Peter had run away in this fashion just when they were to have so much joy of him, and after they had spent so much on his education. The worst of it was that now they had no heir after all. The clerk comforted them as best he could; he also was greatly distressed that Peter should have behaved in such a way just when he should have gained honor from his pupil. Perhaps he had only gone astray, and he would advertise him at church next Sunday, and find out whether anyone had seen him. Then he bade them "Good-bye," and went home and dined on a good fat veal roast.

Now it so happened that the clerk took in a newspaper, and one day he chanced to read in its columns of a new merchant who had settled in a town at some distance, and whose name was "Peter Bull." He put the newspaper in his pocket, and went round to the sorrowing couple who had lost their heir. He read the paragraph to them, and added, "I wonder, now, whether that could be your bull-calf Peter?"

"Yes, of course it is," said the man; "who else would it be?"

His wife then spoke up and said, "You must set out, good man, and see about him, for it *is* him, I am perfectly certain. Take a good sum of money with you, too; for who knows but what he may want some cash now that he has turned a merchant!"

Next day the man got a bag of money on his back and a sandwich in his pocket, and his pipe in his mouth, and set out for the town where the new merchant lived. It was no short way, and he traveled for many days before he finally arrived there. He reached it one morning, just at daybreak, found out the right place, and asked if the merchant was at home. Yes, he was, said the people, but he was not up yet.

"That doesn't matter," said the peasant, "for I am his father. Just show me up to his bedroom."

He was shown up to the room, and as soon as he entered it, and caught sight of the merchant, he recognized him at once. He had the same broad forehead, the same thick neck, and same red hair, but in other respects he was now like a human being. The peasant rushed straight up to him and took a firm hold of him. "Oh Peter," said he, "what a sorrow you have caused us, both myself and your mother, by running off like this just as we had got you well educated! Get up, now, so that I can see you properly, and have a talk with you."

The merchant thought that it was a lunatic who had made his way in to him, and thought it best to take things quietly.

"All right," said he, "I shall do so at once." He got out of bed and made haste to dress himself.

"Ay," said the peasant, "now I can see how clever our clerk is. He has done well by you, for now you look just like a human being. If one didn't know it, one would never think that it was you we got from the red cow; will you come home with me now?"

"No," said the merchant, "I can't find time just now. I have a big business to look after."

"You could have the farm at once, you know," said the peasant, "and we old people would retire. But if you would rather stay in business, of course you may do so. Are you in want of anything?"

"Oh, yes," said the merchant; "I want nothing so much as money. A merchant has always a use for that."

"I can well believe that," said the peasant, "for you had nothing at all to start with. I have brought some with me for that very end." With that he emptied his bag of money out upon the table, so that it was all covered with bright dollars.

When the merchant saw what kind of man he had before him he began to speak him fair, and invited him to stay with him for some days, so that they might have some more talk together.

"Very well," said the peasant, "but you must call me 'Father.'"

"I have neither father nor mother alive," said Peter Bull.

"I know that," said the man; "your real father was sold at Hamburg last Michaelmas, and your real mother died while calving in spring; but my wife and I have adopted you as our own, and you are our only heir, so you must call me 'Father.'"

Peter Bull was quite willing to do so, and it was settled that he should keep the money, while the peasant made his will and left to him all that he had, before he went home to his wife, and told her the whole story.

She was delighted to hear that it was true enough about Peter Bull—that he was no other than their own bull-calf.

"You must go at once and tell the clerk," said she, "and pay him the hundred dollars of his own money that he spent upon our son. He has earned them well, and more besides, for all the joy he has given us in having such a son and heir."

The man agreed with this, and thanked the clerk for all he had done, and gave him two hundred dollars. Then he sold the farm, and removed with his wife to the town where their dear son and heir was living. To him they gave all their wealth, and lived with him till their dying day.

83. MAID LENA
(Denmark)

ONCE UPON A TIME there was a farmer who had three sons. The eldest was called Peter, the second Paul, and the third Esben. Now Peter and Paul were a couple of strong, wide-awake lads; they could hear, and see, and laugh, and play, and sow, and reap, so they were very useful to their father. But the youngest was a poor sort of do-nothing fellow, who never had a word to say, but went mooning about like one in a dream, or sat over the fire and raked up the ashes; so they called him Esben-Ash-rake.

The farm stood amid fertile fields and fair green meadows; but in their midst lay a tract of barren, worthless moorland, strewn over with stones and overgrown with heather. Here Esben loved to lie asleep and dreaming, or staring up at the sky.

Peter and Paul, however, could not bear to see that bit of waste land, so their father gave them leave to see what they could do with it. True, there was an old story about the land belonging to the fairies, but, of course, that was all nonsense. So Peter and Paul set to work with a will; they dug up all the stones, and put them in a heap on one side; and they plowed and sowed their new field. They sowed it with wheat, and it did well all through the winter, and in the spring gave promise of a splendid crop.

Not one of their other fields looked half so well, until Midsummer Eve, when there came a sudden end to all their satisfaction—for on Midsummer Eve the whole crop was utterly destroyed. The entire field looked as if it had been trodden underfoot; every blade of wheat was so crushed and beaten down that it could never recover or lift itself up again.

No one could understand how such a thing had happened. So there remained nothing to do but plow the field afresh, and let the grass grow.

Next spring there was finer and better grass there than in any of their meadows, but just the same thing happened again. On Midsummer Eve all the grass was trodden down and beaten out as if with a flail, so they got no profit out of the field that year. Then they plowed it once more, let it lie fallow through the winter, and in the spring sowed their field with flax. It came up beautifully, and before Midsummer Eve was in full flower. It was a pretty sight, and Peter and Paul surveyed it with pride and joy; but, remembering what had taken place the two former years, they agreed that one of them should keep watch there on Midsummer Eve. Peter, as the eldest, wished to undertake this duty; so, arming himself with a stout cudgel, he sat down on the great bank of stones he had helped to pile up when they cleared the land.

It was a beautifully mild evening, clear and still. Peter quite meant to keep wide awake. For all that, however, he fell asleep, and never woke till midnight, when there came a fearful rushing and roaring overhead, that made the ground beneath him shake and tremble; and when he tried to look about him the whole sky was pitchy black. But in the midst of it all, there shone something red that looked like a fiery dragon, and the whole field seemed to roll from side to side, till he began to feel as if he were being tossed in a blanket; and there was such a roaring and buzzing in his ears that at last he became completely dazed. He could not bear it any longer, but was glad enough to escape with a whole skin, and get safely home.

Next day the flax lay there, trodden down and beaten out, till the whole field looked as smooth and bare as a deal board. So after that neither Peter nor Paul cared to bestow any more labor upon the land, and the next spring the whole place was overgrown with grass and wild flowers. There were white ladysmocks, blue cornflowers, and scarlet poppies; the heather, too, came creeping and peeping up everywhere among the stones and flowers. For while the brothers were working away so hard with plow and harrow, the heather had lain snugly hidden in little nooks and crannies.

And now nobody troubled himself any further about the field except Esben, who liked it far better this year than he had done the three previous summers, and he used to go there oftener than ever and lie staring up at the blue sky.

Late on Midsummer Eve he slipped out of the house (after having slept most of the day), for he meant to keep watch all that night. He wanted to know what it was that went on there every Midsummer Eve, and whether it was the work of fairy folk or other folk.

Close to the heap of stones there stood a tall tree, an old ash that had stood there many hundred years. Esben climbed up into this tree, sat very still, and kept wide awake till midnight. Then he, too, heard a roaring and a rushing that seemed to fill the air, and he, too, saw the sky grow as dark as if a carpet were spread out over it; and out of the black sky he saw a red gleam come. It came nearer and nearer till it took the form of a fiery dragon, with three heads and three long necks. As the dragon drew nearer, the storm increased, and a whirlwind rushed round and round the field, until each single blade and stalk lay there crushed and ground down, as if it had been trampled underfoot. The old ash tree lashed about him with its branches, while its aged trunk swayed to and fro so violently that Esben had to hold on tight, lest the whirlwind should blow him away.

Then all at once it grew quite still and quiet, the sky was clear again, and instead of a dragon with three heads, Esben now saw what looked like three large swans. But as they came nearer he saw they were three young girls, partly disguised in the form and plumage of swans, with great white wings and long, flowing veils; and they sank slowly down through the air to the foot of the old ash where Esben was. Then they cast aside their feathery disguise; the wings folded themselves together, and there, at the foot of the tree, lay three white veils as fine as cobwebs. They themselves, however, rose and danced, hand in hand, round and round the field, singing all the while.

Never had Esben heard anything so enchanting, never had he seen anything so beautiful, as these young girls in their white robes and with golden crowns upon their heads. For a long time he was afraid to move, lest he should frighten them away; but at length he slipped softly down, picked up the three white veils, and climbed as noiselessly up again.

The three swan-princesses had not noticed anything, but went on dancing round and round the meadow until three hours after midnight.

Then they came back to the tree, and wanted to put on their veils again. But there were no veils to be found. They ran about, looking and looking, till at last they saw Esben up in the tree. They spoke to him, and said they were sure he had taken their veils.

"Yes," Esben told them, he had them.

Then they entreated him to let them have them again, or they should be utterly ruined, they said. And they wept and implored, and promised to give him so much money for the veils that he would be richer than any king in the land.

Esben sat and gazed at them. How beautiful they were! So he told them they should not have their veils unless one of them would consent to be his wife.

"Ah, no," said one.

"Certainly not!" cried the second.

But the third and youngest Princess said:

"Yes, only bring us our veils."

Esben gave the other two their veils, but refused to let the third have hers until she gave him her hand and a kiss, and put a ring on his finger, and promised to come and be married to him next Midsummer Eve.

"We are three sisters," answered the Princess, "and were brought up in a castle that used to stand on this very spot. But a long, long time ago we were carried off by a wicked fairy, who keeps us imprisoned ten thousand miles from here, and only on Midsummer Eve are we allowed to revisit our old home. Now you must build a castle on this very spot, where our marriage also can take place, and everything must be arranged on a princely scale. You may invite as many guests as you please, only not the King of the land. You shall not lack money. Break off a twig from the ash tree you climbed, strike the largest of the stones lying at its root, and say, 'For Maid Lena!' The stone will roll back, and under it you will find all you may require. You can open and shut your treasure house, as often as you like to repeat these words, with a stroke of the ash twig. And so farewell till then," she said; and she wound her veil about her head, as her sisters had already done; then it spread out like two white wings, and all three princesses flew away.

At first they looked like three white swans; but they rose higher and higher till they were nothing but little white specks, and then they were lost to sight, and at the same moment the first ray of sunlight fell across the field.

For a long time Esben stood gazing after them, quite stunned with all he had seen and heard. At last he roused himself, tore a twig from the ash tree and struck the stone, with the words, "For Maid Lena!"

Immediately the stone rolled back, and beneath it was the entrance to a royal treasure house, full of silver and gold, and precious stones and costly jewels, and goblets and dishes, and candelabra, all of the most artistic form and design—in short, everything was there that could adorn a king's table.

Esben took as many gold and silver coins as he could carry, struck the stone again, repeating the same words, and then went back to the farm. His father and brothers hardly knew him again, he wasn't like the same man. He walked with head erect, his hair was thrown back from his forehead, his eyes were shining, and he looked full of life and energy.

Then he told them he knew now who it was that had destroyed their harvest the three previous summers. That piece of land was not to be cultivated; but he intended building a castle there, and there his wedding was to take place next Midsummer Eve.

At first they thought he had lost his wits; but when they saw all the silver and gold he had brought with him, they changed their opinions, and let him give what orders he pleased.

And now began a busy time, the like of which was never seen, with ax and saw, and hammer and plane, and line and trowel, so that on Midsummer Eve the castle stood complete, with tower and turret, and roof and pinnacle all glittering with gold.

Now it so happened that just before Midsummer Eve, after all the invitations were out, Esben's father and mother met the King, who had arranged a little trip into the country, and had contrived that his route should take him past the castle of which he had heard so much. Of course the farmer took off his hat to the King, who lifted his in return, and said he had heard of the grand wedding that was being prepared for his youngest son, and added:

"I should like to see him and his young bride."

Well, the farmer did not see that he could do otherwise than say that they would feel it a very great honor if the King would come to the wedding.

So then the King thanked him, and said that it would give him great pleasure, and then he rode on.

The wedding day came, and the guests came, and the King came too.

Esben was there, but as yet no bride had appeared. People began to whisper that things were not quite right, that Esben's bride had come to him in a dream, and vanished with the dream.

About sunset Esben went and stood in front of the castle, and gazed up into the air.

"Oho!" said the folks, "she is to come that road, is she? Then she is neither more nor less than one of the crazy fancies Esben's head is always full of."

But Esben remained quite undisturbed; he had seen the swans coming flying through the air, and now he knew that she was near at hand.

Directly afterward there came rolling up to the castle gates a magnificent golden chariot, drawn by six white horses.

Esben sprang to the carriage door, and there sat the bride, radiantly beautiful. But the first thing she said was:

"Is the King come?" and Esben was obliged to say, "Yes; but he invited himself, we did not ask him."

"That makes no difference," she said. "If I were to become a bride here today, the King would have to be the bridegroom, and it would cost you your life, which would make me most unhappy, for I wish to marry you, and no one else. And now you will have to come to me, if you can, and that before the year is out, or it will be too late. I live ten thousand miles from here, in a castle south of the sun, west of the moon, and in the center of the earth."

When she had thus spoken, she drove off at a tremendous pace, and directly afterward Esben saw a flock of swans rise up in the air and disappear among the clouds.

So he took his staff in his hand, left everything, and set off on his wanderings through the wide, wide world to seek and find his bride. He made straight for the south, and he wandered for days and for weeks, and wherever he came he asked people if they knew the castle, but there was no one who had ever even heard the name.

So at last, one day, out in a wood, he came upon two terribly grim-looking fellows fighting. Esben stopped and asked them what they were fighting about. They told him they were fighting for an old hat that was lying close by; their father was dead, and now they wanted to divide their inheritance, but the hat they could not divide.

"The hat is not worth much," said Esben.

But the dwarfs said this hat was not like other hats, for it possessed this peculiarity: whoever put it on became invisible, and so they both wanted to have it.

And then they fell to again, and fought and struggled.

"Well, fight away till you are friends again," said Esben, as he snatched up the hat, put it on his head, and went his way.

When he had gone some little distance he came upon two other dwarfs, who were fighting savagely. They also wanted to divide their father's property, which consisted solely in a pair of boots, but whoever put them on went a hundred miles with each step, so they both wanted them.

Esben got into conversation with them, and when he had learned the state of affairs he advised them to run a race for the boots.

"Now, I will throw a stone," said he, "and you must run after it, and whoever gets there first shall have the boots."

This they agreed to, so Esben threw the stone, and they set off running.

Meanwhile Esben had put on the boots, and the first step carried him a hundred miles away.

Once again he came upon two dwarfs quarreling over their inheritance, which could not be divided, and which both wanted to have. This was a rusty old clasp-knife. But it possessed this virtue, they said: If you opened it, and just pointed at anyone with it, they fell down dead and then if you shut it up again and touched them with it, they became alive again directly.

"Let me look at the knife," said Esben. "I shall be able to advise you, for I have settled such quarrels before."

When he had got it, he wanted to prove it, so he opened it, and pointed it at the two dwarfs, who immediately fell down dead.

"That's right," said Esben; so he shut up the knife and touched them with it, and they jumped up again directly.

Esben put the knife in his pocket, said good-bye, put the hat on his head, and in another second was a hundred miles away.

He went on and on till evening, when he came to a little house that stood in the middle of a thick wood. A very old woman lived there; she was so old that she was all overgrown with moss.

Esben greeted her politely, and asked if she could tell him where the castle was that stood south of the sun, west of the moon, and in the center of the earth.

"No," she said; she had never heard of such a castle. But she ruled over all the beasts of the field, and she could call them together, and ask if any one of them knew. So she blew her whistle, and wild beasts came gathering round them from all sides. They came running at full speed, all except the fox; he came sneaking behind in a very bad temper, for he was just going to catch a goose when he heard the whistle, and was obliged to come away and leave it. But neither the fox nor any one of the animals knew anything about the castle.

"Well, then, you must go to my sister," said the old woman; "she rules over all the birds of the air. If she cannot help you, no one can. She lives three hundred miles south of this, on the top of a high mountain. You cannot miss your way."

So Esben set off again, and soon came to the bird mountain.

The old woman who lived there had never heard of the castle south of the sun, west of the moon, and in the center of the earth; but she whistled with her pipe, and all the birds came flocking from all four corners of the earth. She asked them if they knew the castle, but there was not one of them who had ever been so far.

"Ah! but the old eagle is not here," she said, and whistled again.

At last the old eagle came sailing heavily along, his wings whirring and whizzing, and he alighted on the top of a tree.

"Where do you come from?" said the old woman. "You come too late; your life must pay the forfeit."

"I come from the castle south of the sun, west of the moon, and in the center of the earth," said the eagle. "I have a nest and young ones there, and I was obliged to see after them a little before I could leave them and fly so far away."

The old woman answered that his life should be spared if he would conduct Esben to the castle.

The eagle thought he could manage that, if he were allowed to stop and rest the night.

Next morning Esben got up on the eagle's back, and the eagle flew away with him—high, high up in the air, and far away over the stormy ocean.

When they had gone a long, long way, the eagle said:

"Do you see anything out yonder?"

"I see something like a high, black wall close upon us!"

"Ah! that is the earth; we have to go through that. Hold fast; for if you were to get killed, my life would have to pay the forfeit."

So they flew straight into the pitch-dark cave. Esben held fast, and almost directly afterward he saw daylight again.

When they had gone a little farther, the eagle said again:

"Do you see anything out yonder?"

"I see something like a great glass mountain," said Esben.

"That is water," said the eagle; "we have to go through that. Hold fast; for if you were to get killed, my life would have to pay the forfeit."

So they plunged right into the water, and got safely through. Then they flew some distance through the air, and then the eagle said again:

"Do you see anything out yonder?"

"I only see flames of fire," said Esben.

"We have to go through that," said the eagle. "Creep well under my feathers, and hold fast; for if you should get killed, my life would have to pay the forfeit."

So they flew straight into the fire, but they got safely through. Then the eagle sank slowly down, and alighted on the land.

"Now," said he, "I must rest awhile; but we have five hundred miles farther to go."

"Ah! now I can carry you," said Esben; so he took the eagle on his back, and with five strides they were there.

"Now we have come too far," said the eagle. "Can you step ten miles backward?"

"No, I can't do that," said Esben.

"Then we must fly those ten miles," said the eagle.

So they arrived safe and sound at the castle south of the sun, west of the moon, and in the center of the earth. That *was* a castle, the like of which was not to be found in all the world. It shone from top to bottom like pure gold.

When Esben came to the castle gate, he sat down, and presently a serving-maid passed him on her way into the castle. He called to her:

"Greet Maid Lena, and beg her for a goblet of wine for a weary wayfarer."

The girl brought the message to the Princess, who ordered her own golden goblet to be filled with wine, and sent the girl out with it.

When Esben had drunk the wine, he threw his ring into the goblet—the ring she had given him the day they first met. The Princess recognized the ring directly, so she ran down and embraced Esben, and led him into the castle.

"Now I have got you, I must let you go again directly," she said; "and you must journey all the long way back in my swan garb, for if the witch who has enchanted us should catch sight of you, she would change you into stone with a single glance."

"There is a remedy for that," said Esben; "only take me to her."

So Esben put on his invisible hat, took his knife in his hand, went up to the old witch, and just pointed at her, and she fell down dead. So he had her buried forty fathoms underground, and then he married his Princess, and he is married to her still.

84. THE OLD WOMAN AND THE TRAMP

or NAIL BROTH

(Sweden)

THERE WAS ONCE a tramp, who went plodding his way through a forest. The distance between the houses was so great that he had little hope of finding a shelter before the night set in. But all of a sudden he saw some lights between the trees. He then discovered a cottage, where there was a fire burning on the hearth. How nice it would be to roast oneself before that fire, and to get a bite of something, he thought; and so he dragged himself toward the cottage.

Just then an old woman came toward him.

"Good evening, and well met!" said the tramp.

"Good evening," said the woman. "Where do you come from?"

"South of the sun, and east of the moon," said the tramp; "and now I am on the way home again, for I have been all over the world with the exception of this parish," he said.

"You must be a great traveler, then," said the woman. "What may be your business here?"

"Oh, I want a shelter for the night," he said.

"I thought as much," said the woman; "but you may as well get away from here at once, for my husband is not at home, and my place is not an inn," she said.

"My good woman," said the tramp, "you must not be so cross and hardhearted, for we are both human beings, and should help one another, it is written."

"Help one another?" said the woman, "help? Did you ever hear such a thing? Who'll help me, do you think? I haven't got a morsel in the house! No, you'll have to look for quarters elsewhere," she said.

But the tramp was like the rest of his kind; he did not consider himself beaten at the first rebuff. Although the old woman grumbled and complained as much as she could, he was just as persistent as ever, and went on begging and praying like a starved dog, until at last she gave in, and he got permission to lie on the floor for the night.

That was very kind, he thought, and he thanked her for it.

"Better on the floor without sleep, than suffer cold in the forest deep," he said; for he was a merry fellow, this tramp, and was always ready with a rhyme.

When he came into the room he could see that the woman was not so badly off as she had pretended; but she was a greedy and stingy woman of the worst sort, and was always complaining and grumbling.

He now made himself very agreeable, of course, and asked her in his most insinuating manner for something to eat.

"Where am I to get it from?" said the woman. "I haven't tasted a morsel myself the whole day."

But the tramp was a cunning fellow, he was.

"Poor old granny, you must be starving," he said. "Well, well, I suppose I shall have to ask you to have something with me, then."

"Have something with you!" said the woman. "You don't look as if you could ask anyone to have anything! What have you got to offer one, I should like to know?"

"He who far and wide does roam sees many things not known at home; and he who many things has seen has wits about him and senses keen," said the tramp. "Better dead than lose one's head! Lend me a pot, granny!"

The old woman now became very inquisitive, as you may guess, and so she let him have a pot.

He filled it with water and put it on the fire, and then he blew with all his might till the fire was burning fiercely all round it. Then he took a four-inch nail from his pocket, turned it three times in his hand and put it into the pot.

The woman stared with all her might.

"What's this going to be?" she asked.

"Nail broth," said the tramp, and began to stir the water with the porridge stick.

"Nail broth?" asked the woman.

"Yes, nail broth," said the tramp.

The old woman had seen and heard a good deal in her time, but that anybody could have made broth with a nail, well, she had never heard the like before.

"That's something for poor people to know," she said, "and I should like to learn how to make it."

"That which is not worth having, will always go a-begging," said the tramp.

But if she wanted to learn how to make it she had only to watch him, he said, and went on stirring the broth.

The old woman squatted on the ground, her hands clasping her knees, and her eyes following his hand as he stirred the broth.

"This generally makes good broth," he said; "but this time it will very likely be rather thin, for I have been making broth the whole week with the same nail. If one only had a handful of sifted oatmeal to put in, that would make it all right," he said. "But what one has to go without, it's no use thinking more about," and so he stirred the broth again.

"Well, I think I have a scrap of flour somewhere," said the old woman, and went out to fetch some, and it was both good and fine.

The tramp began putting the flour into the broth, and went on stirring, while the woman sat staring now at him and then at the pot until her eyes nearly burst their sockets.

"This broth would be good enough for company," he said, putting in one handful of flour after another. "If I had only a bit of salted beef and a few potatoes to put in, it would be fit for gentlefolks, however particular they might be," he said. "But what one has to go without, it's no use thinking more about."

When the old woman really began to think it over, she thought she had some potatoes, and perhaps a bit of beef as well; and these she gave the tramp, who went on stirring, while she sat and stared as hard as ever.

"This will be grand enough for the best in the land," he said.

"Well, I never!" said the woman; "and just fancy—all with a nail!"

He was really a wonderful man, that tramp! He could do more than drink a sup and turn the tankard up, he could.

"If one had only a little barley and a drop of milk, we could ask the king himself to have some of it," he said; "for this is what he has every blessed evening—that I know, for I have been in service under the king's cook," he said.

"Dear me! Ask the king to have some! Well, I never!" exclaimed the woman, slapping her knees. She was quite awestruck at the tramp and his grand connections.

"But what one has to go without, it's no use thinking more about," said the tramp.

And then she remembered she had a little barley; and as for milk, well, she wasn't quite out of that, she said, for her best cow had just calved. And then she went to fetch both the one and the other.

The tramp went on stirring, and the woman sat staring, one moment at him and the next at the pot.

Then all at once the tramp took out the nail.

"Now it's ready, and now we'll have a real good feast," he said. "But to this kind of soup the king and the queen always take a dram or two, and one sandwich at least. And then they always have a cloth on the table when they eat," he said. "But what one has to go without, it's no use thinking more about."

But by this time the old woman herself had begun to feel quite grand and fine, I can tell you; and if that was all that was wanted to make it just as the king had it, she thought it would be nice to have it just the same way for once, and play at being king and queen with the tramp. She went straight to a cupboard and brought out the brandy bottle, dram glasses, butter and cheese, smoked beef and veal, until at last the table looked as if it were decked out for company.

Never in her life had the old woman had such a grand feast, and never had she tasted such broth, and just fancy, made only with a nail!

She was in such a good and merry humor at having learned such an economical way of making broth that she did not know how to make enough of the tramp who had taught her such a useful thing.

So they ate and drank, and drank and ate, until they became both tired and sleepy.

The tramp was now going to lie down on the floor. But that would never do, thought the old woman; no, that was impossible. "Such a grand person must have a bed to lie in," she said.

He did not need much pressing. "It's just like the sweet Christmastime," he said, "and a nicer woman I never came across. Ah, well! Happy are they who meet with such good people," said he, and he lay down on the bed and went asleep.

And next morning when he woke the first thing he got was coffee and a dram.

When he was going the old woman gave him a bright dollar piece.

"And thanks, many thanks, for what you have taught me," she said. "Now I shall live in comfort, since I have learned how to make broth with a nail."

"Well, it isn't very difficult, if one only has something good to add to it," said the tramp as he went his way.

The woman stood at the door staring after him.
"Such people don't grow on every bush," she said.

85. SALT AND BREAD*
(Sweden)

THERE WAS ONCE a King with three daughters. The two older girls were jealous of the youngest, whom the King loved dearly, and they spent much time and effort trying to destroy the King's love for her. They tried to win special favors and privileges from their father, never missing an opportunity to suggest that the youngest girl did not return his affection. Their evil jealousy wouldn't let them rest. At last the King became troubled over the rumors he heard from the older daughters. He even became suspicious of the youngest girl. And one day when the three daughters were with him, he could not refrain from putting their love to a test.

So he asked the oldest girl to tell him how much she loved him, and she replied:

"I value you, my father, as God in Heaven!"

Her answer pleased the King. He then asked the second daughter the same question, and she replied:

"Oh my father, I value you as my own life!"

This answer also pleased the King. And he turned now to the youngest daughter, asking her how she would describe her feelings. She answered:

"Oh my father, I value you as salt and bread."

The King was startled by this reply. Then he became angry that she cared no more for him than the humblest things on a poor man's table. His anger turned to fury that his youngest daughter, on whom he had

---

* From *Ride with the Sun* edited by Harold Courlander for The United Nations Women's Guild. Copyright © 1955 by McGraw-Hill Book Company, Inc. Used with permission.

lavished so much affection, thought so little of him in return. And he ordered his servants to drive her out of his house. They did as they were told, and took her into the woods and abandoned her. Now, at last, the two older daughters were happy.

In the woods, the youngest daughter was miserable and frightened. She cried when she thought about the home and the father she loved. She could not understand his anger, nor why she had been banished. She wandered about the woods helplessly, and at last, in fear of the wild animals, she climbed into a tall tree.

It happened that a King from another country at that moment was hunting in the woods. As he rode along on his horse, he heard his dogs barking with excitement. He hurried after them and found them surrounding the tree where the Princess was hiding. He looked upward, expecting to find a bear. Instead, he saw the beautiful face of the unhappy girl. He spoke to her kindly and asked her to come down.

He put the girl on his horse and took her to his castle. There he fed her and warmed her before a log fire. At last, overcome by his kindness, the Princess poured out her story. The King was impressed with her goodness as well as her beauty. He cared for her in his castle, and at last he asked her to marry him. The girl, too, had fallen in love, and she agreed.

So a date was set for the wedding, and invitations were sent to the royalty of the seven neighboring kingdoms. When the wedding day came, the royal guests arrived. Among them were the young Princess' father and her two older sisters. They did not recognize her, so sure were they that the Princess had disappeared forever in the woods.

When they took their seats at the banquet table, wonderful food of all kinds was set before the guests. But none of the food was salted, and there was no salt on the table. Neither was there bread.

At last the girl's father could not refrain from commenting, and he said, "I don't understand, but it seems to me that two most precious things are missing from this feast."

"Ah?" the Princess, now a Queen, replied. "What can you be speaking of?"

"Why," her father replied, "salt and bread."

"Yes," the girl said. "They are among the most precious things we know. And once because I valued my father as highly as these things was driven out of his house and into the woods to die."

When her father heard these words he was overcome. He recognized her and embraced her with a cry of joy, thankful and happy that she was alive and well. He begged her forgiveness for his misunderstanding of her words of affection and for his having driven her away.

As for the older sisters, their plot against the youngest was now exposed, and it was their turn to be turned out of their father's house. From that day on, no more was ever heard of them. If they were ever rescued from the woods by hunting kings, nobody has ever heard about it.

86. THE SEAL'S SKIN
(Iceland)

THERE WAS ONCE some man from Myrdal in Eastern Iceland who went walking among the rocks by the sea one morning before anyone else was up. He came to the mouth of a cave, and inside the cave he could hear merriment and dancing, but outside it he saw a great many sealskins. He took one skin away with him, carried it home, and locked it away in a chest. Later in the day he went back to the mouth of the cave; there was a young and lovely woman sitting there, and she was stark naked, and weeping bitterly. This was the seal whose skin it was that the man had taken. He gave the girl some clothes, comforted her, and took her home with him. She grew very fond of him, but did not get on so well with other people. Often she would sit alone and stare out to sea.

After some while the man married her, and they got on well together, and had several children. As for the skin, the man always kept it locked up in the chest, and kept the key on him wherever he went. But after many years, he went fishing one day and forgot it under his pillow at home. Other people say that he went to church one Christmas with the rest of his household, but that his wife was ill and stayed at home; he had forgotten to take the key out of the pocket of his everyday clothes when he changed. Be that as it may, when he came home again the chest was open, and both wife and skin were gone. She had taken the key and examined the chest, and there she had found the skin; she had been unable to resist the temptation, but had said farewell to her children, put the skin on, and flung herself into the sea.

Before the woman flung herself into the sea, it is said that she spoke these words:

> "Woe is me! Ah, woe is me!
> I have seven bairns on land,
> And seven in the sea."

It is said that the man was brokenhearted about this. Whenever he rowed out fishing afterward, a seal would often swim round and round his boat, and it looked as if tears were running from its eyes. From that time on, he had excellent luck in his fishing, and various valuable things were washed ashore on his beach. People often noticed, too, that when the children he had had by this woman went walking along the seashore, a seal would show itself near the edge of the water and keep level with them as they walked along the shore, and would toss them jellyfish and pretty shells. But never did their mother come back to land again.

87. THE PIG-HEADED WIFE
(Finland)

WHEN MATTI MARRIED LIISA, he thought she was the pleasantest woman in the world. But it wasn't long before Liisa began to show her real character. Headstrong as a goat she was, and as fair set on having her own way.

Matti had been brought up to know that a husband should be the head of his family, so he tried to make his wife obey. But this didn't work with Liisa. It just made her all the more stubborn and pig-headed. Every time that Matti asked her to do one thing, she was bound to do the opposite, and work as he would she generally got her own way in the end.

Matti was a patient sort of man, and he put up with her ways as best he could, though his friends were ready enough to make fun of him for being henpecked. And so they managed to jog along fairly well.

But one year as harvest time came round, Matti thought to himself, "Here am I, a jolly goodhearted fellow, that likes a bit of company. If only I had a pleasant sort of wife, now, it would be a fine thing to invite all our friends to the house and have a nice dinner and drink and a good time. But it's no good thinking of it, for as sure as I propose a feast, Liisa will declare a fast."

And then a happy thought struck him.

"I'll see if I can't get the better of Liisa, all the same. I'll let on I want to be quiet, and then she'll be all for having the house full of guests."

So a few days later he said, "The harvest holidays will be here soon, but don't you go making any sweetcakes this year. We're too poor for that sort of thing."

"Poor! What are you talking about?" Liisa snapped. "We've never had more than we have this year. I'm certainly going to bake a cake, and a good big one too."

"It works," thought Matti. "It works!" But all he said was, "Well, if you make a cake, we won't need a pudding too. We mustn't be wasteful."

"Wasteful, indeed!" Liisa grumbled. "We shall have a pudding, and a big pudding!"

Matti pretended to sigh, and rolled his eyes. "Pudding's bad enough, but if you take it in your head to serve stuffed pig again, we'll be ruined!"

"You'll kill our best pig," quoth Liisa, "and let's hear no more about it."

"But wine, Liisa," Matti went on. "Promise me you won't open a single bottle. We've barely enough to last us through the winter as it is."

Liisa stamped her foot. "Are you crazy, man? Who ever heard of stuffed pig without wine! We'll not only have wine, but I'll buy coffee too. I'll teach you to call me extravagant by the time I'm through with you!"

"Oh, dear, oh, dear," Matti sighed. "If you're going to invite a lot of guests, on top of everything else, that'll be the end of it. We can't possibly have guests."

"And have all the food spoil with no one to eat it, I suppose?" jeered Liisa. "Guests we'll have, and what's more, you'll sit at the head of the table, whether you like it or not."

"Well, at any rate I'll drink no wine myself," said Matti, growing bolder. "If I don't drink the others won't, and I tell you we'll need that wine to pull us through the winter."

Liisa turned on him, furious. "You'll drink with your guests as a host should, till every bottle is empty. There! Now will you be quiet?"

When the day arrived the guests came, and great was the feasting. They shouted and sang round the table, and Matti himself made more noise than any of his friends. So much so, that long before the feast was over Liisa began to suspect he had played a trick on her. It made her furious to see him so jolly and carefree.

As time went on she grew more and more contrary, until there was no living with her. Now it happened one day in the spring, when all the streams were high, that Matti and Liisa were crossing the wooden bridge over the little river which separated two of their meadows. Matti crossed first, and noticing that the boards were badly rotted, he called out without thinking, "Look where you step, Liisa! The plank is rotten there. Go lightly or you'll break through."

"Step lightly!" shouted Liisa. "I'll do as—"

But for once Liisa didn't finish what she had to say. She jumped with all her weight on the rotted timbers and fell plop into the swollen stream.

Matti scratched his head for a moment; then he started running upstream as fast as he could go.

Two fishermen along the bank saw him and called, "What's the matter, my man? Why are you running upstream so fast?"

"My wife fell in the river," Matti panted, "and I'm afraid she's drowned."

"You're crazy," said the fishermen. "Anyone in his right mind would search downstream, not up!"

"Ah," said Matti, "but you don't know my Liisa! All her life she's been so pig-headed that even when she's dead she'd be bound to go against the current!"

88. THE FOREST BRIDE

(*Finland*)

THERE WAS ONCE a farmer who had three sons. One day, when the boys were grown to manhood, he said to them:

"My sons, it is high time that you were all married. Tomorrow I wish you to go out in search of brides."

"But where shall we go?" the oldest son asked.

"I have thought of that, too," the father said. "Do each of you chop down a tree and then take the direction in which the fallen tree points. I'm sure that each of you, if you go far enough in that direction, will find a suitable bride."

So, the next day the three sons chopped down trees. The oldest son's tree fell pointing north.

"That suits me!" he said, for he knew that to the north lay a farm where a very pretty girl lived.

The tree of the second son when it fell pointed south.

"That suits me!" the second son declared, thinking of a girl that he had often danced with who lived on a farm to the south.

The youngest son's tree—the youngest son's name was Veikko—when it fell pointed straight to the forest.

"Ha! Ha!" the older brothers laughed. "Veikko will have to go courting one of the wolf girls or one of the foxes!"

They meant by this that only animals lived in the forest, and they thought they were making a good joke at Veikko's expense. But Veikko said he was perfectly willing to take his chances and go where his tree pointed.

The older brothers went off gaily and presented their suits to the two farmers whose daughters they admired. Veikko, too, started off with a brave front, but after he had gone some distance in the forest, his courage began to ebb.

"How can I find a bride," he asked himself, "in a place where there are no human creatures at all!"

Just then he came to a little hut. He pushed open the door and went in. It was empty. To be sure, there was a little mouse sitting on the table, daintily combing her whiskers, but a mouse of course doesn't count.

"There's nobody here!" Veikko said aloud.

The little mouse paused in her toilet and, turning toward him, said reproachfully:

"Why, Veikko, I'm here!"

"But you don't count. You're only a mouse!"

"Of course I count!" the little mouse declared. "But tell me, what were you hoping to find?"

"I was hoping to find a sweetheart."

The little mouse questioned him further, and Veikko told her the whole story of his brothers and the trees.

"The two older ones are finding sweethearts easily enough," Veikko said, "but I don't see how I can off here in the forest. And it will shame me to have to go home and confess that I alone have failed."

"See here, Veikko," the little mouse said, "why don't you take me for your sweetheart?"

Veikko laughed heartily.

"But you're only a mouse! Whoever heard of a man having a mouse for a sweetheart!"

The mouse shook her little head solemnly.

"Take my word for it, Veikko, you could do much worse than have me for a sweetheart! Even if I am only a mouse, I can love you and be true to you."

She was a dear, dainty little mouse, and as she sat looking up at Veikko, with her little paws under her chin and her bright little eyes sparkling, Veikko liked her more and more.

Then she sang Veikko a pretty little song, and the song cheered him so much that he forgot his disappointment at not finding a human sweetheart, and as he left her to go home, he said:

"Very well, little mouse, I'll take you for my sweetheart!"

At that the mouse made little squeaks of delight, and she told him that she'd be true to him and wait for him no matter how long he was in returning.

Well, the older brothers when they got home boasted loudly about their sweethearts.

"Mine," said the oldest, "has the rosiest, reddest cheeks you ever saw!"

"And mine," the second announced, "has long yellow hair!"

Veikko said nothing.

"What's the matter, Veikko?" the older brothers asked him, laughing. "Has your sweetheart pretty pointed ears or sharp white teeth?"

You see they were still having their little joke about foxes and wolves.

"You needn't laugh," Veikko said. "I've found a sweetheart. She's a gentle dainty little thing gowned in velvet."

"Gowned in velvet!" echoed the oldest brother with a frown.

"Just like a princess!" the second brother sneered.

"Yes," Veikko repeated, "gowned in velvet like a princess. And when she sits up and sings to me, I'm perfectly happy."

"Huh!" grunted the older brothers not at all pleased that Veikko should have so grand a sweetheart.

"Well," said the old farmer after a few days, "now I should like to know what those sweethearts of yours are able to do. Have them each bake me a loaf of bread so that I can see whether they're good housewives."

"Mine will be able to bake bread—I'm sure of that!" the oldest brother declared boastfully.

"So will mine!" chorused the second brother.

Veikko was silent.

"What about the Princess?" they said with a laugh. "Do you think the Princess can bake bread?"

"I don't know," Veikko answered truthfully. "I'll have to ask her."

Of course he had no reason for supposing that the little mouse could bake bread, and by the time he reached the hut in the forest, he was feeling sad and discouraged.

When he pushed open the door, he found the little mouse as before seated on the table, daintily combing her whiskers. At sight of Veikko she danced about with delight.

"I'm so glad to see you!" she squeaked. "I knew you would come back!"

Then when she noticed that he was silent, she asked him what was the matter. Veikko told her:

"My father wants each of our sweethearts to bake him a loaf of bread. If I come home without a loaf, my brothers will laugh at me."

"You won't have to go home without a loaf!" the little mouse said. "I can bake bread."

Veikko was much surprised at this.

"I never heard of a mouse that could bake bread!"

"Well, I can!" the little mouse insisted.

With that, she began ringing a small silver bell, *tinkle, tinkle, tinkle.* Instantly there was the sound of hurrying footsteps, tiny scratchy footsteps, and hundreds of mice came running into the hut.

The little princess mouse, sitting up very straight and dignified, said to them:

"Each of you go fetch me a grain of the finest wheat."

All the mice scampered quickly away and soon returned one by one, each carrying a grain of the finest wheat. After that it was no trick at all for the princess mouse to bake a beautiful loaf of wheaten bread.

The next day the three brothers presented their father the loaves of their sweethearts' baking. The oldest one had a loaf of rye bread.

"Very good," the farmer said. "For hardworking people like us, rye bread is good."

The loaf the second son had was made of barley.

"Barley bread is also good," the farmer said.

But when Veikko presented his loaf of beautiful wheaten bread, his father cried out:

"What! White bread! Ah, Veikko now must have a sweetheart of wealth!"

"Of course!" the older brothers sneered. "Didn't he tell us she was a princess? Say, Veikko, when a princess wants fine white flour, how does she get it?"

Veikko answered simply:

"She rings a little silver bell, and when her servants come in, she tells them to bring her grains of the finest wheat."

At this the older brothers nearly exploded with envy until their father had to reprove them.

"There! There!" he said. "Don't grudge the boy his good luck! Each girl has baked the loaf she knows how to make, and each in her own way will probably make a good wife. But before you bring them home to me, I want one further test of their skill in housewifery. Let them each send me a sample of their weaving."

The older brothers were delighted at this, for they knew that their sweethearts were skillful weavers.

"We'll see how her ladyship fares this time!" they said, sure in their hearts that Veikko's sweetheart, whoever she was, would not put them to shame with her weaving.

Veikko, too, had serious doubts of the little mouse's ability at the loom.

"Whoever heard of a mouse that could weave?" he said to himself as he pushed open the door of the forest hut.

"Oh, there you are at last!" the little mouse squeaked joyfully.

She reached out her little paws in welcome, and then in her excitement she began dancing about on the table.

"Are you really glad to see me, little mouse?" Veikko asked.

"Indeed I am!" the mouse declared. "Am I not your sweetheart? I've been waiting for you and waiting, just wishing that you would return! Does your father want something more this time, Veikko?"

"Yes, and it's something I'm afraid you can't give me, little mouse."

"Perhaps I can. Tell me what it is."

"It's a sample of your weaving. I don't believe you can weave. I never heard of a mouse that could weave."

"Tut! Tut!" said the mouse. "Of course I can weave! It would be a strange thing if Veikko's sweetheart couldn't weave!"

She rang the little silver bell, *tinkle, tinkle, tinkle,* and instantly there was the faint *scratch-scratch* of a hundred little feet as mice came running in from all directions and sat up on their haunches awaiting their princess' orders.

"Go each of you," she said, "and get me a fiber of flax, the finest there is."

The mice went scurrying off, and soon they began returning one by one each bringing a fiber of flax. When they had spun the flax and carded it, the little mouse wove a beautiful piece of fine linen. It was so sheer that she was able, when she folded it, to put it into an empty nutshell.

"Here, Veikko," she said, "here in this little box is a sample of my weaving. I hope your father will like it."

Veikko, when he got home, felt almost embarrassed, for he was sure that his sweetheart's weaving would shame his brothers. So, at first he kept the nutshell hidden in his pocket.

The sweetheart of the oldest brother had sent as a sample of her weaving, a square of coarse cotton.

"Not very fine," the farmer said, "but good enough."

The second brother's sample was a square of cotton and linen mixed.

"A little better," the farmer said, nodding his head.

Then he turned to Veikko.

"And you, Veikko, has your sweetheart not given you a sample of her weaving?"

Veikko handed his father a nutshell, at sight of which his brothers burst out laughing.

"Ha! Ha! Ha!" they laughed. "Veikko's sweetheart gives him a nut when he asks for a sample of her weaving."

But their laughter died as the farmer opened the nutshell and began shaking out a great web of the finest linen.

"Why, Veikko, my boy!" he cried, "however did your sweetheart get threads for so fine a web?"

Veikko answered modestly:

"She rang a little silver bell and ordered her servants to bring her in fibers of finest flax. They did so, and after they had spun the flax and carded it, my sweetheart wove the web you see."

"Wonderful!" gasped the farmer. "I have never known such a weaver! The other girls will be all right for farmers' wives, but Veikko's sweetheart might be a princess! Well," concluded the farmer, "it's time that you all brought your sweethearts home. I want to see them with my own eyes. Suppose you bring them tomorrow."

"She's a good little mouse and I'm very fond of her," Veikko thought to himself as he went out to the forest, "but my brothers will certainly laugh when they find she is only a mouse! Well, I don't care if they do laugh! She's been a good little sweetheart to me and I'm not going to be ashamed of her!"

When he got to the hut, he told the little mouse at once that his father wanted to see her.

The little mouse was greatly excited.

"I must go in proper style!" she said.

She rang the little silver bell and ordered her coach and five. The coach, when it came, turned out to be an empty nutshell, and the five prancing steeds that were drawing it were five black mice. The little mouse seated herself in the coach with a coachman mouse on the box in front of her and a footman mouse on the box behind her.

"Oh, how my brothers will laugh!" thought Veikko.

But he didn't laugh. He walked beside the coach and told the little mouse not to be frightened, that he would take good care of her. His father, he told her, was a gentle old man and would be kind to her.

When they left the forest, they came to a river that was spanned by a footbridge. Just as Veikko and the nutshell coach reached the middle of the bridge, a man met them coming from the opposite direction.

"Mercy me!" the man exclaimed as he caught sight of the strange little coach that was rolling along beside Veikko. "What's that?"

He stooped down and looked, and then with a loud laugh he put out his foot and pushed the coach, the little mouse, her servants, and her five prancing steeds all off the bridge and into the water below.

"What have you done! What have you done!" Veikko cried. "You've drowned my poor little sweetheart!"

The man, thinking Veikko was crazy, hurried away.

"You poor little mouse!" he said. "How sorry I am that you are drowned! You were a faithful, loving sweetheart, and now that you are gone I know how much I loved you!"

As he spoke, he saw a beautiful coach of gold drawn by five glossy horses go up the far bank of the river. A coachman in gold lace held the reins and a footman in pointed cap sat up stiffly behind. The most beautiful girl in the world was seated in the coach. Her skin was as red as a berry and as white as snow, her long golden hair gleamed with jewels, and she was dressed in pearly velvet. She beckoned to Veikko, and when he came close, she said:

"Won't you come sit beside me?"

"Me? Me?" Veikko stammered, too dazed to think.

The beautiful creature smiled.

"You were not ashamed to have me for a sweetheart when I was a mouse," she said, "and surely now that I am a princess again, you won't desert me!"

"A mouse!" Veikko gasped. "Were you the little mouse?"

The Princess nodded.

"Yes, I was the little mouse under an evil enchantment, which could never have been broken if you had not taken me for a sweetheart and if another human being had not drowned me. Now the enchantment is broken forever. So, come, we will go to your father, and after he has given us his blessing, we will get married and go home to my kingdom."

And that's exactly what they did. They drove at once to the farmer's house, and when Veikko's father and his brothers and his brothers' sweethearts saw the Princess' coach stopping at their gate, they all came out bowing and scraping to see what such grand folk could want of them.

"Father!" Veikko cried, "don't you know me?"

The farmer stopped bowing long enough to look up.

"Why, bless my soul!" he cried, "it's our Veikko!"

"Yes, father, I'm Veikko, and this is the princess that I'm going to marry!"

"A princess, did you say, Veikko? Mercy me, where did my boy find a princess?"

"Out in the forest where my tree pointed."

"Well, well, well," the farmer said, "where your tree pointed! I've always heard that was a good way to find a bride."

The older brothers shook their heads gloomily and muttered:

"Just our luck! If only our trees had pointed to the forest, we, too, should have found princesses instead of plain country wenches!"

But they were wrong. It wasn't because his tree pointed to the forest that Veikko got the Princess; it was because he was so simple and good that he was kind even to a little mouse.

Well, after they had got the farmer's blessing, they rode home to the Princess' kingdom and were married. And they were happy as they should have been, for they were good and true to each other and they loved each other dearly.

89. GOD AND THE DEVIL SHARE THE HARVEST
(Latvia)

THERE WAS A TIME when only God and the Devil lived in the world. When spring came, God harnessed a horse to a plow and went into the fields to plow the soil. When he had finished, he sowed some grain. The Devil, herding cows, watched everything God was doing from the bushes and wondered, "Is this some kind of a joke? What is God up to? I'll have to keep watch from these bushes every day to see what comes of all this."

God's grain grew before one's eyes. In the hot rays of the sun, it ripened. And in the fall God returned to reap. As he's working, the

Devil comes up and asks what he's doing. Thus and so: "In the spring I sowed," God answers, "and now I'm reaping—so I'll have bread for the winter."

The following spring the Devil grows tired of herding cows, and he comes to God to ask if they can work together—half and half. He says to God, "Let's plant crops together this year—I'll take the part that grows above the ground, and you take what grows below ground." Very well. God thinks it over a bit and plants potatoes. In the fall the Devil harvests his share of the crop—the worthless green tops—and God takes his—the potatoes. During the winter the Devil chews and spits his greens, but God eats his potatoes whistling.

The following spring the Devil says to God, "This year I'll take the lower part of the crop and you take the upper." Very well. God thinks it over a bit and sows wheat. In the fall each one harvests his share. During the winter God eats wheatcakes every day, rubbing a full belly— but the Devil, in fits of anger, chews on the stubble.

90. THE BUL-BUL BIRD
(Latvia)

IN A FARAWAY LAND lives a king with three sons. These three sons have learned that nine kingdoms away another king has a bird who can do anything you ask of him. The bird is said to live in a garden, in a golden cage. The cage is said to hang in a triple-forked linden tree. Every evening the bird flies home, to sleep in his golden cage. But most important is this: On a claw of the bird's left foot is a small ring. Whoever can take off this ring will own the bird. Many have gone to get the ring, but all have gone in vain.

The king's sons decide that they will go too. The oldest son will go first—he saddles his horse and prepares for the journey. The two younger sons saddle their horses also, and ride with their brother to the bridge. At the bridge the oldest son jumps off his horse, cuts three grooves in the bridge with his sword, and tells his brothers to be sure to come each day to look at these grooves: If they remain white, then all is well with him; but if they're filled with blood, the brothers should hurry to his aid.

On the ninth day the oldest son arrives at the king's castle nine kingdoms away, and says he has come to get the bird. Hearing this, the king thoughtfully turns his head and answers, "My dear son—what will you do with this bird? He is the magic Bul-Bul Bird himself! So many have come already, so many more will come—all in vain!"

But the oldest son only replies, "Whatever happens, I'm going!"

Very well. At sunset the oldest son enters the garden and starts to search for the triple-forked linden tree. He looks over here—nothing, he looks over there—still nothing. At last he thinks to poke his head into a thicket of birch trees—yes, that should be it. Pleased, he pushes his way through the trees and finds in a small, grassy field a triple-forked linden tree with a golden cage. The grass around the tree is very, very thick. All is still, for the bird isn't home yet. The oldest son hides in the grass and waits. After a while the garden suddenly rings with sound, as if thousands and again thousands of birds had started to sing. The Bul-Bul Bird is home. He alights on his cage and, carefully looking around, asks in a mournful voice, "Everyone else is asleep—isn't there a single soul who will say, 'Bul-Bul Bird, go to sleep too'?"

The oldest son thinks to himself, "If the only trouble is that, why, then, it's nothing!" He answers, "Bul-Bul Bird, go to sleep!" But at that very moment the Bul-Bul Bird strikes him with his wing, and look!—the oldest son turns into a birch tree.

The next morning his brothers go to the bridge and see blood in the grooves cut by the sword. The second son prepares for the journey at once and rides to the land nine kingdoms away to find his brother. He arrives, and the king tells him that his older brother, having gone to look for the Bul-Bul Bird, has remained in the garden. The second son enters the garden, looks over here, looks over there—no brother, no linden tree in sight. At last he thinks to poke his head into the thicket of birch trees—yes, there's the linden, but not his brother. He hides in the thick grass and waits. All is still. Here, a little after sunset, the garden suddenly rings with sound, as if thousands and again thousands of birds had started to sing. And the Bul-Bul Bird is there. He alights on the golden cage, looks around, and then in a mournful voice says, "Everyone else is asleep—isn't there a single soul here who will say, 'Bul-Bul Bird, go to sleep too'?"

The second son doesn't say a thing. But after a while the Bul-Bul

Bird says again, so mournfully, "Everyone else may sleep—except for me. Isn't there a single soul here who will speak these words, 'Bul-Bul Bird, go to sleep'?"

The second son's heart is now moved to pity. He answers, "Bul-Bul Bird, go to sleep!" But at that very moment the Bul-Bul Bird strikes him with his wing, and look!—the second son turns into a birch tree.

The next morning the youngest son goes to the bridge and sees blood in the grooves cut by the sword. He prepares for the journey at once and rides to the land nine kingdoms away to find his brothers. He arrives, and the king tells him that, having gone to look for the Bul-Bul Bird, his brothers have remained in the garden. The youngest son enters the garden, and he looks over here, he looks over there—no brothers, no linden tree in sight. At last he thinks to poke his head into the thicket of birch trees. Yes, there's the linden, but not his brothers—only the grass appears a bit trampled. He hides in the thick grass, but within reach of the golden cage, and waits. All is still. Here, a little after sunset, the garden suddenly rings with sound, as if thousands and again thousands of birds had started to sing. And there is the Bul-Bul Bird. He alights on his golden cage, looks around, and then in a mournful voice says, "Everyone else is asleep—isn't there a single soul here who will say, 'Bul-Bul Bird, go to sleep'?"

The youngest son doesn't say a thing. But after a while the Bul-Bul Bird says again, so mournfully, "Everyone else may sleep—except for me. Isn't there a single soul here who will just speak these words, 'Bul-Bul Bird, go to sleep'?"

The youngest son doesn't say a thing. But after a while, the Bul-Bul Bird starts to cry and, sighing and snuffling, says, "Everyone else is asleep—only I have to stay awake. Isn't there a single soul here who will say these few little words, 'Bul-Bul Bird, go to sleep too'?"

Hearing this, the youngest son can't hold back any longer. He's about to speak the words. But luckily, the Bul-Bul Bird has become bored and hops into his cage. As soon as the bird is inside the cage, the youngest son knows it's better not to speak the words after all. Inside his cage, the Bul-Bul Bird takes a good look around. At last, when he doesn't hear or see anyone, he calmly tucks his beak into his feathers and goes to sleep.

Very, very slowly the youngest son crawls out of the grass, and very, very softly he reaches through the door of the cage for the bird's ring. He slips it off the bird's left foot with his right hand, and with his left hand—slam!—he shuts the door of the cage. The Bul-Bul Bird is awake at once, and he struggles, and kicks, and hops, and screeches as hard as if doom were at hand. He carries on for a long, long time. Only with daylight does he start to calm down, and then, with lowered head, he says, "You have taken my ring—now I am yours."

"But tell me, Bul-Bul Bird—where are my brothers?"

"The two birches beside you, they are your brothers."

"But tell me, Bul-Bul Bird—what sort of creatures are the other birch trees?"

"The others are people too."

"But tell me, Bul-Bul Bird—how can I make them human again?"

"Go deeper into the birch grove and look around well—you will see a pile of sand. If you throw three handfuls of this sand on each birch tree, it will turn back into a person."

Very well. The youngest son first revives his brothers, and his brothers help him revive others. But when the three of them can't manage by themselves any more, the others also help to bring sand, and now, faster and faster, one birch after another disappears, until the entire grove is transformed, and the garden is swarming and humming with a crowd of people. They all gather around the youngest son, so overjoyed they hardly know what to do. But the youngest son wants to make them even happier. He asks the Bul-Bul Bird—can he still sing as he did the evening before? And the Bul-Bul Bird sings and sings for them. Oh, what a voice!

Three days later they all part: The brothers go one way, the others go theirs. At midday, our three brothers are walking along the sea. The older two want to go on, but the youngest is terribly weary. He lies down by the sea and soon falls asleep. Seeing this, the older brothers conspire to steal the Bul-Bul Bird and to throw the youngest son, who has rescued them, into the waves of the sea. Agreed, and done. The Bul-Bul Bird was now in their clutches, but the scoundrels have missed getting the ring—that remains on the finger of their youngest brother. The two older brothers arrive at their father's, and they brag about their long search, their great efforts in getting the Bul-Bul Bird—but as to what has happened to their youngest brother, they say they don't know.

They hoped for many good things from the Bul-Bul Bird—but without the ring, the Bul-Bul Bird obeys neither this nor that command, only stands around with lowered head.

And so it continues for quite some time. The older sons live at their father's with no remorse, and the old father, remembering his youngest son, weeps and grieves now and then. But what can he do?

Yet, the old man wept for nothing, for his beloved son had not drowned in the sea, but had been carried in the light arms of Water Maidens to the beautiful amber palace of the Mistress of the Sea. She likes the handsome youth, and she marries him. They both live happily. But one day a Water Maiden brings news that she has heard the old king bitterly weeping. The youngest son feels great pity for the old man, and he decides at once to leave the amber palace for a few days and to make his old father happy. He rubs the Bul-Bul Bird's ring. Instantly the ring becomes a golden bridge, stretching from the amber palace in the sea to the castle of his father.

The father, seeing his son hale and hearty, is so overjoyed he hardly knows what to do. And the Bul-Bul Bird starts at once to sing again, and tells the king what the older brothers did to the youngest. The oldest two fall on their knees before their father, and before their youngest brother, to ask for mercy. The youngest son has a loving heart and forgives them, and then helps them beseech their father for his forgiveness too.

For three days the youngest son stayed in his father's castle, for three days he rejoiced in his good fortune. But on the fourth day, at sunrise, he took the Bul-Bul Bird and returned to the amber palace. As he opened the amber palace gates, the golden bridge vanished and again became a golden ring.

East Europe

The Fool of the World and the Flying Ship

91. THE FOOL OF THE WORLD AND THE FLYING SHIP
(*Russia*)

THERE WERE ONCE upon a time an old peasant and his wife, and they had three sons. Two of them were clever young men who could borrow money without being cheated, but the third was the Fool of the World. He was as simple as a child, simpler than some children, and he never did anyone a harm in his life.

Well, it always happens like that. The father and mother thought a lot of the two smart young men; but the Fool of the World was lucky if he got enough to eat, because they always forgot him unless they happened to be looking at him, and sometimes even then.

But however it was with his father and mother, this is a story that shows that God loves simple folk, and turns things to their advantage in the end.

For it happened that the Tzar of that country sent out messengers along the highroads and the rivers, even to huts in the forest like ours, to say that he would give his daughter, the Princess, in marriage to anyone who could bring him a flying ship—ay, a ship with wings, that should sail this way and that through the blue sky, like a ship sailing on the sea.

"This is a chance for us," said the two clever brothers; and that same day they set off together, to see if one of them could not build the flying ship and marry the Tzar's daughter, and so be a great man indeed.

And their father blessed them, and gave them finer clothes than ever he wore himself. And their mother made them up hampers of food for the road, soft white rolls, and several kinds of cooked meats, and bottles of vodka. She went with them as far as the highroad, and waved her hand to them till they were out of sight. And so the two clever brothers set merrily off on their adventure, to see what could be done with their cleverness. And what happened to them I do not know, for they were never heard of again.

The Fool of the World saw them set off, with their fine parcels of food, and their fine clothes, and their bottles of vodka.

"I'd like to go too," says he, "and eat good meat, with soft white rolls, and drink vodka, and marry the Tzar's daughter."

"Stupid fellow," says his mother, "what's the good of your going? Why, if you were to stir from the house you would walk into the arms of a bear; and if not that, then the wolves would eat you before you had finished staring at them."

But the Fool of the World would not be held back by words.

"I am going," says he. "I am going. I am going. I am going."

He went on saying this over and over again, till the old woman his mother saw there was nothing to be done, and was glad to get him out of the house so as to be quit of the sound of his voice. So she put some food in a bag for him to eat by the way. She put in the bag some crusts of dry black bread and a flask of water. She did not even bother to go as far as the footpath to see him on his way. She saw the last of him at the door of the hut, and he had not taken two steps before she had gone back into the hut to see to more important business.

No matter. The Fool of the World set off with his bag over his shoulder, singing as he went, for he was off to seek his fortune and marry the Tzar's daughter. He was sorry his mother had not given him any vodka; but he sang merrily for all that. He would have liked white rolls instead of the dry black crusts; but, after all, the main thing on a journey is to have something to eat. So he trudged merrily along the road, and sang because the trees were green and there was a blue sky overhead.

He had not gone very far when he met an ancient old man with a bent back, and a long beard, and eyes hidden under his bushy eyebrows.

"Good day, young fellow," says the ancient old man.

"Good day, grandfather," says the Fool of the World.

"And where are you off to?" says the ancient old man.

"What!" says the Fool; "haven't you heard? The Tzar is going to give his daughter to anyone who can bring him a flying ship."

"And you can really make a flying ship?" says the ancient old man.

"No, I do not know how."

"Then what are you going to do?"

"God knows," says the Fool of the World.

"Well," says the ancient, "if things are like that, sit you down here.

We will rest together and have a bite of food. Bring out what you have in your bag."

"I am ashamed to offer you what I have here. It is good enough for me, but it is not the sort of meal to which one can ask guests."

"Never mind that. Out with it. Let us eat what God has given."

The Fool of the World opened his bag, and could hardly believe his eyes. Instead of black crusts he saw fresh white rolls and cooked meats. He handed them out to the ancient, who said, "You see how God loves simple folk. Although your own mother does not love you, you have not been done out of your share of the good things. Let's have a sip at the vodka. . . ."

The Fool of the World opened his flask, and instead of water there came out vodka, and that of the best. So the Fool and the ancient made merry, eating and drinking; and when they had done, and sung a song or two together, the ancient says to the Fool:

"Listen to me. Off with you into the forest. Go up to the first big tree you see. Make the sacred sign of the cross three times before it. Strike it a blow with your little hatchet. Fall backward on the ground, and lie there, full length on your back, until somebody wakes you up. Then you will find the ship made, all ready to fly. Sit you down in it, and fly off whither you want to go. But be sure on the way to give a lift to everyone you meet."

The Fool of the World thanked the ancient old man, said good-bye to him, and went off to the forest. He walked up to a tree, the first big tree he saw, made the sign of the cross three times before it, swung his hatchet round his head, struck a mighty blow on the trunk of the tree, instantly fell backward flat on the ground, closed his eyes, and went to sleep.

A little time went by, and it seemed to the Fool as he slept that somebody was jogging his elbow. He woke up and opened his eyes. His hatchet, worn out, lay beside him. The big tree was gone, and in its place there stood a little ship, ready and finished. The Fool did not stop to think. He jumped into the ship, seized the tiller, and sat down. Instantly the ship leaped up into the air, and sailed away over the tops of the trees.

The little ship answered the tiller as readily as if she were sailing in water, and the Fool steered for the highroad, and sailed along above it, for he was afraid of losing his way if he tried to steer a course across the open country.

He flew on and on, and looked down, and saw a man lying in the road below him with his ear on the damp ground.

"Good day to you, uncle," cried the Fool.

"Good day to you, Sky-fellow," cried the man.

"What are you doing down there?" says the Fool.

"I am listening to all that is being done in the world."

"Take your place in the ship with me."

The man was willing enough, and sat down in the ship with the Fool, and they flew on together singing songs.

They flew on and on, and looked down, and there was a man on one leg, with the other tied up to his head.

"Good day, uncle," says the Fool, bringing the ship to the ground. "Why are you hopping along on one foot?"

"If I were to untie the other I should move too fast. I should be stepping across the world in a single stride."

"Sit down with us," says the Fool.

The man sat down with them in the ship, and they flew on together singing songs.

They flew on and on, and looked down, and there was a man with a gun, and he was taking aim, but what he was aiming at they could not see.

"Good health to you, uncle," says the Fool. "But what are you shooting at? There isn't a bird to be seen."

"What!" says the man. "If there were a bird that you could see, I should not shoot at it. A bird or a beast a thousand versts away, that's the sort of mark for me."

"Take your seat with us," says the Fool.

The man sat down with them in the ship, and they flew on together. Louder and louder rose their songs.

They flew on and on, and looked down, and there was a man carrying a sack full of bread on his back.

"Good health to you, uncle," says the Fool, sailing down. "And where are you off to?"

"I am going to get bread for my dinner."

"But you've got a full sack on your back."

"That—that little scrap! Why, that's not enough for a single mouthful."

"Take your seat with us," says the Fool.

The Eater sat down with them in the ship, and they flew on together, singing louder than ever.

They flew on and on, and looked down, and there was a man walking round and round a lake.

"Good health to you, uncle," says the Fool. "What are you looking for?"

"I want a drink, and I can't find any water."

"But there's a whole lake in front of your eyes. Why can't you take a drink from that?"

"That little drop!" says the man. "Why, there's not enough water there to wet the back of my throat if I were to drink it at one gulp."

"Take your seat with us," says the Fool.

The Drinker sat down with them, and again they flew on, singing in chorus.

They flew on and on, and looked down, and there was a man walking toward the forest, with a fagot of wood on his shoulders.

"Good day to you, uncle," says the Fool. "Why are you taking wood to the forest?"

"This isn't simple wood," says the man.

"What is it, then?" says the Fool.

"If it is scattered about, a whole army of soldiers leaps up out of the ground."

"There's a place for you with us," says the Fool.

The man sat down with them, and the ship rose up into the air, and flew on, carrying its singing crew.

They flew on and on, and looked down, and there was a man carrying a sack of straw.

"Good health to you, uncle," says the Fool; "and where are you taking your straw?"

"To the village."

"Why, are they short of straw in your village?"

"No; but this is such straw that if you scatter it abroad in the very hottest of the summer, instantly the weather turns cold, and there is snow and frost."

"There's a place here for you too," says the Fool.

"Very kind of you," says the man, and steps in and sits down, and away they all sail together, singing like to burst their lungs.

They did not meet anyone else, and presently came flying up to the palace of the Tzar. They flew down and cast anchor in the courtyard.

Just then the Tzar was eating his dinner. He heard their loud singing, and looked out of the window and saw the ship come sailing down into his courtyard. He sent his servant out to ask who was the great prince who had brought him the flying ship, and had come sailing down with such a merry noise of singing.

The servant came up to the ship, and saw the Fool of the World and his companions sitting there cracking jokes. He saw they were all moujiks, simple peasants, sitting in the ship; so he did not stop to ask questions, but came back quietly and told the Tzar that there were no gentlemen in the ship at all, but only a lot of dirty peasants.

Now the Tzar was not at all pleased with the idea of giving his only daughter in marriage to a simple peasant, and he began to think how he could get out of his bargain. Thinks he to himself, "I'll set them such tasks that they will not be able to perform, and they'll be glad to get off with their lives, and I shall get the ship for nothing."

So he told his servant to go to the Fool and tell him that before the Tzar had finished his dinner the Fool was to bring him some of the magical water of life.

Now, while the Tzar was giving this order to his servant, the Listener, the first of the Fool's companions, was listening and heard the words of the Tzar and repeated them to the Fool.

"What am I to do now?" says the Fool, stopping short in his jokes. "In a year, in a whole century, I never could find that water. And he wants it before he has finished his dinner."

"Don't you worry about that," says the Swift-goer, "I'll deal with that for you."

The servant came and announced the Tzar's command.

"Tell him he shall have it," says the Fool.

His companion, the Swift-goer, untied his foot from beside his head, put it to the ground, wriggled it a little to get the stiffness out of it, ran off, and was out of sight almost before he had stepped from the ship. Quicker than I can tell it you in words he had come to the water of life, and put some of it in a bottle.

"I shall have plenty of time to get back," thinks he, and down he sits under a windmill and goes off to sleep.

The royal dinner was coming to an end, and there wasn't a sign of him. There were no songs and no jokes in the flying ship. Everybody was watching for the Swift-goer, and thinking he would not be in time.

The Listener jumped out and laid his right ear to the damp ground, listened a moment, and said, "What a fellow! He has gone to sleep under the windmill. I can hear him snoring. And there is a fly buzzing with its wings, perched on the windmill close above his head."

"This is my affair," says the Far-shooter, and he picked up his gun from between his knees, aimed at the fly on the windmill, and woke the Swift-goer with the thud of the bullet on the wood of the mill close by his head. The Swift-goer leaped up and ran, and in less than a second had brought the magic water of life and given it to the Fool. The Fool gave it to the servant, who took it to the Tzar. The Tzar had not yet left the table, so that his command had been fulfilled as exactly as ever could be.

"What fellows these peasants are," thought the Tzar. "There is nothing for it but to set them another task." So the Tzar said to his servant, "Go to the captain of the flying ship and give him this message: 'If you are such a cunning fellow, you must have a good appetite. Let you and your companions eat at a single meal twelve oxen roasted whole, and as much bread as can be baked in forty ovens!'"

The Listener heard the message, and told the Fool what was coming. The Fool was terrified, and said, "I can't get through even a single loaf at a sitting."

"Don't worry about that," said the Eater. "It won't be more than a mouthful for me, and I shall be glad to have a little snack in place of my dinner."

The servant came, and announced the Tzar's command.

"Good," says the Fool. "Send the food along, and we'll know what to do with it."

So they brought twelve oxen roasted whole, and as much bread as could be baked in forty ovens, and the companions had scarcely sat down to the meal before the Eater had finished the lot.

"Why," said the Eater, "what a little! They might have given us a decent meal while they were about it."

The Tzar told his servant to tell the Fool that he and his companions were to drink forty barrels of wine, with forty bucketfuls in every barrel.

The Listener told the Fool what message was coming.

"Why," says the Fool, "I never in my life drank more than one bucket at a time."

"Don't worry," says the Drinker. "You forget that I am thirsty. It'll be nothing of a drink for me."

They brought the forty barrels of wine, and tapped them, and the Drinker tossed them down one after another, one gulp for each barrel. "Little enough," says he. "Why, I am thirsty still."

"Very good," says the Tzar to his servant, when he heard that they had eaten all the food and drunk all the wine. "Tell the fellow to get ready for the wedding, and let him go and bathe himself in the bath-house. But let the bath-house be made so hot that the man will stifle and frizzle as soon as he sets foot inside. It is an iron bath-house. Let it be made red hot."

The Listener heard all this and told the Fool, who stopped short with his mouth open in the middle of a joke.

"Don't you worry," says the moujik with the straw.

Well, they made the bath-house red hot, and called the Fool, and the Fool went along to the bath-house to wash himself, and with him went the moujik with the straw.

They shut them both into the bath-house, and thought that that was the end of them. But the moujik scattered his straw before them as they went in, and it became so cold in there that the Fool of the World had scarcely time to wash himself before the water in the cauldrons froze to solid ice. They lay down on the very stove itself, and spent the night there, shivering.

In the morning the servants opened the bath-house, and there were the Fool of the World and the moujik, alive and well, lying on the stove and singing songs.

They told the Tzar, and the Tzar raged with anger. "There is no getting rid of this fellow," says he. "But go and tell him that I send him this message: 'If you are to marry my daughter, you must show that you are able to defend her. Let me see that you have at least a regiment of soldiers.'" Thinks he to himself, "How can a simple peasant raise a troop? He will find it hard enough to raise a single soldier."

The Listener told the Fool of the World, and the Fool began to lament, "This time," says he, "I am done indeed. You, my brothers, have saved me from misfortune more than once, but this time, alas, there is nothing to be done."

"Oh, what a fellow you are!" says the peasant with the fagot of wood. "I suppose you've forgotten about me. Remember that I am the man for this little affair, and don't you worry about it at all."

The Tzar's servant came along and gave his message.

"Very good," says the Fool, "but tell the Tzar that if after this he puts me off again, I'll make war on his country, and take the Princess by force."

And then, as the servant went back with the message, the whole crew on the flying ship set to their singing again, and sang and laughed and made jokes as if they had not a care in the world.

During the night, while the others slept, the peasant with the fagot of wood went hither and thither, scattering his sticks. Instantly where they fell there appeared a gigantic army. Nobody could count the number of soldiers in it—cavalry, foot soldiers, yes, and guns, and all the guns new and bright, and the men in the finest uniforms that ever were seen.

In the morning, as the Tzar woke and looked from the windows of the palace, he found himself surrounded by troops upon troops of soldiers, and generals in cocked hats bowing in the courtyard and taking orders from the Fool of the World, who sat there joking with his companions in the flying ship. Now it was the Tzar's turn to be afraid. As quickly as he could he sent his servants to the Fool with presents of rich jewels and fine clothes, invited him to come to the palace, and begged him to marry the Princess.

The Fool of the World put on the fine clothes, and stood there as handsome a young man as a princess could wish for a husband. He presented himself before the Tzar, fell in love with the Princess and she with him, married her the same day, received with her a rich dowry, and became so clever that all the court repeated everything he said. The Tzar and the Tzaritza liked him very much, and as for the Princess, she loved him to distraction.

92. THE BABA YAGA
(Russia)

ONCE UPON A TIME there was an old couple. The husband lost his wife and married again. But he had a daughter by the first marriage, a young girl, and she found no favor in the eyes of her evil stepmother, who used to beat her, and consider how she could get her killed outright. One day the father went away somewhere or other, so the stepmother said to the girl, "Go to your aunt, my sister, and ask her for a needle and thread to make you a shift."

Now that aunt was a Baba Yaga. Well, the girl was no fool, so she went to a real aunt of hers first, and says she:

"Good morning, auntie!"

"Good morning, my dear! what have you come for?"

"Mother has sent me to her sister, to ask for a needle and thread to make me a shift."

Then her aunt instructed her what to do. "There is a birch tree there, niece, which would hit you in the eye—you must tie a ribbon round it; there are doors which would creak and bang—you must pour oil on their hinges; there are dogs which would tear you in pieces—you must throw them these rolls; there is a cat which would scratch your eyes out—you must give it a piece of bacon."

So the girl went away, and walked and walked, till she came to the place. There stood a hut, and in it sat weaving the Baba Yaga, the Bony-Shanks.

"Good morning, auntie," says the girl.

"Good morning, my dear," replies the Baba Yaga.

"Mother has sent me to ask you for a needle and thread to make me a shift."

"Very well; sit down and weave a little in the meantime."

So the girl sat down behind the loom, and the Baba Yaga went outside, and said to her servant-maid:

"Go and heat the bath, and get my niece washed; and mind you look sharp after her. I want to breakfast off her."

Well, the girl sat there in such a fright that she was as much dead as alive. Presently she spoke imploringly to the servant-maid, saying:

"Kinswoman dear, do please wet the firewood instead of making it burn; and fetch the water for the bath in a sieve." And she made her a present of a handkerchief.

The Baba Yaga waited awhile; then she came to the window and asked:

"Are you weaving, niece? are you weaving, my dear?"

"Oh yes, dear aunt, I'm weaving." So the Baba Yaga went away again, and the girl gave the Cat a piece of bacon, and asked:

"Is there no way of escaping from here?"

"Here's a comb for you and a towel," said the Cat; "take them, and be off. The Baba Yaga will pursue you, but you must lay your ear on the ground, and when you hear that she is close at hand, first of all throw down the towel. It will become a wide, wide river. And if the Baba Yaga gets across the river, and tries to catch you, then you must lay your ear on the ground again, and when you hear that she is close at hand, throw down the comb. It will become a dense, dense forest; through that she won't be able to force her way anyhow."

The girl took the towel and the comb and fled. The dogs would have rent her, but she threw them the rolls, and they let her go by; the doors would have begun to bang, but she poured oil on their hinges, and they let her pass through; the birch tree would have poked her eyes out, but she tied the ribbon around it, and it let her pass on. And the Cat sat down to the loom, and worked away; muddled everything about, if it didn't do much weaving. Up came the Baba Yaga to the window, and asked:

"Are you weaving, niece? are you weaving, my dear?"

"I'm weaving, dear aunt, I'm weaving," gruffly replied the Cat.

The Baba Yaga rushed into the hut, saw that the girl was gone, and took to beating the Cat, and abusing it for not having scratched the girl's eyes out. "Long as I've served you," said the Cat, "you've never given me so much as a bone; but she gave me bacon." Then the Baba Yaga pounced upon the dogs, on the doors, on the birch tree, and on the servant-maid, and set to work to abuse them all, and to knock them about. Then the dogs said to her, "Long as we've served you, you've never so much as pitched us a burned crust; but she gave us rolls to eat." And the doors said, "Long as we've served you, you've never poured even a drop of water on our hinges; but she poured oil on us." The birch tree said, "Long as I've served you, you've never tied a single thread round me; but she fastened a ribbon around me." And the servant-maid said, "Long as I've served you, you've never given me so much as a rag; but she gave me a handkerchief."

The Baba Yaga, bony of limb, quickly jumped into her mortar, sent it flying along with the pestle, sweeping away the while all traces of its flight with a broom, and set off in pursuit of the girl. Then the girl put her ear to the ground, and when she heard that the Baba Yaga was chasing her, and was now close at hand, she flung down the towel. And it became a wide, such a wide river! Up came the Baba Yaga to the river, and gnashed her teeth with spite; then she went home for her oxen, and drove them to the river. The oxen drank up every drop of the river, and then the Baba Yaga began the pursuit anew. But the girl put her ear to the ground again, and when she heard that the Baba Yaga was near, she flung down the comb, and instantly a forest sprang up, such an awfully thick one! The Baba Yaga began gnawing away at it, but however hard she worked, she couldn't gnaw her way through it, so she had to go back again.

But by this time the girl's father had returned home, and he asked: "Where's my daughter?"

"She's gone to her aunt's," replied her stepmother.

Soon afterward the girl herself came running home.

"Where have you been?" asked her father.

"Ah, father!" she said, "mother sent me to aunt's to ask for a needle and thread to make me a shift. But aunt's a Baba Yaga, and she wanted to eat me!"

"And how did you get away, daughter?"

"Why like this," said the girl, and explained the whole matter. As soon as her father had heard all about it, he became wroth with his wife, and shot her. But he and his daughter lived on and flourished, and everything went well with them.

93. THE FIREBIRD, THE HORSE OF POWER AND THE PRINCESS VASILISSA
(*Russia*)

ONCE UPON A TIME a strong and powerful Tzar ruled in a country far away. And among his servants was a young archer, and this archer had a horse—a horse of power—such a horse as belonged to the wonderful men of long ago—a great horse with a broad chest, eyes like fire, and hoofs of iron. There are no such horses nowadays. They sleep with the strong men who rode them, the bogatirs, until the time comes when Russia has need of them. Then the great horses will thunder up from under the ground, and the valiant men leap from the graves in the armor they have worn so long. The strong men will sit those horses of power, and there will be swinging of clubs and thunder of hoofs, and the earth will be swept clean from the enemies of God and the Tzar. So my grandfather used to say, and he was as much older than I as I am older than you, little ones, and so he should know.

Well, one day long ago, in the green time of the year, the young archer rode through the forest on his horse of power. The trees were green; there were little blue flowers on the ground under the trees; the squirrels ran in the branches, and the hares in the undergrowth; but no birds sang. The young archer rode along the forest path and listened for the singing of the birds, but there was no singing. The forest was silent, and the only noises in it were the scratching of four-footed beasts, the dropping of fir cones, and the heavy stamping of the horse of power in the soft path.

"What has come to the birds?" said the young archer.

He had scarcely said this before he saw a big curving feather lying in the path before him. The feather was larger than a swan's, larger than an eagle's. It lay in the path, glittering like a flame; for the sun was on it, and it was a feather of pure gold. Then he knew why there was no singing in the forest. For he knew that the firebird had flown that way, and that the feather in the path before him was a feather from its burning breast.

The horse of power spoke and said:

"Leave the golden feather where it lies. If you take it you will be sorry for it, and know the meaning of fear."

But the brave young archer sat on the horse of power and looked at the golden feather, and wondered whether to take it or not. He had no wish to learn what it was to be afraid, but he thought, "If I take it and bring it to the Tzar my master, he will be pleased; and he will not send me away with empty hands, for no tzar in the world has a feather from the burning breast of the firebird." And the more he thought, the more he wanted to carry the feather to the Tzar. And in the end he did not listen to the words of the horse of power. He leaped from the saddle, picked up the golden feather of the firebird, mounted his horse again, and galloped back through the green forest till he came to the palace of the Tzar.

He went into the palace, and bowed before the Tzar and said:

"O Tzar, I have brought you a feather of the firebird."

The Tzar looked gladly at the feather, and then at the young archer.

"Thank you," says he; "but if you have brought me a feather of the firebird, you will be able to bring me the bird itself. I should like to see it. A feather is not a fit gift to bring to the Tzar. Bring the bird itself, or, I swear by my sword, your head shall no longer sit between your shoulders!"

The young archer bowed his head and went out. Bitterly he wept, for he knew now what it was to be afraid. He went out into the courtyard, where the horse of power was waiting for him, tossing its head and stamping on the ground.

"Master," says the horse of power, "why do you weep?"

"The Tzar has told me to bring him the firebird, and no man on earth can do that," says the young archer, and he bowed his head on his breast.

"I told you," says the horse of power, "that if you took the feather you would learn the meaning of fear. Well, do not be frightened yet, and do not weep. The trouble is not now; the trouble lies before you. Go to the Tzar and ask him to have a hundred sacks of maize scattered over the open field, and let this be done at midnight."

The young archer went back into the palace and begged the Tzar for this, and the Tzar ordered that at midnight a hundred sacks of maize should be scattered in the open field.

Next morning, at the first redness in the sky, the young archer rode out on the horse of power, and came to the open field. The ground was scattered all over with maize. In the middle of the field stood a great oak with spreading boughs. The young archer leaped to the ground, took off the saddle, and let the horse of power loose to wander as he pleased about the field. Then he climbed up into the oak and hid himself among the green boughs.

The sky grew red and gold, and the sun rose. Suddenly there was a noise in the forest round the field. The trees shook and swayed, and almost fell. There was a mighty wind. The sea piled itself into waves with crests of foam, and the firebird came flying from the other side of the world. Huge and golden and flaming in the sun, it flew, dropped down with open wings into the field, and began to eat the maize.

The horse of power wandered in the field. This way he went, and that, but always he came a little nearer to the firebird. Nearer and nearer came the horse. He came close up to the firebird, and then suddenly stepped on one of its spreading fiery wings and pressed it heavily to the ground. The bird struggled, flapping mightily with its fiery wings, but it could not get away. The young archer slipped down from the tree, bound the firebird with three strong ropes, swung it on his back, saddled the horse, and rode to the palace of the Tzar.

The young archer stood before the Tzar, and his back was bent under the great weight of the firebird, and the broad wings of the bird hung on either side of him like fiery shields, and there was a trail of golden feathers on the floor. The young archer swung the magic bird to the foot of the throne before the Tzar; and the Tzar was glad, because since the beginning of the world no tzar had seen the firebird flung before him like a wild duck caught in a snare.

The Tzar looked at the firebird and laughed with pride. Then he lifted his eyes and looked at the young archer, and says he:

"As you have known how to take the firebird, you will know how to bring me my bride, for whom I have long been waiting. In the land of Never, on the very edge of the world, where the red sun rises in flame from behind the sea, lives the Princess Vasilissa. I will marry none but her. Bring her to me, and I will reward you with silver and gold. But if you do not bring her, then, by my sword, your head will no longer sit between your shoulders!"

The young archer wept bitter tears, and went out into the courtyard where the horse of power was stamping the ground with its hoofs of iron and tossing its thick mane.

"Master, why do you weep?" asked the horse of power.

"The Tzar has ordered me to go to the land of Never, and to bring back the Princess Vasilissa."

"Do not weep—do not grieve. The trouble is not yet; the trouble is to come. Go to the Tzar and ask him for a silver tent with a golden roof, and for all kinds of food and drink to take with us on the journey."

The young archer went in and asked the Tzar for this, and the Tzar gave him a silver tent with silver hangings and a gold-embroidered roof, and every kind of rich wine and the tastiest of foods.

Then the young archer mounted the horse of power and rode off to the land of Never. On and on he rode, many days and nights, and came at last to the edge of the world, where the red sun rises in flame from behind the deep blue sea.

On the shore of the sea the young archer reined in the horse of power, and the heavy hoofs of the horse sank in the sand. He shaded his eyes and looked out over the blue water, and there was the Princess Vasilissa in a little silver boat, rowing with golden oars.

The young archer rode back a little way to where the sand ended and the green world began. There he loosed the horse to wander where he pleased, and to feed on the green grass. Then on the edge of the shore, where the green grass ended and grew thin and the sand began, he set up the shining tent, with its silver hangings and its gold-embroidered roof. In the tent he set out the tasty dishes and the rich flagons of wine which the Tzar had given him, and he sat himself down in the tent and began to regale himself, while he waited for the Princess Vasilissa.

The Princess Vasilissa dipped her golden oars in the blue water, and the little silver boat moved lightly through the dancing waves. She sat in the little boat and looked over the blue sea to the edge of the world, and there, between the golden sand and the green earth, she saw the tent standing, silver and gold in the sun. She dipped her oars, and came nearer to see it better. The nearer she came the fairer seemed the tent, and at last she rowed to the shore and grounded her little boat on the golden sand, and stepped out daintily and came up to the tent. She was a little frightened, and now and again she stopped and looked back to where the silver boat lay on the sand with the blue sea beyond it. The young archer said not a word, but went on regaling himself on the pleasant dishes he had set out there in the tent.

At last the Princess Vasilissa came up to the tent and looked in.

The young archer rose and bowed before her. Says he:

"Good day to you, Princess! Be so kind as to come in and take bread and salt with me, and taste my foreign wines."

And the Princess Vasilissa came into the tent and sat down with the young archer, and ate sweetmeats with him, and drank his health in a golden goblet of the wine the Tzar had given him. Now this wine was heavy, and the last drop from the goblet had no sooner trickled down her little slender throat than her eyes closed against her will, once, twice, and again.

"Ah me!" says the Princess, "it is as if the night itself had perched on my eyelids, and yet it is but noon."

And the golden goblet dropped to the ground from her little fingers, and she leaned back on a cushion and fell instantly asleep. If she had been beautiful before, she was lovelier still when she lay in that deep sleep in the shadow of the tent.

Quickly the young archer called to the horse of power. Lightly he lifted the Princess in his strong young arms. Swiftly he leaped with her into the saddle. Like a feather she lay in the hollow of his left arm, and slept while the iron hoofs of the great horse thundered over the ground.

They came to the Tzar's palace, and the young archer leaped from the horse of power and carried the Princess into the palace. Great was the joy of the Tzar; but it did not last for long.

"Go, sound the trumpets for our wedding," he said to his servants, "let all the bells be rung."

The bells rang out and the trumpets sounded, and at the noise of the horns and the ringing of the bells the Princess Vasilissa woke up and looked about her.

"What is this ringing of bells," says she, "and this noise of trumpets? And where, oh, where is the blue sea, and my little silver boat with its golden oars?" And the Princess put her hand to her eyes.

"The blue sea is far away," says the Tzar, "and for your little silver boat I give you a golden throne. The trumpets sound for our wedding, and the bells are ringing for our joy."

But the Princess turned her face away from the Tzar; and there was no wonder in that, for he was old, and his eyes were not kind.

And she looked with love at the young archer; and there was no wonder in that either, for he was a young man fit to ride the horse of power.

The Tzar was angry with the Princess Vasilissa, but his anger was as useless as his joy.

"Why, Princess," says he, "will you not marry me, and forget your blue sea and your silver boat?"

"In the middle of the deep blue sea lies a great stone," says the Princess, "and under that stone is hidden my wedding dress. If I cannot wear that dress I will marry nobody at all."

Instantly the Tzar turned to the young archer, who was waiting before the throne.

"Ride swiftly back," says he, "to the land of Never, where the red sun rises in flame. There—do you hear what the Princess says?—a great stone lies in the middle of the sea. Under that stone is hidden her wedding dress. Ride swiftly. Bring back that dress, or, by my sword, your head shall no longer sit between your shoulders!"

The young archer wept bitter tears, and went out into the courtyard, where the horse of power was waiting for him, champing its golden bit.

"There is no way of escaping death this time," he said.

"Master, why do you weep?" asked the horse of power.

"The Tzar has ordered me to ride to the land of Never, to fetch the wedding dress of the Princess Vasilissa from the bottom of the deep blue sea. Besides, the dress is wanted for the Tzar's wedding, and I love the Princess myself."

"What did I tell you?" says the horse of power. "I told you that there would be trouble if you picked up the golden feather from the firebird's burning breast. Well, do not be afraid. The trouble is not yet; the trouble is to come. Up! into the saddle with you, and away for the wedding dress of the Princess Vasilissa!"

The young archer leaped into the saddle, and the horse of power, with his thundering hoofs, carried him swiftly through the green forests and over the bare plains, till they came to the edge of the world, to the land of Never, where the red sun rises in flame from behind the deep blue sea. There they rested, at the very edge of the sea.

The young archer looked sadly over the wide waters, but the horse of power tossed its mane and did not look at the sea, but on the shore. This way and that it looked, and saw at last a huge lobster moving slowly, sideways, along the golden sand.

Nearer and nearer came the lobster, and it was a giant among lobsters, the tzar of all the lobsters; and it moved slowly along the shore, while the horse of power moved carefully and as if by accident, until it stood between the lobster and the sea. Then when the lobster came close by, the horse of power lifted an iron hoof and set it firmly on the lobster's tail.

"You will be the death of me!" screamed the lobster—as well he might, with the heavy foot of the horse of power pressing his tail into the sand. "Let me live, and I will do whatever you ask of me."

"Very well," says the horse of power, "we will let you live," and he slowly lifted his foot. "But this is what you shall do for us. In the middle of the blue sea lies a great stone, and under that stone is hidden the wedding dress of the Princess Vasilissa. Bring it here."

The lobster groaned with the pain in his tail. Then he cried out in a voice that could be heard all over the deep blue sea. And the sea was disturbed, and from all sides lobsters in thousands made their way toward the bank. And the huge lobster that was the oldest of them all and the tzar of all the lobsters that live between the rising and the setting of the sun, gave them the order and sent them back into the sea. And the young archer sat on the horse of power and waited.

After a little time the sea was disturbed again, and the lobsters in their thousands came to the shore, and with them they brought a golden casket in which was the wedding dress of the Princess Vasilissa. They had taken it from under the great stone that lay in the middle of the sea.

The tzar of all the lobsters raised himself painfully on his bruised tail and gave the casket into the hands of the young archer, and instantly the horse of power turned himself about and galloped back to the palace of the Tzar, far, far away, at the other side of the green forests and beyond the treeless plains.

The young archer went into the palace and gave the casket into the hands of the Princess, and looked at her with sadness in his eyes, and she looked at him with love. Then she went away into an inner chamber, and came back in her wedding dress, fairer than the spring itself.

Great was the joy of the Tzar. The wedding feast was made ready, and the bells rang, and flags waved above the palace.

The Tzar held out his hand to the Princess, and looked at her with his old eyes. But she would not take his hand.

"No," says she, "I will marry nobody until the man who brought me here has done penance in boiling water."

Instantly the Tzar turned to his servants and ordered them to make a great fire, and to fill a great cauldron with water and set it on the fire, and, when the water should be at its hottest, to take the young archer and throw him into it, to do penance for having taken the Princess Vasilissa away from the land of Never.

There was no gratitude in the mind of that Tzar.

Swiftly the servants brought wood and made a mighty fire, and on it they laid a huge cauldron of water, and built the fire round the walls of the cauldron. The fire burned hot and the water steamed. The fire burned hotter, and the water bubbled and seethed. They made ready to take the young archer, to throw him into the cauldron.

"Oh, misery!" thought the young archer. "Why did I ever take the golden feather that had fallen from the firebird's burning breast? Why did I not listen to the wise words of the horse of power?" And he remembered the horse of power, and he begged the Tzar:

"O lord Tzar, I do not complain. I shall presently die in the heat of the water on the fire. Suffer me, before I die, once more to see my horse."

"Let him see his horse," says the Princess.

"Very well," says the Tzar. "Say good-bye to your horse, for you will not ride him again. But let your farewells be short, for we are waiting."

The young archer crossed the courtyard and came to the horse of power, who was scraping the ground with his iron hoofs.

"Farewell, my horse of power," says the young archer. "I should have listened to your words of wisdom, for now the end is come, and we shall never more see the green trees pass above us and the ground disappear beneath us, as we race the wind between the earth and the sky."

"Why so?" says the horse of power.

"The Tzar has ordered that I am to be boiled to death—thrown into that cauldron that is seething on the great fire."

"Fear not," says the horse of power, "for the Princess Vasilissa has made him do this, and the end of these things is better than I thought. Go back, and when they are ready to throw you in the cauldron, do you run boldly and leap yourself into the boiling water."

The young archer went back across the courtyard, and the servants made ready to throw him into the cauldron.

"Are you sure that the water is boiling?" says the Princess Vasilissa.

"It bubbles and seethes," said the servants.

"Let me see for myself," says the Princess, and she went to the fire and waved her hand above the cauldron. And some say there was something in her hand, and some say there was not.

"It is boiling," says she, and the servants laid hands on the young archer; but he threw them from him, and ran and leaped boldly before them all into the very middle of the cauldron.

Twice he sank below the surface, borne round with the bubbles and foam of the boiling water. Then he leaped from the cauldron and stood before the Tzar and the Princess. He had become so beautiful a youth that all who saw cried aloud in wonder.

"This is a miracle," says the Tzar. And the Tzar looked at the beautiful young archer, and thought of himself—of his age, of his bent back, and his gray beard, and his toothless gums. "I too will become beautiful," thinks he, and he rose from his throne and clambered into the cauldron, and was boiled to death in a moment.

And the end of the story? They buried the Tzar, and made the young archer Tzar in his place. He married the Princess Vasilissa, and lived many years with her in love and good fellowship. And he built a golden stable for the horse of power, and never forgot what he owed to him.

94. THE STORY OF KING FROST
(Russia)

THERE WAS ONCE upon a time a peasant woman who had a daughter and a stepdaughter. The daughter had her own way in everything, and whatever she did was right in her mother's eyes; but the poor stepdaughter had a hard time. Let her do what she would, she was always blamed, and got small thanks for all the trouble she took; nothing was right, everything wrong; and yet, if the truth were known, the girl was worth her weight in gold—she was so unselfish and goodhearted. But her stepmother did not like her, and the poor girl's days were spent in weeping; for it was impossible to live peacefully with the woman. The wicked shrew was determined to get rid of the girl by fair means or foul, and kept saying to her father: "Send her away, old man; send her away—anywhere so that my eyes shall not be plagued any longer by the sight of her, or my ears tormented by the sound of her voice. Send her out into the fields, and let the cutting frost do for her."

In vain did the poor old father weep and implore her pity; she was firm, and he dared not gainsay her. So he placed his daughter in a sleigh, not even daring to give her a horsecloth to keep herself warm with, and drove her out on to the bare, open fields, where he kissed her and left her, driving home as fast as he could, that he might not witness her miserable death.

Deserted by her father, the poor girl sat down under a fir tree at the edge of the forest and began to weep silently. Suddenly she heard a faint sound: it was King Frost springing from tree to tree, and cracking his fingers as he went. At length he reached the fir tree beneath which she was sitting, and with a crisp crackling sound he alighted beside her, and looked at her lovely face.

"Well, maiden," he snapped out, "do you know who I am? I am King Frost, king of the red-noses."

"All hail to you, great King!" answered the girl, in a gentle, trembling voice. "Have you come to take me?"

"Are you warm, maiden?" he replied.

"Quite warm, King Frost," she answered, though she shivered as she spoke.

Then King Frost stooped down, and bent over the girl, and the crackling sound grew louder, and the air seemed to be full of knives and darts; and again he asked:

"Maiden, are you warm? Are you warm, you beautiful girl?"

And though her breath was almost frozen on her lips, she whispered gently, "Quite warm, King Frost."

Then King Frost gnashed his teeth, and cracked his fingers, and his eyes sparkled, and the crackling, crisp sound was louder than ever, and for the last time he asked her:

"Maiden, are you still warm? Are you still warm, little love?"

And the poor girl was so stiff and numb that she could just gasp, "Still warm, O King!"

Now her gentle, courteous words and her uncomplaining ways

touched King Frost, and he had pity on her, and he wrapped her up in furs, and covered her with blankets, and he fetched a great box, in which were beautiful jewels and a rich robe embroidered in gold and silver. And she put it on, and looked more lovely than ever, and King Frost stepped with her into his sleigh, with six white horses.

In the meantime the wicked stepmother was waiting at home for news of the girl's death, and preparing pancakes for the funeral feast. And she said to her husband: "Old man, you had better go out into the fields and find your daughter's body and bury her." Just as the old man was leaving the house the little dog under the table began to bark, saying:

> "*Your* daughter shall live to be your delight;
> *Her* daughter shall die this very night."

"Hold your tongue, you foolish beast!" scolded the woman. "There's a pancake for you, but you must say:

> '*Her* daughter shall have much silver and gold;
> *His* daughter is frozen quite stiff and cold.'"

But the doggie ate up the pancake and barked, saying:

> "His daughter shall wear a crown on her head;
> Her daughter shall die unwooed, unwed."

Then the old woman tried to coax the doggie with more pancakes and to terrify it with blows, but he barked on, always repeating the same words. And suddenly the door creaked and flew open, and a great heavy chest was pushed in, and behind it came the stepdaughter, radiant and beautiful, in a dress all glittering with silver and gold. For a moment the stepmother's eyes were dazzled. Then she called to her husband: "Old man, yoke the horses at once into the sleigh, and take my daughter to the same field and leave her on the same spot exactly"; and so the old man took the girl and left her beneath the same tree where he had parted from his daughter. In a few minutes King Frost came past, and, looking at the girl, he said:

"Are you warm, maiden?"

"What a blind old fool you must be to ask such a question!" she answered angrily. "Can't you see that my hands and feet are nearly frozen?"

Then King Frost sprang to and fro in front of her, questioning her, and getting only rude, rough words in reply, till at last he got very angry, and cracked his fingers, and gnashed his teeth, and froze her to death.

But in the hut her mother was waiting for her return, and as she grew impatient she said to her husband: "Get out the horses, old man, to go and fetch her home; but see that you are careful not to upset the sleigh and lose the chest."

But the doggie beneath the table began to bark, saying:

"Your daughter is frozen quite stiff and cold,
And shall never have a chest full of gold."

"Don't tell such wicked lies!" scolded the woman. "There's a cake for you; now say:

'Her daughter shall marry a mighty King.'

At that moment the door flew open, and she rushed out to meet her daughter, and as she took her frozen body in her arms she too was chilled to death.

95. PRINCE HEDGEHOG
(Russia)

ONCE UPON A TIME there was an emperor and an empress who for many years had been childless. One day the empress wished for a son, were he no bigger than a hedgehog. The proverb says, "What one wishes for, that one gets," and so it was with her, for she shortly gave birth to a son who looked exactly like a hedgehog and was covered all over with sharp spines.

Far and wide the news was spread abroad through the world, and the parents were much ashamed of such a son. Nevertheless, they had him educated in all useful knowledge, and he had so clever a head that by the time he was fourteen he knew all knowledge through and through.

By this time his parents could no longer endure him near them, and they assigned to him a great forest as a place of abode, feeling certain that he would then fall prey to a wolf or a fox or some sort of a beast. They strictly commanded him not to return before the expiration of seven years. They gave him permission, however, to take with him anything that he especially cared for; but he would take nothing whatever except a sow and a great cock upon which he was wont to ride. With these he went away into the forest.

Year out, year in, Prince Hedgehog remained in the forest, and he raised so many swine that at last they were too many for even him to count. Finally he thought to himself, "My seven years are up; I will go back home." So he quickly gathered his swine together and drove them to the city of his parents.

When they perceived afar off the immense drove of swine, they thought, "Here comes a wealthy swine-drover." But soon they recognized their son, who was riding upon his cock behind the swine and making straight for the imperial castle. So they received him into the castle and showed him the best of hospitality, dividing his swine among different pens, for they filled every swine-pen in the city.

While they were at table they asked their son how he enjoyed himself in the forest, and said that if he wished to go back there they would give him a goat this time. But he declared that he was not going back, for he had made up his mind to marry.

The astonished parents replied, "Why, what maiden would love you and take you for a husband?" The poor youth knew no answer to this question, so he mounted his cock and rode sadly away.

Now the parents thought he would never come back again. But he was a clever fellow, and he went as a suitor to the king of a neighboring country who had three unmarried daughters.

When he found himself near the city the cock flew up with him to the window of the room in which guests were assembled enjoying themselves. The cock crowed with all his might, until the chamberlain went to the window and asked what he wanted. The Hedgehog answered, "I come a-wooing."

Then the king permitted him to come into the room, and offered him the welcome-cup, according to ancient manner and custom. Then the king again asked him what business brought him, and Hedgehog, the imperial prince, answered him shortly and to the point, "I come a-wooing."

The king immediately assured him that he had only to choose one of the three unmarried daughters. The Hedgehog chose the youngest, but she would not have him for a husband until her father threatened to have her banished unless she gave a cheerful consent.

She saw no help for it, and thought to herself: "I can never get out of this scrape; come what may, I'll take him. We have gold and treasure in abundance, and we shall easily get along through life."

When the Hedgehog had received her consent he went back to his parents and told them what had happened to him. His parents would not believe him, and sent the chamberlain to inquire if it was true that the emperor's son, the Hedgehog, was to marry the king's daughter. When the chamberlain returned and told the emperor that his son had spoken the truth, the emperor ordered his horses to be harnessed, and went with his wife to visit the king, riding in their carriage, while their son rode behind on his cock.

When they arrived they found everything ready for the wedding. But, according to custom, the bridal party were obliged to go to the church a few days before the marriage to pray and confess to the priest. When the young lady came to confession she asked the priest how she might manage to get rid of the prince and not be obliged to marry him.

The priest gave her a sound scolding, and said in conclusion: "Just keep quiet and all will end well. Mark what I say, and remember it well. When you are come into the church and are taking your place in the sacristy, do you follow close behind the others. When you get to the high altar sprinkle your bridegroom thrice with holy-water, and be careful to prick yourself each time with one of his spines. Then three drops of blood will trickle out of your hand, and you must let these also fall upon him."

After confession the bridal pair went home to breakfast. The next day—it was a Sunday—the bridal party went at half past eleven into the church, and the bride did in every respect as the priest had counseled.

And, behold, the Hedgehog was transformed into a beautiful youth whose like was not to be found in all the world. Then the bridal party sat down upon the benches and heard mass, and the priest united them and preached them a sermon how they should cleave to each other all their lives long.

After that they went back to the house, and the wedding-feast lasted until late in the night.

96. SALT
(Russia)

ONCE UPON A TIME there were three brothers, and their father was a great merchant who sent his ships far over the sea, and traded here and there in countries the names of which I, being an old man, can never rightly call to mind. Well, the names of the two elder brothers do not matter, but the youngest was called Ivan the Ninny, because he was always playing and never working; and if there was a silly thing to do, why, off he went and did it. And so, when the brothers grew up, the father sent the two elder ones off, each in a fine ship laden with gold and jewels, and rings and bracelets, and laces and silks, and sticks with little bits of silver hammered into their handles, and spoons with patterns of blue and red, and everything else you can think of that costs too much to buy. But he made Ivan the Ninny stay at home, and did not give him a ship at all. Ivan saw his brothers go sailing off over the sea on a summer morning, to make their fortunes and come back rich men; and then, for the first time in his life, he wanted to work and do something useful. He went to his father and kissed his hand, and he kissed the hand of his little old mother, and he begged his father to give him a ship so that he could try his fortune like his brothers.

"But you have never done a wise thing in your life, and no one could count all the silly things you've done if he spent a hundred days in counting," said his father.

"True," said Ivan; "but now I am going to be wise, and sail the sea and come back with something in my pockets to show that I am not a ninny any longer. Give me just a little ship, father mine—just a little ship for myself."

"Give him a little ship," said the mother. "He may not be a ninny after all."

"Very well," said his father. "I will give him a little ship; but I am not going to waste good roubles by giving him a rich cargo."

"Give me any cargo you like," said Ivan.

So his father gave him a little ship, a little old ship, and a cargo of rags and scraps and things that were not fit for anything but to be thrown away. And he gave him a crew of ancient old sailormen who were past work; and Ivan went on board and sailed away at sunset, like the ninny he was. And the feeble, ancient old sailormen pulled up the ragged, dirty sails, and away they went over the sea to learn what fortune, good or bad, God had in mind for a crew of old men with a ninny for a master.

The fourth day after they set sail there came a great wind over the sea. The feeble old men did the best they could with the ship; but the old, torn sails tore from the masts, and the wind did what it pleased, and threw the little ship on an unknown island away in the middle of the sea. Then the wind dropped, and left the little ship on the beach, and Ivan the Ninny and his ancient old men, like good Russians, praising God that they were still alive.

"Well, children," said Ivan, for he knew how to talk to sailors, "do you stay here and mend the sails, and make new ones out of the rags we carry as cargo, while I go inland and see if there is anything that could be of use to us."

So the ancient old sailormen sat on deck with their legs crossed, and made sails out of rags, of torn scraps of old brocades, of soiled embroidered shawls, of all the rubbish that they had with them for a cargo. You never saw such sails. The tide came up and floated the ship, and they threw out anchors at bow and stern, and sat there in the sunlight, making sails and patching them and talking of the days when they were young. All this while Ivan the Ninny went walking off into the island.

Now in the middle of that island was a high mountain, a high mountain it was, and so white that when he came near it Ivan and Ninny began thinking of sheepskin coats, although it was midsummer and the sun was hot in the sky. The trees were green round about, but there was nothing growing on the mountain at all. It was just a great white mountain piled up into the sky in the middle of a green island. Ivan walked a little way up the white slopes of the mountain, and then, because he felt thirsty, he thought he would let a little snow melt in his mouth. He took some in his fingers and stuffed it in. Quickly enough it came out again, I can tell you, for the mountain was not made of snow but of good Russian salt. And if you want to try what a mouthful of salt is like, you may.

Ivan the Ninny did not stop to think twice. The salt was so clean and shone so brightly in the sunlight. He just turned round and ran back to the shore, and called out to his ancient old sailormen and told them to empty everything they had on board over into the sea. Over it all went, rags and tags and rotten timbers, till the little ship was as empty as a soup bowl after supper. And then those ancient old men were set to work carrying salt from the mountain and taking it on board the little ship, and stowing it away below deck till there was not room for another grain. Ivan the Ninny would have liked to take the whole mountain, but there was not room in the little ship. And for that the ancient old sailormen thanked God, because their backs ached and their old legs were weak, and they said they would have died if they had had to carry any more.

Then they hoisted up the new sails they had patched together out of the rags and scraps of shawls and old brocades, and they sailed away once more over the blue sea. And the wind stood fair, and they sailed before it, and the ancient old sailors rested their backs, and told old tales, and took turn and turn about at the rudder.

And after many days' sailing they came to a town, with towers and churches and painted roofs, all set on the side of a hill that sloped down into the sea. At the foot of the hill was a quiet harbor, and they sailed in there and moored the ship and hauled down their patchwork sails.

Ivan the Ninny went ashore, and took with him a little bag of clean white salt to show what kind of goods he had for sale, and he asked his way to the palace of the Tzar of that town. He came to the palace, and went in and bowed to the ground before the Tzar.

"Who are you?" says the Tzar.

"I, great lord, am a Russian merchant, and here in a bag is some of my merchandise, and I beg your leave to trade with your subjects in this town."

"Let me see what is in the bag," says the Tzar.

Ivan the Ninny took a handful from the bag and showed it to the Tzar.

"What is it?" says the Tzar.

"Good Russian salt," says Ivan the Ninny.

Now in that country they had never heard of salt, and the Tzar looked at the salt, and he looked at Ivan and he laughed.

"Why, this," says he, "is nothing but white dust, and that we can pick up for nothing. The men of my town have no need to trade with you. You must be a ninny."

Ivan grew very red, for he knew what his father used to call him. He was ashamed to say anything. So he bowed to the ground, and went away out of the palace.

But when he was outside he thought to himself, "I wonder what sort of salt they use in these parts if they do not know good Russian salt when they see it. I will go to the kitchen."

So he went round to the back door of the palace, and put his head into the kitchen, and said, "I am very tired. May I sit down here and rest a little while?"

"Come in," says one of the cooks. "But you must sit just there, and not put even your little finger in the way of us; for we are the Tzar's cooks, and we are in the middle of making ready his dinner." And the cook put a stool in a corner out of the way, and Ivan slipped in round the door, and sat down in the corner and looked about him. There were seven cooks at least, boiling and baking, and stewing and toasting, and roasting and frying. And as for scullions, they were as thick as cockroaches, dozens of them, running to and fro, tumbling over each other, and helping the cooks.

Ivan the Ninny sat on his stool, with his legs tucked under him and the bag of salt on his knees. He watched the cooks and the scullions, but he did not see them put anything in the dishes which he thought could take the place of salt. No; the meat was without salt, the kasha was without salt, and there was no salt in the potatoes. Ivan nearly turned sick at the thought of the tastelessness of all that food.

There came the moment when all the cooks and scullions ran out of the kitchen to fetch the silver platters on which to lay the dishes. Ivan slipped down from his stool, and running from stove to stove, from saucepan to frying pan, he dropped a pinch of salt, just what was wanted, no more no less, in every one of the dishes. Then he ran back to the stool in the corner, and sat there, and watched the dishes being put on the silver platters and carried off in gold-embroidered napkins to be the dinner of the Tzar.

The Tzar sat at table and took his first spoonful of soup.

"The soup is very good today," says he, and he finishes the soup to the last drop.

"I've never known the soup so good," says the Tzaritza, and she finishes hers.

"This is the best soup I ever tasted," says the Princess, and down goes hers, and she, you know, was the prettiest princess who ever had dinner in this world.

It was the same with the kasha and the same with the meat. The Tzar and the Tzaritza and the Princess wondered why they had never had so good a dinner in all their lives before.

"Call the cooks," says the Tzar. And they called the cooks, and the cooks all came in, and bowed to the ground, and stood in a row before the Tzar.

"What did you put in the dishes today that you never put before?" says the Tzar.

"We put nothing unusual, your greatness," say the cooks, and bowed to the ground again.

"Then why do the dishes taste better?"

"We do not know, your greatness," say the cooks.

"Call the scullions," says the Tzar. And the scullions were called, and they too bowed to the ground, and stood in a row before the Tzar.

"What was done in the kitchen today that has not been done there before?" says the Tzar.

"Nothing, your greatness," say all the scullions except one.

And that one scullion bowed again, and kept on bowing, and then he said, "Please, your greatness, please, great lord, there is usually none in the kitchen but ourselves; but today there was a young Russian merchant, who sat on a stool in the corner and said he was tired."

"Call the merchant," says the Tzar.

So they brought in Ivan the Ninny, and he bowed before the Tzar, and stood there with his little bag of salt in his hand.

"Did you do anything to my dinner?" says the Tzar.

"I did, your greatness," says Ivan.

"What did you do?"

"I put a pinch of Russian salt in every dish."

"That white dust?" says the Tzar.

"Nothing but that."

"Have you got any more of it?"

"I have a little ship in the harbor laden with nothing else," says Ivan.

"It is the most wonderful dust in the world," says the Tzar, "and I will buy every grain of it you have. What do you want for it?"

Ivan the Ninny scratched his head and thought. He thought that if the Tzar liked it as much as all that it must be worth a fair price, so he said, "We will put the salt into bags, and for every bag of salt you must give me three bags of the same weight—one of gold, one of silver, and one of precious stones. Cheaper than that, your greatness, I could not possibly sell."

"Agreed," says the Tzar. "And a cheap price, too, for a dust so full of magic that it makes dull dishes tasty, and tasty dishes so good that there is no looking away from them."

So all the day long, and far into the night, the ancient old sailormen bent their backs under sacks of salt, and bent them again under sacks of gold and silver and precious stones. When all the salt had been put in the Tzar's treasury—yes, with twenty soldiers guarding it with great swords shining in the moonlight—and when the little ship was loaded with riches, so that even the deck was piled high with precious stones, the ancient old men lay down among the jewels and slept till morning, when Ivan the Ninny went to bid good-bye to the Tzar.

"And where shall you sail now?" asked the Tzar.

"I shall sail away to Russia in my little ship," says Ivan.

And the Princess, who was very beautiful, said, "A little Russian ship?"

"Yes," says Ivan.

"I have never seen a Russian ship," says the Princess, and she begs her father to let her go to the harbor with her nurses and maids, to see the little Russian ship before Ivan set sail.

She came with Ivan to the harbor, and the ancient old sailormen took them on board.

She ran all over the ship, looking now at this and now at that, and Ivan told her the names of everything—deck, mast, and rudder.

"May I see the sails?" she asked. And the ancient old men hoisted the ragged sails, and the wind filled the sails and tugged.

"Why doesn't the ship move when the sails are up?" asked the Princess.

"The anchor holds her," said Ivan.

"Please let me see the anchor," says the Princess.

"Haul up the anchor, my children, and show it to the Princess," says Ivan to the ancient old sailormen.

And the old men hauled up the anchor, and showed it to the Princess; and she said it was a very good little anchor. But, of course, as soon as the anchor was up the ship began to move. One of the ancient old men bent over the tiller, and, with a fair wind behind her, the little ship slipped out of the harbor and away to the blue sea. When the Princess looked round, thinking it was time to go home, the little ship was far from land, and away in the distance she could only see the gold towers of her father's palace, glittering like pinpoints in the sunlight. Her nurses and maids wrung their hands and made an outcry, and the Princess sat down on a heap of jewels, and put a handkerchief to her eyes, and cried and cried and cried.

Ivan the Ninny took her hands and comforted her, and told her of the wonders of the sea that he would show her, and the wonders of the land. And she looked up at him while he talked, and his eyes were kind and hers were sweet; and the end of it was that they were both very well content, and agreed to have a marriage feast as soon as the little ship should bring them to the home of Ivan's father. Merry was that voyage. All day long Ivan and the Princess sat on deck and said sweet things to each other, and at twilight they sang songs, and drank tea, and told stories. As for the nurses and maids, the Princess told them to be glad; and so they danced and clapped their hands, and ran about the ship, and teased the ancient old sailormen.

When they had been sailing many days, the Princess was looking out over the sea, and she cried out to Ivan, "See, over there, far away, are two big ships with white sails, not like our sails of brocade and bits of silk."

Ivan looked, shading his eyes with his hands.

"Why, those are the ships of my elder brothers," said he. "We shall all sail home together."

And he made the ancient old sailormen give a hail in their cracked old voices. And the brothers heard them, and came on board to greet Ivan and his bride. And when they saw that she was a Tzar's daughter, and that the very decks were heaped with precious stones, because there was no room below, they said one thing to Ivan and something else to each other.

To Ivan they said, "Thanks be to God, He has given you good trading."

But to each other, "How can this be?" says one. "Ivan the Ninny bringing back such a cargo, while we in our fine ships have only a bag or two of gold."

"And what is Ivan the Ninny doing with a princess?" says the other.

And they ground their teeth, and waited their time, and came up suddenly, when Ivan was alone in the twilight, and picked him up by his head and his heels, and heaved him overboard into the dark blue sea.

Not one of the old men had seen them, and the Princess was not on deck. In the morning they said that Ivan the Ninny must have walked overboard in his sleep. And they drew lots. The eldest brother took the Princess, and the second brother took the little ship laden with gold and silver and precious stones. And so the brothers sailed home very well content. But the Princess sat and wept all day long, looking down into the blue water. The elder brother could not comfort her, and the second brother did not try. And the ancient old sailormen muttered in their beards, and were sorry, and prayed to God to give rest to Ivan's soul; for although he had been a ninny, and although he had made them carry a lot of salt and other things, yet they loved him, because he knew how to talk to ancient old sailormen.

But Ivan was not dead. As soon as he splashed into the water, he crammed his fur hat a little tighter on his head, and began swimming in the sea. He swam about until the sun rose, and then, not far away, he saw a floating timber log, and he swam to the log, and got astride of it, and thanked God. And he sat there on the log in the middle of the sea, twiddling his thumbs for want of something to do.

There was a strong current in the sea that carried him along, and at last, after floating for many days without ever a bite for his teeth or a drop for his gullet, his feet touched land. Now that was at night, and he left the log and walked up out of the sea, and lay down on the shore and waited for morning.

When the sun rose he stood up, and saw that he was on a bare island, and he saw nothing at all on the island except a huge house as big as a mountain; and as he was looking at the house the great door creaked with a noise like that of a hurricane among the pine forests, and opened; and a giant came walking out, and came to the shore, and stood there, looking down at Ivan.

"What are you doing here, little one?" says the giant.

Ivan told him the whole story, just as I have told it to you.

The giant listened to the very end, pulling at his monstrous whiskers. Then he said, "Listen, little one. I know more of the story than you, for I can tell you that tomorrow morning your eldest brother is going to marry your Princess. But there is no need for you to take on about it. If you want to be there, I will carry you and set you down before the house in time for the wedding. And a fine wedding it is like to be, for our father thinks well of those brothers of yours bringing back all those precious stones, and silver and gold enough to buy a kingdom."

And with that he picked up Ivan the Ninny and set him on his great shoulders, and set off striding through the sea.

He went so fast that the wind of his going blew off Ivan's hat.

"Stop a moment," shouts Ivan, "my hat has blown off."

"We can't turn back for that," says the giant, "we have already left your hat five hundred versts behind us." And he rushed on, splashing through the sea. The sea was up to his armpits. He rushed on, and the sea was up to his waist. He rushed on, and before the sun had climbed to the top of the blue sky he was splashing up out of the sea with the water about his ankles. He lifted Ivan from his shoulders and set him on the ground.

"Now," says he, "little man, off you run, and you'll be in time for the feast. But don't you dare to boast about riding on my shoulders. If you open your mouth about that you'll smart for it, if I have to come ten thousand thousand versts."

Ivan the Ninny thanked the giant for carrying him through the sea, promised that he would not boast, and then ran off to his father's house. Long before he got there he heard the musicians in the courtyard playing as if they wanted to wear out their instruments before night. The wedding feast had begun, and when Ivan ran in, there, at the high board, was sitting the Princess, and beside her his eldest brother. And there were his father and mother, his second brother, and all the guests. And every one of them was as merry as could be, except the Princess, and she was as white as the salt he had sold to her father.

Suddenly the blood flushed into her cheeks. She saw Ivan in the doorway. Up she jumped at the high board, and cried out, "There, there is my true love, and not this man who sits beside me at the table."

"What is this?" says Ivan's father, and in a few minutes knew the whole story.

He turned the two elder brothers out of doors, gave their ships to Ivan, married him to the Princess, and made him his heir. And the wedding feast began again, and they sent for the ancient old sailormen to take part in it. And the ancient old sailormen wept with joy when they saw Ivan and the Princess, like two sweet pigeons, sitting side by side; yes, and they lifted their flagons with their old shaking hands, and cheered with their old cracked voices, and poured the wine down their dry old throats.

There was wine enough and to spare, beer too, and mead—enough to drown a herd of cattle. And as the guests drank and grew merry and proud they set to boasting. This one bragged of his riches, that one of his wife. Another boasted of his cunning, another of his new house, another of his strength, and this one was angry because they would not let

him show how he could lift the table on one hand. They all drank
Ivan's health, and he drank theirs, and in the end he could not bear to
listen to their proud boasts.

"That's all very well," says he, "but I am the only man in the world
who rode on the shoulders of a giant to come to his wedding feast."

The words were scarcely out of his mouth before there were a tremendous trampling and a roar of a great wind. The house shook with
the footsteps of the giant as he strode up. The giant bent down over
the courtyard and looked in at the feast.

"Little man, little man," says he, "you promised not to boast of me. I
told you what would come if you did, and here you are and have
boasted already."

"Forgive me," says Ivan; "it was the drink that boasted, not I."

"What sort of drink is it that knows how to boast?" says the giant.

"You shall taste it," says Ivan.

And he made his ancient old sailormen roll a great barrel of wine
into the yard, more than enough for a hundred men, and after that a
barrel of beer that was as big, and then a barrel of mead that was no
smaller.

"Try the taste of that," says Ivan the Ninny.

Well, the giant did not wait to be asked twice. He lifted the barrel of
wine as if it had been a little glass, and emptied it down his throat. He
lifted the barrel of beer as if it had been an acorn, and emptied it after
the wine. Then he lifted the barrel of mead as if it had been a very
small pea, and swallowed every drop of mead that was in it. And after
that he began stamping about and breaking things. Houses fell to
pieces this way and that, and trees were swept flat like grass. Every step
the giant took was followed by the crash of breaking timbers. Then suddenly he fell flat on his back and slept. For three days and nights he
slept without waking. At last he opened his eyes.

"Just look about you," says Ivan, "and see the damage that you've
done."

"And did that little drop of drink make me do all that?" says the
giant. "Well, well, I can well understand that a drink like that can do a
bit of bragging. And after that," says he, looking at the wrecks of
houses, and all the broken things scattered about—"after that," says he,
"you can boast of me for a thousand years, and I'll have nothing
against you."

And he tugged at his great whiskers, and wrinkled his eyes, and went
striding off into the sea.

That is the story about salt, and how it made a rich man of Ivan the Ninny, and besides, gave him the prettiest wife in the world, and she a Tzar's daughter.

97. THE TREASURE
(*Russia*)

IN A CERTAIN KINGDOM there lived an old couple in great poverty. Sooner or later the old woman died. It was in winter, in severe and frosty weather. The old man went round to his friends and neighbors, begging them to help him to dig a grave for the old woman; but his friends and neighbors, knowing his great poverty, all flatly refused. The old man went to the priest (but in that village they had an awfully grasping priest, one without any conscience) and says he:—

"Lend a hand, reverend Father, to get my old woman buried."

"But have you got any money to pay for the funeral? If so, friend, pay up beforehand!"

"It's no use hiding anything from you. Not a single copeck have I at home. But if you'll wait a little, I'll earn some, and then I'll pay you with interest—on my word, I'll pay you!"

The priest wouldn't so much as listen to the old man.

"If you haven't any money, don't you dare to come here," says he.

"What's to be done?" thinks the old man. "I'll go to the graveyard, dig a grave as I best can, and bury the old woman myself." So he took an ax and a shovel, and went to the graveyard. When he got there he began to prepare a grave. He chopped away the frozen ground on the top with the ax, and then he took to the shovel. He dug and dug, and at last he dug out a metal pot. Looking into it he saw that it was stuffed full of ducats that shone like fire. The old man was immensely delighted, and cried, "Glory be to Thee, O Lord! I shall have where-withal both to bury my old woman, and to perform the rites of remembrance."

He did not go on digging the grave any longer, but took the pot of

gold and carried it home. Well, we all know what money will do—
everything went as smooth as oil! In a trice there were found good folks
to dig the grave and fashion the coffin. The old man sent his daughter-
in-law to purchase meat and drink and different kinds of relishes—
everything that there ought to be at memorial feasts—and he himself
took a ducat in his hand and hobbled back again to the priest's. The
moment he reached the door, out flew the priest at him.

"You were distinctly told, you old lout, that you were not to come
here without money; and now you've slunk back again."

"Don't be angry, Father," said the old man imploringly. "Here's gold
for you. If you'll only bury my old woman, I'll never forget your
kindness."

The priest took the money, and didn't know how best to receive the
old man, where to seat him, with what words to smooth him down.
"Well now, old friend! Be of good cheer; everything shall be done,"
said he.

The old man made his bow, and went home, and the priest and his
wife began talking about him.

"There now, the old hunks!" they say. "So poor, forsooth, so poor!
And yet he's paid a gold piece. Many a defunct person of quality have I
buried in my time, but I never got so much from anyone before."

The priest got under way with all his retinue, and buried the old
crone in proper style. After the funeral the old man invited him to his
house, to take part in the feast in memory of the dead. Well, they entered the cottage, and sat down to table—and there appeared from
somewhere or other meat and drink and all sorts of snacks, everything
in profusion. The (reverend) guest sat down, ate for three people,
looked greedily at what was not his. The (other) guests finished their
meal, and separated to go to their homes; then the priest also rose from
table. The old man went to speed him on his way. As soon as they got
into the farmyard, and the priest saw they were alone at last, he began
questioning the old man: "Listen, friend! confess to me, don't leave so
much as a single sin on your soul—it's just the same before me as before
God! How have you managed to get on at such a pace? You used to be
a poor peasant, and now—marry! where did it come from? Confess,
friend, whose breath have you stopped? whom have you pillaged?"

"What are you talking about, Father? I will tell you the exact truth.
I have not robbed, nor plundered, nor killed anyone. A treasure tumbled into my hands of its own accord."

And he told him how it had all happened. When the priest heard these words he actually shook all over with greediness. Going home, he did nothing by night and by day but think, "That such a wretched lout of a peasant should have come in for such a lump of money! Is there any way of tricking him now, and getting this pot of money out of him?" He told his wife about it, and he and she discussed the matter together, and held counsel over it.

"Listen, mother," says he; "we've a goat, haven't we?"

"Yes."

"All right, then; we'll wait till it's night, and then we'll do the job properly."

Late in the evening the priest dragged the goat indoors, killed it, and took off its skin—horns, beard, and all complete. Then he pulled the goat's skin over himself and said to his wife:

"Bring a needle and thread, mother, and fasten up the skin all round, so that it may not slip off."

So she took a strong needle, and some tough thread, and sewed him up in the goatskin. Well, at the dead of night, the priest went straight to the old man's cottage, got under the window, and began knocking and scratching. The old man heard the noise, jumped up and asked:

"Who's there?"

"The Devil!"

"Ours is a holy spot!" shrieked the peasant, and began crossing himself and uttering prayers.

"Listen, old man," says the priest. "From me thou wilt not escape, although thou may'st pray, although thou may'st cross thyself; much better give me back my pot of money, otherwise I will make thee pay for it. See now, I pitied thee in thy misfortune, and I showed thee the treasure, thinking thou wouldst take a little of it to pay for the funeral, but thou hast pillaged it utterly."

The old man looked out of the window—the goat's horns and beard caught his eye—it was the Devil himself, no doubt of it.

"Let's get rid of him, money and all," thinks the old man; "I've lived before now without money, and now I'll go on living without it."

So he took the pot of gold, carried it outside, flung it on the ground, and bolted indoors again as quickly as possible.

The priest seized the pot of money, and hastened home. When he got back, "Come," says he, "the money is in our hands now. Here, mother, put it well out of sight, and take a sharp knife, cut the thread, and pull the goatskin off me before anyone sees it."

She took a knife and was beginning to cut the thread at the seam, when forth flowed blood, and the priest began to howl:

"Oh! it hurts, mother, it hurts! don't cut, mother, don't cut!"

She began ripping the skin open in another place, but with just the same result. The goatskin had united with his body all round. And all that they tried, all that they did, even to taking the money back to the old man, was of no avail. The goatskin remained clinging tight to the priest all the same. God evidently did it to punish him for his great greediness.

98. WOE
(Russia)

IN A CERTAIN VILLAGE there lived two peasants, two brothers: one of them poor, the other rich. The rich one went away to live in a town, built himself a large house, and enrolled himself among the traders. Meanwhile the poor man sometimes had not so much as a morsel of bread, and his children—each one smaller than the other—were crying and begging for food. From morning till night the peasant would struggle, like a fish trying to break through ice, but nothing came of it all. At last one day he said to his wife:

"Suppose I go to town, and ask my brother whether he won't do something to help us."

So he went to the rich man and said:

"Ah, brother mine! do help me a bit in my trouble. My wife and children are without bread. They have to go whole days without eating."

"Work for me this week, then I'll help you," said his brother.

What was there to be done! The poor man betook himself to work, swept out the yard, cleaned the horses, fetched water, chopped firewood.

At the end of the week the rich man gave him a loaf of bread, and says:

"There's for your work!"

"Thank you all the same," dolefully said the poor man, making his bow and preparing to go home.

"Stop a bit! come and dine with me tomorrow, and bring your wife too: tomorrow is my birthday, you know."

"Ah, brother! how can I? you know very well you'll be having merchants coming to you in boots and pelisses, but I have to go about in bast shoes and a miserable old gray caftan."

"No matter, come! there will be room even for you."

"Very well, brother! I'll come."

The poor man returned home, gave his wife the loaf, and said:

"Listen, wife! we're invited to a party tomorrow."

"What do you mean by a party? who's invited us?"

"My brother! he keeps his birthday tomorrow."

"Well, well! let's go."

Next day they got up and went to the town, came to the rich man's house, offered him their congratulations, and sat down on a bench. A number of the birthday guests were already seated at table. All of these the host feasted gloriously, but he forgot even so much as to think of his poor brother and his wife; not a thing did he offer them; they had to sit and merely look on at the others eating and drinking.

The dinner came to an end; the guests rose from table, and expressed their thanks to their host and hostess; and the poor man did likewise, got up from his bench, and bowed down to his girdle before his brother. The guests drove off homeward, full of drink and merriment, shouting, singing songs. But the poor man had to walk back empty.

"Suppose we sing a song too," he says to his wife.

"What a fool you are!" says she, "people sing because they've made a good meal and had lots to drink; but why ever should you dream of singing?"

"Well, at all events, I've been at my brother's birthday party. I'm ashamed of trudging along without singing. If I sing, everybody will think I've been feasted like the rest."

"Sing away then, if you like; but I won't!"

The peasant began a song. Presently he heard a voice joining in it. So he stopped, and asked his wife:

"Is it you that's helping me to sing with that thin little voice?"

"What are you thinking about! I never even dreamed of such a thing."

"Who is it, then?"

"I don't know," said the woman. "But now, sing away, and I'll listen."

He began his song again. There was only one person singing, yet two voices could be heard. So he stopped, and asked:

"Woe, is that you that's helping me to sing?"

"Yes, master," answered Woe: "it's I that's helping you."

"Well then, Woe! let's all go on together."

"Very good, master! I'll never depart from you now."

When the peasant got home, Woe bid him go to the tavern.

"I've no money," says the man.

"Out upon you, peasant! What do you want money for? why you've got on a sheepskin jacket. What's the good of that? It will soon be summer; anyhow you won't be wanting to wear it! Off with the jacket, and to the tavern we'll go."

So the peasant went with Woe into the tavern, and they drank the sheepskin away.

The next day Woe began groaning—its head ached from yesterday's drinking—and again bade the master of the house have a drink.

"I've no money," said the peasant.

"What do we want money for? Take the cart and the sleigh; we've plenty without them."

There was nothing to be done; the peasant could not shake himself free from Woe. So he took the cart and the sleigh, dragged them to the tavern, and there he and Woe drank them away. Next morning Woe began groaning more than ever, and invited the master of the house to go and drink off the effects of the debauch. This time the peasant drank away his plow and his harrow.

A month hadn't passed before he had got rid of everything he possessed. Even his very cottage he pledged to a neighbor, and the money he got that way he took to the tavern.

Yet another time did Woe come close beside him and say:

"Let us go, let us go to the tavern!"

"No, no, Woe! it's all very well, but there's nothing more to be squeezed out."

"How can you say that? Your wife has got two petticoats: leave her one, but the other we must turn into drink."

The peasant took the petticoat, drank it away, and said to himself:

"We're cleaned out at last, my wife as well as myself. Not a stick nor a stone is left!"

Next morning Woe saw, on waking, that there was nothing more to be got out of the peasant, so it said:

"Master!"

"Well, Woe?"

"Why, look here. Go to your neighbor, and ask him to lend you a cart and a pair of oxen."

The peasant went to the neighbor's.

"Be so good as to lend me a cart and a pair of oxen for a short time," says he. "I'll do a week's work for you in return."

"But what do you want them for?"

"To go to the forest for firewood."

"Well then, take them: only don't overburden them."

"How could you think of such a thing, kind friend!"

So he brought the pair of oxen, and Woe got into the cart with him, and away he drove into the open plain.

"Master!" asks Woe, "do you know the big stone on this plain?"

"Of course I do."

"Well then if you know it, drive straight up to it."

They came to the place where it was, stopped, and got out of the cart. Woe told the peasant to lift the stone; the peasant lifted it, Woe helping him. Well, when they had lifted it, there was a pit underneath chock full of gold.

"Now then, what are you staring at!" said Woe to the peasant, "be quick and pitch it into the cart."

The peasant set to work and filled the cart with gold; cleared the pit to the very last ducat. When he saw there was nothing more left:

"Just give a look, Woe," he said; "isn't there some money left in there?"

"Where?" said Woe, bending down; "I can't see a thing."

"Why there; something is shining in yon corner!"

"No, I can't see anything," said Woe.

"Get into the pit; you'll see it then."

Woe jumped in: no sooner had it got there than the peasant closed the mouth of the pit with the stone.

"Things will be much better like that," said the peasant: "if I were to take you home with me, O Woeful Woe, sooner or later you'd be sure to drink away all this money too!"

The peasant got home, shoveled the money into his cellar, took the oxen back to his neighbor, and set about considering how he should manage. It ended in his buying a wood, building a large homestead, and becoming twice as rich as his brother.

After a time he went into the town to invite his brother and sister-in-law to spend his birthday with him.

"What an idea!" said his rich brother: "you haven't a thing to eat, and yet you ask people to spend your birthday with you!"

"Well, there was a time when I had nothing to eat, but now, thank God! I've as much as you. If you come, you'll see for yourself."

"So be it! I'll come," said his brother.

Next day the rich brother and his wife got ready, and went to the birthday party. They could see that the former beggar had got a new house, a lofty one, such as few merchants had! And the peasant treated them hospitably, regaled them with all sorts of dishes, gave them all sorts of meads and spirits to drink. At length the rich man asked his brother:

"Do tell me by what good luck have you grown rich?"

The peasant made a clean breast of everything—how Woe the Woeful had attached itself to him, how he and Woe had drunk away all that he had, to the very last thread, so that the only thing that was left him was the soul in his body. How Woe showed him a treasure in the open field, how he took that treasure, and freed himself from Woe into the bargain. The rich man became envious.

"Suppose I go to the open field," thinks he, "and lift up the stone and let Woe out. Of a surety it will utterly destroy my brother, and then he will no longer brag of his riches before me!"

So he sent his wife home, but he himself hastened into the plain. When he came to the big stone, he pushed it aside, and knelt down to see what was under it. Before he had managed to get his head down low enough, Woe had already leaped out and seated itself on his shoulders.

"Ha!" it cried, "you wanted to starve me to death in here! No, no! Now will I never on any account depart from you."

"Only hear me, Woe!" said the merchant: "it wasn't I at all who put you under the stone."

"Who was it then, if it wasn't you?"

"It was my brother put you there, but I came on purpose to let you out."

"No, no! that's a lie. You tricked me once; you shall not trick me a second time!"

Woe gripped the rich merchant tight by the neck; the man had to carry it home, and there everything began to go wrong with him. From the very first day Woe began again to play its usual part, every day it called on the merchant to renew his drinking. Many were the valuables which went in the tavern.

"Impossible to go on living like this!" says the merchant to himself. "Surely I've made sport enough for Woe! It's time to get rid of it—but how?"

He thought and thought, and hit on an idea. Going into the large yard, he cut two oaken wedges, took a new wheel, and drove a wedge firmly into one end of its axle box. Then he went to where Woe was:

"Hello, Woe! why are you always idly sprawling there?"

"Why, what is there left for me to do?"

"What is there to do! let's go into the yard and play at hide-and-seek."

Woe liked the idea. Out they went into the yard. First the merchant hid himself; Woe found him immediately. Then it was Woe's turn to hide.

"Now then," says Woe, "you won't find me in a hurry! There isn't a chink I can't get into!"

"Get along with you!" answered the merchant. "Why you couldn't creep into that wheel there, and yet you talk about chinks!"

"I can't creep into that wheel? See if I don't go clean out of sight in it!"

Woe slipped into the wheel; the merchant caught up the oaken wedge, and drove it into the axle box from the other side. Then he seized the wheel and flung it, with Woe in it, into the river. Woe was drowned, and the merchant began to live again as he had been wont to do of old.

99. CLEVER MANKA
(Czechoslovakia)

THERE WAS ONCE a rich farmer who was as grasping and unscrupulous as he was rich. He was always driving a hard bargain and always getting the better of his poor neighbors. One of these neighbors was a humble shepherd who, in return for service, was to receive from the farmer a heifer. When the time of payment came, the farmer refused to give the shepherd the heifer, and the shepherd was forced to lay the matter before the burgomaster.

The burgomaster, who was a young man and as yet not very experienced, listened to both sides, and when he had deliberated, he said:

"Instead of deciding this case, I will put a riddle to you both, and the man who makes the best answer shall have the heifer. Are you agreed?"

The farmer and the shepherd accepted this proposal and the burgomaster said:

"Well, then, here is my riddle: What is the swiftest thing in the world? What is the sweetest thing? What is the richest? Think out your answers and bring them to me at this same hour tomorrow."

The farmer went home in a temper.

"What kind of burgomaster is this young fellow!" he growled. "If he had let me keep the heifer, I'd have sent him a bushel of pears. But now I'm in a fair way of losing the heifer, for I can't think of any answer to his foolish riddle."

"What is the matter, husband?" his wife asked.

"It's that new burgomaster. The old one would have given me the heifer without any argument, but this young man thinks to decide the case by asking us riddles."

When he told his wife what the riddle was, she cheered him greatly by telling him that she knew the answers at once.

"Why, husband," said she, "our gray mare must be the swiftest thing in the world. You know yourself nothing ever passes us on the road. As for the sweetest, did you ever taste honey any sweeter than ours? And I'm sure there's nothing richer than our chest of golden ducats that we've been laying by these forty years."

The farmer was delighted.

"You're right, wife, you're right! That heifer remains ours!"

The shepherd, when he got home, was downcast and sad. He had a daughter, a clever girl named Manka, who met him at the door of his cottage and asked:

"What is it, father? What did the burgomaster say?"

The shepherd sighed.

"I'm afraid I've lost the heifer. The burgomaster set us a riddle, and I know I shall never guess it."

"Perhaps I can help you," Manka said. "What is it?"

The shepherd gave her the riddle, and the next day, as he was setting out for the burgomaster's, Manka told him what answers to make.

When he reached the burgomaster's house, the farmer was already there rubbing his hands and beaming with self-importance.

The burgomaster again propounded the riddle and then asked the farmer his answers.

The farmer cleared his throat and with a pompous air began:

"The swiftest thing in the world? Why, my dear sir, that's my gray mare, of course, for no other horse ever passes us on the road. The sweetest? Honey from my beehives, to be sure. The richest? What can be richer than my chest of golden ducats!"

And the farmer squared his shoulders and smiled triumphantly.

"H'm," said the young burgomaster dryly. Then he asked:

"What answers does the shepherd make?"

The shepherd bowed politely and said:

"The swiftest thing in the world is thought, for thought can run any distance in the twinkling of an eye. The sweetest thing of all is sleep, for when a man is tired and sad, what can be sweeter? The richest thing is the earth, for out of the earth come all the riches of the world."

"Good!" the burgomaster cried. "Good! The heifer goes to the shepherd!"

Later the burgomaster said to the shepherd:

"Tell me now, who gave you those answers? I'm sure they never came out of your own head."

At first the shepherd tried not to tell, but when the burgomaster pressed him, he confessed that they came from his daughter, Manka. The burgomaster, who thought he would like to make another test of

Manka's cleverness, sent for ten eggs. He gave them to the shepherd and said:

"Take these eggs to Manka and tell her to have them hatched out by tomorrow and to bring me the chicks."

When the shepherd reached home and gave Manka the burgomaster's message, Manka laughed and said: "Take a handful of millet and go right back to the burgomaster. Say to him: 'My daughter sends you this millet. She says that if you plant it, grow it, and have it harvested by tomorrow, she'll bring you the ten chicks and you can feed them the ripe grain.'"

When the burgomaster heard this, he laughed heartily.

"That's a clever girl of yours," he told the shepherd. "If she's as comely as she is clever, I think I'd like to marry her. Tell her to come to see me, but she must come neither by day nor by night, neither riding nor walking, neither dressed nor undressed."

When Manka received this message, she waited until the next dawn when night was gone and day not yet arrived. Then she wrapped herself in a fish net and, throwing one leg over a goat's back and keeping one foot on the ground, she went to the burgomaster's house.

Now I ask you: did she go dressed? No, she wasn't dressed. A fish net isn't clothing. Did she go undressed? Of course not, for wasn't she covered with a fish net? Did she walk to the burgomaster's? No, she didn't walk, for she went with one leg thrown over a goat. Then did she ride? Of course she didn't ride, for wasn't she walking on one foot?

When she reached the burgomaster's house, she called out:

"Here I am, Mr. Burgomaster, and I've come neither by day nor by night, neither riding nor walking, neither dressed nor undressed."

The young burgomaster was so delighted with Manka's cleverness and so pleased with her comely looks that he proposed to her at once and in a short time married her.

"But understand, my dear Manka," he said, "you are not to use that cleverness of yours at my expense. I won't have you interfering in any of my cases. In fact, if ever you give advice to anyone who comes to me for judgment, I'll turn you out of my house at once and send you home to your father."

All went well for a time. Manka busied herself in her housekeeping and was careful not to interfere in any of the burgomaster's cases.

Then one day two farmers came to the burgomaster to have a dispute settled. One of the farmers owned a mare that had foaled in the marketplace. The colt had run under the wagon of the other farmer, and thereupon the owner of the wagon claimed the colt as his property.

The burgomaster, who was thinking of something else while the case was being presented, said carelessly:

"The man who found the colt under his wagon is, of course, the owner of the colt."

As the owner of the mare was leaving the burgomaster's house, he met Manka and stopped to tell her about the case. Manka was ashamed of her husband for making so foolish a decision, and she said to the farmer:

"Come back this afternoon with a fishing net and stretch it across the dusty road. When the burgomaster sees you, he will come out and ask you what you are doing. Say to him that you're catching fish. When he asks you how you can expect to catch fish in a dusty road, tell him it's just as easy for you to catch fish in a dusty road as it is for a wagon to foal. Then he'll see the injustice of his decision and have the colt returned to you. But remember one thing: you mustn't let him find out that it was I who told you to do this."

That afternoon, when the burgomaster chanced to look out the window, he saw a man stretching a fish net across the dusty road. He went out to him and asked:

"What are you doing?"

"Fishing."

"Fishing in a dusty road? Are you daft?"

"Well," the man said, "it's just as easy for me to catch fish in a dusty road as it is for a wagon to foal."

Then the burgomaster recognized the man as the owner of the mare, and he had to confess that what he said was true.

"Of course the colt belongs to your mare and must be returned to you. But tell me," he said, "who put you up to this? You didn't think of it yourself."

The farmer tried not to tell, but the burgomaster questioned him until he found out that Manka was at the bottom of it. This made him very angry. He went into the house and called his wife.

"Manka," he said, "did you forget what I told you would happen if you went interfering in any of my cases? Home you go this very day. I don't care to hear any excuses. The matter is settled. You may take with you the one thing you like best in my house, for I won't have people saying that I treated you shabbily."

Manka made no outcry.

"Very well, my dear husband, I shall do as you say: I shall go home to my father's cottage and take with me the one thing I like best in your house. But don't make me go until after supper. We have been very happy together and I should like to eat one last meal with you. Let us have no more words but be kind to each other as we've always been and then part as friends."

The burgomaster agreed to this, and Manka prepared a fine supper of all the dishes of which her husband was particularly fond. The burgomaster opened his choicest wine and pledged Manka's health. Then he set to, and the supper was so good that he ate and ate and ate. And the more he ate, the more he drank until at last he grew drowsy and fell sound asleep in his chair. Then without awakening him, Manka had him carried out to the wagon that was waiting to take her home to her father.

The next morning, when the burgomaster opened his eyes, he found himself lying in the shepherd's cottage.

"What does this mean?" he roared out.

"Nothing, dear husband, nothing!" Manka said. "You know you told me I might take with me the one thing I liked best in your house, so of course I took you! That's all."

For a moment the burgomaster rubbed his eyes in amazement. Then he laughed loud and heartily to think how Manka had outwitted him.

"Manka," he said, "you're too clever for me. Come on, my dear, let's go home."

So, they climbed back into the wagon and drove home.

The burgomaster never again scolded his wife, but thereafter whenever a very difficult case came up, he always said:

"I think we had better consult my wife. You know she's a very clever woman."

100. INTELLIGENCE AND LUCK

(*Czechoslovakia*)

ONCE UPON A TIME Luck met Intelligence on a garden-seat. "Make room for me!" said Luck. Intelligence was then as yet inexperienced, and didn't know who ought to make room for whom. He said: "Why should I make room for you? you're no better than I am." "He's the better man," answered Luck, "who performs most. See you there yon peasant's son who's plowing in the field? Enter into him, and if he gets on better through you than through me, I'll always submissively make way for you, whensoever and wheresoever we meet." Intelligence agreed, and entered at once into the plowboy's head.

As soon as the plowboy felt that he had intelligence in his head, he began to think: "Why must I follow the plow to the day of my death? I can go somewhere else and make my fortune more easily." He left off plowing, put up the plow, and drove home. "Daddy," says he, "I don't like this peasant's life; I'd rather learn to be a gardener." His father said: "What ails you, Vanek? have you lost your wits?" However, he bethought himself, and said: "Well, if you will, learn, and God be with you! Your brother will be heir to the cottage after me."

Vanek lost the cottage, but he didn't care for that, but went and put himself apprentice to the king's gardener. For every little that the gardener showed him, Vanek comprehended ever so much more. Ere long he didn't even obey the gardener's orders as to how he ought to do anything, but did everything his own way. At first the gardener was angry, but, seeing everything thus getting on better, he was content. "I see that you've more intelligence than I," said he, and henceforth let Vanek garden as he thought fit. In no long space of time Vanek made the garden so beautiful that the king took great delight in it, and frequently walked in it with the queen and with his only daughter.

The princess was a very beautiful damsel, but ever since she was twelve years old she had ceased speaking, and no one ever heard a single word from her. The king was much grieved, and caused proclamation to be made, that whoever should bring it to pass that she should speak again should be her husband. Many young kings, princes, and other great lords announced themselves one after the other, but all went away as they had come; no one succeeded in causing her to speak. "Why shouldn't I too try my luck?" thought Vanek; "who knows whether I mayn't succeed in bringing her to answer when I ask her a question?" He at once caused himself to be announced at the palace, and the king and his councilors conducted him into the room where the princess was.

The king's daughter had a pretty little dog, and was very fond of him because he was so clever, understanding everything that she wanted. When Vanek went into the room with the king and his councilors, he made as if he didn't even see the princess, but turned to the dog and said: "I have heard, doggie, that you are very clever, and I come to you for advice. We are three companions in travel, a sculptor, a tailor, and myself. Once upon a time we were going through a forest and were obliged to pass the night in it. To be safe from wolves, we made a fire, and agreed to keep watch one after the other. The sculptor kept watch first, and for amusement to kill time took a log and carved a damsel out of it. When it was finished he woke the tailor to keep watch in his turn. The tailor, seeing the wooden damsel, asked what it meant. 'As you see,' said the sculptor, 'I was weary, and didn't know what to do with myself, so I carved a damsel out of a log; if you find time hang heavy on your hands, you can dress her.' The tailor at once took out his scissors, needle, and thread, cut out the clothes, stitched away, and when they were ready, dressed the damsel in them. He then called me to come and keep watch. I, too, asked him what the meaning of all this was. 'As you see,' said the tailor, 'the sculptor found time hang heavy on his hands and carved a damsel out of a log, and I for the same reason clothed her; and if you find time hanging on your hands, you can teach her to speak.' And by morning dawn I had actually taught her to speak. But in the morning when my companions woke up, each wanted to possess the damsel. The sculptor said, 'I made her'; the tailor, 'I clothed her.' I, too, maintained my right. Tell me, therefore, doggie, to which of us the damsel belongs?"

The dog said nothing, but instead of the dog the princess replied: "To whom can she belong but to yourself? What's the good of the sculptor's damsel without life? What's the good of the tailor's dressing without speech? You gave her the best gift, life and speech, and therefore she by right belongs to you." "You have passed your own sentence," said Vanek; "I have given you speech again and a new life, and you therefore by right belong to me." Then said one of the king's councilors: "His Royal Grace will give you a plenteous reward for succeeding in unloosing his daughter's tongue; but you cannot have her to wife, as you are of mean lineage." The king said: "You are of mean lineage; I will give you a plenteous reward instead of our daughter."

But Vanek wouldn't hear of any other reward, and said: "The king promised without any exception, that whoever caused his daughter to speak again should be her husband. A king's word is a law; and if the king wants others to observe his laws, he must first keep them himself. Therefore the king *must* give me his daughter." "Seize and bind him!" shouted the councilor. "Whoever says the king *must* do anything, offers an insult to His Majesty, and is worthy of death. May it please Your Majesty to order this malefactor to be executed with the sword?" The king said: "Let him be executed." Vanek was immediately bound and led to execution. When they came to the place of execution Luck was there waiting for him, and said secretly to Intelligence, "See how this man has got on through you, that he has to lose his head! Make way, and let me take your place!"

As soon as Luck entered Vanek, the executioner's sword broke against the scaffold, just as if someone had snapped it; and before they brought him another, up rode a trumpeter on horseback from the city, galloping as swift as a bird, trumpeted merrily, and waved a white flag, and after him came the royal carriage for Vanek. This is what had happened: The princess had told her father at home that Vanek had but spoken the truth, and the king's word ought not to be broken. If Vanek were of mean lineage the king could easily make him a prince. The king said: "You're right; let him be a prince!" The royal carriage was immediately sent for Vanek, and the councilor who had irritated the king against him was executed in his stead. Afterward, when Vanek and the princess were going together in a carriage from the wedding, Intelligence happened to be somewhere on the road, and seeing that he couldn't help meeting Luck, bent his head and slipped on one side, just as if cold water had been thrown upon him. And from that time forth it is said that Intelligence has always given a wide berth to Luck whenever he has had to meet him.

101. CZAR TROJAN'S EARS
(*Yugoslavia*)

ONCE UPON A TIME there lived a czar named Trojan. Trojan had ears like those on a goat. Each day he would call a barber to shave him but none ever returned from the palace for after the barber had done his work the czar would ask, "What do you see, my good man?" and the barber would answer, "I see that the czar has the ears of a goat." When he heard the barber's answer, the czar would order the barber's head to be chopped off at once.

One day the turn fell to a barber who was so frightened for his safety that he pretended to be ill. In his place he sent his young apprentice.

When the apprentice appeared before the czar the unhappy monarch demanded to know why the master artisan had not come himself. The apprentice answered sweetly that his master was ill, whereupon the czar was satisfied and sat down to be shaved.

During his work, the apprentice noticed that Trojan's ears were like the ears of a goat but when the czar asked him what he had observed, the apprentice answered, "I see nothing, Sire."

Trojan gave the apprentice twelve gold ducats and ordered him to come regularly to shave him.

When the apprentice returned home, the artisan was curious and asked him about Czar Trojan. The apprentice reported that the czar was courteous and kind and that he had been ordered to come personally each day to shave the ruler. He showed his master the twelve gold ducats but he said nothing about Czar Trojan's goat's ears.

From that time on the apprentice went each day to shave the czar and each day he received twelve gold ducats. He revealed the czar's secret to nobody, but after many months the apprentice began to worry and grieve. The burden of carrying the czar's secret was growing heavier and heavier on his heart. He grew thinner and thinner. He started to pine and became sad and listless.

The artisan, noticing the change in his ordinarily good-natured pupil, started little by little to put questions to the boy. Finally the young man confessed that he carried in his heart a great secret which he was forbidden to tell anyone in the world.

"If only I could tell my secret to someone, I would be much relieved," said the troubled apprentice.

The artisan was kind, and wanting to help, he said, "Tell me and I shall tell no one; if you are afraid to tell me, go to the priest and tell him; if you can't tell him either, then go out into the fields behind the town. Dig a hole. Put your head into it, and say three times to the earth what you know. Then close the hole and come away."

The apprentice chose to tell his secret to the earth. He went out of the town, dug the hole, put his head into it and said three times, "Czar Trojan has the ears of a goat."

Covering the hole once more with earth, he returned home, tranquil in his heart and mind.

In time, an elder tree grew on the spot where the apprentice had told his secret and from the tree grew three branches as fine and straight as candles.

One day some shepherds found the elder tree. One of them cut off a branch and made a fine flute but when the flute began to whistle, instead of a tune, the shepherds heard the flute pipe out "Czar Trojan has the ears of a goat."

With much excitement, the shepherds returned to the town to tell the news. "Czar Trojan has the ears of a goat! Czar Trojan has the ears of a goat!" they whispered to all who would listen.

The news spread like wildfire and soon Czar Trojan himself heard little children in the streets imitating the voice of the flute as it whistled "Czar Trojan has the ears of a goat!"

At once Trojan summoned the apprentice to him and demanded in a fury, "Why did you tell my secret to my people?"

As he was innocent, the poor frightened apprentice was at a loss for words. He implored the monarch to believe that he had told no one and when he saw that the czar would not listen and had drawn his sword in preparation for cutting off his head he cried out in desperation. He confessed that he had told his secret to the earth. He told Czar Trojan how the elder tree had shot up on the spot where he had confided the secret and he recounted the tale of how each flute made from a branch of the tree whistled the secret to the wind.

The czar, being a benevolent man at heart and being exceedingly fond of his young barber, decided to test the truth of the apprentice's words. Calling for his carriage and taking the apprentice with him, Trojan departed in search of the elder tree.

Coming to the spot where the apprentice had told his secret to the earth, they discovered the tree with only one branch left. Czar Trojan ordered the young man to make a flute of the branch and when it was made, he commanded the young man to play upon it. As the czar waited in disbelief, the flute whistled "Czar Trojan has the ears of a goat! Czar Trojan has the ears of a goat!"

Finally Trojan was convinced that on earth nothing can be hidden. He granted life to his barber's apprentice and from that time on gave permission that all men could come to shave him without fear.

102. A STROKE OF LUCK
(*Hungary*)

HE WENT PLOWING. He was a poor man. The plow cut a furrow and turned up a lot of money. When he set eyes on it, he began to speculate about what to say to his wife. He feared that she might blurt it out to the neighbors, and they would be served a summons to appear before the magistrate.

He went and bought a hare and a fish.

When she brought him his midday meal, he said to her after he had dined, "Let's fry a fish."

She said, "What do you think! How could we catch a fish here in the field?"

"Come on, woman, I've just seen a couple of them, when I was plowing around the blackthorn shrub." He led her to the blackthorn shrub.

Says the woman, "Look, old man, there's a fish."

"Haven't I told you so?" And he flung the ox goad at the shrub so that the fish turned out at once.

Then he said, "Let's catch a hare."

"Don't be kidding me. You haven't got a gun."

"Never mind. I'll knock it off with the ox goad."

They were going along when she cried out, "Look! there's a hare on the tree yonder there."

The man flung his goad at the tree and the hare fell down.

They were working till the day drew to a close, and in the evening they made their way home. When they went past the church, they heard an ass braying.

The man said to the woman, "You know what the ass is braying? He is saying, 'The priest says in his sermon that soon a comet will appear and that will be the end of the world!' "

They went on. When they passed the city hall, the ass uttered another loud bray. The man said, "The ass says that 'The magistrate and the town clerk have just been caught embezzling public funds.' "

As time wore on they were making good use of their money.

The neighbors kept asking them, "Where did that lot of money come from?"

Then she said to one of the neighbor women, "I wouldn't mind telling you, but you mustn't pass it on to anyone." And she told her that they had found the money. Their neighbor reported it to the magistrate, and they were summoned to appear before him. And when he was questioned about the money, the man denied it. By no means did they find any money. Not a penny had been found by them.

The magistrate then said, "Your wife will tell me."

"What's the use asking her. She's just a silly woman," he said.

The woman flew into a temper and began to shout at him, "Don't you dare say that again. Didn't we find the money when we caught the fish under the blackthorn bush?"

"Now Your Honor may hear for yourself. Catching a fish in a bush. What next!"

"Can't you remember how you shot down a hare from the tree with the ox goad?"

"Well, haven't I told Your Honor? It's no use asking that fool of a woman."

"A fool you are yourself. Have you forgotten that on our way home we heard an ass braying when we passed the church, and you said that the priest was preaching that a comet would appear and that would be the end of the world."

"Now wasn't I right, Your Honor? It would be better to leave her alone, or she might give offense with her silly talk."

The woman flew into a rage and said, "Don't you remember that when we were passing the city hall and the ass uttered a loud bray you were telling me, 'that the magistrate and the town clerk have been just caught out . . .'" The magistrate jumped to his feet and said to the man, "Take her home, my good man, she seems to have lost her wits."

103. IT COULD ALWAYS BE WORSE
(Yiddish)

THE POOR JEW had come to the end of his rope. So he went to his rabbi for advice.

"Holy Rabbi!" he cried. "Things are in a bad way with me, and are getting worse all the time! We are poor, so poor, that my wife, my six children, my in-laws and I have to live in a one-room hut. We get in each other's way all the time. Our nerves are frayed and, because we have plenty of troubles, we quarrel. Believe me—my home is a hell and I'd sooner die than continue living this way!"

The rabbi pondered the matter gravely. "My son," he said, "promise to do as I tell you and your condition will improve."

"I promise, Rabbi," answered the troubled man. "I'll do anything you say."

"Tell me—what animals do you own?"

"I have a cow, a goat and some chickens."

"Very well! Go home now and take all these animals into your house to live with you."

The poor man was dumbfounded, but since he had promised the rabbi, he went home and brought all the animals into his house.

The following day the poor man returned to the rabbi and cried, "Rabbi, what misfortune have you brought upon me! I did as you told me and brought the animals into the house. And now what have I got? Things are worse than ever! My life is a perfect hell—the house is turned into a barn! Save me, Rabbi—help me!"

"My son," replied the rabbi serenely, "go home and take the chickens out of your house. God will help you!"

So the poor man went home and took the chickens out of his house. But it was not long before he again came running to the rabbi.

"Holy Rabbi!" he wailed. "Help me, save me! The goat is smashing everything in the house—she's turning my life into a nightmare."

"Go home," said the rabbi gently, "and take the goat out of the house. God will help you!"

The poor man returned to his house and removed the goat. But it wasn't long before he again came running to the rabbi, lamenting loudly, "What a misfortune you've brought upon my head, Rabbi! The cow has turned my house into a stable! How can you expect a human being to live side by side with an animal?"

"You're right—a hundred times right!" agreed the rabbi. "Go straight home and take the cow out of your house!"

And the poor unfortunate hastened home and took the cow out of his house.

Not a day had passed before he came running again to the rabbi. "Rabbi!" cried the poor man, his face beaming. "You've made life sweet again for me. With all the animals out, the house is so quiet, so roomy and so clean! What a pleasure!"

104. CHELM JUSTICE
(Yiddish)

A GREAT CALAMITY befell Chelm one day. The town cobbler murdered one of his customers. So he was brought before the judge who sentenced him to die by hanging.

When the verdict was read a townsman arose and cried out, "If your Honor pleases—you have sentenced to death the town cobbler! He's the only one we've got. If you hang him who will mend our shoes?"

"Who? Who?" cried all the people of Chelm with one voice.

The judge nodded in agreement and reconsidered his verdict.

"Good people of Chelm," he said, "what you say is true. Since we have only one cobbler it would be a great wrong against the community to let him die. As there are two roofers in the town let one of them be hanged instead!"

105. SAINT OR HORSE
(Yiddish)

A YOUNG MAN once came to a great rabbi and asked him to make him a rabbi.

It was winter time then. The rabbi stood at the window looking out upon the yard while the rabbinical candidate was droning into his ears a glowing account of his piety and learning.

The young man said, "You see, Rabbi, I always go dressed in spotless white like the sages of old. I never drink any alcoholic beverages; only water ever passes my lips. Also, I perform austerities. I have sharp-edged nails inside my shoes to mortify me. Even in the coldest weather, I lie naked in the snow to torment my flesh. Also daily, the *shammes* gives me forty lashes on my bare back to complete my perpetual penance."

And as the young man spoke, a white horse was led into the yard and to the water trough. It drank, and then it rolled in the snow, as horses sometimes do.

"Just look!" cried the rabbi. "That animal, too, is dressed in white. It also drinks nothing but water, has nails in its shoes and rolls naked in the snow. Also, rest assured, it gets its daily ration of forty lashes on the rump from its master. Now, I ask you, is it a saint, or is it a horse?"

106. WHEN HERSHEL EATS—
(*Yiddish*)

IN A CERTAIN VILLAGE lived a rich man. He was stingy and hardhearted, but he was also clever and knew how to conceal his corruption. Those who didn't know him even got the impression that he was kindhearted. On the Sabbath he would invite some poor traveler to his table, but woe to the unwary victim who fell into his clutches!

As a mark of honor he would place the wretch at the head of the table. Then the cat-and-mouse play began. He would ply the stranger with innumerable questions so that out of politeness he'd have to answer them. This gave him no opportunity to eat. In the meantime his host was enjoying both his food and his own cunning. To add insult to injury, when practically nothing was left on the table the host would turn with solicitude to his guest and upbraid him gently, "Why didn't you eat? Why did you talk so much?"

What was the poor man to do? He had to thank his host like a hypocrite and go to bed hungry.

Once it chanced that Hershel Ostropolier arrived in this village. Hearing of the queer ways of this rich man and his tricks, he decided to take revenge on him for all the poor unfortunates he had maltreated.

When Friday night arrived Hershel asked the *shammes* of the synagogue to arrange that he be invited to this rich man's house as his Sabbath guest. The *shammes* even tried to dissuade him from the step.

"Take my word for it," he said, "this rich man is wicked."

But Hershel insisted. So the *shammes* made the necessary arrangements for his visit.

After the Friday night service in the synagogue Hershel went home with the rich man. When they sat down to supper his host seated him in the place of honor, introduced him to the members of his household and showed him marked attention. After they all had recited the bless-

ings over the wine the servant brought in a tureen of fish. Its aroma
made the already hungry Hershel even hungrier.

The head of the household first stuck his fork into a fine portion of
gefilte fish and put it on his plate. Then, as if absent-minded, he didn't
pass the tureen to Hershel but kept it near himself. He fell into a
revery.

"From where do you come, uncle?" he asked.

"From Vishnitz," answered Hershel, mentioning a name at random.

"From Vishnitz? Then surely you must know Shaiah the miller! How
is he? What's he doing?"

"Shaiah the miller?" echoed Hershel. "He died."

Thereupon, without any further ceremony, Hershel extended his arm
across the table and stuck his fork into a large portion of fish which he
put on his plate. He fell to and ate with zest.

But his host was flabbergasted at what Hershel had told him. He
turned pale and put down his fork.

"Did you hear, Malke?" he cried incredulously to his wife. "My old
friend Shaiah is dead! Why didn't his wife let me know? I wonder what
will happen to his fortune—he must have left a nice little pile! But tell
me—how is Velvel?"

"Which Velvel?"

"Why Shaiah's eldest son, you know, the one who runs the inn in
Vishnitz."

"Oh, you mean Velvel who runs the inn? He died too!" said Hershel
in a matter-of-fact voice, spearing another piece of fish.

"Velvel died?" cried the rich man incredulously. "Did you hear,
Malke—Velvel died! Woe is me. He owes me five hundred rubles! But
tell me how is Velvel's partner, Yoshe the vintner? Is he running the
inn now?"

"No!" sighed Hershel, chewing away at the fish. "He also died."

"What! Yoshe the vintner is also dead! Woe is us, Malke! My
money is lost!"

And as the rich man continued to rave and get excited Hershel went
on eating calmly, smiling into his beard.

"Uncle," the rich man finally ventured with trepidation, "maybe you
know what Shaiah's brother, Avrum the dry-goods merchant, is doing?"

"What Avrum?" asked Hershel innocently, almost choking on a
mouthful of delicious white *chaleh.*

"Why, don't you know—Avrum the dry-goods merchant! He lives
near the lake, in the big white house!"

"Oh, he? I knew him well," answered Hershel. "He's dead too!"

"Have you gone out of your head, uncle?" shrieked the rich man in an unearthly voice, jumping up from his chair. "Surely, you don't mean to tell me that everybody in Vishnitz died?"

"My dear friend," drawled Hershel in his nasal way, "when I eat, everybody is as good as dead for me! But say, my good host, you've been so busy talking you've forgotten to eat! Know what? Your *gefilte fish* is really first rate!"

Middle East

Ali Baba and the Forty Thieves

107. ALADDIN AND THE WONDERFUL LAMP
(Arabian Nights)

THERE ONCE LIVED a poor tailor, who had a son called Aladdin, a careless, idle boy who would do nothing but play all day long in the streets with little idle boys like himself. This so grieved the father that he died; yet, in spite of his mother's tears and prayers, Aladdin did not mend his ways. One day, when he was playing in the streets as usual, a stranger asked him his age, and if he was not the son of Mustapha the tailor. "I am, sir," replied Aladdin; "but he died a long while ago." On this the stranger, who was a famous African magician, fell on his neck and kissed him, saying: "I am your uncle, and knew you from your likeness to my brother. Go to your mother and tell her I am coming."

Aladdin ran home and told his mother of his newly found uncle. "Indeed, child," she said, "your father had a brother, but I always thought he was dead." However, she prepared supper, and bade Aladdin seek his uncle, who came laden with wine and fruit. He presently fell down and kissed the place where Mustapha used to sit, bidding Aladdin's mother not to be surprised at not having seen him before, as he had been forty years out of the country. He then turned to Aladdin, and asked him his trade, at which the boy hung his head, while his mother burst into tears. On learning that Aladdin was idle and would learn no trade, he offered to take a shop for him and stock it with merchandise. Next day he bought Aladdin a fine suit of clothes and took him all over the city, showing him the sights, and brought him home at nightfall to his mother, who was overjoyed to see her son so fine.

Next day the magician led Aladdin into some beautiful gardens a long way outside the city gates. They sat down by a fountain and the magician pulled a cake from his girdle, which he divided between them. They then journeyed onward till they almost reached the mountains. Aladdin was so tired that he begged to go back, but the magician beguiled him with pleasant stories, and led him on in spite of himself.

At last they came to two mountains divided by a narrow valley. "We will go no farther," said the false uncle. "I will show you something wonderful; only do you gather up sticks while I kindle a fire." When it was lit the magician threw on it a powder he had about him, at the same time saying some magical words. The earth trembled a little and opened in front of them, disclosing a square flat stone with a brass ring in the middle to raise it by. Aladdin tried to run away, but the magician caught him and gave him a blow that knocked him down. "What have I done, uncle?" he said piteously; whereupon the magician said more kindly: "Fear nothing, but obey me. Beneath this stone lies a treasure which is to be yours, and no one else may touch it, so you must do exactly as I tell you." At the word treasure Aladdin forgot his fears, and grasped the ring as he was told, saying the names of his father and grandfather. The stone came up quite easily, and some steps appeared. "Go down," said the magician; "at the foot of those steps you will find an open door leading into three large halls. Tuck up your gown and go through them without touching anything, or you will die instantly. These halls lead into a garden of fine fruit trees. Walk on till you come to a niche in a terrace where stands a lighted lamp. Pour out the oil it contains, and bring it me." He drew a ring from his finger and gave it to Aladdin, bidding him prosper.

Aladdin found everything as the magician had said, gathered some fruit off the trees, and, having got the lamp, arrived at the mouth of the cave. The magician cried out in a great hurry: "Make haste and give me the lamp." This Aladdin refused to do until he was out of the cave. The magician flew into a terrible passion, and throwing some more powder onto the fire, he said something, and the stone rolled back into its place.

The magician left Persia forever, which plainly showed that he was no uncle of Aladdin's, but a cunning magician, who had read in his magic books of a wonderful lamp, which would make him the most powerful man in the world. Though he alone knew where to find it, he could only receive it from the hand of another. He had picked out the foolish Aladdin for this purpose, intending to get the lamp and kill him afterward.

For two days Aladdin remained in the dark, crying and lamenting. At last he clasped his hands in prayer, and in so doing rubbed the ring, which the magician had forgotten to take from him. Immediately an enormous and frightful genie rose out of the earth, saying: "What wouldst thou with me? I am the Slave of the Ring, and will obey thee in all things." Aladdin fearlessly replied: "Deliver me from this place!" whereupon the earth opened, and he found himself outside. As soon as his eyes could bear the light he went home, but fainted on the threshold. When he came to himself he told his mother what had passed, and showed her the lamp and the fruits he had gathered in the garden, which were in reality precious stones. He then asked for some food. "Alas! child," she said, "I have nothing in the house, but I have spun a little cotton and will go and sell it." Aladdin bade her keep her cotton, for he would sell the lamp instead. As it was very dirty she began to rub it, that it might fetch a higher price. Instantly a hideous genie appeared, and asked what she would have. She fainted away, but Aladdin, snatching the lamp, said boldly: "Fetch me something to eat!" The genie returned with a silver bowl, twelve silver plates containing rich meats, two silver cups, and two bottles of wine. Aladdin's mother, when she came to herself, said: "Whence comes this splendid feast?" "Ask not, but eat," replied Aladdin. So they sat at breakfast till it was dinnertime, and Aladdin told his mother about the lamp. She begged him to sell it, and have nothing to do with devils. "No," said Aladdin, "since chance hath made us aware of its virtues, we will use it, and the ring likewise, which I shall always wear on my finger." When they had eaten all the genie had brought, Aladdin sold one of the silver plates, and so on until none were left. He then had recourse to the genie, who gave him another set of plates, and thus they lived for many years.

One day Aladdin heard an order from the Sultan proclaiming that everyone was to stay at home and close his shutters while the Princess, his daughter, went to and from the bath. Aladdin was seized by a desire to see her face, which was very difficult, as she always went veiled. He hid himself behind the door of the bath, and peeped through a chink. The Princess lifted her veil as she went in, and looked so beautiful that Aladdin fell in love with her at first sight. He went home so changed that his mother was frightened. He told her he loved the Princess so deeply that he could not live without her, and meant to ask her in marriage of her father. His mother, on hearing this, burst out laughing, but Aladdin at last prevailed upon her to go before the Sultan and carry his request. She fetched a napkin and laid in it the magic fruits from the enchanted garden, which sparkled and shone like the most beautiful jewels. She took these with her to please the Sultan, and set out, trusting in the lamp. The Grand Vizier and the lords of council had just gone in as she entered the hall and placed herself in front of the Sultan. He, however, took no notice of her. She went every day for a week, and stood in the same place. When the council broke up on the sixth day the Sultan said to his Vizier: "I see a certain woman in the audience chamber every day carrying something in a napkin. Call her next time, that I may find out what she wants." Next day, at a sign from the Vizier, she went up to the foot of the throne and remained kneeling till the Sultan said to her: "Rise, good woman, and tell me what you want." She hesitated, so the Sultan sent away all but the Vizier, and bade her speak freely, promising to forgive her beforehand for anything she might say. She then told him of her son's violent love for the Princess. "I prayed him to forget her," she said, "but in vain; he threatened to do some desperate deed if I refused to go and ask your Majesty for the hand of the Princess. Now I pray you to forgive not me alone, but my son Aladdin." The Sultan asked her kindly what she had in the napkin, whereupon she unfolded the jewels and presented them. He was thunderstruck, and turning to the Vizier said: "What sayest thou? Ought I not to bestow the Princess on one who values her at such a price?" The Vizier, who wanted her for his own son, begged the Sultan to withhold her for three months, in the course of which he hoped his son would contrive to make him a richer present. The Sultan granted this, and told Aladdin's mother that, though he consented to the marriage, she must not appear before him again for three months.

Aladdin waited patiently for nearly three months, but after two had elapsed, his mother, going into the city to buy oil, found everyone rejoicing, and asked what was going on. "Do you not know," was the answer, "that the son of the Grand Vizier is to marry the Sultan's daughter tonight?" Breathless, she ran and told Aladdin, who was overwhelmed at first, but presently bethought him of the lamp. He rubbed it, and the genie appeared, saying: "What is thy will?" Aladdin replied: "The Sultan, as thou knowest, has broken his promise to me, and the Vizier's son is to have the Princess. My command is that tonight you bring hither the bride and bridegroom." "Master, I obey," said the genie. Aladdin then went to his chamber, where, sure enough, at midnight the genie transported the bed containing the Vizier's son and the Princess. "Take this newly married man," he said, "and put him outside in the cold, and return at daybreak." Whereupon the genie took the Vizier's son out of bed, leaving Aladdin with the Princess. "Fear nothing," Aladdin said to her; "you are my wife, promised to me by your unjust father, and no harm shall come to you." The Princess was too frightened to speak, and passed the most miserable night of her life, while Aladdin lay down beside her and slept soundly. At the appointed hour the genie fetched in the shivering bridegroom, laid him in his place, and transported the bed back to the palace.

Presently the Sultan came to wish his daughter good morning. The unhappy Vizier's son jumped up and hid himself, while the Princess would not say a word, and was very sorrowful. The Sultan sent her mother to her, who said: "How comes it, child, that you will not speak to your father? What has happened?" The Princess sighed deeply, and at last told her mother how, during the night, the bed had been carried into some strange house, and what had passed there. Her mother did not believe her in the least, but bade her rise and consider it an idle dream.

The following night exactly the same thing happened, and next morning, on the Princess's refusing to speak, the Sultan threatened to cut off her head. She then confessed all, bidding him ask the Vizier's son if it were not so. The Sultan told the Vizier to ask his son, who owned the truth, adding that, dearly as he loved the Princess, he had rather die than go through another such fearful night, and wished to be separated from her. His wish was granted, and there was an end of feasting and rejoicing.

When the three months were over, Aladdin sent his mother to remind the Sultan of his promise. She stood in the same place as before, and the Sultan, who had forgotten Aladdin, at once remembered him, and sent for her. On seeing her poverty the Sultan felt less inclined than ever to keep his word, and asked his Vizier's advice, who counseled him to set so high a value on the Princess that no man living could come up to it. The Sultan then turned to Aladdin's mother, saying: "Good woman, a sultan must remember his promises, and I will remember mine, but your son must first send me forty basins of gold brimful of jewels, carried by forty black slaves, led by as many white ones, splendidly dressed. Tell him that I await his answer." The mother of Aladdin bowed low and went home, thinking all was lost. She gave Aladdin the message, adding: "He may wait long enough for your answer!" "Not so long, mother, as you think," her son replied. "I would do a great deal more than that for the Princess." He summoned the genie, and in a few moments the eighty slaves arrived, and filled up the small house and garden. Aladdin made them set out to the palace, two and two, followed by his mother. They were so richly dressed, with such splendid jewels in their girdles, that everyone crowded to see them and the basins of gold they carried on their heads. They entered the palace, and, after kneeling before the Sultan, stood in a half-circle round the throne with their arms crossed, while Aladdin's mother presented them to the Sultan. He hesitated no longer, but said: "Good woman, return and tell your son that I wait for him with open arms." She lost no time in telling Aladdin, bidding him make haste. But Aladdin first called the genie. "I want a scented bath," he said, "a richly embroidered habit, a horse surpassing the Sultan's, and twenty slaves to attend me. Besides this, six slaves, beautifully dressed, to wait on my mother; and lastly, ten thousand pieces of gold in ten purses." No sooner said than done. Aladdin mounted his horse and passed through the streets, the slaves strewing gold as they went. Those who had played with him in his childhood knew him not, he had grown so handsome. When the Sultan saw him he came down from his throne, embraced him, and led him into a hall where a feast was spread, intending to marry him to the Princess that very day. But Aladdin refused, saying, "I must build a palace fit for her," and took his leave. Once home, he said to the genie: "Build me a palace of the finest marble, set with jasper, agate, and other precious stones. In the middle you shall build me a large hall with a dome, its four walls of massy gold and silver, each side having six windows, whose lattices, all except one which is to be left unfinished, must be set with diamonds and rubies. There must be stables and horses and grooms and slaves; go and see about it!"

The palace was finished by next day, and the genie carried him there and showed him all his orders faithfully carried out, even to the laying of a velvet carpet from Aladdin's palace to the Sultan's. Aladdin's mother then dressed herself carefully, and walked to the palace with her slaves, while he followed her on horseback. The Sultan sent musicians with trumpets and cymbals to meet them, so that the air resounded with music and cheers. She was taken to the Princess, who saluted her and treated her with great honor. At night the Princess said good-bye to her father, and set out on the carpet for Aladdin's palace, with his mother at her side, and followed by the hundred slaves. She was charmed at the sight of Aladdin, who ran to receive her. "Princess," he said, "blame your beauty for my boldness if I have displeased you." She told him that, having seen him, she willingly obeyed her father in this matter. After the wedding had taken place Aladdin led her into the hall, where a feast was spread, and she supped with him, after which they danced till midnight.

Next day Aladdin invited the Sultan to see the palace. On entering the hall with the four-and-twenty windows, with their rubies, diamonds, and emeralds, he cried: "It is a world's wonder! There is only one thing that surprises me. Was it by accident that one window was left unfinished?" "No, sir, by design," returned Aladdin. "I wished your Majesty to have the glory of finishing this palace." The Sultan was pleased, and sent for the best jewelers in the city. He showed them the unfinished window, and bade them fit it up like the others. "Sir," replied their spokesman, "we cannot find jewels enough." The Sultan had his own fetched, which they soon used, but to no purpose, for in a month's time the work was not half done. Aladdin, knowing that their task was vain, bade them undo their work and carry the jewels back, and the genie finished the window at his command. The Sultan was surprised to receive his jewels again, and visited Aladdin, who showed him the window finished. The Sultan embraced him, the envious Vizier meanwhile hinting that it was the work of enchantment.

Aladdin had won the hearts of the people by his gentle bearing. He was made captain of the Sultan's armies, and won several battles for him, but remained modest and courteous as before, and lived thus in peace and content for several years.

But far away in Africa the magician remembered Aladdin, and by his magic arts discovered that Aladdin, instead of perishing miserably in the cave, had escaped, and had married a princess, with whom he was living in great honor and wealth. He knew that the poor tailor's son could only have accomplished this by means of the lamp, and traveled night and day till he reached the capital of China, bent on Aladdin's ruin. As he passed through the town he heard people talking everywhere about a marvelous palace. "Forgive my ignorance," he asked, "what is this palace you speak of?" "Have you not heard of Prince Aladdin's palace," was the reply, "the greatest wonder of the world? I will direct you if you have a mind to see it." The magician thanked him who spoke, and having seen the palace knew that it had been raised by the Genie of the Lamp, and became half mad with rage. He determined to get hold of the lamp, and again plunge Aladdin into the deepest poverty.

Unluckily, Aladdin had gone hunting for eight days, which gave the magician plenty of time. He bought a dozen copper lamps, put them into a basket, and went to the palace, crying: "New lamps for old!" followed by a jeering crowd. The Princess, sitting in the hall of four-and-twenty windows, sent a slave to find out what the noise was about, who came back laughing, so that the Princess scolded her. "Madam," replied the slave, "who can help laughing to see an old fool offering to exchange fine new lamps for old ones?" Another slave, hearing this, said:

"There is an old one on the cornice there which he can have." Now this was the magic lamp, which Aladdin had left there, as he could not take it out hunting with him. The Princess, not knowing its value, laughingly bade the slave take it and make the exchange. She went and said to the magician: "Give me a new lamp for this." He snatched it and bade the slave take her choice, amid the jeers of the crowd. Little he cared, but left off crying his lamps, and went out of the city gates to a lonely place, where he remained till nightfall, when he pulled out the lamp and rubbed it. The genie appeared, and at the magician's command carried him, together with the palace and the Princess in it, to a lonely place in Africa.

Next morning the Sultan looked out of the window toward Aladdin's palace and rubbed his eyes, for it was gone. He sent for the Vizier and asked what had become of the palace. The Vizier looked out too, and was lost in astonishment. He again put it down to enchantment, and this time the Sultan believed him, and sent thirty men on horseback to fetch Aladdin in chains. They met him riding home, bound him, and forced him to go with them on foot. The people, however, who loved him, followed, armed, to see that he came to no harm. He was carried before the Sultan, who ordered the executioner to cut off his head. The executioner made Aladdin kneel down, bandaged his eyes, and raised his scimitar to strike. At that instant the Vizier, who saw that the crowd had forced their way into the courtyard and were scaling the walls to rescue Aladdin, called to the executioner to stay his hand. The people, indeed, looked so threatening that the Sultan gave way and ordered Aladdin to be unbound, and pardoned him in the sight of the crowd. Aladdin now begged to know what he had done. "False wretch!" said the Sultan, "come hither," and showed him from the window the place where his palace had stood. Aladdin was so amazed that he could not say a word. "Where is my palace and my daughter?" demanded the Sultan. "For the first I am not so deeply concerned, but my daughter I must have, and you must find her or lose your head." Aladdin begged for forty days in which to find her, promising if he failed to return and suffer death at the Sultan's pleasure. His prayer was granted, and he went forth sadly from the Sultan's presence. For three days he wandered about like a madman, asking everyone what had become of his palace, but they only laughed and pitied him. He came to the banks of a river, and knelt down to say his prayers before throwing himself in. In so doing he rubbed the magic ring he still wore. The genie he had seen in the cave appeared, and asked his will. "Save my life, genie," said

Aladdin, "and bring my palace back." "That is not in my power," said the genie; "I am only the Slave of the Ring; you must ask him of the lamp." "Even so," said Aladdin, "but thou canst take me to the palace, and set me down under my dear wife's window." He at once found himself in Africa, under the window of the Princess, and fell asleep out of sheer weariness.

He was awakened by the singing of the birds, and his heart was lighter. He saw plainly that all his misfortunes were owing to the loss of the lamp, and vainly wondered who had robbed him of it.

That morning the Princess rose earlier than she had done since she had been carried into Africa by the magician, whose company she was forced to endure once a day. She, however, treated him so harshly that he dared not live there altogether. As she was dressing, one of her women looked out and saw Aladdin. The Princess ran and opened the window, and at the noise she made Aladdin looked up. She called to him to come to her, and great was the joy of these lovers at seeing each other again. After he had kissed her Aladdin said: "I beg of you, Princess, in God's name, before we speak of anything else, for your own sake and mine, tell me what has become of an old lamp I left on the cornice in the hall of four-and-twenty windows, when I went hunting." "Alas!" she said, "I am the innocent cause of our sorrows," and told him of the exchange of the lamp. "Now I know," cried Aladdin, "that we have to thank the African magician for this! Where is the lamp?" "He carries it about with him," said the Princess. "I know, for he pulled it out of his breast to show me. He wishes me to break my faith with you and marry him, saying that you were beheaded by my father's command. He is forever speaking ill of you, but I only reply by my tears. If I persist, I doubt not but he will use violence." Aladdin comforted her, and left her for a while. He changed clothes with the first person he met in the town, and having bought a certain powder returned to the Princess, who let him in by a little side door. "Put on your most beautiful dress," he said to her, "and receive the magician with smiles, leading him to believe that you have forgotten me. Invite him to sup with you, and say you wish to taste the wine of his country. He will go for some and while he is gone I will tell you what to do." She listened carefully to Aladdin and when he left her arrayed herself gaily for the first time since she left China. She put on a girdle and headdress of diamonds, and, seeing in a glass that she was more beautiful than ever, received the magician, saying, to his great amazement: "I have made up my mind that Aladdin is dead, and that all my tears will not bring him back to me, so I am resolved to mourn no more, and have therefore invited you to sup with me; but I am tired of the wines of China, and would fain taste those of Africa." The magician flew to his cellar, and the Princess put the powder Aladdin had given her in her cup. When he returned she asked him to drink her health in the wine of Africa, handing him her cup in exchange for his, as a sign she was reconciled to him. Before drinking the magician made her a speech in praise of her beauty, but the Princess cut him short, saying: "Let us drink first, and you shall say what you will afterward." She set her cup to her lips and kept it there, while the magician drained his to the dregs and fell back lifeless. The Princess then opened the door to Aladdin, and flung her arms round his neck; but Aladdin put her away, bidding her leave him, as he had more to do. He then went to the dead magician, took the lamp out of his vest, and bade the genie carry the palace and all in it back to China. This was done, and the Princess in her chamber only felt two little shocks, and little thought she was at home again.

The Sultan, who was sitting in his closet, mourning for his lost daughter, happened to look up, and rubbed his eyes, for there stood the palace as before! He hastened thither, and Aladdin received him in the hall of the four-and-twenty windows, with the Princess at his side. Aladdin told him what had happened, and showed him the dead body of the magician, that he might believe. A ten days' feast was proclaimed, and it seemed as if Aladdin might now live the rest of his life in peace; but it was not to be.

The African magician had a younger brother, who was, if possible, more wicked and more cunning than himself. He traveled to China to avenge his brother's death, and went to visit a pious woman called Fatima, thinking she might be of use to him. He entered her cell and clapped a dagger to her breast, telling her to rise and do his bidding on pain of death. He changed clothes with her, colored his face like hers, put on her veil, and murdered her, that she might tell no tales. Then he went toward the palace of Aladdin, and all the people, thinking he was the holy woman, gathered round him, kissing his hands and begging his blessing. When he got to the palace there was such a noise going on round him that the Princess bade her slave look out of the window and ask what was the matter. The slave said it was the holy woman, curing people by her touch of their ailments, whereupon the Princess, who had long desired to see Fatima, sent for her. On coming to the Princess the magician offered up a prayer for her health and prosperity. When he had done the Princess made him sit by her, and begged him to stay with her always. The false Fatima, who wished for nothing better, consented, but kept his veil down for fear of discovery. The Princess showed him the hall, and asked him what he thought of it. "It is truly beautiful," said the false Fatima. "In my mind it wants but one thing." "And what is that?" said the Princess. "If only a roc's egg," replied he, "were hung up from the middle of this dome, it would be the wonder of the world."

After this the Princess could think of nothing but the roc's egg, and when Aladdin returned from hunting he found her in a very ill humor. He begged to know what was amiss, and she told him that all her pleasure in the hall was spoiled for the want of a roc's egg hanging from the dome. "If that is all," replied Aladdin, "you shall soon be happy." He left her and rubbed the lamp, and when the genie appeared commanded him to bring a roc's egg. The genie gave such a loud and terrible shriek that the hall shook. "Wretch!" he cried, "is it not enough that I have done everything for you, but you must command me to bring my master and hang him up in the midst of this dome? You and your wife and your palace deserve to be burned to ashes, but that this request does not come from you, but from the brother of the African magician, whom you destroyed. He is now in your palace disguised as the holy woman—whom he murdered. He it was who put that wish into your wife's head. Take care of yourself, for he means to kill you." So saying, the genie disappeared.

Aladdin went back to the Princess, saying his head ached, and requesting that the holy Fatima should be fetched to lay her hands on it. But when the magician came near, Aladdin, seizing his dagger, pierced him to the heart. "What have you done?" cried the Princess. "You have killed the holy woman!" "Not so," replied Aladdin, "but a wicked magician," and told her of how she had been deceived.

After this Aladdin and his wife lived in peace. He succeeded the Sultan when he died, and reigned for many years, leaving behind him a long line of kings.

108. ALI BABA AND THE FORTY THIEVES

(Arabian Nights)

IN A TOWN in Persia there dwelt two brothers, one named Cassim, the other Ali Baba. Cassim was married to a rich wife and lived in plenty, while Ali Baba had to maintain his wife and children by cutting wood in a neighboring forest and selling it in the town. One day, when Ali Baba was in the forest, he saw a troop of men on horseback, coming toward him in a cloud of dust. He was afraid they were robbers, and climbed into a tree for safety. When they came up to him and dismounted, he counted forty of them. They unbridled their horses and tied them to trees. The finest man among them, whom Ali Baba took to be their captain, went a little way among some bushes, and said: "Open, Sesame!" so plainly that Ali Baba heard him. A door opened in the rocks, and having made the troop go in, he followed them, and the door shut again of itself. They stayed some time inside, and Ali Baba, fearing they might come out and catch him, was forced to sit patiently in the tree. At last the door opened again, and the Forty Thieves came out. As the Captain went in last he came out first, and made them all pass by him; he then closed the door, saying: "Shut, Sesame!" Every man bridled his horse and mounted, the Captain put himself at their head, and they returned as they came.

Then Ali Baba climbed down and went to the door concealed among the bushes, and said: "Open, Sesame!" and it flew open. Ali Baba, who expected a dull, dismal place, was greatly surprised to find it large and well lighted, and hollowed by the hand of man in the form of a vault, which received the light from an opening in the ceiling. He saw rich bales of merchandise—silk, stuff-brocades all piled together, and gold and silver in heaps, and money in leather purses. He went in and the door shut behind him. He did not look at the silver, but brought out as many bags of gold as he thought his asses, which were browsing outside, could carry, loaded them with the bags, and hid it all with fagots. Using the words: "Shut, Sesame!" he closed the door and went home.

Then he drove his asses into the yard, shut the gates, carried the moneybags to his wife, and emptied them out before her. He bade her keep the secret, and he would go and bury the gold. "Let me first measure it," said his wife. "I will go borrow a measure of someone, while you dig the hole." So she ran to the wife of Cassim and borrowed a measure. Knowing Ali Baba's poverty, the sister was curious to find out what sort of grain his wife wished to measure, and artfully put some suet at the bottom of the measure. Ali Baba's wife went home and set the measure on the heap of gold, and filled it and emptied it often, to her great content. She then carried it back to her sister, without noticing that a piece of gold was sticking to it, which Cassim's wife perceived directly her back was turned. She grew very curious, and said to Cassim when he came home: "Cassim, your brother is richer than you. He does not count his money, he measures it." He begged her to explain this riddle, which she did by showing him the piece of money and telling him where she found it.

Then Cassim grew so envious that he could not sleep, and went to his brother in the morning before sunrise. "Ali Baba," he said, showing him the gold piece, "you pretend to be poor and yet you measure gold." By this Ali Baba perceived that through his wife's folly Cassim and his wife knew their secret, so he confessed all and offered Cassim a share. "That I expect," said Cassim; "but I must know where to find the treasure, otherwise I will discover all, and you will lose all." Ali Baba, more out of kindness than fear, told him of the cave, and the very words to use. Cassim left Ali Baba, meaning to be beforehand with him and get the treasure for himself. He rose early next morning, and set out with ten mules loaded with great chests. He soon found the place, and the door in the rock. He said: "Open, Sesame!" and the door opened and shut behind him. He could have feasted his eyes all day on the treasures, but he now hastened to gather together as much of it as possible; but when he was ready to go he could not remember what to say for thinking of his great riches. Instead of "Sesame," he said: "Open, Barley!" and the door remained fast. He named several different sorts of grain, all but the right one, and the door still stuck fast. He was so frightened at the danger he was in that he had as much forgotten the word as if he had never heard it.

About noon the robbers returned to their cave, and saw Cassim's mules roving about with great chests on their backs. This gave them the alarm: they drew their sabers, and went to the door, which opened on their Captain's saying: "Open, Sesame!" Cassim, who had heard the trampling of their horses' feet, resolved to sell his life dearly, so when the door opened he leaped out and threw the Captain down. In vain, however, for the robbers with their sabers soon killed him. On entering the cave they saw all the bags laid ready, and could not imagine how anyone had got in without knowing their secret. They cut Cassim's body into four quarters, and nailed them up inside the cave, in order to frighten anyone who should venture in, and went away in search of more treasure.

As night drew on Cassim's wife grew very uneasy, and ran to her brother-in-law, and told him where her husband had gone. Ali Baba did his best to comfort her, and set out to the forest in search of Cassim. The first thing he saw on entering the cave was his dead brother. Full of horror, he put the body on one of his asses, and bags of gold on the other two, and, covering all with some fagots, returned home. He drove the two asses laden with gold into his own yard, and led the other to Cassim's house. The door was opened by the slave Morgiana, whom he knew to be both brave and cunning. Unloading the ass, he said to her: "This is the body of your master, who has been murdered, but whom we must bury as though he had died in his bed. I will speak with you again, but now tell your mistress I am come." The wife of Cassim, on learning the fate of her husband, broke out into cries and tears, but Ali Baba offered to take her to live with him and his wife if she would promise to keep his counsel and leave everything to Morgiana; whereupon she agreed, and dried her eyes.

Morgiana, meanwhile, sought an apothecary and asked him for some lozenges. "My poor master," she said, "can neither eat nor speak, and no one knows what his distemper is." She carried home the lozenges and returned next day weeping, and asked for an essence only given to those just about to die. Thus, in the evening, no one was surprised to hear the wretched shrieks and cries of Cassim's wife and Morgiana, telling everyone that Cassim was dead. The day after Morgiana went to an old cobbler near the gates of the town who opened his stall early, put a piece of gold in his hand, and bade him follow her with his needle and thread. Having bound his eyes with a handkerchief, she took him to the room where the body lay, pulled off the bandage, and bade him sew the quarters together, after which she covered his eyes again and led him home. Then they buried Cassim, and Morgiana his slave followed him to the grave, weeping and tearing her hair, while Cassim's wife stayed at home uttering lamentable cries. Next day she went to live with Ali Baba, who gave Cassim's shop to his eldest son.

The Forty Thieves, on their return to the cave, were much astonished to find Cassim's body gone and some of their moneybags. "We are certainly discovered," said the Captain, "and shall be undone if we cannot find out who it is that knows our secret. Two men must have known it; we have killed one, we must now find the other. To this end one of you who is bold and artful must go into the city dressed as a traveler, and discover whom we have killed, and whether men talk of the strange manner of his death. If the messenger fails he must lose his life, lest we be betrayed." One of the thieves started up and offered to do this, and after the rest had highly commended him for his bravery he disguised himself, and happened to enter the town at daybreak, just by Baba Mustapha's stall. The thief bade him good day, saying: "Honest man, how can you possibly see to stitch at your age?" "Old as I am," replied the cobbler, "I have very good eyes, and you will believe me when I tell you that I sewed a dead body together in a place where I had less light than I have now." The robber was overjoyed at his good fortune, and, giving him a piece of gold, desired to be shown the house where he stitched up the dead body. At first Mustapha refused, saying that he had been blindfolded; but when the robber gave him another piece of gold he began to think he might remember the turnings if blindfolded as before. This means succeeded; the robber partly led him, and was partly guided by him, right in front of Cassim's house, the door of which the robber marked with a piece of chalk. Then, well pleased, he bade farewell to Baba Mustapha and returned to the forest. By and by Morgiana, going out, saw the mark the robber had made, quickly guessed that some mischief was brewing, and fetching a piece of chalk marked two or three doors on each side, without saying anything to her master or mistress.

The thief, meantime, told his comrades of his discovery. The Captain thanked him, and bade him show him the house he had marked. But when they came to it they saw that five or six of the houses were chalked in the same manner. The guide was so confounded that he knew not what answer to make, and when they returned he was at once beheaded for having failed. Another robber was dispatched, and, having won over Baba Mustapha, marked the house in red chalk; but Morgiana being again too clever for them, the second messenger was put to death also. The Captain now resolved to go himself, but, wiser than the others, he did not mark the house, but looked at it so closely that he could not fail to remember it. He returned, and ordered his men to go into the neighboring villages and buy nineteen mules, and thirty-eight leather jars, all empty, except one which was full of oil. The Captain put one of his men, fully armed, into each, rubbing the outside of the jars with oil from the full vessel. Then the nineteen mules were loaded with thirty-seven robbers in jars, and the jar of oil, and reached the town by dusk. The Captain stopped his mules in front of Ali Baba's house, and said to Ali Baba, who was sitting outside for coolness: "I have brought some oil from a distance to sell at tomorrow's market, but it is now so late that I know not where to pass the night, unless you will do me the favor to take me in." Though Ali Baba had seen the Captain of the robbers in the forest, he did not recognize him in the disguise of an oil merchant. He bade him welcome, opened his gates for the mules to enter, and went to Morgiana to bid her prepare a bed and supper for his guest. He brought the stranger into his hall, and after they had supped went again to speak to Morgiana in the kitchen, while the Captain went into the yard under pretense of seeing after his mules, but really to tell his men what to do. Beginning at the first jar and ending at the last, he said to each man: "As soon as I throw some stones from the window of the chamber where I lie, cut the jars open with your knives and come out, and I will be with you in a trice." He returned to the house, and Morgiana led him to his chamber. She then told Abdallah, her fellow-slave, to set on the pot to make some broth for her master, who had gone to bed. Meanwhile her lamp went out, and she had no more oil in the house. "Do not be uneasy," said Abdallah; "go into the yard and take some out of one of those jars." Morgiana thanked him for his advice, took the oil pot, and went into the yard. When she came to the first jar the robber inside said softly: "Is it time?"

Any other slave but Morgiana, on finding a man in the jar instead of the oil she wanted, would have screamed and made a noise; but she, knowing the danger her master was in, bethought herself of a plan, and answered quietly: "Not yet, but soon." She went to all the jars, giving the same answer, till she came to the jar of oil. She now saw that her master, thinking to entertain an oil merchant, had let thirty-eight robbers into his house. She filled her oil pot, went back to the kitchen, and, having lit her lamp, went again to the oil jar and filled a large kettle full of oil. When it boiled she went and poured enough oil into every jar to stifle and kill the robber inside. When this brave deed was done she went back to the kitchen, put out the fire and the lamp, and waited to see what would happen.

In a quarter of an hour the Captain of the robbers awoke, got up, and opened the window. As all seemed quiet he threw down some little pebbles which hit the jars. He listened, and as none of his men seemed to stir he grew uneasy, and went down into the yard. On going to the first jar and saying: "Are you asleep?" he smelled the hot boiled oil, and knew at once that his plot to murder Ali Baba and his household had been discovered. He found all the gang were dead, and, missing the oil out of the last jar, became aware of the manner of their death. He then forced the lock of a door leading into a garden, and climbing over several walls made his escape. Morgiana heard and saw all this, and, rejoicing at her success, went to bed and fell asleep.

At daybreak Ali Baba arose, and, seeing the oil jars there still, asked why the merchant had not gone with his mules. Morgiana bade him look in the first jar and see if there was any oil. Seeing a man, he started back in terror. "Have no fear," said Morgiana; "the man cannot harm you: he is dead." Ali Baba, when he had recovered somewhat from his astonishment, asked what had become of the merchant. "Merchant!" said she, "he is no more a merchant than I am!" and she told him the whole story, assuring him that it was a plot of the robbers of the forest, of whom only three were left, and that the white and red chalk marks had something to do with it. Ali Baba at once gave Morgiana her freedom, saying that he owed her his life. They then buried the bodies in Ali Baba's garden, while the mules were sold in the market by his slaves.

The Captain returned to his lonely cave, which seemed frightful to him without his lost companions, and firmly resolved to avenge them by killing Ali Baba. He dressed himself carefully, and went into the town, where he took lodgings in an inn. In the course of a great many journeys to the forest he carried away many rich stuffs and much fine linen, and set up a shop opposite that of Ali Baba's son. He called himself Cogia Hassan, and as he was both civil and well dressed he soon made friends with Ali Baba's son, and through him with Ali Baba, whom he was continually asking to sup with him. Ali Baba, wishing to return his kindness, invited him into his house and received him smiling, thanking him for his kindness to his son. When the merchant was about to take his leave Ali Baba stopped him, saying: "Where are you going, sir, in such haste? Will you not stay and sup with me?" The merchant refused, saying that he had a reason; and, on Ali Baba's asking him what that was, he replied: "It is, sir, that I can eat no victuals that have any salt in them." "If that is all," said Ali Baba, "let me tell you that there shall be no salt in either the meat or the bread that we eat tonight." He went to give this order to Morgiana, who was much surprised. "Who is this man," she said, "who eats no salt with his meat?" "He is an honest man, Morgiana," returned her master; "therefore do as I bid you." But she could not withstand a desire to see this strange man, so she helped Abdallah to carry up the dishes, and saw in a moment that Cogia Hassan was the robber Captain, and carried a dagger under his garment. "I am not surprised," she said to herself, "that this wicked man, who intends to kill my master, will eat no salt with him; but I will hinder his plans."

She sent up the supper by Abdallah, while she made ready for one of the boldest acts that could be thought on. When the dessert had been served, Cogia Hassan was left alone with Ali Baba and his son, whom he thought to make drunk and then to murder them. Morgiana, meanwhile, put on a headdress like a dancing girl's, and clasped a girdle round her waist, from which hung a dagger with a silver hilt, and said to Abdallah: "Take your tambourine, and let us go and divert our master and his guest." Abdallah took his tambourine and played before Morgiana until they came to the door, where Abdallah stopped playing and Morgiana made a low curtsy. "Come in, Morgiana," said Ali Baba, "and let Cogia Hassan see what you can do"; and, turning to Cogia Hassan, he said: "She's my slave and my housekeeper." Cogia Hassan was by no means pleased, for he feared that his chance of killing Ali Baba was gone for the present; but he pretended great eagerness to see Morgiana, and Abdallah began to play and Morgiana to dance. After she had performed several dances she drew her dagger and made passes with it, sometimes pointing it at her own breast, sometimes at her master's, as if it were part of the dance. Suddenly, out of breath, she snatched the tambourine from Abdallah with her left hand, and, holding the dagger in her right, held out the tambourine to her master. Ali Baba and his son put a piece of gold into it, and Cogia Hassan, seeing that she was coming to him, pulled out his purse to make her a present, but while he was putting his hand into it Morgiana plunged the dagger into his heart.

"Unhappy girl!" cried Ali Baba and his son, "what have you done to ruin us?" "It was to preserve you, master, not to ruin you," answered Morgiana. "See here," opening the false merchant's garment and showing the dagger; "see what an enemy you have entertained! Remember, he would eat no salt with you, and what more would you have? Look at him! he is both the false oil merchant and the Captain of the Forty Thieves."

Ali Baba was so grateful to Morgiana for thus saving his life that he offered her to his son in marriage, who readily consented, and a few days after the wedding was celebrated with great splendor. At the end of a year Ali Baba, hearing nothing of the two remaining robbers, judged they were dead, and set out to the cave. The door opened on his saying: "Open, Sesame!" He went in, and saw that nobody had been there since the Captain left it. He brought away as much gold as he could carry, and returned to town. He told his son the secret of the cave, which his son handed down in his turn, so the children and grandchildren of Ali Baba were rich to the end of their lives.

109. THE FISHERMAN AND THE GENIE
(Arabian Nights)

THERE ONCE WAS an aged fisherman, who was so poor that he could scarcely earn as much as would maintain himself, his wife, and three children. He went early every day to fish in the morning, and imposed it as a law upon himself not to cast his nets above four times a day. He went one morning before the moon had set, and, coming to the seaside, undressed himself. Three times did he cast his net, and each time he made a heavy haul. Yet, to his indescribable disappointment and despair, the first proved to be an ass, the second a basket full of stones, and the third a mass of mud and shells.

As daylight now began to appear he said his prayers and commended himself and his needs to his Creator. Having done this, he cast his nets the fourth time, and drew them as formerly, with great difficulty. But, instead of fish, he found nothing in them but a vessel made of yellow copper, having the impression of a seal upon its leaden cover.

This turn of fortune rejoiced him. "I will sell it," said he, "to the smelter, and with the money buy a measure of corn."

He examined the vessel on all sides, and shook it, to see if its contents made any noise, but heard nothing. This circumstance, together with the impression of the seal upon the leaden cover, made him think it enclosed something precious. To satisfy himself, he took his knife and pried open the lid. He turned the mouth downward, but to his surprise, nothing came out. He placed it before him, and while he sat gazing at it attentively, there came forth a very thick smoke, which made him step back two or three paces.

The smoke rose to the clouds, and, spreading itself along the sea and upon the shore, formed a great mist, which we may well imagine filled the fisherman with astonishment. When the smoke was all out of the vessel, it re-formed, and became a solid mass, which changed before his eyes into a genie twice as high as the greatest of giants. At the sight of such a monster, the fisherman would have fled, but was so frightened that he could not move.

The genie regarded the fisherman with a fierce look, and exclaimed in a terrible voice, "Prepare to die, for I will surely kill thee."

"Ah!" replied the fisherman, "why would you kill me? Did I not just now set you at liberty, and have you already forgotten my kindness?"

"Yes, I remember it," said the genie, "but that shall not save thy life. I have only one favor to grant thee."

"And what is that?" asked the fisherman.

"It is," answered the genie, "to give thee thy choice, in what manner thou wouldst have me put thee to death."

"But how have I offended you?" demanded the fisherman. "Is that your reward for the service I have rendered you?"

"I cannot treat thee otherwise," said the genie. "And that thou mayest know the reason, listen to my story.

"I am one of those rebellious spirits that opposed the will of Heaven.

"Solomon, the son of David, commanded me to acknowledge his power, and to submit to his commands. I refused, and told him I would rather expose myself to his resentment than swear fealty as he required. To punish me, he shut me up in this copper vessel. And that I might not break my prison, he himself stamped upon this leaden cover his seal with the great name of God engraved upon it. He then gave the vessel to a genie, with orders to throw me into the sea.

"During the first hundred years of my imprisonment, I swore that if anyone should deliver me before the expiration of that period I would make him rich.

"During the second, I made an oath that I would open all the treasures of the earth to anyone that might set me at liberty.

"In the third, I promised to make my deliverer a potent monarch, to be always near him in spirit and to grant him every day three requests, of whatsoever nature they might be.

"At last, being angry to find myself a prisoner so long, I swore that if anyone should deliver me I would kill him without mercy, and grant him no other favor than to choose the manner of his death. And therefore, since thou hast delivered me today, I give thee that choice."

The fisherman was extremely grieved, not so much for himself, as on account of his three children; and bewailed the misery to which they must be reduced by his death. He tried to appease the genie, and said, "Alas! take pity on me in consideration of the service I have done you."

"I have told thee already," replied the genie, "it is for that very reason I must kill thee. Do not lose time. All thy reasonings shall not divert me from my purpose. Make haste, and tell me what manner of death thou preferrest?"

Necessity is the mother of invention. The fisherman bethought himself of a stratagem. "Since I must die then," said he to the genie, "I submit to the will of Heaven. But before I choose the manner of my death, I conjure you by the great name which was engraved upon the seal of the prophet Solomon, the son of David, to answer me truly the question I am going to ask you."

The genie, finding himself obliged to make a positive answer by this adjuration, trembled. Then he replied to the fisherman, "Ask what thou wilt, but make haste."

"I wish to know," asked the fisherman, "if you were actually in this vessel. Dare you swear it by the name of the great God?"

"Yes," replied the genie, "I do swear, by that great name, that I was."

"In good faith," answered the fisherman, "I cannot believe you. The vessel is not capable of holding one of your stature, and how is it possible that your whole body could lie in it?"

"Is it possible," replied the genie, "that thou dost not believe me after the solemn oath I have taken?"

"Truly not I," said the fisherman. "Nor will I believe you, unless you go into the vessel again."

Thereupon the body of the genie dissolved and changed itself into smoke, extending as before upon the seashore. And at last, being collected, it began to re-enter the vessel, which it continued to do till no part remained outside. Immediately the fisherman took the cover of lead, and speedily replaced it on the vessel.

"Genie," cried he, "now it is your turn to beg my favor. But I shall throw you into the sea, whence I took you. Then I will build a house upon the shore, where I will live and tell all fishermen who come to throw in their nets, to beware of such a wicked genie as you are, who has made an oath to kill the person who sets you at liberty."

110. THE DONKEY DRIVER AND THE THIEF
(Arabia)

ONE DAY TWO THIEVES walking down a deserted country road came upon a farmer slowly leading his donkey by the harness. Because the farmer looked rather simpleminded one of the thieves decided to play a trick on him.

"I am going to steal that donkey!" he declared.

"What! In broad daylight?" exclaimed the other. "How can you?"

"You'll see."

Very quietly, while the farmer jogged along half asleep, completely unaware of what was happening, the thief crept up to the donkey, disconnected the harness, and put it on his own head. Then he motioned his friend to hide the donkey in the forest.

After the animal was safely hidden, the thief suddenly stopped in his tracks. The farmer, still in a dreamy state, did not look up but merely yanked on the harness of the beast to get him going. When nothing happened, he yanked even harder. *Still* nothing happened. Furious, his eyes flew open and he turned to beat the donkey when he discovered with astonishment a man inside his animal's harness.

"Who . . . who . . . are you?" stammered the farmer.

"Why, I'm the donkey," replied the thief.

"But . . . but . . ."

Raising a hand, the thief attempted to calm the trembling man.

"Please," he said, "let me explain." Lifting the harness from his head, he settled himself comfortably upon a stone and begged the farmer to do the same.

"Several years ago I was human—just as you. But I became very lazy and would not do my chores. My mother grew extremely cross with me, and rightfully so. One day she discovered that along with all my other bad habits I had turned into a thief. She became so angry she put a hex on me, transforming me into a donkey for seven years. But today the curse is over and I am free to be human once again."

Astounded by the story, the farmer reproached himself for having worked the donkey so hard.

"Please allow me to congratulate you on your freedom, and to apologize for any bad behavior on my part. If I had known . . . But what is done, is done. Here," offered the farmer earnestly, "let me give you some money. It will give you a new start."

The thief thanked the farmer, and then bade him a pleasant good-bye. A little later he rejoined the second thief, who was hiding in the woods with the donkey. He complimented his friend on his fine performance, and the two scoundrels laughed heartily for some time over the ridiculous episode. Afterward, since they had no need of him, they sold the donkey in the nearest town.

A few days later the farmer came to town to buy a new beast. While examining the animals for sale, he suddenly came across one that looked strangely familiar.

"It is . . . No! Can it be . . . ?" Carefully studying the beast, he abruptly recognized his own brand mark burnished on its back.

"Good heavens!" shouted the farmer. "You scoundrel! Just a few days as a human being and you're at it again. No wonder your mother transformed you! When will you give up stealing and conniving?"

The donkey lifted its head and bared its teeth in a merry bray.

"That does it!" the farmer exclaimed. "You know perfectly well you understand every word I say. Well!" he cried, backing away in triumph, "I'll show you. This time I won't buy you. I'll leave the likes of you to another master."

Quite pleased with himself, the stupid farmer walked away.

111. THE FARMER AND HIS HIRED HELP

(Afghanistan)

ONCE THERE LIVED two brothers who were so poor that they had barely enough to eat. Discouraged with their lot, they sat down together and tried to think of some way to improve their situation. At last the older brother decided it would be best if he went away and tried to find work elsewhere. If he proved successful, he would send his wages to his brother, who would remain at home looking after the family affairs.

The very next morning the older brother set out. He had not traveled far when he came upon a prosperous farm. On the gatepost out front hung a large sign asking for hired help. Immediately he went to the farm building, knocked on the door, and asked to see the farmer.

"I understand you need some help," he said.

"Why yes," answered the farmer cordially. He looked the boy over carefully and then said, "You look like a strong, healthy lad. I think you'll do."

Though pleased to have found work so easily, the boy became a bit concerned when he heard the conditions of the job.

"I will hire you as a helper," said the farmer, "only if you agree to stay until springtime when the first cuckoo calls. If you should shirk your work, however, or become ill-tempered at any time, you will have to pay me a penalty of fifty pieces of gold. On the other hand," he added, "if I should become angry or ill-tempered at any time, then I will pay you a thousand rubles."

"But where will I get the pieces of gold?" asked the boy. "I haven't a penny to my name."

"Oh, that doesn't matter," replied the farmer generously. "If you have no money, you will just have to work for me for seven years without receiving any wages."

The lad considered the bargain very strange. Seven years was a long, long time. Still, he needed the job desperately. "And," he reasoned, "I am a good worker. I shall just have to be extremely careful not to lose my temper. And I should be able to do that for the few months between now and spring."

Agreeing to the conditions, the boy signed the contract the farmer had drawn up.

On the following day, at the first light of dawn, the farmer awakened the new hand and led him to a broad meadow.

"Mow this meadow as long as there is light," he said.

All day long the lad mowed the field and did not return home until late in the evening. By this time he was thoroughly exhausted.

"What?" the farmer exclaimed upon seeing him, "are you back already?"

Somewhat confused by this strange question, the boy replied, "But the sun has been down for several hours now."

"Aha," said the farmer, amused by this reply, "apparently you have misunderstood the terms of our agreement. It is true that the sun is down," he smirked, "but there is still plenty of light. If you'll notice," he continued, pointing to the sky, "there is a brilliantly shining moon tonight."

"This must be a joke," the lad thought to himself, and he could not restrain himself from frowning.

"You are not angry?" asked the farmer, his face contorted by a large grin.

"No, no. Not at all," replied the lad quietly. "But I am very tired and I would like to rest."

The farmer insisted, however, that the hired hand return to the fields, claiming that otherwise he would be shirking his duty. Not wanting to break his agreement, the boy went back to his mowing and he worked all through the night. And hours later the setting moon was followed by the rising sun. By this time, the boy had reached the limit of his strength. In sheer exhaustion he dropped to the ground. As soon as the farmer arrived in the meadow and saw his sleeping farmhand, he urged him up again.

"Can't you see? The sun is up. It's a fine new day."

In his despair, the lad cried out in anger, "Curse your field and curse your bread and money! This is inhuman treatment!"

"You are cursing me," said the farmer. "No doubt you are angry."

Trapped, the boy sobbed with anguish. From where could he get the fifty gold pieces with which to buy his contract? How could he work for seven years for such a man without killing himself? Then he hit upon a solution. Signing a new contract, he promised the farmer that he would pay off his debt in installments. Dejected, hungry and haggard-looking, he took his leave and returned home to his brother.

"What has happened to you?" his brother asked when he observed the terrible state in which his brother had entered the house.

"I have been duped by a villain," he said, and he went on to explain his bitter experience with the farmer.

"It is a good lesson," replied the younger brother, "and don't be too angry. I believe I shall go and look for some work. And don't be too surprised if I turn up at the farm of that very same scoundrel."

The next morning he set off down the road, a mysterious smile curving around his lips. In the late afternoon he arrived at the home of the rich farmer and asked for work. The farmer agreed to take him on and offered him the same proposal he had made his older brother a few days before. However, the young man refused, saying that the offer was not big enough.

"What do you mean?" asked the farmer, somewhat surprised.

"Let us make it a hundred gold pieces or fourteen years of work without pay, if I fail to live up to the agreement."

Delighted with this arrangement, the farmer promptly produced a contract and both he and the hired hand signed it. Each seemed extremely pleased with the stipulations of the agreement.

Cordially the farmer provided the new helper with a good dinner, and then immediately sent him to bed so that he would be fresh for the morning's chores.

As soon as dawn peeped over the horizon, the farmer was up, waiting for the new hired hand to appear so that he could instruct him in his duties. As the sun gew higher and higher in the sky and the boy still did not arrive, the farmer began to get very impatient. Finally, he knocked on the boy's door.

"The morning is well started and you lie in bed dreaming away!" he cried. "Do you think the grass will mow itself?"

"Are you slightly angry?" asked the boy.

Taken aback by the quickness of the reply, the farmer said, "No, no. Of course I'm not angry. I just wanted to remind you that there is work to be done."

"Very well," answered the lad, "I shall start dressing right away." Slowly he put on his pants and shirt, and then laced his boots at a snail's pace. To the farmer standing outside the door, every minute of waiting seemed like an hour.

Anxiously he called out, "Hurry, lad, hurry! I can't wait all day."

"Are you getting angry again?" quizzed the boy.

"No, no, nothing of the kind," replied the farmer, exercising great self-control. "But we have a lot of work to do."

At last, when the sun was very high in the heavens, the lad came out of his room and went with the farmer to the meadow. Upon their arrival there, the new hand noticed that all the other workers were having their lunch.

"Is it worthwhile starting now?" he asked. "Everyone else is eating. Why don't we have our lunch, too?"

Finding it hard to refuse, the farmer agreed reluctantly. It turned out that the young boy was a very slow eater with a very hearty appetite. At last, patting his full stomach, he turned to the farmer and said, "Since there is a lot of hard work ahead of us, I think we need a nap to help gather our strength for the job." With that he lay down on the grass and fell dead asleep until evening.

Shaking his fist in frustration, the farmer cried, "It's getting dark, boy, can't you see? All the other workers have mowed their fields. Wake up! Wake up!" But the lad did not stir.

Finally the farmer shrieked, "May the one who sent you here break his neck."

Suddenly the lad rubbed his drowsy eyes and looked straight at the farmer.

"Are you angry?" he asked.

Forced to protest, the farmer replied, "No, no. I only wished to say that it is dark and time for us to go home."

Instantly the boy jumped to his feet.

"That's different," he said. "Let's go."

When the two arrived at the house, the farmer discovered that he had visitors. Turning to the lad, he ordered him to slaughter a goat for dinner.

"Which one?" asked the boy, feigning total bewilderment.

"Any you find along the path," replied the farmer with annoyance.

Without another word, the lad set out on his assignment.

A short time later all of the farmer's neighbors came running to his house in great excitement.

"What is the matter?" the farmer demanded.

"Your helper has gone crazy!" they exclaimed.

"How do you mean?"

"He has slaughtered every one of your goats! Your entire flock is destroyed!"

"*What!*" screamed the farmer, and he rushed into the yard, where he confronted the farmhand. "What have you done, you idiot?" he roared.

"Why," exclaimed the boy, wide-eyed, "I have done exactly what you have asked me to do. You told me to kill *any* sheep along the path and *all of them* were along the path. I merely followed your orders." Looking directly at the farmer, he continued innocently, "Why, have I done anything wrong? You're not angry, are you?"

"No," replied the farmer through half-clenched teeth, "I'm not angry. It is just a pity that my flock is ruined."

At the end of the month the villainous farmer had lost all his patience. He began to plot a way that would release him from his contract without having to pay the penalty. Reflecting that spring was not too far away, he decided that he would speed up the first call of the cuckoo. Helping his wife into a tall tree, he instructed her to call out like a cuckoo as soon as she saw him and the hired hand enter the woods. Next, he invited the lad to go hunting with him. As they entered the forest, the farmer's wife caught sight of the two and she called out in a clear voice, "Coo-koo, coo-koo."

"Good heavens!" exclaimed the farmer, stopping dead in his tracks, "listen to that!"

"Coo-koo, coo-koo."

"Strange," the farmer said, acting surprised, "spring is here already. Well, this means that our agreement is terminated. The cuckoo calls, and you're free to go."

But the boy, immediately sensing the farmer's plot, was not taken in by such wiles.

"It is unbelievable," he said, "a cuckoo's call in the middle of the winter. That's rather odd, don't you think? I believe I'll look into this."

Quietly stalking through the woods, he stopped directly in front of the tree from where the call had come, and raised his gun as if ready to fire.

"No, no," shrieked the farmer, throwing himself in front of the boy. "Don't shoot, don't shoot!"

Grinning with amusement, the boy lowered his gun.

The farmer, now completely ruined, turned on the boy and screamed,

"Go away, get away from here as fast as you can! Get out of my sight! You've driven me out of my mind!"

Very quietly the boy said, "Why, I believe you're angry."

"Yes, yes! I *am* angry. I'll pay you the money. It's worth it to get rid of a scoundrel like you!"

Boiling with rage, the farmer rushed to the house and from a secret place took out a hundred pieces of gold.

"There!" he said, flinging the money at the boy. "Now go, and never come near here again."

"I won't leave until you tear up the contract as well," the boy replied with caution. The farmer did this immediately. Then the boy paid him the fifty gold coins owed by his brother, and the farmer tore up that contract as well. With that accomplished, the young man promptly took his leave, heading home with a joyous heart and richer by fifty gold coins.

The farmer, after surveying his losses, finally decided that he had learned a lesson. Never again did he trick hired hands into unfair contracts, but on the contrary he began to offer better working conditions. He noticed with surprise that a lot more work got done when his men were happy because they were well treated. Eventually, he became known in the area as a kind and just employer, and many people were eager for the chance to work for him.

112. DON'T THROW STONES FROM NOT-YOURS TO YOURS*
(Israel)

THERE WAS ONCE a rich man with a large house surrounded by beautiful gardens. He had many servants, and he had them constantly

---

* From *Ride with the Sun* edited by Harold Courlander for The United Nations Women's Guild. Copyright © 1955 by McGraw-Hill Book Company, Inc. Used with permission.

working at beautifying his estate. As they worked in the gardens, they dug up many stones, and the rich man ordered them to fling the stones over the wall into the road. Every day it was this way. All the stones that the servants gathered they threw over the wall into the road where people walked.

One day the rich man was standing at this gate while his workmen were dumping stones this way. An old man of the nearby village was passing. He stopped and protested to the rich man.

"Why do you throw stones from not-yours to yours?" he asked.

"What are you talking about?" the rich man said. "Don't you know that this great house and the grounds all around it are mine? My land extends to this very wall, and the road on the other side has nothing to do with me."

The old villager shook his head.

"God has been so good to you that you have lost the power to see that nothing in life is permanent," the villager said. And he went away, leaving the rich man to ponder on his words. But the rich man did not ponder long. Soon he was walking among his workmen, encouraging them to clear more stones out of the garden and to fling them over the wall.

The years passed. The gardens were cleared of stones. And somehow the rich man's fortunes began to change. Little by little he lost his wealth. A time came when he had to sell a little of his precious gardens. Again he had to sell, and again. At last he gave up the house itself. He became shabby and poor. He was no better off than the most unfortunate and miserable of beggars.

Then one day, when he was old, he walked along the road past the great estate that had once been his. As he walked he stumbled among the stones that lay in his path. His feet were bare, and the stones cut them and bruised them.

He stopped and looked at the wall he remembered so well. And he sat at the roadside to rest his sore and tired feet. And then he recalled the words of the villager who had said long ago, "Why do you throw stones from not-yours to yours?"

113. THE THREE HARES
(Turkey)

ONCE UPON A TIME, or so they say, there lived three baby hares, who dwelt with their father and mother in a deep and narrow hole. When they were just a month old their father called them all before him.

"My little ones," he said, "pay attention to what I am going to say to you."

The three little hares pricked up their ears, and began to listen very carefully.

"You are now," said their father, "quite well grown. This very day your first month of life is at an end, and your second month is beginning. Tonight or tomorrow your brothers will be born, and this hole of ours is narrow: we cannot all take refuge in it. Each one of you, therefore, must go out, and dig his own run, and make his own nest. It is the custom of hares. Your mother and I, when we were a month old, also left our father's home. But settle somewhere very near to us: let us keep close to each other."

Father Hare, when he had finished his talk, went away, and left his children alone. For a little while they talked about what they should do, and then they said good-bye to their mother and father, came up from the hole, and left it.

The first little hare said to himself, he said:

"I am not going to stay in this place, or dig any such hole. That dark, drain-like den of Father's simply made me sick. I have had enough of it. The weather's lovely, too. I shall build a beautiful little cottage in the nicest place I can find, somewhere near the woods and the meadows; and there I shall live. Whenever I like I shall go out and eat my fill, and I shall sit and look out of my windows and enjoy myself."

So this little hare did just as he said. He collected leaves, moss, sticks, brushwood and tufts of bushes and whatever else he could find, and piled them up and arranged them into a lovely little house. Then he went inside and settled down. Presently he felt hungry, so he went out to look for food. And while he was sitting in a meadow a fox came up to him and said:

"Hare, hare, little downy hare, stop, let us talk to each other. Don't run away from me, I wouldn't hurt you."

But the little hare answered:

"Fox, fox, cunning-eyed fox, you would like to catch and eat me, but you shall not!"

And with these words away he went, leaping and bounding, into his house, and hid himself. But in a few minutes the fox was there and had pulled down the house and had eaten the poor little hare, scrunch, munch. Such was the price this heedless one paid for his folly.

The second young hare, likewise, said to himself:

"I know what I shall do. How tired I had grown of a life in dark lairs and dens! Now let me make a nest for myself, in the roots of a tree."

And he, too, did just as he said he would do. He carried twigs and straw and moss, and scraps of everything that he could find, to the roots of a tree, crept inside, and sat. When he began to feel hungry out he came to find some food, and while he was grazing in a meadow along came the fox.

"Hare, hare," called the cunning fox, "little downy hare, don't run away from me. I mean no harm to you! Stay, let us talk to each other."

This put the little hare into a fright.

"Fox, fox, cunning-eyed fox," he cried, "I know well enough what you are after. You would like to eat me if you could, but you'll never catch me!"

And off he ran, leaping and bounding, into his nest. But when the fox saw the nest he began to laugh.

"Hare, hare, silly little hare," he cried, "now you shall see! I am going to eat you up and swallow you down in a single gulp!"

In a few minutes he had torn down the nest of sticks and straws, and had eaten the poor little hare, scrunch, munch. And so this one, too, was lost by his own foolish act. Alas! he had not stopped to think that homes made like birds' nests are of no use to hares.

The third little hare said to himself:

"I shall dig a hole somewhere near my father's den, but I shall make it deeper and longer than his. Then I shall get inside it and make myself at home."

So he set to work at a great pace, and day and night he dug. In a few days he had made a winding run, which was deep and long and safe, and when it was finished he went inside and hid himself. As soon as he felt in need of food he came out again, and went to a field, and there, sure enough, he met the fox. To this hare, too, the crafty fox called out:

"Hare, hare, little downy hare, do come and talk to me. I wouldn't hurt you."

But this little hare was wiser than his brothers.

"Fox, fox, cunning-eyed, sharp-nosed fox, I know your tricks!" said he. "Do you think I didn't hear that only yesterday you gobbled up one of my brothers? But you won't catch me!"

And straightway off he ran, leaping and bounding, and so into his narrow twisty lair, and sat. Along came the fox, but try as he might he could not get into the hole. He waited awhile, but at last he had to take himself off, and that was the end of him. And this is how the third little hare proved himself cleverer than his brothers. From all foxes, dogs, and hunters, may he live safely forever!

Asia

The Wife's Portrait

114. MOMOTARO or THE PEACH-BOY

(Japan)

IF YOU'LL BELIEVE ME there was a time when the fairies were none so shy as they are now. That was the time when beasts talked to men, when there were spells and enchantments and magic every day, when there was great store of hidden treasure to be dug up, and adventures for the asking.

At that time, you must know, an old man and an old woman lived alone by themselves. They were good and they were poor and they had no children at all.

One fine day, "What are you doing this morning, good man?" says the old woman.

"Oh," says the old man, "I'm off to the mountains with my billhook to gather a fagot of sticks for our fire. And what are you doing, good wife?"

"Oh," says the old woman, "I'm off to the stream to wash clothes. "It's my washing day," she adds.

So the old man went to the mountains and the old woman went to the stream.

Now, while she was washing the clothes, what should she see but a fine ripe peach that came floating down the stream? The peach was big enough, and rosy red on both sides.

"I'm in luck this morning," said the dame, and she pulled the peach to shore with a split bamboo stick.

By and by, when her good man came home from the hills, she set the peach before him. "Eat, good man," she said. "This is a lucky peach I found in the stream and brought home for you."

But the old man never got a taste of the peach. And why did he not?

All of a sudden the peach burst in two and there was no stone to it, but a fine boy baby where the stone should have been.

"Mercy me!" says the old woman.

"Mercy me!" says the old man.

The boy baby first ate up one half of the peach and then he ate up the other half. When he had done this he was finer and stronger than ever.

"Momotaro! Momotaro!" cries the old man. "The eldest son of the peach."

"Truth it is indeed," says the old woman. "He was born in a peach."

Both of them took such good care of Momotaro that soon he was the stoutest and bravest boy of all that countryside. He was a credit to them, you may believe. The neighbors nodded their heads and they said, "Momotaro is the fine young man!"

"Mother," says Momotaro one day to the old woman, "make me a good store of *kimi-dango*" (which is the way that they call millet dumplings in those parts).

"What for do you want *kimi-dango?*" says his mother.

"Why," says Momotaro, "I'm going on a journey, or as you may say, an adventure, and I shall be needing the *kimi-dango* on the way."

"Where are you going, Momotaro?" says his mother.

"I'm off to the Ogres' Island," says Momotaro, "to get their treasure, and I should be obliged if you'd let me have the *kimi-dango* as soon as may be," he says.

So they made him the *kimi-dango*, and he put them in a wallet, and he tied the wallet to his girdle and off he set.

"*Sayonara*, and good luck to you, Momotaro!" cried the old man and the old woman.

"*Sayonara! Sayonara!*" cried Momotaro.

He hadn't gone far when he fell in with a monkey.

"Kia! Kia!" says the monkey. "Where are you off to, Momotaro?"

Says Momotaro, "I'm off to the Ogres' Island for an adventure."

"What have you got in the wallet hanging at your girdle?"

"Now you're asking me something," says Momotaro. "Sure, I've some of the best millet dumplings in all Japan."

"Give me one," says the monkey, "and I will go with you."

So Momotaro gave a millet dumpling to the monkey, and the two of them jogged on together. They hadn't gone far when they fell in with a pheasant.

"Ken! Ken!" said the pheasant. "Where are you off to, Momotaro?"

Says Momotaro, "I'm off to the Ogres' Island for an adventure."

"What have you got in your wallet, Momotaro?"

"I've got some of the best millet dumplings in all Japan."

"Give me one," says the pheasant, "and I will go with you."

So Momotaro gave a millet dumpling to the pheasant, and the three of them jogged on together.

They hadn't gone far when they fell in with a dog.

"Bow! Wow! Wow!" says the dog. "Where are you off to, Momotaro?"

Says Momotaro, "I'm off to the Ogres' Island."

"What have you got in your wallet, Momotaro?"

"I've got some of the best millet dumplings in all Japan."

"Give me one," says the dog, "and I will go with you."

So Momotaro gave a millet dumpling to the dog, and the four of them jogged on together. By and by they came to the Ogres' Island.

"Now, brothers," says Momotaro, "listen to my plan. The pheasant must fly over the castle gate and peck the Ogres. The monkey must climb over the castle wall and pinch the Ogres. The dog and I will break the bolts and bars. He will bite the Ogres, and I will fight the Ogres."

Then there was the great battle.

The pheasant flew over the castle gate: "Ken! Ken! Ken!"

Momotaro broke the bolts and bars, and the dog leaped into the castle courtyard. "Bow! Wow! Wow!"

The brave companions fought till sundown and overcame the Ogres. Those that were left alive they took prisoners and bound with cords—a wicked lot they were.

"Now, brothers," says Momotaro, "bring out the Ogres' treasure."

So they did.

The treasure was worth having, indeed. There were magic jewels there, and caps and coats to make you invisible. There was gold and silver, and jade and coral, and amber and tortoise-shell and mother-of-pearl.

"Here's riches for all," says Momotaro. "Choose, brothers, and take your fill."

"Kia! Kia!" says the monkey. "Thanks, my Lord Momotaro."

"Ken! Ken!" says the pheasant. "Thanks, my Lord Momotaro."

"Bow! Wow! Wow!" says the dog. "Thanks, my dear Lord Momotaro."

115. THE OLD WOMAN WHO LOST HER DUMPLINGS

(*Japan*)

LONG, LONG AGO there was a funny old woman, who liked to laugh and to make dumplings of rice-flour.

One day, while she was preparing some dumplings for dinner, she let one fall; and it rolled into a hole in the earthen floor of her little kitchen and disappeared. The old woman tried to reach it by putting her hand down the hole, and all at once the earth gave way, and the old woman fell in.

She fell quite a distance, but was not a bit hurt; and when she got up on her feet again, she saw that she was standing on a road, just like the road before her house. It was quite light down there; and she could see plenty of rice-fields, but no one in them. How all this happened, I cannot tell you. But it seems that the old woman had fallen into another country.

The road she had fallen upon sloped very much: so, after having looked for her dumpling in vain, she thought that it must have rolled farther away down the slope. She ran down the road to look, crying:

"My dumpling, my dumpling! Where is that dumpling of mine?"

After a little while she saw a stone *Fizō* standing by the roadside, and she said:

"O Lord *Fizō*, did you see my dumpling?" *Fizō* answered:

"Yes, I saw your dumpling rolling by me down the road. But you had better not go any farther, because there is a wicked *Oni* living down there, who eats people."

But the old woman only laughed, and ran on further down the road, crying: "My dumpling, my dumpling! Where is that dumpling of mine?" And she came to another statue of *Fizō*, and asked it:

"O kind Lord *Fizō*, did you see my dumpling?"

And *Fizō* said:

"Yes, I saw your dumpling go by a little while ago. But you must not run any further, because there is a wicked *Oni* down there, who eats people."

But she only laughed, and ran on, still crying out: "My dumpling, my dumpling! Where is that dumpling of mine?" And she came to a third *Fizō*, and asked it:

"O dear Lord *Fizō*, did you see my dumpling?"

But *Fizō* said:

"Don't talk about your dumpling now. Here is the *Oni* coming. Squat down here behind my sleeve, and don't make any noise."

Presently the *Oni* came very close, and stopped and bowed to *Fizō*, and said:

"Good day, *Fizō San!*"

Fizō said good day, too, very politely.

Then the *Oni* suddenly snuffed the air two or three times in a suspicious way, and cried out: "*Fizō San, Fizō San!* I smell a smell of mankind somewhere—don't you?"

"Oh!" said *Fizō*, "perhaps you are mistaken."

"No, no!" said the *Oni* after snuffing the air again, "I smell a smell of mankind."

Then the old woman could not help laughing—"*Te-he-he!*"—and the *Oni* immediately reached down his big hairy hand behind *Fizō's* sleeve, and pulled her out, still laughing, "*Te-he-he!*"

"Ah! ha!" cried the *Oni*.

Then *Fizō* said:

"What are you going to do with that good old woman? You must not hurt her."

"I won't," said the *Oni*. "But I will take her home with me to cook for us."

"*Te-he-he!*" laughed the old woman.

"Very well," said *Fizō*; "but you must really be kind to her. If you are not, I shall be very angry."

"I won't hurt her at all," promised the *Oni*; "and she will only have to do a little work for us every day. Good-bye, *Fizō San*."

Then the *Oni* took the old woman far down the road, till they came to a wide deep river, where there was a boat. He put her into the boat, and took her across the river to his house. It was a very large house. He led her at once into the kitchen, and told her to cook some dinner for himself and the other *Oni* who lived with him. And he gave her a small wooden rice-paddle, and said:

"You must always put only one grain of rice into the pot, and when you stir that one grain of rice in the water with this paddle, the grain will multiply until the pot is full."

So the old woman put just one rice-grain into the pot, as the *Oni* told her, and began to stir it with the paddle; and, as she stirred, the one grain became two,—then four,—then eight,—then sixteen, thirty-two, sixty-four, and so on. Every time she moved the paddle the rice increased in quantity; and in a few minutes the great pot was full.

After that, the funny old woman stayed a long time in the house of the *Oni*, and every day cooked food for him and for all his friends. The *Oni* never hurt or frightened her, and her work was made quite easy by the magic paddle—although she had to cook a very, very great quantity of rice, because an *Oni* eats much more than any human being eats.

But she felt lonely, and always wished very much to go back to her own little house, and make her dumplings. And one day, when the *Oni* were all out somewhere, she thought she would try to run away.

She first took the magic paddle, and slipped it under her girdle; and then she went down to the river. No one saw her; and the boat was there. She got into it, and pushed off; and as she could row very well, she was soon far away from the shore.

But the river was very wide; and she had not rowed more than one fourth of the way across, when the *Oni*, all of them, came back to the house.

They found that their cook was gone, and the magic paddle, too. They ran down to the river at once, and saw the old woman rowing away very fast.

Perhaps they could not swim: at all events they had no boat; and they thought the only way they could catch the funny old woman would be to drink up all the water of the river before she got to the other bank. So they knelt down, and began to drink so fast that before the old woman had got half way over, the water had become quite low.

But the old woman kept on rowing until the water had got so shallow that the *Oni* stopped drinking, and began to wade across. Then she dropped her oar, took the magic paddle from her girdle, and shook it at the *Oni*, and made such funny faces that the *Oni* all burst out laughing.

But the moment they laughed, they could not help throwing up all the water they had drunk, and so the river became full again. The *Oni* could not cross; and the funny old woman got safely over to the other side, and ran away up the road as fast as she could.

She never stopped running until she found herself at home again.

After that she was very happy; for she could make dumplings whenever she pleased. Besides, she had the magic paddle to make rice for her. She sold her dumplings to her neighbors and passengers, and in quite a short time she became rich.

116. THE SPARROW WITH THE SLIT TONGUE
(Japan)

A LONG LONG time ago, an old couple dwelt in the very heart of a high mountain. They lived together in peace and harmony, although they were very different in character, the man being good-natured and honest, and the wife being greedy and quarrelsome when anyone came her way that she could possibly quarrel with.

One day the old man was sitting in front of his cottage, as he was very fond of doing, when he saw flying toward him a little sparrow, followed by a big black raven. The poor little thing was very much frightened and cried out as it flew, and the great bird came behind it terribly fast, flapping its wings and craning its beak, for it was hungry and wanted some dinner. But as they drew near the old man, he jumped up, and beat back the raven, which mounted, with hoarse screams of disappointment, into the sky, and the little bird, freed from its enemy, nestled into the old man's hand, and he carried it into the house. He stroked its feathers, and told it not to be afraid, for it was quite safe; but as he still felt its heart beating, he put it into a cage, where it soon plucked up courage to twitter and hop about. The old man was fond of all creatures, and every morning he used to open the cage door, and the sparrow flew happily about until it caught sight of a cat or a rat or some other fierce beast, when it would instantly return to the cage, knowing that there no harm could come to it.

The woman, who was always on the lookout for something to grumble at, grew very jealous of her husband's affection for the bird, and would gladly have done it some harm had she dared. At last, one morning her opportunity came. Her husband had gone to the town some miles away down the mountain, and would not be back for several hours, but before he left he did not forget to open the door of the cage. The sparrow hopped about as usual, twittering happily, and thinking no evil, and all the while the woman's brow became blacker and blacker, and at length her fury broke out. She threw her broom at the bird, who was perched on a bracket high up on the wall. The broom missed the bird, but knocked down and broke the vase on the bracket, which did not soothe the angry woman. Then she chased it from place to place, and at last had it safe between her fingers, almost as frightened as on the day that it had made its first entrance into the hut.

By this time the woman was more furious than ever. If she had dared, she would have killed the sparrow then and there, but as it was she only ventured to slit its tongue. The bird struggled and piped, but there was no one to hear it, and then, crying out loud with the pain, it flew from the house and was lost in the depths of the forest.

By and by the old man came back, and at once began to ask for his pet. His wife, who was still in a very bad temper, told him the whole story, and scolded him roundly for being so silly as to make such a fuss over a bird. But the old man, who was much troubled, declared she was a bad, hardhearted woman, to have behaved so to a poor harmless bird; then he left the house, and went into the forest to seek his pet. He walked many hours, whistling and calling for it, but it never came, and he went sadly home, resolved to be out with the dawn and never to rest till he had brought the wanderer back. Day after day he searched and called; and evening after evening he returned in despair. At length he gave up hope, and made up his mind that he should see his little friend no more.

One hot summer morning, the old man was walking slowly under the cool shadows of the big trees, and without thinking where he was going, he entered a bamboo thicket. As the bamboos became thinner, he found himself opposite to a beautiful garden, in the center of which stood a tiny spick-and-span little house, and out of the house came a lovely maiden, who unlatched the gate and invited him in the most hospitable way to enter and rest. "Oh, my dear old friend," she exclaimed, "how glad I am you have found me at last! I am your little sparrow, whose life you saved, and whom you took such care of."

The old man seized her hands eagerly, but no time was given him to ask any questions, for the maiden drew him into the house, and set food before him, and waited on him herself.

While he was eating, the damsel and her maids took their lutes, and sang and danced to him, and altogether the hours passed so swiftly that the old man never saw that darkness had come, or remembered the scolding he would get from his wife for returning home so late.

Thus, in dancing and singing, and talking over the days when the maiden was a sparrow hopping in and out of her cage, the night passed away, and when the first rays of sun broke through the hedge of bamboo, the old man started up, thanked his hostess for her friendly welcome, and prepared to say farewell. "I am not going to let you depart like that," said she; "I have a present for you, which you must take as a sign of my gratitude." And as she spoke, her servants brought in two chests, one of them very small, the other large and heavy. "Now choose which of them you will carry with you." So the old man chose the small chest, and hid it under his cloak, and set out on his homeward way.

But as he drew near the house his heart sank a little, for he knew what a fury his wife would be in, and how she would abuse him for his absence. And it was even worse than he expected. However, long experience had taught him to let her storm and say nothing, so he lit his pipe and waited till she was tired out. The woman was still raging, and did not seem likely to stop, when her husband, who by this time had forgotten all about her, drew out the chest from under his cloak, and opened it. Oh, what a blaze met his eyes! gold and precious stones were heaped up to the very lid, and lay dancing in the sunlight. At the sight of these wonders even the scolding tongue ceased, and the woman approached, and took the stones in her hand, setting greedily aside those that were the largest and most costly. Then her voice softened, and she begged him quite politely to tell her where he had spent his evening, and how he had come by these wonderful riches. So he told her the whole story, and she listened with amazement, till he came to the choice which had been given him between the two chests. At this her tongue broke loose again, as she abused him for his folly in taking the little one, and she never rested till her husband had described the exact way which led to the sparrow-princess's house. When she had got it into her head, she put on her best clothes and set out at once. But in her blind haste she often missed the path, and she wandered for several hours before she at length reached the little house. She walked boldly up to the door and entered the room as if the whole place belonged to her, and quite frightened the poor girl, who was startled at the sight of her old enemy. However, she concealed her feelings as well as she could, and bade the intruder welcome, placing before her food and wine, hoping that when she had eaten and drunk she might take her leave. But nothing of the sort.

"You will not let me go without a little present?" said the greedy wife, as she saw no signs of one being offered her. "Of course not," replied the girl, and at her orders two chests were brought in, as they had been before. The old woman instantly seized the bigger, and staggering under the weight of it, disappeared into the forest, hardly waiting even to say good-bye.

It was a long way to her own house, and the chest seemed to grow heavier at every step. Sometimes she felt as if it would be impossible for her to get on at all, but her greed gave her strength, and at last she arrived at her own door. She sank down on the threshold, overcome with weariness, but in a moment was on her feet again, fumbling with the lock of the chest. But by this time night had come, and there was no light in the house, and the woman was in too much hurry to get to her treasures, to go and look for one. At length, however, the lock gave way, and the lid flew open, when, O horror! instead of gold and jewels, she saw before her serpents with glittering eyes and forky tongues. And they twined themselves about her and darted poison into her veins, and she died, and no man regretted her.

117. THE TALE OF THE OKI ISLANDS
(Japan)

MANY HUNDREDS OF YEARS ago—about the year 1320 to be exact—the Emperor Hojo Takatoki ruled Japan with absolute power. A samurai, a noble soldier by the name of Oribe Shima, accidentally displeased the ruler and was banished from the land. Oribe was sent to a wild rocky group of islands off the coast of Japan called the Oki Islands. There he led a lonely, miserable life, for he had left behind his beautiful young daughter, Tokoyo, and he missed her terribly. She, too, felt unbearably sad, and at last, unable to stand the separation any longer, decided to try to reach her father or die in the attempt. She was a brave girl and knew no fear. As a child she had loved to dive with the women whose job it was to collect oyster shells deep down under the sea. She risked her life as they did, though she was of higher birth and frailer body.

After selling all her property, Tokoyo set out for the coast and at last reached a place called Akasaki, from where on clear days the islands of Oki could be seen. She tried to persuade the fishermen of the town to take her to the islands, but no one would, for it was a long and difficult journey. Besides, no one was allowed to visit those who had been banished there.

Although discouraged, Tokoyo refused to give up. With the little money she had left, she bought some food. Then, in the dark of night, she went down to the sea, and finding a light boat, she set sail all alone for the islands. Fortune sent her a strong breeze, and the current also helped her. The following evening, chilled and half dead, she arrived at the rocky shore of one of the islands. Scrambling out of the boat, she made her way up the beach to a sheltered spot and lay down to sleep for the night. She awoke in the morning quite refreshed, and after eating the rest of her food, she decided immediately to search for her father.

On the road she met a fisherman.

"Do you know my father?" she asked. Then she told him her story.

"No," said the fisherman, "I have never heard of him." Then he cautioned her earnestly. "Take my advice and do not ask for him. Your questions may get you into trouble, and may send your father to his death."

After that, Tokoyo wandered from place to place, hoping to hear word of her father, but fearful of asking anyone about him. She managed to stay alive by begging food from kindly people she met here and there along the way.

One evening she came to a shrine which stood on a rocky ledge. After praying to Buddha to help her find her father, she lay down in a small grove nearby and went to sleep. In a little while she was awakened by the sound of a girl's sobs, and a curious clapping of hands. She looked up into the bright moonlight and was startled to see a beautiful young girl of about fifteen crying bitterly. Beside her stood a priest, who clapped his hands and murmured over and over:

"*Namu Amida Butsu's.*"

Both were dressed in white gowns. After the prayer was over, the priest led the girl to the edge of the rocks, and was about to push her into the sea when Tokoyo ran out and caught hold of her just in time to save her from falling over the cliff.

The old priest was completely astonished, but in no way cross.

"I judge from this action," he said, "that you are a stranger to this island. Otherwise you would know that this ceremony is not to my liking. Unfortunately, on this island we are cursed by an evil god called Yofune-Nushi. He lives at the bottom of the sea, and each year demands that we sacrifice one girl under fifteen years of age to his kingdom. We make this offering on June thirteenth, the Day of the Dog, between eight and nine o'clock at night. If we do not appease him, the evil god becomes angry and causes great storms at sea and many of our fishermen drown."

Tokoyo listened gravely, then spoke.

"Holy monk, let this young girl go and I will take her place. I am the sad daughter of Oribe Shima, a noble samurai who has been banished to these islands. It is in search of my father that I have come here; but he is so closely guarded, I cannot get to him, or even find out where he is. My heart is broken and I no longer wish to live. Let me sacrifice myself. All I ask is that you deliver this letter to my father if you can find him."

After she had finished speaking, Tokoyo removed the white robe from the girl and placed it on herself. She then knelt at the shrine and prayed for courage to kill the evil god, Yofune-Nushi. Upon rising, she withdrew from her clothes a beautiful dagger that belonged to her family, and placing it between her teeth, she dived into the roaring sea and disappeared. The priest and the young girl stood at the ledge looking after Tokoyo, overcome with wonder at her courage.

Tokoyo, an excellent swimmer, headed straight downward through the clear water, which was illuminated by the moonlight. Down, down she swam, passing schools of silvery fish, until she reached the very bottom. There she found herself opposite an enormous cave which glittered with marvelous shells. Peering in, she thought she saw a man seated in the cave. She grasped her dagger, and bravely entered the cave, planning to battle and kill the evil god. When she got close, she was surprised to see that what she thought was a man was only a

wooden statue of Hojo Takatoki, the emperor who had exiled her father. Angry and disappointed, she started to strike the statue, but then
she changed her mind. "What good would it do? I'd rather do good
than evil," she thought to herself. Deciding to rescue the statue, Tokoyo undid her sash and tied the statue to herself. Then she began
swimming upward.

As she came out of the cave, an enormous glowing snakelike creature
covered with horrible scales and waving tiny legs swam up in front of
her. Its fiery eyes convinced Tokoyo that she was face to face with the
evil sea god that terrorized the island. Determined to kill the dreadful
monster, Tokoyo courageously swam close and with her dagger struck
out his right eye. The evil god, surprised with pain, tried to re-enter his
cave, but because he was so enormous and at that moment half-blind,
he could not find his way. Swiftly taking advantage of the situation,
Tokoyo struck him in the heart. With monstrous gasps and heavings
the evil beast slowly died.

Tokoyo, happy to have rid the island of the dreadful god which
demanded the life of a young girl each year, decided that she must raise
the monster to the surface so that the island people would know once
and for all he was dead. Struggling slowly and painfully, she at last
managed to swim to the top, bringing along also the wooden statue of
the emperor.

The priest and the girl, still lingering at the ledge, were astonished to
see Tokoyo emerge suddenly from the water.

Rushing down to greet her, they cried out in amazement when they
saw what she carried with her. Carefully they led the exhausted girl to a
dry spot of beach where she lay down.

When assistance came, everything was brought to town—the body of
the evil god, the wooden statue of the emperor, and Tokoyo herself.
Word had already spread in the village, and the brave young girl was
given a heroine's welcome. After that there were many ceremonies celebrating her extraordinary courage. The lord who ruled the island informed the emperor Takatoki directly of what had passed.

The emperor, who had long been suffering from an unknown dis-
ease, suddenly found himself well again. It was clear to him that he had
been laboring under the curse of someone to whom he had behaved
unjustly—someone who had carved his figure, cursed it, and sunk it in
the sea. Now that the statue had been raised, the curse was over and he
was well again. When he discovered that the person who had freed him
from his spell was none other than the daughter of Oribe Shima, he im-

mediately ordered the release of the noble samurai from the island prison.

Tokoyo and her father, once again happily reunited, went back to their native village, where they were hailed and feted. Oribe Shima's lands were returned to him and he was soon as prosperous as ever.

On the islands of Oki a shrine was built to commemorate the wonderful event, and all across Japan the name of Tokoyo became forever famous.

118. THE STONECUTTER
(Japan)

ONCE UPON A TIME there lived a stonecutter, who went every day to a great rock in the side of a big mountain and cut out slabs for gravestones or for houses. He understood very well the kinds of stones wanted for the different purposes, and as he was a careful workman he had plenty of customers. For a long time he was quite happy and contented, and asked for nothing better than what he had.

Now in the mountain dwelt a spirit which now and then appeared to men, and helped them in many ways to become rich and prosperous. The stonecutter, however, had never seen this spirit, and only shook his head, with an unbelieving air, when anyone spoke of it. But a time was coming when he learned to change his opinion.

One day the stonecutter carried a gravestone to the house of a rich man, and saw there all sorts of beautiful things, of which he had never even dreamed. Suddenly his daily work seemed to grow harder and heavier, and he said to himself: "Oh, if only I were a rich man, and could sleep in a bed with silken curtains and golden tassels, how happy I should be!"

And a voice answered him: "Your wish is heard; a rich man you shall be!"

At the sound of the voice the stonecutter looked round, but could see nobody. He thought it was all his fancy, and picked up his tools and went home, for he did not feel inclined to do any more work that day. But when he reached the little house where he lived, he stood still with amazement, for instead of his wooden hut was a stately palace filled with splendid furniture, and most splendid of all was the bed, in every respect like the one he had envied. He was nearly beside himself with joy, and in his new life the old one was soon forgotten.

It was now the beginning of summer, and each day the sun blazed more fiercely. One morning the heat was so great that the stonecutter could scarcely breathe, and he determined he would stop at home till the evening. He was rather dull, for he had never learned how to amuse himself, and was peeping through the closed blinds to see what was going on in the street, when a little carriage passed by, drawn by servants dressed in blue and silver. In the carriage sat a prince, and over his head a golden umbrella was held, to protect him from the sun's rays.

"Oh, if I were only a prince!" said the stonecutter to himself, as the carriage vanished round the corner. "Oh, if I were only a prince, and could go in such a carriage and have a golden umbrella held over me, how happy I should be!"

And the voice of the mountain spirit answered: "Your wish is heard; a prince you shall be."

And a prince he was. Before his carriage rode one company of men and another behind it; servants dressed in scarlet and gold bore him along, the coveted umbrella was held over his head, everything heart could desire was his. But yet it was not enough. He looked round still for something to wish for, and when he saw that in spite of the water he poured on his grass the rays of the sun scorched it, and that in spite of the umbrella held over his head each day his face grew browner and browner, he cried in his anger: "The sun is mightier than I; oh, if I were only the sun!"

And the mountain spirit answered: "Your wish is heard; the sun you shall be."

And the sun he was, and felt himself proud in his power. He shot his beams above and below, on earth and in heaven; he burned up the grass in the fields and scorched the faces of princes as well as of poorer folk. But in a short time he began to grow tired of his might, for there seemed nothing left for him to do. Discontent once more filled his soul, and when a cloud covered his face, and hid the earth from him, he cried in his anger: "Does the cloud hold captive my rays, and is it mightier than I? Oh, that I were a cloud, and mightier than any!"

And the mountain spirit answered: "Your wish is heard; a cloud you shall be!"

And a cloud he was, and lay between the sun and the earth. He caught the sun's beams and held them, and to his joy the earth grew green again and flowers blossomed. But that was not enough for him, and for days and weeks he poured forth rain till the rivers overflowed their banks, and the crops of rice stood in water. Towns and villages were destroyed by the power of the rain, only the great rock on the mountainside remained unmoved. The cloud was amazed at the sight, and cried in wonder: "Is the rock, then, mightier than I? Oh, if I were only the rock!"

And the mountain spirit answered: "Your wish is heard; the rock you shall be!"

And the rock he was, and gloried in his power. Proudly he stood, and neither the heat of the sun nor the force of the rain could move him. "This is better than all!" he said to himself. But one day he heard a strange noise at his feet, and when he looked down to see what it could be, he saw a stonecutter driving tools into his surface. Even while he looked a trembling feeling ran all through him, and a great block broke off and fell upon the ground. Then he cried in his wrath: "Is a mere child of earth mightier than a rock? Oh, if I were only a man!"

And the mountain spirit answered: "Your wish is heard. A man once more you shall be!"

And a man he was, and in the sweat of his brow he toiled again at his trade of stonecutting. His bed was hard and his food scanty, but he had learned to be satisfied with it, and did not long to be something or somebody else. And as he never asked for things he had not got, or desired to be greater and mightier than other people, he was happy at last, and heard the voice of the mountain spirit no longer.

119. THE WIFE'S PORTRAIT

(Japan)

VERY, VERY LONG AGO in a certain place there lived a rather slow-witted man named Gombei. He became thirty, then forty years old, but there was no one who would become his wife. He lived all alone in a dirty little hut.

One evening a beautiful woman, such as he had never seen before, came to his hut. "Tonight, please let me stay overnight here," she requested. Gombei was very surprised, but he gladly agreed to let her stay.

As night came, the woman said to him, "You are all alone in the world, and so am I; please take me as your wife." Gombei joyfully agreed, and she became his wife.

Gombei was so in love with his new wife that he hardly knew what he was doing. When he would sit down to make straw sandals, he was constantly looking at her, so that sometimes he would make the sandals five or six *shaku* [five or six feet] long, and they would be unfit for anyone to wear. Or when he would start to make straw rain capes, he could not take his eyes off his wife, and the capes would become longer and longer, one or two *jo* [ten to twenty feet], and no one could wear them. Then again, when he would go out to work in the fields, he would begin to wonder if his wife were all right and, after making one furrow, would run home to see her, then return to his work; but he would only get one more furrow made before he would again start thinking about his wife so much that he would have to run home again to see her. In this way he was hardly able to get any work done at all.

Since her husband could not get his work done, the wife went to the village and had an artist paint her portrait. She brought it home and gave it to Gombei, saying, "Here, this is just like me; please take it and hang it on a branch of a mulberry tree near the field. You can look at it as much as you want as you do your work."

Gombei took the picture and hung it near the field, and from then on he would work every day in the field, always looking at the picture. One day, however, a great wind came and, picking up the picture, whirled it high up into the air. Gombei was grief-stricken. Crying bitterly, he returned home to tell his wife what had happened. She comforted him, saying, "Do not worry so about it. I can easily have another painted just like it."

The wind carried the picture about here and there, finally letting it fall in the garden of the lord of the province. When the lord saw the picture, he thought it so beautiful that he greatly desired to marry the woman whose portrait it was. He commanded his retainers, saying, "Since this picture has been painted, this beautiful woman must surely exist somewhere. You must go and find her for me."

The retainers took the picture and went about from village to village, asking everyone they met if they knew where the woman whose portrait it was might be found. Finally they came to the village where Gombei lived. There they asked, "Do you know the woman who is painted here?" The villagers replied, "Yes, that woman is the wife of Gombei." The retainers went to the hut where Gombei lived, and there they found that the woman was exactly like the picture.

"The lord of the province has commanded us to take this woman with us," said the retainers, forcing her to go with them.

"Have mercy on me, please. Please have mercy on me," Gombei pleaded, but to no avail, and his wife was taken away. Gombei, stricken with grief, cried endlessly. His nose began to run. The mucus mixed with his tears and made a stream reaching clear to the ground. His wife too cried and cried. "Gombei," she sobbed, "there is no way out; I must go. But when the end of the year comes, you must come to the lord's castle and sell pine trees for the new year's gate decorations. If you do that, we can surely meet again." Saying this, she was taken away.

Soon the end of the year drew near. Gombei took a large bundle of young pine trees on his back and merrily set off for the lord's castle. When he came to the front gate of the castle, he called out in a loud voice, "Gate pines for sale! Gate pines for sale!"

As soon as she heard Gombei's voice outside, his wife, who until then had never even smiled, broke into merry laughter. The lord was so happy to see her laugh that he ordered his retainers to bring in the man selling pine trees. When Gombei was brought in, the woman again laughed happily.

The lord was overjoyed and said, "If you enjoy the pine tree peddler so much, I shall become one, and you shall be happier than ever." Saying this, he put his own robes on Gombei and took Gombei's dirty rags and put them on. He loaded the pine trees on his back and danced about calling, "Gate pines for sale! Gate pines for sale!"

When she saw this, the woman looked happier than ever before and again burst out in laughter. The lord was so pleased that he went through the gates and outside the castle, walking along calling, "Gate pines for sale! Gate pines for sale!"

As soon as he was gone, the woman ordered the retainers to close the iron gates securely and lock them. After a short while the lord returned. When he found that the gates were shut, he was very surprised. Pounding on the doors of the gate, he called, "The lord is outside, the lord is outside," but no one would open the gates.

Inside the castle, Gombei and his wife, surrounded by many servants, spent the rest of their lives in peace and luxury.

Ichigo buranto kudatta. "The market was good; everything sold out."

120. URASHIMA
(*Japan*)

MANY YEARS AGO a boy lived down by the sea, where the great green waves came riding in to break on the shore in clouds of salty spray. This boy, Urashima, loved the water as a brother, and was often out in his boat from purple dawn to russet evening. One day as he was fishing, something tugged at his line, and he pulled in. It was not a fish, as he expected, but a wrinkled old turtle.

"Well," said Urashima, "if I cannot get a fish for my dinner, at least I will not keep this old fellow from all the dinners he has yet to come." For in Japan they say that all the turtles live to be a thousand years old.

So the kindhearted Urashima tumbled him back into the water, and what a splash he made! But from the spray there seemed to rise a beautiful girl who stepped into the boat with Urashima. She said to him: "I am the daughter of the sea-god. I was that turtle you just threw back into the water. My father sent me to see if you were as kind as you seemed, and I see that you are. We who live under the water say that those who love the sea can never be unkind. Will you come with us to the dragon palace far below the green waves?"

Urashima was very glad to go, so each took an oar and away they sped.

Long before the sun had sunk behind the purple bars of evening, Urashima and the Dragon Princess had reached the twilight depths of the under sea. The fishes scudded about them through branches of coral and trailing ropes of seaweed. The roar of the waves above came to them only as a trembling murmur, to make the silence sweeter.

Here was the dragon palace of seashell and pearl, of coral and emerald. It gleamed with all the thousand lights and tints that lurk in the depths of the water. Fishes with silver fins were ready to come at their wish. The daintiest foods that the ocean holds for her children were served to them. Their waiters were seven dragons, each with a golden tail.

Urashima lived in a dream of happiness with the Dragon Princess for four short years. Then he remembered his home, and longed to see his father and his kindred once again. He wished to see the village streets and the wave-lapped stretch of sand where he used to play.

He did not need to tell the princess of his wish, for she knew it all, and said: "I see that you long for your home once more; I will not keep you, but I fear to have you go. Still I know you will wish to come back, so take this box and let nothing happen to it, for if it is opened you can never return."

She then placed him in his boat and the lapping waves bore him up and away until his prow crunched on the sand where he used to play.

Around that bend in the bay stood his father's cottage, close by the great pine tree. But as he came nearer he saw neither tree nor house. He looked around. The other houses, too, looked strange. Strange children were peering at him. Strange people walked the streets. He wondered at the change in four short years.

An old man came along the shore. To him Urashima spoke.

"Can you tell me, sir, where the cottage of Urashima has gone?"

"Urashima?" said the old man. "Urashima! Why, don't you know that he was drowned four hundred years ago, while out fishing? His brothers, their children, and their children's children have all lived and died since then. Four hundred years ago it was, on a summer day like this, they say."

Gone! His father and mother, his brothers and playmates, and the cottage he loved so well. How he longed to see them; but he must hurry back to the dragon palace, for now that was his only home. But how should he go? He walked along the shore, but could not remember the way to take. Forgetting the promise he had made to the princess, he took out the little pearl box and opened it. From it a white cloud seemed to rise, and as it floated away he thought he saw the face of the Dragon Princess. He called to her, reached for her, but the cloud was already floating far out over the waves.

As it floated away he suddenly seemed to grow old. His hands shook and his hair turned white. He seemed to be melting away to join the past in which he had lived.

When the new moon hung her horn of light in the branches of the pine tree, there was only a small pearl box on the sandy rim of shore, and the great green waves were lifting white arms of foam as they had done four hundred years before.

121. THE MAGIC KETTLE
(Japan)

RIGHT IN THE MIDDLE of Japan, high up among the mountains, an old man lived in his little house. He was very proud of it, and never tired of admiring the whiteness of his straw mats, and the pretty papered walls, which in warm weather always slid back, so that the smell of the trees and flowers might come in.

One day he was standing looking at the mountain opposite, when he heard a kind of rumbling noise in the room behind him. He turned round, and in the corner he beheld a rusty old iron kettle, which could not have seen the light of day for many years. How the kettle got there the old man did not know, but he took it up and looked it over carefully, and when he found that it was quite whole he cleaned the dust off it and carried it into his kitchen.

"That was a piece of luck," he said, smiling to himself; "a good kettle

costs money, and it is as well to have a second one at hand in case of
·need; mine is getting worn out, and the water is already beginning to
come through its bottom."

Then he took the other kettle off the fire, filled the new one with
water, and put it in its place.

No sooner was the water in the kettle getting warm than a strange
thing happened, and the man, who was standing by, thought he must
be dreaming. First the handle of the kettle gradually changed its shape
and became a head, and the spout grew into a tail, while out of the
body sprang four paws, and in a few minutes the man found himself
watching, not a kettle, but a tanuki! The creature jumped off the fire,
and bounded about the room like a kitten, running up the walls and
over the ceiling, till the old man was in an agony lest his pretty room
should be spoiled. He cried to a neighbor for help, and between them
they managed to catch the tanuki, and shut him up safely in a wooden
chest. Then, quite exhausted, they sat down on the mats, and consulted
together what they should do with this troublesome beast. At length
they decided to sell him, and bade a child who was passing send them a
certain tradesman called Jimmu.

When Jimmu arrived, the old man told him that he had something
which he wished to get rid of, and lifted the lid of the wooden chest,
where he had shut up the tanuki. But, to his surprise, no tanuki was
there, nothing but the kettle he had found in the corner. It was certainly very odd, but the man remembered what had taken place on the
fire, and did not want to keep the kettle any more, so after a little bargaining about the price, Jimmu went away carrying the kettle with him.

Now Jimmu had not gone very far before he felt that the kettle was
getting heavier and heavier, and by the time he reached home he was so
tired that he was thankful to put it down in the corner of his room, and
then forgot all about it. In the middle of the night, however, he was
awakened by a loud noise in the corner where the kettle stood, and
raised himself up in bed to see what it was. But nothing was there except the kettle, which seemed quiet enough. He thought that he must
have been dreaming, and fell asleep again, only to be roused a second
time by the same disturbance. He jumped up and went to the corner,
and by the light of the lamp that he always kept burning he saw that
the kettle had become a tanuki, which was running round after his tail.
After he grew weary of that, he ran on the balcony, where he turned
several somersaults, from pure gladness of heart. The tradesman was
much troubled as to what to do with the animal, and it was only to-

ward morning that he managed to get any sleep; but when he opened his eyes again there was no tanuki, only the old kettle he had left there the night before.

As soon as he had tidied his house, Jimmu set off to tell his story to a friend next door. The man listened quietly, and did not appear so surprised as Jimmu expected, for he recollected having heard, in his youth, something about a wonder-working kettle. "Go and travel with it, and show it off," said he, "and you will become a rich man; but be careful first to ask the tanuki's leave, and also to perform some magic ceremonies to prevent him from running away at the sight of the people."

Jimmu thanked his friend for his counsel, which he followed exactly. The tanuki's consent was obtained, a booth was built, and a notice was hung up outside it inviting the people to come and witness the most wonderful transformation that ever was seen.

They came in crowds, and the kettle was passed from hand to hand, and they were allowed to examine it all over, and even to look inside. Then Jimmu took it back, and setting it on the platform, commanded it to become a tanuki. In an instant the handle began to change into a head, and the spout into a tail, while the four paws appeared at the sides. "Dance," said Jimmu, and the tanuki did his steps, and moved first on one side and then on the other, till the people could not stand still any longer, and began to dance too. Gracefully he led the fan dance, and glided without a pause into the shadow dance and the umbrella dance, and it seemed as if he might go on dancing forever. And so very likely he would, if Jimmu had not declared he had danced enough, and that the booth must now be closed.

Day after day the booth was so full it was hardly possible to enter it, and what the neighbor foretold had come to pass, and Jimmu was a rich man. Yet he did not feel happy. He was an honest man, and he thought that he owed some of his wealth to the man from whom he had bought the kettle. So, one morning, he put a hundred gold pieces into it, and hanging the kettle once more on his arm, he returned to the seller of it. "I have no right to keep it any longer," he added when he had ended his tale, "so I have brought it back to you, and inside you will find a hundred gold pieces as the price of its hire."

The man thanked Jimmu, and said that few people would have been as honest as he. And the kettle brought them both luck, and everything went well with them till they died, which they did when they were very old, respected by everyone.

122. A TAOIST PRIEST
(*China*)

ONCE UPON A TIME there was a Mr. Han, who belonged to a wealthy family and was fond of entertaining people. A man named Hsü, of the same town, frequently joined him over the bottle; and on one occasion when they were together a Taoist priest came to the door with his alms bowl in his hand. The servants threw him some money and food, but the priest would not accept them, neither would he go away; and at length the servants took no more notice of him. Mr. Han finally heard the noise of the priest knocking his bowl and asked his servants what was the matter; and they had hardly told him when the priest himself walked in. Mr. Han begged him to be seated; whereupon the priest bowed to both gentlemen and took his seat.

On making the usual inquiries, they found that he lived in an old tumbledown temple to the east of the town, and Mr. Han expressed regret at not having heard sooner of his arrival, so that he might have shown him the proper hospitality of a resident. The priest said that he had only recently arrived and had no friends in the place; but hearing that Mr. Han was a jovial fellow, he had been very anxious to take a glass with him. Mr. Han then ordered wine, and the priest soon distinguished himself as a hard drinker; Mr. Hsü treated him with a certain amount of disrespect in consequence of his shabby appearance, but Mr. Han made allowances for him as being a traveler. When he had drunk over twenty large cups of wine, the priest took his leave, returning subsequently whenever any jollification was going on, no matter whether it was eating or drinking. Even Han began to tire a little of him; and on one occasion Hsü said to him in raillery, "Good priest, you seem to like being a guest; why don't you play the host sometimes for a change?"

"Ah," replied the priest, "I am much the same as yourself—a mouth carried between a couple of shoulders."

This put Hsü to shame, and he had no answer to make; so the priest continued, "But although that is so, I have been revolving the question with myself for some time, and when you visit me I shall do my best to repay your kindness with a cup of my own poor wine."

When they had finished drinking, the priest said he hoped he should have the pleasure of their company the following day at noon; and at the appointed time the two friends went together, not expecting, however, to find anything ready for them. But the priest was waiting for them in the street; and, passing through a handsome courtyard, they beheld long suites of elegant apartments stretching away before them. In great astonishment, they remarked to the priest that they had not visited this temple for some time and asked when it had been thus repaired; to which he replied that the work had been only lately completed. They then went inside, and there was a magnificently decorated apartment, such as would not be found even in the houses of the wealthy. This made them begin to feel more respect for their host; and no sooner had they sat down than wine and food were served by a number of boys, all about sixteen years of age, and dressed in embroidered coats, with red shoes. The drink and the food were delicious, and very nicely served; and when the dinner was taken away, so many rare fruits were put on the table that it would be impossible to mention the names of all of them. They were arranged in dishes of crystal and jade, the brilliancy of which lighted up the surrounding furniture; and the goblets in which the wine was poured were of glass, and more than a foot in circumference.

The priest here cried out, "Call the Shih sisters," whereupon one of the boys went out and in a few moments two elegant young ladies walked in. The first was tall and slim like a willow wand; the other was short and very young. Both were exceedingly pretty. Being told to sing while the company were drinking, the younger beat time and sang a song, while the elder accompanied her on the flageolet. They acquitted themselves admirably; and, when the song was over, the priest, holding his goblet bottom upward in the air, challenged his guests to follow his example, bidding his servants pour out more wine all round. He then turned to the girls and, remarking that they had not danced for a long time, asked if they were still able to do so; upon which a carpet was spread by one of the boys, and the two young ladies proceeded to dance, their long robes waving about and perfuming the air around. The dance concluded, they leaned against a painted screen, while the two guests gradually became more and more befuddled and were at last completely drunk.

The priest took no notice of them; but when he had finished drinking, he got up and said, "Pray, go on with your wine; I am going to rest awhile and will return by and by." He then went away and lay down on a splendid couch at the other end of the room; at which Hsü was very angry and shouted out, "Priest, you are a rude fellow," at the same time making toward him with a view to rousing him. The priest then ran out, and Han and Hsü lay down to sleep, one at each end of the room, on elaborately carved couches covered with beautiful mattresses.

When they woke up they found themselves lying in the road, Mr. Hsü with his head in a dirty drain. Hard by were a couple of rush huts; but everything else was gone.

123. SIMPLE WANG
(China)

NOW I MUST TELL you of Simple Wang. He once lived in a village whose name is no longer even remembered. Only a rough path led to this village, and it led no farther. So no travelers passed through, no caravans of merchants, no cavalcades of officials. The villagers lived in an insignificant way, cut off from the benefits of refined conversation.

They were a simple people, but among them Wang was renowned for being simple to the point of stupidity.

Very early one summer morning, when the scent of the gwehwa tree sweetened the dewy air, he stood manfully outside his modest home, about to make a journey to the city. He had already shouldered his long carrying pole, and from it, before him and behind, hung wide bamboo baskets stacked high with charcoal. He had never before been to the city, or for that matter anywhere else. His wife had urged him to undertake this adventure. She hoped that a fine profit might be made from selling charcoal to prudent citizens who had the coming winter's bleakness in mind.

Wang, with a desperate heave, took up the weight of his load and set off briskly, with the little tripping steps of those who carry great burdens. For a short way his young wife ran beside him. "Go safely," she begged. "Return prosperous, and bring me back a present."

She was very pretty. So Wang, grunting a little under his load, asked what he should bring.

"A new comb," cried the little, twinkling wife.

"A comb?" said Wang, not being able to think in a moment, full as he was of importance and excitement, exactly what a comb was.

The combs they used in those times were of wood and were curved. His wife pointed with a long finger to the crescent moon which still showed palely in the morning sky. "Like that," she told him, and then, ashamed at having run so far along the public street in daylight, dropped behind and left Wang to pursue his journey.

He, having looked dully at the moon for some time so as to impress it on his mind, now made great haste away from his home toward the unknown city.

On his way, you may be sure, he both saw and heard things too strange to be imagined. That is not so remarkable as the fact that he did arrive safely at the city gates and did after a few days sell all his charcoal at a good price.

In the early evening, relieved of his burden and made bold by the possession of a weighty string of cash, he wandered in the jostling city street, where banners of red and yellow, blue and green, hung from shop fronts and balconies, and where the frantic hubbub of clamoring shopmen and shouting buyers made everyone smile with happiness.

Suddenly, out of nowhere, Wang remembered his wife's present. He stood stock still, while hurrying people pushed round him, jolted against him, and all but trod over him. Wang did not even notice them. Now, what did I say I would buy? he was anxiously asking himself. He had not the least idea what it was—until he remembered the moon. With a chuckle of relief, he looked upward to where a thin strip of sky could be seen between the close-leaning shop roofs. Looking down toward the street's end, he saw the moon. It was full now and hung low and white in the evening light.

"Something round," thought Wang, a little bewildered. The idea of roundness did not suggest anything to him. Scratching his head in perplexity, he edged along by the open shops. Almost at once he saw what he wanted. It was quite round. It could not be any rounder, thought Wang, almost hugging himself with satisfaction.

So without haggling over the price and without inspecting his purchase, he paid what was asked, and wrapping it in a piece of cotton cloth, hurried off, with only a casual bow to the shopkeeper.

What Wang had bought was a mirror. He did not even know what a mirror was. No person in his village had ever owned one or seen one; nor had any of them heard of such a thing.

The same favorable spirits who had protected Wang in his going must also have presided over his homecoming, for he reached his own village after a journey of many days, unhurt, unplundered, and still clutching the gift for his wife.

Alone with her, he produced the present. Trembling with excitement, the little wife seized the parcel and opened it. Her cry of dismay when she perceived that this was not a comb changed to lamentation when, looking into the mirror, she saw her own pretty face.

"*Ayee-ah!*" she wailed. "My husband has brought back a beautiful new wife." (For I must tell you that in these parts at this time a man might have more than one wife.)

The poor girl's unhappiness was extreme. Crying and complaining, she ran off to the house of her father, which, happily, was but a short distance down the street.

There she flung herself at her mother's feet.

"My husband has brought home a new wife," she wailed, handing her mother the mirror.

The mother took up the strange thing with great caution. Then, looking in it, she saw her own face.

"Well, Daughter," she said, "if your honorable husband had to bring home a second wife, he need not, surely, have chosen an ugly old hag like this one."

Who can tell where this sad misunderstanding might have led them all, had not it been decided to take the strange matter to the village magistrate?

He, as simple as any of them, took up the mirror. He looked at it. How could he know that it was his own image that he saw there? He thought at once that some waggish person had dressed up to look like him.

"Impertinent creature!" he said with cold anger. "With what shameless freedom do you show your contempt for the law when in coming before me you make a mock of my appearance?"

And he ordered them all—Wang, the pretty wife, and mother-in-law —to be whipped.

That was bad. But while they all three resisted this punishment with great strugglings and loud lamentations, the mirror was broken.

And that was good, wasn't it?

124. FAITHFUL EVEN IN DEATH
(*China*)

THE VILLAGE OF THE Liang family and that of the Chu family were close together. The inhabitants were well-to-do and content. Old excellency Liang and old excellency Chu were good friends. A son was born to the Liang family, who was given the name Hsienpo. Being an unusually quick and clever child, he was sent to the school in the town.

At the same time a daughter was born to the Chu family, who, besides being very clever, was particularly beautiful. As a child she loved to read and study, and only needed to glance at a book to know a whole sentence by heart. Old Chu simply doted on her. When she grew up, she wanted to go away and study. Her father tried in vain to dissuade her, but eventually he arranged for her to dress as a boy and study with Hsienpo.

The two lived together, worked together, argued together, and were the best of friends. The eager and zealous Hsienpo did not notice that Yingt'ai was really a girl, and therefore he did not fall in love with her. Yingt'ai studied so hard and was so wrapped up in her work that her fellow students paid no attention to her. Being very modest, and never taking part in the children's jokes, she exercised a calming influence over even the most impudent. When she slept with Hsienpo, each lay on one side of the bed, and between them stood a bowl of water. They had arranged that whoever knocked over the bowl must pay a fine; but the serious little Hsienpo never touched it.

When Yingt'ai changed her clothes, she never stood about naked but pulled on her clean clothes under the old ones, which she then took off and finished dressing. Her fellow students could not understand why she did this, and asked her the reason. "Only peasants expose the body they have received from their parents," she said; "it should not be done." Then the boys began to copy her, not knowing her real reason was to prevent their noticing that she was a girl.

Then her father died, and her sister-in-law, who did not approve of Yingt'ai's studying, ordered her to come home and learn housework. But Yingt'ai refused and continued to study.

The sister-in-law, fearing that Yingt'ai had fallen in love with Hsienpo, used to send her from time to time babies' things, swaddling clothes, children's clothes and covers, and many other things. The students became curious when they saw the things, and Yingt'ai could tell them only that they were the things she herself had used as a child, which her sister-in-law was now sending her to keep.

The time passed quickly. Soon Yingt'ai and Hsienpo were grown up. Yingt'ai still dressed as a man, and being a well-brought-up girl, she did not dare to ask Hsienpo to marry her; but when she looked at him, her heart was filled with love. His delicate manner attracted her irresistibly, and she swore to marry him and none other.

She proposed the marriage to her sister-in-law, who did not consider it suitable, because after her father's death they had lost all their money. Against Yingt'ai's will the sister-in-law arranged a match with a Dr. Ma, of a newly rich family in the village. Yingt'ai objected strongly, but she could do nothing about it. Day after day she had to listen to complaints: she was without filial piety, she was a shameless, decadent girl, a disgrace to the family. Her sister-in-law still feared she might secretly marry Hsienpo, and she urged the Ma family to appoint a day for the wedding. Then she cut off Yingt'ai's school money, which forced her to return home.

Yingt'ai was obliged to hide her misery. Weeping bitterly, she said good-bye to Hsienpo, who accompanied her part of the way home. As they separated, Yingt'ai sang a song which revealed that she was a girl and that she wanted to marry him. But the good, dense Hsienpo did not understand her hints. He did not see into Yingt'ai's heart, and tried to comfort her by telling her that one must return home some time and that they would soon meet again. Yingt'ai saw that everything was hopeless, and went home in tears.

Hsienpo felt very lonely without his companion, with whom he had lived day and night for many years. He kept on writing letters to Yingt'ai, begging her to come back to school, but he never received a reply.

Finally he could bear it no longer, and went to visit her. "Is Mr.

Yingt'ai at home?" he asked. "Please tell him his school friend, Hsienpo, has come and wants to see him."

The servant looked at him curiously, and then said curtly, "There is no Mr. Yingt'ai here—only a Miss Yingt'ai. She is to be married soon, and naturally she can't leave her room. How could she speak to a man? Please go away, sir, for if the master discovers you, he will make a complaint against you for improper behavior."

Suddenly everything was clear to Hsienpo. In a state of collapse he crept home. There he found, under Yingt'ai's books, a bundle of letters and essays which showed him clearly how deeply Yingt'ai loved him and also that she did not want to marry any other man. Through his own stupidity, his lack of understanding, the dream had come to nought.

Overcome by remorse, he spent the days lost in tears. Yingt'ai was always before his eyes, and in his dreams he called her name, or cursed her sister-in-law and Dr. Ma, himself, and all the ways of society. Because he ceased to eat or drink, he fell ill and gradually sank into the grave.

Yingt'ai heard the sad news. Now she had nothing more to live for. If she had not been so carefully watched, she would have done herself some injury. In this state of despair the wedding day arrived. Listlessly she allowed herself to be pushed into the red bridal chair and set off for the house of her bridegroom, Dr. Ma. But when they passed the grave of Hsienpo, she begged her attendants to let her get out and visit it, to thank him for all his kindness. On the grave, overcome by grief, she flung herself down and sobbed. Her attendants urged her to return to her chair, but she refused. Finally, after great persuasion, she got up, dried her tears, and, bowing several times in front of the grave, she prayed as follows: "You are Hsienpo, and I am Yingt'ai. If we were really intended to be man and wife, open your grave three feet wide."

Scarcely had she spoken when there came a clap like thunder and the grave opened. Yingt'ai leaped into the opening, which closed again before the maids could catch hold of her, leaving only two bits of her dress in their hands. When they let these go, they changed into two butterflies which flew up into the air.

Dr. Ma was furious when he heard that his wife had jumped into the grave of Hsienpo. He had the grave opened, but the coffin was empty except for two white stones. No one knew where Hsienpo and Yingt'ai had gone. In a rage the grave violators flung the two stones onto the road, where immediately a bamboo with two stems shot up. They were shimmering green, and swayed in the wind. The grave robbers knew that this was the result of magic, and cut down the bamboo with a knife; but as soon as they had cut down one, another shot up, until finally several people cut down the two stems at the same time. Then these flew up to heaven and became rainbows.

Now the two lovers have become immortals. If they ever want to be together, undisturbed and unseen, so that no one on earth can see them or even talk about them, they wait until it is raining and the clouds are hiding the sky. The red in the rainbow is Hsienpo, and the blue is Yingt'ai.

125. THE YOUNG HEAD OF THE FAMILY
(China)

THERE WAS ONCE a family consisting of a father, his three sons, and his two daughters-in-law. The two daughters-in-law, wives of the two elder sons, had but recently been brought into the house, and were both from one village a few miles away. Having no mother-in-law living, they were obliged to appeal to their father-in-law whenever they wished to visit their former homes, and as they were lonesome and homesick they perpetually bothered the old man by asking leave of absence.

Vexed by these constant petitions, he set himself to invent a method of putting an end to them, and at last gave them leave in this wise: "You are always begging me to allow you to go and visit your mothers, and thinking that I am very hardhearted because I do not let you go. Now you may go, but only upon condition that when you come back you will each bring me something I want. The one shall bring me some fire wrapped in paper, and the other some wind in a paper. Unless you promise to bring me these, you are never to ask me to let you go home; and if you go, and fail to get these for me, you are never to come back."

The old man did not suppose that these conditions would be accepted, but the girls were young and thoughtless, and in their anxiety to get away did not consider the impossibility of obtaining the articles required. So they made ready with speed, and in great glee started off on foot to visit their mothers. After they had walked a long distance, chatting about what they should do and whom they should see in their native village, the high heel of one of them slipped from under her foot, and she fell down. Owing to this mishap both stopped to adjust the misplaced footgear, and while doing this the conditions under which alone they could return to their husbands came to mind, and they began to cry.

While they sat there crying by the roadside a young girl came riding along from the fields on a water buffalo. She stopped and asked them what was the matter, and whether she could help them. They told her she could do them no good; but she persisted in offering her sympathy and inviting their confidence, till they told her their story, and then she at once said that if they would go home with her she would show them a way out of their trouble. Their case seemed so hopeless to themselves, and the child was so sure of her own power to help them, that they finally accompanied her to her father's house, where she showed them how to comply with their father-in-law's demand.

For the first a paper lantern only would be needed. When lighted it would be a fire, and its paper surface would compass the blaze, so that it would truly be "some fire wrapped in paper." For the second a paper fan would suffice. When flapped, wind would issue from it, and the "wind wrapped in paper" could thus be carried to the old man.

The two young women thanked the wise child, and went on their way rejoicing. After a pleasant visit to their old homes, they took a lantern and a fan, and returned to their father-in-law's house. As soon as he saw them he began to vent his anger at their light regard for his commands, but they assured him that they had perfectly obeyed him, and showed him that what they had brought fulfilled the conditions prescribed. Much astonished, he inquired how it was that they had suddenly become so astute, and they told him the story of their journey, and of the little girl who had so opportunely come to their relief. He inquired whether the little girl was already betrothed, and, finding that she was not, engaged a go-between to see if he could get her for a wife for his youngest son.

Having succeeded in securing the girl as a daughter-in-law, he brought her home, and told all the rest of the family that as there was no mother in the house, and as this girl had shown herself to be possessed of extraordinary wisdom, she should be the head of the household.

The wedding festivities being over, the sons of the old man made ready to return to their usual occupations on the farm; but, according to their father's order, they came to the young bride for instructions. She told them that they were never to go to or from the fields empty-handed. When they went they must carry fertilizers of some sort for the land, and when they returned they must bring bundles of sticks for fuel. They obeyed, and soon had the land in fine condition, and so much fuel gathered that none need be bought. When there were no more sticks, roots, or weeds to bring, she told them to bring stones instead; and they soon accumulated an immense pile of stones, which were heaped in a yard near their house.

One day an expert in the discovery of precious stones came along, and saw in this pile a block of jade of great value. In order to get possession of this stone at a small cost, he undertook to buy the whole heap, pretending that he wished to use them in building. The little head of the family asked an exorbitant price for them, and, as he could not induce her to take less, he promised to pay her the sum she asked, and to come two days later to bring the money and to remove the stones. That night the girl thought about the reason for the buyer's being willing to pay so large a sum for the stones, and concluded that the heap must contain a gem. The next morning she sent her father-in-law to invite the buyer to supper, and she instructed the men of her family in regard to his entertainment. The best of wine was to be provided, and the father-in-law was to induce him to talk of precious stones, and to cajole him into telling in what way they were to be distinguished from other stones.

The head of the family, listening behind a curtain, heard how the valuable stone in her heap could be discovered. She hastened to find and remove it from the pile; and, when her guest had recovered from the effect of the banquet, he saw that the value had departed from his purchase. He went to negotiate again with the seller and she conducted the conference with such skill that she obtained the price originally agreed upon for the heap of stones, and a large sum besides for the one in her possession.

The family, having become wealthy, built an ancestral hall of fine design and elaborate workmanship, and put the words "No Sorrow" as an inscription over the entrance. Soon after, a mandarin passed that way, and, noticing this remarkable inscription, had his sedan-chair set down, that he might inquire who were the people that professed to have no sorrow. He sent for the head of the family, was much surprised on seeing so young a woman thus appear, and remarked: "Yours is a singular family. I have never before seen one without sorrow, nor one with so young a head. I will fine you for your impudence. Go and weave me a piece of cloth as long as this road."

"Very well," responded the little woman; "so soon as your Excellency shall have found the two ends of the road, and informed me as to the number of feet in its length, I will at once begin the weaving."

Finding himself at fault, the mandarin added, "And I also fine you as much oil as there is water in the sea."

"Certainly," responded the woman; "as soon as you shall have measured the sea, and sent me correct information as to the number of gallons, I will at once begin to press out the oil from my beans."

"Indeed," said the mandarin, "since you are so sharp, perhaps you can penetrate my thoughts. If you can, I will fine you no more. I hold this pet quail in my hand; now tell me whether I mean to squeeze it to death, or to let it fly in the air."

"Well," said the woman, "I am an obscure commoner, and you are a famed magistrate; if you are no more knowing than I, you have no right to fine me at all. Now I stand with one foot on one side my threshold and the other foot on the other side; tell me whether I mean to go in or come out. If you cannot guess my riddle, you should not require me to guess yours."

Being unable to guess her intention the mandarin took his departure, and the family lived long in opulence and good repute under its chosen head.

126. THE MOST FRUGAL OF MEN
(China)

A MAN WHO WAS considered the most frugal of all the dwellers in a certain kingdom heard of another man who was the most frugal in the whole world. He said to his son thereupon: "We, indeed, live upon little, but if we were more frugal still, we might live upon nothing at all. It will be well worthwhile for us to get instructions in economy from the Most Frugal of Men." The son agreed, and the two decided that the son should go and inquire whether the master in economic science would take pupils. An exchange of presents being a necessary preliminary to closer intercourse, the father told the son to take the smallest of coins, one farthing, and to buy a sheet of paper of the cheapest sort. The boy, by bargaining, got two sheets of paper for the farthing. The father put away one sheet, cut the other sheet in halves, and on one half drew a picture of a pig's head. This he put into a large covered basket, as if it were the thing which it represented—the usual gift sent in token of great respect. The son took the basket, and after a long journey reached the abode of the most frugal man in the world.

The master of the house was absent, but his son received the traveler, learned his errand, and accepted the offering. Having taken from the basket the picture of the pig's head, he said courteously to his visitor: "I am sorry that we have nothing in the house that is worthy to take the place of the pig's head in your basket. I will, however, signify our friendly reception of it by putting in four oranges for you to take home with you."

Thereupon the young man, without having any oranges at hand, made the motions necessary for putting the fruit into the basket. The son of the most frugal man in the kingdom then took the basket and went to his father to tell of thrift surpassing his own.

When the most frugal man in the world returned home, his son told him that a visitor had been there, having come from a great distance to take lessons in economy. The father inquired what offering he brought as an introduction, and the son showed the small outline of the pig's head on thin brown paper. The father looked at it, and then asked his son what he had sent as a return present. The son told him he had merely made the motions necessary for transferring four oranges, and showed how he had clasped the imaginary fruit and deposited it in the visitor's basket. The father immediately flew into a terrible rage and boxed the boy's ears, exclaiming: "You extravagant wretch! With your fingers thus far apart you appeared to give him large oranges. Why didn't you measure out small ones?"

127. THE MAGIC BROCADE

(*China*)

ONCE UPON A TIME, long, long ago, there lived in a small village in the southern part of China a mother and her three sons. Since the poor woman was a widow, she had to support her growing family as best she could. Fortunately she was very skilled at weaving fine brocade. This material was a specialty of the Chuang area where they lived and it was made of rich fabric with designs of silver, gold, and silk woven upon it. The widow was quite famous in the surrounding countryside for her brocades, as she had a special talent for making the birds and other animals and the flowers that she wove into her cloth appear lifelike. Some people even said that her flowers and animals and birds were even *more* beautiful than real ones.

One day the widow had to go into the market place to sell some cloth she had just finished. It took her no time at all to get rid of it, for everyone was anxious to buy her work. When she had completed her business she strolled among the stalls, looking at all the interesting objects for sale. Suddenly her glance was caught by a beautiful picture and she paused. In the painting was a marvelous white house surrounded by vast fields and grand walks which led to glorious gardens bursting with fruit and flowers. Between the stately trees in the background could be glimpsed some smaller buildings, and among the fluttering leaves flew rare brightly plumed birds of all kinds. Instantly the widow fell in love with the picture and bought it. When she got home she showed it to her three sons, who also thought it was very beautiful.

"Oh," sighed the widow, "wouldn't it be wonderful if we lived in such a place!"

The two elder sons shook their heads and laughed.

"My dear mother, that's only an idle dream," said the eldest.

"Perhaps it might happen in the next world," agreed the second son, "but not in this one."

Only the youngest son comforted her.

"Why don't you weave a copy of the picture into a brocade?" he suggested. With a gentle smile on his face, he added, "That will be nearly as good as living in it."

This thought made the mother very happy. Right away she went out and bought all the colored silk yarns she needed. Then she set up her loom and began to weave the design of the painting into the brocade.

Day and night, month after month, the mother sat at her loom weaving her silks. Though her back ached and her eyes grew strained from the exacting work, still she would not stop. She worked as if possessed. Gradually the two elder sons became annoyed.

One day the eldest one said with irritation, "Mother, you weave all day but you never sell anything."

"Yes!" grumbled the second. "And we have to earn money for the rice you eat by chopping wood. We're tired of all this hard work."

The youngest son didn't want his mother to be worried. He told his brothers not to complain and promised that he would look after everything. From then on, every morning he went up the mountain by himself and chopped enough wood to take care of the whole family.

Day after day the mother continued her weaving. At night she burned pine branches to make enough light. The branches smoked so much that her eyes became sore and bloodshot. But still she would not stop.

A year passed.

Tears from the mother's eyes began to drop upon the picture. She wove the crystal liquid into a bright clear river and also into a charming little fish pond.

Another year went by.

Now the tears from the mother's eyes turned into blood and dropped like red jewels upon the cloth. Quickly she wove them into a flaming sun and into brilliant red flowers.

Hour after hour, without a moment's stop, the widow went on weaving.

Finally, at the end of the third year, her brocade was done. The mother stepped away from her work and smiled with pride and with great happiness. There it all was: the beautiful house, the breathtaking gardens filled with exotic flowers and fruit, the brilliant birds, and beyond in the vast fields sheep and cattle grazing contentedly upon the grass.

Suddenly a great wind from the west howled through the house. Catching up the rare brocade it sped through the door and disappeared over the hill. Frantically the mother chased after her beautiful treasure, only to see it blown high into the sky, far beyond her reach. It flew straight toward the east and in a twinkling it had completely vanished.

The heartbroken mother, unable to bear such a calamity, fell into a deep faint. Carefully her three sons carried her into the house and laid her upon the bed. Hours later, after sipping some ginger broth, the widow slowly came to herself.

"My son," she implored her eldest, "go to the east and find my brocade for me. It means more to me than life."

The boy nodded and quickly set out on his journey. After traveling eastward for more than a month, he came to a mountain pass where an old white-haired woman sat in front of a stone house. Beside her stood a handsome stone horse which looked as though it longed to eat the red fruit off the pretty tree that grew next to it. As the eldest boy passed by, the old lady stopped him.

"Where are you going, young man?" she asked.

"East," he said, and told her the story of the brocade.

"Ah!" she said, "the brocade your mother wove has been carried away by the fairies of the Sun Mountain because it was so beautifully made. They are going to copy it."

"But, tell me, how can I recover it?" begged the boy.

"That will be very difficult," said the old woman. "First, you have to knock out two of your front teeth and put them into the mouth of my stone horse. Then he will be able to move and to eat the red fruit hanging from this tree. When he has eaten ten pieces, then you can mount him. He will take you directly to the Sun Mountain. But first you will have to pass through the Flame Mountain which burns with a continuous fierceness." Here the old lady offered a warning. "You must not utter a word of complaint, for if you do you will instantly be burned to ashes. When you have arrived at the other side, you must then cross an icy sea." With a grave nod she whispered, "And if you give the slightest shudder, you will immediately sink to the bottom."

After hearing all this, the eldest son felt his jaw and thought anxiously of the burning fire and lashing sea waves. He went white as a ghost.

The old woman looked at him and laughed.

"You won't be able to stand it, I can see," she said. "Don't go. I'll give you a small iron box full of gold. Take it and live comfortably."

She fetched the box of gold from the stone house and gave it to the boy. He took it happily and went away. On his way home he began thinking about all the money he now had. "This gold will enable me to live very well. If I take it home, I will have to share it. Spending it all on myself will be much more fun than spending it on four people." He decided right then and there not to go home and turned instead to the path which led to a big city.

At home the poor mother waited two months for her eldest son to return, but he did not come back. Gradually her illness got worse. At length she sent her second son to bring the brocade back.

When the boy reached the mountain pass he came upon the old woman at the stone house, who told him the same things she had told his older brother. As he learned all that he must do in order to obtain the brocade, he became frightened and his face paled. Laughing, the woman offered him a box of gold, just as she had his brother. Greatly relieved, the boy took it and went on his way, deciding also to head for the city instead of returning home.

After waiting and waiting for the second son to return home, the widow became desperately ill. At last she turned blind from weeping. Still neither of her sons ever came back.

The youngest son, beside himself with worry, begged his mother to let him go in search of the brocade.

"I'll bring it back to you, Mother, I promise."

Faint with exhaustion and despair, the widow nodded weakly.

Traveling swiftly, the youngest son took only half a month to arrive at the mountain pass. There he met the old woman in front of the stone house. She told him exactly the same things that she had told his two brothers, but added, "My son, your brothers each went away with a box of gold. You may have one, too."

With steady firmness the boy refused. "I shall not let these difficulties stop me," he declared. "I am going to bring back the brocade that took my mother three years to weave."

Instantly he knocked two teeth out of his mouth and put them into the mouth of the handsome stone horse. The stone horse came alive and went to the tall green tree and ate ten pieces of red fruit hanging from its branches. As soon as it had done this, the horse lifted its elegant head, tossed its silver mane, and neighed. Quickly the boy mounted its back, and together they galloped off toward the east.

After three days and nights the young son came to Flame Mountain. On every side fires spit forth wildly. The boy stared for a moment at the terrifying sight, then spurring his horse he dashed courageously up the flaming mountain, enduring the ferocious heat without once uttering a sound.

Once on the other side of the mountain, he came to a vast sea. Great waves frosted with chunks of ice crashed upon him as he made his way painfully across the freezing water. Though cold and aching, he held the horse's mane tightly, persisting in his journey without allowing himself to shudder.

Emerging on the opposite shore, he saw at once the Sun Mountain. Warm light flooded the air and flowers blossomed everywhere. On top of the mountain stood a marvelous palace and from it he could hear sounds of girlish laughter and singing.

Quickly the boy tapped his horse. It reared up and flew with great speed to the door of the palace. The boy got down and entered the front hall. There he found one hundred beautiful fairies, each sitting at a loom and weaving a copy of his mother's brocade.

The fairies were all very surprised to see him. One came forth at last and spoke.

"We shall finish our weaving tonight and you may have your mother's brocade tomorrow. Will it please you to wait here for the night?"

"Yes," said the son. He sat down, prepared to wait forever if necessary for his mother's treasure. Several fairies graciously attended him, bringing delicious fruit to refresh him. Instantly all his fatigue disappeared.

When dusk fell, the fairies hung from the center of the ceiling an enormous pearl which shone so brilliantly it lit the entire room. Then, while they went on weaving, the youngest son went to sleep.

One fairy finally finished her brocade, but it was not nearly as well done as the one the widow had made. The sad fairy felt she could not part with the widow's brocade and longed to live in that beautiful human world, so she embroidered a picture of herself on the original work.

When the young son woke up just before daylight, the fairies had all gone, leaving his mother's cloth under the shining pearl. Not waiting for daybreak the boy quickly clasped it to his chest and, mounting his horse, galloped off in the waning moonlight. Bending low upon the stallion's flowing mane and clamping his mouth tightly shut, he passed again through the icy sea and up and down the flaming mountain. Soon he reached the mountain pass where the old woman stood waiting for him in front of her stone house. Smiling warmly, she greeted him.

"Young man, I see you have come back."

"Yes, old woman." After he dismounted, the woman took his teeth from the horse and put them back into his mouth. Instantly the horse turned back to stone. Then she went inside the house and returned with a pair of deerskin shoes.

"Take these," she said, "they will help you get home."

When the boy put them on he found he could move as though he had wings. In a moment he was back in his own house. He entered his mother's room and unrolled the brocade. It gleamed so brightly that the widow gasped and opened her eyes, finding her sight entirely restored. Instantly cured of all illness, she rose from her bed. Together she and her son took the precious work outside to see it in the bright light. As they unrolled it, a strange, fragrant breeze sprang up and blew upon the brocade, drawing it out longer and longer and wider and wider until at last it covered all the land in sight. Suddenly the silken threads trembled and the picture burst into life. Scarlet flowers waved in the soft wind. Animals stirred and grazed upon the tender grasses of the vast fields. Golden birds darted in and out of the handsome trees and about the grand white house that commanded the landscape. It was all exactly as the mother had woven it, except that now there was a beautiful girl in red standing by the fish pond. It was the fairy who had embroidered herself into the brocade.

The kind widow, thrilled with her good fortune, went out among her poor neighbors and asked them to come to live with her on her new land, and share the abundance of her fields and gardens.

It will not surprise you to learn that the youngest son married the beautiful fairy girl and that they lived together very happily for many, many years.

One day two beggars walked slowly down the road. They were the two elder sons of the widow, and it was clear from their appearance that they had long ago squandered all the gold they had. Astonished to see such a beautiful place, they decided to stop and beg something from the owner. But when they looked across the fields, they suddenly recognized that the people happily picnicking by the pretty stream were none other than their very own mother and brother—and a beautiful lady who must be their brother's wife. Blushing with shame, they quickly picked up their begging sticks and crept silently away.

128. PLANTING A PEAR TREE
(*China*)

A COUNTRY MAN was one day selling his pears in the market. They were unusually sweet and fine flavored, and the price he asked was high. A Taoist priest in rags and tatters stopped at the barrow and begged one of them. The country man told him to go away, but when he did not do so the country man began to curse and swear at him. The priest said, "You have several hundred pears on your barrow; I ask for a single one, the loss of which, sir, you would not feel. Why then get angry?"

The lookers-on told the country man to give the man an inferior one and let him go, but this he obstinately refused to do. Thereupon the beadle of the place, finding the commotion too great, purchased a pear and handed it to the priest. The latter received it with a bow and, turning to the crowd, said, "We who have left our homes and given up all that is dear to us are at a loss to understand selfish, niggardly conduct in others. Now I have some exquisite pears which I shall do myself the honor to put before you."

Here somebody asked, "Since you have pears yourself, why don't you eat those?"

"Because," replied the priest, "I wanted one of these pips to grow them from." So saying, he munched the pear; and when he had finished took a pip in his hand, unstrapped a pick from his back, and proceeded to make a hole in the ground, several inches deep, wherein he deposited the pip, filling in the earth as before. He then asked the bystanders for a little hot water to water it with, and one among them who loved a joke fetched him some boiling water from a neighboring shop. The priest poured this over the place where he had made the hole, and every eye was turned upon him when sprouts were seen shooting up and gradually growing larger and larger. By and by there was a tree with branches sparsely covered with leaves; then flowers, and last of all fine, large, sweet-smelling pears hanging in great profusion. These the priest picked and handed round to the assembled crowd until all were gone, whereupon he took his pick and hacked away for a long time at the tree, finally cutting it down. This he shouldered, leaves and all, and sauntered quietly away.

Now, from the very beginning, our friend the country man had been among the crowd, straining his neck to see what was going on and forgetting all about his business. At the departure of the priest he turned round and discovered that every one of his pears was gone. He then knew that those the old fellow had been giving away so freely were really his own pears. Looking more closely at the barrow, he also found that one of the handles was missing, evidently having been newly cut off. Boiling with rage, he set out in pursuit of the priest, but just as he turned the corner he saw the lost barrow handle lying under the wall, being in fact the very pear tree the priest had cut down. But there were no traces of the priest—much to the amusement of the crowd in the market place.

129. THE GROOM'S CRIMES
(China)

LORD CHING, THE MARQUIS of Ch'i, assigned a groom to care for his favorite horse. But the horse died suddenly, and the lord was furious. He ordered his men to cut off the groom's limbs.

It happened that Yen Tzu was attending the lord, and when the lord's men entered, their swords at the ready, Yen Tzu stopped them. He said to Lord Ching, "In the time of the sage-kings Yao and Shun, who ruled by example only, if anyone was to be dismembered, whose limbs would they begin with?"

"With the king's own limbs," said Lord Ching. And he canceled the punishment. Instead he gave orders to have the groom condemned to death by due process.

"In that case," said Yen Tzu, "the man will die ignorant of his

the approaching fish struck at insects. He took up his net and got several, each a foot long.

Delighted, Hsü thanked the young man and started home. Then he turned to offer his benefactor some fish, but the young man declined, saying, "I have often enjoyed your delicious brew. For my trifling assistance it's not worth speaking of reciprocity. In fact, if you wouldn't refuse my company, I'd like to make a custom of it."

"We have spent only an evening together," answered Hsü. "What do you mean by 'often enjoyed'? But it would be a pleasure if you kept visiting me, though I'm afraid I don't have anything to repay your kindness." Then he asked the young man his name.

"I am a Wang," was the reply, "but have no given name. You could call me 'Liu-lang,' or 'Sixth-born,' when we meet." And thus they parted.

Next day Hsü sold his fish and bought more wine. In the evening the young man was already there when Hsü arrived at the riverbank, so they had the pleasure of drinking together again. And again after several rounds the young man suddenly whisked away to drive the fish for Hsü.

Things went on agreeably like this for half a year when out of the blue Liu-lang announced to Hsü, "Ever since I had the honor of your acquaintance, we have been closer than closest kin. But the day of parting has come." His voice was filled with sadness.

Hsü was surprised and asked why. The young man started to speak and then stopped several times until he said at last, "Close as we are, the reason may shock you. But now that we are to part, there's no harm in telling you the plain truth: I'm a ghost, one with a weakness for wine. I died by drowning when I was drunk, and I have been here for several years. The reason you always caught more fish than anyone else is that I was secretly driving them toward you in thanks for your libations. But tomorrow my term of karma ends, and a replacement for me will be coming. I'm to be reborn into another life on earth. This evening is all that remains for us to share, and it is hard not to feel sad."

Hsü was frightened at first, but they had been close friends for so long that his fear abated. He sighed deeply over the news, poured a drink, and said, "Liu-lang, drink this up and don't despair. If our ways must part, that's reason enough for regret; but if your karmic lot is fulfilled and your term of suffering relieved, that's cause for congratulation, not sorrow." And together they shared a deep swig of wine. "Who will replace you?" asked Hsü.

"You'll see from the riverbank. At high noon a woman will drown as she crosses the river. That will be the one!" As the roosters in the hamlet called forth the dawn, the two drinkers parted, shedding tears.

The next day Hsü watched expectantly from the edge of the river. A woman came carrying a baby in her arms. As she reached the river, she fell. She tossed the child to shore, then began crying and flailing her hands and feet. She surfaced and sank several times until she pulled herself out, streaming water. Then she rested a little while, took her child in her arms, and left.

When the woman was sinking, Hsü could not bear it and wished he could rush to her rescue. He held back only because he remembered that she was to replace Liu-lang. But when the woman got herself out he began to doubt what Liu-lang had told him.

At dusk Hsü went fishing in the usual spot. Again his friend came and said to him, "Now we are together again and need not speak of parting for the time being." When Hsü asked why, Liu-lang replied, "The woman had already taken my place, but I had pity for the child in her arms. Two should not be lost for one, and so I spared them. When I will be replaced is not known, and so it seems that the brotherhood between us shall continue."

Hsü sighed with deep feeling. "Such a humane heart should be seen by the Highest in Heaven." And so they had the pleasure of each other's company as before.

Several days later, however, Liu-lang came to say good-bye again. Hsü thought he had found another replacement, but Liu-lang said, "No, my compassionate thought for the drowning woman actually reached to heaven, and I have been rewarded with a position as local deity in Wu township of Chauyüan county. I assume office tomorrow. Please remember our friendship and visit me; don't worry about the length or difficulty of the journey."

"What a comfort to have someone as upright as you for a deity," said Hsü, offering his congratulations. "But no road connects men and gods. Even if the distance did not daunt me, how could I manage to go?"

"Simply go; don't think about it," replied the young man. After repeating the invitation, he left.

Hsü went home to put his things in order and set out at once, though his wife mocked him. "You're going hundreds of miles? Even if this place exists, I don't think you can hold a conversation with a clay idol!" she sneered. Hsü paid no attention. He started off and eventually arrived in Chauyüan county, where he learned that there really was a Wu township. On his way there he stopped at a hostel and asked for directions to the temple. The host said with an air of pleasant surprise, "By any chance is our guest's surname Hsü?"

"Yes, how did you know?"

The host left abruptly without making a reply. Presently a mixed throng approached and circled Hsü like a wall; men carried their babies, women peeped around their doors. The crowd announced to an amazed Hsü, "Several nights ago we had a dream in which our deity said that a friend named Hsü would be coming and that we should help him out with his traveling expenses. We have been respectfully awaiting you." Marveling at this reception, Hsü went to sacrifice at the temple.

"Since we parted," he prayed, "my thoughts have dwelled on you night and day. I have come far to keep our agreement, and I am both favored and deeply moved by the sign you gave the local people. But I am embarrassed to have come without a fitting gift. All I brought was a flask of wine. If it is acceptable, let us drink as we used to on the river-bank." His prayer done, Hsü burned paper money. Shortly he saw a wind arise behind the shrine. The smoke swirled around for a time and then disappeared.

That night Liu-lang, looking altogether different now that he was capped and garbed in finery, entered Hsü's dreams. Expressing his appreciation, Liu-lang said, "For you to come so far to see me moves me to tears, but I am unable to meet you directly because I hold such a trivial position. It saddens me to be so near to the living and yet so far. The people here have some meager presents for you as a token of our past association. Whenever you are to return home, I shall see you off myself."

Hsü remained in Wu township a few more days before preparing to leave. The people of Wu tried to keep him longer, making earnest appeals and inviting him to daylong feasts with different hosts. But Hsü was set on returning home. The people outdid themselves in generosity, and before the morning passed his bags were filled with gifts. The gray-haired and the young gathered to see him out of the village. And a whirlwind followed him some three or four miles farther. Hsü bowed again and again. "Take care of yourself, Liu-lang," he said. "Don't bother coming so far. With your humane and loving heart, you can surely bring good fortune to this township without advice from old friends." The wind swirled around for a time and then was gone. The villagers, exclaiming in wonder at these events, also went to their homes.

When Hsü arrived back in his own village, his family's circumstances

had improved so much that he did not return to fishing. Later he saw
people from Chauyüan county who told him that the deity was working
miracles and had become widely known.

The Recorder of Things Strange says: To attain the heights of ambi-
tion without forgetting the friends one made when poor and lowly—that
is what made Wang Liu-lang a god! Nowadays, when do the high and
noble in their carriages recognize those still wearing a bamboo hat?

—*P'u Sung-ling*

133. THE KING'S FAVORITE
(*China*)

IN ANCIENT TIMES the beautiful woman Mi Tzu-hsia was the
favorite of the lord of Wei. Now, according to the law of Wei, anyone
who rode in the king's carriage without permission would be punished
by amputation of the foot. When Mi Tzu-hsia's mother fell ill, someone brought the news to her in the middle of the night. So she took the
king's carriage and went out, and the king only praised her for it. "Such
filial devotion!" he said. "For her mother's sake she risked the punishment of amputation!"

Another day she was dallying with the lord of Wei in the fruit garden. She took a peach, which she found so sweet that instead of finishing it she handed it to the lord to taste. "How she loves me," said the
lord of Wei, "forgetting the pleasure of her own taste to share with
me!"

But when Mi Tzu-hsia's beauty began to fade, the king's affection
cooled. And when she offended the king, he said, "Didn't she once take
my carriage without permission? And didn't she once give me a peach
that she had already chewed on?"

—*Han Fei Tzu*

134. THE CLEVER THIEF
(Korea)

IN KOREA, MANY YEARS ago, there once lived an old thief who was known throughout the country as a very clever person—far too clever to be captured. However, one morning he was so careless and overconfident that he was caught stealing some spices from a shopkeeper. With great satisfaction the police brought the thief before an extremely severe judge who fined the old man very heavily. Unable to pay the sum, the thief had to submit instead to a very lengthy jail sentence. When he arrived at the prison he examined with great thoroughness his cell and the building itself, looking for a means of escape. Finding none, he soon gave up the idea of escape and instead decided upon another way of getting out of jail. Early one morning he called for the jailkeeper.

"Yes," the keeper inquired gruffly, "what do you want?"

"Take me before the king," demanded the thief.

"The king!" The jailkeeper threw back his head and gasped with laughter. "Why should the king see *you?*"

The thief ignored the jailkeeper's scorn.

"Tell him I have a gift for him—of extraordinary value."

The jailkeeper, impressed with the old man's seriousness, finally agreed to arrange the interview.

The next afternoon the thief was taken to the royal quarters. There the king sat upon an enormous throne, looking very impressive and stern.

"Well, well, what is it? What do you have for me?" asked the king. "I don't have all day to spend on the likes of you, you know."

Before replying, the thief noted that the prime minister, the secretary of state, the general of the army, and the head jailkeeper were also present.

"Your Majesty," said the thief, "I have come here to present you with a rare and valuable gift."

Slipping his hand into his pocket, he carefully withdrew a tiny box, elegantly wrapped in gold paper with silver ribbons.

The king took the package and swiftly opened it. Examining the contents, his face suddenly flushed red with rage and his voice filled the room with a series of royal bellows.

"What is the meaning of this? How dare you bring me an ordinary plum pit!"

"True," admitted the old thief quietly, "it is a plum pit." Here he paused for emphasis. "But by no means an ordinary one."

"What do you mean by that?" stormed the king.

"He who plants this pit," stated the old man, "will reap nothing but golden plums."

A moment of astonished silence greeted this news.

Finally the king said, "Well, if that's the case, why haven't you planted it yourself?"

"For a very good reason, Your Majesty," answered the thief. "Only people who have never stolen or cheated can reap the benefit. Otherwise, the tree will bear only ordinary plums. That is why," and the old thief smiled in his most winning way, "I have brought the pit to you. Certainly, Your Majesty has never stolen anything or cheated."

"Alas," declared the king with great regret in his voice—for he was an honest man no matter what other faults he had—"I am afraid I am not the right person."

"What do you mean?" cried the others present.

But the king remained silent, remembering how he had once stolen some pennies from his mother's purse when he was a little boy.

"Well, how about the prime minister?" suggested the thief. "Perhaps he—"

But the old thief got no further with his sentence.

"Impossible!" blustered the prime minister with a very red face. He had often accepted bribes from people who wanted fine positions in the government. Surely, the pit would never work for him.

"You then, General?" asked the thief, turning to the head of the army.

"No, no," muttered the general with lowered eyes. He had become an enormously rich man by cheating his soldiers of part of their pay.

"Well then, Mr. Secretary of State?" offered the thief.

"I'm afraid not," sputtered the honorable old man, whose conscienc:

was obviously troubling him. Like the prime minister, he had at times accepted money in return for favors.

"Then the head jailkeeper must be our man," said the thief solemnly as he turned to the last candidate.

Silently the jailkeeper shook his head and shrugged his shoulders. "I'm afraid I'm not right either," he said at last. He was remembering how he was always treating new prisoners, sending those who gave him money to the best quarters and reserving the worst cells for the poor and unfortunate.

Refusing to give up, the thief suggested several other officials. Each of the fine gentlemen, however, rejected in his turn the offer of the plum pit that would bear him golden fruit forever.

When the room was entirely still, each official trying to hide his embarrassment, the old thief suddenly burst out laughing.

"You gentlemen," he exclaimed, "you embezzle and you steal, and yet you never end up in jail!" He searched their faces earnestly, and then in a quiet voice, he added, "I have done nothing more than steal some spices, and for this I have been condemned to serve five years in jail."

For quite some time the king and his officials remained silent with shame.

At last the king stirred.

"I would suggest," he said in a low voice, looking at each of his ministers one by one, "that we all contribute to this man's fine, so that he will not go back to jail."

Immediately the necessary money was gathered and placed at the monarch's feet. Calling the old thief to him, the king gave him the money.

"Go, my good man," he said. "You are free. You have spent enough time in prison. From your experience you have instructed us wisely. Ministers and kings sometimes forget themselves. We will remember your lesson well."

And so, with nothing more than a plum pit to help him, the very clever old thief left jail a free man.

135. THE TIGER'S WHISKER*
(*Korea*)

A YOUNG WOMAN by the name of Yun Ok came one day to the house of a mountain hermit to seek his help. The hermit was a sage of great renown and a maker of charms and magic potions.

When Yun Ok entered his house, the hermit said, without raising his eyes from the fireplace into which he was looking: "Why are you here?"

Yun Ok said: "Oh, Famous Sage, I am in distress! Make me a potion!"

"Yes, yes, make a potion! Everyone needs potions! Can we cure a sick world with a potion?"

"Master," Yun Ok replied, "if you do not help me, I am truly lost!"

"Well, what is your story?" the hermit said, resigned at last to listen.

"It is my husband," Yun Ok said. "He is very dear to me. For the past three years he has been away fighting in the wars. Now that he has returned, he hardly speaks to me, or to anyone else. If I speak, he doesn't seem to hear. When he talks at all, it is roughly. If I serve him food not to his liking, he pushes it aside and angrily leaves the room. Sometimes when he should be working in the rice field, I see him sitting idly on top of the hill, looking toward the sea."

"Yes, so it is sometimes when young men come back from the wars," the hermit said. "Go on."

"There is no more to tell, Learned One. I want a potion to give my husband so that he will be loving and gentle, as he used to be."

"Ha, so simple, is it?" the hermit said. "A potion! Very well; come back in three days and I will tell you what we shall need for such a potion."

---

* From *The Tiger's Whisker and Other Tales and Legends from Asia and the Pacific*, © 1959 by Harold Courlander. Reprinted by permission of Harcourt Brace Jovanovich, Inc.

Three days later Yun Ok returned to the home of the mountain sage. "I have looked into it," he told her. "Your potion can be made. But the most essential ingredient is the whisker of a living tiger. Bring me this whisker and I will give you what you need."

"The whisker of a living tiger!" Yun Ok said. "How could I possibly get it?"

"If the potion is important enough, you will succeed," the hermit said. He turned his head away, not wishing to talk any more.

Yun Ok went home. She thought a great deal about how she would get the tiger's whisker. Then one night when her husband was asleep, she crept from her house with a bowl or rice and meat sauce in her hand. She went to the place on the mountainside where the tiger was known to live. Standing far off from the tiger's cave, she held out the bowl of food, calling the tiger to come and eat. The tiger did not come.

The next night Yun Ok went again, this time a little bit closer. Again she offered a bowl of food. Every night Yun Ok went to the mountain, each time a few steps nearer the tiger's cave than the night before. Little by little the tiger became accustomed to seeing her there.

One night Yun Ok approached to within a stone's throw of the tiger's cave. This time the tiger came a few steps toward her and stopped. The two of them stood looking at one another in the moonlight. It happened again the following night, and this time they were so close that Yun Ok could talk to the tiger in a soft, soothing voice. The next night, after looking carefully into Yun Ok's eyes, the tiger ate the food that she held out for him. After that when Yun Ok came in the night, she found the tiger waiting for her on the trail. When the tiger had eaten, Yun Ok could gently rub his head with her hand. Nearly six months had passed since the night of her first visit. At last one night, after caressing the animal's head, Yun Ok said:

"Oh, Tiger, generous animal, I must have one of your whiskers. Do not be angry with me!"

And she snipped off one of the whiskers.

The tiger did not become angry, as she had feared he might. Yun Ok went down the trail, not walking but running, with the whisker clutched tightly in her hand.

The next morning she was at the mountain hermit's house just as the sun was rising from the sea. "Oh, Famous One!" she cried, "I have it! I have the tiger's whisker! Now you can make me the potion you promised so that my husband will be loving and gentle again!"

The hermit took the whisker and examined it. Satisfied that it had really come from a tiger, he leaned forward and dropped it into the fire that burned in his fireplace.

"Oh, sir!" the young woman called in anguish. "What have you done with it!"

"Tell me how you obtained it," the hermit said.

"Why, I went to the mountain each night with a little bowl of food. At first I stood afar, and I came a little closer each time, gaining the tiger's confidence. I spoke gently and soothingly to him, to make him understand I wished him only good. I was patient. Each night I brought him food, knowing that he would not eat. But I did not give up. I came again and again. I never spoke harshly. I never reproached him. And at last one night he took a few steps toward me. A time came when he would meet me on the trail and eat out of the bowl that I held in my hands. I rubbed his head, and he made happy sounds in his throat. Only after that did I take the whisker."

"Yes, yes," the hermit said, "you tamed the tiger and won his confidence and love."

"But you have thrown the whisker in the fire!" Yun Ok cried. "It is all for nothing!"

"No, I do not think it is all for nothing," the hermit said. "The whisker is no longer needed. Yun Ok, let me ask you, is a man more vicious than a tiger? Is he less responsive to kindness and understanding? If you can win the love and confidence of a wild and bloodthirsty animal by gentleness and patience, surely you can do the same with your husband?"

Hearing this, Yun Ok stood speechless for a moment. Then she went down the trail, turning over in her mind the truth she had learned in the house of the mountain hermit.

136. HATS TO DISAPPEAR WITH
(Korea)

ONCE UPON A TIME in Korea there lived a bandit who was very ambitious but very unlucky. Every time he was about to steal something he would be discovered and have to make a quick getaway. Several times he had even been caught and ended up in prison.

"If only I could somehow become invisible," the bandit thought, "then all my problems would be solved." After thinking about this problem for some time he remembered that the goblins of Korea wore magic caps called Horang Gamte which had the power of making them invisible. "If only I could get my hands on one of those hats," the bandit thought and began to make plans for finding one.

He knew the goblins wore the hats when they stole food from people to take to feed the dead. So he decided he would go and wait at the graveyard until the goblins came with food. He climbed up into a tree and waited. At midnight the goblins came. Although they were invisible they made a lot of noise talking and it was still possible to see the food they carried, so the bandit began to fish for a hat wherever he saw food moving around.

At last he caught a hat on the end of his stick. As soon as the hat was off the goblin's head the bandit could see it so he had no trouble securing it. He could also see the goblin which was a very exciting thing for a human.

The goblins, however, were very frightened when one of their number lost his hat. They thought perhaps some evil spirit was after them. So they dropped all their food and ran away.

As soon as the goblins had gone, the bandit took his hat and went home.

Now he wore the hat every time he went out to steal and he became very successful. Things seemed to disappear before people's eyes and the only thing they could think of to blame it on was the goblins.

The bandit was very careful to stay away from places he thought the goblins might go in search of food. Anyway he was only interested in stealing riches and jewels. He hoped to get rich quickly and retire for he knew his luck would not hold out forever. It would only be a matter of time until the goblins started looking for their lost hat.

At first the goblins thought some evil spirit had taken their hat. But then they began to hear humans blaming them for robberies of all kinds of things they had never even thought of taking. If there was some invisible bandit out stealing things it had to be the man who took their hat.

So they began to plot how they might find the bandit and recover their hat. Perhaps they could surprise him on one of his thieving missions, grab the hat and run.

Each night the goblins would gather outside a different rich man's house hoping they might surprise the bandit. But months went by and they never saw him.

Then one day some goblins were hanging around near a jewelry merchant when the bandit came and started picking up jewels right in front of the jeweler's eyes. The jeweler couldn't figure out what was going on and thought the goblins must be after him. But the goblins could see the bandit since they had hats on too. So they simply grabbed his hat and ran away laughing about what would happen to the bandit.

All of a sudden the bandit was visible again and he was caught red-handed with the jewels and sent to jail.

When people heard the story they said the bandit deserved his bad luck because no good would ever come to a human who tried to outsmart the goblins.

137. WHY THE PARROT REPEATS MAN'S WORDS*

(Thailand)

IN ANCIENT TIMES it was not the parrot which was kept in the house by man and taught to speak, but the lorikeet. For people had found that this small bird was a very intelligent creature, and he needed very little teaching. If he heard a word he could repeat it easily. Not only that, he often spoke his own thoughts to man instead of merely imitating the sounds he heard around him.

But it happened one time that all this changed.

One day, it is said, a farmer saw a buffalo wandering in his rice field. It was his neighbor's animal, but the farmer took the buffalo, killed it, cut up the meat, cooked some and ate it, and the remainder he hid. Part of the meat the man hid on the top of the rice house. The rest he hid in the rice bin.

The next day the neighbor came looking for his animal, saying to the farmer, "Have you seen my lost buffalo?"

The farmer replied, "No, I have seen no lost buffalo."

But just then the farmer's lorikeet spoke up. "My master killed it. He ate some and hid some. Part he hid in the rice bin and part he hid over the rice house."

When the neighbor heard this, he looked in the places the bird had mentioned, and there he found the buffalo meat.

But the farmer said, "Yes, this is where I always keep meat. But I did not see your buffalo. This is the meat of another animal."

The lorikeet called out again: "He killed it. Part he hid in the rice bin and part he hid over the rice house."

---

* From *Ride with the Sun* edited by Harold Courlander for The United Nations Women's Guild. Copyright © 1955 by McGraw-Hill Book Company, Inc. Used with permission.

The neighbor was perplexed. He didn't know whether to accept the word of the man or the bird. And so he took the matter to court. The trial was set for the following day.

The farmer who had stolen the meat said to himself, "Why should the word of a lorikeet be taken, rather than my word?"

That night he took the bird from its cage and placed it in a large brass pot. He covered the pot with a cloth, so that it was dark inside. Outside, the night was clear and bright. The moon was full. But inside the pot, the lorikeet could see nothing of this. The man began to beat on the pot, softly at first, then more loudly, until it sounded like thunder. He took a dipper of water, dripping a little of it on the cloth now and then so that it sounded like rain. All night long he pounded on the pot and dripped water, and he stopped only when dawn came. Then he took the lorikeet and put it back in its cage.

When it was time for the trial, the farmer took his bird and went to court. The neighbor who had lost the buffalo told how the lorikeet had instructed him where to find the stolen meat. The judge asked the lorikeet for his testimony. The bird repeated what he had said before: "He killed the buffalo. Part he hid in the rice bin and part he hid over the rice house."

The man who had stolen the buffalo spoke, saying, "The meat that was in the rice bin and over the rice house was that of another animal. How can it be that you give more weight to the words of this stupid bird than to my words?"

"The lorikeet is indeed intelligent," the judge said.

"He speaks more often with nonsense than with sense," the farmer replied. "Ask him another question. Ask him what kind of a night we had last night."

So the judge asked the lorikeet, which replied, "Last night was dark and stormy. The wind blew, the rain poured down, and the thunder roared."

"If you remember," the farmer said, "last night was calm and clear, and the moon shone with all its brightness. Can you now condemn me for a crime on the testimony of this bird?"

The people were convinced, and the judge was convinced. They said: "No, you are innocent, and your life was endangered by the witless testimony of the lorikeet. Henceforth we will not keep this bird in our houses and care for him as though he were one of us."

So the man who stole the buffalo was freed, and the lorikeet was expelled and sent back into the forest. The lorikeet lived as he had before he had known man, fending for himself and caring for his own needs.

But one day the lorikeet saw a new bird in the forest, larger than himself and covered with brilliant red and green feathers. He spoke to the new bird, asking him who he was.

"I am the parrot," the bird answered. "I have come from the South, and now I am going to live in this country. I speak the language of man."

Then the lorikeet said, "Welcome to the country. As you are a stranger here, accept my advice and warning. I too speak the language of man. For many years I was kept in man's house and cared for. I saw with my eyes and heard with my ears. I spoke not only words that man spoke, but what was in my own mind as well. But when I said what was in my own mind it displeased man, and I was driven away. This is my warning: When man learns that you can speak his language, he will capture you and bring you into his house. Say nothing but what he teaches you. Repeat his words and nothing more. For man loves to hear only his own thoughts repeated. He is not interested in truth or wisdom from any other source."

The parrot listened to the lorikeet and thanked him. And it came about as the lorikeet had predicted. Man learned of the arrival of the talking parrot, and the parrot was captured and brought to man's house. He was fed and cared for, as once the lorikeet had been cared for, and he was taught the things that man wanted him to say.

But fearful of ever saying his true thoughts lest man resent them, the parrot only echoes the words that he hears from man's lips.

138. MISTER LAZYBONES
(Laos)

UNDER A WILD fig tree there lived a man called Mister Lazybones. He had received this name from his neighbors because he was never known to have worked a day in his life. He did not even plant or hunt his food, but rather would lie all day under the fig tree and wait for the fruit to fall into his mouth. All the people scorned him and would sometimes throw rocks and dirt at him, but he was too lazy to defend himself.

One day a great wind blew some of his figs into a nearby stream. They floated downstream. The king's niece was sitting by the water and when she saw the figs float by she picked one up and ate it. It was the most delicious fruit she had ever tasted and she vowed she would marry the man to whom the figs belonged.

She told her uncle of the vow and he promised her they would try to find the man who owned the tree so she could marry. The king ordered all fig growers to bring a sample of their fruit to the court. The king's niece tasted all the figs that were brought to court, but none tasted like the one she had found in the stream. The king then inquired whether there were any fig trees in the land that had not been sampled by his niece. The people told him that the only other fig tree in the land was that of Mister Lazybones, who was too lazy to make the journey to court.

When the niece heard this she decided she would go herself and taste Mister Lazybones' figs. When she had tasted the fruit, she knew at once that this was the tree and the man she sought.

The king was very upset that his niece was going to marry such a lazy good-for-nothing, but he had given his word so he could not object. He allowed his niece to marry Mister Lazybones, but he refused to let them live at the palace and he cut off his niece's inheritance.

So they were married, and lived happily for a time. The girl was very kind to her husband and together they lived under the fig tree and enjoyed the delicious fruit.

But then one day misfortune struck. The fig tree stopped bearing fruit and the wife became very ill. Mister Lazybones was very upset because he realized he had come to love his wife very much. Never before had anyone been so kind to him or taken such good care of him.

He knew he would have to work to keep his wife alive, but he did not care because for the first time in his life he had something to work for. He tried very hard to make his wife comfortable and then set to planting new fig trees. Many new fig trees began to grow, the land prospered, and his wife got well.

When the king learned of the work that Mister Lazybones had done and of the loving care he had shown his niece, he restored his niece's inheritance and asked the couple to come and live with him at the palace.

At the palace Mister Lazybones was able to live a life of ease and comfort and once again did not have to work. He would of often think to himself, "When I was poor and lazy they called me Mister Lazybones and scorned me, but now that I am rich and lazy they call me prince and revere me." And when this thought came into his head Mister Lazybones would laugh quietly to himself at the foolishness of life.

139. THE FISHERMAN AND THE GATEKEEPER

(*Burma*)

THERE ONCE LIVED a king who, in order to celebrate the birth of his first child, decided to give a great banquet. Kings and noblemen from all the surrounding lands were invited to attend, and the event promised to be one of the most spectacular ever seen in that kingdom.

As the day approached, the court was bursting with activity in preparation for the feast. All the food except the fish was prepared days in advance. The fish was to be the main course, and had to be caught at the last moment so that it would be fresh.

The day before the banquet, after all the guests had arrived, there arose a great storm at sea. None of the fishing boats was able to go out and it seemed as though the king's banquet would be ruined. All the other food would seem like nothing without the main course and the king was very sad at the thought of being disgraced in front of all the visiting nobility.

All seemed lost until the gatekeeper announced that the king had a visitor. The visitor was allowed to enter and in walked a fisherman with a huge net filled to the brim with large and delicious-looking fresh fish. The fisherman had heard of the king's plight and had risked his life and braved the storm to provide fish for the royal banquet.

The king was overcome with happiness at this news. He had the cook prepare the fish at once, and then offered the fisherman any reward he should ask for.

Much to the king's surprise, the fisherman asked for one hundred lashes of the whip. The king was so shocked at this he told the fisherman he could not possibly punish a man who had performed such a brave and wonderful task. But the fisherman insisted that this was the reward he desired, and the king had but to comply. And so the king ordered the one hundred lashes, but he instructed his servants to be very gentle in carrying out the fisherman's strange request.

The servants thought the man must indeed be a fool to ask for such a reward, and they were so gentle that they did not in any way harm the man. After he had received fifty lashes of the whip the fisherman told the servants to stop. He then informed them that the remaining fifty lashes were to go to the gatekeeper with whom he had promised to share his reward.

The servants immediately sent for the king and the fisherman then explained why he wanted to share his reward with the gatekeeper. When the fisherman arrived at the gate with his catch the gatekeeper would not allow him to enter until he promised to share of his reward. And so the fisherman, in order that he might not be delayed in delivering the fish to the king, had immediately agreed to the gatekeeper's request.

The king was very angry when he heard this story. He ordered the servants to give the gatekeeper the fifty remaining lashes, but this time without gentleness. He then had the gatekeeper banished from the kingdom.

As for the fisherman, he was rewarded generously and given a place of honor at the king's banquet. The banquet was a complete success and all agreed that the fish was the most delicious they had ever tasted.

140. THE LITTLE LIZARD'S SORROW

(*Vietnam*)

THERE IS IN VIETNAM a certain species of small lizard only three inches long with webbed feet and a short, round head. They are often seen indoors, running swiftly upside down on the ceiling or along the walls, emitting little snapping cries that sound like "Tssst . . . tssst!" Suppose that you drop an egg on the kitchen floor; the kind of sound you would make then, with the tip of your tongue between your teeth, is like the cry of these harmless, funny little lizards. Sounds of mild sorrow, of genuine shock but somehow humorous regret that seem to say, "Oh, if only I had been . . . If only I had known . . . Oh, what a pity, what a pity . . . Tssst! Tssst!"

THERE was once a very rich man whose house was immense and filled with treasures. His land was so extensive that, as the Vietnamese say, "Cranes fly over it with outstretched wings," for cranes only do so over very long distances. Wealth breeding vanity, one of the rich man's greatest pleasures was beating other rich men at a game he himself had invented. One player would announce one of his rare possessions, the other would counter the challenge by saying that he, too—if he really did—owned such a treasure. "A stable of fifty buffalos," one man would say. The other would reply, "Yes, I also have fifty of them." It was then his turn to announce, "I sleep in an all-teak bed encrusted with mother-of-pearl." The first player would lose if he slept on cherry planks!

One day, a stranger came to the rich man's house. Judging from his appearance, the gatekeeper did not doubt that the visitor was a madman. He wanted, he said, to play the famous game with the mansion's master. Yet dressed in clothes that looked as if they had been mended hundreds of times, and wearing broken straw sandals, the stranger appeared to be anything but a wealthy man. Moreover, his face was gaunt and pale as if he had not had a good meal in days. But there was such proud, quiet dignity to the stranger that the servant did not dare shut the gates in his face. Instead, he meekly went to inform his master of the unlikely visitor's presence. Intrigued, the man ordered that the pauper be ushered in.

Trying to conceal his curiosity and surprise, the rich man offered his visitor the very best chair and served him hot, perfumed tea.

"Well, stranger, is it true that you have deigned to come here to play a game of riches with me?" he began inquiringly.

The visitor was apparently unimpressed by the rich surroundings, giving them only a passing, casual look. Perfectly at ease, sipping his tea from the rare porcelain cup, he answered in a quiet though self-assured voice, "Yes, sir, that is if you, too, so wish."

"Naturally, naturally," the rich man raised his hand in a sweeping motion. "But, may I ask, with your permission, where you reside and what is your honorable occupation?"

The stranger gave a little chortle, visibly amused. "Sir, would you gain any to know about these? I came here simply to play your game; only, I have two conditions, if you are so generous as to allow them."

"By all means! Pray, tell me what they are," the rich man readily inquired.

The visitor sat farther back on the brocaded chair, his voice soft and confidential. "Well, here they are. A game is no fun if the winner does not win anything and the loser does not lose anything. Therefore I would suggest that if I win I would take everything in your possession— your lands, your stables, your servants, your house and everything contained in it. But if you win—" Here the stranger paused, his eyes narrowed ever so slightly, full of humorous malice, "If you win, you would become the owner of everything that belongs to me." The stranger paused again. "And what belongs to me, sir, you will have no idea of. I am one of the most fortunate men alive, sir. . . . And besides that," he added with a knowing look, "I would remain in this house to serve you as a domestic the rest of my life."

For a long moment, the rich man sat back in silence. Another long moment went by, then the rich man spoke: "That's agreed. But, please tell me your other condition."

Eyes dreamy, the stranger looked out of the window. "My second condition, sir, is not so much a condition as a request. I hope you would not mind giving me, a visitor, an edge over you. May I be allowed to ask the first question?"

The rich man thought for a long second, then said, "That is also agreed. Let's begin."

"Do I really understand that you have agreed to both my conditions?" the stranger asked thoughtfully.

Something in the visitor's manner and voice hurt the rich man's pride. He was ready to stake his very life on this game that he himself had created. There was no way out. "Yes," he said. "Yes, indeed I have. Now tell me, please, what do you have that I have not got?" The stranger smiled. Reaching to his feet, he took up his traveling bag, a coarse cotton square tied together by the four ends. Opening it slowly, ceremoniously, he took out an object and handed it to his host without a word. It was an empty half of a coconut shell, old and chipped, the kind poor people use as a container to drink water from.

"A coconut-shell cup!" the rich man exclaimed. One could not know whether he was merely amused or completely shattered.

"Yes, sir, a coconut-shell cup. A *chipped* shell cup. I use it to drink from on my wanderings. I am a wanderer," the visitor said quietly.

Holding the shell between his thumb and his forefinger and looking as if he had never seen such an object before, the rich man interrupted, "But, but you don't mean that I do not have a thing like this?"

"No, sir, you have not. How could you?" the stranger replied.

Turning the residence upside down, the man and his servants discovered odds and ends of one thousand and one kinds, but they were unable to produce a drinking cup made from a coconut shell. In the servants' quarters, however, they found a few such utensils, but they were all brand new, not chipped. One could imagine that the servants of such a wealthy man would not deign to drink from a chipped cup. Even a beggar would throw it away. . . .

"You see, sir," the stranger said to the rich man once they were again seated across the tea table, "you see, I am a wanderer, as I have said. I am a free man. This cup here is several years old and my only possession besides these poor clothes I have on. If you do not think me too immodest, I would venture that I treasure it more than you do all your collections of fine china. But, from this day, I am the owner and lone master of all that belongs to you. . . ."

Having taken possession of the rich man's land, houses, herds and all his other treasures, the stranger began to give them away to the poor and needy people. Then, one day, taking up his old cotton bag, he left the village and no one ever saw him again.

As for the dispossessed rich man, it is believed that he died of grief and regret and was transformed into this small lizard. Curiously, one sees him scurrying about only indoors. Running up and down the walls, crossing the ceiling, staring at people and furniture, he never stops his "Tssst, tssst." Vietnamese children, in particular, are very fond of him for he looks so harassed, so funny.

But, oh, such sorrow, such regret, such self-pity.

141. THE FLY
(Vietnam)

EVERYONE IN THE VILLAGE knew the usurer, a rich and smart man. Having accumulated a fortune over the years, he settled down to a life of leisure in his big house surrounded by an immense garden and guarded by a pack of ferocious dogs. But still unsatisfied with what he had acquired, the man went on making money by lending it to people all over the county at exorbitant rates. The usurer reigned supreme in the area, for numerous were those who were in debt to him.

One day, the rich man set out for the house of one of his peasants. Despite repeated reminders, the poor laborer just could not manage to pay off his long-standing debt. Working himself to a shadow, the peasant barely succeeded in making ends meet. The moneylender was therefore determined that if he could not get his money back this time, he would proceed to confiscate some of his debtor's most valuable belongings. But the rich man found no one at the peasant's house but a small boy of eight or nine playing alone in the dirt yard.

"Child, are your parents home?" the rich man asked.

"No, sir," the boy replied, then went on playing with his sticks and stones, paying no attention whatever to the man.

"Then, where are they?" the rich man asked, somewhat irritated, but the little boy went on playing and did not answer.

When the rich man repeated his query, the boy looked up and answered, with deliberate slowness, "Well, sir, my father has gone to cut living trees and plant dead ones and my mother is at the market place selling the wind and buying the moon."

"What? What in heaven are you talking about?" the rich man commanded. "Quick, tell me where they are, or you will see what this stick can do to you!" The bamboo walking stick in the big man's hand looked indeed menacing.

After repeated questioning, however, the boy only gave the same reply. Exasperated, the rich man told him, "All right, little devil, listen to me! I came here today to take the money your parents owe me. But if you tell me where they really are and what they are doing, I will forget all about the debt. Is that clear to you?"

"Oh, sir, why are you joking with a poor little boy? Do you expect me to believe what you are saying?" For the first time the boy looked interested.

"Well, there is heaven and there is earth to witness my promise," the rich man said, pointing up to the sky and down to the ground.

But the boy only laughed. "Sir, heaven and earth cannot talk and therefore cannot testify. I want some living thing to be our witness."

Catching sight of a fly alighting on a bamboo pole nearby, and laughing inside because he was fooling the boy, the rich man proposed, "There is a fly. He can be our witness. Now, hurry and tell me what you mean when you say that your father is out cutting living trees and planting dead ones, while your mother is at the market selling the wind and buying the moon."

Looking at the fly on the pole, the boy said, "A fly is a good enough witness for me. Well, here it is, sir. My father has simply gone to cut down bamboos and make a fence with them for a man near the river. And my mother . . . oh, sir, you'll keep your promise, won't you? You will free my parents of all their debts? You really mean it?"

"Yes, yes, I do solemnly swear in front of this fly here." The rich man urged the boy to go on.

"Well, my mother, she has gone to the market to sell fans so she can buy oil for our lamps. Isn't that what you would call selling the wind to buy the moon?"

Shaking his head, the rich man had to admit inwardly that the boy was a clever one. However, he thought, the little genius still had much to learn, believing as he did that a fly could be a witness for anybody. Bidding the boy good-bye, the man told him that he would soon return to make good his promise.

A few days had passed when the moneylender returned. This time he found the poor peasant couple at home, for it was late in the evening. A nasty scene ensued, the rich man claiming his money and the poor peasant apologizing and begging for another delay. Their argument awakened the little boy who ran to his father and told him, "Father, father, you don't have to pay your debt. This gentleman here has promised me that he would forget all about the money you owe him."

"Nonsense," the rich man shook his walking stick at both father and son. "Nonsense, are you going to stand there and listen to a child's inventions? I never spoke a word to this boy. Now, tell me, are you going to pay or are you not?"

The whole affair ended by being brought before the mandarin who governed the county. Not knowing what to believe, all the poor peasant and his wife could do was to bring their son with them when they went to court. The little boy's insistence about the rich man's promise was their only encouragement.

The mandarin began by asking the boy to relate exactly what had happened between himself and the moneylender. Happily, the boy hastened to tell about the explanations he gave the rich man in exchange for the debt.

"Well," the mandarin said to the boy, "if this man here has indeed made such a promise, we have only your word for it. How do we know that you have not invented the whole story yourself? In a case such as this, you need a witness to confirm it, and you have none." The boy remained calm and declared that naturally there was a witness to their conversation.

"Who is that, child?" the mandarin asked.

"A fly, Your Honor."

"A fly? What do you mean, a fly? Watch out, young man, fantasies are not to be tolerated in this place!" The mandarin's benevolent face suddenly became stern.

"Yes, Your Honor, a fly. A fly which was alighting on this gentleman's nose!" The boy leaped from his seat.

"Insolent little devil, that's a pack of lies!" The rich man roared indignantly, his face like a ripe tomato. "The fly was *not* on my nose; *he was on the housepole* . . ." But he stopped dead. It was, however, too late.

The majestic mandarin himself could not help bursting out laughing. Then the audience burst out laughing. The boy's parents too, although timidly, laughed. And the boy, and the rich man himself, also laughed.

With one hand on his stomach, the mandarin waved the other hand toward the rich man:

"Now, now, that's all settled. You have indeed made your promises, dear sir, to the child. *Housepole or no housepole, your conversation did happen after all!* The court says you must keep your promise."

And still chuckling, he dismissed all parties.

142. THE VALIANT CHATTEE-MAKER
(*India*)

LONG, LONG AGO, in a violent storm of thunder, lightning, wind, and rain, a Tiger crept for shelter close to the wall of an old woman's hut. This old woman was very poor, and her hut was but a tumbledown place, through the roof of which the rain came *drip, drip, drip*, on more sides than one. This troubled her much, and she went running about from side to side, dragging first one thing and then another out of the way of the leaky places in the roof, and as she did so, she kept saying to herself, "Oh, dear! oh, dear! how tiresome this is! I'm sure the roof will come down! If an elephant, or a lion, or a tiger were to walk in, he wouldn't frighten me half as much as this perpetual dripping."

And then she would begin dragging the bed and all the other things in the room about again, to get them out of the way of the rain. The Tiger, who was crouching down just outside, heard all that she said, and thought to himself, "This old woman says she would not be afraid of an elephant, or a lion, or a tiger, but that this perpetual dripping frightens her more than all. What can this 'perpetual dripping' be? It must be something very dreadful." And, hearing her immediately afterward dragging all the things about the room again, he said to himself, "What a terrible noise! Surely that must be the '*perpetual dripping*.'"

At this moment a chattee-maker, that is, a potter, who was in search of his donkey, which had strayed away, came down the road. The night being very cold, he had, truth to say, taken a little more toddy than was good for him, and seeing, by the light of a flash of lightning, a large animal lying down close to the old woman's hut, mistook it for the donkey he was looking for. So, running up to the Tiger, he seized hold of it by one ear, and commenced beating, kicking, and abusing it with all his might and main.

"You wretched creature," he cried, "is this the way you serve me, obliging me to come out and look for you in such pouring rain, and on such a dark night as this? Get up instantly, or I'll break every bone in your body"; and he went on scolding and thumping the Tiger with his utmost power, for he had worked himself up into a terrible rage. The Tiger did not know what to make of it all, but he began to feel quite frightened, and said to himself, "Why, this must be the 'perpetual dripping'; no wonder the old woman said she was more afraid of it than of an elephant, a lion, or a tiger, for it gives most dreadfully hard blows."

The Chattee-maker, having made the Tiger get up, got on his back, and forced him to carry him home, kicking and beating him the whole way (for all this time he fancied he was on his donkey), and then he tied his fore feet and his head firmly together, and fastened him to a post in front of his house, and when he had done this he went to bed.

Next morning, when the Chattee-maker's wife got up and looked out of the window, what did she see but a great big Tiger tied up in front of their house, to the post to which they usually fastened the donkey; she was very much surprised, and running to her husband, awoke him, saying, "Do you know what animal you fetched home last night?"

"Yes, the donkey, to be sure," he answered.

"Come and see," said she, and she showed him the great Tiger tied to the post. The Chattee-maker at this was no less astonished than his wife, and felt himself all over to find out if the Tiger had not wounded him. But no! there he was, safe and sound, and there was the Tiger tied to the post, just as he had fastened it up the night before.

News of the Chattee-maker's exploit soon spread through the village, and all the people came to see him and hear him tell how he had caught the Tiger and tied it to the post; and this they thought so wonderful, that they sent a deputation to the Rajah, with a letter to tell him how a man of their village had, alone and unarmed, caught a great Tiger, and tied it to a post.

When the Rajah read the letter he also was much surprised, and determined to go in person and see this astonishing sight. So he sent for his horses and carriages, his lords and attendants, and they all set off together to look at the Chattee-maker and the Tiger he had caught.

Now the Tiger was a very large one, and had long been the terror of all the country round, which made the whole matter still more extraordinary; and this being represented to the Rajah, he determined to confer every possible honor on the valiant Chattee-maker. So he gave him houses and lands, and as much money as would fill a well, made him lord of his court, and conferred on him the command of ten thousand horses.

It came to pass, shortly after this, that a neighboring Rajah, who had long had a quarrel with this one, sent to announce his intention of going instantly to war with him; and tidings were at the same time brought that the Rajah who sent the challenge had gathered a great army together on the borders and was prepared at a moment's notice to invade the country.

In this dilemma no one knew what to do. The Rajah sent for all his generals, and inquired which of them would be willing to take command of his forces and oppose the enemy. They all replied that the country was so ill-prepared for the emergency, and the case was apparently so hopeless, that they would rather not take the responsibility of the chief command. The Rajah knew not whom to appoint in their stead. Then some of his people said to him, "You have lately given command of ten thousand horses to the valiant Chattee-maker who caught the Tiger. Why not make him Commander-in-Chief? A man who could catch a Tiger and tie him to a post must surely be more courageous and clever than most."

"Very well," said the Rajah, "I will make him Commander-in-Chief." So he sent for the Chattee-maker and said to him, "In your hands I place all the power of the kingdom; you must put our enemies to flight."

"So be it," answered the Chattee-maker, "but, before I lead the whole army against the enemy, suffer me to go by myself and examine their position; and, if possible, find out their numbers and strength."

The Rajah consented, and the Chattee-maker returned home to his wife, and said, "They have made me Commander-in-Chief, which is a very difficult post for me to fill, because I shall have to ride at the head of all the army, and you know I never was on a horse in my life. But I have succeeded in gaining a little delay, as the Rajah has given me permission to go first alone, and reconnoiter the enemy's camp. Do you, therefore, provide a very quiet pony, for you know I cannot ride, and I will start tomorrow morning."

But before the Chattee-maker had started, the Rajah sent over to him a most magnificent charger, richly caparisoned, which he begged he would ride when going to see the enemy's camp.

The Chattee-maker was frightened almost out of his life, for the charger that the Rajah had sent him was very powerful and spirited, and he felt sure that, even if he ever got on it, he should very soon tumble off; however, he did not dare to refuse it, for fear of offending the Rajah by not accepting his present. So he sent him back a message of dutiful thanks, and said to his wife, "I cannot go on the pony now that the Rajah has sent me this fine horse, but how am I ever to ride it?"

"Oh, don't be frightened," she answered; "you've only got to get upon it, and I will tie you firmly on, so that you cannot tumble off, and if you start at night no one will see that you are tied on."

"Very well," he said.

So that night his wife brought the horse that the Rajah had sent him to the door. "Indeed," said the Chattee-maker, "I can never get into that saddle, it is so high up."

"You must jump," said his wife.

Then he tried to jump several times, but each time he jumped he tumbled down again.

"I always forget when I am jumping," said he, "which way I ought to turn."

"Your face must be toward the horse's head," she answered.

"To be sure, of course," he cried, and giving one great jump he jumped into the saddle, but with his face toward the horse's tail.

"This won't do at all," said his wife as she helped him down again, "try getting on without jumping."

"I never can remember," he continued, "when I have got my left foot in the stirrup, what to do with my right foot, or where to put it."

"That must go in the other stirrup," she answered; "let me help you."

So, after many trials, in which he tumbled down very often, for the horse was fresh and did not like standing still, the Chattee-maker got into the saddle; and no sooner had he got there than he cried, "O wife, wife, tie me very firmly as quickly as possible, for I know I shall jump down again if I can." Then she fetched some strong rope and tied his feet firmly into the stirrups, and fastened one stirrup to the other, and put another rope round his waist, and another round his neck, and fastened them to the horse's body, and neck, and tail.

When the horse felt all these ropes about him he could not imagine what queer creature had got upon his back, and he began rearing, and kicking, and prancing, and at last set off full gallop, as fast as he could tear, right across country.

"Wife, wife," cried the Chattee-maker, "you forgot to tie my hands."

"Never mind," said she, "hold on by the mane." So he caught hold of the horse's mane as firmly as he could. Then away went horse, away went Chattee-maker, away, away, away, over hedges, over ditches, over rivers, over plains, away, away, like a flash of lightning, now this way, now that, on, on, on, gallop, gallop, gallop, until they came in sight of the enemy's camp.

The Chattee-maker did not like his ride at all, and when he saw where it was leading him he liked it still less, for he thought the enemy would catch him and very likely kill him. So he determined to make one desperate effort to be free, and stretching out his hand as the horse shot past a young banyan tree, seized hold of it with all his might, hoping the resistance it offered might cause the ropes that tied him to break. But the horse was going at his utmost speed, and the soil in which the banyan tree grew was loose, so that when the Chattee-maker caught hold of it and gave it such a violent pull, it came up by the roots, and on he rode as fast as before, with the tree in his hand.

All the soldiers in the camp saw him coming, and having heard that an army was to be sent against them, made sure that the Chattee-maker was one of the vanguard. "See," cried they, "here comes a man of gigantic stature on a mighty horse! He rides at full speed across the country, tearing up the very trees in his rage! He is one of the opposing force; the whole army must be close at hand. If they are such as he, we are all dead men." Then, running to their Rajah, some of them cried again, "Here comes the whole force of the enemy" (for the story had by this time become exaggerated); "they are men of gigantic stature mounted on mighty horses; as they come they tear up the very trees in their rage; we can oppose men, but not monsters such as these." These were followed by others, who said, "It is all true," for by this time the Chattee-maker had got pretty near the camp, "they're coming! they're coming! let us fly! let us fly! fly, fly for your lives!"

And the whole panic-stricken multitude fled from the camp (those who had seen no cause for alarm going because the others did, or because they did not care to stay by themselves) after having obliged their Rajah to write a letter to the one whose country he was about to invade, to say that he would not do so, and propose terms of peace, and to sign it, and seal it with his seal. Scarcely had all the people fled from the camp, when the horse on which the Chattee-maker was came galloping into it, and on his back rode the Chattee-maker, almost dead from fatigue, with the banyan tree in his hand. Just as he reached the camp the ropes by which he was tied broke, and he fell to the ground. The horse stood still, too tired with its long run to go further. On recovering his senses, the Chattee-maker discovered, to his surprise, that the whole camp, full of rich arms, clothes, and trappings, was entirely deserted. In the principal tent, moreover, he found a letter addressed to his Rajah, announcing the retreat of the invading army, and proposing terms of peace.

So he took the letter, and returned home with it as fast as he could, leading his horse all the way, for he was afraid to mount him again.

It did not take him long to reach his house by the direct road, for while riding he had gone a more circuitous journey than was necessary, and he got there just at nightfall. His wife ran out to meet him, overjoyed at his speedy return. As soon as he saw her, he said, "Ah, wife, since I saw you last I've been all round the world, and had many wonderful and terrible adventures. But never mind that now, send this letter quickly to the Rajah by a messenger, and also the horse that he sent for me to ride. He will then see, by the horse looking so tired, what a long ride I've had, and if he is sent on beforehand, I shall not be obliged to ride him up to the palace door tomorrow morning, as I otherwise should, and that would be very tiresome, for most likely I should tumble off."

So his wife sent the horse and the letter to the Rajah, and a message that her husband would be at the palace early next morning, as it was then late at night. And next day he went down there as he had said he would, and when the people saw him coming, they said, "This man is as modest as he is brave; after having put our enemies to flight, he walks quite simply to the door, instead of riding here in state, as any other man would." (For they did not know that the Chattee-maker walked because he was afraid to ride.)

The Rajah came to the palace door to meet him, and paid him all possible honor. Terms of peace were agreed upon between the two countries, and the Chattee-maker was rewarded for all he had done by being given twice as much rank and wealth as he had before, and he lived very happily all the rest of his life.

143. THE TIGER, THE BRAHMAN, AND THE JACKAL
(India)

ONCE UPON A TIME, a tiger was caught in a trap. He tried in vain to get out through the bars, and rolled and bit with rage and grief when he failed.

By chance a poor Brahman came by.

"Let me out of this cage, oh, pious one!" cried the tiger.

"Nay, my friend," replied the Brahman mildly, "you would probably eat me if I did."

"Not at all!" swore the tiger with many oaths; "on the contrary, I should be forever grateful, and serve you as a slave!"

Now when the tiger sobbed and sighed and wept and swore, the pious Brahman's heart softened, and at last he consented to open the door of the cage. Out popped the tiger, and, seizing the poor man, cried, "What a fool you are! What is to prevent my eating you now, for after being cooped up so long I am just terribly hungry!"

In vain the Brahman pleaded for his life; the most he could gain was a promise to abide by the decision of the first three things he chose to question as to the justice of the tiger's action.

So the Brahman first asked a pipal tree what it thought of the matter, but the pipal tree replied coldly: "What have you to complain about? Don't I give shade and shelter to everyone who passes by, and don't they in return tear down my branches to feed their cattle? Don't whimper—be a man!"

Then the Brahman, sad at heart, went farther afield till he saw a buffalo turning a well-wheel; but he fared no better from it, for it answered: "You are a fool to expect gratitude! Look at me! While I gave milk they fed me on cottonseed and oil-cake, but now I am dry they yoke me here, and give me refuse as fodder!"

The Brahman, still more sad, asked the road to give him its opinion.

"My dear sir," said the road, "how foolish you are to expect anything else! Here am I, useful to everybody, yet all, rich and poor, great and small, trample on me as they go past, giving me nothing but the ashes of their pipes and the husks of their grain!"

On this the Brahman turned back sorrowfully, and on the way he met a jackal, who called out: "Why, what's the matter, Mr. Brahman? You look as miserable as a fish out of water!"

The Brahman told him all that had occurred. "How very confusing!" said the jackal, when the recital was ended; "would you mind telling me over again, for everything has got so mixed up?"

The Brahman told it all over again, but the jackal shook his head in a distracted sort of way, and still could not understand.

"It's very odd," said he, sadly, "but it all seems to go in at one ear and out at the other! I will go to the place where it all happened, and then perhaps I shall be able to give a judgment."

So they returned to the cage, by which the tiger was waiting for the Brahman, and sharpening his teeth and claws.

"You've been away a long time!" growled the savage beast, "but now let us begin our dinner."

"*Our* dinner!" thought the wretched Brahman, as his knees knocked together with fright; "what a remarkably delicate way of putting it!"

"Give me five minutes, my lord!" he pleaded, "in order that I may explain matters to the jackal here, who is somewhat slow in his wits."

The tiger consented, and the Brahman began the whole story over again, not missing a single detail, and spinning as long a yarn as possible.

"Oh, my poor brain! oh, my poor brain!" cried the jackal, wringing its paws. "Let me see! how did it all begin? You were in the cage, and the tiger came walking by——"

"Pooh!" interrupted the tiger, "what a fool you are! *I* was in the cage."

"Of course!" cried the jackal, pretending to tremble with fright; "yes! I was in the cage—no I wasn't—dear! dear! where are my wits? Let me see—the tiger was in the Brahman, and the cage came walking by—no, that's not it, either! Well, don't mind me, but begin your dinner, for I shall never understand!"

"Yes, you shall!" returned the tiger, in a rage at the jackal's stupidity; "I'll *make* you understand! Look here—I am the tiger——"

"Yes, my lord!"

"And that is the Brahman——"

"Yes, my lord!"

"And that is the cage——"

"Yes, my lord!"

"And I was in the cage—do you understand?"

"Yes—no— Please, my lord——"

"Well?" cried the tiger impatiently.

"Please, my lord!—how did you get in?"

"How!—why in the usual way, of course!"

"Oh, dear me!—my head is beginning to whirl again! Please don't be angry, my lord, but what is the usual way?"

At this the tiger lost patience, and, jumping into the cage, cried: "This way! Now do you understand how it was?"

"Perfectly!" grinned the jackal, as he dexterously shut the door, "and if you will permit me to say so, I think matters will remain as they were!"

144. HOW THE RAJA'S SON WON THE PRINCESS LABAM
(India)

IN A COUNTRY there was a Raja who had an only son who every day went out to hunt. One day the Rani, his mother, said to him, "You can hunt wherever you like on these three sides; but you must never go to the fourth side." This she said because she knew if he went on the fourth side he would hear of the beautiful Princess Labam, and that then he would leave his father and mother and seek for the Princess.

The young Prince listened to his mother, and obeyed her for some time; but one day, when he was hunting on the three sides where he was allowed to go, he remembered what she had said to him about the fourth side, and he determined to go and see why she had forbidden him to hunt on that side. When he got there, he found himself in a jungle, and nothing in the jungle but a quantity of parrots, who lived in it. The young Raja shot at some of them, and at once they all flew away up to the sky. All, that is, but one, and this was their Raja, who was called Hiraman parrot.

When Hiraman parrot found himself alone, he called out to the other parrots: "Don't fly away and leave me alone when the Raja's son shoots. If you desert me like this, I will tell the Princess Labam."

Then the parrots all flew back to their Raja, chattering. The Prince was greatly surprised, and said, "Why, these birds can talk!" Then he said to the parrots: "Who is the Princess Labam? Where does she live?" But the parrots would not tell him where she lived. "You can never get to the Princess Labam's country." That is all they would say.

The Prince grew very sad when they would not tell him anything more; and he threw his gun away and went home. When he got home, he would not speak or eat, but lay on his bed for four or five days, and seemed very ill.

At last he told his father and mother that he wanted to go and see the Princess Labam. "I must go," he said; "I must see what she is like. Tell me where her country is."

"We do not know where it is," answered his father and mother.

"Then I must go and look for it," said the Prince.

"No, no," they said, "you must not leave us. You are our only son. Stay with us. You will never find the Princess Labam."

"I must try and find her," said the Prince. "Perhaps God will show me the way. If I live and I find her, I will come back to you; but perhaps I shall die, and then I shall never see you again. Still I must go."

So they had to let him go, though they cried very much at parting with him. His father gave him fine clothes to wear, and a fine horse. And he took his gun, and his bow and arrows, and a great many other weapons; "For," he said, "I may want them." His father, too, gave him plenty of rupees.

Then he himself got his horse all ready for the journey, and he said good-bye to his father and mother; and his mother took her handkerchief and wrapped some sweetmeats in it, and gave it to her son. "My child," she said to him, "when you are hungry eat some of these sweetmeats."

He then set out on his journey, and rode on and on till he came to a jungle in which were a tank and shady trees. He bathed himself and his horse in the tank, and then sat down under a tree. "Now," he said to himself, "I will eat some of the sweetmeats my mother gave me, and I will drink some water, and then I will continue my journey." He opened his handkerchief and took out a sweetmeat. He found an ant in it. He took out another. There was an ant in that one too. So he laid the two sweetmeats on the ground, and he took out another and another and another, until he had taken them all out; but in each he found an ant. "Never mind," he said, "I won't eat the sweetmeats; the ants shall eat them." Then the Ant-Raja came and stood before him and said: "You have been good to us. If ever you are in trouble, think of me and we will come to you."

The Raja's son thanked him, mounted his horse and continued his journey. He rode on and on until he came to another jungle, and there he saw a tiger who had a thorn in his foot, and was roaring loudly from the pain.

"Why do you roar like that?" said the young Raja. "What is the matter with you?"

"I have had a thorn in my foot for twelve years," answered the tiger, "and it hurts me so; that is why I roar."

"Well," said the Raja's son, "I will take it out for you. But perhaps, as you are a tiger, when I have made you well, you will eat me."

"Oh, no," said the tiger, "I won't eat you. Do make me well."

Then the Prince took a little knife from his pocket and cut the thorn out of the tiger's foot; but when he cut, the tiger roared louder than ever—so loud that his wife heard him in the next jungle, and came bounding along to see what was the matter. The tiger saw her coming, and hid the Prince in the jungle, so that she should not see him.

"What man hurt you that you roared so loud?" said the wife.

"No one hurt me," answered the husband; "but a Raja's son came and took the thorn out of my foot."

"Where is he? Show him to me," said his wife.

"If you promise not to kill him, I will call him," said the tiger.

"I won't kill him; only let me see him," answered his wife.

Then the tiger called the Raja's son, and when he came the tiger and his wife made him a great many salaams. Then they gave him a good dinner and he stayed with them for three days. Every day he looked at the tiger's foot, and the third day it was quite healed. Then he said good-bye to the tigers, and the tiger said to him, "If ever you are in trouble, think of me, and we will come to you."

The Raja's son rode on and on till he came to a third jungle. Here he found four fakirs whose teacher and master had died, and had left four things: a bed, which carried whoever sat on it wherever he wished to go; a bag, that gave its owner whatever he wanted, jewels, food or clothes; a stone bowl that gave its owner as much water as he wanted, no matter how far he might be from a tank; and a stick and rope, to which its owner had only to say, if any one came to make war on him, "Stick, beat as many men and soldiers as are here," and the stick would beat them and the rope would tie them up.

The four fakirs were quarreling over these four things. One said, "I want this"; another said, "You cannot have it, for I want it"; and so on.

The Raja's son said to them: "Do not quarrel for these things. I will shoot four arrows in four different directions. Whichever of you gets to my first arrow, shall have the first thing—the bed. Whoever gets to the second arrow, shall have the second thing—the bag. He who gets to the third arrow, shall have the third thing—the bowl. And he who gets to the fourth arrow, shall have the last things—the stick and rope." To this they agreed. And the Prince shot off his first arrow. Away raced the fakirs to get it. When they brought it back to him he shot off the second, and when they had found and brought it to him he shot off his third, and when they had brought him the third he shot off the fourth.

While they were away looking for the fourth arrow the Raja's son let his horse loose in the jungle and sat on the bed, taking the bowl, the stick and rope, and the bag with him. Then he said, "Bed, I wish to go to the Princess Labam's country." The little bed instantly rose up into the air and began to fly, and it flew and flew till it came to the Princess Labam's country, where it settled on the ground. The Raja's son asked some men he saw, "Whose country is this?"

"The Princess Labam's country," they answered. Then the Prince went on till he came to a house where he saw an old woman.

"Who are you?" she said. "Where do you come from?"

"I come from a far country," he said; "do let me stay with you tonight."

"No," she answered, "I cannot let you stay with me; for our King has ordered that men from other countries may not stay in his country. You cannot stay in my house."

"You are my aunty," said the Prince; "let me remain with you for this one night. You see it is evening, and if I go into the jungle, then the wild beasts will eat me."

"Well," said the old woman, "you may stay here tonight; but tomorrow morning you must go away, for if the King hears you have passed the night in my house, he will have me seized and put into prison."

Then she took him into her house, and the Raja's son was very glad. The old woman began preparing dinner, but he stopped her. "Aunty," he said, "I will give you food." He put his hand into his bag, saying, "Bag, I want some dinner," and the bag gave him instantly a delicious dinner, served up on two gold plates. The old woman and the Raja's son then dined together.

When they had finished eating, the old woman said, "Now I will fetch some water."

"Don't go," said the Prince. "You shall have plenty of water directly." So he took his bowl and said to it, "Bowl, I want some water," and then it filled with water. When it was full, the Prince cried out, "Stop, bowl!" and the bowl stopped filling. "See, aunty," he said, "with this bowl I can always get as much water as I want."

By this time night had come. "Aunty," said the Raja's son, "why don't you light a lamp?"

"There is no need," she said. "Our King has forbidden the people in his country to light any lamps; for, as soon as it is dark, his daughter, the Princess Labam, comes and sits on her roof, and she shines so that she lights up all the country and our houses, and we can see to do our work as if it were day."

When it was quite black night the Princess got up. She dressed herself in her rich clothes and jewels, and rolled up her hair, and across her head she put a band of diamonds and pearls. Then she shone like the moon and her beauty made night day. She came out of her room and sat on the roof of her palace. In the daytime she never came out of her house; she only came out at night. All the people in her father's country then went about their work and finished it.

The Raja's son watched the Princess quietly, and was very happy. He said to himself, "How lovely she is!"

At midnight, when everybody had gone to bed, the Princess came down from her roof and went to her room; and when she was in bed and asleep, the Raja's son got up softly and sat on his bed. "Bed," he said to it, "I want to go to the Princess Labam's bedroom." So the little bed carried him to the room where she lay fast asleep.

The young Raja took his bag and said, "I want a great deal of betel leaf," and it at once gave him quantities of betel leaf. This he laid near the Princess's bed, and then his little bed carried him back to the old woman's house.

Next morning all the Princess's servants found the betel leaf, and began to eat it. "Where did you get all that betel leaf?" asked the Princess.

"We found it near your bed," answered the servants. Nobody knew the Prince had come in the night and put it all there.

In the morning the old woman came to the Raja's son. "Now it is morning," she said, "and you must go; for if the King finds out all I have done for you, he will seize me."

"I am ill today, dear aunty," said the Prince; "do let me stay till tomorrow morning."

"Good," said the old woman. So he stayed, and they took their dinner out of the bag, and the bowl gave them water.

When night came the Princess got up and sat on her roof, and at twelve o'clock, when everyone was in bed, she went to her bedroom, and was soon fast asleep. Then the Raja's son sat on his bed and it carried him to the Princess. He took his bag and said, "Bag, I want a most lovely shawl." It gave him a splendid shawl, and he spread it over the Princess as she lay asleep. Then he went back to the old woman's house and slept till morning.

In the morning, when the Princess saw the shawl she was delighted. "See, mother," she said; "Khuda must have given me this shawl, it is so beautiful." Her mother was very glad too.

"Yes, my child," she said; "Khuda must have given you this splendid shawl."

When it was morning the old woman said to the Raja's son, "Now you must really go."

"Aunty," he answered, "I am not well enough yet. Let me stay a few days longer. I will remain hidden in your house, so that no one may see me." So the old woman let him stay.

When it was black night, the Princess put on her lovely clothes and jewels and sat on her roof. At midnight she went to her room and went to sleep. Then the Raja's son sat on his bed and flew to her bedroom. There he said to his bag, "Bag, I want a very, very beautiful ring." The bag gave him a glorious ring. Then he took the Princess Labam's hand gently to put on the ring, and she started up very much frightened.

"Who are you?" she said to the Prince. "Where do you come from? Why do you come to my room?"

"Do not be afraid, Princess," he said; "I am no thief. I am a great Raja's son. Hiraman parrot, who lives in the jungle where I went to hunt, told me your name, and then I left my father and mother and came to see you."

"Well," said the Princess, "as you are the son of such a great Raja, I will not have you killed, and I will tell my father and mother that I wish to marry you."

The Prince then returned to the old woman's house; and when morning came the Princess said to her mother, "The son of a great Raja has come to this country, and I wish to marry him." Her mother told this to the King.

"Good," said the King; "but if this Raja's son wishes to marry my daughter, he must first do whatever I bid him. If he fails I will kill him. I will give him eighty pounds' weight of mustard seed, and out of this he must crush the oil in one day. If he cannot do this he shall die."

In the morning the Raja's son told the old woman that he intended to marry the Princess. "Oh," said the old woman, "go away from this country, and do not think of marrying her. A great many Rajas and Rajas' sons have come here to marry her, and her father has had them all killed. He says whoever wishes to marry his daughter must first do whatever he bids him. If he can, then he shall marry the Princess; if he cannot, the King will have him killed. But no one can do the things the King tells him to do; so all the Rajas and Rajas' sons who have tried have been put to death. You will be killed too, if you try. Do go away." But the Prince would not listen to anything she said.

The King sent for the Prince to the old woman's house, and his servants brought the Raja's son to the King's courthouse and to the King. There the King gave him eighty pounds of mustard seed, and told him to crush all the oil out of it that day, and bring it next morning to him to the courthouse. "Whoever wishes to marry my daughter," he said to the Prince, "must first do all I tell him. If he cannot, then I have him killed. So if you cannot crush all the oil out of this mustard seed you will die."

The Prince was very sorry when he heard this. "How can I crush the oil out of all this mustard seed in one day?" he said to himself; "and if I do not, the King will kill me." He took the mustard seed to the old woman's house, and did not know what to do. At last he remembered the Ant-Raja, and the moment he did so, the Ant-Raja and his ants came to him. "Why do you look so sad?" said the Ant-Raja.

The Prince showed him the mustard seed, and said to him: "How can I crush the oil out of all this mustard seed in one day? And if I do not take the oil to the King tomorrow morning, he will kill me."

"Be happy," said the Ant-Raja; "lie down and sleep; we will crush all the oil out for you during the day, and tomorrow morning you shall take it to the King." The Raja's son lay down and slept, and the ants crushed out the oil for him. The Prince was very glad when he saw the oil.

The next morning he took it to the courthouse to the King. But the King said: "You cannot yet marry my daughter. If you wish to do so, you must first fight with my two demons, and kill them." The King a long time ago had caught two demons, and then, as he did not know what to do with them, he had shut them up in a cage. He was afraid to let them loose for fear they would eat up all the people in his country; and he did not know how to kill them. So all the Kings and Kings' sons who wanted to marry the Princess Labam had to fight with these demons; "For," said the King to himself, "perhaps the demons may be killed, and then I shall be rid of them."

When he heard of the demons the Raja's son was very sad. "What can I do?" he said to himself. "How can I fight with these two demons?" Then he thought of his tiger: and the tiger and his wife came to him and said, "Why are you so sad?" The Raja's son answered: "The King has ordered me to fight with his two demons and kill them. How can I do this?" "Do not be frightened," said the tiger. "Be happy. I and my wife will fight with them for you."

Then the Raja's son took out of his bag two splendid coats. They were all gold and silver, and covered with pearls and diamonds. These he put on the tigers to make them beautiful, and he took them to the King, and said to him, "May these tigers fight your demons for me?" "Yes," said the King, who did not care in the least who killed his demons, provided they were killed. "Then call your demons," said the Raja's son, "and these tigers will fight them." The King did so, and the tigers and the demons fought and fought until the tigers had killed the demons.

"That is good," said the King. "But you must do something else before I give you my daughter. Up in the sky I have a kettledrum. You must go and beat it. If you cannot do this, I will kill you."

The Raja's son thought of his little bed; so he went to the old woman's house and sat on his bed. "Little bed," he said, "up in the sky is the King's kettledrum. I want to go to it." The bed flew up with him, and the Raja's son beat the drum, and the King heard him. Still, when he came down, the King would not give him his daughter. "You have," he said to the Prince, "done the three things I told you to do;

but you must do one thing more." "If I can, I will," said the Raja's son.

Then the King showed him the trunk of a tree that was lying near his courthouse. It was a very, very thick trunk. He gave the Prince a wax hatchet, and said, "Tomorrow morning you must cut this trunk in two with this wax hatchet."

The Raja's son went back to the old woman's house. He was very sad, and thought that now the Raja would certainly kill him. "I had his oil crushed out by the ants," he said to himself. "I had his demons killed by the tigers. My bed helped me to beat his kettledrum. But now what can I do? How can I cut that thick tree trunk in two with a wax hatchet?"

At night he went on his bed to see the Princess. "Tomorrow," he said to her, "your father will kill me." "Why?" asked the Princess.

"He has told me to cut a thick tree trunk in two with a wax hatchet. How can I ever do that?" said the Raja's son. "Do not be afraid," said the Princess; "do as I bid you, and you will cut it in two quite easily."

Then she pulled out a hair from her head and gave it to the Prince. "Tomorrow," she said, "when no one is near you, you must say to the tree trunk, 'The Princess Labam commands you to let yourself be cut in two by this hair.' Then stretch the hair down the edge of the wax hatchet's blade."

The Prince next day did exactly as the Princess had told him; and the minute the hair that was stretched down the edge of the hatchet blade touched the tree trunk it split into two pieces.

The King said, "Now you can marry my daughter." Then the wedding took place. All the Rajas and Kings of the countries round were asked to come to it, and there were great rejoicings. After a few days the Prince's son said to his wife, "Let us go to my father's country." The Princess Labam's father gave them a quantity of camels and horses and rupees and servants; and they traveled in great state to the Prince's country, where they lived happily.

The Prince always kept his bag, bowl, bed, and stick; only, as no one ever came to make war on him, he never needed to use the stick.

145. HOW SUN, MOON, AND WIND WENT OUT TO DINNER

(*India*)

ONE DAY SUN, Moon, and Wind went out to dine with their uncle and aunt Thunder and Lightning. Their mother (one of the most distant Stars you see far up in the sky) waited alone for her children's return.

Now both Sun and Wind were greedy and selfish. They enjoyed the great feast that had been prepared for them, without a thought of saving any of it to take home to their mother—but the gentle Moon did not forget her. Of every dainty dish that was brought round, she placed a small portion under one of her beautiful long fingernails, that Star might also have a share in the treat.

On their return, their mother, who had kept watch for them all night long with her little bright eye, said, "Well, children, what have you brought home for me?" Then Sun (who was eldest) said: "I have brought nothing home for you. I went out to enjoy myself with my friends—not to fetch a dinner for my mother!" And Wind said, "Neither have I brought anything home for you, mother. You could hardly expect me to bring a collection of good things for you, when I merely went out for my own pleasure." But Moon said, "Mother, fetch a plate, see what I have brought you." And shaking her hands she showered down such a choice dinner as never was seen before.

Then Star turned to Sun and spoke thus, "Because you went out to amuse yourself with your friends, and feasted and enjoyed yourself, without any thought of your mother at home—you shall be cursed. Henceforth, your rays shall ever be hot and scorching, and shall burn all that they touch. And men shall hate you, and cover their heads when you appear."

(And that is why the Sun is so hot to this day.)

Then she turned to Wind and said, "You also who forgot your mother in the midst of your selfish pleasures—hear your doom. You shall always blow in the hot dry weather, and shall parch and shrivel all living things. And men shall detest and avoid you from this very time."

(And that is why the Wind in the hot weather is still so disagreeable.)

But to Moon she said, "Daughter, because you remembered your mother, and kept for her a share in your own enjoyment, from henceforth you shall be ever cool, and calm, and bright. No noxious glare shall accompany your pure rays, and men shall always call you 'blessed.'"

(And that is why the Moon's light is so soft, and cool, and beautiful even to this day.)

146. THE MONKEY AND THE CROCODILE
(India)

A MONKEY LIVED in a great tree on a riverbank. In the river there were many Crocodiles.

A Crocodile watched the Monkeys for a long time, and one day she said to her son: "My son, get one of those Monkeys for me. I want the heart of a Monkey to eat."

"How am I to catch a Monkey?" asked the little Crocodile. "I do not travel on land, and the Monkey does not go into the water."

"Put your wits to work, and you'll find a way," said the mother.

And the little Crocodile thought and thought.

At last he said to himself: "I know what I'll do. I'll get that Monkey that lives in a big tree on the riverbank. He wishes to go across the river to the island where the fruit is so ripe."

So the Crocodile swam to the tree where the Monkey lived. But he was a stupid Crocodile.

"Oh, Monkey," he called, "come with me over to the island where the fruit is so ripe."

"How can I go with you?" asked the Monkey. "I do not swim."

"No—but I do. I will take you over on my back," said the Crocodile.

The Monkey was greedy, and wanted the ripe fruit, so he jumped down on the Crocodile's back.

"Off we go!" said the Crocodile.

"This is a fine ride you are giving me!" said the Monkey.

"Do you think so? Well, how do you like this?" asked the Crocodile, diving.

"Oh, don't!" cried the Monkey, as he went under the water. He was afraid to let go, and he did not know what to do under the water.

When the Crocodile came up, the Monkey sputtered and choked. "Why did you take me under water, Crocodile?" he asked.

"I am going to kill you by keeping you under water," answered the Crocodile. "My mother wants Monkey heart to eat, and I'm going to take yours to her."

"I wish you had told me you wanted my heart," said the Monkey, "then I might have brought it with me."

"How queer!" said the stupid Crocodile. "Do you mean to say that you left your heart back there in the tree?"

"That is what I mean," said the Monkey. "If you want my heart, we must go back to the tree and get it. But we are so near the island where the ripe fruit is, please take me there first."

"No, Monkey," said the Crocodile, "I'll take you straight back to your tree. Never mind the ripe fruit. Get your heart and bring it to me at once. Then we'll see about going to the island."

"Very well," said the Monkey.

But no sooner had he jumped onto the bank of the river than— whisk! up he ran into the tree.

From the topmost branches he called down to the Crocodile in the water below:

"My heart is way up here! If you want it, come for it, come for it!"

147. TIT FOR TAT

(*India*)

THERE ONCE LIVED a Camel and Jackal who were great friends. One day the Jackal said to the Camel, "I know that there is a fine field of sugarcane on the other side of the river. If you will take me across I'll show you the place. This plan will suit me as well as you. You will enjoy eating the sugarcane, and I am sure to find many crabs, bones, and bits of fish by the riverside, on which to make a good dinner."

The Camel consented, and swam across the river, taking the Jackal, who could not swim, on his back. When they reached the other side, the Camel went to eat the sugarcane, and the Jackal ran up and down the riverbank devouring all the crabs, bits of fish, and bones he could find.

But being so much smaller an animal, he had made an excellent meal before the Camel had eaten more than two or three mouthfuls; and no sooner had he finished his dinner, than he ran round and round the sugarcane field, yelping and howling with all his might.

The villagers heard him; and thought, "There is a Jackal among the sugarcanes; he will be scratching holes in the ground, and spoiling the roots of the plants." And they went down to the place to drive him away. But when they got there, they found to their surprise not only a Jackal, but a Camel who was eating the sugarcanes! This made them very angry, and they caught the poor Camel, and drove him from the field, and beat him till he was nearly dead.

When they had gone, the Jackal said to the Camel, "We had better go home." And the Camel said, "Very well, then, jump upon my back as you did before."

So the Jackal jumped upon the Camel's back, and the Camel began to recross the river. When they had got well into the water, the Camel said, "This is a pretty way in which you have treated me, friend Jackal. No sooner had you finished your own dinner than you must go yelping about the place loud enough to arouse the whole village, and bring all the villagers down to beat me black and blue, and turn me out of the field before I had eaten two mouthfuls! What in the world did you make such a noise for?"

"I don't know," said the Jackal. "It is a custom I have. I always like to sing a little after dinner."

The Camel waded on through the river. The water reached up to his knees—then above them—up, up, up, higher and higher, until he was obliged to swim. Then turning to the Jackal, he said, "I feel very anxious to roll." "Oh, pray don't; why do you wish to do so?" asked the Jackal. "I don't know," answered the Camel; "it is a custom I have. I always like to have a little roll after dinner."

So saying, he rolled over in the water, shaking the Jackal off as he did so. And the Jackal was drowned, but the Camel swam safely ashore.

The Pacific

How Ma-ui Fished Up the Great Island

148. HOW MA-UI FISHED UP THE GREAT ISLAND

(Hawaii)

NOW, ALTHOUGH MA-UI HAD done many great deeds, he was not thought so very much of in his own house. His brothers complained that when he went fishing with them he caught no fish, or, if he drew one up, it was a fish that had been taken on a hook belonging to one of them and that Ma-ui had managed to get tangled on to his own line. And yet Ma-ui had invented many things that his brothers made use of. At first they had spears with smooth heads on them: if they struck a bird, the bird was often able to flutter away, drawing away from the spearhead that had pierced a wing. And if they struck through a fish, the fish was often able to wriggle away. Then Ma-ui put barbs upon his spear, and his spearhead held the birds and the fish. His brothers copied the spearhead that he made, and after that they were able to kill and secure more birds and fish than ever before.

He made many things that they copied, and yet his brothers thought him a lazy and a shiftless fellow, and they made their mother think the same about him. They were the better fishermen—that was true; indeed, if there were no one but Ma-ui to go fishing, Hina-of-the-Fire, his mother, and Hina-of-the-Sea, his sister, would often go hungry.

At last Ma-ui made up his mind to do some wonderful fishing; he might not be able to catch the fine fish that his brothers desired—the u-lua and the pi-mo-e—but he would take up something from the bottom of the sea that would make his brothers forget that he was the lazy and the shiftless one.

He had to make many plans and go on many adventures before he was ready for this great fishing. First he had to get a fishhook that was different from any fishhook that had ever been in the world before. In those days fishhooks were made out of bones—there was nothing else to make fishhooks out of—and Ma-ui would have to get a wonderful bone to form into a hook. He went down into the underworld to get that bone.

He went to where his ancestress was. On one side she was dead and on the other side she was a living woman. From the side of her that was dead Ma-ui took a bone—her jawbone—and out of this bone he made his fishhook. There was never a fishhook like it in the world before, and it was called "Ma-nai-i-ka-lani," meaning "made fast to the heavens." He told no one about the wonderful fishhook he had made for himself.

He had to get a different bait from any bait that had ever been used in the world before. His mother had sacred birds, the alae, and he asked her to give him one of them for bait. She gave him one of her birds.

Then Ma-ui, with his bait and his hook hidden, and with a line that he had made from the strongest olona vines, went down to his brothers' canoe. "Here is Ma-ui," they said when they saw him, "here is Ma-ui, the lazy and the shiftless, and we have sworn that we will never let him come again with us in our canoe." They pushed out when they saw him coming; they paddled away, although he begged them to take him with them.

He waited on the beach. His brothers came back, and they had to tell him that they had caught no fish. Then he begged them to go back to sea again and to let him go this time in their canoe. They let him in, and they paddled off. "Farther and farther out, my brothers," said Ma-ui; "out there is where the u-lua and the pi-mo-e are." They paddled far out. They let down their lines, but they caught no fish. "Where are the u-lua and the pi-mo-e that you spoke of?" said his brothers to him. Still he told them to go farther and farther out. At last they got tired with paddling, and they wanted to go back.

Then Ma-ui put a sail upon the canoe. Farther and farther out into the ocean they went. One of the brothers let down a line, and a great fish drew on it. They pulled. But what came out of the depths was a shark. They cut the line and let the shark away. The brothers were very tired now. "Oh, Ma-ui," they said, "as ever, thou art lazy and shiftless. Thou hast brought us out all this way, and thou wilt do nothing to help us. Thou hast let down no line in all the sea we have crossed."

It was then that Ma-ui let down his line with the magic hook upon it, the hook that was baited with the struggling alae bird. Down, down went the hook that was named "Ma-nai-i-ka-lani." Down through the waters the hook and the bait went. Ka-uni ho-kahi, Old One Tooth who holds fast the land to the bottom of the sea, was there. When the sacred bird came near him he took it in his mouth. And the magic hook that Ma-ui had made held fast in his jaws.

Ma-ui felt the pull upon the line. He fastened the line to the canoe, and he bade his brothers paddle their hardest, for now the great fish was caught. He dipped his own paddle into the sea, and he made the canoe dash on.

The brothers felt a great weight grow behind the canoe. But still they paddled on and on. Weighty and more weighty became the catch; harder and harder it became to pull it along. As they struggled on, Ma-ui chanted a magic chant, and the weight came with them.

> "O Island, O great Island,
> O Island, O great Island!
> Why art thou
> Sulkily biting, biting below?
> Beneath the earth
> The power is felt,
> The foam is seen:
> Come,
> O thou loved grandchild
> Of Kanaloa."

On and on the canoe went, and heavier and heavier grew what was behind them. At last one of the brothers looked back. At what he saw he screamed out in affright. For there, rising behind them, a whole land was rising up, with mountains upon it. The brother dropped his paddle when he saw what had been fished up; as he dropped his paddle the line that was fastened to the jaws of old Ka-uni ho-kahi broke.

What Ma-ui fished up would have been a mainland, only that his brother's paddle dropped and the line broke. Then only an island came up out of the water. If more land had come up, all the islands that we know would have been joined in one.

There are people who say that his sister, Hina-of-the-Sea, was near at the time of that great fishing. They say she came floating out on a calabash. When Ma-ui let down the magic hook with their mother's sacred bird upon it, Hina-of-the-Sea dived down and put the hook into the mouth of Old One Tooth, and then pulled at the line to let Ma-ui know that the hook was in his jaws. Some people say this, and it may be the truth. But whether or not, everyone, on every island in the Great Ocean, from Kahiki-mo-e to Hawaii nei, knows that Ma-ui fished up a great island for men to live on.

149. WHY THERE ARE NO TIGERS IN BORNEO

(Indonesia)

THOUGH TIGERS PROWL the jungles of Java and Sumatra and many other islands of Indonesia, there are none whatever in the forests of Borneo. An old folk story tells the reason for this.

It seems that the Rajah of All the Tigers, who lived on Java, found that food was getting so scarce that he and his subjects were threatened with starvation. So he decided that he would send word to the inhabitants of Borneo that they must send him food, or he would come with his army and conquer the land.

He selected three messengers to carry his ultimatum to Borneo, and they traveled over the sea and came to the island, weary and hot. They searched everywhere for the rajah of Borneo but could not find him. When they were about to give up, they met a tiny mouse-deer.

"Where is your rajah?" the tigers demanded. "We have an important message to deliver to him."

"He is hunting," the mouse-deer replied. "What is your important message?"

"We bring word from our rajah that your ruler must surrender. Take us to your rajah so that we can deliver our message."

The mouse-deer thought quickly. "Would it not be better if you rested here in the shade, after your long journey, and let me carry the message for you? I promise to find the rajah and deliver your message promptly, and I will bring you his answer."

The messengers looked at one another and decided, since it was so hot and they were so tired, to let the mouse-deer do as he suggested.

"Very well," said the spokesman, "but be quick about it. Go and tell him that the Rajah of All the Tigers demands food, in great quantiies which we shall specify. It must be given to us at once or our rajah will send his army to destroy you. What is more," he said, stepping forward and nearly knocking down the tiny mouse-deer, "give him this, as a token of our rajah's might." He drew out a tiger's whisker and gave it to the mouse-deer.

"This is from the royal face," he said importantly. "The rajah himself plucked it from his whiskers, to show how strong he is."

The mouse-deer took the royal whisker and held it away from him. "It is very large," he said, in a tiny voice. "Your rajah must be strong and fierce."

"Begone!" said the messenger imperiously. "We will wait here . . . but not too long."

The mouse-deer turned and fled. His thoughts raced as he ran. If the Rajah of All the Tigers in Java needed food he must be desperate for meat. "I am meat," thought the little mouse-deer, "and so are all the creatures on Borneo. If the Rajah of All the Tigers sends an army, he will destroy us . . . and then he will remain in Borneo. I must think!"

He ran through the woods and leaped the streams. Suddenly there was a rustling sound in the leaves and his quick eyes spied his friend the porcupine.

The porcupine peered up at him. "What is your hurry, kanchil?" he asked. "It is too hot to run so fast."

"I am worried . . . but seeing you has solved my problem. Give me one of your quills, friend, and save Borneo for all of us!"

"I'll gladly give you a quill," said the porcupine. "Surely I have enough and to spare—at least one for my good friend the mouse-deer. But can't you tell me why you need it?"

"Later," said the mouse-deer. "You are a good friend indeed. You have saved our country."

And off he bounded, bearing the quill in his teeth.

He ran as fast as he could back to the spot where he had left the tigers. They were pacing back and forth, looking annoyed and fierce.

"Well, you've been gone a long time!" the oldest one cried angrily.

"I had to find our rajah," said the mouse-deer breathlessly. "And I had to wait till he woke from his nap after his hunting. Then I had to wait for an audience. And then I had to wait for his answer."

"Well, what is it?" the messengers demanded. "Did you tell him what our rajah said?"

"Word for word, as you told it to me," the mouse-deer answered. "I told him that your rajah demanded food at once, and surrender, or he would come with his great army and destroy us."

"Yes, yes. And he said . . . ?"

The mouse-deer replied, "He said, 'Very well, let the Rajah of All the Tigers in Java come and fight us. He will find that we can fight better than he. In fact,' he said, 'I am weary of peace and would welcome a battle in which we could prove our might once more.'"

"Did you give him the whisker from the royal face?" the oldest tiger asked.

"I gave it to him," the mouse-deer replied. "And do you see this whisker I hold in my teeth?"

"Is that a whisker?" the tigers asked. "It is larger than you are, longer by a foot, and thicker than your leg."

"It is from the royal face of our rajah," the mouse-deer said. He took the quill from his teeth and handed it to the oldest messenger. "Feel it; see how thick it is. Our rajah plucked it from his face and said that I was to give it to you to take to your rajah."

"Nothing more?" the messengers asked, turning pale.

"Nothing more. . . . Oh, you are going?"

The oldest tiger said hurriedly, "We must return at once. Our rajah waits for your rajah's answer."

"Of course. And it is hot here, and you have a long way to go. Be sure to take good care of the whisker . . . although, if need be, our rajah can always send another one."

The oldest tiger took the big quill carefully in his paws, and all the messengers started back to Java. They crossed the land and then the water and then the land again, and came at last to the spot where their rajah waited impatiently.

"You have been gone far too long," the rajah rumbled in his throat. "What word do you bring?"

The messengers trembled at the terrible tone of his voice, thinking of the message they had to deliver. They looked to the oldest one, and he swallowed hard, and said, "Oh mighty one, the miserable rajah of Borneo said he would welcome war and sent you this."

He stepped forward fearfully and held out the big, thick quill of the porcupine. "It comes from his royal face," he quavered.

The Rajah of All the Tigers in Java gazed at it long and hard, stroking his own whiskers the while. He could not help feeling the difference. He said nothing for a long time.

Then he looked blandly at the trembling messengers. "I have de cided," he said, "that it would be better to demand food of the elephants of Sumatra."

Whether the elephants of Sumatra ever sent the food the story does not tell, but it is a fact that from that day to this there have been no tigers in Borneo.

150. HOW PLATYPUSES CAME TO AUSTRALIA
(*Australia*)

A YOUNG DUCK used to swim away by herself in the creek. Her tribe told her that Mulloka the water devil would catch her some day if she were so venturesome. But she did not heed them.

One day after having swum down some distance she landed on a bank where she saw some young green grass. She was feeding about when suddenly Biggoon, an immense water rat, rushed out from a hidden place and seized her.

She struggled and struggled, but all in vain. "I live alone," he said. "I want a wife."

"Let me go," said the duck. "I am not for you. My tribe has a mate for me."

"You stay quietly with me, and I will not hurt you. I am lonely here. If you struggle more, or try to escape, I will knock you on the head, or spear you with this little spear I always carry."

"But my tribe will come and fight you, and perhaps kill me."

"Not they. They will think Mulloka has got you. But even if they do come, let them. I am ready." And again he showed his spear.

The duck stayed. She was frightened to go while the rat watched her. She pretended that she liked her new life, and meant to stay always; while all the time she was thinking how she would escape. She knew her tribe came to look for her, for she heard them. But Biggoon kept her imprisoned in his hole in the side of the creek all day, only letting her out for a swim at night, when he knew her tribe would not come for fear of Mulloka.

She hid her feelings so well that at last Biggoon thought she really was content with him, and gradually he gave up watching her, taking his long day sleep as of old. Then came her chance.

One day, when Biggoon was sound asleep, she slunk out of the burrow, slid into the creek and swam away up it, as quickly as she could, toward her old camp.

Suddenly she heard a sound behind her. She thought it must be Biggoon, or perhaps the dreaded Mulloka, so, stiff as her wings were, she raised herself on them and flew the rest of the way, alighting at length very tired among her tribe.

They all gabbled around her at once, hardly giving her time to answer them. When they heard where she had been, the old mother ducks warned all the younger ones to swim only upstream in the future, for Biggoon would surely have vowed vengeance against them all now, and they must not risk meeting him.

How that little duck enjoyed her liberty and being with her tribe again! How she splashed as she pleased in the creek in the daytime and flew about at night if she wished! She felt as if she never wanted to sleep again.

It was not long before the laying season came. The ducks all chose their nesting places, some in hollow trees, and some in mirria bushes. When the nests were all nicely lined with down feathers, the ducks laid their eggs. Then they sat patiently on them until at last the little fluffy, downy ducks came out. Then in a little time the ducks in the trees took the ducklings on their backs and in their bills, and flew into the water with them, one at a time. Those in the mirria bushes waddled out with their young ones after them.

In due course the duck who had been imprisoned by Biggoon hatched out her young, too. Her friends came swimming around the mirria bush she was in, and said, "Come along. Bring out your young ones, too. Teach them to love the water as we do."

Out she came, only two children after her. And what were they? Such a quacking gabble her friends set up, shrieking, "What are those?"

"My children," she said proudly.

She would not show that she, too, was puzzled at her children's being quite different from those of her tribe. Instead of down feathers they had a soft fur. Instead of two feet they had four. Their bills were those of ducks, and their feet were webbed, and on the hind ones were just showing the points of a spear, like Biggoon always carried to be in readiness for his enemies.

"Take them away," cried the ducks, flapping their wings and making a great splash. "Take them away. They are more like Biggoon than us. Look at their hind feet; the tip of his spear is sticking from them already. Take them away, or we shall kill them before they grow big and kill us. They do not belong to our tribe. Take them away. They have no right here."

And such a row they made that the poor little mother duck went off with her two little despised children, of whom she had been so proud despite their peculiarities.

She did not know where to go. If she went down the creek Biggoon might catch her again, and make her live in the burrow, or kill her children because they had webbed feet, a duck's bill, and had been hatched out of eggs. He would say they did not belong to his tribe. No one would own them. There would never be anyone but herself to care for them. The sooner she took them right away the better.

So thinking, away upstream she went until she reached the mountains. There she could hide from all who knew her, and bring up her children. On and on she went, until the creek grew narrow and scrubby on its banks, so changed from the broad streams which used to flow placidly between large unbroken plains that she scarcely knew it. She lived there for a little while, then pined away and died, because even her children, as they grew, saw how different they were from her, and kept away by themselves, until she felt too lonely and miserable to live, too unhappy to find food. Thus pining she soon died, away on the mountains, far from her old noorumba, or hereditary hunting ground, which was hers by right of birth.

The children lived on and throve, laid eggs and hatched out more children just like themselves, until at last, pair by pair, they so increased that before long all the mountain creeks had some of them. And there they still live, the Gayadari, or platypus, quite a tribe apart—for when did ever a rat lay eggs? Or a duck have four feet?

151. THE BUNYIP
(Australia)

LONG, LONG AGO, some young men left the camp where they lived to get some food for their wives and children. The sun was hot, but they liked heat, and as they went they ran races and tried who could hurl his spear the farthest, or was cleverest in throwing a weapon called a boomerang, which always returns to the thrower. They did not get on very fast at this rate, but presently they reached a flat place that in time of flood was full of water, but was now, in the height of summer, only a set of pools, each surrounded with a fringe of plants, with bulrushes standing in the inside of all. In that country the people are fond of the roots of bulrushes, which they think as good as onions, and one of the young men said that they had better collect some of the roots and carry them back to the camp. It did not take them long to weave the tops of the willows into a basket, and they were just going to wade into the water and pull up the bulrush roots when a youth suddenly called out: "After all, why should we waste our time in doing work that is only fit for women and children? Let them come and get the roots for themselves; but we will fish for eels and anything else we can get."

This delighted the rest of the party, and they all began to arrange their fishing lines, made from the bark of the yellow mimosa, and to search for bait for their hooks. Most of them used worms, but one, who had put a piece of raw meat for dinner into his skin wallet, cut off a little bit and baited his line with it, unseen by his companions.

For a long time they cast patiently, without receiving a single bite; the sun had grown low in the sky, and it seemed as if they would have to go home empty-handed, not even with a basket of roots to show; when the youth, who had baited his hook with raw meat, suddenly saw his line disappear under the water. Something, a very heavy fish he supposed, was pulling so hard that he could hardly keep his feet, and for a few minutes it seemed either as if he must let go or be dragged into the pool. He cried to his friends to help him, and at last, trembling with fright at what they were going to see, they managed between them to land on the bank a creature that was neither a calf nor a seal, but something of both, with a long, broad tail. They looked at each other with horror, cold shivers running down their spines; for though they had never beheld it, there was not a man among them who did not know what it was—the cub of the awful Bunyip!

All of a sudden the silence was broken by a low wail, answered by another from the other side of the pool, as the mother rose up from her den and came toward them, rage flashing from her horrible yellow eyes. "Let it go! let it go!" whispered the young men to each other; but the captor declared that he had caught it, and was going to keep it. "He had promised his sweetheart," he said, "that he would bring back enough meat for her father's house to feast on for three days, and though they could not eat the little Bunyip, her brothers and sisters should have it to play with." So, flinging his spear at the mother to keep her back, he threw the little Bunyip onto his shoulders, and set out for the camp, never heeding the poor mother's cries of distress.

By this time it was getting near sunset, and the plain was in shadow, though the tops of the mountains were still quite bright. The youths had all ceased to be afraid, when they were startled by a low rushing sound behind them, and, looking round, saw that the pool was slowly rising, and the spot where they had landed the Bunyip was quite covered. "What could it be?" they asked one of another; "there was not a cloud in the sky, yet the water had risen higher already than they had ever known it do before." For an instant they stood watching as if they were frozen, then they turned and ran with all their might, the man with the Bunyip running faster than all. When he reached a high peak overlooking all the plain he stopped to take breath, and turned to see if he was safe yet. Safe! why only the tops of the trees remained above that sea of water, and these were fast disappearing. They must run fast indeed if they were to escape. So on they flew, scarcely feeling the ground as they went, till they flung themselves on the ground before the holes scooped out of the earth where they had all been born. The old men were sitting in front, the children were playing, and the women chattering together, when the little Bunyip fell into their midst, and there was scarcely a child among them who did not know that something terrible was upon them. "The water! the water!" gasped one of the young men; and there it was, slowly but steadily mounting the ridge itself. Parents and children clung together, as if by that means they could drive back the advancing flood; and the youth who had caused all this terrible catastrophe, seized his sweetheart, and cried: "I will climb with you to the top of that tree, and there no waters can reach us." But, as he spoke, something cold touched him, and quickly he glanced down at his feet. Then with a shudder he saw that they were feet no longer, but bird's claws. He looked at the girl he was clasping, and beheld a great black bird standing at his side; he turned to his friends, but a flock of great awkward flapping creatures stood in their place. He put up his hands to cover his face, but they were no more hands, only the ends of wings; and when he tried to speak, a noise such as he had never heard before seemed to come from his throat, which had suddenly become narrow and slender. Already the water had risen to his waist, and he found himself sitting easily upon it, while its surface reflected back the image of a black swan, one of many.

Never again did the swans become men; but they are still different from other swans, for in the nighttime those who listen can hear them talk in a language that is certainly not swan's language; and there are even sounds of laughing and talking, unlike any noise made by the swans whom we know.

The little Bunyip was carried home by its mother, and after that the waters sank back to their own channels. The side of the pool where she lives is always shunned by everyone, as nobody knows when she may suddenly put out her head and draw him into her mighty jaws. But people say that underneath the black waters of the pool she has a house filled with beautiful things, such as mortals who dwell on the earth have no idea of. Though how they know I cannot tell you, as nobody has ever seen it.

Africa

Why There Are Cracks in Tortoise's Shell

152. TALK*
(Africa—Ashanti Tribe)

ONCE, NOT FAR from the city of Accra on the Gulf of Guinea, a country man went out to his garden to dig up some yams to take to market. While he was digging, one of the yams said to him, "Well, at last you're here. You never weeded me, but now you come around with your digging stick. Go away and leave me alone!"

The farmer turned around and looked at his cow in amazement. The cow was chewing her cud and looking at him.

"Did you say something?" he asked.

The cow kept on chewing and said nothing, but the man's dog spoke up. "It wasn't the cow who spoke to you," the dog said. "It was the yam. The yam says leave him alone."

The man became angry, because his dog had never talked before, and he didn't like his tone besides. So he took his knife and cut a branch from a palm tree to whip his dog. Just then the palm tree said, "Put that branch down!"

The man was getting very upset about the way things were going, and he started to throw the palm branch away, but the palm branch said, "Man, put me down softly!"

He put the branch down gently on a stone, and the stone said, "Hey, take that thing off me!"

This was enough, and the frightened farmer started to run for his village. On the way he met a fisherman going the other way with a fish trap on his head.

"What's the hurry?" the fisherman asked.

"My yam said, 'Leave me alone!' Then the dog said, 'Listen to what the yam says!' When I went to whip the dog with a palm branch the tree said, 'Put that branch down!' Then the palm branch said, 'Do it softly!' Then the stone said, 'Take that thing off me!'"

---

* From *The Cow-Tail Switch* by Harold Courlander and George Herzog. © 1947 by Holt, Rinehart & Winston, © 1965 by Harold Courlander and George Herzog.

"Is that all?" the man with the fish trap asked. "Is that so frightening?"

"Well," the man's fish trap said, "did he take it off the stone?"

"Wah!" the fisherman shouted. He threw the fish trap on the ground and began to run with the farmer, and on the trail they met a weaver with a bundle of cloth on his head.

"Where are you going in such a rush?" he asked them.

"My yam said, 'Leave me alone!' " the farmer said. "The dog said, 'Listen to what the yam says!' The tree said, 'Put that branch down!' The branch said, 'Do it softly!' And the stone said, 'Take that thing off me!' "

"And then," the fisherman continued, "the fish trap said, 'Did he take it off?' "

"That's nothing to get excited about," the weaver said. "No reason at all."

"Oh, yes it is," his bundle of cloth said. "If it happened to you you'd run too!"

"Wah!" the weaver shouted. He threw his bundle on the trail and started running with the other men.

They came panting to the ford in the river and found a man bathing. "Are you chasing a gazelle?" he asked them.

The first man said breathlessly, "My yam talked at me, and it said, 'Leave me alone!' And my dog said, 'Listen to your yam!' And when I cut myself a branch the tree said, 'Put that branch down!' And the branch said, 'Do it softly!' And the stone said, 'Take that thing off me!' "

The fisherman panted, "And my trap said, 'Did he?' "

The weaver wheezed, "And my bundle of cloth said, 'You'd run too!' "

"Is that why you're running?" the man in the river asked.

"Well, wouldn't you run if you were in their position?" the river said.

The man jumped out of the water and began to run with the others. They ran down the main street of the village to the house of the chief. The chief's servant brought his stool out, and he came and sat on it to listen to their complaints. The men began to recite their troubles.

"I went out to my garden to dig yams," the farmer said, waving his arms. "Then everything began to talk! My yam said, 'Leave me alone!' My dog said, 'Pay attention to your yam!' The tree said, 'Put that branch down!' The branch said, 'Do it softly!' And the stone said, 'Take it off me!' "

"And my fish trap said, 'Well, did he take it off?'" the fisherman said.

"And my cloth said, 'You'd run too!'" the weaver said.

"And the river said the same," the bather said hoarsely, his eyes bulging.

The chief listened to them patiently, but he couldn't refrain from scowling. "Now this is really a wild story," he said at last. "You'd better all go back to your work before I punish you for disturbing the peace."

So the men went away, and the chief shook his head and mumbled to himself, "Nonsense like that upsets the community."

"Fantastic, isn't it?" his stool said. "Imagine, a talking yam!"

153. ANANSI'S HAT-SHAKING DANCE*
(Africa—Ashanti Tribe)

IF YOU LOOK CLOSELY, you will see that Kwaku Anansi, the spider, has a bald head. It is said that in the old days he had hair, but that he lost it through vanity.

It happened that Anansi's mother-in-law died. When word came to Anansi's house, Aso, his wife, prepared to go at once to her own village for the funeral. But Anansi said to Aso: "You go ahead; I will follow."

When Aso had gone, Anansi said to himself: "When I go to my dead mother-in-law's house, I will have to show great grief over her death. I will have to refuse to eat. Therefore, I shall eat now." And so he sat in his own house and ate a huge meal. Then he put on his mourning clothes and went to Aso's village.

First there was the funeral. Afterward there was a large feast. But Anansi refused to eat, out of respect for his wife's dead mother. He

* From *The Hat-shaking Dance and Other Ashanti Tales from Ghana.* © 1957 by Harold Courlander. Reprinted by permission of Harcourt Brace Jovanovich, Inc.

said: "What kind of man would I be to eat when I am mourning for my mother-in-law? I will eat only after the eighth day has passed."

Now this was not expected of him, because a man isn't required to starve himself simply because someone has died. But Anansi was the kind of person that when he ate, he ate twice as much as others, and when he danced, he danced more vigorously than others, and when he mourned, he had to mourn more loudly than anybody else. Whatever he did, he didn't want to be outdone by anyone else. And although he was very hungry, he couldn't bear to have people think he wasn't the greatest mourner at his own mother-in-law's funeral.

So he said: "Feed my friends, but as for me, I shall do without." So everyone ate—the porcupine, the rabbit, the snake, the guinea fowl, and the others. All except Anansi.

On the second day after the funeral they said to him again: "Eat, there is no need to starve."

But Anansi replied: "Oh no, not until the eighth day, when the mourning is over. What kind of man do you think I am?"

So the others ate. Anansi's stomach was empty, and he was unhappy.

On the third day they said again: "Eat, Kwaku Anansi, there is no need to go hungry."

But Anansi was stubborn. He said: "How can I eat when my wife's mother has been buried only three days?" And so the others ate, while Anansi smelled the food hungrily and suffered.

On the fourth day, Anansi was alone where a pot of beans was cooking over the fire. He smelled the beans and looked in the pot. At last he couldn't stand it any longer. He took a large spoon and dipped up a large portion of the beans, thinking to take it to a quiet place and eat it without anyone's knowing. But just then the dog, the guinea fowl, the rabbit, and the others returned to the place where the food was cooking.

To hide the beans, Anansi quickly poured them in his hat and put it on his head. The other people came to the pot and ate, saying again: "Anansi, you must eat."

He said: "No, what kind of man would I be?"

But the hot beans were burning his head. He jiggled his hat around with his hands. When he saw the others looking at him, he said: "Just at this very moment in my village the hat-shaking festival is taking place. I shake my hat in honor of the occasion."

The beans felt hotter than ever, and he jiggled his hat some more. He began to jump with pain, and he said: "Like this in my village they are doing the hat-shaking dance."

He danced about, jiggling his hat because of the heat. He yearned to take off his hat, but he could not because his friends would see the beans. So he shouted: "They are shaking and jiggling the hats in my village, like this! It is a great festival! I must go!"

They said to him: "Kwaku Anansi, eat something before you go."

But now Anansi was jumping and writhing with the heat of the beans on his head. He shouted: "Oh no, they are shaking hats, they are wriggling hats and jumping like this! I must go to my village! They need me!"

He rushed out of the house, jumping and pushing his hat back and forth. His friends followed after him saying: "Eat before you go on your journey!"

But Anansi shouted: "What kind of man do you think I am, with my mother-in-law just buried?"

Even though they all followed right after him, he couldn't wait any longer, because the pain was too much, and he tore the hat from his head. When the dog saw, and the guinea fowl saw, and the rabbit saw, and all the others saw what was in the hat, and saw the hot beans sticking to Anansi's head, they stopped chasing him. They began to laugh and jeer.

Anansi was overcome with shame. He leaped into the tall grass, saying: "Hide me." And the grass hid him.

That is why Anansi is often found in the tall grass, where he was driven by shame. And you will see that his head is bald, for the hot beans he put in his hat burned off his hair.

All this happened because he tried to impress people at his mother-in-law's funeral.

154. ANANSI AND HIS VISITOR, TURTLE
(Africa—Ashanti Tribe)
West Africa Ghana

IT WAS ALMOST TIME for Sun to sink to his resting place when Turtle, tired and dusty from hours of wandering, came to Anansi's house in the middle of a clearing in the woods. Turtle was hungry and the appetizing aroma of freshly cooked fish and yams drew him to approach Anansi's door and to knock. Anansi jerked the door open. When he saw the tired stranger he was inwardly annoyed, but it was an unwritten law of his country that one must never, no never, refuse hospitality to a passer-by.

Anansi smiled grimly and said, "Come in, come in, and share my dinner, Mr. Turtle."

As Turtle stretched out one paw to help himself from the steaming platter Anansi almost choked on a mouthful of food. In a shocked voice he said, "Turtle, I must remind you that in my country it is ill-mannered to come to the table without first washing. Please go to the stream at the foot of the hill and wash your dusty paws."

Turtle waddled down the hill and waded in the water for a while. He even washed his face. By the time he had trudged back up the trail to Anansi's house, the platter of fish was half empty. Anansi was eating at a furious rate.

Turtle stretched out one paw to help himself to food, but again Anansi stopped him. "Turtle, your paws are still dusty. Please, go wash them."

"It is the dust from the long trail up the hill," Turtle explained in a meek voice. Clearly, it was not Turtle's place to argue if he expected to share the delectable meal, so he crawled down the hill a second time and rewashed his paws. Turtle was careful to walk on the grass beside the dusty trail on the climb back to Anansi's house. He hurried, for by now he was ravenous.

But, oh dear! Anansi had scraped the platter bare of fish and yams.

"My, that was a good dinner," he said, wiping the last drop of gravy from his chin.

"Thank you for your wonderful hospitality, Anansi. Some day you must visit me." And Turtle, in a huff, went on home.

Some months later Anansi visited Turtle. After creepy crawling all day from one tall grass stem to the next he found Turtle snoozing beside the river.

"Well, well," exclaimed Turtle. "So you have come to share my dinner. Make yourself comfortable, my dear Anansi, while I go below and prepare the food." He plunged into the river with a splash. Anansi was hungry. He paced the shore line and watched for Turtle's reappearance.

At last Turtle's head popped above the water. "Dinner is ready," he called as he bit into a huge clam. "Come on down." Then he disappeared from sight.

Anansi dived head first into the water, sank a few inches, then floated to the surface. His spindly legs and tiny body prevented him from sinking. He flipped and flapped his puny arms, tried swallow dives and belly flops, but he could not reach the bed of the river.

Then that cunning spider schemed. He filled the pockets of his jacket with small round pebbles, dived into the river, and sank with a bump that landed him right at the dinner table. Before him was spread the most delicious meal he had ever seen. There were oysters and clams, mussels, slices of eel, and crabs. As a centerpiece, sprays of watercress rested against large pink shrimp. Anansi's eyes widened with pleasure, his stomach rumbled in anticipation.

Turtle, already seated at the table, swallowed a piece of eel, looked at Anansi and said, "Oh, Anansi, I must remind you that in my country it is ill-mannered to come to the table wearing a jacket. Please take it off."

Very slowly Anansi removed his jacket. Very slowly Anansi left the table. Without the weight of the pebbles to hold him down he floated straight up through the green water and out of sight.

When you set out to outsmart another person to your own advantage, there is usually someone who can outsmart you.

155. HOW SPIDER OBTAINED THE SKY-GOD'S STORIES
(Africa—Ashanti Tribe)

KWAKU ANANSI, THE SPIDER, once went to Nyankonpon, the sky-god, in order to buy the sky-god's stories. The sky-god said, "What makes you think *you* can buy them?" The spider answered and said, "I know I shall be able." Thereupon the sky-god said, "Great and powerful towns like Kokofu, Bekwai, Asumengya, have come, but they were unable to purchase them, and yet you who are but a mere masterless man, you say you will be able?"

The spider said, "What is the price of the stories?" The sky-god said, "They cannot be bought for anything except Onini, the python; Osebo, the leopard; Mmoatia, the fairy; and Mmoboro, the hornets." The spider said, "I will bring some of all these things, and, what is more, I'll add my old mother, Nsia, the sixth child, to the lot."

The sky-god said, "Go and bring them then." The spider came back, and told his mother all about it, saying, "I wish to buy the stories of the sky-god, and the sky-god says I must bring Onini, the python; Osebo, the leopard; Mmoatia, the fairy; and Mmoboro, the hornets; and I said I would add you to the lot and give you to the sky-god." Now the spider consulted his wife, Aso, saying, "What is to be done that we may get Onini, the python?" Aso said to him, "You go off and cut a branch of a palm tree, and cut some string-creeper as well, and bring them." And the spider came back with them. And Aso said, "Take them to the stream." So Anansi took them; and, as he was going along, he said, "It's longer than he is, it's not so long as he; you lie, it's longer than he."

The spider said, "There he is, lying yonder." The python, who had overheard this imaginary conversation, then asked, "What's this all about?" To which the spider replied, "Is it not my wife, Aso, who is arguing with me that this palm branch is longer than you, and I say she is a liar." And Onini, the python, said, "Bring it, and come and measure me." Anansi took the palm branch and laid it along the python's body. Then he said, "Stretch yourself out." And the python stretched himself out, and Anansi took the rope-creeper and wound it and the sound of the tying was *nwenene! nwenene! nwenene!* until he came to the head.

Anansi, the spider, said, "Fool, I shall take you to the sky-god and receive the sky-god's tales in exchange." So Anansi took him off to Nyame, the sky-god. The sky-god then said, "My hand has touched it, there remains what still remains." The spider returned and came and told his wife what had happened, saying, "There remain the hornets." His wife said, "Look for a gourd, and fill it with water and go off with it." The spider went along through the bush, when he saw a swarm of hornets hanging there, and he poured out some of the water and sprinkled it on them. He then poured the remainder upon himself and cut a leaf of plantain and covered his head with it. And now he addressed the hornets, saying, "As the rain has come, had you not better come and enter this, my gourd, so that the rain will not beat you; don't you see that I have taken a plantain leaf to cover myself?" Then the hornets said, "We thank you, Aku, we thank you, Aku." All the hornets flew, disappearing into the gourd, *fom!* Father Spider covered the mouth, and exclaimed, "Fools, I have got you, and I am taking you to receive the tales of the sky-god in exchange."

And he took the hornets to the sky-god. The sky-god said, "My hand has touched it; what remains still remains."

The spider came back once more, and told his wife, and said, "There remains Osebo, the leopard." Aso said, "Go and dig a hole." Anansi said, "That's enough, I understand." Then the spider went off to look for the leopard's tracks, and, having found them, he dug a very deep pit, covered it over, and came back home. Very early next day, when objects began to be visible, the spider said he would go off, and when he went, lo, a leopard was lying in the pit. Anansi said, "Little father's child, little mother's child, I have told you not to get drunk, and now, just as one would expect of you, you have become intoxicated, and that's why you have fallen into the pit. If I were to say I would get you out, next day, if you saw me, or likewise any of my children, you would go and catch me and them." The leopard said, "O! I could not do such a thing."

Anansi then went and cut two sticks, put one here, and one there, and said, "Put one of your paws here, and one also of your paws here."

And the leopard placed them where he was told. As he was about to climb up, Anansi lifted up his knife, and in a flash it descended on his head, *gao!* was the sound it made. The pit received the leopard and *fom!* was the sound of the falling. Anansi got a ladder to descend into the pit to go and get the leopard out. He got the leopard out and came back with it, exclaiming, "Fool, I am taking you to exchange for the stories of the sky-god." He lifted up the leopard to go and give to Nyame, the sky-god. The sky-god said, "My hands have touched it; what remains still remains."

Then the spider came back, carved an Akua's child, a black flat-faced wooden doll, tapped some sticky fluid from a tree and plastered the doll's body with it. Then he made *eto*, pounded yams, and put some in the doll's hand. Again he pounded some more and placed it in a brass basin; he tied string round the doll's waist, and went with it and placed it at the foot of the odum tree, the place where the fairies come to play. And a fairy came along. She said, "Akua, may I eat a little of this mash?" Anansi tugged at the string, and the doll nodded her head. The fairy turned to one of the sisters, saying, "She says I may eat some." She said, "Eat some, then." And she finished eating, and thanked her. But when she thanked her, the doll did not answer. And the fairy said to her sister, "When I thank her, she does not reply." The sister of the first fairy said, "Slap her crying-place." And she slapped it, *pa!* And her hand stuck there. She said to her sister, "My hand has stuck there." She said, "Take the one that remains and slap her crying-place again." And she took it and slapped her, *pa!* and this one, too, stuck fast. And the fairy told her sister, saying, "My two hands have stuck fast." She said, "Push it with your stomach." She pushed it and her stomach stuck to it. And Anansi came and tied her up, and he said, "Fool, I have got you, I shall take you to the sky-god in exchange for his stories." And he went off home with her.

Now Anansi spoke to his mother, Ya Nsia, the sixth child, saying, "Rise up, let us go, for I am taking you along with the fairy to go and give you to the sky-god in exchange for his stories." He lifted them up, and went off there to where the sky-god was. Arrived there he said, "Sky-god, here is a fairy and my old woman whom I spoke about, here she is, too." Now the sky-god called his elders, the Kontire and Akwam chiefs, the Adonten, the Gyase, the Oyoko, Ankobea, and Kyidom. And he put the matter before them, saying, "Very great kings have come, and were not able to buy the sky-god's stories, but Kwaku Anansi, the spider, has been able to pay the price: I have received from him Osebo, the leopard; I have received from him Onini, the python; and of his own accord, Anansi has added his mother to the lot; all these things lie here." He said, "Sing his praise." "*Eee!*" they shouted. The sky-god said, "Kwaku Anansi, from today and going on forever, I take my sky-god's stories and I present them to you, *kose! kose! kose!* my blessing, blessing, blessing! No more shall we call them the stories of the sky-god, but we shall call them spider-stories."

This, my story, which I have related, if it be sweet, or if it be not sweet, take some elsewhere, and let some come back to me.

156. YOUNDE GOES TO TOWN
(West Africa)

ONCE IN THE COUNTRY of Akim, in the hills far back from the coast, there was a man named Younde. He was a simple man who had never been far from home, and he spent his time at farming and hunting like the other people of the village. He had often heard talk about the big town of Accra by the ocean, and all the wonderful things to be found there, but he had never seen it. He had never been farther from his village than the river.

But one day Younde had to go to Accra. He put on his best clothes, and took his knife and put it in his belt. He wrapped some food in a cloth and put it on his head and started out. He walked for many days, and the road was hot and dusty. After a while he was out of his own country, and people didn't speak Akim, which was his language, any more. He came closer and closer to Accra. There were many people and donkeys on the way, all going to town or coming back from town, more people than he had ever seen on the road before.

Then he saw a great herd of cows grazing by the edge of the road. He had never seen so many cows in his life. He stopped and looked at them in wonder. He saw a little boy herding the cows and he went up to him and said, "Who is the owner of all these cattle?"

But the boy didn't understand Younde, because Younde spoke Akim, while in Accra they spoke the Ga language, and he replied, "Minu," which meant "I don't understand."

"Minu! What a rich man he must be to own so many cows!" Younde said.

He continued his way into the town. He was very impressed with everything he saw.

He came to a large building and stopped to look at it. It was made of stone, and it was very high. He shook his head. There was nothing like this back in the hills. When a woman came by on her way to market Younde spoke to her.

"What a tremendous house!" he said. "What rich person can own such a building?"

But the woman didn't know what Younde was saying, because he talked Akim and she knew only Ga, so she replied to him:

"Minu."

"Minu! That man again!"

Younde was overcome. No one back in Akim had ever been so wealthy as Minu. As he went farther and farther into the town he kept seeing more wonders. He came to the market. It covered a space larger than all the houses in Younde's village. He walked through the center of it, and saw the women selling things that were rare in his village, like iron pots and iron spoons.

"Where do all these things come from?" Younde asked a little girl. She smiled at him.

"Minu," she replied.

Younde was silent. Everything was Minu. Minu everywhere.

The crowd was very great. People pushed and shoved, for it was the big market day and everyone within walking distance had come to sell or buy. Younde had never seen so many people in one place. The stories he had heard about Accra hadn't done it justice. He stopped an old man with a drum under his arm and said:

"So many people, all at one time! What makes so many people all come to Accra?"

"Minu," the old man said.

Younde was overwhelmed. What influence that Minu had! People came to Accra in great crowds just because of him. How ignorant folks back in the village were of this great personage.

He went out of the market down to the ocean's edge. Lying in the water were many little fishing boats with sails, the first Younde had ever seen.

"Wah! To whom do all those boats belong?" he asked a fisherman standing on the beach.

"Minu," the fisherman replied.

Younde walked away, and came to where a large iron cargo ship was being loaded with palm oil and fruit. Smoke came out of its stacks in huge black clouds, and hundreds of men swarmed over its decks.

"Hah!" Younde said in great excitement to a man carrying a stalk of bananas on his head. "This must be the largest boat in the world!"

"Minu," the man said.

"Yes, I know, that much I guessed," Younde said. "But where is all the fruit going?"

"Minu," the man said, and went up onto the deck of the ship.

Younde was overcome. Minu was indeed a great man. He owned everything. He ate everything. You couldn't ask a question but what people would answer "Minu." Minu here, there, everywhere.

"I wouldn't have believed it if I hadn't seen it," Younde said. "They ought to call Accra 'Minu's Town.' How wonderful it would be to have Minu's great wealth!"

Younde then transacted his business in Accra, and again he wrapped food in his cloth and set it on his head and started out for home.

When he came to the edge of the town he saw a great procession and heard the beating of drums. He came close and saw it was a funeral. Men were carrying a coffin and women were crying out in mourning. It was the most impressive funeral Younde had ever seen. He pushed his way into the crowd and looked. And to one of the mourners he said:

"Who is this person who has died?"

And the mourner replied sadly:

"Minu."

"What! The great Minu is dead?" Younde said. "The man who owned the cattle and the tall house, the sailing boats and the iron steamship? The man whose reputation has crowded the market place beyond belief? Oh, poor Minu! He had to leave all his wealth behind. He has died just like an ordinary person!"

Younde continued his way out of the city, but he couldn't get the tragedy of Minu from his mind.

"Poor Minu!" he said over and over again. "Poor Minu!"

157. HOW FROG LOST HIS TAIL
(Africa—Sukuma Tribe)

FROG SQUATTED IN HIS muddy home on the edge of the water hole. He felt miserable. He knew he was ugly, with a mouth like a black cave and protruding eyes like doorknobs. And his figure! Frog worried because he thought he resembled nothing better than an old potato that has gone to seed. Frog's chief grievance was that he had no tail.

Each day at sundown when the forest and savanna animals came to drink, they swished their tails and jeered at Frog because he was ugly. So Frog went to the Sky God. He implored the great spirit to improve his appearance. "At least, give me a tail," Frog begged.

"Very well," the Sky God declared. "I will give you a tail if you will be watchman for my special well that never dries up."

Frog replied, "I will guard the well closely. Now, please, give me a tail."

Frog showed off his long, tapering tail by hopping to and fro before his new home beside the special well. Unfortunately, having such a magnificent tail as well as his responsible position made Frog conceited —and very bossy. And he never forgot or ever forgave the animals for their previous unfriendliness. Frog's arrogance became unbearable when every other water hole and well but his special charge dried up.

"Who comes to this muddy well?" Frog demanded when the animals crawled weakly in search of water to quench their thirst. Then he would shout rudely, "Go away! Go away! There is no water here. The well is dry."

The Sky God heard of Frog's behavior. He came quietly to the well and he received the same unkind treatment. The Sky God shook with anger. He punished Frog. He took away his tail and he drove him from the well.

The Sky God keeps reminding Frog of the misery he caused. Every springtime when Frog is born as a tadpole, he has a long, beautiful tail.

But as he grows, his tail shrinks. It shrinks and shrinks and then it disappears.

The Sky God takes the tail away because Frog was once spiteful and unforgiving.

158. THE RUBBER MAN
(Africa—Hausa Tribe)

SPIDER WAS A LAZY fellow. The rainy season had come and everybody except Spider was working on the farms—hoeing, digging, and planting. Every morning Spider lay long in bed, only rising at midday, to eat a leisurely meal and spend the afternoon resting under a shady tree.

Now his wife knew that the other people in the village had almost finished their planting, and each day she would say hesitantly:

"Don't forget to tell me when you want my help on the farm," for she dared say no more than that.

Spider would reply, "Oh, there's plenty of time yet. The rains have scarcely begun."

But as the days went by and people passing on the road called out to Spider, asking him when he was going to begin work on his farm, he decided on a plan.

"Today I shall begin clearing the weeds and tomorrow I shall plant groundnuts," he said to his wife one morning. "Go to the market and buy a sackful, then roast them and salt them and have them ready for me to plant in the morning."

"But husband," objected his wife, "whoever heard of groundnuts being roasted and salted except for eating?"

"Don't argue with me, woman," said Spider. "I know what I am doing. Surely you understand that if we plant groundnuts prepared in this way, then the fresh crop they produce will be already roasted and salted and we shall be able to eat them as soon as they are ripe, without cooking them at all."

"How clever you are," said his simple wife, as she set off for the market, while Spider went deep into the bush where no one could see him, and had a good sleep.

That evening Spider returned and told his wife how hard he had worked on the farm, while he watched her shelling, roasting, and salting the groundnuts.

As soon as the sun rose, Spider took the sack of nuts and pretended to go to his farm. Along the little winding paths he went, until he was far away from the village and the farms. Then, sitting down beneath a tree, he had a wonderful feast and ate every single nut. He followed this with a drink of water from a nearby stream, then, curling up in the shade of a tree, slept soundly until sunset.

Hurrying home he called to his wife, "Isn't supper ready yet? We men have a hard life! Here have I been working all day in the fields and you, with nothing to do except cook my supper, haven't even got it ready yet!"

"It's just coming," replied his wife, as she brought him his meal. "And I will put some water on the fire now, so that you can wash with warm water before you go to bed."

Every day the same thing happened. Spider said good-bye to his wife in the morning and pretended to go to his farm, but instead of hoeing and weeding like the other men he found a quiet, lonely spot and went to sleep. When evening came, he went back to his wife, complaining of his tired limbs and aching back, and after a well-cooked supper and a good wash he went to bed.

Time passed until, one by one, the other husbands began to bring home their harvest. But Spider brought nothing. At last his wife said:

"Surely our groundnuts are ready by now? Nearly everyone in the village is harvesting."

"Ours are slower than the others," replied Spider. "Wait a little longer."

At last his wife changed her tactics and suggested:

"I'll come to the farm with you tomorrow and help with the harvest. I'm sure our nuts are ready now."

"I don't want you working on the farm like a poor man's wife," replied Spider. "Have patience for a few more days and I'll harvest the groundnuts myself and bring them home."

Now Spider was indeed in a fix! How could he bring home groundnuts to his wife when he had not even got a farm? There was only one solution. He must steal some.

That night, when his wife was asleep, he crept out of the house and made his way to the biggest farm of all, the chief's farm which still had row upon row of groundnuts unharvested. As quietly as he could, he filled his leather bag with nuts which he dug from the ground, and hiding the bag in a tree some distance away, he returned home.

Early next morning he announced cheerfully to his wife:

"Aha! Today I go to the farm to harvest the first of our nuts. Mind you have a good supper waiting for me when I come home tired and weary."

"Oh yes, husband, I will," exclaimed his delighted wife, little knowing that Spider was going straight to the tree where he had hidden his bag and would sleep there all day. She had supper ready for him when he came home, complaining of exhaustion and describing how hard he had worked digging up the nuts, which he handed to her.

Joyfully she cracked open a nut and put it in her mouth. Then her face fell and she cried:

"But these are ordinary nuts! Did you not say that they would grow already roasted and salted?"

"I remember saying no such thing," replied Spider. "The reason we salted the nuts was to keep the ants from eating them, once I had planted them in the soil. What a stupid woman you are to think nuts can grow which are roasted and salted already!"

"I see," said his wife. "I must have misunderstood you," and being a very simple woman she thought no more about it.

That night, and a number of following nights, Spider went back to the chief's farm, stole a bagful of groundnuts and hid them in a tree. Then when morning came he pretended to go to his farm, had a long, deep sleep and returned to his wife with the stolen goods in the evening.

But alas! the chief's servant soon noticed that somebody was stealing his master's nuts and was determined to catch him, so taking several large calabashes, he went into the bush until he found some guttapercha trees. Then, making long slashes in the bark, he left a calabash at the foot of each tree to catch the sap as it trickled out, and next day when he returned he found they were full of sticky, brown rubber. This he took back to the farm and made into the shape of a man which he placed in the middle of the chief's groundnut field. Then he rubbed his hands together with glee and said to himself, "Aha! Now I shall soon know who the thief is!"

When all was dark and the villagers were asleep in bed, Spider crept out of his house as usual and made his way silently to the chief's farm. He was just about to begin digging when he saw what he thought was the figure of a man, only a few yards away.

"Oh!" he gasped. "What do you want here?" But there was no reply.

"Who are you?" Spider demanded a little louder. "What are you doing on the chief's farm in the middle of the night?" But there was still no reply.

Spider became frightened and angry, so lifting his hand he struck the man a hard blow on the cheek, saying:

"Why don't you answer me?"

Now the rubber man had been standing in the sun all day and was still extremely sticky, and Spider found that he could not pull his hand away from the man's face.

"Let me go at once!" he spluttered. "How dare you hold on to me like that!" And he hit him with the other hand. Now Spider really was in a fix as *both* hands were stuck, and he began to realize that this was no ordinary man. Lifting his knees he tried to free himself by pushing them against the man's body, only to find that they too were held fast.

Frantically he battered his head against the man's chest—and now he could not move at all!

"How foolish I am," he said to himself. "I shall have to stay here all night and everybody will know I am a thief."

Sure enough when the morning came, the chief's servant hurried to the farm to see who had been caught. How he laughed when he saw Spider stuck to the rubber man—head, hands, knees, and all.

"So you were the thief!" he exclaimed. "I might have guessed it."

Poor Spider! How ashamed he was when the chief's servant managed to get him away from the sticky rubber and brought him before the chief. For weeks afterward he hid among the rafters of his house seeing and speaking to nobody, and ever since that day his descendants have always hidden in corners.

159. THE ORIGIN OF DEATH
(*Africa—Akamba Tribe*)

AND HOW DID it happen?

It is God who created men. And since God had pity, He said, "I do not wish men to die altogether. I wish that men, having died, should rise again." And so He created men and placed them in another region. But He stayed at home.

And then God saw the chameleon and the weaver-bird. After He had spent three days with the chameleon and the weaver-bird, He recognized that the weaver-bird was a great maker of words compounded of lies and truth. Now of lies there were many, but of the words of truth there were few.

Then He watched the chameleon and recognized that he had great intelligence. He did not lie. His words were true. So he spoke to the chameleon, "Chameleon, go into that region where I have placed the men I created, and tell them that when they have died, even if they are altogether dead, still they shall rise again—that each man shall rise again after he dies."

The chameleon said, "Yes, I will go there." But he went slowly, for it is his fashion to go slowly. The weaver-bird had stayed behind with God.

The chameleon traveled on, and when he had arrived at his destination, he said, "I was told, I was told, I was told. . . ." But he did not say what he had been told.

The weaver-bird said to God, "I wish to step out for a moment."

And God said to him, "Go!"

But the weaver-bird, since he is a bird, flew swiftly, and arrived at the place where the chameleon was speaking to the people and saying, "I was told. . . ." Everyone was gathered there to listen. When the weaver-bird arrived, he said, "What was told to us? Truly, we were told that men, when they are dead, shall perish like the roots of the aloe."

Then the chameleon exclaimed, "But we were told, we were told, we were told, that when men are dead, they shall rise again."

Then the magpie interposed and said, "The first speech is the wise one."

And now all the people left and returned to their homes. This was the way it happened.

And so men become old and die; they do not rise again.

160. MAN CHOOSES DEATH
(Madagascar)

ONE DAY GOD ASKED the first human couple who then lived in heaven what kind of death they wanted, that of the moon or that of the banana. Because the couple wondered in dismay about the implications of the two modes of death, God explained to them: the banana puts forth shoots which take its place and the moon itself comes back to life. The couple considered for a long time before they made their choice. If they elected to be childless they would avoid death, but they would also be very lonely, would themselves be forced to carry out all the work, and would not have anybody to work and strive for. Therefore they prayed to God for children, well aware of the consequences of their choice. And their prayer was granted. Since that time man's sojourn is short on this earth.

161. THE WOMAN AND THE CHILDREN OF THE SYCAMORE TREE

(Africa—Masai Tribe)

THERE WAS ONCE a woman who had no husband, and she lived for many days in trouble. One day she said to herself, "Why do I always feel so troubled? It is because I have neither children nor husband. I shall go to the medicine-man and get some children."

She went to the medicine-man and told him she was unhappy owing to the fact that although she had now grown old, she had neither husband nor children. The medicine-man asked her which she wanted, husband or children, and she told him she wanted children.

She was instructed to take some cooking pots—three, or as many as she could carry—and to search for a fruit-bearing sycamore, to fill the pots with the fruit, to put them in her hut, and to go for a walk.

The woman followed these instructions carefully. She gathered the fruit, filled the pots, placed them in her hut, and went for a walk until the evening.

On arriving near the kraal, she heard the sound of voices and asked herself, "Why does one hear the voices of children in the kraal?" She went nearer, and found her hut filled with children, all her work finished, the boys herding the cattle, the hut swept clean by the girls, the warriors singing and dancing on the common, and the little children waiting to greet her. She thus became a rich woman, and lived happily with her children for many days.

One day, however, she scolded the children, and reproached them for being children of the tree. They remained silent and did not speak to her; then, while she went to visit her friends in the other kraals, the children returned to the sycamore tree, and became fruit again. On her return to her own kraal, the woman wept bitterly when she found it empty, and paid another visit to the medicine-man, whom she taxed with having spirited away her children.

The medicine-man told her that he did not know what she should do now, and when she proposed to go and look at the sycamore tree, he recommended her to try.

She took her cooking pots to the tree and climbed up into it. But when she reached the fruit they all put forth eyes and stared at her. This so startled her that she was unable to descend, and her friends had to come and help her down.

She did not go to the tree again to search for her children.

162. THE WISE DOG
(Africa—Yoruba Tribe)

A STRANGE THING once occurred in the Country of the Animals. There came a period of great strife and trouble, with many bitter fights and much hardship. Everything seemed to go wrong. It was as if a great curse had descended on all of them.

The king of the animals called a great meeting. Something must be done to put things right. All the animals were agreed on this point, but what were they to do, and what was the cause of their misfortunes? They argued over the matter for a very long time; many suggestions were put forward, but no conclusions were reached. Then somebody (nobody afterward could say who had made the suggestion in the first place) suggested that all their troubles could be traced back to the days of their early youth, and if anybody were to be blamed it must be their mothers. Yes, their mothers were to blame for the whole thing. Had they not been responsible for bringing them up? Had they not allowed them to play about when they should have been doing other things? Were their mothers not always interfering with them in the days of their youth? They had been a handicap all through. So the animals, seeking for a scapegoat on which to pin all their subsequent misfortunes, found one ready to hand in their mothers. The idea spread like a bush fire in the dry season. "We must kill all our mothers to punish them for our misfortunes and appease the gods," they all screamed. Every animal was to kill his own mother.

There was only one animal who was not carried away with this evil idea. He was the dog, who greatly respected his mother. He was too wise an animal to be carried away by their foolish words, but he had sufficient intelligence to see that it was hopeless to go against the wishes of all the other animals. So the dog quietly acquiesced to the idea of everybody killing off his own mother. The great slaughter of mothers commenced. The dog, fearing that if he hid his mother the other animals would discover her hiding place and slaughter them both, sent her to Heaven.

The dog's mother was very grateful for her son's kindness and consideration. When she was about to depart, she told him that if ever he was in any trouble or want, he had only to call on her and she would help him. She then taught him a little song to sing when in trouble.

The animals were soon to know that the killing of their mothers had not helped matters very much, for the next season brought a terrible famine to the land. The water holes dried up, and there was no meat, and all the crops failed, and many animals died.

The dog, remembering his mother's parting words, went out to a quiet and unfrequented part of the bush and sang:

> "O Mother, O Mother, send down your cord,
> Take your son up to Heaven and feed him today.
> For he needs your help now and remembers your words,
> O please Mother, O Mother, O Mother!"

Immediately a cord descended from Heaven and on the end of it hung a tiny bench. The dog sat himself down on the little bench and was pulled up through the clouds to Heaven. When he reached Heaven, his mother feasted him and did everything she could to make him happy, and when evening came he was let down again into the starving Country of the Animals.

Each day while the famine lasted, the dog would go and sing his song, and the cord would descend and take him up to visit his mother in Heaven.

One day, the tortoise, who was a friend of the dog, met him.

"My friend," the tortoise remarked, "how is it that you manage to look so sleek and fat in such a dry and unhappy time? There is a severe famine, the worst in living memory, and we are all growing thin and feeble, yet you, I notice, are getting fatter. Please tell me the reason for it."

Now the dog was afraid that the tortoise might remark on his good health to the other animals, so he decided to let the tortoise in on his secret. "Tortoise, if you promise never to tell any of the other animals, I will let you into my great secret." The tortoise, like all people who are promised a share in a great secret, swore that he would tell nobody else. Alas, nature is a frail thing and probably the tortoise's intentions were as good as those of human beings who find themselves in a similar situation.

"Meet me at this place tomorrow morning at sunrise and I will show you," continued the dog.

At sunrise, the tortoise was waiting for the dog, and the dog came and sang to his mother as before, and again the cord with the tiny bench descended from Heaven and the dog and the tortoise sat on it and were hauled up into the sky by the dog's mother.

At sundown they descended, looking well fed and happy, the tortoise swearing by all things in Heaven and on earth that he would not divulge the dog's secret to any living animal.

A few days later the tortoise paid a visit to the king of the animals. "O great king, may I have a word with you privately?" he asked. The lion rose from his throne and motioned all the other animals to depart and leave them alone. "I have just come, great lion, from a place where there is no famine, and one can eat to satisfaction," whispered the tortoise.

"Where is this place? I have not eaten a good meal for days, and I begin to hate this cursed country," replied the king.

"If you are willing to advance my position and interests in your kingdom, king of all animals, I will gladly tell you how we can reach this wonderful place," replied the tortoise as he peeped out at the king from under his shell.

"It shall be done, provided you keep your word. Make all the necessary arrangements for our departure, but keep it secret, tortoise," added the lion.

So the tortoise told the king to meet him at sunrise at a certain place. Needless to say the dog knew nothing about this arrangement. The following morning, the tortoise did not have to wait long at the rendezvous. In the gray light of dawn he saw the king coming and was greatly annoyed to find that he did not come alone. The king had brought not only his favorite wife, but also all his personal friends and followers. There was, in fact, quite a crowd of other animals.

"This is the last thing I wanted or expected," said the tortoise to himself, "but there is nothing I can do about it now, even if I take only the king up, all the others will witness it."

When the king arrived, the tortoise greeted him and all his followers. Then he sang the dog's song and the cord with the tiny bench descended from the pale morning sky.

"How are we all going to sit on this tiny bench?" asked the king.

"We aren't," said the tortoise hurriedly. "There is only room for you and myself I fear; the others must remain behind."

"So be it," said the king, and he threw himself down onto the bench, and with great difficulty the tortoise was able to squeeze himself onto it too. The favorite wife and the king's followers were of a different opinion, however, for, as they saw the king and the tortoise ascending, they all rushed forward and as many as could flung themselves onto the rope.

Then there followed the most undignified scene imaginable. While the lion and the tortoise roared at them all to let go, the starving animals hung on with grim determination and took no notice of their king's orders. Some managed to clutch the cord, others, not so fortunate, hung on to the tails of the animals higher up, some even clutched at the lion's mane and others sat on the tortoise. A twisting, wriggling mass of angry, shouting animals slowly ascended into the sky.

The dog's mother, perceiving that something was amiss with the cord, peeped down from Heaven and saw all the animals ascending. "Mercy, they are all coming up to kill me," she declared, so quickly seizing a large knife, she cut the cord when they were halfway up to Heaven. There followed a great crash as they all fell to earth and were killed, with the exception of the tortoise, whose thick shell saved his life.

The animals from a nearby village, hearing the great crash of falling bodies, came out to investigate. They soon discovered that all the animals except the tortoise were dead, and it was not long before they recognized the dead body of the king. The tortoise was taken to the town to answer for the king's death. He told the whole story concerning the dog's mother and the cord that pulled them up to Heaven.

The animals would not believe his wonderful story, however, so he was led out to the spot where the king had died and beheaded for supposed crimes.

The dog later went back to sing to his mother to let down the cord. Alas, there was now no cord to let down. It only extended halfway, and so the dog was never again able to visit Heaven.

As the famine continued in the Country of the Animals, the dog took himself off to the Country of Man, and ever since that time the dog has relied on man to feed him. Many men and animals have spent their lives wondering how the dog was able to send his mother to Heaven. Some suggested that he killed her as the other animals did, while others hold the view that somebody in Heaven must have let the cord down at his request. Alas, we shall never know the answer now, for the dog, having once shared a secret with fatal results, has never been caught out a second time.

163. THE HUNTER AND HIS MAGIC FLUTE
(*Africa—Yoruba Tribe*)

THERE ONCE LIVED a mighty hunter called Ojo, and it was his custom, like all Yoruba hunters, to go off into the forest for long periods, sometimes for as much as three months. Ojo used to build a camp for himself with sticks and palm fronds in the center of the area he had chosen to hunt. He then set out each day with his bow and arrows for a day's hunting, returning later with the day's kill to the forest camp. Before settling down to sleep for the night, Ojo used to cut up the flesh and dry it over a fire. The camp served as a store as well as a place of refuge at night. When his store of dried flesh was sufficient, Ojo returned home to his wife, and she sold the dried meat to the villagers in exchange for their daily requirements.

Ojo had three dogs and he had given them strange names: "Cut to Pieces," "Swallow Up," and "Clear the Remains." His other possession was a very old flute, which Ojo claimed possessed very great magical powers. "For," said Ojo, "however far I go when hunting in the forest, if I blow on this flute 'Cut to Pieces,' 'Swallow Up,' and 'Clear the Remains,' will hear it and come to wherever I am."

When the next time came for Ojo to set out on his long hunting expedition, he decided to leave the three dogs behind, tied up with stout ropes in his compound. He asked his wife to look after them and, if they suddenly showed signs of great nervousness and agitation, to release them immediately and let them follow him to the forest. His wife having agreed, Ojo set out.

After three days' journey, Ojo came to the place in the forest where he had decided to build his camp. He had never been in that region before, and, as far as he knew, none of the other hunters had been there either, but his experienced eyes and ears told him that the thick forest he now found himself in was full of game.

Ojo set to work and soon his camp was taking shape. However, for some reason or other Ojo felt worried. He had the feeling that all the time he was being watched, not by animals, but by some powerful evil spirit. When he was a boy he had often been told about the spirits of the forest, and he was afraid of them, although he had never seen any of them during all the years he had been hunting. Other hunters had claimed to have seen them; they had even seen the great Mother of the Forest, Iyabomba herself. Iyabomba, they had told him, was the size of ten full-grown men and her body was covered with hungry mouths.

When Ojo had completed his camp, he lay down inside to watch; the feeling of fear and of being watched never left him. He had the impression that something evil was drawing nearer to him and so Ojo was not altogether surprised when a huge monster suddenly appeared before him. Ojo immediately recognized it as the Mother of the Forest. The great Iyabomba stood before him. Ojo was too sick with fear to run away, he just stood rooted to the ground gazing at Iyabomba.

Suddenly, Iyabomba was speaking to him, "Have no fear, hunter. I know why you come to my domain and I will not devour you if you do me no harm." Then the Mother of the Forest departed as suddenly as she had come.

It was time for Ojo to hunt and he was more than thankful to get away from the terrifying Iyabomba. "Can Iyabomba's promise be relied on?" he asked himself. Ojo had a successful day's hunting, and when he returned later to his camp with the day's kill, his fear of the Mother of the Forest had abated. Ojo set to work to cut up the meat and then to light a fire and dry it. Afterward he prepared his own meal and then settled down for a night's rest.

The following day, Ojo set off to hunt again. It was another successful day for him and he returned once again to his forest camp laden with meat. As he approached, the hunter was quick to notice that there had been a visitor to his camp during his absence. It did not require the expert eye of a hunter to recognize the great foot marks of Iyabomba in the grass, and when Ojo entered his hut, he found she had taken all the meat he had prepared the day before. "Never mind," thought Ojo to himself, "I have had a good day's hunting and now perhaps the Mother of the Forest is satisfied." So he prepared the meat as before.

Iyabomba was not satisfied, however, for each time Ojo returned he found that she had stolen all that he had killed the previous day. The hunter was afraid to inquire from her why she took his meat, in case she ate him too, but after the sixth day Ojo still had nothing to show for all his skillful hunting. What annoyed Ojo still more was the fact that it was the best area in which he had ever hunted and it was all a waste of time because of Iyabomba's greed. "If I stay here for a year, the old hag will still continue to steal my meat," he thought to himself. Ojo did not go hunting the following day, instead he moved his camp to a distant part of the forest and commenced his work all over again. Here he was no more successful than before, for Iyabomba had followed him and continued to steal his meat. At last Ojo's anger overcame his fear and he decided to remain behind in his camp and wait for Iyabomba to come. She did not come all that day, however, so at last Ojo struck his camp and tied up all his loads. As he was departing Ojo called out in a loud tone, "Why have you eaten all my meat, you old hag? Do you steal from every poor hunter who enters your forest?" Hardly had he spoken these words when there was an angry roar from Iyabomba and she came crashing through the forest toward him with all her mouths open as if to devour him. Ojo took to his heels and fled. Now Iyabomba was calling him with all her mouths to come back and be eaten, but Ojo ran faster. It was no use. She was much bigger than he and could have soon outpaced him long before he was clear of the forest. Seeing a great tree, Ojo hurriedly climbed up into its topmost branches as the Mother of the Forest came rushing up.

Not being able to climb up, she set to work with her great mouths and started to tear the bottom of the tree away, piece by piece. It was then that Ojo remembered his magic flute, which still hung from his shoulder. Picking it up, he blew a tune on it. Far away in his compound, "Cut to Pieces," "Swallow Up," and "Clear the Remains" heard the sounds and commenced to howl. Before Ojo's wife had time to release them, the dogs had snapped the ropes that tied them, and with one great leap they had cleared the mud walls of the compound and were racing toward Ojo.

In the meantime, however, Iyabomba was eating her way through the tree with great rapidity. Ojo waited until she had nearly eaten through and it was beginning to sway. Then, taking a small leather packet, which contained a fine magic powder, he sprinkled it on the tree and immediately it became whole again. Iyabomba was very surprised. She stopped and looked up at Ojo; then, turning another part of her body toward the tree she attacked it with her many mouths again. Each time the tree was nearly cut through Ojo sprinkled a little more of the magic powder on the tree and it immediately became whole again. In this way Ojo and Iyabomba continued for a long time, until at last all the magic powder had been used up, and the tree was nearly cut through again.

Ojo was beginning to think that his battle with the Mother of the Forest was nearly finished when to his great relief, "Cut to Pieces," "Swallow Up," and "Clear the Remains" suddenly appeared, and with a great noise, they threw themselves onto Iyabomba. There was a long and bitter fight, but at last they killed her and the three dogs, living up to their strange names, devoured everything that had once been the Mother of the Forest.

Ojo then climbed down the tree, and collecting up his things and his three dogs, he was about to return home and relate all these strange happenings to his wife when, greatly to his surprise, for they were in a very desolate spot, he saw a very beautiful woman standing close by.

"I have been held a prisoner by Iyabomba: now that you have killed her and rescued me, will you take me home, Ojo, and let me become your wife?" she asked the hunter.

Ojo was surprised that this beautiful woman should know his name, but he gladly consented to take her back with him and marry her. When they reached home Ojo's wife was very pleased to see them all, and there was great feasting and celebrations when the village was told that the Mother of the Forest was dead and that this beautiful woman, who was to become Ojo's second wife, had been rescued from the clutches of Iyabomba.

That night, when all was quiet and the people had returned home to sleep, a strange thing happened. Ojo's second wife, who had pretended to sleep, suddenly got up and commenced to change herself into a great creature with many mouths. She was in actual fact the sister of Iyabomba and had witnessed the killing of her sister by the hunter's dogs. She had made up her mind to revenge her sister's death and had changed herself into a beautiful woman as a disguise, knowing that Ojo would never suspect her, and would take her home with him. Now the time for her revenge had come. She would kill the hunter, his wife, and their three dogs, and then return to rule in the place of her sister, as Mother of the Forest.

"Cut to Pieces," "Swallow Up," and "Clear the Remains" were in the compound. They sensed the change that was taking place inside the house and started to bark. This barking woke Ojo and his wife and before Iyabomba's sister could kill the hunter, they had rushed into the house and torn her to pieces too.

Thus perished Iyabomba, the Mother of the Forest, and her sister. Ojo often went to hunt afterward in that part of the forest where he had first met Iyabomba, but he was never again disturbed by forest spirits and always returned from his hunting expeditions fully laden.

He lived with his wife, "Cut to Pieces," "Swallow Up," "Clear the Remains," and the magic flute, but he never took to himself a second wife.

164. THE FUNERAL OF THE HYENA'S MOTHER
(Africa—Yoruba Tribe)

TODAY, ALL THE WILD animals in the world fear each other. This was not always the case, however, for long ago they used to like to meet together on ceremonial occasions for feasting and dancing, just in the same way as human beings do today. The change came suddenly and unexpectedly, and it was all due to the death of the hyena's mother.

In those far-off days, the animal world was divided up into many groups over which various animals ruled as chiefs, similar, in fact, to the way we are ruled in our country today. One such group was the Flesh-Eating Community, over which the hyena ruled. He was a most powerful ruler and thought a great deal of himself, and he was immensely proud of his family and of its great name and traditions.

Now Chief Hyena's father had died when Chief Hyena was very young, and so Mother Hyena had to train her son. This she had proceeded to do with great care and diligence. She taught him how to track and stalk and kill, to follow scents, and to conceal himself when danger was about. All this she taught him and much more besides. In fact everything that any young hyena should know was imparted to the young chief by his mother, until he was a very cunning animal indeed. So it was not surprising that Chief Hyena was very fond of his mother, and treated her with great respect when he grew up and became a full chief.

Then one day, when her time on earth was up, Mother Hyena died. Chief Hyena was much upset and he decided that his mother must have the finest burial that had ever been seen in the land. He called the animals together and told them that they must make preparations for a great funeral. There was to be great feasting and dancing after the burial ceremony, and it was to last many days. The details of the ceremony were arranged by the council, and when they had been explained to the chief, he seemed pleased and told them to make sure that all the important individuals from the various other animal groups were invited to take part in the ceremonies.

In actual fact, Chief Hyena was far from satisfied with his council's arrangements. He felt that something much more grand and spectacular was required for the last rites of such an important person as his late mother. So he called two of his particular old friends, the lion and the leopard, and suggested that they should round off the ceremonies by sacrificing ten of the animals from among the guests. By so doing they would have a good feast themselves, the gods would be appeased, and the spirit of Mother Hyena would have rest. The lion and the leopard thought that this was a most excellent suggestion. And so it was decided that during the singing and dancing on the way to the burial ground, the three of them should pounce simultaneously on the animals selected, and kill them.

The following day, the funeral of Mother Hyena took place. All the animals came and there was great singing and drumming as the procession made its way to the burial ground. None of the animals knew or suspected anything about the proposed ten sacrifices, and so, when Chief Hyena and his friends the lion and the leopard suddenly pounced on their victims, there was great consternation among all the guests.

Chief Hyena killed a sheep, the lion killed a bird, and the leopard killed a goat. This caused much commotion and all the animals fled in terror, with the result that the other seven proposed victims were able to escape while the first killings were taking place.

When the three victims were dead, the killers found themselves alone with the body of Mother Hyena. Chief Hyena proposed that they should continue the ceremonies without the others, but lust for killing had been roused in the lion and leopard, and they told Chief Hyena to complete the ceremonies himself, while they went off to look for more victims to sacrifice.

From that day to this the animals have never again gathered together for social functions. The hyena family members are disliked and feared by the other animals, and they live apart. The lion and leopard families are equally disliked and feared. They still roam the countryside, looking for victims to sacrifice for Mother Hyena, or so they say.

The peaceful and the bloodthirsty can never mix freely.

165. ONI AND THE GREAT BIRD
(Africa—Yoruba Tribe)

THERE WAS ONCE a strange boy called Oni who was born wearing a pair of boots. As Oni grew, the boots grew also. When he was a boy of eighteen years of age, war broke out between his people and another village. It was during the battle that Oni made a second discovery about himself, which separated him from his fellow men and made him different. The enemy arrows did not seem to harm him. Many pierced his body which in the ordinary course of events should have slain him. The other young men noticed this too. They already regarded Oni as strange because of his wonderful boots, but when they discovered that he could not be killed they were afraid to have him near them. When he returned from the war, several people tried to kill him in various ways, but without any success. Finding this did not work, it was decided to find an excuse to banish him. He was accused of setting a house on fire in the village, and although Oni had nothing to do with the fire, he was found guilty and banished.

Oni wandered alone on foot for a long time. One afternoon he came to the banks of a great river and finding an empty canoe and feeling tired of walking, he got into the boat and made his way downstream. Toward evening, when it was growing dark, Oni reached a town, and decided to pull into the bank and spend the night there. There were the sounds of many bells being rung and people seemed to be in a hurry. Oni tied up the canoe and climbed the bank, and as he did so he met an old man. "Good evening, my friend. My name is Oni. I am a stranger to your town and have nowhere to spend the night. Will you take me to your house?" Oni asked the old man.

"Yes, certainly, come along with me, but we must go quickly because the bells are ringing and it is growing dusk," replied the old man.

"What is the name of your town and why do your people ring bells on the approach of darkness?" asked Oni.

"People call this place Ajo, but hurry up, we must get indoors. I will explain the bells to you when we are inside," replied the old man.

When they reached the old man's house, they found his people waiting anxiously for him at the door. The bells had now stopped ringing and they were hurried inside and the door was securely fastened.

"Now," said the old man, "sit down and eat with us and I will explain. For many years now we, the people of Ajo, have been troubled by the nightly arrival of a giant eagle. We call it Anodo. It always appears on the approach of darkness and stays until the approach of dawn. Anybody who is unfortunate enough to be out of doors at the time of its appearance is sure to be killed by it. You were very fortunate, young man, to reach Ajo before darkness. Our king has ordered the ringing of bells to warn the people to return to their homes and lock the doors. None of us knows where the eagle comes from, or where it goes when it leaves us at dawn. It is a terrible curse and in the past it has killed many of our people."

The old man had hardly finished speaking before Oni heard the sound of great wings flapping over the house. It sounded like a great wind, and the windows and doors shook in their frames.

"It must be a very great bird," remarked Oni. After Oni had been fed, the old man gave him a mat and a cloth and he lay down to sleep in the corner of the room. Sleep would not come to Oni, however, for he heard the constant noise of the great eagle's wings as it flew to and fro over Ajo.

When morning had come and the eagle had departed, Oni thanked the old man for his kindness and set out to find the King of Ajo and to ask for an audience. It was granted.

"My name is Oni and I am a stranger to your town. I have come to offer my services in helping to rid this town of the eagle Anodo," said Oni.

"And what makes you think you will succeed where so many others have tried and failed?" asked the king.

"I have certain powers and juju," said Oni.

"So had the others. One by one all my hunters have been killed or carried off by Anodo. Strangers have come from time to time to offer their services, but they too have perished. It is some time now since anybody has tried to kill Anodo, and I have issued orders to my remaining hunters not to try, as enough of them have been killed already," said the king.

"Have you ever offered a reward to anybody who could succeed in killing the bird?" asked Oni.

"Indeed yes. The man who succeeds will have half my kingdom. I made that offer long ago," replied the king.

"Then I will try tonight," answered Oni, and he paid his respects to the king and departed.

Oni returned to the old man's house and told him what had happened, and of his intention to challenge Anodo. The old man was very frightened and implored him to give up the idea, for he would only perish and perhaps all those in the house too. But Oni was not frightened. He took his bow and arrows and knives and examined them carefully.

It seemed ages to Oni before he heard the bells ringing. Never had he known a longer day in his life. The old man was uneasy and his people were almost hostile toward Oni. When they heard the bells ringing at last, they lost no time in fastening the doors and windows and ordered Oni to lie down on his mat and keep quiet.

Presently they heard the noise of a great wind which heralded the approach of Anodo. Soon the great wings were above the house. Oni waited till the great bird was overhead and then he commenced to sing:

> "Tonight Oni will be at war with Anodo,
> The eagle, whose talons are sharper than knives,
> For now the knives of nature and man will meet.
> Oni is invincible; his knife is sharp."

Anodo heard the challenge as he hovered over the house, and circling slowly round he came back and sang:

> "Ah fortune, I have found a victim tonight,
> I have lived many months without a kill,
> Will the singer come out and feel the sharpness
> Of my talons and of my beak? It will take me
> A moment to tear him to pieces. Come out."

All the people in the house were terrified. They seized Oni and threw him out of the house, fearing the vengeance of Anodo on them all.

As they threw Oni out into the road, Anodo swooped down and seizing him in his talons drew him upward. Oni slashed the eagle in the chest with his knife and the eagle dropped him with a scream. Oni fell to the ground, dazed. He picked himself up as the huge bird descended once again. He had time to use his bow and discharge an arrow into Anodo before the wounded bird beat him to the ground with his great wings and pecked him severely. Again Oni's knife tore at the eagle, and he buried it twice in Anodo. Slowly the eagle beat his great wings and rose slowly into the air; then he hovered for a last terrible dive on Oni. Oni watched him and, putting an arrow in his bow, took aim. The great bird hovered, then with a terrible noise he tore down on the boy, gathering speed as he came. There was a great roar of wind as he came down. Oni discharged a second arrow, then another and another in quick succession, but still the bird came on. A moment later it had hit Oni and knocked him over. The boy rolled over, a thousand lights dancing before his eyes; then all went blank, and he felt himself sinking down and down into a bottomless pit. He was knocked unconscious and had not seen that the great bird was already dead before it struck him. Its great wings swept the boy to one side, and it plunged on into a cotton tree, which snapped like a twig, and came crashing down to bury the eagle and Oni under a mass of leaves.

When Oni recovered, he felt very weak, and it was all he could do to free himself from the great wing of the dead Anodo and the cotton tree leaves. As he struggled, one of his magic boots came off and remained stuck beneath the dead bird. He was very weak and with great difficulty staggered along till he reached the edge of the river; then Oni fainted again.

Early next morning the people came out to see the dead Anodo lying in the broken cotton tree. There was great rejoicing and drumming and the king soon appeared with his chiefs to view the wonderful sight. "Who is the great man who killed Anodo?" he asked. One of his hunters stepped forward and prostrating himself on the ground claimed that he was responsible for the deed.

"Then you will be rewarded generously, for I have promised to give half my kingdom to the man who killed Anodo and it is yours," replied the king.

There was great rejoicing and dancing and the hunter was carried to the king's palace and feasted. A very bedraggled figure then appeared; his clothes were torn and one of his boots was missing. It was Oni.

"Ah," said the king, "here is the stranger who calls himself Oni and who came yesterday to announce his intention of killing the eagle. You come too late, my friend, I fear."

"I killed Anodo. This man is an imposter and a liar," said Oni.

There was whispering between the king and his chiefs. At last he said, "Very well, you claim to have killed Anodo. What proof have you got to offer?"

"You see my condition," replied Oni, "but if you require further proof, send your men out to clear away the dead eagle and the broken cotton tree. Somewhere underneath you will find one of my boots."

The king ordered his men to go at once and search for the boot. After some little time the men returned. They carried Oni's magic boot. "We found it underneath the dead eagle's wing," they announced to the king.

"Now if you are still undecided and disbelieve my story, will you ask everybody to try on the boot and see if it fits?" said Oni.

The king ordered everybody to try and see if they could fit the boot to their feet. Strange to relate, although it looked a perfectly normal boot, nobody could manage to put it on. When they had all tried without success, the boot was placed before the king and Oni stepped forward and said:

> "Boot from Heaven—boot from Heaven,
> Go on to your master's foot."

Immediately, the boot started to move from before the king and fitted itself onto Oni's foot of its own accord. The people and the king were convinced of the truth of Oni's claims and marveled greatly and were very delighted and grateful for his brave deed. The dishonest hunter was taken out and executed, and Oni received the promised reward.

That night, for the first time in many years, the bells of Ajo did not sound the curfew. Instead, the streets were full of happy, dancing people.

166. THE WOODEN SPOON AND THE WHIP
(Africa—Yoruba Tribe)

WHEN FAMINE ONCE CAME to the land a certain man called Ajayi, finding there was nothing to eat in or near to his town, went farther afield in search of food. He came to a river and wandered along its bank till he came to an oil palm that overhung the river. Ajayi was overjoyed to find some palm nuts growing over the water. He climbed up the tree and out over the water and was just about to pick the palm nuts when they fell into the river. They all sank immediately except for one, which continued to float and was carried downstream. Ajayi climbed down from the tree and followed along the bank, all the time watching for the palm nut to be carried close in to the bank. However, it remained, bobbing up and down in the middle of the stream, and was slowly carried down to the sea.

Seeing that he was about to lose the one remaining nut, Ajayi took off his clothes and jumped into the sea, but as he reached it, the nut sank, and Ajayi, more determined than ever, dived down after it. The next moment a wonderful thing happened, for he suddenly found himself in a great palace under the sea, and there before him, in magnificent robes, sat Olokun, god of the sea.

"What brings you to my palace, Ajayi?" asked the Sea God.

Ajayi explained how he had gone out to search for food and had found and followed a palm nut, which had led him before Olokun.

"Stay with me and I will see that you are fed," said Olokun.

"My family is starving at home," replied Ajayi.

The Sea God stood up and going to a wooden chest, which stood in one corner of his room, he opened it and brought out a strange-looking wooden spoon.

"Ajayi," he said, "take this wooden spoon back to your family and keep it safely, and you and your family will never want for food. All you have to do is to ask the spoon what its duty is, and it will always provide you with food."

Ajayi thanked the Sea God for his great kindness, and having paid his respects, he was led out through one of the many passages that led off from Olokun's hall. Presently Ajayi found himself outside and standing on the seashore. He went home as quickly as he could and showed his family the wonderful spoon. "What is your duty?" Ajayi asked the spoon.

"To feed," replied the spoon, and immediately there was plenty of food prepared and ready for eating, and Ajayi and his family ate to satisfaction.

Ajayi was a good man and wanted to help his people. He went to the king and showed him the spoon. The king called all his people together and they all came and sat down in his compound and had as much food as they required.

Having fed all the people, the king and Ajayi next decided to feed all the starving animals, so all the animals were summoned to the palace, and they all came and ate till their great hunger was satisfied.

At the end of the feast, a tortoise came up to Ajayi and asked him how he had managed to get the wonderful spoon. Ajayi related the story of the palm nut and how it had led him eventually to the Sea God Olokun. The tortoise thanked Ajayi and then went off to the spoon and said, "What is your duty?"

"To feed," replied the spoon.

"Then get me a palm nut," replied the tortoise. Immediately a palm nut was placed before the tortoise. He picked it up, and having thanked the king, he left the palace.

The tortoise set out for the river, and when he reached the water's edge he threw the palm nut in and watched it as it floated slowly down toward the sea. The tortoise followed.

When the nut reached the sea, the tortoise dived in after it and followed it down as it sank. The next minute the tortoise found himself standing before the Sea God Olokun.

"What brings you here, tortoise?" asked Olokun.

The tortoise related how he had seen some palm nuts growing on a tree by the river, and feeling hungry, he had tried to pick them, but they had suddenly fallen from the tree into the water and one had continued to float downstream till it had led him before the Sea God.

"Having come before me, what do you want?" demanded Olokun.

"I want you to give me a wooden spoon so that I can feed my starving family," replied the tortoise.

"I have no spoons left," replied the Sea God, getting up and opening his wooden chest. "However, since you have taken so much trouble to see me, I will give you a whip instead, and it will help you and your family for the rest of your lives."

The tortoise thanked Olokun for his great kindness and, taking the whip, he was led out through the passage till he found himself standing outside on the seashore. He hurried home, and going inside with his family, he locked the door to keep people from seeing his magic whip. "Now," said the tortoise, "I have as good a gift as Ajayi. This whip will provide us with everything. Whip, what is your duty?" asked the tortoise.

"To flog," replied the whip, and immediately it commenced to flog the tortoise and his family. The tortoise was very sorry he had locked the door and it was a long time before he could escape from the whip.

The next day, he determined to have his revenge, and took the whip to the king. He explained that it was as good as Ajayi's spoon and could work wonders. He presented the whip to the king. The king then summoned all the people to a great feast, and when they had gathered, he explained that Olokun had sent them another gift. Then turning to the whip he said, "What is your duty, whip?"

"To flog," replied the whip, and it commenced to flog everybody present including the king.

The tortoise had in the meantime concealed himself in a mortar in the corner of the king's compound and was safe. He greatly enjoyed the joke as the people ran around crying for help and trying to escape from the whip. At last the whip lay down and was still. The sore and angry people heard somebody laughing in the mortar and they went and dragged the tortoise out of his hiding place and took him before the king. He was promptly executed for his great impudence.

167. WHY THERE ARE CRACKS IN TORTOISE'S SHELL
(Africa—Baila Tribe)

MR. TORTOISE, WHO WAS married to Mrs. Tortoise, had in Vulture a friend who was constant in visiting him. But, having no wings, Tortoise was unable to return the visits, and this upset him. One day he bethought himself of his cunning and said to his wife, "Wife!"

Mrs. Tortoise answered, "Hello, husband! What is it?"

Said he, "Don't you see, wife, that we are becoming despicable in Vulture's eyes?"

"How despicable?"

"Despicable, because it is despicable for me not to visit Vulture. He is always coming here and I have never yet been to his house—and he is my friend."

Mrs. Tortoise replied, "I don't see how Vulture should think us despicable unless we could fly as he does and then did not pay him a visit."

But Mr. Tortoise persisted: "Nevertheless, wife, it is despicable."

Said his wife, "Very well, then, sprout some wings and fly and visit your friend Vulture."

Mr. Tortoise answered, "No, I shan't sprout any wings because I was not born that way."

"Well," said Mrs. Tortoise, "what will you do?"

"I shall find a way," he replied.

"Find it then," said Mrs. Tortoise, "and let us see what you will do."

Later Tortoise said to his wife, "Come and tie me up in a parcel with a lump of tobacco and, when Vulture arrives, give it to him and say that it is tobacco to buy grain for us." So Mrs. Tortoise took some palm leaf and made him into a parcel and put him down in the corner.

THE FIRE ON THE MOUNTAIN

At his usual time, Vulture came to pay his visit and said, "Where's your husband gone, Mrs. Tortoise?"

"My husband has gone some distance to visit some people, and he left hunger here. We have not a bit of grain in the house."

Vulture said, "You are in trouble indeed, not having any grain."

Mrs. Tortoise replied, "We are in such trouble as human beings never knew." And she went on: "Vulture, at your place is there no grain to be bought?"

"Yes," said he, "any amount, Mrs. Tortoise."

She brought the bundle and said, "My husband left this lump of tobacco thinking you would buy some grain with it for us and bring it here."

Vulture willingly took it and returned to his home in the heights. As he was nearing his native town he was surprised to hear a voice saying, "Untie me, I am your friend Tortoise. I said I would pay a visit to you."

But Vulture, in his surprise, let go his hold of the bundle and down crashed Tortoise to the earth, *pididi-pididi*, his shell smashed to bits, and he died. And so the friendship between Tortoise and Vulture was broken: and you can still see the cracks in Tortoise's shell.

168. THE FIRE ON THE MOUNTAIN*
(*Ethiopia*)

PEOPLE SAY THAT in the old days in the city of Addis Ababa there was a young man by the name of Arha. He had come as a boy from the country of Gurage, and in the city he became the servant of a rich merchant, Haptom Hasei.

Haptom Hasei was so rich that he owned everything that money

---

* From *The Fire on the Mountain* by Harold Courlander and Wolf Leslau, © 1950 by Holt, Rinehart & Winston, © 1978 by Harold Courlander and Wolf Leslau.

could buy, and often he was very bored because he had tired of everything he knew, and there was nothing new for him to do.

One cold night, when the damp wind was blowing across the plateau, Haptom called to Arha to bring wood for the fire. When Arha was finished, Haptom began to talk.

"How much cold can a man stand?" he said, speaking at first to himself. "I wonder if it would be possible for a man to stand on the highest peak, Mount Intotto, where the coldest winds blow, through an entire night without blankets or clothing and yet not die?"

"I don't know," Arha said. "But wouldn't it be a foolish thing?"

"Perhaps, if he had nothing to gain by it, it would be a foolish thing to spend the night in that way," Haptom said. "But I would be willing to bet that a man couldn't do it."

"I am sure a courageous man could stand naked on Mount Intotto throughout an entire night and not die of it," Arha said. "But as for me, it isn't my affair since I've nothing to bet."

"Well, I'll tell you what," Haptom said. "Since you are so sure it can be done, I'll make a bet with you anyway. If you can stand among the rocks on Mount Intotto for an entire night without food or water or clothing or blankets or fire and not die of it, then I will give you ten acres of good farmland for your own, with a house and cattle."

Arha could hardly believe what he had heard.

"Do you really mean this?" he asked.

"I am a man of my word," Haptom replied.

"Then tomorrow night I will do it," Arha said, "and afterward, for all the years to come, I shall till my own soil."

But he was very worried, because the wind swept bitterly across that peak. So in the morning Arha went to a wise old man of his own tribe and told him of the bet he had made. The old man listened quietly and thoughtfully, and when Arha had finished he said:

"I will help you. Across the valley from Intotto is a high rock which can be seen in the daytime. Tomorrow night, as the sun goes down, I shall build a fire there, so that it can be seen from where you stand on the peak. All night long you must watch the light of my fire. Do not close your eyes or let the darkness creep upon you. As you watch my fire, think of its warmth, and think of me, your friend, sitting there tending it for you. If you do this you will survive, no matter how bitter the night wind."

Arha thanked the old man warmly and went back to Haptom's house with a light heart. He told Haptom he was ready, and in the afternoon

Haptom sent him, under the watchful eyes of other servants, to the top of Mount Intotto. There, as night fell, Arha removed his clothes and stood in the damp cold wind that swept across the plateau with the setting sun. Across the valley, several miles away, Arha saw the light of his friend's fire, which shone like a star in the blackness.

The wind turned colder and seemed to pass through his flesh and chill the marrow in his bones. The rock on which he stood felt like ice. Each hour the cold numbed him more, until he thought he would never be warm again, but he kept his eyes upon the twinkling light across the valley and remembered that his old friend sat there tending a fire for him. Sometimes wisps of fog blotted out the light, and then he strained to see until the fog passed. He sneezed and coughed and shivered and began to feel ill. Yet all night through he stood there, and only when the dawn came did he put on his clothes and go down the mountain back to Addis Ababa.

Haptom was very surprised to see Arha, and he questioned his servants thoroughly.

"Did he stay all night without food or drink or blankets or clothing?"

"Yes," his servants said. "He did all of these things."

"Well, you are a strong fellow," Haptom said to Arha. "How did you manage to do it?"

"I simply watched the light of a fire on a distant hill," Arha said.

"What! You watched a fire? Then you lose the bet, and you are still my servant, and you own no land!"

"But this fire was not close enough to warm me, it was far across the valley!"

"I won't give you the land," Haptom said. "You didn't fulfill the conditions. It was only the fire that saved you."

Arha was very sad. He went again to his old friend and told him what had happened.

"Take the matter to the judge," the old man advised him.

Arha went to the judge and complained, and the judge sent for Haptom. When Haptom told his story, and the servants said that Arha had watched a distant fire across the valley, the judge said, "No, you have lost, for Haptom Hasei's condition was that you must be without fire."

Once more Arha went to his old friend with the sad news that he was doomed to the life of a servant, as though he had not gone through the ordeal on the mountaintop.

"Don't give up hope," the old man said. "More wisdom grows wild in the hills than in any city judge."

He got up from where he sat and went to find a man named Hailu, in whose house he had been a servant when he was young. He explained to the good man about the bet between Haptom and Arha and asked if something couldn't be done.

"Don't worry about it," Hailu said after thinking for a while. "I will take care of it for you."

Some days later Hailu sent invitations to many people in the city to come to a feast at his house. Haptom was among them, and so was the judge who had ruled that Arha had lost the bet.

When the day of the feast arrived, the guests came riding on mules with fine trappings, their servants strung out behind them on foot. Haptom came with twenty servants, one of whom held a silk umbrella over his head to shade him from the sun, and four drummers played music that signified the great Haptom was here.

The guests sat on soft rugs laid out for them and talked. From the kitchen came the odors of wonderful things to eat: roast goat, roast corn and durra, pancakes called injera, and many tantalizing sauces. The smell of the food only accentuated the hunger of the guests. Time passed. The food should have been served, but they didn't see it, only smelled vapors that drifted from the kitchen. The evening came, and still no food was served. The guests began to whisper among themselves. It was very curious that the honorable Hailu had not had the food brought out. Still the smells came from the kitchen. At last one of the guests spoke out for all the others.

"Hailu, why do you do this to us? Why do you invite us to a feast and then serve us nothing?"

"Why, can't you smell the food?" Hailu asked with surprise.

"Indeed we can, but smelling is not eating; there is no nourishment in it!"

"And is there warmth in a fire so distant that it can hardly be seen?" Hailu asked. "If Arha was warmed by the fire he watched while standing on Mount Intotto, then you have been fed by the smells coming from my kitchen."

The people agreed with him; the judge now saw his mistake, and Haptom was shamed. He thanked Hailu for his advice, and announced that Arha was then and there the owner of the land, the house, and the cattle.

Then Hailu ordered the food brought in, and the feast began.

169. WHY THE SUN AND THE MOON LIVE IN THE SKY

(Africa—Efik-Ibibio)

MANY YEARS AGO the sun and the water were great friends, and both lived on the earth together. The sun very often used to visit the water, but the water never returned his visits. At last the sun asked the water why it was that he never came to see him in his house. The water replied that the sun's house was not big enough, and that if he came with his people he would drive the sun out.

The water then said, "If you wish me to visit you, you must build a very large compound; but I warn you that it will have to be a tremendous place, as my people are very numerous and take up a lot of room."

The sun promised to build a very big compound, and soon afterward he returned home to his wife, the moon, who greeted him with a broad smile when he opened the door. The sun told the moon what he had promised the water, and the next day he commenced building a huge compound in which to entertain his friend.

When it was completed, he asked the water to come and visit him the next day.

When the water arrived, he called out to the sun and asked him whether it would be safe for him to enter, and the sun answered, "Yes, come in, my friend."

The water then began to flow in, accompanied by the fish and all the water animals.

Very soon the water was knee-deep, so he asked the sun if it was still safe, and the sun again said, "Yes," so more water came in.

When the water was level with the top of a man's head, the water said to the sun, "Do you want more of my people to come?"

The sun and the moon both answered, "Yes," not knowing any better, so the water flowed in, until the sun and moon had to perch themselves on the top of the roof.

Again the water addressed the sun, but, receiving the same answer, and more of his people rushing in, the water very soon overflowed the top of the roof, and the sun and the moon were forced to go up into the sky, where they have remained ever since.

170. A TUG-OF-WAR
(Africa—Fan Tribe)

TORTOISE CONSIDERED HIMSELF a great personage. He went about calling attention to his greatness. He said to people, "We three, Elephant, Hippopotamus, and I, are the greatest, and we are equal in power and authority."

Thus he boasted, and his boasts came to the ears of Elephant and Hippopotamus. They listened and then they laughed. "Pooh, that's nothing. He is a small person of no account, and his boasting can only be ignored."

The talebearer returned to Tortoise telling him what the two great ones had said. Tortoise grew very vexed indeed. "So, they despise me, do they? Well, I will just show them my power. I am equal to them, and they will know it before long! They will yet address me as Friend." And he set off.

He found Elephant in the forest, lying down; and his trunk was eight miles long, his ears as big as a house, and his four feet large beyond measure. Tortoise approached him and boldly called out, "Friend, I have come! Rise and greet me. Your Friend is here."

Elephant looked about astonished. Then spying Tortoise he rose up and asked indignantly, "Tortoise, small person, whom do you address as Friend?"

"You. I call you Friend. And are you not, Elephant?"

"Most certainly I am not," replied Elephant in anger. "Besides, you have been going about and saying certain things about your great power

—that it is equal to mine. How do you come to talk in such a way?"

Tortoise then said, "Elephant, don't get angry. Listen to me. True, I addressed you as Friend and said we were equal. You think that because you are of such a great size, you can surpass me, just because I am small? Let us have a test. Tomorrow morning we will have a tug-of-war."

Said Elephant, "What is the use of that? I can mash you with one foot."

"Be patient. At least try the test." And when Elephant unwillingly consented, Tortoise added, "When we tug, if one pulls over the other, he shall be considered greater, and if neither overpulls, then we are equal, and will call each other Friend."

Then Tortoise cut a very long vine and brought one end to Elephant. "This end is yours. I will go off with my end to a certain spot; and we will begin to tug, and neither of us will stop to eat or sleep, until one pulls the other over, or the vine breaks." And he went off with the other end of the vine and hid it on the outskirts of the town where Hippopotamus lived.

Hippopotamus was bathing in the river and Tortoise shouted to him, "Friend, I have come! You! Come ashore! I am visiting you!"

There was a great splashing as Hippopotamus came to shore, bellowing angrily, "You are going to get it now! Whom do you call Friend?"

"Why, you, of course. There is no one else here, is there?" answered Tortoise. "But do not be so quick to fight. I do not fear your size. I say we are equals, and if you doubt me, let us have a trial. Tomorrow morning we will have a tug-of-war. He who shall overcome the other, shall be the superior. But if neither is found superior, then we are equals and will call each other Friend." Hippopotamus thought the plan was absurd, but finally he consented.

Tortoise then brought his end of the vine to Hippopotamus and said, "This end is yours. And now I go. Tomorrow when you feel a pull on the vine, know that I am ready at the other end. Then you begin to tug, and we will not eat or sleep until the test is ended."

In the morning, Tortoise went to the middle of the vine and shook it. Elephant immediately grabbed his end, Hippopotamus caught up his end, and the tugging began. Each pulled at the vine mightily and it remained taut. At times it was pulled in one direction, and then in the other, but neither was overpulling the other.

Tortoise watched the quivering vine, laughing in his heart. Then he went away to seek for food, leaving the two at their tug, and hungry.

He ate his belly full of mushrooms and then went comfortably to sleep.

Late in the afternoon he rose and said, "I will go and see whether those fools are still pulling." When he went there the vine was still stretched taut, with neither of them winning. At last, Tortoise nicked the vine with his knife. The vine parted, and at their ends Elephant and Hippopotamus, so suddenly released, fell with a great crash back onto the ground.

Tortoise started off with one end of the broken vine. He came on Elephant looking doleful and rubbing a sore leg. Elephant said, "Tortoise, I did not know you were so strong. When the vine broke I fell over and hurt my leg. Yes, we are really equals. Strength is not because the body is large. We will call each other Friend."

Most pleased with this victory over Elephant, Tortoise then went off to visit Hippopotamus, who looked sick and was rubbing his head. Hippopotamus said, "So, Tortoise, we are equal. We pulled and pulled and despite my great size I could not surpass you. When the vine broke I fell and hurt my head. Indeed, strength has no greatness of body. We will call each other Friend."

After that, whenever they three and others met in council, the three sat together on the highest seats. And always they addressed each other as Friend.

Do you think they were really equal?

North America

Paul Bunyan's Cornstalk

171. PEOPLE WHO COULD FLY
(Black American)

IT HAPPENED LONG, long ago, when black people were taken from their homes in Africa and forced to come here to work as slaves. They were put onto ships, and many died during the long voyage across the Atlantic Ocean. Those that survived stepped off the boats into a land they had never seen, a land they never knew existed, and they were put into the fields to work.

Many refused, and they were killed. Others would work, but when the white man's whip lashed their backs to make them work harder, they would turn and fight. And some of them killed the white men with the whips. Others were killed by the white men. Some would run away and try to go back home, back to Africa where there were no white people, where they worked their own land for the good of each other, not for the good of white men. Some of those who tried to go back to Africa would walk until they came to the ocean, and then they would walk into the water, and no one knows if they did walk to Africa through the water or if they drowned. It didn't matter. At least they were no longer slaves.

Now when the white man forced Africans onto the slave ships, he did not know, nor did he care, if he took the village musicians, artists, or witch doctors. As long as they were black and looked strong, he wanted them—men, women, and children. Thus, he did not know that sometimes there would be a witch doctor among those he had captured. If he had known, and had also known that the witch doctor was the medium of the gods, he would have thought twice. But he did not care. These black men and black women were not people to him. He looked at them and counted each one as so much money for his pocket.

It was to a plantation in South Carolina that one boatload of Africans was brought. Among them was the son of a witch doctor who had not completed by many months studying the secrets of the gods from his father. This young man carried with him the secrets and powers of the generations of Africa.

One day, one hot day when the sun singed the very hair on the head, they were working in the fields. They had been in the fields since before the sun rose, and, as it made its journey to the highest part of the sky, the very air seemed to be on fire. A young woman, her body curved with the child that grew deep inside her, fainted.

Before her body struck the ground, the white man with the whip was riding toward her on his horse. He threw water in her face. "Get back to work, you lazy nigger! There ain't going to be no sitting down on the job as long as I'm here." He cracked the whip against her back and, screaming, she staggered to her feet.

All work had stopped as the Africans watched, saying nothing.

"If you niggers don't want a taste of the same, you'd better get to work!"

They lowered their heads and went back to work. The young witch doctor worked his way slowly toward the young mother-to-be, but before he could reach her, she collapsed again, and the white man with the whip was upon her, lashing her until her body was raised from the ground by the sheer violence of her sobs. The young witch doctor worked his way to her side and whispered something in her ear. She, in turn, whispered to the person beside her. He told the next person, and on around the field it went. They did it so quickly and quietly that the white man with the whip noticed nothing.

A few moments later, someone else in the field fainted, and, as the white man with the whip rode toward him, the young witch doctor shouted, "Now!" He uttered a strange word, and the person who had fainted rose from the ground, and moving his arms like wings, he flew into the sky and out of sight.

The man with the whip looked around at the Africans, but they only stared into the distance, tiny smiles softening their lips. "Who did that? Who was that who yelled out?" No one said anything. "Well, just let me get my hands on him."

Not too many minutes had passed before the young woman fainted once again. The man was almost upon her when the young witch doctor shouted, "Now!" and uttered a strange word. She, too, rose from the ground and, waving her arms like wings, she flew into the distance and out of sight.

This time the man with the whip knew who was responsible, and as he pulled back his arm to lash the young witch doctor, the young man yelled, "Now! Now! Everyone!" He uttered the strange word, and all of the Africans dropped their hoes, stretched out their arms, and flew away, back to their home, back to Africa.

That was long ago, and no one now remembers what word it was that the young witch doctor knew that could make people fly. But who knows? Maybe one morning someone will awake with a strange word on his tongue and, uttering it, we will all stretch out our arms and take to the air, leaving these blood-drenched fields of our misery behind.

172. BABY IN THE CRIB
(*Black American*)

JOHN STOLE A PIG from Old Marsa. He was on his way home with him and his Old Marsa seen him. After John got home he looked out and seen his Old Marsa coming down to the house. So he put this pig in a cradle they used to rock the babies in in them days (some people called them cribs), and he covered him up. When his Old Marsa come in John was sitting there rocking him.

Old Marsa says, "What's the matter with the baby, John?"

"The baby got the measles."

"I want to see him."

John said, "Well you can't; the doctor said if you uncover him the measles will go back in on him and kill him."

So his Old Marsa said, "It doesn't matter; I want to see him, John." He reached down to uncover him.

John said, "If that baby is turned to a pig now, don't blame me."

173. THE WONDERFUL TAR-BABY STORY
(Uncle Remus)

ONE DAY BRER FOX went to work and got him some tar and mixed it with some turpentine and fixed up a contraption what he called a Tar-Baby, and he took this here Tar-Baby and he set her in the big road, and then he lay off in the bushes for to see what the news was going to be. And he didn't have to wait long, neither, 'cause by and by here come Brer Rabbit pacin' down the road—lippity-clippity, clippity-lippity—just as sassy as a jay-bird.

Brer Fox he lay low. Brer Rabbit come prancin' 'long till he spy the Tar-Baby, and then he fetched up on his behind legs like he was 'stonished. The Tar-Baby, she set there, she did, and Brer Fox, he lay low.

"Mawnin'," says Brer Rabbit, says 'ee. "Nice weather this mawnin'," says 'ee.

Tar-Baby ain't sayin' nothin', and Brer Fox, he lay low.

"How does your symptoms seem to segashuate?" says Brer Rabbit, says 'ee.

Brer Fox, he wink his eye slow, and lay low, and the Tar-Baby, she ain't sayin' nothin'.

"How you come on, then? Is you deaf?" says Brer Rabbit, says 'ee. "'Cause if you is, I can holler louder," says 'ee.

Tar-Baby stay still, and Brer Fox, he lay low.

"You're stuck up, that's what you is," says Brer Rabbit, says 'ee, "and I'm going to cure you, that's what I'm going to do," says 'ee.

Brer Fox, he sorter chuckle in his stomach, he did, but Tar-Baby ain't sayin' nothin'.

"I'm going to learn you how to talk to 'spectable folks, if it's the last act," says Brer Rabbit, says 'ee. "If you don't take off that hat and tell me howdy, I'm going to bust you wide open," says 'ee.

Tar-Baby stays still, and Brer Fox, he lay low.

Brer Rabbit keep on askin' him, and the Tar-Baby, she keep on sayin' nothin' till presently Brer Rabbit draw back with his fist, he did, and blip he took her side of the head. Right there's where he broke his molasses jug. His fist stuck and he can't pull loose. The tar held him. But Tar-Baby, she stay still, and Brer Fox, he lay low.

"If you don't let me loose, I'll knock you again," says Brer Rabbit, says 'ee, and with that he fetched her a wipe with the other hand, and that stuck. Tar-Baby, she ain't sayin' nothin', and Brer Fox, he lay low.

"Turn me loose, before I kick the natural stuffin' out of you," says Brer Rabbit, says 'ee, but the Tar-Baby, she ain't sayin' nothin'. She just held on, and then Brer Rabbit lost the use of his feet in the same way. Brer Fox, he lay low.

Then Brer Rabbit squalled out that if the Tar-Baby don't turn him loose, he'll butt her cranksided. And then he butted, and his head got stuck. Then Brer Fox, he sauntered forth, lookin' as innocent as one of your mother's mockin'-birds.

"Howdy, Brer Rabbit," says Brer Fox, says 'ee. "You look sorter stuck up this mawnin'," says 'ee, and then he rolled on the ground and laughed and laughed till he couldn't laugh no more. "I expect you'll take dinner with me this time, Brer Rabbit. I done laid in some calamus root, and I ain't going to take no excuse," says Brer Fox, says 'ee.

Then Brer Fox looks at Brer Rabbit again, and he starts feelin' mighty good. "Well, I expect I got you this time, Brer Rabbit," says 'ee. "You been runnin' round here sassin' after me a mighty long time, but I expect you done come to the end of the row. You been cuttin' up your capers and bouncin' round in this neighborhood until you come to believe you're the boss of the whole gang. And then you're always somewhere where you got no business," says Brer Fox, says 'ee. "Who asked you for to come and strike up an acquaintance with this here Tar-Baby? And who stuck you up where you is? Nobody in the round world. You just took and jammed yourself on that Tar-Baby without waitin' for any invite," says Brer Fox, says 'ee, "and there you is and there you'll stay till I fixes up a brush-pile and fires her up, 'cause I'm going to barbecue you this day sure," says Brer Fox, says 'ee.

Then Brer Rabbit talk mighty humble.

"I don't care what you do with me, Brer Fox," says 'ee, "just so you don't fling me in that brier-patch. Roast me, Brer Fox," says 'ee, "but don't fling me in that brier-patch," says 'ee.

"It's so much trouble to kindle a fire," says Brer Fox, says 'ee, "that I expect I'll have to hang you," says 'ee.

"Hang me just as high as you please, Brer Fox," says Brer Rabbit, says 'ee, "but do for the Lord's sake, don't fling me in that brier-patch," says 'ee.

"I ain't got no string," says Brer Fox, says 'ee, "and now I expect I'll have to drown you," says 'ee.

"Drown me just as deep as you please, Brer Fox," says Brer Rabbit, says 'ee, "but don't fling me in that brier-patch," says 'ee.

"There ain't no water nigh," says Brer Fox, says 'ee, "and now I expect I'll have to skin you," says 'ee.

"Skin me, Brer Fox," says Brer Rabbit, says 'ee, "snatch out my eyeballs, tear out my ears by the roots, and cut off my legs," says 'ee, "but do please, Brer Fox, don't fling me in that brier-patch," says 'ee.

Course Brer Fox wanted to hurt Brer Rabbit bad as he can, so he catch him by the behind legs and slung him right in the middle of the brier-patch. There was a considerable flutter where Brer Rabbit struck the bushes, and Brer Fox sort of hang around for to see what was going to happen. By and by he hear somebody call him, and way up the hill he see Brer Rabbit settin' cross-legged on a chinkapin log combin' the pitch outen his hair with a chip. Then Brer Fox know that he been swop off mighty bad. Brer Rabbit was pleased for to fling back some of his sass, and he holler out:

"Bred and born in a brier-patch, Brer Fox—bred and born in a brier-patch!" and with that he skip out just as lively as a cricket in the embers.

174. PAUL BUNYAN'S CORNSTALK*
(Western United States)

PAUL BUNYAN WAS the fellow who invented the ax with two edges so a man could stand between two trees and chop them both down at the same time. As it turned out, Paul was the only man who

---

* By permission of Harold Courlander.

could do that trick, but the other lumberjacks used the double-bitted ax anyway, because they didn't have to sharpen the blades so often. Paul Bunyan also had other tricks. Most lumberjacks used to cut off the tops of the pines before they felled them. But when Paul was in a hurry, he'd wait till a tree started falling; then he'd get set with his ax and lop off the top of the tree as it came down.

Nothing Paul Bunyan ever did was small. He had an ox named Babe, who used to help him with his logging work. Babe was just about the most phenomenal ox in Michigan. His color was blue, and he stood ninety hands high. If you happened to hang on the tip of one horn, it's doubtful if you could have seen the tip of the other, even on a clear day. One day when Paul had Babe out plowing, the ox was stung by a Michigan deer fly about the size of a bushel basket. Babe took off across the country dragging the plow behind him, right across Indiana, Illinois, and Missouri, with the deer fly bringing up the rear. After a while Babe veered south and didn't stop till he got to the Rio Grande. The plow that Babe was hitched to dug a furrow four miles wide and two hundred miles long. You can check it in your own geography book. They call it Grand Canyon nowadays.

Even the storms that Paul was in were big. The biggest of all was the one they call the Big Blue Snow. It snowed for two months straight, and the way the drifts piled up only the tops of the tallest pines were showing. Lumberjacks went out that winter on their snowshoes and cut off all the pine tops. It saved them a lot of time when spring came around. Babe the blue ox didn't get a wink of sleep, though, from December till the first of March. It seems that standing out there in the weather the way he was, the snow that fell on his back melted and ran down his tail, and once it got there it froze into ice. Babe's tail kept getting heavier and heavier, and it drew on his hide so hard it just pulled his eyelids wide open and kept them that way. Babe never did get his eyes closed until the spring thaw came and melted the ice off his tail.

But the Big Blue Snow wasn't anything compared to the big drouth that started in Saginaw County and spread out as far as the Alleghenies in the East and the Rockies in the West. It all started with Paul Bunyan's vegetable garden. Paul planted some corn and some pumpkins. One of those cornstalks was six feet high before the others had sprouted. In two weeks it was tall as a house and growing like crazy. About the time it was as big as a fifty-year-old pine, people began to come in from all over the county to see it. It was growing out of the ground so fast it was pulling up stones that even the frost couldn't heave out. Same kind of thing, more or less, happened to one of the pumpkin vines. It grew so fast it just darted around like a Massauga rattlesnake. It climbed into any place where there was an opening. People had to keep their windows closed. The ones that didn't had to cut their way out of their beds with a brush knife. Sometimes that vine would grow into one window and out another between sunset and sunrise. Things weren't too bad until the vine blossomed and the pumpkins came out. They were about the size of hogsheads—the *little* pumpkins, that is—and when the vine whipped back and forth looking for someplace to grow it just snapped the pumpkins around like crab apples on a string. People had to be mighty alert to keep from getting hit by those pumpkins. One man lost a team of horses that way, and half a dozen good barns and one silo were stoved in.

But the real problem started when the corn and pumpkin roots began to soak up all the water out of the ground. Farms for sixty miles around went dry—fields, springs, and wells. The pine woods turned yellow from lack of moisture. The Au Sable River just turned into a trickle, and pretty soon there wasn't anything there but dry mud. The next thing that happened was that the water in the Great Lakes began to go down. It went down so fast in Lake Huron it left the fish hanging in the air. When things began to look real bad, folks came and told Paul Bunyan he'd just have to get rid of his corn and pumpkins. Paul was reasonable about it. First he went after the pumpkin vine. He spent four hours racing around trying to catch hold of the end, and finally did it by trapping it in a barn. He hitched Babe up to the end of the vine, but as fast as Babe pulled the vine grew. Babe ran faster and faster, and he was near Lake Ontario before he had the vine tight enough to pull it out.

Then Paul sized up his cornstalk. He figured he'd have to chop it down. He sharpened up his ax and spit on his hands. He made a good deep cut in that stalk, but before he could chip out a wedge the stalk grew up six feet, cut and all. Every time he made a cut it would shoot up out of reach before he could swing his ax again. Pretty soon he saw there wasn't any use going on this way. "Only way to kill this stalk is to cut off the top," he said. He hung his ax in his belt and started climbing. In about two hours he was completely out of sight. People just stood around and waited. They stood around two and a half days without any sight of Paul. Lars Larson called, "Paul!" but there was no answer. Erik Erikson and Hans Hanson called, "Paul!" But there wasn't any word from Paul Bunyan. So they waited some more. Two more days went by. No word from Paul. They decided that if everyone yelled at once maybe the sound would carry. So all together the two thousand eight hundred men and boys hollered, "Paul!" And sure enough, they heard his faint voice from up above.

"When you going to top that cornstalk?" they yelled back at him.

"Hasn't that top come down yet?" Paul hollered back. "I cut it off three days ago!"

And it was the truth, too. The stalk stopped growing, the water in the Great Lakes stopped falling, the Au Sable River began to run, the springs began to flow again, and things came back to normal. But it was a narrow escape.

175. THE TWO OLD WOMEN'S BET
(Southern United States)

ONE TIME THERE WERE two old women got to talkin' about the men folks: how foolish they could act, and what was the craziest fool thing their husbands had ever done. And they got to arguin', so fin'ly they made a bet which one could make the biggest fool of her husband.

So one of 'em said to her man when he come in from work that evenin', says, "Old man, do you feel all right?"

"Yes," he says, "I feel fine."

"Well," she told him, "you sure do look awful puny."

Next mornin' she woke him up, says, "Stick out your tongue, old man." He stuck his tongue out, and she looked at it hard, says, "Law me! you better stay in the bed today. You must be real sick from the look of your tongue."

Went and reached up on the fireboard, got down all the bottles of medicine and tonic was there and dosed the old man out of every bottle. Made him stay in the bed several days and she kept on talkin' to him about how sick he must be. Dosed him every few minutes and wouldn't feed him nothin' but mush.

Came in one mornin', sat down by the bed, and looked at him real pitiful, started in snifflin' and wipin' her eyes on her apron, says, "Well, honey, I'll sure miss ye when you're gone." Sniffed some more, says, "I done had your coffin made."

And in a few days she had 'em bring the coffin right on in beside the old man's bed. Talked at the old man till she had him thinkin' he was sure 'nough dead. And fin'ly they laid him out, and got everything fixed for the buryin'.

Well, the day that old woman had started a-talkin' her old man into his coffin, the other'n she had gone on to her house and about the time her old man came in from work she had got out her spinnin' wheel and went to whirlin' it. There wasn't a scrap of wool on the spindle, and the old man he fin'ly looked over there and took notice of her, says, "What in the world are ye doin', old woman?"

"Spinnin'," she told him, and 'fore he could say anything she says, "Yes, the finest thread I ever spun. Hit's wool from virgin sheep, and they tell me anybody that's been tellin' his wife any lies can't see the thread."

So the old man he come on over there and looked at the spindle, says, "Yes, indeed, hit surely is mighty fine thread."

Well, the old woman she'd be there at her wheel every time her old man come in from the field—spin and wind, spin and wind, and every now and then take the shuck off the spindle like it was full of thread and lay it in a box. Then one day the old man come in and she was foolin' with her loom, says, "Got it all warped off today. Just got done threadin' it on the loom." And directly she sat down and started in weavin'—step on the treadles, throwin' the shuttle and hit empty. The old man he'd come and look and tell her what fine cloth it was, and the old woman she 'uld weave right on. Made him think she was workin' day and night. Then one evenin' she took hold on the beam and made the old man help her unwind the cloth.

"Lay it on the table, old man— Look out! You're a-lettin' it drag the floor."

Then she took her scissors and went to cuttin'.

"What you makin', old woman?"

"Makin' you the finest suit of clothes you ever had."

Got out a needle directly and sat down like she was sewin'. And there she was, every time the old man got back to the house, workin' that needle back and forth. So he come in one evenin' and she says to him, "Try on the britches, old man. Here." The old man he shucked off hi overalls and made like he was puttin' on the new britches.

"Here's your new shirt," she told him, and he pulled off his old one and did his arms this-a-way and that-a-way gettin' into his fine new shirt. "Button it up, old man." And he put his fingers up to his throat and fiddled 'em right on down.

"Now," she says, "let's see does the coat fit ye." And she come at him with her hands up like she was holdin' out his coat for him, so he backed up to her and stuck his arms in his fine new coat.

"Stand off there now, and let me see is it all right.—Yes, it's just fine. You sure do look good."

And the old man stood there with nothin' on but his shoes and his hat and his long underwear.

Well, about that time the other old man's funeral was appointed and everybody in the settlement started for the buryin' ground. The grave was all dug and the preacher was there, and here came the coffin in a wagon, and fin'ly the crowd started gatherin'. And pretty soon that old man with the fine new suit of clothes came in sight. Well, everybody's eyes popped open, and they didn't know whether they ought to laugh or not but the kids went to gigglin' and about the time that old man got fairly close one feller laughed right out, and then they all throwed their heads back and laughed good. And the old man he 'uld try to tell somebody about his fine new suit of clothes, and then the preacher busted out laughin' and slappin' his knee—and everybody got to laughin' and hollerin' so hard the dead man sat up to see what was goin' on. Some of 'em broke and ran when the corpse rose up like that, but they saw him start in laughin'—laughed so hard he nearly fell out the coffin—so they all came back to find out what-'n-all was goin' on.

The two old women had started in quarrelin' about which one had won the bet, and the man in the coffin heard 'em; and when he could stop laughin' long enough he told 'em, says, "Don't lay it on me, ladies! He's got me beat a mile!"

176. JACK IN THE GIANTS' NEWGROUND
(Southern United States)

I

ONE TIME AWAY BACK years ago there was a boy named Jack. He and his folks lived off in the mountains somewhere and they were awful poor, just didn't have a thing. Jack had two brothers, Will and Tom, and they are in some of the Jack Tales, but this one I'm fixin' to tell you now, there's mostly just Jack in it.

Jack was awful lazy sometimes, just wouldn't do ary lick of work. His mother and his daddy kept tryin' to get him to help, but they couldn't do a thing with him when he took a lazy spell.

Well, Jack decided one time he'd pull out from there and try his luck in some other section of the country. So his mother fixed him up a little snack of dinner, and he put on his old raggedy hat and lit out.

Jack walked on, walked on. He eat his snack 'fore he'd gone very far. Sun commenced to get awful hot. He traveled on, traveled on, till he was plumb out of the settlement what he knowed. Hit got to be about twelve, sun just a-beatin' down, and Jack started gettin' hungry again.

He came to a fine smooth road directly, decided he'd take that, see where it went, what kind of folks lived on it. He went on, went on, and pretty soon he came to a big fine stone house up above the road. Jack stopped. He never had seen such a big house as that before. Then he looked at the gate and saw it was made out of gold. Well, Jack 'lowed some well-doin' folks must live there, wondered whether or no they'd give him his dinner. Stepped back from the gate, hollered, "Hello!"

A man came to the door, says, "Hello, stranger. What'll ye have?"

"I'm a-lookin' for a job of work."

"Don't know as I need to hire anybody right now. What's your name?"

"Name's Jack."

"Come on up, Jack, and sit a spell. Ain't it pretty hot walkin'?"

"Pretty hot," says Jack.

"Come on up on the porch and cool off. You're not in no hurry, are ye?"

Jack says, "Well, I'll stop a little while, I reckon."

Shoved back that gold gate and marched on in. The man reached in the door and pulled out a couple of chairs. Jack took one and they leaned back, commenced smokin'. Directly Jack says to that man, "What did you say your name was, mister?"

"Why, Jack, I'm the King."

"Well, now, King," says Jack, "hit looks like you'd be a-needin' somebody with all your land. I bet you got a heap of land to work."

"Are ye a hard worker, Jack?"

"Oh, I'm the workin'est one of all back home yonder."

"You a good hand to plow?"

"Yes sir!"

"Can ye clear newground?"

"Why, that's all I ever done back home."

"Can ye kill giants?"

"Huh?" says Jack, and he dropped his pipe. Picked it up, says, "Well, I reckon I could try."

The old King sort of looked at Jack and how little he was, says, "Well, now, Jack, I have got a little piece of newground I been tryin' for the longest to get cleared. The trouble is there's a gang of giants live over in the next holler, been disputin' with me about the claim. They kill ever' Englishman goes up there, kill 'em and eat 'em. I reckon I've done hired about a dozen men claimed to be giant-killers, but the giants killed them, ever' last one."

"Are these here giants very big 'uns?" says Jack.

"Well, they're all about six times the size of a natural man, and there's five of 'em. The old man has got four heads and his old woman has got two. The oldest boy has got two heads, and there's a set of twins has got three heads a-piece."

Jack didn't say nothin', just kept studyin' about how hungry he was.

King says, "Think ye can clear that patch, Jack?"

"Why, sure!" says Jack. "All I can do is get killed, or kill them, one."

"All right, son. We'll make arrangements about the work after we eat. I expect my old woman's about got dinner ready now. Let's us go on in to the table."

"Thank ye, King," says Jack. "I hope it won't put ye out none."

"Why, no," says the King. "Hit ain't much, but you're welcome to what we got."

Well, Jack eat about all the dinner he could hold, but the King's old woman kept on pilin' up his plate till he was plumb foundered. His dish set there stacked up with chicken and cornbread and beans and greens and pie and cake, and the Queen had done poured him milk for the third time. The old King kept right on, and Jack didn't want them to think he couldn't eat as much as anybody else, so directly he reached down and took hold on the old leather apron he had on and doubled that up under his coat. Then he'd make like he was takin' a bite, but he'd slip it down in that leather apron. He poured about four glasses of milk down there, too. Had to fasten his belt down on it so's it'uld hold.

Well, directly the King pushed his chair back, and then he and Jack went on out and sat down again, leaned back against the house and lit their pipes.

King says to Jack, says, "If you get that patch cleared, Jack, I'll pay ye a thousand dollars a-piece for ever' giant's head you bring down, and pay ye good wages for gettin' that patch cleared: ten cents a hour."

Jack said that suited him all right, and he got the King to point him out which ridge it was. Then Jack says to the King, "You say them giants live over in the other holler?"

King said they did.

Jack says, "Can they hear ye when ye start hackin'?"

"They sure can," says the King.

Jack didn't say nothin'.

The King says to him, "You don't feel uneasy now, do ye, Jack?"

"Why, no, bedads!" says Jack. "Why, I may be the very giant-killer you been lookin' for. I may not kill all of 'em today, but I'll try to get a start anyhow."

So the King told him maybe he'd better go on to work. Said for him to go on out past the woodpile and get him a ax, says, "You might get in a lick or two 'fore them giants come. You'll find a tree up there where them other men have knocked a couple of chips out'n. You can just start in on that same tree."

So Jack started on out to the woodpile. The King watched him, saw him lean over and pick up a little old Tommy hatchet, says, "Hey, Jack! You'll need the ax, won't ye?"

"Why, no," says Jack. "This here'll do me all right." He started on off, turned around, says, "I'll be back about time for supper."

The old King just grinned and let him go on.

When Jack fin'ly got up on that ridge, he was scared to death. He sat down on a log and studied awhile. He knowed if he started in cuttin', them giants would come up there; and he knowed if he didn't, the King 'uld know he hadn't done no work and he'd likely get fired and wouldn't get no supper. So Jack thought about it some more, then he picked out the tallest poplar he could see, and cloomb up in it, started in choppin' on the limbs way up at the very top . . .

Hack! Hack! Hack!

Heard a racket directly, sounded like a horse comin' up through the bresh. Jack looked down the holler, saw a man about thirty foot high comin' a-stompin' up the mountain, steppin' right over the laurel bushes and the rock-clifts. Jack was so scared he like to slipped his hold.

The old giant came on up, looked around till he fin'ly saw where Jack was settin', came over there under him, says, "Hello, stranger."

"Howdy do, daddy."

"What in the world you a-doin' up there?"

"I'm a-clearin' newground for that man lives back down yonder."

"Clearin' land? Well, I never seen such a fool business, start in clearin' newground in the top of a tree! Ain't ye got no sense?"

"Why, that's allus the way we start in clearin' back home."

"What's your name, son?"

"My name's Jack."

"Well, you look-a-here, Jack. This patch of land is ours and we don't aim to have it cleared. We done told the King so."

"Oh, well, then," says Jack, "I didn't know that. If I'd 'a knowed that I'd 'a not started."

"Come on down, Jack. I'll take ye home for supper."

Didn't think Jack 'uld know what he meant. Jack hollered back, says, "All right, daddy. I'll be right down."

Jack cloomb down a ways, got on a limb right over the old giant's head, started in talkin' to him, says, "Daddy, they tell me giants are awful stout. Is that so?"

"Well, some," says the old giant. "I can carry a thousand men before me."

"Well, now, daddy, I bet I can do somethin' you can't do."

"What's that, Jack?"

"Squeeze milk out'n a flint rock."

"I don't believe ye."

"You throw me up a flint rock here and I'll show ye."

So while the old giant hunted him up a flint rock, Jack took his knife and punched a little hole in that old leather apron. The giant chunked the rock up to him and Jack squeezed down on it, pushed up against his apron, and the milk commenced to dreen out . . .

Dreep, dreep, dreep.

"Do it again, Jack!"

So Jack pushed right hard that time, and hit just went like milkin' a cow.

The old giant hollered up to Jack, says, "Throw me down that rock."

He took the rock and squeezed and squeezed till fin'ly he got so mad he mashed down on it and they tell me he crumbled that flint rock plumb to powder.

Then Jack hollered down to him again, says, "I can do somethin' else you can't do."

"What's that, Jack?"

"I can cut myself wide open and sew it back up. And it won't hurt me none."

"Aw, shucks, Jack. I know you're lyin' now."

"You want to see me do it?"

"Go ahead."

Jack took his knife and ripped open that leather apron, took a piece of string he had, punched some holes, and sewed it back up, says, "See, daddy? I'm just as good as I ever was."

Well, the old giant just couldn't stand to let Jack outdo him, so he hollered up, says, "Hand here the knife, Jack."

Took Jack's knife and cut himself wide open, staggered around a little and fin'ly querled over on the ground dead. Well, Jack, he scaled down the tree and cut off the old giant's heads with that little Tommy hatchet, took 'em on back to the King's house.

II

The King paid Jack two thousand dollars like he said he would. Jack eat him a big supper and stayed the night. Next mornin', after he eat his breakfast, Jack told the King he reckoned he'd have to be a-gettin' on back home. Said his daddy would be a-needin' him settin' out tobacco.

But the King says, "Oh, no, Jack. Why, you're the best giant-killer I ever hired. There's some more of that giant gang yet, and I'd like awful well to get shet of the whole crowd of 'em."

Jack didn't want to do it. He figgered he'd done made him enough money to last him awhile, and he didn't want to get mixed up with them giants any more'n he could help. But the King kept on after him till Jack saw he couldn't get out of it very handy. So he went and got the Tommy hatchet, started on up to the newground again.

Jack hadn't hardly got up there that time 'fore he heard somethin' comin' up the holler stompin' and breakin' bresh, makin' the awfulest racket. He started to climb him a tree like he done before, but the racket was gettin' closer and closer, and Jack looked and saw it was them twin giants that had three heads a-piece.

"Law, me!" says Jack. "I can't stand that! I'll hide."

He saw a big holler log down the hill a ways, grabbed him up a shirt-tail full of rocks and shot in that log like a ground squirrel. Hit was pretty big inside there. Jack could turn right around in it.

The old giants fin'ly got there. Jack heard one of 'em say to the other'n, "Law! Look a-yonder! Somebody's done killed brother."

"Law, yes! Now, who you reckon could 'a done that? Why, he could 'a carried a thousand Englishmen before him, single-handed. I didn't hear no racket up here yesterday, did you?"

"Why, no, and the ground ain't trompled none, neither. Who in the world you reckon could 'a done it?"

Well, they mourned over him awhile, then they 'lowed they'd have to take him on down and fix up a buryin'. So they got hold on him, one by the hands and the other by the feet, started on down.

"Poor brother!" says one of 'em. "If we knowed who it was killed him, we'd sure fix them!"

The other'n stopped all at once, says, "Hold on a minute. There ain't a stick of wood to the house. Mother sent us up here after wood; we sure better not forget that. We'll have to have plenty of wood too, settin' up with brother tonight."

"We better get about the handiest thing we can find," says the other'n. "Look yonder at that holler log. Suppose'n we take that down."

Well, they laid the old dead giant down across the top of that log and shouldered it up. Jack got shook around right considerable inside the log, but after he got settled again, he looked and saw the old giant in front had the log restin' right betwixt his shoulders. And directly Jack happened to recollect he had all them rocks. So after they'd done gone down the holler a little piece, Jack he picked him out a rock and cut-drive at the giant in front—fumped him right in the back of the head. Old giant stumbled, and stopped and hollered back at his brother, says, "You look-a-here! What you a-throwin' rocks at me for?"

"I never so throwed no rocks at you."

"You did so! You nearly knocked me down!"

"Why, I never done it!"

They argued awhile, fin'ly started on down again.

Jack waited a minute or two, then he cut loose with another good-sized rock. *Wham!*

"You confounded thing! You've done hit me again!"

"I never done no such a thing!"

"You did too!"

"I never teched ye!"

"You're the very one. You needn't try to lie out of it neither. You can see as good as I can there ain't nobody else around here to throw no rocks. You just hit me one other time now, and I'll come back there and smack the fire out-a you!"

They jawed and cussed a right smart while till fin'ly they quit and got started on down again.

Well, this time Jack picked out the sharpest-edged rock he had, drew back and clipped him again right in the same place. *Pow!* The old giant in front hollered so loud you could 'a heard him five miles, throwed that log off'n his shoulder and just made for the other'n, says, "That makes three times you've done rocked me! And you'll just take a beatin' from me now or know I can't do it!"

Them twin giants started in to fightin' like horses kickin'. Beat any fightin' ever was seen: pinchin' and bitin' and kickin' and maulin' one another; made a noise like splittin' rails. They fit and scratched and scratched and fit till they couldn't stand up no more. Got to tumblin' around on the ground, knockin' down trees and a-kickin' up rocks and dirt. They were clinched so tight couldn't neither one break loose from the other'n, and directly they were so wore out they just lay there all tangled up in a pile, both of 'em pantin' for breath.

So when Jack saw there wasn't no danger in 'em, he crawled out from that log and chopped off their heads, put 'em in a sack and pulled on back to the King's house.

III

Well, the old King paid Jack six thousand dollars for that load of heads. Then Jack said he just had to get on in home. Said his folks would be uneasy about him, and besides that they couldn't get the work done up unless he was there.

But the King says to him, says, "Why, Jack, there ain't but two more of 'em now. You kill them for me and that'll wind 'em up. Then we won't have no trouble at all about that newground."

Jack said he'd see what he could do: went on back that same evenin'. This time Jack didn't climb no tree or nothin'. Went to work makin' him a bresh pile, made all the racket he could. The old four-headed giant come a-tearin' up there in no time. Looked around, saw the other giants lyin' there dead, came over to where Jack was, says, "Hello, stranger."

"Hello, yourself."

"What's your name, buddy?"

"My name's Jack—Mister Jack."

"Well, Mister Jack, can you tell me how come all my boys layin' here dead?"

"Yes, bedads, I can tell ye," says Jack. "They came up here cussin' and 'busin' me, and I had to haul off and kill 'em. You just try and sass me ary bit now, and I'll kill you too!"

"Oh pray, Jack, don't do that! There's only me and the old woman left now, and she's got to have somebody to get in her stovewood and tote up water."

"You better be careful what ye say then. I ain't goin' to take nothin' off nobody."

"Well, now, I don't want to have no racket with ye at all, Mister Jack. You come on down and stay the night with us, help set up with our dead folks, and we'll get fixed to have a buryin' tomorrow."

"Well, I'll go," says Jack, "but you sure better watch out what you say."

"Oh, I'll not say nothin'," says the old giant. Says, "Law, Jack, you must be the awfulest man!"

So the old giant stuck the dead 'uns under his arm and he and Jack started on down. When they got close to the house, the giant stopped, says to Jack, "Now, Jack, you better wait till I go and tell the old lady you've come down for supper. She might cut a shine. She'll be mad enough already about her boys bein' killed."

He went on in and shut the door. Jack slipped up and laid his ear to the keyhole so's he could hear what they said. Heard him tell his old lady, says, "I've got Jack here, claims to be a giant-killer. I found the boys up yonder at the newground with their heads cut off, and this here Jack says he's the one done it."

The old woman just carried on. Fin'ly the old giant got her hushed, says, "He don't look to me like he's so stout as all that. We'll have to test him out a little, and see whe'er he's as bad as he claims he is."

Directly Jack heard him a-comin' to the door rattlin' buckets. So he stepped back from the house and made like he was just comin' up. The old giant came on out, says, "There ain't a bit of water up, Jack. The old woman wants you and me to tote her some from the creek."

Jack saw he had four piggins big as wash tubs, had rope bails fixed on 'em, had 'em slung on one arm. So they went on down to the creek and the old giant set the piggins down. Stove his two in, got 'em full and started on back. Jack knowed he couldn't even tip one of them things over and hit empty. So he left his two piggins a-layin' there, waded out in the creek and started rollin' up his sleeves. The old giant stopped and looked back, saw Jack spit in his hands and start feelin' around under the water.

"What you goin' to do, Jack?"

"Well, daddy," says Jack, "just as soon as I can find a place to ketch a hold, I'm a-goin' to take the creek back up there closer to the house where your old woman can get her water everwhen she wants it."

"Oh, no, Jack! Not take the creek back. Hit'll ruin my cornfield. And besides that, my old lady's gettin' sort-a shaky on her feet; she might fall in and get drownded."

"Well, then," says Jack, "I can't be a-wastin' my time takin' back them two little bitty bucketfulls. Why, I'd not want to be seen totin' such little buckets as them."

"Just leave 'em there, then, Jack. Come on, let's go back to the house. Mind, now, you come on here and leave the creek there where it's at."

When they got back, he told his old woman what Jack had said. Says, "Why, Law me! I had a time gettin' him to leave that creek alone."

He came on out again, told Jack supper wasn't ready yet, said for him to come on and they'd play pitch-crowbar till it was time to eat. They went on down to the level field, the old giant picked up a crowbar from the fence corner. Hit must 'a weighed about a thousand pounds. Says, "Now, Jack, we'll see who can pitch this crowbar the furthest. That's a game me and the boys used to play."

So he heaved it up, pitched it about a hundred yards, says, "You run get it now, Jack. See can you pitch it back here to where I'm at."

Jack ran to where it fell, reached down and took hold on it. Looked up 'way past the old giant, put his hand up to his mouth, hollers, "Hey, Uncle! Hey, Uncle!"

The old giant looked all around, says, "What you callin' me Uncle for?"

"I ain't callin' you.—Hey! *Uncle!*"

"Who are ye hollerin' at, Jack?"

"Why, I got a uncle over in Virginia," says Jack. "He's a blacksmith and this old crowbar would be the very thing for him to make up into horseshoes. Iron's mighty scarce over there. I thought I'd just pitch this out there to him.—Hey! UNCLE!"

"Oh, no, Jack. I need that crowbar. Pray don't pitch it over in Virginia."

"Well, now," says Jack, "I can't be bothered with pitchin' it back there just to where you are. If I can't pitch it where I want, I'll not pitch it at all."

"Leave it layin' then, Jack. Come on let's go back to the house.—You turn loose of my crowbar now."

They got back, the giant went in and told his old woman he couldn't find out nothin' about Jack. Said for her to test him awhile herself. Says, "I'll go after firewood. You see can't you get him in the oven against I get back, so's we can eat."

Went on out, says to Jack, "I got to go get a turn of wood, Jack. You can go on in the house and get ready for supper."

Jack went on in, looked around, didn't see a thing cookin', and there set a big old-fashioned clay oven with red-hot coals all across it, and the lid layin' to one side.

The old giant lady came at him, had a wash rag in one hand and a comb in the other'n, says, "Come here now, Jacky. Let me wash ye and comb ye for supper."

"You've no need to bother," says Jack. "I can wash."

"Aw, Jack. I allus did wash my own boys before supper. I just want to treat ye like one of my boys."

"Thank ye, m'am, but I gen'ally wash and comb myself."

"Aw, please, Jack. You let me wash ye a little now, and comb your head. Come on, Jacky, set up here on this shelf so's I won't have to stoop over."

Jack looked and saw that shelf was right on one side of the big dirt oven. He cloomb on up on the scaffle, rockled and reeled this-a-way and that-a-way. The old woman kept tryin' to get at him with the rag and comb, but Jack kept on teeterin' around till he slipped off on the wrong side. He cloomb back up and he'd rockle and reel some more. The old woman told him, says, "Sit straight now, Jack. Lean over this way a little. Sakes alive! Don't ye know how to sit up on a shelf?"

"I never tried sittin' on such a board before," says Jack. "I don't know how you mean."

"You get down from there a minute. I reckon I'll have to show ye."

She started to climb up there on the scaffle, says, "You put your shoulder under it, Jack. I'm mighty heavy and I'm liable to break it down."

Jack put his shoulder under the far end, and when the old woman went to turn around and sit, Jack shoved up right quick, fetched her spang in the oven. Grabbed him up a hand-spike and prized the lid on. Then he went and hid behind the door.

Old giant came in directly. Heard somethin' in the oven just a-crackin' and a-poppin'.

"Old woman! Hey, old woman! Jack's a-burnin'."

When she didn't answer, the old giant fin'ly lifted the lid off and there was his old lady just about baked done, says, "Well, I'll be confounded! That's not Jack!"

Jack stepped out from behind the door, says, "No, hit sure ain't. And you better mind out or I'll put you in there too."

"Oh, pray, Jack, don't put me in there. You got us licked, Jack. I'm the only one left now, and I reckon I better just leave this country for good. Now, you help me get out of here, Jack, and I'll go off to some other place and I'll promise not to never come back here no more."

"I'd sure like to help ye, daddy, but I don't think we got time now. Hit's too late."

"Too late? Why, how come, Jack?"

"The King told me he was goin' to send a army of two thousand men down here to kill ye this very day. They ought to be here any minute now."

"Two thousand! That many will kill me sure. Law, what'll I do? Pray, Jack, hide me somewhere."

Jack saw a big chest there in the house, told the old giant to jump in that. Time he got in it and Jack fastened the lid down on him, Jack ran to the window and made out like that army was a-comin' down the holler, says, "Yonder they come, daddy. Looks to me like about three thousand. I'll try to keep 'em off, though. You keep right still now and I'll do my best not to let 'em get ye."

Jack ran outside the house and commenced makin' a terrible racket, bangin' a stick on the walls, rattlin' the windows, shoutin' and a-hollerin', a-makin'-out like he was a whole army. Fin'ly he ran back in the house, knocked over the table and two or three chairs, says, "You quit that now and get on out of here! I done killed that old giant! No use in you a-breakin' up them chairs. He ain't here I tell ye!"

Then Jack 'uld tumble over some more chairs and throw the dishes around considerable, says, "You all leave them things alone now, 'fore I have to knock some of ye down."

Then he'd run by that chest and beat on it, says, "He ain't in there. You all leave that chest alone. He's dead just like I told ye. Now you men march right on back to the King and tell him I done got shet of them giants and there ain't ary one left."

Well, Jack fin'ly made like he'd done run the army off. Let the old giant out the chest. He was just a-shakin', says, "Jack, I sure do thank ye for not lettin' all them men find out where I was at."

So Jack took the old giant on down to the depot, put him on a freight train, and they hauled him off to China.

The King paid Jack two thousand dollars for bakin' the old giant lady, but he said he couldn't allow him nothin' on the old giant because the trade they'd made was that Jack had to bring in the heads.

Jack didn't care none about that, 'cause his overhall pockets were just a-bulgin' with money when he got back home. He didn't have to clear that newground for the King, neither. He paid his two brothers, Will and Tom, to do it for him.

And the last time I went down to see Jack he was a-doin' real well.

177. SEÑOR COYOTE AND THE DOGS
(Mexico)

THIS IS A STORY of Señor Coyote, the trickster and the num-skull. Of this creature the other animals truly say that his cleverness is equaled only by his stupidity.

One day when Señor Coyote was walking along the level valley between two mountains, two large dogs that had been trying for a long time to catch him sprang from behind a large stone. The coyote tried to run to the woods, but the dogs had seen to it that he would have to take to the open country. As he ran around the bushes and jumped across rocks and across dry arroyos, making the dust fly, he thought that he was getting away from the dogs behind. Their yelps of *yo! yo! yo!* were getting a little fainter, he thought. Gasping for breath, he looked around for the best direction to take.

But while he was trying to make up his mind, two other dogs rose up out of nowhere and made up his mind for him. He was forced to turn back in the direction from which he had come. The dogs had planned to take turns racing the coyote back and forth across the desert until he was too tired to go any further. The dogs behind him were coming closer, and the coyote knew he was running toward the other two, who were waiting. He knew that he would have to act fast.

Upon the side of the mountain he saw something dark and round that made him take heart. He wished that it were closer. It was a cave. And now he saw two dogs in front of him and heard two dogs behind. He made a sharp turn and raced for the foot of the mountain. Now all four dogs were behind him, but they were running faster and coming closer. They were so close that Señor Coyote could hear them argue about which one would get him. He saw the cave in front of him and a chill of fear went through his body as the thought came to him that maybe the cave opening was big enough for the dogs to enter after him. But the dogs were so close now that they were snapping hairs out of the end of Señor Coyote's tail. And so with a flying dive, he landed inside the mouth of the cave.

Señor Coyote was lucky. The hole was too small for the dogs. Inside the cave he ran as far back as he could. Outside, the dogs complained and whined and pawed around the cave awhile and then were heard no more.

This was easily the worst fright the coyote ever had. But once safe inside the cave, he began to feel brave again. He began to think he was quite a fellow to be able to get rid of the dogs. As his weary limbs became rested, a desire to boast and brag stole over him. There was no one in the cave to talk to, so he began chatting with the various parts of his body which had had some part in the race against the dogs.

"*Patas*," he said, looking at his four feet one at a time, "what did you do?"

"We carried you away," said the feet. "We kicked up dust to blind the bad dogs. We jumped the rocks and bushes and brought you here."

"*Bueno, bueno*," the coyote said, "good, good! You feet did very well." Then he spoke to his ears.

"Ears, what did you do?"

"We listened to the right and the left. We listened to know how far behind the dogs were, so that feet would know how fast to run."

"Splendid!" said the coyote. "And eyes, what did you do?"

"We pointed out the road through the rocks and brush and canyons. We were on the lookout for your safety. We saw this cave."

"Marvelous!" said the coyote with a great laugh. "What a great fellow I am to have such fine eyes, feet, and ears." And so overcome was Señor Coyote with his own self and the great things he had done in his life that he reached over to pat himself on the back. And it was then that he saw his tail back there.

"Aha, my tail," he said, "I had almost forgotten about you. Come, tell me what you did in this battle with the dogs."

The tail could tell by the tone of the coyote's voice that he did not think too highly of him and so did not answer.

"About all you did was add extra load," said the coyote. "More than anything else, you held me back. Almost got me caught, too. You let the dogs grab the end of you. But let's hear from you. Speak up!"

"What did I do?" asked the tail. "I motioned to the dogs, like this, telling them to come on and get you. While you were running I was back there urging the dogs to come on. Through the dust they could see me in my whiteness waving."

Señor Coyote's scowl was becoming darker and darker.

"*Silencio!*" he shouted, stuttering and stammering with anger. "What do you mean?" And he reached back and gave a slap at his tail, and then reached around and bit at it.

"You do not belong here in this cave with the rest of us, you traitor!" And the coyote was backing his tail toward the door of the cave. "Out you go," he said. "Outside! There is no room in here for you. You belong outside. You are on the side of the dogs. You tried to help them catch me, and then you brag about it! Outside!"

And the coyote pointed to his tail with one hand, and to the round piece of daylight, which was the cave door, he pointed with the other hand. "Get out!"

And the coyote backed his tail out the door into the open air. The dogs, who had been listening to the talk inside, were waiting hidden outside. When the coyote's tail appeared through the cave door, the dogs grabbed it. And of course Señor Coyote was jerked out of the cave by his tail. And what the dogs did to him is another story.

178. THE TALKING CAT
(*French Canada*)

ONCE IN ANOTHER TIME, my friends, a great change came into Tante Odette's life although she was already an old woman who thought she had finished with such nonsense as changing one's habits.

It all happened because of a great change that came over Chouchou. The gray cat was a good companion because he seemed quite content to live on bread crusts and cabbage soup. Tante Odette kept a pot of soup boiling on the back of the stove. She added a little more water and a few more cabbage leaves to it each day. In this way, she always had soup on hand and she never had to throw any of it away.

She baked her own bread in her outdoor oven once a week, on Tuesday. If the bread grew stale by Saturday or Sunday, she softened it in the cabbage soup. So nothing was wasted.

As Tante Odette worked at her loom every evening, Chouchou would lie on the little rug by the stove and steadily stare at her with his big green eyes.

"If only you could talk," Tante Odette would say, "what company you would be for me."

One fall evening, Tante Odette was busy at her loom. Her stubby fingers flew among the threads like pigeons. Thump, thump went the loom.

Suddenly there was a thump, thump that didn't come from the loom. It came from the door.

The old woman took the lamp from the low table and went to the door. She opened it slowly. The light from the lamp shone on a queer old man who had the unmistakable look of the woods. He wore a bright red sash around his waist and a black crow feather in his woolen cap. He had a bushy mustache like a homemade broom and a brown crinkled face.

"Pierre Leblanc at your service," said the old man, making a deep bow.

"What do you want?" asked Tante Odette sharply. "I can't stand here all night with the door open. It wastes heat and firewood."

"I seek shelter and work," answered Pierre Leblanc. "I am getting too old to trap for furs or work in the lumber camps. I would like a job on just such a cozy little place as this."

"I don't need any help," snapped Tante Odette. "I am quite able to do everything by myself. And I have my cat."

She was beginning to close the door, but the man put his gnarled hand against it. He was staring at Chouchou.

"A very smart cat he looks to be," he said. "Why don't you ask him if you should take me in? After all, you need pay me nothing but a roof over my head and a little food."

Tante Odette's eyes grew bigger.

"How ridiculous!" she said. "A cat can't talk. I only wish—"

To her great surprise, Chouchou started to talk.

"Oh, indeed I can," he told her, "if the matter is important enough. This Pierre Leblanc looks to me like a very fine man and a good worker. You should take him in."

Tante Odette stood with her mouth open for two minutes before she could make any sound come out of it. At last she said, "Then come in. It is so rare for a cat to be able to talk that I'm sure one should listen to him when he does."

The old man walked close to the stove and stretched his fingers toward it. He looked at the pot of soup bubbling on the back.

Chouchou spoke again.

"Pierre looks hungry," he said. "Offer him some soup—a big, deep bowl of it."

"Oh, dear," sighed Tante Odette, "at this rate, our soup won't last out the week. But if you say so, Chouchou."

Pierre sat at the wooden table and gulped down the soup like a starved wolf. When he had finished, Tante Odette pointed to the loft where he would sleep. Then she took the big gray cat on her lap.

"This is a most amazing thing that you should begin talking after all these years. Whatever came over you?"

But Chouchou had nothing more to say. He covered his nose with the tip of his tail, and there was not another word out of him all night.

Tante Odette decided that the cat's advice had been good. No longer did she have to go to the barn and feed the beasts. And no more skunks crawled into her oven because Pierre saw to it that the door was kept closed. He was indeed a good worker. He seemed quite satisfied with his bed in the loft and his bowls of cabbage soup and chunks of bread.

Only Chouchou seemed to have grown dissatisfied since his arrival.

"Why do you feed Pierre nothing but cabbage soup and bread?" he asked one day. "A workingman needs more food than that. How about some headcheese and pork pie?"

Tante Odette was startled, but Pierre went on drinking his soup.

"But meat is scarce and costs money," she told the cat.

"Pouf!" said the cat. "It is well worth it. Even I am getting a little tired of cabbage soup. A nice pork pie for dinner tomorrow would fill all the empty cracks inside me."

So when Pierre went out to the barn to water the beasts, Tante Odette stealthily lifted the lid of the chest, fished out a torn woolen sock and pulled a few coins out of it. She jumped in surprise when she raised her head and saw Pierre standing in the open doorway watching her.

"I forgot the pail," said Pierre. "I will draw some water from the well while I am about it."

The old woman hastily dropped the lid of the chest and got the pail from behind the stove.

"After Pierre has done his chores," said Chouchou, "he will be glad to go to the store and buy the meat for you."

Tante Odette frowned at the cat.

"But I am the thriftiest shopper in the parish," she said. "I can bring old Henri Dupuis down a few pennies on everything I buy."

"Pierre is a good shopper, too," said Chouchou. "In all Canada, there is not a better judge of meat. Perhaps he will even see something that you would not have thought to buy. Send him to the store."

It turned out that the old man was just as good a shopper as Chouchou had said. He returned from the village with a pinkish piece of pork, a freshly dressed pig's head, a bag of candy, and some tobacco for himself.

"But my money," said Tante Odette. "Did you spend all of it?"

"What is money for but to spend?" asked Chouchou from his rug by the stove. "Can you eat money or smoke it in a pipe?"

"No," said Tante Odette.

"Can you put it over your shoulders to keep you warm?"

"No."

"Would it burn in the stove to cook your food?"

"Oh, no, indeed!"

Chouchou closed his eyes.

"Then what good is money?" he asked. "The sooner one gets rid of it, the better."

Tante Odette's troubled face smoothed.

"I never saw it that way before," she agreed. "Of course, you are right, Chouchou. And you are right, too, Pierre, for choosing such fine food."

But when Pierre went out to get a cabbage from the shed, Tante Odette walked to the chest again and counted her coins.

"I have a small fortune, Chouchou," she said. "Now explain to me again why these coins are no good."

But Chouchou had nothing more to say about the matter.

One Tuesday when Pierre Leblanc was cutting trees in the woods and Tante Odette was baking her loaves of bread in the outdoor oven, a stranger came galloping down the road on a one-eyed horse. He stopped in front of the white fence. He politely dismounted and went over to Tante Odette.

The old woman saw at a glance that he was a man of the woods. His blouse was checked and his cap red. Matching it was the red sash tied around his waist. He looked very much like Pierre Leblanc.

"Can you tell me, madame," he asked, "if a man named Pierre Leblanc works here?"

"Yes, he does," answered Tante Odette, "and a very good worker he is."

The stranger did not look satisfied.

"Of course, Canada is full of Pierre Leblancs," he said. "It is a very common name. Does this Pierre Leblanc wear a red sash like mine?"

"So he does," said Tante Odette.

"On the other hand," said the man, "many Pierre Leblancs wear red sashes. Does he have a mustache like a homemade broom?"

"Yes, indeed," said the woman.

"But there must be many Pierre Leblancs with red sashes and mustaches like brooms," continued the stranger. "This Pierre Leblanc who now works for you, can he throw his voice?"

"Throw his voice!" cried Tante Odette. "What witchcraft is that?"

"Haven't you heard of such a gift?" asked the man. "But of course only a few have it—probably only one Pierre Leblanc in a thousand. This Pierre with you, can he throw his voice behind trees and in boxes and up on the roof so it sounds as if someone else is talking?"

"My faith, no!" cried the woman in horror. "I wouldn't have such a one in my house. He would be better company for the *loup-garou*, that evil one who can change into many shapes."

The man laughed heartily.

"My Pierre Leblanc could catch the *loup-garou* in a wolf trap and lead him around by the chain. He is that clever. That is why I am trying to find him. I want him to go trapping with me in the woods this winter. One says that never have there been so many foxes. I need Pierre, for he is smarter than any fox."

The creak of wheels caused them both to turn around. Pierre Leblanc was driving the ox team in from the woods. He stared at the man standing beside Tante Odette. The man stared back at Pierre. Then both men began bouncing on their feet and whooping in their throats. They hugged each other. They kissed each other on the cheek.

"Good old Pierre!"

"Georges, my friend, where have you kept yourself all summer? How did you find me?"

Tante Odette left them whooping and hugging. She walked into the house with a worried look on her face. She sat down at her loom. Finally she stopped weaving and turned to Chouchou.

"I am a little dizzy, Chouchou," she said. "This *loup-garou* voice has upset me. What do you make of it all?"

Chouchou said nothing.

"Please tell me what to do," pleaded Tante Odette. "Shall we let him stay here? It would be very uncomfortable to have voices coming from the roof and the trees."

Chouchou said nothing.

"Is he maybe in league with the *loup-garou?*"

Chouchou said nothing. Tante Odette angrily threw the shuttle at him.

"Where is your tongue?" she demanded. "Have you no words for me when I need them most?"

But if a cat will not speak, who has got his tongue?

Pierre Leblanc came walking in.

"Such a man!" he roared gleefully. "Only the woods are big enough for him."

"Are you going away with him?" asked the woman, not knowing whether she wanted him to say "yes" or "no." If only Chouchou hadn't been so stubborn.

"That makes a problem," said Pierre. "If I go into the woods this winter, it will be cold and I will work like an ox. But there will be much money in my pocket after the furs are sold. If I stay here, I will be warm and comfortable but—"

He pulled his pockets inside out. Nothing fell from them.

"What is this business about your being able to throw your voice to other places?" asked Tante Odette.

"Did Georges say I could do that?"

Tante Odette nodded.

"Ha! Ha!" laughed Pierre. "What a joker Georges is!"

"But perhaps it is true," insisted the woman.

"If you really want to know," said Pierre, "ask Chouchou. He would not lie. Can I throw my voice, Chouchou?"

Chouchou sank down on his haunches and purred.

"Of course not!" he answered. "Whoever heard of such nonsense?"

Tante Odette sighed in relief. Then she remembered that this did not fix everything.

"Will you go with him?" she asked Pierre. "I have made it very comfortable for you here. And now it is only for supper that we have cabbage soup."

Chouchou spoke up.

"Tante Odette, how can you expect such a good man as Pierre Leblanc to work for only food and shelter? If you would pay him a coin from time to time, he would be quite satisfied to stay."

"But I can't afford that," said the woman.

"Of course you can," insisted Chouchou. "You have a small fortune in the old sock in your chest. Remember what I told you about money?"

"Tell me again," said Tante Odette. "It is hard to hold on to such a thought for long."

"Money is to spend," repeated the cat. "Can it carry hay and water to the beasts? Can it cut down trees for firewood? Can it dig paths through the snow when winter comes?"

"I have caught it again," said Tante Odette. "If you will stay with me, Pierre, I will pay you a coin from time to time."

Pierre smiled and bowed.

"Then I shall be very happy to stay here with you and your wise cat," he decided. "Now I will unload my wood and pile it into a neat stack by the door."

He briskly stamped out. Tante Odette sat down at her loom again.

"We have made a good bargain, haven't we, Chouchou?" She smiled contentedly.

But Chouchou tickled his nose with his tail and said nothing.

That is the way it was, my friends. It would have been a different story if Pierre had not been such a good worker. So remember this: If you must follow the advice of a talking cat, be sure you know who is doing the talking for him.

179. THE INDIAN CINDERELLA
(*Canadian Indian*)

ON THE SHORES of a wide bay on the Atlantic coast there dwelt in old times a great Indian warrior. It was said that he had been one of Glooskap's best helpers and friends, and that he had done for him many wonderful deeds. But that, no man knows. He had, however, a very wonderful and strange power; he could make himself invisible; he could thus mingle unseen with his enemies and listen to their plots. He was known among the people as Strong Wind, the Invisible. He dwelt with his sister in a tent near the sea, and his sister helped him greatly in his work. Many maidens would have been glad to marry him, and he was much sought after because of his mighty deeds; and it was known that Strong Wind would marry the first maiden who could see him as he came home at night. Many made the trial, but it was a long time before one succeeded.

Strong Wind used a clever trick to test the truthfulness of all who sought to win him. Each evening as the day went down, his sister walked on the beach with any girl who wished to make the trial. His sister could always see him, but no one else could see him. And as he came home from work in the twilight, his sister as she saw him drawing near would ask the girl who sought him, "Do you see him?" And each girl would falsely answer "Yes." And his sister would ask, "With what does he draw his sled?" And each girl would answer, "With the hide of a moose," or "With a pole," or "With a great cord." And then his sister would know that they all had lied, for their answers were mere guesses. And many tried and lied and failed, for Strong Wind would not marry any who were untruthful.

There lived in the village a great chief who had three daughters. Their mother had long been dead. One of these was much younger than the others. She was very beautiful and gentle and well beloved by all, and for that reason her older sisters were very jealous of her charms and treated her very cruelly. They clothed her in rags that she might be ugly; and they cut off her long black hair; and they burned her face with coals from the fire that she might be scarred and disfigured. And they lied to their father, telling him that she had done these things herself. But the young girl was patient and kept her gentle heart and went gladly about her work.

Like other girls, the chief's two eldest daughters tried to win Strong Wind. One evening, as the day went down, they walked on the shore with Strong Wind's sister and waited for his coming. Soon he came home from his day's work, drawing his sled. And his sister asked as usual, "Do you see him?" And each one, lying, answered "Yes." And she asked, "Of what is his shoulder strap made?" And each, guessing, said "Of rawhide." Then they entered the tent where they hoped to see Strong Wind eating his supper; and when he took off his coat and his moccasins they could see them, but more than these they saw nothing.

And Strong Wind knew that they had lied, and he kept himself from their sight, and they went home dismayed.

One day the chief's youngest daughter with her rags and her burned face resolved to seek Strong Wind. She patched her clothes with bits of birch bark from the trees, and put on the few little ornaments she possessed, and went forth to try to see the Invisible One as all the other girls of the village had done before. And her sisters laughed at her and called her "fool"; and as she passed along the road all the people laughed at her because of her tattered frock and her burned face, but silently she went her way.

Strong Wind's sister received the little girl kindly, and at twilight she took her to the beach. Soon Strong Wind came home drawing his sled. And his sister asked, "Do you see him?" And the girl answered "No," and his sister wondered greatly because she spoke the truth. And again she asked, "Do you see him now?" And the girl answered, "Yes, and he is very wonderful." And she asked, "With what does he draw his sled?" And the girl answered, "With the Rainbow," and she was much afraid. And she asked further, "Of what is his bowstring?" And the girl answered, "His bowstring is the Milky Way."

Then Strong Wind's sister knew that because the girl had spoken the truth at first her brother had made himself visible to her. And she said, "Truly, you have seen him." And she took her home and bathed her, and all the scars disappeared from her face and body; and her hair grew long and black again like the raven's wing; and she gave her fine clothes to wear and many rich ornaments. Then she bade her take the wife's seat in the tent. Soon Strong Wind entered and sat beside her, and called her his bride. The very next day she became his wife, and ever afterward she helped him to do great deeds. The girl's two elder sisters were very cross and they wondered greatly at what had taken place. But Strong Wind, who knew of their cruelty, resolved to punish them. Using his great power, he changed them both into aspen trees and rooted them in the earth. And since that day the leaves of the aspen have always trembled, and they shiver in fear at the approach of Strong Wind, it matters not how softly he comes, for they are still mindful of his great power and anger because of their lies and their cruelty to their sister long ago.

180. THE DESERTED CHILDREN

(American Indian—Gros Ventre Tribe of Montana)

ONE DAY A LITTLE boy and his sister, returning from play, found only smoldering campfires where their village had been. Deep in the distance the people could still be seen, traveling farther and farther away. As they hurried to catch up, the children found a tepee pole that had been dropped by their parents. "Mother!" they shouted. "Here is one of your poles!" But the parents were moving to a new camp and had left the children on purpose, not caring for them, and from far away came the faint answer, "Never mind, you are not my child!"

The sister kept stopping to help her little brother, who was too young to keep going, and the two were soon left far behind. She led him to a thicket and, making him a bed of boughs, left him there to rest while she cut brush and built a small shelter. From then on they lived in this shelter, eating berries and roots gathered by the child-mother. Many summers passed. The children grew older.

One day, as the girl was looking out of their little lodge, she saw a herd of elk going by, and she exclaimed, "Brother, look at the elk! So many!"

The boy was sitting with his head bowed. His eyes were cast downward, because he was now old enough to feel ashamed of living alone with his sister, and without looking up he replied, "Sister, it will do us no good if I look at them."

But she insisted. Then the boy raised his head and looked at the elk, and they all fell dead in their tracks.

The girl went out, skinned and butchered the elk, and carried the flesh and hides into the lodge. Looking at the pile of meat, she said, "I wish this meat were dried," and no sooner were the words out of her mouth than it was all perfectly dried. Lifting a hide and shaking it, she said, "I wish these hides were tanned," and so they were. She spread a number of them on the ground and murmured to herself, "I wish these were sewn into a tepee cover," and behold! there was a fine large tepee cover lying where the unsewn skins had been. Later the same day a herd of buffalo appeared, and she cried, "Brother! Look at the buffalo!"

"Why do you want me to look at those buffalo?" he protested peevishly. But she insisted, and when at last he raised his head, they too fell dead. Then she skinned them and brought the hides into the brush lodge, where she spread out a few and said, "I wish these hides were tanned into fine robes." Immediately they became what she wished. Then to the other skins she addressed the same magic words, and they became soft robes decorated with paintings. Now that she had everything she needed, she built and arranged her tepee.

One day the girl saw a raven flying by, and she called out, "Raven, take this piece of buffalo fat and go to the camp of my tribe, and when you fly over, drop it in the center of the camp circle and say, 'There is plenty to eat at the old campsite!'"

The raven took the fat and flew to the faraway camp. There he saw all the young men playing the wheel game, and dropping his burden, he croaked, "There is plenty to eat at the old campsite!" It happened that at this time there was a famine in the village, and when the words of the raven were heard, the head chief ordered some young men to go to the old camp to see what they could find. The scouts set forth, and where the old camp had been they saw a fine elk-skin lodge with racks of meat swinging in the wind and buffalo grazing on the surrounding hills. When the chief heard their report, he immediately told his crier to give the order to break camp.

When a new camp had been made near the elk-skin tepee, the father and the mother of the girl quickly discovered that it belonged to their daughter, and they went to her, calling, "My daughter! My daughter!" But she answered, "Keep back! You are not my father, and you are not my mother, for when I found the lodge poles and cried out to you not to leave me, you went on, saying that I was no daughter of yours!"

After a while, however, she seemed to forgive them, and calling all the people around her, she divided among them a large quantity of boiled buffalo tongues. She asked her parents to sit by her side. Meanwhile, her brother had been sitting with his head bowed.

Suddenly the girl cried, "Brother, look at these people! They are the ones who deserted us!"

She repeated her words twice, but the boy would not look up. At the fourth command he raised his head slowly, and as he looked around, the people fell lifeless.

Then the girl said, "Let a few of the men and women return to life, so that the tribe may grow again, but let their characters be changed. Let the people be better than they were." Immediately some of them came to life, and the tribe increased, and their hearts were good.

181. THE GIRL WHO MARRIED A GHOST
(American Indian—The Nisqualli Tribe of Southern Washington)

IN THE ANCIENT DAYS, on a sheltered bay not far from the ocean, there lived a rich man who had three daughters.

This man was a chief and well known for his thrift and his strong character, but he was equally famous for the beauty of his daughters, especially the eldest, who was the most beautiful of all. From far and near came parents and other relatives of eager young men, hoping the chief might consent to the marriage of one or another of his daughters. But to all their promises of lavish gifts, the old man turned a deaf ear. He was happy with his family just as it was, and as for money, he needed no more than he had already.

Again and again he said no, until at last he aroused the hatred and ill will of the neighboring villages. It became an openly expressed wish that something dreadful might happen to the stubborn chief. And once, when he declined to give up his eldest daughter, the visitors angrily denounced him, saying they hoped that ghosts would come and buy her and carry her off to the land of the dead.

To this the old man gave no heed. But not long afterward, from out on the ocean one night, came the sound of many voices singing gay, rollicking songs. As the sound drew nearer, the chief and his family saw many canoes filled with people—a bridegroom's wedding party.

When they had landed and made known their desire, so great were their numbers and so rich their gifts that the chief was unable to refuse, and without hesitation he gave his consent to the marriage of his eldest daughter to a handsome, richly dressed young man.

The wedding ceremony lasted the greater part of the night, yet long before dawn the visitors, accompanied by the bride, set off in their canoes and paddled away into the darkness, singing exultantly. Out onto the ocean they paddled, until they could no longer be seen or heard. Where they were headed, or who they truly were, the chief and his family did not know, yet strangely they felt no misgivings.

The wedding guests paddled on and on—until suddenly a dark, mysterious land loomed up before them. They drew quickly to shore, hauled their canoes onto the beach, and went off in various directions. Although it was not yet daylight, the girl found that she could see without difficulty. Everywhere there were groups of people playing games, some gambling with marked bones, others with wooden discs, some playing shinny, and others shooting arrows at a rolling hoop. As far as she could see there were people, all boisterously happy.

She followed her husband to a great house, in which he and many others dwelled. Side by side on the raised platform around the base of the walls slept great numbers of children. The portion of the house to which her husband led her was screened off by broad rush mats. Soft mats and many blankets covered their bed. It was time to sleep, her husband said. And indeed, after the long night of excitement and travel she was glad to retire.

When the young wife awoke, the sun was already high in the sky, but not a sound greeted her. She thought this odd, recalling the crowds of people she had seen the night before, and turned to look at her husband, whose head rested on her arm. To her horror she found herself gazing into the empty sockets of a grinning skull. What had been a handsome young man was now a skeleton.

Without moving her arm she raised herself on her elbow and peered about. The rows of sleeping children were now rows of whitened bones. Was she dreaming? The bedding that had been so fine was now dirty and old and worn to shreds. The great house was blackened by smoke and almost ready to fall. Only her own clothing remained as it had been when she went to sleep.

Slowly it dawned on her that she had been trapped by some evil magic, and she began to think of escape. She feared to look again at what had been her husband, nor dared to disturb it. Yet she must escape. Slowly, carefully, she moved her arm until it was free, and as the skull slipped from the crook of her elbow it dropped upon the blanket and turned on its side.

She arose, dressed hurriedly, and began to pick her way among the bones and the musty utensils and clothing. When she reached the doorway, she was greeted by another gruesome sight. Strewn about in groups were endless numbers of skeletons—bones, everywhere bones, up and down the shore as far as she could see—in all sorts of positions and still at the various games the people had been playing when daylight had overtaken them.

But the sight of the water gave her hope. She would take a canoe and paddle away, and eventually she would find her home. So thick were the bones on the ground that occasionally she had to push them aside with her foot to avoid walking on them. She could see the prows of canoes above the line of beach gravel, and toward these she carefully threaded her way.

But alas, she found that the boats were old, weather-beaten, decayed, grown over with moss, and full of holes. One after another she pushed them into the water, only to see them fill and sink. Overcome by despair, she collapsed on the gravel and sobbed bitterly.

The crying relieved her feelings. She bathed and dried her face, then looked about. Far down the beach, where a point of land jutted into the water, a wisp of smoke curled upward. Somewhat encouraged, she began walking toward it. The bones of the dead lay all about her. But the thought that human life might still exist in this terrifying place, and that she might soon find companionship, emboldened the girl as she plodded along. She became more careless of how she stepped on the bones or moved them aside.

She made her way slowly, however, and the distance was greater than she expected. The sun had already been traveling a considerable time on its downward course before she reached the place where the smoke was rising. When at last she got there, she found a tiny old woman sitting with her back turned, weaving baskets from hair. The girl hesitated, wondering what she should say. "Come, child," said the little woman without turning around. "You are the one they brought down yesterday."

The woman was Screech Owl. As she spoke, she went right on with her work, for she had not been in the least surprised. Being as much a person of the spirit land as of the earth, she passed back and forth whenever she wished and knew everything that happened in either world. She assured the girl that there was nothing to fear and that she was perfectly safe from harm.

"You do not understand," said the little woman. "You do not know where you are or what to do. This is the land of the ghost people. Those who die on earth come here. When you came, it was night on the earth, and that is the time when the ghosts are active. At sunrise they go to sleep. They have no real bodies at night, and by day they lie about as bones. You must do but one thing: sleep when they sleep and wake when they wake, and all will be well for you. Your only mistake is that you woke too soon. You should have slept. All these people whose skeletons you have seen will begin to move at sunset. You had better stay with me until you see."

So the girl spent the rest of the afternoon with Screech Owl, learning much about the people among whom she had married. As the sun sank below the horizon and shadows deepened into twilight, the sound of faint voices came from the distance, swelling gradually into great choruses of singing and gleeful shouting. But the ghosts soon noticed that something was wrong and that the bride they had brought home the night before was missing. Knowing that Screech Owl was the only person she might find to keep her company in daylight, they came running down that way. Some of them were furious and waved their arms wildly.

Their anger, the girl soon discovered, was due to the fact that she had wounded many of them on her way from the village to the home of Screech Owl. Every time she had moved a bone she had severely injured a ghost, and where she had pushed aside a whole skeleton, that ghost had died. A threatening crowd surrounded her. Not satisfied with injuring innumerable people, they cried, she had thoughtlessly pushed into the water many fine canoes, which had drifted away on the tide. Worst of all, she had nearly killed her own husband by half twisting off his head.

To all these threats and cries for vengeance Screech Owl replied by scolding the ghosts for their failure to tell the girl who they were and what she must do while living among them. Silenced, the angry ones turned to go, and the girl accompanied them. As they went along, they passed many anxious groups attending to the wounded. Some were beyond help. Others had knees twisted, ribs displaced, arms disjointed, feet missing. Her husband she found recovering from what had seemed an almost fatal injury. From that time on, the girl was careful to do as Screech Owl had advised.

Time passed happily, and one day the young wife gave birth to a baby boy, of whom she was very proud. But the ghosts were troubled by this arrival of a child neither properly a ghost nor a human being. They insisted upon taking the mother and her baby back to her earthly home, and so those who had made up the wedding party again voyaged to the earth.

It was dark when they reached the shore where her people lived, but her parents had heard the distant sound of singing and had built a great fire, which lighted the whole house. They were delighted to see their daughter and her child. A fine baby, a pretty boy, everyone said as they passed him from one to another. Then the ghosts told the child's mother that for twelve days she must not unwrap him on his cradleboard by daylight, or he would change and would have to be returned to ghost land. After this warning, the ghost people silently withdrew.

For eleven days the young mother watched her little boy. Each day she went to the woods to gather moss and cedar bark, which she shredded and used to pad the baby on his cradleboard. On the twelfth day she remained absent a long time, and her mother, curious to see if this child brought from ghost land were like other children, unlaced the wrapping.

Raising the blanket, she was shocked to discover the bones of a little skeleton, and indignantly cast bones and cradleboard out of the house. At that instant the baby's mother began to feel ill. Sensing that something had happened to her child, she hurried home to see what was the matter. When she got there and found the cradleboard on the ground and the little bones scattered in the sunlight, she flew into a rage and rebuked her mother severely. One more day and she and her child might have lived happily on earth.

As it was, when darkness fell, the ghosts came for her and the child. Before she departed, the young mother told her parents that she would return to earth once more, though not to their home, nor to remain as much as a day, for they had driven her from them.

Just as she had promised, she came again one night with many of her ghost people, and after singing out on the water for a while they paddled away. Neither the girl nor her child was ever seen again. They themselves had at last become ghosts.

From that time on, no living creature has been able to travel to ghost land, nor do we know what the ghosts are doing or what they are saying there. No living creature, that is, but Screech Owl, who still flies back and forth whenever she chooses. She does not reveal herself to us in human form, however, nor will she speak our language, though sometimes at night we may hear her cry or see her shadow above the smoke hole.

182. THE LOST WOMAN
(American Indian—Blackfeet Tribe)

I

A LONG TIME AGO the Blackfeet were camped on Backfat Creek. There was in the camp a man who had but one wife, and he thought a great deal of her. He never wanted to have two wives. As time passed they had a child, a little girl. Along toward the end of the summer, this man's wife wanted to get some berries, and she asked her husband to take her to a certain place where berries grew, so that she could get some. The man said to his wife: "At this time of the year, I do not like to go to that place to pick berries. There are always Snake or Crow war parties traveling about there." The woman wanted very much to go, and she coaxed her husband about it a great deal; and at last he said he would go, and they started, and many women followed them.

When they came to where the berries grew, the man said to his wife: "There are the berries down in that ravine. You may go down there and pick them, and I will go up on this hill and stand guard. If I see anyone coming, I will call out to you, and you must all get on your horses and run." So the women went down to pick berries.

The man went up on the hill and sat down and looked over the country. After a little time, he looked down into another ravine not far off, and saw that it was full of horsemen coming. They started to gallop up toward him, and he called out in a loud voice, "Run, run, the enemy is rushing on us." The women started to run, and he jumped on his horse and followed them. The enemy rushed after them, and he drew his bow and arrows, and got ready to fight and defend the women. After they had gone a little way, the enemy had gained so much that they were shooting at the Blackfeet with their arrows, and the man was riding back and forth behind the women, and whipping up the horses, now of one, now of another, to make them go faster. The enemy kept getting closer, and at last they were so near that they were beginning to thrust at him with their lances, and he was dodging them and throwing himself down, now on one side of his horse, and then on the other.

At length he found that he could no longer defend all the women, so he made up his mind to leave those that had the slowest horses to the mercy of the enemy, while he would go on with those that had the faster ones. When he found that he must leave the women, he was excited and rode on ahead; but as he passed, he heard someone call out to him, "Don't leave me," and he looked to one side, and saw that he was leaving his wife. When he heard his wife call out thus to him, he said to her: "There is no life for me here. You are a fine-looking woman. They will not kill you, but there is no life for me." She answered: "No, take pity on me. Do not leave me. My horse is giving out. Let us both get on one horse and then, if we are caught, we will die together." When he heard this, his heart was touched and he said: "No, wife, I will not leave you. Run up beside my horse and jump on behind me." The enemy were now so near that they had killed or captured some of the women, and they had come up close enough to the man so that they got ready to hit at him with their war clubs. His horse was now wounded in places with arrows, but it was a good, strong, fast horse.

His wife rode up close to him, and jumped on his horse behind him. When he started to run with her, the enemy had come up on either side of him, and some were behind him, but they were afraid to shoot their arrows for fear of hitting their own people, so they struck at the man with their war clubs. But they did not want to kill the woman, and they did not hurt him. They reached out with their hands to try to pull the woman off the horse; but she had put her arms around her husband and held on tight, and they could not get her off, but they tore her clothing off her. As she held her husband, he could not use his arrows, and could not fight to defend himself. His horse was now going very slowly, and all the enemy had caught up to them, and were all around them.

The man said to his wife: "Never mind, let them take you: they will not kill you. You are too handsome a woman for them to kill you." His wife said, "No, it is no harm for us both to die together." When he saw that his wife would not get off the horse and that he could not fight, he said to her: "Here, look out! You are crowding me onto the neck of the horse. Sit further back." He began to edge himself back, and at last, when he got his wife pretty far back on the horse, he gave a great push and shoved her off behind. When she fell off, his horse had more speed and began to run away from the enemy, and he would shoot back his arrows; and now, when they would ride up to strike him with their hatchets, he would shoot them and kill them, and they began to be afraid of him, and to edge away from him. His horse was very long-winded; and now, as he was drawing away from the enemy, there were only two who were yet able to keep up with him. The rest were being left behind, and they stopped, and went back to where the others had killed or captured the women; and now only two men were pursuing.

After a little while, the Blackfoot jumped off his horse to fight on foot, and the two enemies rode up on either side of him, but a long way off, and jumped off their horses. When he saw the two on either side of him, he took a sheaf of arrows in his hand and began to rush, first toward the one on the right, and then toward the one on the left. As he did this, he saw that one of the men, when he ran toward him and threatened to shoot, would draw away from him, while the other would stand still. Then he knew that one of them was a coward and the other a brave man. But all the time they were closing in on him. When he saw that they were closing in on him, he made a rush at the brave man. This one was shooting arrows all the time; but the Blackfoot did not shoot until he got close to him, and then he shot an arrow into him and ran up to him and hit him with his stone ax and killed him. Then he turned to the cowardly one and ran at him. The man turned to run, but the Blackfoot caught him and hit him with his ax and killed him.

After he had killed them, he scalped them and took their arrows, their horses, and the stone knives that they had. Then he went home, and when he rode into the camp he was crying over the loss of his wife. When he came to his lodge and got off his horse, his friends went up to him and asked what was the matter. He told them how all the women had been killed, and how he had been pursued by two enemies, and had fought with them and killed them both, and he showed them the arrows and the horses and the scalps. He told the women's relations that they had all been killed; and all were in great sorrow, and crying over the loss of their friends.

The next morning they held a council, and it was decided that a party should go out and see where the battle had been, and find out what had become of the women. When they got to the place, they found all the women there dead, except this man's wife. Her they could not find. They also found the two Indians that the man had said that he had killed, and, besides, many others that he had killed when he was running away.

II

When he got back to the camp, this Blackfoot picked up his child and put it on his back, and walked round the camp mourning and crying, and the child crying, for four days and four nights, until he was exhausted and worn out, and then he fell asleep. When the rest of the people saw him walking about mourning, and that he would not eat nor drink, their hearts were very sore, and they felt very sorry for him and for the child, for he was a man greatly thought of by the people.

While he lay there asleep, the chief of the camp came to him and woke him, and said: "Well, friend, what have you decided on? What is your mind? What are you going to do?" The man answered: "My child is lonely. It will not eat. It is crying for its mother. It will not notice anyone. I am going to look for my wife." The chief said, "I cannot say anything." He went about to all the lodges and told the people that this man was going away to seek his wife.

Now there was in the camp a strong medicine man, who was not married and would not marry at all. He had said, "When I had my dream, it told me that I must never have a wife." The man who had lost his wife had a very beautiful sister, who had never married. She was very proud and very handsome. Many men had wanted to marry her, but she would not have anything to do with any man. The medicine man secretly loved this handsome girl, the sister of the poor man. When he heard of this poor man's misfortune, the medicine man was in great sorrow, and cried over it. He sent word to the poor man, saying: "Go and tell this man that I have promised never to take a wife, but that if he will give me his beautiful sister, he need not go to look for his wife. I will send my secret helper in search of her."

When the young girl heard what this medicine man had said, she sent word to him, saying, "Yes, if you bring my brother's wife home, and I see her sitting here by his side, I will marry you, but not before." But she did not mean what she said. She intended to deceive him in some way, and not to marry him at all. When the girl sent this message to him, the medicine man sent for her and her brother to come to his lodge. When they had come, he spoke to the poor man and said, "If I bring your wife here, are you willing to give me your sister for my wife?"

The poor man answered, "Yes." But the young girl kept quiet in his presence, and had nothing to say. Then the medicine man said to them: "Go. Tonight in the middle of the night you will hear me sing." He sent everybody out of his lodge, and said to the people: "I will close the door of my lodge, and I do not want anyone to come in tonight, nor to look through the door. A spirit will come to me tonight." He made the people know, by a sign put out before the door of his lodge, that no one must enter it, until such time as he was through making his medicine. Then he built a fire, and began to get out all his medicine. He unwrapped his bundle and took out his pipe and his rattles and his other things. After a time, the fire burned down until it was only coals and his lodge was dark, and on the fire he threw sweet-scented herbs, sweet grass, and sweet pine, so as to draw his dream-helper to him.

Now in the middle of the night he was in the lodge singing, when suddenly the people heard a strange voice in the lodge say: "Well, my chief, I have come. What is it?" The medicine man said, "I want you to help me." The voice said, "Yes, I know it, and I know what you want me to do." The medicine man asked, "What is it?" The voice said, "You want me to go and get a woman." The medicine man answered: "That is what I want. I want you to go and get a woman—the lost woman." The voice said to him, "Did I not tell you never to call me, unless you were in great need of my help?" The medicine man answered, "Yes, but that girl that was never going to be married is going to be given to me through your help." Then the voice said, "Oh!" and it was silent for a little while. Then it went on and said: "Well, we have a good feeling for you, and you have been a long time not married; so we will help you to get that girl, and you will have her. Yes, we have great pity on you. We will go and look for this woman, and will try to find her, but I cannot promise you that we will bring her; but we will try. We will go, and in four nights I will be back here again at this same time, and I think that I can bring the woman; but I will not promise. While I am gone, I will let you know how I get on. Now I am going away." And then the people heard in the lodge a sound like a strong wind, and nothing more. He was gone.

Some people went and told the sister what the medicine man and the voice had been saying, and the girl was very downhearted, and cried over the idea that she must be married, and that she had been forced into it in this way.

III

When the dream person went away, he came late at night to the camp of the Snakes, the enemy. The woman who had been captured was always crying over the loss of her man and her child. She had another husband now. The man who had captured her had taken her for his wife. As she was lying there, in her husband's lodge, crying for sorrow for her loss, the dream person came to her. Her husband was asleep. The dream-helper touched her and pushed her a little, and she looked up and saw a person standing by her side; but she did not know who it was. The person whispered in her ear, "Get up, I want to take you home." She began to edge away from her husband, and at length got up, and all the time the person was moving toward the door. She followed him out, and saw him walk away from the lodge, and she went after. The person kept ahead, and the woman followed him, and they went away, traveling very fast. After they had traveled some distance, she called out to the dream person to stop, for she was getting tired. Then the person stopped, and when he saw the woman sitting, he would sit down, but he would not talk to her.

As they traveled on, the woman, when she got tired, would sit down, and because she was very tired, she would fall asleep; and when she awoke and looked up, she always saw the person walking away from her, and she would get up and follow him. When day came, the shape would be far ahead of her, but at night it would keep closer. When she spoke to this person, the woman would call him "young man." At one time she said to him, "Young man, my moccasins are all worn out, and my feet are getting very sore, and I am very tired and hungry." When she had said this, she sat down and fell asleep, and as she was falling asleep, she saw the person going away from her. He went back to the lodge of the medicine man.

During this night the camp heard the medicine man singing his song, and they knew that the dream person must be back again, or that his chief must be calling him. The medicine man had unwrapped his bundle, and had taken out all his things, and again had a fire of coals, on which he burned sweet pine and sweet grass. Those who were listening heard a voice say: "Well, my chief, I am back again, and I am here to tell you something. I am bringing the woman you sent me after. She is very hungry and has no moccasins. Get me those things, and I will take them back to her." The medicine man went out of the lodge, and called to the poor man, who was mourning for his wife, that he wanted to see him. The man came, carrying the child on his back, to hear what the medicine man had to say. He said to him: "Get some moccasins and something to eat for your wife. I want to send them to her. She is coming." The poor man went to his sister, and told her to give him some moccasins and some pemmican. She made a bundle of these things, and the man took them to the medicine man, who gave them to the dream person; and again he disappeared out of the lodge like a wind.

IV

When the woman awoke in the morning and started to get up, she hit her face against a bundle lying by her, and when she opened it, she found in it moccasins and some pemmican; and she put on the moccasins and ate, and while she was putting on the moccasins and eating, she looked over to where she had last seen the person, and he was sitting there with his back toward her. She could never see his face. When she had finished eating, he got up and went on, and she rose and followed. They went on, and the woman thought, "Now I have traveled two days and two nights with this young man, and I wonder what kind of a man he is. He seems to take no notice of me." So she made up her mind to walk fast and to try to overtake him, and see what sort of a man he was. She started to do so, but however fast she walked, it made no difference. She could not overtake him. Whether she walked fast, or whether she walked slow, he was always the same distance from her. They traveled on until night, and then she lay down again and fell asleep. She dreamed that the young man had left her again.

The dream person had really left her, and had gone back to the medicine man's lodge, and said to him: "Well, my chief, I am back again. I am bringing the woman. You must tell this poor man to get on his horse, and ride back toward Milk River (the Teton). Let him go in among the high hills on this side of the Muddy, and let him wait there until daylight, and look toward the hills of Milk River; and after the sun is up a little way, he will see a band of antelope running toward him, along the trail that the Blackfeet travel. It will be his wife who has frightened these antelope. Let him wait there for a while, and he will see a person coming. This will be his wife. Then let him go to meet her, for she has no moccasins. She will be glad to see him, for she is crying all the time."

The medicine man told the poor man this, and he got on his horse and started, as he had been told. He could not believe that it was true. But he went. At last he got to the place, and a little while after the sun had risen, as he was lying on a hill looking toward the hills of the Milk River, he saw a band of antelope running toward him, as he had been told he would see. He lay there for a long time, but saw nothing else come in sight; and finally he got angry and thought that what had been told him was a lie, and he got up to mount his horse and ride back. Just then he saw, away down, far off on the prairie, a small black speck, but he did not think it was moving, it was so far off—barely to be seen. He thought maybe it was a rock. He lay down again and took sight on the speck by a straw of grass in front of him, and looked for a long time, and after a while he saw the speck pass the straw, and then he knew it was something. He got on his horse and started to ride up and find out what it was, riding way around it, through the hills and ravines, so that he would not be seen. He rode up in a ravine behind it, pretty near to it, and then he could see it was a person on foot. He got out his bow and arrows and held them ready to use, and then started to ride up to it. He rode toward the person, and at last he got near enough to see that it was his wife. When he saw this, he could not help crying; and as he rode up, the woman looked back, and knew first the horse, and then her husband, and she was so glad that she fell down and knew nothing.

After she had come to herself and they had talked together, they got on the horse and rode off toward camp. When he came over the hill in sight of camp, all the people began to say, "Here comes the man"; and at last they could see from a distance that he had someone on the horse behind him, and they knew that it must be his wife, and they were glad to see him bringing her back, for he was a man thought a great deal of, and everybody liked him and liked his wife and the way he was kind to her.

Then the handsome girl was given to the medicine man and became his wife.

183. THE THEFT OF FIRE
(American Indian—Chippewa Tribe)

ONE DAY IN EARLY winter, soon after Manabozho had grown to manhood, he stood before his grandmother's wigwam shivering in the bitter wind. The lake was frozen. The sun, a pale yellow disk, had lost its heat. He shivered again, knowing that for many months his lodge would be cold, his food frozen, his drinking water underneath four feet of solid ice.

"Nakomis, old grandmother," he said sadly, "I have heard that once, long ago, people had heat within their wigwams all the year. Is it true?"

"You have heard of fire," his grandmother replied.

"What is it like, this fire," asked Manabozho, "that it keeps men warm in winter?"

His grandmother waited, thought a moment before she tried to answer. "It is a little like the sun," she said at last. "It is a little like having a small sun inside the lodge. But one must gather wood to keep it burning. When it is small it needs tinder such as birchbark, twigs, and sticks. When it grows larger it eats great logs from birch trees."

"How can I get this fire to warm us?"

"You cannot get it, Manabozho."

"Where is it kept, that I may try? If I try I shall surely get it!"

"It is far across the ice. It is guarded by an old man and his daughters."

"How do you know of this fire, grandmother?"

"Once, long ago, all men had it. Now one old cripple watches what is left and swears that no other lodge shall have it."

"Where is this old man?"

"On the other side of our lake. He lives there with two daughters. Since he is almost blind, and crippled too, they bring wood for his fire. They fish and set snares for his food. All their care is to feed the fire and him."

"It should not be hard to get fire from a crippled blind man and two squaws who are not always in the wigwam."

"It is so hard that it can never be."

"I do not think so. I shall get some fire. I shall bring it to our wigwam. You shall keep it always burning brightly so that it will warm us through the winters."

"You shall fail, Manabozho. The fire is guarded. Though the old man can barely walk, the fire is well guarded. All day he sits beside it, and as he waits, he weaves a net to take in anyone who comes to see him or his daughters."

"Nevertheless, I shall get some fire," said Manabozho. "Go and gather what is needed to feed it after I have brought it to you."

Manabozho went outside and looked across the frozen lake. He could not see the other shore. While he had been inside, the air had grown colder. Shivering, he wrapped his rabbitskin robe about him, bowed his head into the wind, and started across the ice in the direction of the old man's wigwam.

The freshly frozen ice stretched out, smooth and slippery to his moccasins except where an occasional air hole had opened and let the water underneath flow out to freeze around the edges in a rougher, whitish stretch. Sometimes his weight sent zigzag fractures running out from where he set his feet. The cracking ice boomed beneath him like thunder from a near-struck bolt of lightning. But Manabozho did not fear, knowing that the ice was already four fingers thick and that it was growing thicker every hour. If he took care to avoid air holes, the ice would hold him.

He had traveled only a little while when snow began to fall. The wind made the white flakes dance around him. Soon there were so many that Manabozho could not see the shore behind him. He wondered how near he was to the old man's wigwam. It could not be much farther. It must not be much farther! He was beginning to lose his sense of direction. The wind was blowing harder, getting colder.

And then at last he knew that he was near! He had reached the hole in the lake ice from which the old man's daughters dipped their drinking water.

"Now," said Manabozho, "I must be very near their lodge. I must change myself to something that a young squaw will wish to take inside the wigwam!"

And as he spoke, his rabbitskin robe turned into live rabbitskin! He hopped across the ice and hunched himself up beside the water hole in one of his favorite disguises—Manabozho the manitou, the miracle worker, had become Manabozho the great hare. But there was nothing very great about his appearance as he shivered beside the half-open hole in the ice. He was apparently just a cold, small, timid, frightened rabbit.

After what seemed a very long time a woman came out of the lodge carrying a birchbark bucket. Before she could possibly have seen him, Manabozho jumped into the water, broke through the half-formed ice, sputtered, and pretended he was drowning.

The squaw heard and ran quickly, looked into the hole, and, using her pail, dipped him from the water. "Oh! You poor rabbit!" she said, pressing him close against her.

Manabozho choked and coughed and shivered. In truth, he did not find it hard to shiver. He was really extremely cold, and it was far better to be pressed against the squaw's warm body than to be floundering around in the icy water hole.

"I shall help you, poor, small rabbit," said the woman. "Here, get inside my robe. I will take you to the lodge. My sister and I will make you dry and warm before our fire." With one hand she held him carefully against her, using the other to draw her bucket full of water. Then she carried Manabozho to her father and sister in the wigwam.

As she entered she looked across the lodge, seemingly relieved to see the old man fast asleep. Quickly she turned to the sister. "Look," she said, "I found this rabbit drowning in our water hole. We must dry him. Here, you hold him." So saying, she reached out and put Manabozho into the older woman's hands.

Though the lodge was only dimly lighted, Manabozho could see that this squaw was neither so young nor so pretty as the one who had rescued him from the water. Neither did she draw him close against her as her sister had done. Rather, with her arms partly outstretched in front of her, she held him loosely, with her fingers. She turned half fearfully toward the far side of the wigwam. Manabozho looked, too, and saw that the father continued sleeping. "He will not like it," the older woman said, twitching her head in the direction of the sleeper. She drew her lips together quite severely and unconsciously pinched Manabozho.

"But he is such a very wet, cold, helpless rabbit," the younger sister said, extending her arms as if to take him back.

Not liking the way he was being held, Manabozho began to tremble, then to squirm and wriggle. Surprisingly, the older woman neither dropped him nor returned him to her sister. Instead, she drew him close and cradled him against her. Then, slowly, she began to stroke his trembling wet fur. At last she smiled. "Oh!" she said. "Stop your shaking!" She turned toward her sister. "Perhaps our father will let us keep him." She continued to smile as she petted Manabozho.

Knowing he was safe for now, Manabozho looked about the lodge and understood why it was light inside: He saw the fire he had come to steal. Lying between two logs, it glowed a dull red, the color of the sun at evening; now and then it shot up yellow arrows, the color of the sun at noonday. When it did so, Manabozho could see clearly everything within the wigwam.

Then, as he looked, the old man stirred uneasily on his bed of skin robes. The sleeper woke, pulled a pair of crippled legs up under him, and looked about, seeming to sense a stranger in the lodge.

"Who has been here while I have been sleeping?" he asked crossly. Without waiting for an answer, he picked up his great net and began to weave a new strand across it, then to knot it firmly. "I must make the net bigger and throw it over him when he comes again."

"No one has walked into the wigwam," said the older sister calmly, watching her father as she spoke.

"I think a stranger has." The old man looked about him, then turned to meet his daughter's gaze again. "I think he is here still," he said quite forcefully.

The elder sister held the rabbit out before her. "Is this the one you fear, our father?" she asked in a tone not so soft that it lacked a note of ridicule.

"It is just a rabbit, wet and cold and hungry," said the younger daughter. "You need not fear this rabbit, father."

The old man stopped his work to look up at Manabozho. "I thought it was a man," he said slowly, his voice softening as he spoke. Then it hardened and once again became suspicious. "But the manitous can take on the voices and the shapes of animals! This may be one who has turned himself into a rabbit. He may have come into our lodge to steal our fire!"

"Oh! Father!" cried the two girls, almost together.

Manabozho looked down at the sometimes glowing, sometimes dancing fire on the floor below him. He almost smiled, thinking how he would steal a spark from it and take it home to Nakomis. It would make their lodge warm and comfortable like this one.

"He is really just a rabbit," said the elder daughter.

"He is just a cold, wet rabbit," repeated the younger. "Let us keep him by the fire and warm him!"

Again Manabozho squirmed a little in the elder sister's arms, so anxious was he to get a bit of fire and to be away.

"I do not like his being here at all," the old man said. But Manabozho caught a note of uncertainty in his voice.

"But you will let him stay here, won't you, father?" the younger pleaded.

"Well, if he really is a rabbit . . . But if he steals our fire . . ."

"Him?" The older woman held Manabozho out as she had done before. "How can he steal anything at all?" The glowing coals were just beneath Manabozho now. He wondered if his fur was dry enough to take a spark.

"Even if he took some fire—even if he could—we should have much left," the second daughter added.

"But then the others would have it as well as we," observed the father.

"Why would that matter?"

"Listen. You are but a girl. Yet you should know that when you have something that another wants, you have a power over him. But warm your rabbit if you must, and hope that he is just a rabbit."

"I still do not see—" began the younger daughter stubbornly.

"Of course you do not! Listen again, woman. The people of another lodge, if they get any of our fire, will not sit and watch the flame in comfort. Soon they will recall that we have other things, and they will come and try to take them from us, as they did our fire. But go ahead and keep this rabbit. I have said enough."

The girls laid Manabozho down before the lodge fire. They warmed his back until his fur was once again soft to touch. They warmed his underside until he was white, fluffy, and completely dry. They petted and stroked him.

"He is very soft," said the elder.

"We shall keep him to play with," said the younger.

"You had better plan to eat him!" said the father.

Just then Manabozho rolled over to the embers and picked up a spark in the soft, dry fur of his back. He had no sooner made sure that it was burning than he was out of the lodge, streaking his way across the ice, letting the cold wind and the speed of his flight fan the spark into flame.

The old man struggled to his feet, hobbled to the doorway of his wigwam, and stood watching the tiny blue light disappear across the frozen lake.

"See," he said sadly. "It was a manitou and not a rabbit, as I feared. The manitous are very powerful and will take odd shapes to gain the things they want. Now some other lodge will have a fire again."

Across the ice Manabozho was nearing his grandmother's wigwam. The flame had now worked most of the way to his tail. His back was hurting. He wanted to stop and roll in the snow. But despite the pain he kept running onward, calling loudly as he came.

"Noko! Noko!" he screamed. "Have your tinder ready, for I come aflame!"

His grandmother held the skin door aside for him to enter. She rubbed some of the burning fur off onto a bit of cedar bark, blew upon it, added shreds of birchbark, tiny splinters, and as the flame appeared, began to lay on twigs and branches.

Manabozho had no time to watch her. He was rolling on the earth floor, putting out the other sparks that still clung smoldering to his hide.

When his grandmother had the fire burning briskly she turned aside for a look at her grandson. He was still rubbing the burned spots up and down his backbone.

"Well," she said, "you did it. I did not think you could."

"Of course I did!" said Manabozho. "Now I would think you would try to help me. My back is scorched and sore. And most of my fur is gone! Why do you just stand there staring at me? Do you think I look different?"

"You're a fool!" said his grandmother, turning away from him as if very much amused.

"Why do you say I'm a fool when I—"

"You're a fool because it's just a rabbitskin that's burned."

"I don't see—"

"Are you Manabozho or a rabbit?"

"I'm Manabozho! Of course I'm Manabozho! Don't I look like Manabozho?"

"No."

"I don't?"

"No. You still look like a rabbit. Why don't you change yourself back into Manabozho? Then your back won't hurt."

Manabozho knew now why he looked foolish. He turned himself back into an Indian very quickly. Sure enough, his skin didn't hurt. His hair wasn't scorched any more. In fact, like most Indians, he didn't have much hair at all! What he did have was a slightly scorched rabbitskin draped around his shoulders.

He sat down on a robe before the lodge fire. Already Nakomis's wigwam was becoming warm and comfortable. He began to think of what else he had seen in the old man's lodge that he could get for himself and his grandmother. There had been the net; it might be used for fishing. He recalled the pile of skin robes in the corner; they would be very good for sleeping upon. And then he remembered the younger daughter: He had never seen a young squaw before. If he ever had his own lodge he would need someone like her to make it comfortable and pleasant. Manabozho smiled slyly as he began to plan for her to leave her father and her sister and to come to live with him and old Nakomis.

184. MANABOZHO AND HIS TOE
(American Indian)

MANABOZHO, THE GREAT WIZARD of the Indians, was so powerful that he began to think there was nothing he could not do. Very wonderful were many of his feats, and he grew more conceited day by day. Now, it chanced that one day he was walking about amusing himself by exercising his extraordinary powers, and at length he came to an encampment where one of the first things he noticed was a child lying in the sunshine, curled up with its toe in its mouth.

Manabozho looked at the child for some time, and wondered at its extraordinary posture.

"I have never seen a child before lie like that," said he to himself, "but I could lie like it."

So saying, he put himself down beside the child, and, taking his right foot in his hand, drew it toward his mouth. When he had brought it as near as he could, it was yet a considerable distance away from his lips.

"I will try the left foot," said Manabozho. He did so, and found that he was no better off; neither of his feet could he get to his mouth. He curled and twisted, and bent his large limbs, and gnashed his teeth in rage to find that he could not get his toe to his mouth. All, however, was vain.

At length he rose, worn out with his exertions and passion, and walked slowly away in a very ill humor, which was not lessened by the sound of the child's laughter, for Manabozho's efforts had awakened it.

"Ah, ah!" said Manabozho, "shall I be mocked by a child?"

He did not, however, revenge himself on his victor, but on his way homeward, meeting a boy who did not treat him with proper respect, he transformed him into a cedar tree.

"At least," said Manabozho, "I can do something."

185. THE RAVEN BRINGS LIGHT
(Alaskan Indian)

IN THE FIRST DAYS there was light. Then the sun and the moon disappeared, and people were left with no light but the shining of the stars. The shamans made their strongest charms, but the darkness continued.

At this time in a village of the lower Yukon there lived an orphan boy who always sat upon the bench with the humble people over the entranceway to the kashim. The people of the village thought he was a foolish boy, and he was despised and ill treated by everyone. But after the shamans had tried very hard to bring back the sun and the moon and had failed, the boy began to mock them, saying, "What fine shamans you must be, not to be able to bring back the light. Even I could do it."

At this the shamans became very angry and beat the boy and drove him out of the kashim. Now it happened that this poor orphan was like any other boy until he put on a black coat which he had. Then he was at once magically transformed into a raven, and kept that form until he took off the coat again.

When the shamans drove the boy away, he went to the house of his aunt and told her what he had said and how he had been beaten and driven out. Then he asked her to tell him where the sun and the moon had gone, for he wished to go after them. At first she was loath to tell him, but after a long time he prevailed upon her, and she said to him, "Well, if you wish to find the light you must take off your snowshoes and go far to the south, to a place you will recognize as the right place when you get there."

The Raven boy at once took off his snowshoes and set out for the south. He traveled for many days, but everywhere the darkness was the same. At last, when he had gone a very great distance, he saw far off in front of him a ray of light, and felt encouraged. As he hurried on, the light showed up again, plainer than before, and then vanished and appeared at intervals. At last he came to a large hill, one side of which was in bright light while the other was lost in the blackness of night. In front of him and close to the hill the boy saw a hut, with a man shoveling snow from in front of it. The man was tossing the snow high into the air, and each time he did so the light was obscured, thus causing the alternations of light and darkness the boy had seen as he approached. Close beside the house he saw the light he had come in search of, looking like a great ball of fire. Then the boy paused and began to plan how to get the light and the shovel away from the man.

After a time he walked up to the man and said, "Why are you throwing up the snow and cutting off the light from our village?" The man stopped, looked up, and said, "I am only cleaning away the snow from my door; I am not hiding the light. But who are you, and whence did you come?" "It is so dark in our village that I did not want to live there," said the boy, "so I came here to live with you." "What—all the time?" asked the man. "Yes," replied the boy.

The man then said, "It is well. Come into the house with me." He dropped his shovel on the ground, and, stooping down, led the way through the underground passage, letting the curtain fall over the doorway as he passed, thinking the boy was close behind him. The moment the door flap fell behind the man, the boy caught up the ball of light and put it in the turned-up flap of his fur coat; then, picking up the shovel, he fled away to the north. He ran until his feet became tired. Then by means of his magic coat he changed into a raven and flew as fast as wings could carry him. Behind him he heard the frightful shrieks and cries of the old man who pursued him. At last, when the old man saw that he could not overtake the raven, he cried out, "Never mind; you may keep the light, but give me my shovel."

To this Raven answered, "No, you made our village dark and you may not have your shovel," and he left the old man behind.

As Raven traveled homeward he broke off a piece of the light and threw it away, thus making day. He went on for a long time through the darkness before he broke off another piece of light and made day again. This he continued to do at intervals until he reached the outside of the *kashim* in his own village, when he threw away the last piece. Then he went into the *kashim* and said, "See, you good-for-nothing shamans, I have brought back the light. Now there will be light and then dark, and we will have day and night." And the shamans could not answer him.

Thereafter in Raven's village day and night followed each other as he told them it would, but the length of each varied, for sometimes Raven had traveled a long time without throwing out any light, and at other times he had thrown out the light at frequent intervals, so that sometimes the nights are very short and sometimes they are very long.

186. THE SEDNA LEGEND
(*Eskimo*)

LONG AGO, THERE WERE no seals or walruses for Eskimos to hunt. There were reindeer and birds, bears and wolves, but there were no animals in the sea. There was, at that time, an Eskimo girl called Sedna who lived with her father in an igloo by the seashore. Sedna was beautiful, and she was courted by men from her own village, and by others who came from faraway lands. But none of these men pleased her and she refused to marry.

One day, a handsome young hunter from a strange far-off country paddled his kayak across the shining sea toward the shores of Sedna's home. He wore beautiful clothes and carried an ivory spear.

He paused at the shore's edge, and called to Sedna, "Come with me! Come to the land of the birds, where there is never hunger and where my tent is made of the most beautiful skins. You will rest on soft bear skins, your lamp will always be filled with oil, and you will always have meat."

Sedna at first refused. Again he told her of the home in which they would live, the rich furs and ivory necklaces that he would give her. Sedna could no longer resist. She left her father's home and joined the young hunter.

When they were out at sea, the young man dropped his paddle into the water. Sedna stared with fright as he raised his hands toward the sky, and, before her eyes, they were transformed into huge wings—the wings of a Loon. He was no man at all, but a spirit bird, with the power to become a human being.

Sedna sat on the Loon's back and they flew toward his home. When they landed on an island in the sea, Sedna discovered that the Loon had lied to her. Her new home was cold and windy, and she had to eat fish brought to her by the Loon and by the other birds that shared their island.

Soon she was lonesome and afraid, and she cried sadly, "Oh father, if you knew how sad I am, you would come to me and carry me away in your kayak. I am a stranger here. I am cold and miserable. Please come, and take me back."

When a year had passed and the sea was calm, Sedna's father set out to visit her in her far-off land. She greeted him joyfully and begged him to take her back. He lifted her onto his boat, and raced across the sea toward home.

When the Loon spirit returned, he found his wife gone. The other birds on the island told him that she had fled with her father. He immediately took the shape of a man, and followed in his kayak. When Sedna's father saw him coming, he covered his daughter with the furs he kept in his boat.

Swiftly the Loon spirit rushed alongside in his kayak.

"Let me see my wife," he cried.

Sedna's father refused.

"Sedna," he called out, "come back with me! No man could love you as much as I do."

But Sedna's kayak flashed across the water. The Loon-man stopped paddling. Sadly, slowly, he raised his hands toward the sky and once again they became wings. He flew over the kayak that carried his Sedna away from him. He hovered over the boat, crying the strange, sad call of the Loon. Then he plunged down into the sea.

The moment the Loon spirit disappeared, the sea waves began to swell up in fury. The sea gods were angry that Sedna had betrayed her husband. The kayak rose and fell as huge waves lashed against it. Sedna's father was terrified, and to save himself he pushed Sedna overboard. Sedna rose to the surface and her fingers gripped the edge of the kayak. But her father, frenzied with fear that he would be killed by the vengeful sea spirits, pulled out a knife and stabbed her hands.

Then, it is said, an astonishing thing happened, perhaps because the Loon spirit or the sea spirits had willed it: the blood that flowed from Sedna's hands congealed in the water, taking different shapes, until suddenly two seals emerged from it. Sedna fell back into the sea, and coming back again, gripped the boat even more tightly. Again her father stabbed her hands and the blood flowed, and this time walruses emerged from the blood-red sea. In desperate fear for his life, he stabbed her hands a third time, and the blood flowed through the water, congealed, and the whales grew out of it.

At last the storm ended. Sedna sank to the bottom of the sea, and all the sea animals that were born from her blood followed her.

Sedna's father, exhausted and bitter, at last arrived home. He entered his igloo and fell into a deep sleep. Outside, Sedna's dog, who had been her friend since childhood, howled as the wind blew across the land.

That night, Sedna commanded the creatures of the sea that emerged from her blood to bring her father and her dog to her. The sea animals swam furiously in front of her father's igloo. The tides ran higher and higher. They washed up the beach until they demolished the igloo, and they carried Sedna's father and her dog down to the depths of the sea. There they joined Sedna, and all three have lived ever since in the land of the waters.

To this day, Eskimo hunters pray to Sedna, goddess of the seas, who commands all the sea animals. She is vengeful and bitter, and men beg her to release the animals that were born of her so that they might eat. By her whim, a man successfully harpoons seals and walruses or is swept away from land by the stormy seas. The spirits of the great Medicine Men swim down to her home and comb her hair because her hand still hurts. And if they comb her hair well, she releases a seal, a walrus, or a whale.

Caribbean and West Indies

The Magic Orange Tree

187. THE MAGIC ORANGE TREE
(*Haiti*)

THERE WAS ONCE a girl whose mother died when she was born. Her father waited for some time to remarry, but when he did, he married a woman who was both mean and cruel. She was so mean there were some days she would not give the girl anything at all to eat. The girl was often hungry.

One day the girl came from school and saw on the table three round ripe oranges. *Hmmmm.* They smelled good. The girl looked around her. No one was there. She took one orange, peeled it, and ate it. *Hmmm-mmm.* It was good. She took a second orange and ate it. She ate the third orange. Oh-oh, she was happy. But soon her stepmother came home.

"Who has taken the oranges I left on the table?" she said. "Whoever has done so had better say their prayers now, for they will not be able to say them later."

The girl was so frightened she ran from the house. She ran through the woods until she came to her own mother's grave. All night she cried and prayed to her mother to help her. Finally she fell asleep.

In the morning the sun woke her, and as she rose to her feet something dropped from her skirt onto the ground. What was it? It was an orange pit. And the moment it entered the earth a green leaf sprouted from it. The girl watched, amazed. She knelt down and sang:

> "Orange tree,
> Grow and grow and grow.
> Orange tree, orange tree.
> Grow and grow and grow,
> Orange tree.
> Stepmother is not real mother,
> Orange tree."

The orange tree grew. It grew to the size of the girl. The girl sang:

> "Orange tree,
> Branch and branch and branch.

> Orange tree, orange tree,
> Branch and branch and branch,
> Orange tree.
> Stepmother is not real mother,
> Orange tree."

And many twisting, turning, curving branches appeared on the tree. Then the girl sang:

> "Orange tree,
> Flower and flower and flower.
> Orange tree, orange tree,
> Flower and flower and flower,
> Orange tree.
> Stepmother is not real mother,
> Orange tree."

Beautiful white blossoms covered the tree. After a time they began to fade, and small green buds appeared where the flowers had been. The girl sang:

> "Orange tree,
> Ripen and ripen and ripen.
> Orange tree, orange tree,
> Ripen and ripen and ripen,
> Orange tree.
> Stepmother is not real mother,
> Orange tree."

The oranges ripened, and the whole tree was filled with golden oranges. The girl was so delighted she danced around and around the tree, singing:

> "Orange tree,
> Grow and grow and grow.
> Orange tree, orange tree,
> Grow and grow and grow,
> Orange tree.
> Stepmother is not real mother,
> Orange tree."

But then when she looked, she saw the orange tree had grown up to the sky, far beyond her reach. What was she to do? Oh she was a clever girl. She sang:

> "Orange tree,
> Lower and lower and lower.

> Orange tree, orange tree,
> Lower and lower and lower,
> Orange tree.
> Stepmother is not real mother,
> Orange tree."

When the orange tree came down to her height, she filled her arms with oranges and returned home.

The moment the stepmother saw the gold oranges in the girl's arms, she seized them and began to eat them. Soon she had finished them all.

"Tell me, my sweet," she said to the girl, "where have you found such delicious oranges?"

The girl hesitated. She did not want to tell. The stepmother seized the girl's wrist and began to twist it.

"Tell me!" she ordered.

The girl led her stepmother through the woods to the orange tree. You remember the girl was very clever? Well, as soon as the girl came to the tree, she sang:

> "Orange tree,
> Grow and grow and grow.
> Orange tree, orange tree,
> Grow and grow and grow,
> Orange tree.
> Stepmother is not real mother,
> Orange tree."

And the orange tree grew up to the sky. What was the stepmother to do then? She began to plead and beg.

"Please," she said. "You shall be my own dear child. You may always have as much as you want to eat. Tell the tree to come down and *you* shall pick the oranges for me." So the girl quietly sang:

> "Orange tree,
> Lower and lower and lower.
> Orange tree, orange tree,
> Lower and lower and lower,
> Orange tree.
> Stepmother is not real mother,
> Orange tree."

The tree began to lower. When it came to the height of the step-mother, she leaped on it and began to climb so quickly you might have thought she was the daughter of an ape. And as she climbed f branch to branch, she ate every orange. The girl saw that there would soon be no oranges left. What would happen to her then? The girl sang:

"Orange tree,
Grow and grow and grow.
Orange tree, orange tree,
Grow and grow and grow,
Orange tree.
Stepmother is not real mother,
Orange tree."

The orange tree grew and grew and grew and grew. "Help!" cried the stepmother as she rose into the sky. "H-E-E-lp. . . ."

The girl cried: *"Break!* Orange tree, *Break!"*

The orange tree broke into a thousand pieces . . . and the stepmother as well.

Then the girl searched among the branches until she found . . . a tiny orange pit. She carefully planted it in the earth. Softly she sang:

"Orange tree,
Grow and grow and grow.
Orange tree, orange tree,
Grow and grow and grow,
Orange tree.
Stepmother is not real mother,
Orange tree."

The orange tree grew to the height of the girl. She picked some oranges and took them to market to sell. They were so sweet the people bought all her oranges.

Every Saturday she is at the marketplace selling her oranges. Last Saturday, I went to see her and asked her if she would give me a free orange. "What?" she cried. "After all I've been through!" And she gave me such a kick in the pants that that's how I got here today, to tell you the story—"The Magic Orange Tree."

188. GREEDY MARIANI
(Haiti)

ON A HIGH ROAD, far from any village, lived Mariani. Alone. And little wonder. Mariani was a woman, the possessor of a quick temper, a scolding tongue, a greedy disposition, a . . . But you will see.

Travelers on the high road, surprised by nightfall, would approach Mariani's hut with thankfulness. "If you could spare but a crumb of hospitality . . ." they would beg.

And a crumb was what they received. No more, no less. A mere corner of the hut in which to curl up. No bed. No blanket. A pillow? Ha, ha, a good jest, that. As for food, a bean, a grain or two of rice— and this only if Mariani were in an unaccountably good humor. Which happened, oh, once in ten years.

To bring her entertainment to a proper close, Mariani would awaken her guests at dawn. Equipped with two hefty arms, she would strip them of their valuables and drive them on their way. At least they had an early start on the day's journey. But were they grateful for that? Indeed not. Away they stumbled, shaking their fists, shrieking bad words. "Miser! Witch! Thief!" But probably true. Very likely true.

One stormy night Mariani was occupied pouring cane-sugar syrup into a huge cauldron. A knock at the door.

"*Honneur.*"

"Respect," replied Mariani, and opened the door.

A man stood there eying the doorsill. Timidly he requested shelter to await the end of the tempest. As the lizard greets the ant, so Mariani welcomed the traveler.

This one turned back into the rain and wind, then returned with a sack stuffed to its mouth. He let it fall to the floor with a clink. No doubt about it. Only silver clinks so clinkily. Mariani watched with interest.

The man politely excused himself, backed out the door. Again h came, bearing a second bag. This one also clinked. Back and forth he went, twice more; each time returning with another sack. All stuffed as plumply as a roasted turkey. All clinking beautifully.

Mariani, missing not a clink, set the cauldron over the fire. She busied herself shelling peanuts for the making of cane-syrup *tablettes*, all the while dreaming of those sacks of silver, which would, if she had her way, soon be stashed away under the *mapou* tree in her garden.

Soon the rain ended. A star appeared. The man raised himself from the bench and prepared to load his mules. He did not forget to thank his hostess with much courtesy. But thanks are a matter of nothing to a miser, a witch, a thief.

"Not so fast, my dear sir," spoke Mariani. "Are these then your manners? You shield yourself from the rain under my roof. Now you think to leave without paying me a centime. Shame!"

The traveler, his head bowed, murmured pardons. "*Non*, but *non*, madame, I thought to leave you in return for your gracious hospitality" —he must have been joking—"a sack of silver. If you yourself would care to choose one bag from the four . . ."

"*One* from the four? All four of the four! Is it my fault that my lodging costs so dear? To be exact, four sacks of silver. And fortunate you are that the price is not five or six sacks. The idea! Only one bag of silver for an entire hour's shelter. Actually, closer to an hour and a quarter. . . ."

The stranger did not reply (clever stranger). He loaded the mules with three bags of silver. Not an easy thing to do in the black dark. Then he urged the beasts before him with the tune of his snapping whip:

> *Kalinda, ding ding ding daou,*
> *Kalinda, ding ding ding daou,*
> *Kalinda, ding ding ding daou,*
> *Kalinda, ding ding ding ding daou.*

Mariani stood on her doorstep and cried, "Thief! Render me my due!"

The stranger seemed not to hear. Maybe he was deaf, which at the moment would have been a blessing. He flicked the mules with the ʳing whip.

ʳiani ran after him, tossing insults and abuse with a free tongue. ᵒnse. The man stared at the ground as if in deep thought. Thus they journeyed for some time, the mules and the man mute, Mariani railing and ranting.

Finally, having screeched herself out of breath, the old woman panted, "Monsieur, the syrup boils, the syrup boils, I must prepare my *tablettes*. Give me my money!"

Sang the stranger:

> "Mariani, I begin to hear you now.
>   Better to turn back now,
>   Poor Mariani."

He flipped his whip, and in their sacks the silver tinkled a tune:

> *Kalinda, ding ding ding daou,*
> *Kalinda, ding ding ding daou,*
> *Kalinda, ding ding ding daou,*
> *Kalinda, ding ding ding ding daou.*

"I mock your counsel! Counsel I wish not. I wish my money!" howled Mariani. Still she followed the little band, the mules and the man.

For a long time, a long, long time they marched. In silence. In darkness. Along the long lonely road without encountering a soul. Not one soul.

Weary and out of patience, Mariani threatened, "Thief, I will escort you to the judge. You shall not escape me. Certain it is that my syrup scorches to cinders. You shall pay me for that as well as for lodging."

The driver-of-mules repeated his song:

> "Mariani, I hear you now, I hear you now.
>   Better to turn back, turn back,
>   Poor Mariani."

But Mariani, along with a quick temper, scolding tongue, and greedy disposition, possessed a stubborn nature. Return home while three bags of silver clinked just beyond her fingers? An absurdity. They continued the journey. On and on.

At last, as they approached a village, dawn announced itself. A cock crowed.

The mules vanished. The man faced about and gazed directly at Mariani. *Hélas!* What did she see?

A skull with empty sockets. Bared teeth. Bones clinking, clink clinking in the wind.

Mariani fell, stone dead of shock. And the zombi—for so he was—disappeared among the tombs of a nearby cemetery.

189. UNCLE BOUQUI AND LITTLE MALICE
(Haiti)

THERE WAS A KING in Haiti, and he had a fat sheep he loved more than silver and gold. This sheep was his pet, and he had it near him all the time. He played with it as if it were his child. He combed its fleece and put red ribbons on it, and called it My Joy.

Day and night he watched his sheep because he was afraid someone would steal it. More than anyone else he was afraid of the trickster Malice, the smartest and most cunning fellow in all Haiti.

Now, little Malice had seen that fine fat sheep, and he had a fine fat appetite. Besides, he loved sheep meat more than any other kind of meat. He had made up his mind he was going to eat the king's sheep, and he could think of nothing else except how he could get it.

Well, believe it or not, it didn't take too long. Soon the king's sheep was in Malice's yard, in Malice's pot, and, before you could count five, in Malice's mouth. He enjoyed a great feast of sheep stew.

When the king missed his sheep, he ran around the palace wildly roaring, "Where is My Joy?" But nobody knew where My Joy was. So the king sent for the very best *houngan* (witch doctor) in all Haiti.

When the witch doctor arrived, the king shouted, "Find me My Joy! Find me the thief!"

"I'll find the thief," said the *houngan*. "Give me a candle, a pot of ᵃter, and money."

ᵂhen these things were brought to him, he lit the candle, made a and th the money, and put the water in front of it. Then he prayed nd danced.

Finally he said, "King, My Joy is dead. A thief stole it and ate it."

"Who was the thief? Tell me his name quickly!" roared the king. "Where is he? Who is he? He'll never steal again!" he screamed, stamping and shouting at the top of his voice.

"I can't tell you his name," the witch doctor said, "but I can tell you that he is the smartest man in all Haiti, and you know who that is. Now, pay me. I must go to a fisherman who can't catch fish."

The king paid him. He knew who the smartest man in Haiti was, and he was determined to catch him.

"Chief of the guards, come here!" he shouted.

The chief of the guards came running. "Go and find Malice," said the king. "Put him in chains and bring him here."

"You know, King, it's hard to catch that scoundrel. He is a crafty fellow," mourned the chief of the guards.

"You bring him here in three days or I'll do to you what I want to do to him," warned the king darkly.

Sadly the chief of the guards went out to look for Malice.

The king was still unhappy, so he decided to hold a prayer meeting and give a feast in honor of the dead My Joy. He invited every important person to come to the feast.

You can be sure that Malice knew all about what had happened: that the king had sent the chief of the guards to look for him and bring him back in chains. He was very worried and kept thinking hard how to get his neck out of that noose.

"I'm an honest man until I'm caught," he said, and went where the guard could not see him. He went to the house of Bouqui, that stupid Bouqui of Haiti, who loved to eat more than anyone in the world. Bouqui came to the door.

"Honor!" cried Malice.

"Respect!" answered Bouqui.

That was the proper manner of greeting in Haiti.

"Uncle Bouqui," said Malice with an innocent expression on his face, "Uncle Bouqui, have you heard of the great prayer and feast the king is offering for his lost sheep?"

"No, I have not, Malice."

"Everybody must come in carnival clothes. There will be a song contest, too. He who sings the best song and wears the finest costume will receive as a prize three big fat oxen, five sheep, and other good things. That is a prize for you!"

"Really?" cried Bouqui, his eyes as big as saucers.

"Yes, it is exactly as I tell you," Malice assured him.

"Ah, my dear Nephew Malice! You know how much I love you. Three fat oxen! Five sheep! You know how I love ox and sheep meat. You said three oxen and five sheep, didn't you?"

"That's exactly what I said."

"Here is money, Nephew Malice. Go and buy me the finest costume and teach me the finest song, so that I can win that prize. I promise you half of all the king gives me."

Malice took the money. Then he took the skin of the sheep he had stolen from the king, and from it he made a fancy coat for Bouqui. He brought it to him and put it on his back, and looked at Bouqui with the greatest admiration.

"That coat looks fine on you, *Nonc* Bouqui. Now I'll teach you a song nobody can beat, and you are sure to win the prize."

"Teach me, teach me quickly, Malice. I want to win those oxen and sheep."

"Now, listen carefully while I sing, *Nonc* Bouqui," and Malice began to sing:

> "I am Bouqui the Great,
> who took My Joy
> in the king's palace.
> In the king's palace
> I took My Joy.
> You can see the proof right on my back.
> I ate My Joy
> in the king's palace.
> In the king's palace
> I ate My Joy."

"That is a wonderful song," cried stupid Bouqui. "I'll learn it and I'll win the prize."

"Don't forget that half is for me," said Malice slyly.

"How can I forget, my dear Nephew Malice, after all you have done for me?"

Bouqui learned the song, and when he knew it well, he and Malice went to the king's palace. The building was all lighted up and there was a grand company of important people. Bouqui went in, but Malice stayed out in the bushes, saying he did not feel well.

Bouqui walked around with his head high in the air. Everybody was talking about the terrible loss of the king's sheep and how the thief would be punished, and everybody ate stew and yams and plantains, deliciously cooked by the king's own cook. And they also drank the king's fine rum.

Bouqui ate more and drank more than anyone there. He felt very happy and sang the song Malice had taught him, hoping the king would hear it and that he would win the prize. It did not take long for his song to reach the king's ears.

"What's that song I hear?" shouted the king. "What's that song? Who is singing it?"

"It's me, King!" cried Bouqui. "I'm the one who's singing that song. Listen!" And again he sang:

> "I am Bouqui the Great,
>   who took My Joy
>   in the king's palace.
> In the king's palace
>   I took My Joy.
> You can see the proof right on my back.
> I ate My Joy
>   in the king's palace.
> In the king's palace
>   I ate My Joy."

"Turn around!" roared the king at Bouqui.

Bouqui turned around, and the king saw My Joy's skin on his back.

"Oh, my poor sheep!" cried the king. "So you are the thief and the robber! Ah! You won't ever steal sheep again. Guards, take him, beat him, and broil him! Be quick!"

The guards took poor Bouqui away. Then Malice came out of the bushes and said in an innocent voice, "King, you must pay me the prize because I helped you to find the thief who stole your sheep."

"Hm!" said the king. "A snake is not far from its hole, and Malice is not far from my chief of guards. Maybe the saying is true: Set a thief to catch a thief. You are too smart, Malice. Maybe you had a hand in all this. The witch doctor said the smartest man in my land did this, and Bouqui is *not* the smartest man in my land. Guards, take Malice, also. It will do no harm to punish him a little, too."

So the guards took Malice and bound him in chains, and there were Malice and Bouqui in the same prison, waiting to be punished.

"It's you who got me into this mess, Malice, you scoundrel!" cried Bouqui.

"I know I did, Bouqui, and I'm very sorry for it. I love you even when I do such things. But now I'll get you out of here. Let us both leave and live happily together."

Malice knew how Haitian guards were, so he gave a little money to some, and presents to others, and before long they were both free.

Bouqui swore he would never listen to Malice again.

Do you think he kept that promise?

Of course not!

190. BOUKI RENTS A HORSE*
(Haiti)

IT WAS TIME to dig up the yams and take them to market. Bouki went out with his big hoe and dug up a big pile of yams and left them in the sun to dry. While they were drying, he began to consider how he would get them to the city. "I think I will borrow Moussa's donkey," he said at last. "As long as I have the donkey, I might as well dig up some more yams."

So he dug up some more yams, and then he went to Moussa's house for the donkey. But Moussa said, "Bouki, my donkey ran away yesterday, and we haven't found him yet. Why don't you rent a horse from Mr. Toussaint?"

"Toussaint!" Bouki said. "He'll charge more than I can get for the yams! He'll charge me even for *talking* to him!"

But finally Bouki went to Toussaint's house to see if he could rent a horse.

Toussaint said, "This is a good horse. He's too good to carry yams. But you can have him for one day for fifteen gourdes."

Bouki had only five gourdes.

"I'll take the five now," Toussaint said. "You can give me ten more tomorrow when you come for the horse."

---

*From *The Piece of Fire and Other Haitian Tales*. © 1964 by Harold Courlander. Reprinted by permission of Harcourt Brace Jovanovich, Inc.

Bouki went home. He went to sleep. In the morning when he got up to go to market, Moussa was in front of his house with the donkey.

"Here's the donkey," Moussa said. "He came home in the middle of the night."

Bouki said, "But I already rented Toussaint's horse!"

"Never mind, go tell Toussaint you don't need the horse," Moussa said.

"But I already gave him five gourdes," Bouki complained. "I'll never get my money back!"

Just then Ti Malice came along. He listened to the talk. He said, "Take me along to Toussaint's. I'll get your money back for you."

Bouki and Ti Malice went together to Toussaint's place.

"We've come for the horse," Ti Malice said.

"There he is under the tree," Toussaint said. "But first give me the ten gourdes."

"Not so fast," Ti Malice said. "First we have to see if he's big enough."

"He's big enough," Toussaint said. "He's the biggest horse around here. So give me the ten gourdes."

"First we have to measure him," Ti Malice said. He took a measuring tape from his pocket and stretched it over the horse's back. "Let's see, now," he said to Bouki. "You need about eighteen inches, and you can sit in the middle. I need about fifteen inches, and I can sit here. Madame Malice needs about eighteen inches, and she can sit behind me. Madame Bouki needs about twenty inches, and she can sit in the front."

"Wait!" Toussaint said. "You can't put four people on that horse!"

"Then," Ti Malice said, "Tijean Bouki can go here on the horse's neck. Boukino can sit in his lap, and we can tie Boukinette right here if we're careful."

"Listen!" Toussaint said, starting to sweat. "You must be crazy. A horse can't carry so many people!"

"He can try," Ti Malice said.

"You'll kill him!" Toussaint said.

"We can put my children *here*," Ti Malice said, measuring behind the horse's ears, "but they'll have to push together."

"Just a minute!" Toussaint shouted. "You can't have the horse at all!"

"Oh yes, we can," Ti Malice said, still measuring. "You rented him to us, and today we are going to use him. Bouki, where will we put the baby?"

"Baby?" Bouki said. "Baby?"

"We'll put the baby here," Ti Malice said. "Madame Bouki can hold him. Then over here we can hang the saddle bags to carry the pigs."

"The deal is off!" Toussaint shouted. "This animal isn't a steamship!"

"Now don't try to back out of the deal," Ti Malice said, "or we'll take the matter to the police."

"Here!" Toussaint said. "Here's your five gourdes back!"

"Five gourdes!" Ti Malice said. "You rented him to us for *fifteen*, and now you want to give *five* back? What do you take us for?"

"Yes," Bouki said, "what for?"

"But Bouki only *gave* me five!" Toussaint said.

Ti Malice looked the horse over carefully.

"Where will we put Grandmother?" Bouki asked suddenly.

"Here!" Toussaint shouted. "Here!" He pushed fifteen gourdes into Ti Malice's hands. "And get away from my horse!" He jumped on its back and rode away.

Bouki and Ti Malice watched him go. Then they fell on the ground and began to laugh. They laughed so hard that they had to gasp for air.

Suddenly Bouki stopped laughing. He looked worried. He sat up.

"What's the matter?" Ti Malice asked.

"I don't think we could have done it," Bouki said.

"Done what?" Ti Malice asked.

"Put Grandmother on the horse," Bouki said.

191. ANANSI PLAY WITH FIRE, ANANSI GET BURNED

(Jamaica)

> "I go away, I go away,
> Perhaps I come another day."

THERE WAS GREAT RUNNING around all over in the woods, for Tiger was getting married. Everyone, leaping, walking, crawling, and flying, was invited. Only one was not asked, and that was Anansi. Anansi—sometimes a spider, sometimes a man, sometimes half a man and half a spider—Anansi with a spider face who was always playing tricks and making trouble and cheating everyone in the forest and village. No, Anansi was not invited by Tiger to the wedding feast, because Tiger was angry at Anansi for playing so many mean tricks and cheating him so often.

Anansi was very angry, for he liked eating and dancing most of all. "I must do something about this," he said.

He walked up to Tiger's house, where Tiger was busy cooking and cleaning and getting everything ready.

"Good day, Bredda Tiger, it's a fine day and I see you are cooking fine-smelling food."

"Grrrrrrr," Tiger growled, not even looking at Anansi.

"Heard you were getting married tomorrow to a fine girl."

"Grrrrrrr," Tiger growled again.

"Heard you invited everybody, but you didn't invite me, your friend," and Anansi smiled sweetly.

"Grrrrrrr," Tiger growled louder at Anansi, the troublemaker.

Anansi made believe he did not hear.

"Never thought you would treat me that bad, and I am such a good friend to you."

"Get out of my eyes, you cheat, you thief, you liar," roared Tiger. "Get away from here before I tear you to pieces for the many times you cheated me. I don't want to spoil my wedding day."

That was too much for Anansi—he was boiling with anger. "I'll spoil your wedding day good and strong. If you want fire, you'll get it. I'll give you plenty trouble. I'll put a spell on you. You'll remember me all your life for this insult."

Then he ran away, for Tiger was getting ready to go for him.

Tiger growled and kept on working. Pretty soon he began worrying and thinking. "Folks say Anansi is a magician man. He can put curses on folks. He might put a curse on me. Maybe I should have invited him, even though he has lied to me and cheated me so many times. I better go to see my bride and talk things over with her."

Tiger went to his bride and talked to her of such nice things that he forgot all about Anansi.

But Anansi did not forget. Every one of his thin legs was shaking with anger. "I must fix that mean Tiger so that he remembers me all his life. I'll show him how to insult me! Not to invite me to the feast! When everybody'll be eating good food, I won't. I'll teach him something. But how? . . . How? . . . I know! I know!"

Anansi went back to Tiger's house. But he did not go straight—he was the kind that couldn't go straight. He went round about till he came to Tiger's house. He stopped and looked all around on all sides. Not a sound from the house.

"Just fine. Just what I wanted," Anansi said.

He ran in back of the house where there were trees and bushes, looking for the cowitch creeper. That's a creeper growing on trees. It has nice, soft, fluffy-velvety pods. But look out! If you touch those pods, your skin will burn and itch so you'll want to jump in the river. And you'll scratch and scratch until the blood runs, and then you'll scratch more and more.

"Those cowitch creepers will fix Mr. Tiger so he won't forget me," said Anansi as he climbed up a tree that had plenty of cowitch creepers hanging from it. He cut some of the streamers, holding them in his hands, in which he had put some leaves.

When he came down he went into Tiger's house holding the poison plant far away from him. On the table lay Tiger's wedding clothes nice and ready. Then mean Anansi rubbed the fluffy pods all over Tiger's clothes so that when he put them on, the fluffy things would rub his skin and make him itch to beat Carnival. When he had finished that mean work, he ran off.

After Tiger had talked with his bride and come back to his house, he was still worried. Even when he went to sleep, he kept thinking and worrying about Anansi and what he would do.

Early next morning Tiger put on his wedding clothes, and soon all his animal friends started to come: Dog, Horse, Cat, Monkey, birds, frogs, land turtles—everybody came except Anansi. Tiger was beginning to itch. Guests were greeting him and talking, but poor Tiger was itching terribly. Soon he couldn't stand it. He tore his clothes off and looked at them. So did all the animals, and they saw the cowitch plant all over those clothes.

"That was that devil Anansi. That's the revenge he said he'd take," roared Tiger, and then he told the animals what had happened.

Now, all the animals had a great grudge against Anansi for he had done some wrong to each of them, and they decided they would take revenge on him.

"Let's pay him back for what he has done to us. Let's finish him so he can't do any more harm," shouted each one, from the ant to the horse.

"We'll invite him to the wedding, and when he's here we'll . . ."

"I'll bring him," zoomed Bee, "I'll bring him quick." She flew off, but she did not have to fly far. There was Mr. Anansi hopping around not far from Tiger's house, hoping to be asked to the feast.

Bee told him quickly that he could come: Everyone was waiting for him, and there was plenty left to eat. Anansi was such a glutton he did not smell anything wrong, so he went to Tiger's house. Yes, everybody was waiting for him. Anansi looked at Mr. Tiger, now dressed in different clothes, and thought everything was fine.

All the animals gathered around Anansi, and when there wasn't a hole the size of sand for him to get through, Tiger roared: "Now we have you and we'll show you how to put cowitch on my wedding clothes. You just wait!"

Anansi turned as white as chalk. He looked around and saw there was no place to run, for all the animals were gathered close. Tiger and Horse and Cat ran out to the trees and came back with heaps and heaps of cowitch creeper and laid them on the ground. They brought more and more and made a thick bed of it. Anansi looked on, shaking like a leaf in the wind.

"Now you'll get some of your own medicine," Snake hissed. "We'll put you on the bed of cowitch and roll you around and around in it. That'll pay you for trying to put it on Tiger's wedding clothes."

"You can't do that," Anansi howled. "It'll kill me. I'm your old friend, Mr. Tiger. I just played a little joke."

"Now I'll play a little joke," Tiger roared. "You put the cowitch on my clothes, and now I'll put it on you."

"Bredda Tiger, please don't do that. It'll hurt terribly. I was just playing a little joke."

"You didn't mind hurting me, did you? Now I'll play the same little joke on you."

Then the animals threw Anansi down on the cowitch and rolled him over and over and over. Anansi began to burn and itch like dry grass on fire, and when he saw they were not going to stop, he began thinking fast how he could escape. Even with the terrible burning and itching he had an idea.

"Bredda Tiger," he cried, "the Queen is coming down the road. Do you hear that noise far off? That's her coming this way."

"You are lying. You are up to some old trick," the animals cried.

"I'm not lying. It was in all the papers. You were too busy with the wedding to listen to it."

And though the animals doubted Anansi's word, some of them began to think he might be telling the truth and looked toward the road.

The wind was blowing high in the trees, making a lot of noise in the leaves.

"Don't you hear the noise of the people?" Anansi cried, for he couldn't stand the itching any longer. "That's the folks coming with the Queen!" he screamed so you could hear him from one end of the island to the other. (But he really screamed because of the pain from the cowitch.) "There she is coming on the road! Run quick if you want to see her."

All the animals ran to see the Queen who was not there, and Anansi, he ran the other way to scratch himself. So you see, Anansi got paid what he deserved, but he got away just the same. That was just like Anansi.

Jack Mondory, me no choose none.

192. HOW EL BIZARRÓN FOOLED THE DEVIL

(Cuba)

THERE WAS ONCE a man called El Bizarrón who wandered about looking for work. A restless fellow. He wandered here. He wandered there. But more often there than here.

One day he was told that in the house of the Devil there was need for a servant. "*Pues, ten cuidado!*" they warned. (A forceful way of saying, "Watch out!") Two servants the Devil had already slain. He was a mean one. All who worked for him ended up dead. Much sooner than later, too. Clearly a recommendation to avoid *that* house.

But El Bizarrón retorted, "I'm on my way. The Devil won't frighten *me*."

So, to the Devil's front door he went. And knocked.

Who should open the door but the Devil himself.

"Have you work for a strong man?"

"Work enough for six strong men. You are sure there are not five more of you? Ah, well. *Pase adentro.*"

In walked El Bizarrón. The Devil led him to the room where he was to sleep. "Rest," he said. "Tomorrow you will begin your chores."

El Bizarrón stretched himself on the bed. Before long, healthy snores were livening up that corner of the house.

The next day the Devil sent him to fetch water.

But El Bizarrón demanded, "Give me a pick and shovel."

The Devil without any fuss gave them.

El Bizarrón went down to the river. He began digging a ditch from the stream to the Devil's house. Like six men he toiled. Well . . . like three anyway.

At eleven o'clock came the Devil to check up on El Bizarrón. "Water I wish. Not a ditch. Explain yourself," he commanded.

"I am digging a canal to your house. Then there will be no need to go for water. Water will flow to you."

The Devil reflected. This man can dig. The trench is already the depth of a pitchfork. (The Devil knew his pitchforks.) Moreover, this man can *think*. He didn't like that at all. It was such a distasteful thought that he went off home.

A few days later the Devil ordered El Bizarrón to fetch a load of wood. El Bizarrón demanded, "Give me a length of rope. A long length."

Without much ado the Devil gave it.

El Bizarrón took the rope on his shoulder and went off to the mountain. There he set himself to wind the rope around the trees—around the whole forest. The rope was a lengthy length all right. With all his tramping, the heels of El Bizarrón's shoes were worn to a fraction of a millimeter; not enough sole remained to measure a fraction of anything. At eleven o'clock when the Devil came to see what El Bizarrón was up to, he found him with the rope looped around the mountain as a collar wreathes a neck.

Of course he wanted to know, "What are you doing?"

El Bizarrón answered, "Securing this mountain of woods so I can carry it back in one trip."

What a barbarian, thought the Devil. And he directed El Bizarrón to return to the house. Without the mountain. No room for *that* in the backyard.

Soon after, there was a throwing contest on the beach, with metal bars. The Devil thought, ah, I shall send this strong fellow as a competitor. With his muscles he must surely win me a prize. And he led El Bizarrón to the shore, El Bizarrón with a bar balanced on his shoulder.

At the beach everyone was practicing and preparing himself for the match. Except El Bizarrón. That one curled himself on the sunny sand and took a snooze.

The day peeled off its hours. The contest began. Came the turn of El Bizarrón.

Loudly he cried out, "Order those faraway boats to sail away. Otherwise I will sink them with my shot!"

As this was impossible they would not permit him to throw. It was a disappointment to all. In particular to the Devil, who felt more and more uneasy about El Bizarrón's strength. *And* his acuteness. Too dangerous is this ox with his fox's brain, he decided. I must rid myself of him.

The two made their way back to the Devil's house. In a buttery manner the Devil suggested that since he desired to spend that night stretched out on the iron grill of the barbecue, El Bizarrón might wish to sleep beneath.

"Why not?" asked El Bizarrón in an offhand way.

So it was arranged. The Devil then hid two heavy, heavy rocks that he planned to drop on El Bizarrón during the night.

Evening fell, and both lay down in their places: the Devil on the high grill and El Bizarrón underneath. But El Bizarrón noticed that the Devil appeared much bulkier than usual. A suspicious sign. Hmmmmmmm. Unknown to the Devil, El Bizarrón changed his bed to a corner, a far corner. And waited.

At midnight he heard the clangor of falling rocks. At once he shouted, "Ay, what a mosquito has bitten me!"

Naturally the Devil thought, two boulders have dropped on him and to this fellow they are no more than an insect bite. He was impressed. Disturbed. Shaken to his red marrow.

He climbed down to note exactly El Bizarrón's condition. This one was now sitting under the barbecue, unbruised, unscratched, unmarked. And there lay the smashed rocks.

"Ah," said El Bizarrón in a voice of wonder, "I believed it was a mosquito and instead it was these stones. How came they here?"

Now the Devil's teeth clacked with fright. Speaking between clacks he declared, "Fellow, I shall give you a burro loaded with silver if you will leave here—if you leave for a destination far, far away. Preferably the moon. Or farther."

El Bizarrón accepted the offer. Why not? He brought up the burro. The Devil filled the saddlebags with money, till they bulged like sacks of potatoes.

"There you have it. Now go."

El Bizarrón went. After he had been gone awhile, the Devil's wife said to him, "That ninny deceived you. He is not so strong as all that." She flung sneers against the Devil as if she were hurling stones at a stray dog.

Her scorn convinced her husband. So, saddling a horse, he set out to find El Bizarrón and take from him the donkey and the riches.

Looking back, El Bizarrón glimpsed the Devil approaching at a distance. Quickly he hid the donkey in a field of sugarcane. Then he lay on his back in the middle of the road with his legs in the air.

The Devil came up. In astonishment he asked, "And what ails *you?*"

"Ah, nothing. That stubbornness of a donkey refused to walk. So I gave him a kick that sent him above the clouds. . . ."

The Devil, his teeth clattering again, wanted to know, "But why are you lying here kicking at the wind?"

"I don't want the donkey killed when he drops back to earth. This way I'll ease his fall with my feet."

At that the palsy of the Devil's teeth affected the rest of him. He might have been a flag lashed by a gale. Swiftly he spurred his horse and galloped home.

His wife asked, "Did you catch him?"

"Catch him! Should I want to? There he was. No sign of the burro— he had kicked it to Heaven. And if I had waited to recover the money he might have booted *me* to Heaven. And what place is that for the Devil? Glad am I to be free of him."

193. THE STORY OF THE SMART PARROT
(*Puerto Rico*)

THERE LIVED A MAN in Puerto Rico who had a wonderful parrot. There was not another like him. He was smart, and he could say anything in Spanish as clearly as any Puerto Rican. But there was just one word he could *not* say—the name of the town in which he was born: Cataño. The master of the parrot tried everything to teach the bird that word, but all his trying was of no use. The parrot just couldn't say it.

One day a man from San Juan saw and heard the parrot and tried to buy him. Since the owner of the bird needed money very badly at the time, he sold him the bird for a good sum. But he told the man about the one word the parrot could not say.

"I'll buy your bird anyway," said the man. "I'll teach him to say 'Cataño.' You can take my word for that."

He took the parrot home with him to San Juan and immediately set about trying to teach the bird to say "Cataño." He tried and he tried and he tried, but it was no use; the parrot simply would not say the word. After a while, the man began to lose his patience and became angry.

"You stupid bird! What's the matter with you? Why can't you learn that one word, when you can say so many others? You say 'Cataño' or I'll kill you!"

But the parrot still would not say it, although the man spent hours trying to teach it to him. Finally the man became so angry that he screamed and ranted at the bird. "You say 'Cataño' or I'll kill you!" he repeated. But he might as well have been speaking to a stone wall.

One day, after trying again for hours to make the parrot say the word, the man became very, very angry. He picked up the bird and threw him into an old chicken house in which he kept the fowl to be eaten.

"You are more stupid than the chickens, and soon I'll finish you as I finish them."

In the chicken house were four old chickens that were to be eaten the following Sunday.

The next morning the master came into the chicken house to get the parrot and the chickens. He opened the door and stopped, astounded at the sight he saw.

There were three chickens lying dead, and the parrot was standing in front of the fourth one, screaming over and over again, "Say 'Cataño' or I'll kill you! Say 'Cataño' or I'll kill you!" The other chickens had not been able to say "Cataño," so the parrot had killed them.

The man looked and looked, then he began to laugh. "This is one time I was fooled by a parrot," he said.

He prepared the fourth chicken for dinner and had a fine meal. He never called that parrot a fool again, for a wise master knows a smart servant.

Central and South America

How the Devil Constructed a Church

194. HOW THE DEVIL CONSTRUCTED A CHURCH
(*Honduras*)

THE TOWN OF Curarén is one of the most ancient in Honduras. It was who knows how many years old when the Spanish arrived from across the sea. And that was—let me think—over four centuries ago. Today Curarén still stands, the home of a famous church. The story of this church bears telling.

Some years after the Conquest, the Curarenes (which is another way of saying the inhabitants of Curarén) were ordered by the Spanish governor to build a church in their village. The townsmen were quite content at the thought of a fine church. At the thought of constructing it—piling stone upon stone upon stone upon—they quite contentedly fell asleep.

Time after time they put off the construction. At last, in a fit of rage, the governor decreed that if the church were not completed within a week, inside and out, upside and down, the town would be destroyed—totally destroyed.

It was a distressful business. "An impossible task," groaned the mayor. The members of the town council beat their heads against the ground. Without doubt it was farewell to Curarén—Curarén the ancient, the beautiful, Curarén their home. A pity!

There loomed one hope. Their Indian neighbors to the north informed the town that the *Enemigo Malo*, the Devil, had himself fashioned the Bridge of Slaves in Guatemala. Surely the Curarenes could reach an agreement with him to build their church?

The townsmen shuddered. But—a decree is a decree. The church—or destruction.

It was done. The Devil wrote the contract, and the mayor signed it with the blood of his veins. Both parties were committed. On the one hand, the Devil was to construct the church, even to applying a coat of plaster both inside and out. On the other hand, as his tribute, he would be presented annually with a certain number of unbaptized babies.

During the night of construction the Curarenes were under strict orders to stay inside their homes; only the mayor and town council would remain on watch to make sure the work was well done. The walls would be of stone masonry and the stone would be unadorned. No carving. No embellishment. Even at a price, the Devil had his limits. Of course, the church must be completed before the most diligent cock could crow his morning song, "Christ is born"; otherwise, the work was forfeit.

One councillor rubbed his hands together. "No one can build a church in one night," he whispered. "Even the *Enemigo Malo*. We are quite safe."

But the mayor was troubled. "He's a shrewd one. You don't often hear of *him* losing a bet. And if he wins . . ." The mayor shivered. "I'm afraid he'll manage. And then what?"

The councillors were silent. The "then what?" was too horrible to consider.

On the agreed-on night the work began at dusk. Enormous stones were heard to roll down from the hills. The demon workers hammered and cracked and chipped and smashed, making an infernal racket. Children cried. Dogs howled. Women wept. The uproar within nearly equaled the uproar without. The hours passed, as stone was sandwiched on stone, with lime smeared in between.

The Devil stood by, grimly counting the minutes. The walls rose—but not too quickly. Impatiently the Evil Enemy ordered that to save time larger stones be used at the top to complete the walls. On went the roof and belfry. Up swung the bell. Splash went the plaster as it was mixed.

The race was as good as lost. The number of industrious demons guaranteed that. Already the interior of the church was plastered. Only the outside walls remained.

Where was morning? Was it lost among the shadowy hills of night? The councillors trembled from skull to tarsus, thinking of the terrible promise they had made. Better that the Spanish had razed the village.

But just when the workers began slapping the plaster on the outside stones, there sounded that loveliest and most welcome of songs, the "*Quiquiriqui,* Christ is born!" A moment later it was followed by a thunderous clap as the enraged Devil fled to the Inferno with his legions.

The Curarenes sighed with tremendous relief. Then they looked about. "Why is it so dark?" whispered one.

Perplexed, the mayor answered, "I don't understand it. Not one silver thread of dawn do I see. The east is as black as the west, and both are as black as—well, as night."

"So they are, so they are," croaked a voice from nearby. "I always wanted the chance to outsmart that old rascal."

Holding a candle, Tía Luisa hobbled into view. Between cackles of laughter she told of her trick.

In her hut, which stood close to the church, she had remained awake throughout the night. In one hand she held a candle and in the other a cock. When, well before dawn, the swishing sound of paintbrushes reached her ears, Tía Luisa had lit the candle. Then, naturally, the rooster had crowed.

The gruff old governor, visiting Curarén, approved the church. (He was not informed of either the bargain or the builders.) His only objections were that the largest stones were set at the top of the wall rather than at the bottom, and the church was well painted inside but not out.

The mayor explained that they had tried to plaster the walls, but the plaster refused to adhere and peeled away. As for the large stones, the governor could understand—the laborers had been in a hurry, a fiendish hurry (the mayor winked slowly), so that some of the stones were set helter-skelter, here instead of there. But so what, the church had resulted altogether well, no?

"Oh, altogether," replied the governor. Surely the laborers had toiled night and day? The work had gone particularly quickly at night, the mayor admitted.

And that is the story of the church of Curarén. Except that not long ago a bolt of lightning struck the church, singeing the image of St. Luke.

"Ah," exclaimed an old lady, chuckling, "Satan has never pardoned us for winning *that* bet."

195. THREE MAGIC ORANGES
(*Costa Rica*)

IN THE OLD TIMES there was a king who had a son. And as this king was getting on in years, he wished very much for his son to marry, that he might the sooner see his daughter-in-law. And so he held a great feast. And to this feast he invited all the beautiful princesses from far and near, in the hope that his son would fall in love with one of them. But since the prince was in no hurry to take a wife, he found none to his liking.

Now as you may well imagine, this put the old king in a fine temper, and he ordered his son to set out at once and find himself a wife. And he told him that if he fancied ever to wear the crown upon his head, he had better not return without a suitable bride.

Well then, since he knew he must, the prince mounted a fine horse and rode out into the world, in search of a wife. Presently he came to a green forest, at the edge of which he saw an orange tree with three golden oranges. He plucked the oranges and continued on his way. And he went on, on, and on.

The sun was hot and there was not a single cloud in the sky. And the road was very dusty, for along it rolled many brightly colored oxcarts going to the marketplace with bananas, brown-sugar cakes, and coffee berries. He grew very thirsty; but there was no stream or spring in sight, for it was the summer season and it had not rained for a long time. Just then he remembered the oranges in his pocket. How bright and golden, how full of sweet juice! One, at least, may cool my lips, he thought; so he reined in his horse and cut one in two with his long, sharp knife.

Wonder of wonders! No sooner had he done this than there appeared before him, as if sprung from the earth, a very beautiful maiden with eyes the color of the sky and hair the color of the sun. She begged him for a drink of water, if only a little drop. But he could not give what he had not, and she vanished in the same fashion as she had come.

He stared and wondered, then stroked his chin and said to himself, Well, now I know what sort of oranges these are, and I shall not open them so readily. Then he ate the orange. M-m-m . . . it was sweet! He had never tasted an orange so sweet. And when he had eaten it he felt refreshed and went on his way.

However, it was not long before he was again tormented by thirst, and still there was no water in sight. An hour or more passed by, and still no sign of a stream. And so, since thirst is stronger than good sense, he drew the second orange from his pocket and cut it open. And no sooner had he done this than it was the same thing all over again. But this time the maiden's eyes were green, like a pool of water, and her hair was flaming, like a red hibiscus. She also called for water. But as he had none to offer her, she vanished in the same manner.

"Well," said he, "I still have one orange, and that I will not open unless I have some water handy." And so he ate the second orange and continued along his way.

He had not traveled far when suddenly he was startled by a faint sound, a gentle rippling sound like the murmur of running water. He gave his horse the spur and galloped around a bend in the road, where the sound seemed to be coming from. Then he gasped, for not far off he beheld a lively spring, as clear as the air itself.

He jumped off his horse, filled the hollow of his hand with the cool water, and drank till he was refreshed. When he had done this, he mopped the sweat from his brow and sat down to rest on a convenient grassy bank.

But just then he felt the third orange in his pocket and drew it out. And as he turned it over in his hand he thought, Why, this is the very place to open it! He did so, and on the instant there appeared before him a maiden. Her eyes and her long flowing hair were black as a raven's wing, and her face was soft and white as a jasmine flower. She was beautiful!

Like the others, she asked for water. And losing not a moment, the prince scooped up some water in the hollow of his hand and raised it to her lips. She did not vanish like the others, for the spell was broken.

So beautiful was she and so charmed was the prince that he fell in love with her at sight and immediately asked her to become his wife. She smiled (her little teeth were as white as rice grains), and she consented. Then, being a true princess, she thanked him beyond measure for breaking the cruel enchantment. "You know," she said, "I was once a king's daughter, but an evil witch cast a spell upon me and imprisoned me in that magic orange—until such time as a king's son should break the spell. You are the king's son, and I am set free!"

Full of joy, the prince gently lifted her upon his horse and together they rode home to the royal palace. As they drew near they were followed by many cheering people who came after them, throwing flowers and sombreros in the air. And hearing the cries of the people, the king and all the court came running out of doors.

The prince rode up to them, leaped to the ground as nimbly as you please, and helped the princess down. Then he bowed and said to the king, "Father, here is the maiden of my choice."

Well, the marriage was celebrated at once by a most sumptuous *fiesta*, and everyone rejoiced.

Now the old king's wish to see his daughter-in-law had come true. As time went on he lived out his span of years and died. And the prince and his beautiful princess became king and queen, and wore golden crowns upon their heads.

But misfortune was on their track. Tidings of all these events reached the wicked witch who had enchanted the princess and imprisoned her in the magic orange. Now this witch was exceedingly put out, and to vent her rage she thought of a plan. Disguised as a poor old woman, with a basket full of fruits and fancy pins upon her head, she started for the royal palace without losing any time. And when she arrived there she began to walk up and down the patio, shouting: "Here I bring oranges! . . . Sweet lemons! . . . See what fine mangos! . . . Pins! . . . Pins! . . . Who will buy my fine pins!"

On hearing her cry her wares, the queen looked out of the window. Seeing the old woman standing in the patio with the basket on her head, she asked her to come in, so that she might see the pins. And the witch, who wished for nothing better, went in as fast as she could lay her legs to the ground.

"Here, Señora Queen," she said, as she picked out a pretty hairpin crested with a white pearl. "This will look very fine by your golden crown. Do try it!"

The queen graciously bowed down, and the old woman quickly thrust the pin deep into her head. In a flash the lovely queen was turned into a little white dove and took wing. Through the open window she flew, and on she went till she vanished into a green forest far away. Well, it was that way in those days of magic!

Now all this happened while the young king was out hunting in that same forest. And as he was aiming his arrow at a bright-plumed macaw, suddenly there was a rustle of wings close by. He looked up and saw a little white dove on a treetop. The king thought the dove so remarkably beautiful that immediately he wished to capture her as a present for his wife, the queen. So with all speed he dispatched an arrow. It brushed one of the dove's white wings, making her lose her perch and flutter to the ground. Whereupon she was quickly and gently picked up by his men.

When the king reached his castle he placed the little dove in a golden cage and took her to the queen's chamber. But the queen was nowhere to be found, and the whole of the court soon began to buzz with excitement. Questions were asked and answered, up and down they searched, but to no avail—the queen could not be found. She had disappeared as if she had sunk into the earth. All were very sad, but the king was the most wretched man in his kingdom. Day and night he mourned over the loss of his beloved queen, and nothing could comfort him.

Time passed as swiftly as the wind in those days, and two years and more went by, till one certain day when the unhappy king—in no mood for pleasures—withdrew into his garden, away from the others. Noticing the little dove, forgotten in her golden cage, he opened the cage door and ran his fingers gently over the bird's head. But as he did this he suddenly felt the pearl, so he brushed the feathers apart and discovered the head of the magic pin. Who could have been so cruel, he wondered, as to stick a pin in such a lovely creature.

Then he pulled out the pin as gently as he could. Behold, the dove vanished, and before him stood the queen, as beautiful and radiant as ever she was in all her life. The king was struck dumb. When he had recovered from his astonishment, she told him all that had happened through the treachery of the wicked witch.

Immediately the king ordered his men to set out and find the witch and bring her to the royal palace so that she might be punished for her evil doings.

But of this there was no need. The witch had made a huge fire in her clay stove that day, planning to make a big lot of tamales. Upon hearing the news of the queen's return, she forgot to tend to her work, and the mighty fire she had built spread through her hut. Both the hut and the witch together went up in smoke, which the wind blew away over the treetops.

And so, from this time forth, the king and his beautiful queen lived in peace and love, and nothing ever again marred their happiness.

196. THE LUCKY TABLE
(Costa Rica)

THERE ONCE LIVED in Costa Rica an old widow, and she had two sons. The youngest was called a bobo, or simpleton, because he had not the least idea of the value of money and was sure to spend it buying things of no use at all. And he was just as bad when he wanted to sell something, for he would take whatever price was offered for his goods— no matter how low it was.

Although the old woman and her sons were very poor, they were able to manage for a good long while, but at last there came a bad year. All things went wrong. Their little patch of corn dried up, so they had no corn meal with which to make *tortillas*. The bean vines were blighted, so they had no black beans to eat with their rice. The *yuca* roots spoiled. The pig ran away and could not be found, and the hens would not lay eggs. Yes, everything went wrong.

Then the mother called her sons and said, "Boys, take the cow to the marketplace and sell her! But don't take anything but the best price for her."

"Don't worry, Mama," said the bobo. "We'll sell her as easy as easy and get a lot of pesos for her."

The next day, accordingly, the two sons put on their wide straw sombreros, hung their long, sharp machetes from their belts, said good-bye, and set off together toward the marketplace, leading the cow by a rope. They walked and walked, uphill and downhill, meeting with many brightly painted oxcarts, which were also journeying to the market, carrying brown-sugar cakes and yellow bananas.

When they reached the market, the elder brother left the bobo, charging him to keep his eyes peeled and mind the cow, while he himself went to do an errand for their mother.

Now then, while the brother was away, there came up the street a young lad carrying a big table upon his head. As he drew near he recognized the simple son of the widow. After each had said good day to the other, the lad asked the bobo what he might be doing with that cow. To which the bobo replied that he intended to sell her.

"Don't sell her," said the lad, who knew of the bobo's weak points and had it in mind that he might as well get all he could out of him. "You'll do much better to trade her, for plainly anyone can see with half an eye that she is a sorry beast, old and bare-boned—hardly worth her feed."

"Nothing could be truer," agreed the bobo.

"Tell you what. I'll trade you my table for her."

"Done!" said the bobo. "You take the cow and let me have the table."

"Done! It's yours!" said the lad, and without another word he put down the table. Then he took hold of the rope, gave the cow a flick with the knotted end, and marched off home with her.

Beaming happily over his trade, the bobo then said to himself, "What pleasure my brother will have when he hears of the pretty piece of work I have done!"

By and by the brother returned, and seeing the bobo and not the cow, and fearing some folly, he immediately asked, "Where is the cow? Did you sell her? How much did you get for her? And where is the money?"

"Hold, brother! Don't be so hasty. I'm coming to that. Just give me half a chance and I'll tell you all about it," said the bobo. "See! I traded her for this table here!"

The brother was thunderstruck. "Wh-what? For a t-table?" he stuttered, passing his hand across his brow. "What is this you've done? Traded her for a table! And what good is that to us? Did our mother not charge us to sell her only for the highest sum? Now what'll we do? What'll we do? Oh, evil day! I never thought you would be such a great fool as to give away our cow for a paltry table. Take that, and that." And he gave his brother two slaps. Then in vexation and grief he dropped down upon the ground, weeping.

But the mischief was done and tears could not undo it, and so at length the brother grew calmer and stopped weeping. Seeing that there was nothing to be done but go home, this they did.

"But," said the brother to the bobo, "since you made the trade, you shall carry the table home for your pains."

Now it so befell that on their way back they had to pass through a dark forest of tall trees. They had made their way along very slowly, on account of the table the bobo carried on his shoulders, and they reached the forest just as the night birds, the messengers of twilight, began their songs. Night was almost upon them.

The path was now empty, with not an oxcart or a soul in sight, and the forest ahead looked dark and forbidding. So they resolved to spend the night right where they were. For better protection against the prowling pumas, they decided to climb up and hide in a tall spreading tree, thick with leaves, which stood by the side of the road. They did not dare leave the table on the ground, for fear it might be stolen. So the brother managed to boost the bobo up into the tree with the table still on his back.

Scarcely had they settled themselves on a strong bough when they heard a great noise of voices, as if a large gathering of people were approaching. The noise grew louder as it came near the tree.

"Sh-h! Be still," whispered the elder brother. "Those may be robbers. Let us be very quiet, for if they discover us they'll surely skin us alive."

"Ugh! I wouldn't like that," said the bobo, and he began to shiver and shake so much he almost dropped the table.

"Sh-h! Keep quiet, I say. Don't let another word out of you!"

Robbers they were indeed, just as the brothers feared, and great rascally fellows all. They approached the tree, and since they were tired they sat down beneath it and built a fire. Then they spread out on the ground a cloth and began to count and divide the silver pesos they had stolen. "Ten for Tomás, ten for Paco, ten for Perico. . . ."

Before long, the bobo, who still had the table on his back, began to tire of his load, and so he said softly, "Brother! This table is very heavy!"

"Hush! I can't help that," whispered the brother. "Stay quiet, and don't let that table drop if you value your life."

By and by the bobo called softly again, "Brother! Brother! This table is very, very heavy and I must drop it!"

"No!" whispered the brother. "They'll discover us!"

Then a little while afterward the bobo called a third time. "Brother! This is the end. I cannot hold this table any longer. It's slipping!"

"Zounds!" cried the brother. "Let it fall then, but this is the end for us."

After which the bobo said a silent prayer and let go of the table altogether. Down, down it tumbled with a terrible clatter, right in the midst of all the robbers. Away ran every mother's son of them, leaving their booty behind.

When they were sure that the thieves were not coming back for their money, the two brothers came down from the tree. They gathered the treasure together in the cloth and carried it home, together with their lucky table. They had become rich, and the family lived happily for many years. But the bobo, being a *bobo*, played a mad trick or two every now and then.

197. BRER RABBIT, BUSINESSMAN
(*Costa Rica*)

ONCE BRER RABBIT RAISED a crop of a bushel of corn and a bushel of beans, and as he was such a rascal he made up his mind to sell them for as much as he could get.

So early one Wednesday morning he put on his big straw hat, slung his coat over his shoulder, and started down the road. He came to Sis Roach's house, and knock, knock. Sis Roach was roasting coffee, and she came out, throwing her shawl over her head to keep from taking a chill.

"Who's there? Oh, Brer Rabbit! How are things going with you? Come in and sit down." And Sis Roach wiped off the end of the bench with her apron.

"Can't complain," answered Brer Rabbit. "I was just going by and thought I'd drop in to see if we could do a little business. What would you say if I told you I was selling a bushel of corn and a bushel of beans for two dollars? Did you ever hear the like? But needs must when the devil drives!"

"Well, I'll think it over, Brer Rabbit. If I decide to take you up I'll come over and let you know."

"Oh, no, Sis Roach. You'll have to make up your mind right now, or I'll look for another customer. I came here first because you know how much I think of you. If you want them, come to my house on Saturday around seven in the morning, for I have to go to town."

"What the devil, it's a deal. I'll be over for them on Saturday with my wagon. But don't go. The coffee is almost ready, and I have some tamales I just took out of the oven."

Brer Rabbit sat down, and in a little while Sis Roach was back with a pot of fresh coffee and a nice chunk of tamale. With this to prop up his stomach, Brer Rabbit went on his way. He came to Sis Hen's house, and went knock, knock.

"Who's there?" called out Sis Hen, who was busy getting lunch.

"It's me, Brer Rabbit. I've come to see if we can do a little business."

"Come in, come in, and sit down. Now, what kind of business is this?"

"I'm selling a bushel of corn and a bushel of beans for two dollars. Can you beat it? Just throwing the corn and the beans into the street, you might say. But I'm in a tight spot and I have to take what I can get. I came right over to your place, Sis Hen, because, when all is said and done, we're good friends, and I always like to favor a friend."

Sis Hen got up to turn the tortilla on the griddle, and as she went back and forth she decided it was a good bargain, and she promised Brer Rabbit she would be over on Saturday about eight o'clock for her corn and beans. And she gave him a cheese she had made to taste.

Brer Rabbit went on his way and came to the house of Sis Fox, who was picking some chickens.

"Morning, Sis Fox. How's the world treating you?"

"Bless my soul if it isn't Brer Rabbit! Shanks' mare is right lively this morning. Come in, come in. We're just getting ready to eat."

Brer Rabbit came in, told Sis Fox the same yarn about the corn and the beans, saying that she was the first one he had thought of, and here and there, and that if she wanted them she was to come around nine on Saturday, because he had to go to town. Sis Fox said all right, she would be there on Saturday with her money.

After a fine meal Brer Rabbit said good-bye and went on his way. He came to the house of Brer Coyote, who was just taking a big kettle of preserves off the stove.

"Hi there, Brer Coyote. What you know?"

"Why, Brer Rabbit, haven't seen you in a coon's age. It's better to walk in at the right time than be invited. Come on in and taste these preserves."

While he licked up the dish of preserves, Brer Rabbit offered Brer

Coyote his bushel of corn and beans for two dollars. They made the deal, and Brer Coyote was to come for them with his wagon on Saturday at ten o'clock.

Brer Rabbit said good-bye and went on his way. He came to the house of Hunter Man, who was sitting on the porch cleaning his gun.

"Hunter Man, you're going to think I've gone plumb-dumb crazy, offering you a bushel of corn and a bushel of beans for two dollars. But I'm in debt up to my ears."

Hunter Man thought it over and said he'd be over on Saturday with his two mules for the corn and the beans. Brer Rabbit told him to come about noon, because he had to go to town without fail that morning, and he wouldn't be back until around one. Then Brer Rabbit moseyed along home. Saturday he got up bright and early and sat himself on the fence. The sun was hardly up when he saw Sis Roach coming down the road with her wagon.

Brer Rabbit told her to leave the wagon at the back of the house. He showed her the corn and the beans; Sis Roach pulled out her handkerchief with the two dollars tied in it, untied it, and handed him the money. Then Brer Rabbit invited Sis Roach in, got down the hammock, which was hanging from one of the crossbeams, and said, "Come on, Sis Roach, and have yourself a little swing while you smoke this nice Havana cigar." And Sis Roach stretched herself out in the hammock and began to puff away.

Brer Rabbit was first in and then out of the house. Suddenly he rushed in with his hands to his head. "Lord have mercy, Sis Roach! Sis Hen is coming down the road, and she's headed this way!"

"Don't say that, Brer Rabbit," said Sis Roach, leaping out of the hammock. "God help me if she finds out I'm here! Hide me, hide me, Brer Rabbit! Oh, I can see myself in Sis Hen's craw!"

Brer Rabbit hid her in the oven and went out to meet Sis Hen. He told her to put her wagon in the shed, showed her the bushel of corn and beans, and received her two dollars. Then, winking and making signs, he pointed to the oven, and when she opened it, there was Sis Roach, who was down her crop before you could say amen. Then he invited her into the sitting room, had her get into the hammock, and gave her a Havana cigar.

Sis Hen was having a high old time when in rushed Brer Rabbit with his hands to his head. "Lord have mercy on us, Sis Hen! Guess who's coming down the road?"

"Who, Brer Rabbit?"

"Sis Fox, and I don't know if she's coming for you or for me."

"For me, Brer Rabbit! Who would she be after? For mercy's sake, hide me!" And poor Sis Hen, scared out of her wits, rushed around, not knowing what to do.

Brer Rabbit hid her in the oven and went out to meet Sis Fox. He took her to the barn to leave her wagon, so she would not see the others, got her two dollars, and then did the same as before. Like the sly rascal he was, he kept pointing to the oven till Sis Fox opened it and finished off Sis Hen in the twinkling of an eye. While she lay rocking in the hammock, smoking a Havana cigar, Brer Rabbit was in and out, in and out, like a shuttle. One of these times he came in pretending he was scared to death.

"My God, Sis Fox, guess who's coming down the road!"

Sis Fox jumped out of the hammock. "Who, Brer Rabbit?"

"Brer Coyote. And I don't know if he's after you or after me."

"How can you be so dumb, Brer Rabbit? It's me he's after. Hide me, and please God he don't smell me!"

Brer Rabbit hid her in the oven and went out to meet Brer Coyote. After he got his two dollars he took him into the house.

"Stretch out in that hammock, Brer Coyote, and rest yourself while you smoke this nice little Havana. No need to be in a rush. You know how it is, we're here today and gone tomorrow, and nobody knows when the reaper cometh. For that reason I never hurry."

While he was puffing his cigar Brer Rabbit whispered in his ear, "Go take a look in the oven and see what I've got for you." Brer Coyote opened it, and there was Sis Fox playing possum. In a minute she was really dead, and Brer Coyote ate her up. He was still licking his chops when Brer Rabbit rushed in. "God be merciful to sinners, Brer Coyote! Guess who's coming down the road?"

"Who, Brer Rabbit?" yelled Brer Coyote, trembling at the look on Brer Rabbit's face.

"It's Hunter Man, with a gun this long. And I don't know if he's after you or after me!"

"Oh, Brer Rabbit, he's after me. He's got it in for me. For pity's sake, hide me!"

"Well, get in the oven, and I'll shut the door."

Brer Coyote crawled in, with his heart going like a trip-hammer, while Brer Rabbit went out to the gate to meet Hunter Man.

"I was beginning to think you weren't coming, Hunter Man," said the old whited sepulcher. "Come in, come in, and rest yourself in this hammock, for you must be worn out. Have a cigar, and then you can look at the corn and the beans."

After Hunter Man had rested himself, Brer Rabbit whispered in his ear, "Take your gun, Hunter Man, and have a look in the oven."

Hunter Man went to the oven, and what did he find there but Brer Coyote, whose shanks were knocking together so he couldn't stand up. Hunter Man took aim—bang—and good-bye, Brer Coyote.

Then they went out and loaded the corn and beans on the mules, and Hunter Man was the only customer who got what he had paid for. Brer Rabbit had seven dollars and a half for his bushel of corn and beans, and four wagons and four yoke of oxen, and he felt very proud of himself.

198. THE SEARCH FOR THE MAGIC LAKE
(*Ecuador*)

LONG AGO THERE WAS a ruler of the vast Inca Empire who had an only son. This youth brought great joy to his father's heart but also a sadness, for the prince had been born in ill health.

As the years passed the prince's health did not improve, and none of the court doctors could find a cure for his illness.

One night the aged emperor went down on his knees and prayed at the altar.

"O Great Ones," he said, "I am getting older and will soon leave my people and join you in the heavens. There is no one to look after them but my son, the prince. I pray you make him well and strong so he can be a fit ruler for my people. Tell me how his malady can be cured."

The emperor put his head in his hands and waited for an answer. Soon he heard a voice coming from the fire that burned constantly in front of the altar.

"Let the prince drink water from the magic lake at the end of the world," the voice said, "and he will be well."

At that moment the fire sputtered and died. Among the cold ashes lay a golden flask.

But the emperor was much too old to make the long journey to the end of the world, and the young prince was too ill to travel. So the emperor proclaimed that whosoever should fill the golden flask with the magic water would be greatly rewarded.

Many brave men set out to search for the magic lake, but none could find it. Days and weeks passed and still the flask remained empty.

In a valley, some distance from the emperor's palace, lived a poor farmer who had a wife, two grown sons, and a young daughter.

One day the older son said to his father, "Let my brother and me join in the search for the magic lake. Before the moon is new again, we shall return and help you harvest the corn and potatoes."

The father remained silent. He was not thinking of the harvest, but feared for his sons' safety.

When the father did not answer, the second son added, "Think of the rich reward, Father!"

"It is their duty to go," said his wife, "for we must all try to help our emperor and the young prince."

After his wife had spoken, the father yielded.

"Go if you must, but beware of the wild beasts and evil spirits," he cautioned.

With their parents' blessing, and an affectionate farewell from their young sister, the sons set out on their journey.

They found many lakes, but none where the sky touched the water.

Finally the younger brother said, "Before another day has passed we must return to help father with the harvest."

"Yes," agreed the other, "but I have thought of a plan. Let us each carry a jar of water from any lake along the way. We can say it will cure the prince. Even if it doesn't, surely the emperor will give us a small reward for our trouble."

"Agreed," said the younger brother.

On arriving at the palace, the deceitful youths told the emperor and his court that they brought water from the magic lake. At once the prince was given a sip from each of the brothers' jars, but of course he remained as ill as before.

"Perhaps the water must be sipped from the golden flask," one of the high priests said.

But the golden flask would not hold the water. In some mysterious way the water from the jars disappeared as soon as it was poured into the flask.

In despair the emperor called for his magician and said to him, "Can you break the spell of the flask so the water will remain for my son to drink?"

"I cannot do that, your majesty," replied the magician. "But I believe," he added wisely, "that the flask is telling us that we have been deceived by the two brothers. The flask can be filled only with water from the magic lake."

When the brothers heard this, they trembled with fright, for they knew their falsehood was discovered.

So angry was the emperor that he ordered the brothers thrown into chains. Each day they were forced to drink water from their jars as a reminder of their false deed. News of their disgrace spread far and wide.

Again the emperor sent messengers throughout the land pleading for someone to bring the magic water before death claimed him and the young prince.

Súmac, the little sister of the deceitful youths, was tending her flock of llamas when she heard the sound of the royal trumpet. Then came the voice of the emperor's servant with his urgent message from the court.

Quickly the child led her llamas home and begged her parents to let her go in search of the magic water.

"You are too young," her father said. "Besides, look at what has already befallen your brothers. Some evil spirit must have taken hold of them to make them tell such a lie."

And her mother said, "We could not bear to be without our precious Súmac!"

"But think how sad our emperor will be if the young prince dies," replied the innocent child. "And if I can find the magic lake, perhaps the emperor will forgive my brothers and send them home."

"Dear husband," said Súmac's mother, "maybe it is the will of the gods that we let her go."

Once again the father gave his permission.

"It is true," he murmured, "I must think of our emperor."

Súmac was overjoyed, and went skipping out to the corral to harness one of her pet llamas. It would carry her provisions and keep her company.

Meanwhile her mother filled a little woven bag with food and drink for Súmac—toasted golden kernels of corn and a little earthen jar of *chicha*, a beverage made from crushed corn.

The three embraced each other tearfully before Súmac set out bravely on her mission, leading her pet llama along the trail.

The first night she slept, snug and warm against her llama, in the shelter of a few rocks. But when she heard the hungry cry of the puma, she feared for her pet animal and bade it return safely home.

The next night she spent in the top branches of a tall tree, far out of reach of the dreadful puma. She hid her provisions in a hole in the tree trunk.

At sunrise she was aroused by the voices of gentle sparrows resting on a nearby limb.

"Poor child," said the oldest sparrow, "she can never find her way to the lake."

"Let us help her," chorused the others.

"Oh please do!" implored the child, "and forgive me for intruding in your tree."

"We welcome you," chirped another sparrow, "for you are the same little girl who yesterday shared your golden corn with us."

"We shall help you," continued the first sparrow, who was the leader, "for you are a good child. Each of us will give you a wing feather, and you must hold them all together in one hand as a fan. The feathers have magic powers that will carry you wherever you wish to go. They will also protect you from harm."

Each sparrow then lifted a wing, sought out a special feather hidden underneath, and gave it to Súmac. She fashioned them into the shape of a little fan, taking the ribbon from her hair to bind the feathers together so none would be lost.

"I must warn you," said the oldest sparrow, "that the lake is guarded by three terrible creatures. But have no fear. Hold the magic fan up to your face and you will be unharmed."

Súmac thanked the birds over and over again. Then, holding up the fan in her chubby hands, she said politely, "Please, magic fan, take me to the lake at the end of the world."

A soft breeze swept her out of the top branches of the tree and through the valley. Then up she was carried, higher and higher into the sky, until she could look down and see the great mountain peaks covered with snow.

At last the wind put her down on the shore of a beautiful lake. It was, indeed, the lake at the end of the world, for, on the opposite side from where she stood, the sky came down so low it touched the water.

Súmac tucked the magic fan into her waistband and ran to the edge of the water. Suddenly her face fell. She had left everything back in the forest. What could she use for carrying the precious water back to the prince?

"Oh, I do wish I had remembered the jar!" she said, weeping.

Suddenly she heard a soft thud in the sand at her feet. She looked down and discovered a beautiful golden flask—the same one the emperor had found in the ashes.

Súmac took the flask and kneeled at the water's edge. Just then a hissing voice behind her said, "Get away from my lake or I shall wrap my long, hairy legs around your neck."

Súmac turned around. There stood a giant crab as large as a pig and as black as night.

With trembling hands the child took the magic fan from her waistband and spread it open in front of her face. As soon as the crab looked at it, he closed his eyes and fell down on the sand in a deep sleep.

Once more Súmac started to fill the flask. This time she was startled by a fierce voice bubbling up from the water.

"Get away from my lake or I shall eat you," gurgled a giant green alligator. His long tail beat the water angrily.

Súmac waited until the creature swam closer. Then she held up the fan. The alligator blinked. He drew back. Slowly, quietly, he sank to the bottom of the lake in a sound sleep.

Before Súmac could recover from her fright, she heard a shrill whistle in the air. She looked up and saw a flying serpent. His skin was red as blood. Sparks flew from his eyes.

"Get away from my lake or I shall bite you," hissed the serpent as it batted its wings around her head.

Again Súmac's fan saved her from harm. The serpent closed his eyes and drifted to the ground. He folded his wings and coiled up on the sand. Then he began to snore.

Súmac sat for a moment to quiet herself. Then, realizing that the danger was past, she sighed with great relief.

"Now I can fill the golden flask and be on my way," she said to herself.

When this was done, she held the flask tightly in one hand and clutched the fan in the other.

"Please take me to the palace," she said.

Hardly were the words spoken, when she found herself safely in front of the palace gates. She looked at the tall guard.

"I wish to see the emperor," Súmac uttered in trembling tones.

"Why, little girl?" the guard asked kindly.

"I bring water from the magic lake to cure the prince."

The guard looked down at her in astonishment.

"Come!" he commanded in a voice loud and deep as thunder.

In just a few moments Súmac was led into a room full of sadness. The emperor was pacing up and down in despair. The prince lay motionless on a huge bed. His eyes were closed and his face was without color. Beside him knelt his mother, weeping.

Without wasting words, Súmac went to the prince and gave him a few drops of magic water. Soon he opened his eyes. His cheeks became flushed. It was not long before he sat up in bed. He drank some more.

"How strong I feel!" the prince cried joyfully.

The emperor and his wife embraced Súmac. Then Súmac told them of her adventurous trip to the lake. They praised her courage. They marveled at the reappearance of the golden flask and at the powers of the magic fan.

"Dear child," said the emperor, "all the riches of my empire are not enough to repay you for saving my son's life. Ask what you will and it shall be yours."

"Oh, generous emperor," said Súmac timidly, "I have but three wishes."

"Name them and they shall be yours," urged the emperor.

"First, I wish my brothers to be free to return to my parents. They have learned their lesson and will never be false again. I know they were only thinking of a reward for my parents. Please forgive them."

"Guards, free them at once!" ordered the emperor.

"Secondly, I wish the magic fan returned to the forest so the sparrows may have their feathers again."

This time the emperor had no time to speak. Before anyone in the room could utter a sound, the magic fan lifted itself up, spread itself wide open, and floated out the window toward the woods. Everyone watched in amazement. When the fan was out of sight, they applauded.

"What is your last wish, dear Súmac?" asked the queen mother.

"I wish that my parents be given a large farm and great flocks of llamas, vicuñas, and alpacas, so they will not be poor any longer."

"It will be so," said the emperor, "but I am sure your parents never considered themselves poor with so wonderful a daughter."

"Won't you stay with us in the palace?" ventured the prince.

"Yes, stay with us!" urged the emperor and his wife. "We will do everything to make you happy."

"Oh thank you," said Súmac blushing happily, "but I must return to my parents and to my brothers. I miss them as I know they have missed me. They do not even know I am safe, for I came directly to your palace."

The royal family did not try to detain Súmac any longer.

"My own guard will see that you get home safely," said the emperor.

When she reached home, she found that all she had wished for had come to pass: her brothers were waiting for her with their parents; a beautiful house and huge barn were being constructed; her father had received a deed granting him many acres of new, rich farmland.

Súmac ran into the arms of her happy family.

At the palace, the golden flask was never empty. Each time it was used, it was refilled. Thus the prince's royal descendants never suffered ill health and the kingdom remained strong.

But it is said that when the Spanish conqueror of the ancient Incas demanded a room filled with golden gifts, the precious flask was among them. Whatever happened to this golden treasure is unknown, for the conqueror was killed and the Indians wandered over the mainland in search of a new leader. Some say the precious gifts—including the golden flask—are buried at the bottom of the lake at the end of the world, but no one besides Súmac has ever ventured to go there.

199. THE DEER AND THE JAGUAR SHARE A HOUSE*
(Brazil)

ONE DAY A DEER was wandering along a riverbank, and he said: "I have led a hard life, wandering here and there, never having a house of my own. I would like to have a house, and where would I ever find a better place than here? This is where I will build." And he went away.

A jaguar also said one day: "My life is full of trouble and cares. I shall look for a place to build a house, and I shall settle down comfortably." He went out to find a place, and he came to the same spot that the deer had chosen. When he saw it he exclaimed, "Wherever would I find a better spot for a house than this? Here is where I will live." And he went away, making plans to return.

The deer came back the following day to begin work on his house. It was great labor, but he cleared the ground of brush and trees and made it smooth and clean. Then he left, to return when he could.

The next day the jaguar came to begin work on his house, and he saw that the ground had already been cleared. "Ah!" he said. "The God Tupan is helping me with my work! What good fortune!" So he went to work on the floor of the house, and when the floor was finished it was nearly night and the jaguar went away.

The following morning the deer came and saw the floor completed. He said, "Ah, the God Tupan is helping me build my house! What good luck!" And he built the walls of the house and returned to the forest.

The next day the jaguar came again and saw the walls finished. "Thank you, Tupan!" he said, and he put on the roof. Then he went back to the forest.

---

* From the collection of Harold Courlander. Found in an anonymous manuscript in the New York Public Library.

When the deer came back, he found the roof was finished. He said, "Thank you, Tupan, for all your help!" And in gratitude to the God Tupan, the deer made two rooms in the house, one for Tupan and one for himself. Then he entered one of the rooms and went to sleep.

That night the jaguar came once more. He went into the empty room to sleep, thinking he was sharing the house with Tupan, who had helped him build.

In the morning the deer and the jaguar got up at the same time. The jaguar asked in surprise, "Is it you who helped me build?"

The deer said, "Yes, is it you who helped me build?"

The jaguar said, "Yes. Since we have built this house together, let us share it."

The deer agreed, and they lived together, one in one room, the other in the other room.

One day the jaguar said, "I am going out hunting. I will bring food, so get everything ready, the pots, the water, and the wood for a fire."

He went out in the forest, while the deer prepared for the cooking. The jaguar killed a deer in the forest and brought it back. When the deer who was sharing the house saw what the food was, he became very sad. The jaguar cooked the food, but the deer wouldn't eat. After the jaguar had had his supper, they went to bed. But the deer was thinking with horror about the jaguar's diet, and he couldn't sleep. He feared that the jaguar would come in the night and eat him also.

In the morning the deer said to the jaguar, "Get the pots and the water and the wood ready. I am going hunting."

He went out in the forest and he saw another jaguar there sharpening his claws on the bark of a tree. The deer went on until he found an ant-eater, known as the tamandua. He said to the tamandua, "The jaguar over there has been saying evil things about you."

When the tamandua heard this he became angry. He went to where the jaguar was and, creeping up silently behind him, seized him and killed him. Then he went away.

The deer took the carcass of the jaguar and carried it home. The pots and the water and the wood were ready. But when the jaguar with whom he was living saw what the deer had brought, he lost his appetite. Though the deer cooked the food, the jaguar couldn't eat a thing.

That night, neither the deer nor the jaguar could sleep. The jaguar feared that the deer might come for jaguar meat, and the deer feared that the jaguar would come for deer meat. They lay silently awake as the hours passed. When it was very late, they began to nod. In spite of his nervousness, the jaguar's eyes began to close a little. And so did the deer's. Suddenly the deer's eyes closed completely for a moment, and his head nodded. As he nodded, his antlers hit the wall with a loud noise.

When the jaguar heard the noise he awoke in fright, thinking the deer was coming after him, and he screamed. When the deer heard the scream he was terrified, thinking the jaguar was coming to get him. Both animals leaped to their feet and fled from the house into the forest, one going in one direction and one in another.

And since that time, the jaguar and the deer have never lived together.

200. THE FIVE BROTHERS
(Chile)

THERE WAS ONCE, my dear gentleman, a certain landlord who had five sons. Their names were Pedro, Diego, José, Juan, and Manuel. These boys were so brotherly that if they found even a tiny loaf of bread, they would split it among all five of them. They had two hundred acres of grazing land, animals, nice little houses—everything they needed. But that wasn't enough for these lads. They always wanted to have just a little bit more. One day, Pedro, being the oldest, asked Diego if he would like to make a little trip. It seemed like a good idea and very soon all five brothers had agreed to set out together. Even little Manuel was to go. His brothers loved him very dearly, for he was a brave and manly lad. They were all boys with good manners and a nice way about them. When the plans were made, they went to confer with their father.

"Listen, taitita" [affectionate diminutive of "father"], they said (for in those days you called your father by that name), "we'd like very much to make a little trip for a year to see if we can't perhaps bring home a charm that might please you."

"All right, my lads," said their father, "I'll give you my permission." Then he called to Anita, the boys' pretty little sister. "Daughter, make your brothers something to take with them on their journey."

The following day, the old gentleman gave them his blessing. At the end of a year's time they had to return to their father's house alive and well. He wouldn't have any dead men on his hands! But God will help them, for with the parents' blessing, the young ones make out well. The five brothers set out on the way and came about noontime to a fork of five roads, just like the fingers on your hand. Pedro assigned a road to each of the five of them and said, "We're going to take a little snack before we part. After one year, we'll all meet here to return to our parents' house with something for our sister, who will surely be praying for us." Each of the brothers set out on his own road.

Pedro came to the house of a man who was, by profession, an excellent thief. This man hired him for a companion, for he noticed that the boy had just the right kind of build for slick robberies. The thief began to teach the boy all his trade, boasting that he had no equal and had never been caught. After six months Pedro knew three times what his master did, for he would go and take something right from under your nose. When you looked, he didn't have a blessed thing. Imagine how light-fingered he must have been!

The second brother, Diego, arrived at the cabin of a great hunter. This man took him in as a companion to hunt birds in the forest. After five days, Diego had become a better hunter than his master. What an eye he had for that business! After six months, he knew so much that he didn't even have to look before he aimed. Diego, king of the hunters!

Meanwhile the third brother, José, came to the house of an old bonesetter. People came to this man all broken and falling apart to get treatment. José stopped there and learned from this true master. After six months he too was better than the teacher himself. A man would come in with fractured bones and José would leave him like new, as if he'd never had a break in his life. What hands the boy had!

Juan arrived at the dwelling of an old man who raised the dead. The cadavers came in every day, and after little Juan had been at this job for three months, he raised them better than the old resuscitator himself. Now there was nothing more to teach him of this art.

Manuel, the youngest brother, ended up at the house of a fortune-teller, who taught the boy his trade. Manuel learned to know where his father, his family, and his brothers were and what profession they had. He soon did all this even better than the master, for Manuel felt it as a gift in his head. When a year was up, he said, "My brother Pedro is on his way to the little tree where the five roads part." Can you imagine?

He knew even then that his brothers were headed home. He bade good-bye to the old man, and went to join them.

They all arrived at the junction, each one with his suitcase full of money and dressed to the teeth. When Manuel shuffled in, he asked, "Tell me, what professions do you bring, brothers? If you wish, I'll tell you myself. You, Pedro, are an excellent thief. Diego has become a great hunter, José a fine bonesetter, and Juanito an expert at raising the dead. In case you haven't guessed, I'm a fortune-teller. Now then, in this tree there's a partridge. Kill it, my good hunter." Diego took aim and shot down the bird with ease. "All right, José," added Manuel, "now arrange the bird." As José was busy taking the bird to pieces and dressing it, Pedro slipped over and stole one of the wings. The partridge was all dressed except for the one missing wing. Manuel turned to Pedro and said, "Give it over now, brother."

"It's true enough that you're a professional at this," answered Pedro, for he realized that Manuel could divine just about anything. When the partridge was whole again, with its wing restored, Manuel continued, "Come on, Juan, bring this bird to life." And there on the spot Juan did it. "Pi-pi-pi! Pi-pi-pi!" squawked the bird as it flew into the brush. Now that each of the brothers had made a test of his gift, they all went to present themselves before their father.

"Here they come!" shouted the rest of the family from the front door. The five brothers were received in fitting style, each one coming in well groomed and carrying his great suitcase full of belongings.

"Well, well, my lads," said their father, "let's see what professions you have brought home."

"I," spoke up Pedro proudly, "I am a fine thief."

"Then be off with you," roared the father. "I want no thieves in my house."

"But Our Lord died between two thieves," said the others, "and the good thief is our brother, Pedro."

"What's your profession, Diego?" continued the old man.

"I'm a great hunter."

"And you, José?"

"I'm a bonesetter."

"Ah, very fine," said their father. "It just happens that I want my leg set, and you're the one to do it." When the father had asked Juan, he turned to Manuel, who had been standing by watching quietly.

"And you, little Manuel, what have you brought home to me?"

"Why, I'm a fortune-teller," answered the boy calmly.

"A fortune-teller?"

"Yes, I was just foreseeing the things you were going to say to my brothers."

"How did you know?" asked his father, gaping at his youngest son.

"Each one has his profession, and you should be thankful," answered Manuel.

Now it so happened that there was a king who lived nearby and had heard that the sons of such and such a gentleman had come home with some exceptional gifts and great riches. Someone had stolen a princess from this king five years ago and he had no idea where she was to be found. He knew that one of the brothers was reputed to have become a fortune-teller and it occurred to him that this might be the solution to his problem.

At the same time, Manuel was divining and announced to his brothers, "The king is thinking, boys, and a voyage is going to befall us soon."

"Why is that?" they all chorused, astounded.

"Because the one who has this princess is Old Long Arms, who lives in the sea's current on the other side of the Island of Ivories. This tremendous giant is guarding her there, and we've got to go to search for her. The king will arrive to get us at ten o'clock."

"I'll believe that when I see it," scoffed the father in a huff.

When the king did arrive, it was two minutes before ten.

"Good day, my good man," he called to the boys' father. "Are these five fellows your sons? I want to know which one is the fortune-teller."

"I'm the one," spoke up Manuel. "Are you he that comes in search of his daughter?"

The king marveled at the boy's foresight and asked if the brothers dared to look for his girl.

"Why not? Of course, your Highness," they all answered. "We shall go to the Island of Ivories."

"As soon as you bring her home, the one of you who works the most on this task shall be her husband." The king offered to give them a crew for the long trip, but the five brothers preferred to go alone, for they knew well enough how to work together and manage a boat. Without losing a moment, they set out for the Island of Ivories, sailing straight as an arrow on their course. Those boys were no fools!

"Look, Pedro," said Manuel as they sailed up to the island, "you'll be the one to steal the princess from Old Long Arms. I'll tell you where she is hidden. Diego can take a shot at the giant if necessary."

So Pedro slipped into the castle and grabbed the princess so fast that she didn't know what was happening until they had her in the boat.

They were all sailing away from the island when Manuel cried out, "Take aim, Diego, Old Long Arms is about to fall upon us!" The giant was following them, planning to crush the little boat, which was still just off shore. As the giant loomed into view, Diego took a quick shot and broke one of his arms. The brothers sailed on in peace. Soon Manuel began to relax with the rolling of the waves and forgot all about his duty. Suddenly Old Long Arms dropped his good arm on the little boat and smashed it to splinters. But José, the bonesetter, reconstructed the ship in a few minutes, leaving it as good as new. The brothers climbed back aboard with the princess and were sailing on, when the girl fainted and died on the floor of the little craft. Right away, Juan, who had learned to raise the dead, came and revived her. As they sailed on, Old Long Arms came into sight once more, but this time Diego took careful aim and shot the giant down for good. There were no more misadventures, and they landed with the true princess of the realm. It had been five years since she was carried away by the wicked giant from the Island of Ivories. The king was leaping with joy at the arrival of his long-lost daughter. When she told her father all the adventures of the trip, it appeared that all five brothers claimed to have worked the hardest and to have gained her hand in marriage.

"She's mine, she's mine," shouted Manuel. "I knew where she was."

"And what about the boat which I repaired?" answered José.

"And if it weren't for my killing Old Long Arms, we'd never have gotten here," put in Diego.

"Without me," added Pedro, "you never would have stolen her."

"And I, after all, brought her back to life," concluded Juan.

"Just a minute. Hold your horses," intervened the king. "Each of you is going to shoot an arrow so that you can realize your folly. Five men can hardly marry one woman."

The deal was on. Pedro took up the bow first and shot the arrow fifty yards. Diego came for his turn and shot it sixty yards, José a few inches more, and Juan just a step further.

"Let's see mine," shouted Manuel as he shot. "There it goes beyond the others. The lady is mine!" Manuel had won by a good twenty-five yards.

"I have five daughters," announced the king, "and each of them is going to marry one of you boys."

That was the end of the squabble. The king himself married them all, baptized them, and gave the five true men his blessing. Manuel became their king, and all lived happily together as true Christians in this life.

INDEX OF CATEGORIES OF TALES

(Numbers in parentheses refer to tale numbers in text.)

■ Humorous Tales

■ *Men and Boys*

■ *Wise Men and Judges*

■ *Enchanted or Animal Sweethearts and Spouses*

■ *Married Couples*

INDEX OF TITLES